Also by
JENNIFER ROBERSON

THE SWORD-DANCER SAGA
SWORD-DANCER
SWORD-SINGER
SWORD-MAKER
SWORD-BREAKER
SWORD-BORN
SWORD-SWORN

CHRONICLES OF THE CHEYSULI
Omnibus Editions
SHAPECHANGER'S SONG
LEGACY OF THE WOLF
CHILDREN OF THE LION
THE LION THRONE

THE GOLDEN KEY
(with Melanie Rawn and Kate Elliott)

ANTHOLOGIES
(as editor)
RETURN TO AVALON
HIGHWAYMEN: ROBBERS AND ROGUES

And coming in hardcover in April 2006:
KARAVANS
A new series from Jennifer Roberson

JENNIFER ROBERSON

The Novels of Tiger and Del
Volume #2

DAW BOOKS, INC.

DONALD A. WOLLHEIM, FOUNDER

375 Hudson Street, New York, NY 10014

ELIZABETH R. WOLLHEIM
SHEILA E. GILBERT
PUBLISHERS

http://www.dawbooks.com

First Trade Paperback Printing, March 2006

4   5   6   7   8   9

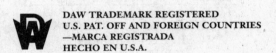

DAW TRADEMARK REGISTERED
U.S. PAT. OFF AND FOREIGN COUNTRIES
—MARCA REGISTRADA
HECHO EN U.S.A.

PRINTED IN THE U.S.A.

Sword-Maker

Acknowledgment

As any author with spouse or significant other can attest, no book is written completely independent of that person. There are things that person does: answers the phone, brings in the mail (telling you if there's a royalty check), goes out for more milk, gets the cat off the computer, tells the barking dog to be quiet, plus myriad other tasks. These things are all important; concentration is occasionally a very delicate thing. But this person also contributes a great deal to the actual creation of a book. He reads, rereads, re-rereads. Tells you what works, and what doesn't. Drives you completely bonkers. But he also improves the book.

Mark O'Green had much to do with *Sword-Maker*. Without him, it wouldn't exist. For this, and other things, I give him my gratitude.

Prologue

She is not a woman for idle conversation, having little patience for small talk, and even less for excuses and explanations. Including those dealing with life and death; mine, or her own. And yet I resorted to both: excuses, explanations. Somehow, I had to.

"It wasn't my fault," I declared. "It wasn't. Did I have any choice? Did you *leave* me any choice?" I snorted in derision. "No, of course not—not *you* . . . you leave no choice or chance to anyone, least of all me . . . you just stare me down across the circle and *dare* me to take you, to cut you, to chop you down with my blade, because it's the only thing that will make you admit you're just as human as anyone else, and just as vulnerable. Just as fragile as anyone, man or woman, made of flesh and blood . . . and you *bleed*, Del . . . just like anyone else—just like *me*—you bleed."

She said nothing. Fair hair shone white in firelight, but blue eyes were nothing more than blackened pockets in a shadow-clad face lacking definition or expression. The beauty remained, but changed. Altered by tension, obsession, pain.

Behind me, tied to a tree, the stud snorted, stomped, pawed a thin layer of slush away from winter-brown turf. Pawing again and again, stripping away even the turf until what he dug was a hole.

Horses can't talk, not like humans; they do what they can with ears, teeth, hooves. What he told me now was he didn't want to eat. Didn't want to sleep. Didn't want to spend the night tied to a bare-branched tree, chilled to the bone by a Northern wind that wouldn't—quite—quit. What he wanted was to leave. To go on. To head south toward his desert homeland where it is never, ever cold.

"Not my fault," I repeated firmly. "Hoolies, bascha, you and that storm-born sword of yours . . . what did you *expect* me to do? I'm a sword-dancer. Put me in a circle with a sword in my hands, and I dance. For pay, for show, for honor—for all those things most men are afraid to name, for fear of showing too much . . . well, I'm *not* afraid, Del—all I know is you left me no choice but to cut you, coming at me like that with that magicked sword of yours—what did you *expect?* I did what I had to. What was needed, for both of us, if for different reasons." I scratched angrily at the scars in my right cheek: four deep-scored claw marks, now white with age, cutting through the beard. "I tried like hoolies to make you quit, to make you leave that thrice-cursed island before it came to something we'd both regret, but you left me no choice. You stepped into that circle all on your own, Del . . . and you paid the price. You found out just how good the Sandtiger is after all, didn't you?"

No answer. Of course not; she still thought she was better. But I had proven which of us was superior in the most eloquent fashion of all.

Swearing at the cold, I resettled the wool cloak I wore, wrapping it more closely around shoulders. Brown hair uncut for far too long blew into my eyes, stinging, and my mouth. It also caught on my short-cropped beard repeatedly, no matter how many times I stripped it back. Even the hood didn't help; the wind tore it from my head again and again and again, until I gave up and left it puddled on my shoulders.

"You and that butcher's blade," I muttered.

Still Del said nothing.

Wearily I scrubbed at brows, eyes, face. I was tired, too tired; the wound in my abdomen ached unremittingly, reminding me with each twinge I'd departed Staal-Ysta far sooner than was wise, in view of the sword thrust I'd taken. The healing was only half done, but I'd departed regardless. There was nothing left for me in Staal-Ysta. Nothing at all, and no one.

Deep in the cairn, flame whipped. Smoke eddied, tangled, shredded on the air. Wind carried it away, bearing word of my presence to the beasts somewhere northeast of me in darkness. The hounds of hoolies, I called them; it fit as well as any other.

I waited for her to speak, even to accuse, but she made no sound at all. Just sat there looking at me, *staring* at me, holding the *jivatma* across wool-trousered thighs. The blade was naked in the darkness, enscribed with runes I couldn't—wasn't meant to—read, speaking of blood and forbidden power too strong for anyone else to key, or to control, with flesh, will, voice.

Del could control it. It was part of her personal magic; the trappings of a sword-singer.

Sword-*singer.* More than sword-dancer, my own personal trade. Something that made her different. That made her *alien.*

Whose name was Boreal.

"Hoolies," I muttered aloud in disgust, and raised the leather bota yet again to squirt Northern *amnit* deep into my throat. I sucked it down, gulp after gulp, pleased by the burning in my belly and the blurring of my senses. And waited for her to say something about drink curing nothing. About how a drinking man is nothing more than a puppet to the bota. About how dangerous it is for a sword-dancer, a man who lives by selling sword and skill, to piss away his edge when he pisses liquor in the morning.

But Del said none of those things.

I wiped *amnit* from my mouth with the back of a hand. Glared at her blearily across the guttering fire. "Not my fault," I told her. "Do you think I *wanted* to cut you?" I coughed, spat, drew in breath too deep for the half-healed wound. It brought me up short, sweating, until I could breathe again, so carefully, meticulously measuring in- and exhalations. "Hoolies, bascha—"

But I broke it off, confused, because she wasn't there.

Behind me, the stud dug holes. And he, like me, was alone.

I released all my breath at once, ignoring the clutch of protest from my ribs. The exhalation was accompanied by a string of oaths as violent as I could make them in an attempt to overcome the uprush of black despair far worse than any I'd ever known.

I dropped the bota and rose, turning my back on the cairn.

Went to the stud, so restless, checking rope and knots. He snorted, rubbed a hard head against me, ignored my grunt of pain, seeking release much as I did. The darkness painted him black; by day he is bay: small, compact, strong, born to the Southron desert.

"I know," I said, "I know. We shouldn't even be here." He nibbled at a cloak brooch: garnet set in gold. I pushed his head away to keep curious teeth from wandering to my face. "We should go home, old son. Just head south and go home. Forget all about the cold and the wind and the snow. Forget all about those hounds."

One day he *would* forget; horses don't think like men. They don't remember much, except what they've been taught. Back home again in the South, in the desert called the Punja, he would recall only the grit of sand beneath his hooves and the beating heat of the day. He'd forget the cold and the wind and the snow. He'd forget the hounds. He'd even forget Del.

Hoolies, I wish *I* could. Her and the look on her face as I'd thrust home the steel in her flesh.

I was shaking. Abruptly I turned from the stud and went back to the cairn. Leaned down, caught up the sheath and harness, closed my fist around the hilt. In my hand the cold metal warmed at once, sweet and seductive; gritting teeth, I yanked the blade free of sheath and bared it in firelight, letting flame set steel to glowing. It ran down the blade like water, pausing only briefly to pool in the runes I now knew as well as I knew my name.

I was shaking. With great care, I took the sword with me to one of the massive piles of broken boulders, found a promising fissure, wedged the blade into it. Tested the seating: good. Then locked both hands around the hilt, meaning to snap it in two. Once and for all, to break it, for what it had done to Del.

Samiel sang to me. A small, private song.

He was hungry, still so hungry, with a thirst that knew no bounds. If I broke him, I would kill him. Was I willing to run that risk?

I tightened my hands on the hilt. Gritted teeth—shut my eyes—

And slid the blade, ringing, very carefully out of the fissure.

I turned. Sat. Slumped, leaning against the boulders. Cradling the deadly *jivatma;* the one I had made my own.

I rested my temple against the pommel of the twisted-silk hilt. It was cool and soothing, as if it sensed my anguish.

"I must be getting old," I muttered. "Old—and tired. What am I now—thirty-four? Thirty-five?" I stuck out a hand and, one by one, folded thumb and fingers absently. "Let's see . . . the Salset found me when I was half a day old . . . kept me for—sixteen years? Seventeen? Hoolies, who can be sure?" I scowled into distance. "Hard to keep track of years when you don't even have a name." I chewed my lip, thinking. "Say, sixteen years with the Salset. Easiest. Seven years as an apprentice to my shodo, learning the sword . . . and thirteen years since then, as a professional sword-dancer." The shock was cold water. "I could be thirty-*six!*"

I peered the length of my body, even slumped as I was. Under all the wool I couldn't see anything, but I knew what was there. Long, powerful legs, but also aching knees. They hurt when I walked too much, hurt after a sword-dance. Hurt when I rode too long, all thanks to the Northern cold. I didn't heal as fast as the old days, and I felt the leftover aches longer.

Was I getting soft around the middle?

I pressed a stiff hand against my belly.

Not so you could tell, though the wound had sucked weight and tone. And then there was the wound itself: bad, yes, and enough to put anyone down for a couple of weeks, but I'd been down for nearly a month and *still* was only half-healed.

I scratched the bearded cheek riven by scars. Old, now; ancient. Four curving lines graven deeply into flesh. For months in the beginning they'd been livid purple, hideous reminders of the cat who had nearly killed me, but I hadn't minded at all. Not even when people stared. Certainly not when women fussed, worried about the cause. Because the scars had been the coinage that bought my freedom from the Salset. I'd killed a marauding sandtiger who was eating all the children. No more the nameless chula. A man, now, instead, who named himself the Sandtiger in celebration of his freedom.

So long ago. Now the scars were white. But the memories were still livid.

So many years alone, until Del strode into my life and made a mockery of it.

I scratched the scars again. Bearded. Long-haired. Unkempt. Dressed in wool instead of silk, to ward off Northern wind. So the aches wouldn't hurt so much.

The sword, in my hands, warmed against my flesh, eerily seductive. The blade bled light and runes. Also the promise of power; it flowed up from tip to quillons, then took the twisted-silk grip as well. Touched my fingers, oh so gently, lingering at my palm. Soft and sweet as a woman's touch: as Del's, even Del's, who was woman enough to be soft and sweet when the mood suited her, knowing it something other than weakness. An honest woman, Delilah; in bed and in the circle.

I flung the sword across the cairn into the darkness. Saw the flash of light, the arc; heard the dull ringing thump as it landed on wind-frosted turf.

"I wish you to hoolies," I told it. "I want no part of you."

And in the dark distances far beyond the blade, one of the beasts bayed.

Part 1

Chapter 1

Only fools make promises. So I guess you can call me a fool.

At the time, it had seemed like a good idea. The hounds that dogged Del and me to Staal-Ysta, high in Northern mountains, were vicious, magic-made beasts, set upon our trail by an unknown agency. For weeks they merely stayed with us, doing nothing other than playing dogs to sheep, herding us farther north. Once there, they'd done much more; they attacked a settlement on the lakeshore, killing more than thirty people. Some of them were children.

Now, I'm no hero. I'm a sword-dancer, a man who sells his sword and services to the highest bidder. Not really a glorious occupation when you think about it; it's a tough, demanding job not every man is suited for. (Some may think they are. The circle makes the decision.) But it's a job that often needs doing, and I'm very good at it.

But it doesn't make me a hero.

Men, I figure, are pretty good at taking care of themselves. Women, too, unless they stick their pretty noses into the middle of something that doesn't concern them; more often than not it doesn't, and they do. But children, on the other hand, don't deserve cruelty. What they deserve is time, so they can grow up enough to make their own decisions about whether to live or die. The hounds had stolen that time from too many settlement children.

I owed nothing to Staal-Ysta, Place of Swords, which had, thanks to Del, tried to steal a year of my life in the guise of honorable service. I owed nothing to the settlement on the lakeshore, except thanks for tending the stud. But no one owed *me* anything, either, and some had died for me.

Besides, my time on the island was done. I was more than ready to leave, even with a wound only halfway healed.

No one protested. They were as willing to see me go as I was to depart. They even gave me gifts: clothing, a little jewelry, money. The only problem was I still needed a sword.

To a Northerner, trained in Staal-Ysta, a *jivatma*—a blooding-blade—is a sacred thing. A sword, but one forged of old magic and monstrous strength of will. There are rituals in the Making, and countless appeals to gods; being Southron, and apostate, I revered none of them. And yet it didn't seem to matter that I held none of the rituals sacred, or disbelieved (mostly) in Northern magic. The swordsmith had fashioned a blade for me, invoking the rituals, and Samiel was mine.

But he didn't—quite—live. Not as the others lived. Not as Del's Boreal.

To a Northerner, he was only half-born, because I hadn't properly keyed him, hadn't *sung* to forge the control I needed in order to wield the power promised by the blessing, by the rituals so closely followed. But then, clean, well-made steel is deadly enough on its own. I thought Northern magic redundant.

And yet some of it existed. I felt it living in the steel each time I unsheathed the weapon. Tasting Del's blood had roused the beast in the blade, just as her blade, free of the sheath, had roused the trailing hounds.

I did not leave the sword lying in dirt and turf throughout the night. Old habits are hard to break; much as I hated the thing, I knew better than to ignore it. So I fetched it, felt the ice replaced with warmth, shoved it home in its sheath. I slept poorly, when at all, wondering what the hounds would do once I caught up to them, and if I'd be called on to use the sword. It was the last thing I wanted to do, after what Del and others had told me.

She had said it so plainly, trying to make me see: *"If you go out there tomorrow and kill a squirrel, that is a true blooding, and your sword will take on whatever habits that squirrel possesses."*

It had, at that moment, amused me; a blade with the heart of a squirrel? But my laughter had not amused her, because she knew what it could mean. Then, I hadn't believed her. Now, I knew much better.

In the darkness, in my bedding, I stared bitterly at the sword. "You're gone," I told it plainly, "the moment I find another."

Unspoken were the words: "*Before* I have to use you."

A man may hate his magic, but takes no chances with it.

The stud had his greeting ready as I prepared to saddle him. First he sidled aside, stepping neatly out from under the saddle, then shook his head violently and slapped me with his tail. Horsehair, lashed hard, stings; it caught me in an eye, which teared immediately, and gave me cause to apply every epithet I could think of to the stud, who was patently unimpressed. He flicked ears, rolled eyes, pawed holes in turf. Threatened with tail again.

"I'll cut it off," I promised. "As far as that goes, maybe I'll cut more than your *tail* off . . . it might be the making of you."

He eyed me askance, blowing, then lifted his head sharply. Ears cut the air like blades. He quivered from head to toe.

"Mare?" I asked wryly.

But he was silent except for his breathing. A stallion, scenting a mare, usually sings a song loud enough to wake even the dead. He'd do the same for another stallion, only the noise would be a challenge. This was something different.

I saddled him quickly, while he was distracted, untied and mounted before he could protest. Because of his alarm I nearly drew the sword, but thought better of it. Better to let the stud run than to count on an alien sword; the stud at least I could trust.

"All right, old man, we'll go."

He was rigid but quivering, breathing heavily. I urged him with rein, heels, and clicking tongue to vacate the clearing, but he was having none of it.

It was not, I thought, the beasts I'd christened hounds. The stink of them was gone; had been ever since I'd left Staal-Ysta.

Something else, then, and close, but nothing I could name. I'm not a horse-speaker, but I know a little of equine habits; enough to discard humans or other horses as the cause of the stud's distress. Wolves, maybe? Maybe. One had gone for him before, though he hadn't reacted like this.

"*Now,*" I suggested mildly, planting booted heels.

He twitched, quivered, sashayed sideways, snorted. But at least he was moving; insisting, I aimed him eastward. He skittered out of the clearing and plunged through sparse trees, splattering slush and mud. Breathing like a bellows through nostrils opened wide.

It was an uneasy peace. The stud was twitchy, jumping at shapes and shadows without justification. Most times, he is a joy, built to go on forever without excess commentary. But when he gets a bug up his rump he is a pain in *mine*, and his behavior deteriorates into something akin to war.

Generally, the best thing to do is ride it out. The stud has been a trustworthy companion for nearly eight years, and worth more than many men. But his actions now jarred the half-healed wound, putting me decidedly out of sorts. I am big but not heavy-handed; he had no complaints of his mouth. But there were times he tempted me, and this was one of them.

I bunched reins, took a deeper seat, and slammed heels home. He jumped in surprise, snorting, then bent his head around to slew a startled eye at me.

"That's right," I agreed sweetly. "Are you forgetting who's boss?"

Which brought back, unexpectedly, something I'd heard before; something someone had said regarding the stud and me. A horse-speaker, a Northerner: Garrod. He'd said too much of our relationship was taken up in eternal battling over which of us was master.

Well, so it was. But I hate a predictable life.

The stud swished his tail noisily, shook his head hard enough to clatter brasses hanging from his headstall, then fell out of his stiff-legged, rump-jarring gait into a considerably more comfortable long-walk.

Tension eased, pain bled away; I allowed myself a sigh. "Not so hard, is it?"

The stud chose not to answer.

East, and a little north. Toward Ysaa-den, a settlement cradled high in jagged mountains, near the borderlands. It was from Ysaa-den that reports of beast-caused deaths had been brought to Staal-Ysta, to the *voca*, who had the duty to send sword-dancers when Northerners were in need.

Others had wanted the duty. But I, with my shiny new Northern title, outranked those who requested the duty. And so it was given to me. To the Southron sword-dancer who was now also a *kaidin*, having earned the rank in formal challenge.

I tracked the hounds by spoor, though with slush dwindling daily there was little left to find. Prints in drying mud were clear, but snowmell shifted still-damp mud and carried the tracks away. I rode with my head cocked sideways, watching for alterations, but what I saw was clear enough: the beasts cut the countryside diagonally northeast with no thought to their backtrail, or anything set on it. Ysaa-den was their target as much as Del had been.

We had come down from above the timberline, now skirting the hem of upland forests, slipping down from bare-flanked peaks. Uplands, downlands; all terms unfamiliar to me, desert-born and bred, until Del had brought me north. Only two months before; it seemed much longer to me. Years, maybe longer. Too long for either of us.

The turf remained winter-brown and would, I thought, for a while. Spring in the uplands was soft in coming, tentative at best. I knew it could still withdraw its favor, coyly turning its back to give me snow in place of warmth. It had happened once before, all of a week ago, when a storm had rendered the world white again and my life a misery.

The trees were still bare of leaves, except for those with spiky green needles. The sky between them was blue, a brighter, richer blue, promising warmer weather. Beyond lay jagged mountains scraping color out of the sky. Pieces of the peaks lay tumbled on the ground, rounded by time into boulders scattered loosely here and there, or heaped into giant cairns like piles of oracle bones. Chips and rubble fouled the track, making it hard to read. The stud picked his way noisily, hammering iron on stone. Stone, as always, gave.

In the South, spring is different. Warmer, certainly. Quicker with its favors. But much too short for comfort; in weeks it would be summer, with the Punja set to blazing beneath the livid eye of the sun. It was enough to burn a man black; me, it baked copper-brown.

I lifted a hand and looked at it. My right hand, palm down. Wide across the palm, with long, strong fingers; creased and ridged with sinew. Knuckles were enlarged; two of them badly scarred. The thumbnail was spatulate, corroded by weeks in a goldmine when I'd been chained to a wall. In places I could see bits of ore trapped in flesh; my days in the North had bleached some of the color out, but beneath it I was still darker than a Northern-born man or woman. Sunburned skin, bronze-brown hair, eyes green in place of blue. Alien to the North, just as Del had been to me.

Ah, yes, Delilah: alien to us all.

Men are fools when it comes to women. It doesn't matter how smart you are, or how shrewd, or how much experience you've had. They're all born knowing just what it takes to find a way to muddle up your head. And given the chance, they do.

I've known men who bed only whores, wanting to make no better commitment, saying it's the best way to avoid entanglements. I've known men who marry women so as not to buy the bedding. And I've known men who do both: bed whores and wives; sometimes, with the latter, their own.

I've even known men who swear off women altogether, out of zeal for religious purity or desire for other men; neither appeals to me, but I'll curse no man for it. And certainly, in the South, I've known men who have no choice in the matter of bedding women, having been castrated to serve tanzeers or anyone else who buys them.

But I've known no man who, drunk or sober, will not, at least once, curse a woman, for sins real or imagined. *A* woman; or even women.

With me, it was singular.

But it wasn't Del I cursed. It was me, for being a fool.

It was me, for proving once and for all which of us was better.

Bittersweet victory. Freedom bought with blood.

* * *

The stud stiffened, snorted noisily, then stopped dead in his tracks.

I saw movement in the trees, coming down from tumbled gray rocks. Nothing more, just movement; something flowing through oracle throws made of stone instead of bone. I caught whipping tail, fixed eyes, teeth bared in a snarl. Heard the wail of something hunting.

Too late the stud tried to run. By then the cat was on him.

It took us down, both of us. It sprang, landed, sprawled, throwing the stud over. I felt him buckle and break, felt him topple. I had time only to draw my left leg up, out of the way; he'd trap it, landing on it. Maybe even break it.

I rolled painfully as the stud went down. Grunted, then caught my breath sharply as my abdomen protested. And ignored it, thinking of the stud.

I came up scrambling, swearing at the cat. A big, heavy-fleshed male. White, splotched with ash, like a man come down with pox.

I picked up a rock and threw it.

It struck a flank, bounced off. The cat barely growled.

Another rock, another strike. This time I shouted at it.

Teeth sank into horseflesh. The stud raked turf with forelegs, screaming in pain and terror.

My hand closed around the hilt. "Oh, hoolies, bascha—not a squirrel, a *cat*—"

And the sword was alive in my hands.

Chapter 2

Hungry. It was *hungry.*

And so very thirsty.

I had felt it before, in the sword. Felt *them* before: hunger and thirst both, with equal dominance. Nearly inseparable, indivisible from one another.

Felt them before, in the circle. When I'd run the sword through Del.

Oh, hoolies, bascha.

No. Don't think about Del.

Hot. It was *hot*—

Better than thinking of Del.

Was it?

Hot as hoolies, I swear.

Sweat broke from pores and ran down forehead, armpits, belly. Beneath hair and wool, it itched.

The cat. Think of the cat.

Hoolies, it is *hot*—

And the sword is so very thirsty.

Oh, bascha, help me.

No—Del isn't here.

Think of the cat, you fool.

Think only of the *cat*—

The sword is warm in my hands. All I can think of is thirst, and the need to quench it with blood.

Sweating, still sweating—

Oh, hoolies, why me?

Thrice-cursed son of a Salset goat—

Watch the cat, you fool!

In my head I hear a song.

Can the cat hear it, too?

Hoolies, it sees me now. Sees the sword. Knows what I want. Turns from the stud—poor stud—to me . . .

Oh, hoolies, here it comes—lift the sword, you fool . . . *do something*, sword-dancer—

But I don't want this sword. And this isn't a real circle—

Real enough, Punja-mite. Are you ready for the cat?

Am I ready for the *sword?*

It has happened before, the slowing. The near stoppage of motion in everything I look at, as if it waits for me. It happened now, as before, though this time the slowing was nearly a true *halt,* clean and pure, leaving me time and room to work, to pick and choose my method; to give the best death to the cat before he gave it to me.

It has happened to me before. But never quite like this.

I smelled blood, musk, extremity, as well as morbid fear. Felt nerves twinge in my belly as the half-healed wound contracted. I wondered, swiftly and uneasily, what the sword was doing. But as I heard the stud's screaming, fear bled away.

Slowly, oh so slowly, the cat looked up from the stud. There was blood in his mouth, blood in his claws, as well as gobbets of horsehair.

In my head, I heard a song. A small, private song, hinting at powerful things.

Beneath the cat, the stud was thrashing, legs flailing. I heard his grunts of extremity.

And the sword sang me a promise: the stud would be released if I gave it the power it needed.

Except I ought to be able to take the cat without using any

magic. The sword was, after all, a *sword,* and effective enough on its own.

But the stud squealed and thrashed, and in my head I heard the song. A soft, subtle song. Yet too powerful to ignore.

I didn't exactly give in to it. I just ignored it. I was too worried about the stud to waste any more time on the noise rolling around in my head. And so, impatiently, I let go of it altogether.

Not for long. Just long enough to think about something else. To stop suppressing it. To rescue my poor horse.

And so, all unwittingly, I let it have its moment. I let it have its lifetime in the shadow of an instant.

Noise rushed in even as I rushed the cat. No, not noise: *music.* Something far more eloquent than anything so commonplace as noise. More powerful than sound. And abruptly I recalled what I had heard on the overlook by the lakeshore, kneeling with the sword. When the music of the Cantéada had crowded into my skull.

How they could sing, the Cantéada. A race born of dreams, given substance by belief. Who had, Del told me once, given music to the world.

Just as they'd given *me* some for the moment of the Naming.

For the stud, I thought, it's worth it. The risk is worth the taking for all the times he's saved *my* skin.

Only the thought, for a moment. And a moment was all that was needed.

The cat flowed aside. The stud lurched up, staggered, ran.

The mouth curled back and opened to display impressive fangs. But slowly, oh so slowly; didn't he know I sang his death?

White cat with gray-irised eyes, and dappled, silver-splotched coat. The pelt would be worth a fortune; I'd take it once he was dead.

—*the sword was alive in my hands*—

"What's mine is mine," I told him, so he would understand.

The sword was *alive.*

The cat peeled back lips and screamed.

The sword invited him in. *Come closer,* it said. *Come closer.*

It made it all so *easy.*

The leap was effortlessly smooth. Smiling, I watched it, admiring his grace. Watched the hind legs coil up to rake; saw the front paws reach out, claws unsheathed; saw the mouth stretch open, the gleam of ivory fangs. Laughing aloud in anticipation, I let him think he'd win.

Then took him in the back of his throat and drove the blade through the base of his skull.

Elation. *Elation*. And a powerful satisfaction.

Not mine. Not *mine;* someone else's. *Something* else's—wasn't it? It wasn't me, was it?

Something inside me laughed. Something inside me *stirred*, like awareness awakening.

Oh, hoolies, what is it?

I smelled burning flesh. Thought it was the cat's. Realized it was my own.

I shouted something. Something appropriate. Something *explicit*. To release shock and rage and pain.

Wrenched my hands from the hilt as the metal burned white-hot.

Oh, hoolies, Del, you never warned me about *this*.

I staggered back, hands crossed at the wrists, mouthing obscenities. Tripped, fell, rolled, sprawled flat on my back, afraid to block with my hands. Hoolies, but they hurt!

I smelled burning flesh. Not my own, the cat's.

Well, that's something, at least. Except he's too dead to feel it.

I lay on my back, still swearing, letting the stream of obscenities take precedence over pain. Anything was welcome, so long as it blocked the fire.

Finally I ran out of breath, if not out of pain, and opened my eyes to look at my hands. It was easy to see them; they were stuck up in the air on the end of painfully rigid arms, elbows planted in the ground.

Hands. Not charred remains. *Hands*. With a thumb and four fingers on each.

Sweat dried on my body. Pain sloughed away. I breathed again normally and decided to stop swearing; there seemed no point in it, now.

Still on my back, I wiggled fingers carefully. Gritted teeth, squinting—and was immensely relieved to discover the flesh remained whole and the bones decently clad. No blisters. No weeping underskin, only normal, everyday hands, though the scars and enlarged knuckles remained. *My* hands, then, not some magical replacements.

I felt better. Sat up slowly, wincing at the protest in my abdomen, and wiggled fingers and thumbs yet again, just to be sure. No pain. No stiffness. Normal flexibility, as if nothing had ever happened.

Scowling, I peered at the sword. "What in hoolies are you?"

In my mind was a word: *jivatma.*

Oh, hoolies, bascha . . . what do I do now?

What I did was get up. Everything appeared to be in working order, if a trifle stiff. Through wool I massaged the sore scar below my short ribs, then forgot it immediately; the cat was worth more attention. The cat—and the sword.

I went over to both. I'd stuck the cat pretty good: through his open mouth and on through the back of his skull. He lay sprawled on his side, but the hilt, thrust into dirt, propped up his head so it was level with the ground.

Two sockets stared up at me. The eyes in them had melted.

For longer than I care to remember, I couldn't look away. Couldn't even move. All I could do was stare, remembering the heat of the hilt. I'd begun to believe it imagined; now I knew better.

Swords don't melt eyes. Nor do they singe whiskers or char lips into a rictus. Swords slice, thrust, cut open; on occasion they will hack, if the swordsman has no skill. But never do they *melt* things.

Something inside me whispered: *Maybe jivatmas do.*

I looked again at my hands. Still whole. Grimy and callused, but whole.

Only the cat had burned.

Well, parts of him. The parts the sword had touched.

Empty eyesockets were black. I realized there was no blood; the sword had swallowed it all.

Oh, hoolies, bascha, I've done what I swore I wouldn't.

In the distance, beasts bayed. Like a pack of hounds, they belled. As they had for Boreal whenever Del had keyed.

And in answer, the stud snorted.

Stud—

I left the cat and the sword and went at once to the stud. He hadn't gone far, just far enough to put distance between himself and the cat, and now he waited quietly, sweat running down flanks and shoulders.

Sweat mixed with blood.

"Oh, hoolies," I said aloud, "he got you good, didn't he?"

The stud nosed me as I came up to him. Grimly I peeled ragged dark mane off his withers—down South, we crop manes short; up North, they leave them long—and saw the cat had dug in pretty deep across brown withers, though the saddle had helped protect the stud a little. I found teeth and claw marks, carving gouges in his hide. There were more claw marks low on the stud's right shoulder from the cat's hind legs, and a few others here and there. All in all, the stud was lucky; the cat had been distracted, by me or the sword. I've seen half-grown sandtigers, in the Punja, take down larger horses much as this cat had done. But they finished the job more quickly by tearing open the jugular.

Then again, I—or the sword—hadn't given the cat the chance to finish the job properly.

Something like fear pinched deep in my belly. But I ignored it with effort, purposefully turning my attention to the stud. "Well, old man," I consoled him, "looks like we'll make a pair. You match my cheek, now—maybe I should name you Snowcat. To go with the Sandtiger."

The stud snorted messily.

"Maybe not," I agreed.

The death-stink of the cat—and the smell of burned flesh—made the stud uneasy, so I tied him to the nearest tree and unsaddled him there, taking weight off his sore hide. I knew I'd do no more riding for a day or two, so I set up camp.

When a horse is the only thing between you and a long walk—or death—a man learns to value his mount, and the stud's health and safety came first. If it slowed us down, too bad; the hounds, I knew, would wait, and the South wasn't going anywhere. So I picked up the remaining bota of *amnit*. I didn't dare risk infection; liquor leaches well enough.

I paused to pat the stud gently, and to check the strength of rope and knot. "Easy, old man. I won't lie—this'll hurt. Just don't take it out on me."

I aimed carefully and squirted, hitting every stripe and bite I could see. Ruthless, maybe, but sponging each wound gently would clean out only one, because the stud wouldn't let me near enough to do any more once he'd felt the bite of the *amnit*. At least this way I got almost all of them at once.

Squealing, he bunched himself and kicked. A horse—especially a stallion—cutting loose with both hind hooves is a dangerous, deadly creature capable of murder. Prudently I moved another pace away, just to be sure, and grinned as he slewed an angry eye around to find me. Once found, he tried a scooping sideways kick with a single hind hoof, hoping to catch me on the sly. When that one missed, he pawed testily, digging craters in the turf.

"You dig a hole, you stand in it," I told him. "I know you're mad—I'd be, too—but it's better than dying, you know. So just stand there like a quiet old ladies' mare and think about what you'd be facing if I didn't have this stuff." I paused, checking the contents. "Good waste of liquor, if you ask me. Might as well drink the rest."

The stud blinked a baleful eye.

I relented. "Tell you what, old son—I'll give you extra grain. That ought to make you feel better."

I dug into one of the pouches and pulled out a fistful of grain, moving within striking range to offer it. But the stud wasn't hungry. He lipped listlessly at the grain, spilling most of it between slack lips. He didn't even want sweetgrass, which was beginning to show signs of life now that most of the snow was going.

Something pinched again inside my belly. "Better not sicken on me," I warned, "after all that *amnit* I wasted." While thinking instead of the sword.

But the stud made no answer.

It came swift and clear and sharp: *If he up and dies on me—*

No. I cut it off. No sense in borrowing grief.

The stud shifted restlessly, knocking stone against stone. I didn't want to leave him just yet, so I leaned against his tree and squirted *amnit* into my throat.

"You've just been out of the South too long, old man . . . like me. *Just* like me; you're a sandtiger dragged out of his desert, swallowing snow instead of sand . . . best get yourself right back home before the cold stiffens all your joints."

Well, it already had stiffened some of mine. In the North, bones age faster. In the South, skin does.

Which means, I guess, I'm growing old inside *and* out.

Gack. What a thought.

I moved off the tree and rubbed a hand down the stud's backbone, smoothing coarse, thick hair. He quivered, expecting *amnit;* I soothed him with a few words. Over his rump I stared at the cat with its alien steel tongue.

I recalled the emotions I'd felt. The *need* to quench the sword; how it had sung its private song. How I, too easily seduced in my moment of fear for the stud, had turned my back on self-made wards and let the song commence. Giving the blade its freedom.

For the stud.

Worth it? Maybe. For that moment. For that *particular* moment.

But what was I to do now? I didn't need it. I didn't *want* it. Not now. Not ever. I'd tasted too much of its power.

"Leave it," I said aloud. "You can get another sword."

Well, so I could. Somewhere. Someday. Meanwhile, I needed a weapon.

"Leave it," I repeated.

Hoolies, I wish I could.

Chapter 3

A *small, soft song. A private, intimate song. Powerful in its prom-*
ise, weakened by neglect.

Deep in sleep, I muttered.

A small, sad song; a trace of desire only hinted at, too shy to speak of
need.

Memories of both.

The stud, stirring, woke me. I sat up, stared hard into darkness,
oriented myself. Got up and went to the stud, who pawed listlessly
at turf.

His head drooped, hanging heavily on the end of a slackened
neck. He shifted from hoof to hoof. When I touched him, he barely
took note.

I was, abruptly, afraid.

Singlestroke and this horse were all I'd ever had. And Singlestroke was gone.

A small, soft, seductive song, promising me companionship such as no
one had ever known.

Companionship—and *power.*

Beneath my hand, he stiffened. I felt the tension in his body;
heard it in his rattling snort, in the crunching of gravel beneath shod
hooves. His ears lanced erect, then slapped back against his head.

"Hey—" But abruptly I shut it off.

I hadn't felt it for weeks. At first it was so alien I didn't recognize it, and then the strangeness slid away and familiarity took its place. A man doesn't forget what it's like to be sick.

Not *sick* sick. I've been that before, from wound fever or the Northern malady called a "cold." And not sick from too much liquor; I've been that, too, more often than I care to recall. No. This sickness wasn't of the body but of the soul, all wrapped up like a nameday gift in a sash called fear.

And even that was different.

All the hair stood up on my arms. Tickled the back of my neck. Tightened scalp against skull. I shivered involuntarily, cursing myself for a fool, then felt nausea knot my belly.

Don't ask me what it is. Del called it an affinity for magic. Kem, the sword-maker, said I was sensitive to the *essence* of it, whatever that means. All I know is it makes me sick and uncomfortable, and very sour in my outlook. Being a conspicuously lighthearted, good-humored soul—or at least one lacking in personal demons—I don't much like having my sensibilities mangled by something as dark and erratic as magic.

If it just didn't make me feel *sick.*

Maybe it was the cat. I'd eaten too much cat. Too much Northern cat stuffed into a Southroner's belly.

But the stud hadn't had any, and he wasn't happy, either.

Or, more likely, the sword. Trust it to make my life miserable in more ways than one.

Then again—

"Ah, hoolies," I muttered, as I smelled the stink of the hounds.

I'd forgotten what it was to be up close, to see white eyes ashine in the darkness. To smell their stink. To sense the press of numbers crowding so close to me.

I had played tracker. Now they hunted me.

The stud knew the stench, too. He, like me, had killed, smashing furred bodies beneath cold Southron iron, but liked it no better than I. We weren't made for magic, either of us, being bred only to travel the sands beneath a Southron sun. *Without* benefit of magic.

The sword lay sheathed by the fire, set beside my bedding. It was, I thought grimly, a mark of decay in habits that I had left my weapon to go to the stud. It displayed an unaccustomed trend toward worrying, which has never been my vice, as well as pointing up my distinct dislike for the Northern sword. I mean, it *was* a sword, like it or not; it could save my life even if I disliked it. But at the moment it couldn't do anything, because I'd left it behind. All I had was a knife, and no horse to use for escape. Or attack, if it came to that; I'd have to do it on foot.

White eyes shone bright in darkness. In silence the hounds gathered, wearing shadows in place of clothes. Black and gray on gray and black; I couldn't count their numbers.

It crossed my mind that maybe the stud could be ridden after all, pain or no pain. Not far, not far enough to injure him, just far *enough*; enough to leave beasts behind.

But retreat wasn't what I'd come for. It wasn't the promise I'd made.

I sucked in a guts-deep breath. "Come on," I said, "try me."

Sheer bravado, maybe. Nothing more than noise. But it's always worth a try, because sometimes it will work.

*Some*times.

They crept out of the shadows into the red-gray glow of dying coals. Maned, gray, dappled beasts: part dog, part wolf, part nightmare. Without a shred of beauty, or a trace of independence. What they did was at someone's bidding, not a decision of their own.

The stud shifted uneasily. He stamped, breaking stone.

"Try me," I repeated. "Have I come too close to the lair?"

They came all at once, like a wave of slushy water. In spate, they swallowed the campsite, then ebbed back toward the trees.

But the tide had taken the sword.

Gaping in disbelief, I saw the glint of the pommel, a flash of moonlight off the hilt. Saw teeth close on the sheath and shed it, leaving it behind; apparently the warding magic inherent in a named blade made no difference to equally magical beasts.

Which made me wonder why it existed at all, if it was useless against the hounds.

Two of them mouthed the sword awkwardly. One held the hilt, the other the blade, busily growling at one another like two dogs fighting over a stick. But this stick was made of steel. Magicked, gods-blessed steel.

The others surrounded them like a tanzeer's phalanx of guards. They headed for the trees, for the shadows I couldn't pierce.

Hoolies, they wanted the *sword*.

So much for my own value.

I very nearly laughed. If they wanted the thrice-cursed thing *that* much, let them have it. I didn't want it. It was one way of getting rid of it.

Except I knew better than that. The beasts could never use it, but the man who made them could. And that I couldn't risk, since he was the one I sought.

Very calmly I drew the ward-whistle from beneath my woolen tunic and stuck it between my lips. Such a tiny, inconsequential geegaw, but made by beings I still had trouble believing in, even though I'd seen—and heard—them myself. Cantéada. I recalled their silvery skin, feathery scalp crests, nimble fingers and froglike throats. And I recalled their music.

Music was in the whistle, as was power. And so I waited a moment, to build up false hopes, then blew an inaudible blast.

It did its job, as always. They dropped the sword and fled.

Grinning around the whistle, I went over and picked up the blade.

And wished I hadn't touched it.

Shame flooded me. Shame and anger and grief, that I had treated the sword so poorly when it was deserving of so much better. What had it done to me?

In disbelief, I spat out the whistle. *I* hadn't thought those thoughts. And wouldn't; of that I was certain. But the thoughts had come from somewhere. The *feelings* had come from somewhere.

I threw the sword down again. It thumped dully against turf, glinting red-white in coals and moonlight. "Look, you," I said, "you may not be like any sword I've ever known, but it doesn't give you the right to tell me what to think. It doesn't give you the right to make me feel guilty, or ashamed, or angry—or *anything*, hear me? Magic, schmagic—I want nothing to do with you and nothing will ever change that. As far as I'm concerned, the hounds can have you . . . except I'm not about to let you fall into the hands of someone who can tap into whatever power you possess—"

I broke it off abruptly. I realized precisely how stupid I sounded, talking to a sword.

Well, talking to a sword isn't so bad; I think we all do it from time to time, before we step into a circle. But talking to a magicked blade made me most distinctly uneasy; I was afraid it might understand.

I wiped sweaty palms on my clothing. I hadn't imagined the feelings. I hadn't imagined the *shame*.

And, most definitely, I hadn't imagined the power demanding to be unleashed.

Coiling itself so tightly, like a cat before it springs.

In my head, I heard a song. A small, soft song, promising health and wealth and longevity, as if it were a god.

"*Jivatmas* die," I said hoarsely. "I've seen it before, twice. You aren't invincible, and you don't make *us* immortal. Don't promise me what you can't."

Notes wavered, then died away. I bent and scooped up the sword.

In my hands, it burned.

"*Hoolies*—" Flesh fused itself to steel. "Let go!" I shouted. "You thrice-cursed son of a goat—*let go of my hands!*"

Steel clung, caressed, absorbed. I thought again of melted eyes in a blade-riven skull.

"Hoolies take you!" I yelled. "What do you want, my *soul?*"

Or was it trying to *give* one?

—on my knees, now—

—hoolies, oh, hoolies—stuck to a sword . . . oh, hoolies, *stuck* to a sword—

—and for how *long?*

Sweat ran down my body. In the cold night air, I steamed. "No one ever told me—no one ever said—no one *warned* me about this—"

Well, maybe they had. I just didn't listen much.

Sweat stung my eyes. I blinked, ducked my head into a shoulder, rubbed wet hair away. I stank of sweat, old wool and grime, with the acrid tang of fear.

I drew in a ragged breath. "What in hoolies am I—"

Fire lit up the sky.

At least, I *think* it was fire. It was something. Something bright and blinding. Something that damped the moon and the stars with a delicate, lace-edged beauty.

And beauty it was, like nothing I've ever seen. Nothing I've ever dreamed. Kneeling with the sword clutched in my hands—or the sword clutching *me*—I stared, mouth open, and let my head tip back so I could see the glory of Northern lights. The magic of sky-born steel, rune-wrought by the gods, baptised in human blood.

Celebrated by song.

Dancing in the sky was a curtain of luminescence. The colors were muted magnificence, flowing one into the other. They rippled. Dripped. Changed places. Met and melted together, forming other colors. Bright, burning colors, like fire in the sky. The night was alive with it.

In my head I heard a song. A new and powerful song. It wasn't one I knew. It wasn't from my sword, too new to sing like that. From a sword with a little age. From a sword who understood *power*, being cognizant of its own, and how to guard the gift. A sword born of the North, born of ice and snow and storm; of the cold winter wailing of a keen-edged banshee-storm.

A sword who knew my name; whose name I knew as well.

Samiel fell out of my hands. "Hoolies," I croaked, "she's alive."

Chapter 4

I denied it. Immediately. Vehemently. With everything I had; I did not *dare* allow myself to believe it might be true, because hopes hauled up too high have that much farther to fall.

Oh, bascha. *Bascha.*

I denied it. Desperately. All the way down through the darkness, picking my way with care. All the way down through boulders, slipping and skidding on rubble. Through the shadows of looming trees.

Choking on painful certainty: Del is dead. I killed her.

Fire filled the sky. Such clean, vivid colors, rippling like Southron silks. Boreal's doing, no other: steel brush against black sky, with artistry born of magic.

Doubts, like smoke, blew away, leaving me empty of breath.

—*Delilah is alive*—

I stopped walking. Stopping sliding. Stopped cursing myself for a fool. And stood awkwardly, rigidly clutching a tree. Trying to breathe again. Trying to comprehend. Trying to sort out a welter of feelings too complex to decipher.

—*Delilah is alive*—

Sweat bathed me. I leaned against the tree and shut my eyes, shivering, releasing the air I'd finally gulped. Sucking it back in even more loudly. Nearly choking. Ignoring the knot in my belly, the cramping of my guts, the trembling in my hands.

Trying to understand.

Relief. Shock. Amazement. An overwhelming joy. But also compelling guilt and an odd, swelling fear. A deep and abiding despair.

Delilah is alive.

Gods of valhail, help me.

Colors poured out of the sky like layers of ruffled silks: rose, red, violet, emerald, a hint of Southron yellow, traces of amber-gold. The blush of burnished orange. The richness of blue on black and all the shadings in between.

I scrubbed sweat off my face. Took pains to steady my breathing. Then silently followed the brightness down and stepped out of a tree-striped, hollow darkness into frost and fog and rainbow, where a sword held dominance. Alien, rune-wrought steel, naked in Del's bare hands.

Delilah was alive.

She stood as I have seen her stand before, paying homage to the North, or to the sword herself. With legs spread, braced; with arms stretched wide above her head, balancing blade across flattened palms. Three feet of deadly steel, shining whitely in the night; a foot of knotted silver twisted carefully into a hilt. Ornate and yet oddly plain, with a magnificent symmetry. Simplistic in promised power, lethal in promises kept.

All in white, Delilah. Tunic, trews, hair. And the stark, ravaged face, devoid of all save desperation.

Thin fog purled down from the blade. Streamers licked Del's hands, face, clothing, frothed around her ankles, spilled out across the ground. Drops of moisture glistened, reflecting sword-born rainbows. All in white, Delilah; uncompromising white. A blank, stark canvas. Behind her was the night; uncompromising black. But arrayed above us both were the colors of the world, summoned by rune-wrought steel.

White on black, and light. A brilliant, blinding light that made me want to squint.

Ghost, I thought; wraith. A spirit made of shadows, lent light by a playful demon. Nothing more than a fetch, or a trick of imagination. It wasn't really Del. It couldn't *really* be Del.

Gods, let it be Del—

I felt the touch of wind. It blew softly across the clearing, shredding sword-born fog, and gently touched my face. The testing fingers of a blind man; the subtle caress of a lover's touch. A cold, winter wind, bordering on banshee. Letting me taste its strength. Letting me sense its power.

Believe, it told me plainly. *I am born of Boreal, and only one commands her. Only one can summon her power. To key it, and control it. To make me substance out of nothing; to give me life out of proper season.*

Winter was in the clearing. It numbed my ears, my nose; stiffened aging joints. Lifted the hem and folds of my cloak and snapped it away from my body, stripping hair out of my face. Threatening beard with frost-rime and my lungs with frigid breath.

Del sang on. A small, soft song. A song of infinite power.

She had traded her soul for that song. As well as humanity.

I turned my back on her. I turned my back on her power. On winter and on the wind, fixing my eyes on spring. Thinking of things to come, not on what had passed.

Walked out of her light into darkness. Into things I could understand.

Thinking: Del is *alive.*

Which meant I could be angry.

And so I was, when at last she came riding into my camp. Hoolies, six weeks. And all that time: *alive.*

Me thinking her dead.

Me thinking I'd killed her.

All those days and nights.

Delilah is alive.

I squatted by the fire cairn and warmed hands over the coals. I didn't really need to, since Del's sword-summoned winter was banished, but at least it was something to do. It gave me something to look at instead of staring at her.

Oh, I looked. I looked—and swallowed hard. Glanced away again in forced, false negligence, staring blindly at hands that tried repeatedly to tremble; they didn't because I wouldn't let them. It took all the strength I had.

She rode a dark dappled horse; roan, I thought, blue, though in the darkness it was hard to tell. A tall dark-eyed gelding stepping daintily through storm-strewn rubble.

The stud, less concerned with pride and appearances, peeled back his lip and squealed. He'd teach the gelding his place or know the reason why.

Moonbleached hair was white, scraped back from a too-pale face showing keen edges of too-sharp bone. The skull, now strongly visible, was flawless in its beauty, but I preferred more flesh on it. She had lost too much to the circle, and to its aftermath.

The fire was gone from the sky like so much wine spilled from a cup. The blade rode her back in its customary harness, slanting left to right. From the downward curve of ornate quillons to the carefully crafted pommel knot, nearly a foot of shining steel rose beside her head.

Boreal: *jivatma*. A sword-singer's blooding-blade.

With it, she'd killed the man who had taught her how to fight. With mine, I'd nearly killed her.

Delilah is alive.

The stud stomped, pawed, squealed, arching neck and raising tail. I was relieved to see it, because even though, for him, it was muted, the show of dominance nonetheless meant he was feeling better. Maybe I'd worried for naught.

About the stud *and* Del; here she was before me.

With customary prudence, Del reined in her gelding at the edge of the cairn's sphere of meager light. Not far enough to calm the stud, but enough to tell him the gelding offered no threat to his dominance.

Or did she do it to tell me the same?

Hoolies, that was done with. The circle had made its choice.

All in white, Delilah: in the South, the color of mourning; in the North, I didn't know. Belted tunic, baggy trousers. Heavy cloak, free of all adornment, save for the moonwashed silver of fur gaiters cross-gartered around her shins, and brown leather bracers warding most of her forearms. They shone with silver bosses, as did her belt; silver brooches clasped the cloak. Loose hair tumbled over her shoulders.

I thought: *I can't do this.*

And knew somehow I would.

"Well," I said lightly, "what do you offer a wraith?"

"*Amnit,*" she said, "if you have it."

There was nothing in her tone except familiar quietude. No trace of emotion; I hoped mine showed the same.

"Oh, a bota or two." I pulled one up from the ground, let it dangle from my hand. The leather bag twisted on its thong, then unwound in the other direction in a slow, predictable spiral.

She sat silently in her saddle, watching the bota spin. In the poor light her eyes were black. Too black in a too-white face.

Oh, hoolies, bascha. What do we do now?

She watched the bota spin.

Wondering what to say?

No, not Del. She hones words as well as weapons, but uses them less often.

She finally looked at me. "I came because I need you."

Deep in my gut, something spasmed.

Del's voice was steady; she gives little away in speech. "No one will dance with me."

Of course. That. Nothing else, for her. Her needs are different from mine.

The wound ached afresh. I set the bota down, carefully exhaling. "Oh?"

"No one," she repeated. This time I heard it clearly: pain, anguish, grief. In Del, always muted. Nearly always hidden. Often not present at all.

Anger stirred. I suppressed it instantly, idly rubbing a bearded chin. "But you think *I* will."

The gelding stomped. Del sat it out, hands only loosely holding reins across the pommel of her saddle. Her eyes were very steady. "You are the Sandtiger. Southron, not Northern. My dishonor means nothing to you." For only a moment, she paused. "After all, you were the victor."

I made no answer at first, letting the words settle. Victor, was I? In a way; I had won the dance, and therefore won my freedom.

But winning is often losing; the taste of victory, in this case, was decidedly bittersweet.

I stared hard at the glow of the cairn. Coals and color ran together, filling up my eyes. Quietly, I said, "I very nearly died."

Softly, when she could, "I traveled farther than you."

I looked at her sharply. The residue of fireglow overlay her face, hiding expression from me. And then it faded, slowly, and I saw the expression. Saw the determination.

I wanted to laugh. Here we were arguing over which of us had come closer to dying, and each of us responsible for the other's circumstances.

I wanted to laugh. I wanted to cry. And then both emotions spilled away. In their place was anger. "I nearly killed you, Del. I stepped into that circle hoping only to beat you, to *stop* you, and yet I nearly killed you." I shook my head. "It's different now. Nothing can be the same."

"Sameness remains," she countered quietly. "There are still things I must do before my song is sung."

"Like what?" I demanded. "Hunt down Ajani and kill him?"

"Yes," Del answered simply.

Rising so abruptly pulled the new skin around my wound. But it didn't stop me. It didn't stop me at all. I took the shortest route: straight across the fire cairn directly to her gelding, where I reached up and caught Del's left wrist before she could react.

It isn't easy to take Del unaware. She knows me well enough to predict much of what I will do, but not so well as to predict *everything* I will do. And this time, she couldn't.

I heard her blurt of shock as I jerked her down out of the saddle. Heard my grunt of effort mingled with her sound.

It was awkward. It was painful. She is tall and strong and quick, but now weakened by her own wound. She came free in a tangle of stirrups, cloak, harness and sword, arms and legs awry. I knew it would hurt; I *meant* it to hurt. But at least it hurt us both.

She came down hard. The gelding snorted and sidled away, leaving us room as he avoided further hostilities. I grunted again as my half-healed wound protested. Sweat broke out afresh.

Hoolies, this hurts.

But I didn't regret it at all.

The pommel knot of her sword knocked me in the chin, though not hard enough to do damage. Not hard enough to loosen my grip. Not hard enough to stop me as I dumped her on the ground.

Breathing hard, I stood over her, tucking down toward the right a little to ward the wound from more pain. "You stupid, sand-sick, selfish little fool, haven't you learned *anything?*"

Del was sprawled on her back with the sword trapped under her. Instead she went for her knife.

"Uh-uh, bascha—I don't think so." I slammed her wrist down with my foot and put some weight on it. Enough to hold it still. The knife glinted in moonlight but a handspan away. "What—are you going to kill me because I insulted you? Because I called you a fool? Or selfish?" I laughed at her expression. "You *are* a fool, bascha . . . a silly, selfish, sandsick girl feeding off dreams of revenge."

Fair hair slipped free of her throat. I saw fragile flesh move as she swallowed heavily. Tendons stood out tautly.

"*Oh*, no," I said sharply, and bent to snatch her from the ground.

It aborted her efforts entirely, if without any grace. Having felt the results of her brothers' teaching before, I wasn't about to allow her the chance again. I pivoted hips aside and took the kick she meant for my groin on the shin instead, which hurt, but not as much as it might have. Then I filled my hands with cloak, tunic and harness leather and yanked her up from the ground, half-dragging, half-carrying her thirty or forty feet, where I pressed her back against one of the tumbled boulders. I restrained her the only way I knew how, which was with all of my weight. Caught between me and stone, Del had nowhere to go.

No knife. No sword. Now all she had was words.

"You're *scared*," she accused. "Swear at me if you like—call me all the names you can think of, if it makes you feel better. It doesn't change a thing. I see it in your face, in your eyes . . . I feel it in your *hands*. You're scared to death, Tiger. Scared because of me."

It was not what I expected.

"Scared." Less vehemence, but no less certainty. "I know you,

Tiger—you've spent the last six weeks punishing yourself for what you did . . . I *know* you, Tiger—you've spent every day and every night of the past six weeks scared I was dead, and scared I was alive. Because if I was dead, you couldn't live with it—with killing your Northern bascha?" Only once, she shook her head. "Oh, no, not you . . . not the *Sandtiger,* who is not quite the uncaring, unfeeling killer he likes people to think he is. So you prayed—yes *you,* just in case—you prayed I was alive so you wouldn't have to hate yourself, and yet the whole time you've been scared I *was* alive. Because if I was, and we ever came face-to-face again, you'd have to explain why. You'd have to *tell* me why. You'd have to find a way to justify what you did."

I took my weight from her. Turned. Took two disjointed steps away from her. And stopped.

Oh, hoolies, bascha. Why does it always hurt so?

Her voice was unrelenting. "So, Tiger . . . we are face-to-face. There is time now for the explaining, the telling, for the justifying—"

I cut her off curtly. "Is that why you came?"

She sounded a little breathless, if no less definite. "I told you why I came. No one will dance with me. Not in Staal-Ysta, certainly . . . and I think nowhere else, as well. Women are freer in the North than in the South, but few men will dance against a woman, even in practice bouts. And I need it. Badly. I have lost strength, speed, fitness . . . I need you to dance with me. If I am to kill Ajani, I must be strong enough to do it."

I swung, intending to say something, but let it die as I saw how she clung to the boulder. There was no color in her face, none at all, even in her lips. She pressed one arm across her abdomen, as if to hold in her guts. She sagged against the stone.

Oh, hoolies, bascha.

"Don't touch me," she said sharply.

I stopped short of her and waited.

She drew in a noisy breath. "Say you will dance with me."

I spread my hands. "And if I don't, you won't let me touch you—is that it? You won't let me pick you up from the ground—which is where you'll be in a moment—and carry you to the fire, where there's food and *amnit*—"

"Say it," she said, "and we won't have to find out that you *can't* carry me, which would hurt your pride past repairing."

"Del, this is ridiculous—"

"Yes," she agreed. "But we've both been that before."

"If you think I'm going to step into a circle with you after what happened the last time—"

"Just say it!" she cried, and something at last broke. She crossed both arms against her ribs and hugged herself hard, standing only by dint of braced legs and sheer determination. "If I don't go after him—if I don't kill Ajani—if I don't honor my oath . . ." She grimaced, loosened hair hanging, obscuring much of her face but not the ragged tone in her voice. "I have to, I *have* to . . . there is nothing left for me . . . nothing at all left for me . . . no parents, no brothers, no aunts and uncles and cousins . . . not even Kalle is mine—not even my *daughter* is mine—" She sucked in a painful whooping breath. "Ajani is all I have. His death is all I have. It's all the honor that's left."

I wondered briefly who she was talking to: me or to herself? But I let it go, thinking of something else. "There's more to honor than that." I intended to explain thoroughly, but broke it off to catch her as her legs buckled and she slid down the boulder to huddle against cold stone. And discovered she was right: I couldn't pick her up. So the two of us sat there, cursing private pain, hiding it from one another behind sweaty, muttered curses and denials to half-gasped questions.

"Dance with me," she said. "Do you want me to beg?"

I gritted it out through tight-shut teeth. "I don't want you to beg. I don't want you to dance. I don't want you to do anything but heal."

Del curled one hand into a fist and thumped herself weakly in the chest. "It's all I have—it's all I *am* . . . if I don't kill Ajani—"

I turned toward her awkwardly, trying not to twist sore flesh. "We'll talk about that later."

Her voice was startled. "What are you doing?"

"Trying to peel back some of your layers so I can get a look at your wound."

"Leave it," she said, "leave it. It is healing without your help.

Do you think they would have let me go if I was in danger of dying?"

"Yes," I answered bluntly. "Telek and Stigand? And all the rest of the *voca?* Stupid question, bascha . . . I'm surprised they didn't kick you out before this. I'm surprised they didn't kick you out the day *I* left."

"To do that would have dishonored Staal-Ysta," she said faintly. "I was the chosen champion—"

"—who was meant to die in the circle, dancing with me," I finished. "Telek and Stigand threw you to the sandtigers, bascha—no joke intended—and they had no intention of you surviving the dance. Your death would have satisfied the honor of Staal-Ysta, and my victory bought me out of the year you pledged me to. In the South we call it two goat kids for a single breeding . . . it's what the *voca* wanted. You dead and me gone. As it is, we're *both* gone."

"And Kalle stays behind." Her tone was bitter as she twisted away from me and sat up very straight, easing the layers of rucked up wool binding her sore ribs. "So, they got what they wanted. I have lost a daughter, who was perhaps not meant to be mine . . . but there is still her father. And Ajani I will kill."

"Which means we're back where we started." I drew in a deep breath, caught it sharply on a twinge, let it out slowly again. "What I started to say earlier—"

"I did not come for your advice." Del pushed herself up awkwardly, straightened with infinite care, walked very slowly toward the roan.

The abruptness of it stunned me. *"What?"*

She caught the gelding's reins, led him to a tree safely distant from the stud, tied him. "I did not come for advice. Only for your dancing."

So cool and clipped. So much like the old Del, with no time for other's feelings. Full circle, I thought. Back where it all started.

But not quite, bascha. I'm not the same man. Because—or in spite—of you, I'm not the same man.

Chapter 5

I sat on my bedding by the fire cairn, scratching sandtiger scars, drinking *amnit*, thinking. *Thinking; what in hoolies happens now?*

So, she wanted to ride with me. For a while. To dance with me in the circle, until she was fit enough to challenge Ajani. Which meant she'd intended all along to leave me, once she found me. Once she was fit again.

Which meant she was using me.

Well, we all use one another. One way or another.

But Del was using *me*.

Again.

Without, apparently, considering my own feelings. Or else she *had* considered them, and thought I'd be happier without her. Once she was ready to leave.

Or else she was merely concocting a wild tale to cover up the real reason she'd tracked me down, which had less to do with Ajani and more to do with me.

No. Not Del. She's nothing if not determined.

Nothing if not *obsessed*.

Which meant Ajani was still the most important issue, and I was merely a means to make her fit enough to kill him.

Which came back to me being used.

Again.

A little part of me suggested it didn't matter, that having Del around was enough compensation. Because, of course, she would share my bed again, and that ought to be enough to make any man overlook certain things.

Maybe, once, it would've been. But not anymore. I could overlook nothing. Because a bigger part of me didn't like being reduced to a *means*. I deserved better.

And a still larger part reminded me with exquisite clarity that Del hadn't thought twice about offering me as bait to the *voca* on Staal-Ysta to buy a year off her exile.

Well, she might have *thought* twice. But she'd still offered easily enough without even consulting me.

And it rankled. Oh, it rankled.

I sat on my bedding by the cairn, scratching, drinking, staring. Waiting for Delilah.

She puttered with her gelding, unsaddling him, wiping him down, talking softly, settling him for the night. Wasting time? Stalling? Maybe. But probably not; Del knows what she does and why, and spends no time on what-might-have-beens after the fact.

I watched her: white wraith in the cairnglow, white specter against black trees; so white-on-white, Delilah: tunic, trews, hair, except for flashing silver. Bosses on belt and bracers. Two heavy cloak brooches weighting each wool-swathed shoulder.

And the twisted sword hilt, slashed across her back.

Hoolies, what do I do?

Hoolies, what *don't* I do?

Having no answer for either, I sat by the cairn and sucked *amnit*, waiting for Delilah.

Eventually, she came. With arms full of gear and bedding, she came at last toward the cairn. Toward me. And at last I could tell her.

"No," I said calmly.

In mid-step, she hesitated. Then halted altogether. "No?" she echoed blankly, clearly confused. Thinking about something else.

"You asked me to dance with you. Well, I can give it to you in Southron, in Desert, in Northern. Even in uplander." Humorlessly, I smiled. "Which 'no' do you want? Which one will you believe?"

Her face was white as ice. Only her eyes were black.

With exquisite care, I set aside my bota. "Did you think I was so well-trained that I'd lie down and show you my belly so you could feel good again?"

She stood very still, clutching blankets.

I kept my tone even. Perfectly expressionless, so she would know what it was like. "You came fully expecting me to agree. Not to ask, not to request—to *tell.* 'Dance with me, Sandtiger. Step into the circle.'" Slowly I shook my head. "I don't disagree with your reasons for wanting Ajani dead. I understand revenge as well as or better than anyone. But you forfeited your right to expect me to do anything just for the asking. You forfeited the *asking.*"

Del said nothing at all for a very long moment. The meager light from the cairn carved lines into her face, but showed me no expression. No expression at all.

I waited. The circle teaches patience, many kinds of patience. But never have I felt the waiting so intensely. Never have I wanted it to end so badly. And afraid to know the answer, to know how the ending would be.

Her voice was very low. "Do you want me to leave?"

Yes. No. I don't know.

I swallowed painfully. "You were wrong," I told her.

Del clutched bedding.

"Wrong," I repeated softly. "And until you can see it, until you can admit it, I don't think I can help you. I don't *want* to help you."

Breath rushed out of her mouth. With it, her answer. Her explanation. Her *excuse,* for something requiring none because none could be enough. "It was for Kalle—"

"It was for you."

"It was for kin—"

"It was for you."

A painful desperation: "It was for *honor,* Tiger—"

"It was for you, Delilah."

The full name made her flinch. The movement made her wince. Her defenses were coming down: against pain, against truth, against me. The latter, I thought, was what counted. It might yet make her whole.

"Pride," I said, "is powerful. You threw mine away very easily. Will you do the same with your own?"

Her face was slack with shock. "How did I throw away your pride?"

I was on my feet, oblivious to the pain of a wrenched abdomen. Yanking her out of the saddle had taken its toll on us both. "Hoolies, Del, have you forgotten entirely? I was a *slave* for half my life! Not an innocent young Northern girl playing at swords and knives, well-loved by her kin, but a human beast of burden. A chula. A *thing*. Something with no name, no identity, no reason for being alive except to serve others. Except to *service* others—what do you think I did at night in the hyorts with the women?"

I saw the shock in her face, but it hardly slowed me down. "Do you think it was always for pleasure? Do you think it was always merely a man using a woman?" I shook hair out of my eyes. "Let me tell you, Delilah, it isn't always a woman who gets used . . . it isn't always a woman who feels dirty and used and without value other than what she offers in bed. *It isn't always a woman—*"

Oh, hoolies, I hadn't meant to say so much, or so brutally. But I finished it anyway, since it was begging to be said; since it *had* to be said, if we were ever to recover even a trace of the old relationship. Even that of the circle.

I steadied my voice with effort. "I won my freedom—and my name—through desperation and sheer dumb luck, Del, not to mention pain both physical and emotional . . . and yet you were willing to throw it all away again just to buy yourself some time. Is that what I was to you? A means to an end? The coin to buy your daughter? A body to barter away? Is that what I was, Delilah?"

She was strung so taut she twitched. And then, jerkily, she bent. Set down bedding and gear. Shuddered once, deeply, then caught the hilt of her sword in both hands and whipped it out of the sheath.

For a moment, for one incredulous, painful moment, I thought she meant to kill me. That I'd gone too far, though I'd barely gone far enough.

The moment passed. Del cradled Boreal. Vertically, and carefully, pressing blade between breasts. Briefly, oh so briefly, she closed her eyes, murmured something, then slowly, painfully lowered herself to one knee. Then brought down the other.

Del knelt before me in the dirt. She bent, placed Boreal flat on the ground, then crossed her arms across her chest, making fists of her hands. In deep obeisance, she bowed, resting forehead against the blade.

She held herself in perfect stillness for a moment of rigid silence, then raised herself again. Her eyes were black in the cairnglow, empty of all save the knowledge of need. Hers as well as my own.

With frequent checks and taut swallows, she spoke to me in Northern. It was a dialect I didn't know, probably born of Staal-Ysta and precise, required rituals meant to enhance the mystery of the *jivatma.* I've never been much impressed with the trappings of such things, preferring straightforward, unadorned talk, but I made no move to stop her. Clearly she needed it.

Eventually she stopped. Bowed again. Then straightened to look at me, and repeated it all in Southron so I could understand.

Appalled, I cut her off almost immediately. "That's not necessary."

She waited. Swallowed. Began again.

I spat out an oath. "I *said*—"

She raised her voice and overrode me.

"Hoolies, Del, do you think this is what I want? Abasement? Atonement? I'm not asking any such thing, you fool . . . I just want you to understand what it is you did. I just want you to realize—" But I broke it off in disgust because she wasn't listening.

She ran down eventually. All the forms were followed, the requirements satisfied. She was a true daughter of Staal-Ysta, no matter what anyone said; no matter that she was exiled. She completed the ritual.

She bowed over Boreal once again. Then picked up her sword, rose, turned awkwardly from me and walked toward the roan. Stumbling a little. Catching herself with effort. All of her grace was banished, yet none of her dignity.

She had thrown away her pride. Now both of us were even.

Chapter 6

*S*he broke through, thrust, cut into me, just above the wide belt. I felt the brief tickle of cold steel separate fabric and flesh, sliding through both with ease, then catch briefly on a rib, rub by, cut deeper, pricking viscera. There was no pain at all, consumed by shock and ice, and then the cold ran through my bones and ate into every muscle.

Deep in sleep, I twitched.

I lunged backward, running myself off the blade. The wound itself wasn't painful, too numb to interfere, but the storm was inside my body. The blood I bled was ice.

I drew a knee up toward my belly, trying to ward the wound. Trying to turn the blade that had already pierced my flesh.

"Yield!" she shouted. "Yield!" Shock and residual anger made her tone strident.

I wanted to. But I couldn't. Something was in me, in my sword; something crept into blood and bones and sinew and the new, bright steel. Something that spoke of need. That spoke of ways to win. That sang of ways to blood—

I woke up sweating, breathing like a bellows; like the stud run too hard. The fire was reduced to coals with only the moon for light, and it offered little enough. I looked for Del in the darkness. Saw nothing but deeper shadows.

Hoolies, did I dream it? Did I dream the whole thing?

I sat up rigidly and immediately wished I hadn't. Deep inside, I ached. I'd twisted in my sleep and the half-healed wound protested.

My sword was screaming for blood.

Did I dream the whole thing? Or only part of it?

A twig snapped. Movement. Maybe I didn't dream it.

Hoolies, make it real.

I stared into darkness. So hard my eyes burned, trying to define the narrow line between dream and reality.

"I'll make you," she gasped. "Somehow—" And she was coming at me, at me, breaking through my weakened guard and showing me three feet of deadly jivatma. "Yield!" she cried again.

My sword was screaming for blood.

Del was gone. That I was certain of, hating it. Hating myself for the wash of fear, of anguish; the uprush of painful guilt. What I'd said to her needed saying. I didn't regret a word of it. But none of what I'd told her was intended to chase her away.

Only to give her a choice.

Del always makes her own choices, no matter how painful they are. No matter how demanding. She shirks nothing I am aware of, counting the finished task more important than the doing. For my angry, obsessed Delilah, the end was always more important than how it was accomplished.

Which meant she might well have left, since I'd given her my answer.

Had I? I didn't recall refusing to dance with her, so long as she admitted her wrongdoing.

She'd conducted an atonement ritual. Begged my forgiveness. Spoken freely of dishonor, and how hers had tainted me. But not once, not *once*, had she admitted she was wrong.

Hoolies, she is stubborn!

Cursing softly, I untangled blankets and pelts from legs, stood stiffly, cursed some more. Then heard the roan gelding blowing in the darkness and realized Del wasn't really *gone*, she simply wasn't present.

Well, a woman is due her privacy.

And then I saw the light.

Oh, hoolies, bascha, what are you doing now?

Boreal, of course. Del went nowhere without her. She didn't always use her, being disinclined to show off, but when she did it showed. Like now, with the light.

Del was up to something.

I am big, but I can move quietly. I learned in childhood, in slavery, how to stay motionless for long periods of time. How to be *invisible,* so no one notices you. It saved me from extra whippings, from cuffs and slaps and blows. It was something I cultivated out of a need for self-preservation, and it served me even in freedom. It served me even now.

Silently I moved, muffling myself in my cloak, and slipped easily through the shadows. Pausing now and then, emulating trees; some say I am tall enough. And at last I found Delilah kneeling in the darkness. Singing softly to her sword.

Regardless of what had happened with my sword while killing the cat, music is still alien to me. I don't understand it. And I didn't, really, now, though the words were clear enough, if sung in Northern instead of Southron. But the song was a private song, composed solely for Boreal.

Del sings to her sword a lot. Northerners do that; don't ask me why. In the South, we merely dance, letting movement speak for itself. But on Staal-Ysta I'd learned it was customary—no, *necessary*—for a sword-dancer to sing. A variation of the dance. Music for the circle.

For Del, it was more than that. It was music for the sword. With it she keyed the power and used it, depending on the song to harness Boreal's magic.

Del sang softly, and Boreal came alive.

I've seen it before. Drop by drop, bead by bead, running the length of the blade from tip to hilt until the steel is aflame. But this time the light was dull, private, as if she purposely damped it down. Her song was barely a whisper, and the answer that came the same.

Guilt flickered. Clearly this was a private, personal ritual, meant for Del alone. But I didn't leave. I couldn't. Magic I've always distrusted; now I distrusted Del.

Deep inside, something spasmed. Something that spoke of unease. Something that spoke of fear.

Would it ever be the same? Or had we gone too far?

Del sang her song and the sword came alive.

"Help me," she whispered. "Oh, help me—"

It was Northern speech, not Southron, but I've learned enough to understand. Necessity had made me; this moment was no different.

Del drew in a breath. "Make me strong. I need to be *strong*. Make me hard. I *need* to be hard. Don't let me be so soft. Don't let me be so weak."

She was the strongest woman I knew.

"I have a need," she whispered, "a great and powerful need. A task that must be finished. A song that must be ended. But now I am afraid."

Light shirred up the sword. It pulsed as if it answered.

"Make me strong," she asked. "Make me hard again. Make me what I must be, if I am to end my song."

Easy enough to ask. Harder, I thought, to live with.

Lastly, softly, she begged: *"Make me not care what he thinks."*

Oh, hoolies, bascha. Don't do this to yourself.

But it was already done. Boreal was quiescent. Delilah had her answer.

And I had a sword to hate.

Chapter 7

Something bad woke me. Something snatched me out of a dreamless sleep and forced me into wakefulness. Into an abrupt, unpleasant awareness.

Something bad that smelled. Something in my *face*—

I don't know what I shouted. Something loud. Something angry. And, I'll admit, something frightened. But then I don't know a man alive who wouldn't feel afraid if he woke up from a sound sleep to discover a beast standing over his head.

Even as I exploded out of my bedding, the hound lunged at my throat. I smelled its stench, felt its breath, saw the white glint of shining eyes. Flailed out with both arms as I tried to thrust it away.

The hound lunged again, still trying for my throat. Dimly I heard Del, on the other side of the cairn, crying out in Northern. She sounded startled *and* furious; I made no answer, having no time to make the effort, but hoped she'd do something other than shout. Which, of course, she did, with Boreal at her beck.

My own sword was buried beneath tumbled bedding. Now I lay on dirt, hard, cold dirt, with my head at the cairn stones. The hound might take my throat; the coals might take my hair.

No one wants to die. But least of all with no hair.

The beast made no sound. But Del did, and loudly, as she told me to flatten myself.

I tried. I mean, no man aware of Boreal's power risks himself so readily. But even as I kicked over and tried to dig myself into the dirt, the hound evaded the blade. Del's skill was better than that, but my head was in the way. So were my flailing hands, locking themselves at a furred throat. I wanted nothing more than to try for my knife, but dared not take a hand off the hound, or I'd lose my brief advantage.

I felt teeth at my own throat. Snapping, grasping, grabbing. The stench was overwhelming. It smelled of rotting bodies.

Something snugged taut against the back of my neck. Something like wire, or thong. And then I realized it was my necklet. My string of sandtiger claws.

Hoolies, it wanted my *claws?*

But I had no time to wonder beyond my initial surprised response. I heard Del's muttered order to watch my head, which I couldn't actually do since my eyes were *in* it, and ducked. But she missed again, though barely; I heard Boreal's whisper as steel sang past my head.

"Just *do* it—" I blurted.

And then the beast was lunging away, evading the blade yet again. It left me in the darkness and fled away into the trees.

I lay sprawled on my back, one hand at my throat busily digging through woolen wrappings to see if I was whole. To feel if my flesh was bleeding. I yanked wool away with some violence, then heaved a sigh of relief as nothing but skin met my fingers. No blood or torn flesh at all; only whole, unbitten skin.

Meanwhile, Del ignored me entirely and stepped across my body to follow the spoor of the beast. Just in case it might double back. Just in case it might have companions. Not a bad idea, but she might have thought of me. After all, for all *she* knew I could be bleeding to death right there on the ground, dwindling bit by bit— or bucket by bucket—before her eyes.

Except she wasn't looking. Which sort of ruined the effect.

I felt the thong at my neck, heard the rattle of claws, felt relief wash quickly through me. Which meant I was perfectly entitled to be testy, since there was nothing wrong with me.

I let Del get four steps. "Don't bother," I said. "It got what it came for."

She swung back, sword aglint. "What do you mean, 'what it came for'?"

I sat up slowly, still massaging the flesh of my throat. It felt bruised; no surprise. "The whistle," I told her hoarsely. "The Cantéada ward-whistle. That's what it wanted." Not my claws after all, though I didn't tell her that. I didn't think she'd understand why I'd worried about it at all.

Del glanced back into the shadows. I knew the beast was gone; the stink of it had faded. But she waited, sword at the ready, until her own suspicions died. And then she came to me.

"Let me see," she said.

Finally. But I shrugged negligence as she knelt down, setting Boreal close at hand. "I'm all right. It didn't even break the skin."

Del's hands were insistent. She peeled back wrappings, shoved my hand aside, carefully examined flesh in the thin light of the moon.

It was odd having her so close to me after so long a separation. I smelled her familiar scent, felt her familiar touch, saw her familiar face; the faint frown between her brows. At moments like this it was hard to recall just what had come between us.

And then there were other moments when I remembered all too well.

Ah, hoolies, bascha . . . too much sand blown out of the desert.

If Del was aware of my scrutiny, she made no sign of it. She simply examined my throat carefully, nodded slightly, then took her hands away. "So," she said, "they have learned. And we are back where we started."

"Not quite," I muttered. "Too much sand blown out of the desert."

Del frowned. "What?"

For some reason, I was irritated. "We're not back where we started because too many things have changed." I shifted position, felt the pull of newly stretched scar tissue, tried to hide the discomfort from her. Just as she hid her own from me. "Go back to sleep, Del. I'll take first watch."

"You're in no shape for that."

"Neither of us are, but we'll each of us have to do it. I just thought I might as well start."

She considered protesting, but didn't. She knew better; I was right. And so she went back to her bedding on the other side of the cairn and wrapped herself in pelts. All I could see of her was the dim pale glow of her hair.

I sorted out my own tumbled bedding and made sense of it again. And then I settled carefully, snugging deep into cloak and pelts, and prepared to wait through the night. I wanted to give her till dawn; she'd done the same for me.

Trouble was, I couldn't.

It didn't take much. Just a glance at Del on the far side of the cairn, all bound up in pelts and blankets. The glow of the moon in her hair. The sound of her even breathing. And all the feelings recalled.

I sat there rigidly, half sick. Joints ached, my wound throbbed, the flesh of my throat complained. Even my head hurt. Because I gritted my teeth so hard my jaw threatened to crack.

Just tell her, you fool. Tell her the truth.

Across the cairn, she settled. Hurting at least as much as I, inside *and* out.

Deep in my belly, something tightened. Not desire. Something more powerful yet: humiliation. And more than a little discomfort. Of the spirit as well as the flesh.

Oh, hoolies, fool, just tell her the truth.

Just open your mouth and talk; it's never been very hard.

You made Del ask for atonement. She's at least due an explanation.

But that she hadn't asked for one made me feel even worse.

Something inside of me quailed. Guilt. Regret. Remorse. Enough to break a man.

But the woman was due the words.

I stared hard out into the darkness. The night was quiet, save for its normal song. It was cold—colder in bed alone—but spring promised warmer nights. Already the color was different.

You're avoiding the truth, old man.

The woman is due the words. The least you can do is say them out loud where she can hear them, instead of inside your head.

Easier thought than said.

I looked at Del again. And knew all too well that even though she was—and had been—wrong, I shared the responsibility of putting things to rights. Of admitting my own faults. Because when things have gone awry, it takes two to straighten them out.

I drew in a deep breath, so deep it made me lightheaded, then blew it out again. And finally opened my mouth. This time the words would be spoken instead of locked away.

"I *was* afraid," I told her. "I was scared to death. I was everything you accused me of earlier. And it was why I left Staal-Ysta."

I knew she was still awake. But Del said nothing.

"I left on purpose," I continued stolidly. "I wasn't driven out, or invited out, or even asked to leave; I was a *kaidin,* according to all the customs, and they had no right to ask it. I could have stayed. They would have let me stay, to see if you lived or died . . . but I couldn't. I saw you lying there in the circle, cut open by my sword, and I left you behind on purpose."

Del was very still.

I scraped a tongue across too-dry lips. "They put you in Telek's lodge—in *Telek's!*—because it was the closest. Because they thought you would die, and that your daughter deserved to watch. To hear the funeral songs."

Her breath rasped faintly.

"They stitched me back together—you carved me up pretty good—and gave me the gifts bestowed upon a new *kaidin.* I had, they said, conducted myself honorably, and was therefore due the tribute as well as the rank. They patched me up, gave me gifts, rowed me across the lake." I swallowed painfully; it was much harder than I'd imagined. "I knew you were alive. When I left. I knew. But I thought you would die. I thought you would *die.* I thought—I *did*—I just . . . and I couldn't—I just *couldn't*—" I let it trail off. The emptiness was incredible. "Oh, hoolies, Del . . . of all the lives I've taken, I couldn't face taking yours."

Silence. It hadn't come out the way I'd wanted it to. I hadn't said everything that needed saying, that I *wanted* to say; I couldn't. How could I explain what I'd experienced when I'd felt my own sword cut into her body? How could I tell her what it was to see her lying on hardpacked dirt like a puppeteer's broken toy, bisected by my sword? How could I tell her how frightened I had been, how *sickened* I had been? How much in that moment I had wished myself in her place?

How could I tell her I was absolutely *certain* she would die—and I couldn't bear to watch it?

And so I had left her. While she lived. So I could remember her *alive*.

For me, it was very important. It was necessary. It was *required*, as so many things have been required of me. Required by myself.

Silence, while I sat there waiting for her to say something about my cowardice. My lack of empathy. My willingness to leave her on Staal-Ysta before her fate was known. I'd made her ask my forgiveness; now I needed hers.

And then, at last, a response. But her tone was oddly detached. "You should have killed me. You should have finished it. Blooding and Keying in me would have made you invincible." Del sighed a little. "The magic of the North and all the power of the South. Invincibility, Sandtiger. A man to be reckoned with."

I drew in a steadying breath. The worst, for me, was over. I think. "I'm already that," I said dryly. "I'm everything I want to be right now, this minute, here. I don't need magic for that. Certainly not the kind of magic that comes from killing people."

Del tightened wrappings, locking the cold away. Locking herself inside, as she did so very often. "You should have killed me," she said. "Now I have no name. A blade without a name."

There was grief. Anguish. Bitterness. The painful yearning of an exile for a land no longer hers. For a world forever denied, except in memories.

I stared blindly into the dark. "And a song that never ends?"

Clearly, it stung. "I will end it," she declared. "I *will* end my song. Ajani will die by my hand."

I let a moment go by. "What then, Delilah?"

"There is Ajani. Only Ajani."

She was cold, hard, relentless. Focused on her task. Her sword had answered her plea.

But how much of it was the sword? How much merely Del?

How responsible are *any* of us for what we do to survive, to make our way in the world?

How hard do we make ourselves to accomplish the hardest goal?

Quietly, I said, "I'm not going South."

Huddled in bedding, Del was little more than an indistinguishable lump of shadow against the ground. But now she sat up.

The moonlight set her aglow as blankets fell back from her shoulders: pristine white against dappled darkness. Her hair, unbraided, was tousled, tumbling over her shoulders. Curtaining the sides of her face.

She stared at me, frowning. "I did wonder why they told me you were going to Ysaa-den. I thought at first perhaps they lied, merely to trouble me—it was far out of my way, and yours, if I was to go to the South—but then I found your tracks, and it was true." She shook her head. "But I don't understand why. You've been complaining about the snow and the cold ever since we crossed the border."

I listened to her tone, hearing echoes and nuances; her fight to maintain balance. "I don't like it," I agreed. "I didn't like it *before* we crossed the border. But there's something I have to do."

I also didn't like the look of her. The intensity. She was too thin, too drawn, too obsessed with Ajani. The sword had cut her flesh, but the man had hurt her more.

Del's tone was carefully modulated so as not to show too much. All the same, it showed enough. "I thought you'd go south at once."

"No. Not this time."

"I thought the Sandtiger roamed wherever he wanted, unbound by other desires." She paused. "At least, he used to."

I shut my eyes, waited a beat, answered her quietly. "It won't work, Del. You've pushed me this way and that way like an oracle bone for months, now. No more. There are things I have to do."

"*I* have to go south."

"Who's stopping you? Weren't you the one who spent five years apprenticing on Staal-Ysta just so you *could* go south all by yourself? Weren't you the one who went hunting the Sandtiger with only a storm-born sword for companionship? Weren't you—"

"Enough, Tiger. Yes, I did all those things. And I have done this thing: I have come to you asking your help in making me fit again. But if you are unwilling to give it—"

"I'll give it," I interrupted. "I said that already, after you did your little ritual. But I can't go south right away, which means if you really want my help, you'll have to come along."

"Something has happened," she said suspiciously. "Did Telek and Stigand force you to swear oaths? Did they give you a task? Did you make promises to the *voca* in exchange for tending me?"

"No. I have every intention of going home as soon as I've tracked them to their lair. It has nothing to do with oaths to Telek and Stigand, or promises to the *voca*. It's just something I want to do." I paused. "And if you don't like it, you don't have to come."

"Tracked *who*—?" She broke it off. "Those beasts? The hounds? Oh, Tiger, you don't mean—"

"I made a promise, Del. To myself. I intend to keep it."

Wide-eyed, she stared at me, which didn't make me feel any better. No man likes having it thrown in his face that he's lacked responsibility throughout much of his life; me making this promise exhibited a new side of the Sandtiger. Del didn't exactly *say* anything, but then she didn't have to. All she had to do was stare at me in exactly the way she was.

"Tiger—"

"It's why I'm out here in the middle of a Northern nowhere, Del; why else? I'm tracking those hounds. To Ysaa-den or wherever. To *whoever*—I intend to find the sorcerer who set them loose."

"And kill him," she clarified.

"I imagine so," I agreed. "Unless, of course, he's polite enough to stop on my say-so."

She hooked hair behind her ears. "So. You're tracking the hounds in order to kill their master, and I'm tracking Ajani with much the same end in mind. What is the difference, Tiger? Why are you right and I'm wrong?"

"I don't want to argue about this—"

"I'm not arguing. I'm asking."

"My reasons are a bit different from yours," I said testily. "Aside from hounding us for more months than I care to remember, those beasts have also killed people. And some were children."

"Yes," Del agreed, "as Ajani killed my kin . . . including all the babies."

"Oh, hoolies, Del—" I shifted position, wished I hadn't. "What you're after is revenge, pure and simple. I'm not saying it's *wrong*— what Ajani did was horrible—but I think you've lost sight of reality. What's driving you now is misplaced pride and utter obsession—and that's not healthy for anyone."

"You think I'd be better off in some man's bed, or in some man's house, bearing him fourteen sons."

I blinked. "Fourteen might be a bit much. Hard on the woman, I'd think."

Del bit back a retort. "Tiger, do you deny it? Wouldn't you rather see me in some man's bed instead of in the circle?" She paused delicately. "In *your* bed, maybe, instead of in your circle?"

"You've been in my bed," I answered bluntly, "*and* you've been in my circle. I don't know what the first one got you, but the second nearly killed you."

That she hurt was obvious; that I'd cut too deep equally so. "So it did," she sighed finally. "Yes, so it did. As for the first? I don't know. I don't know what it got me. I don't know what it *should* have—do we put a price on bedding?"

"I'm going north," I told her. "Or wherever it is the hounds go. You can come, or not. It's up to you. But if you do, we'll put a price on nothing. No bedding, Del. Will that make you happy?"

She stared back at me. "I thought that would be your price."

"For sparring with you?" I shook my head. "Once, yes. Back when we first met, and you promised me a bedding in place of coin you didn't have. And you paid, bascha. You paid very nicely, eventually . . . except by that time I wasn't exactly counting. Neither, I think, were you—so that debt we'll call forgiven." I shrugged. "If you want to come along with me now to get your practice in so you can face Ajani, that's fine with me. But things can't be the same, not after all that's happened."

"You won't last," she predicted. "This could take weeks, and you don't do days very well."

"Bet me," I said.

Slowly Del smiled. "I know you, Tiger. This isn't a fair wager. Not for you. I *know* you."

"Do you? Really? Then let me tell you why it *is* a fair wager." I held her eyes with my own. "When a man's been made a fool of, he doesn't much feel like going to bed with the woman who did it. When a man has been *used*—without his permission or knowledge— he doesn't much feel like going to bed with the woman who did the using." With effort, I kept my tone uninflected. "And when that woman, faced with the truth of what she did, adamantly refuses to admit she was wrong, he doesn't really care about the bedding any more. Because what he likes in that woman is more than just her body and what it can do for him in bed. What he likes in that woman is her loyalty and honesty and honor."

Del said nothing. I don't think she could.

"But then you've sort of set aside all those useless attributes in the last year, haven't you, Delilah? So I guess what I feel doesn't matter so much any more."

Del's face was colorless. "Tiger—"

"Think about it," I said. "And think about *me* for a change, in- stead of your oaths of honor. Instead of your obsession."

Shock receded slowly. I'd struck a number of chords within her, but clearly she was unprepared to deal with what I'd said. And so she returned to the original topic. "I still say—I *still* say—the bet is a waste of time."

I shrugged. "So let's test it."

Her eyes were assessive. "How much are you willing to wager?"

I stared hard at her for a moment. Then pulled my sword from its sheath.

It felt right. Warm and good and *right*, like a woman hugging your neck.

Like a fully quenched *jivatma* making promises to protect you.

All the hairs stood up on my arms. It took all the strength I had to put the sword down. In fitful, tarnished moonlight, the new-made *jivatma* gleamed.

Color drained from her face. I nodded confirmation of the question she wouldn't ask. "Now you know how serious I am."

"But—you can't. You can't wager your *sword*."

"I just did."

She stared at the weapon lying mutely in front of my knees. "What would I do with it?"

"*If* you won—and you won't—anything you want. He'd be your sword."

"I have a sword." Her left hand went out to touch the harness and sheath lying at her side. "I have a sword, Tiger."

"Then sell it. Give it away. Break it. Melt it down." I shrugged. "I don't care, Del. If you win, you can do whatever you want."

Slowly she shook her head. "You have no respect for things you don't understand."

I cut her off. "Respect must be earned, bascha, not bought. Not even trained, as it is in Staal-Ysta. Because until tested, respect is nothing but a word. Emptiness, Del. Nothing more than that."

Still she shook her head. "That sword was made for you—made *by* you—"

"It's a piece of steel," I said curtly.

"You completed the rituals, asked the blessing—"

"—and stuck it into you." I shocked her into silence. "Do you really think I want a sword that tried to kill you?"

Del looked at Boreal, sheathed by her side. Remembering the circle. Remembering the dance.

Her tone was oddly hollow. "I would have killed you."

"You tried. I made you mad, and you tried. Fair enough—it was what I meant to do, to throw you out of your pattern." I shrugged. "But I didn't want to kill you. I didn't intend to do it. The *sword* wanted to do it . . . that bloodthirsty, angry sword."

"Angry," she echoed.

"It was," I told her. "I could feel it. *Taste* it. I could hear it in my head."

She heard something in my tone. "But—now it isn't angry?"

I smiled grimly. "Not so much anymore. Just like that hound, it got what it came for."

Del nodded slowly. "You killed someone, then. After all. You've quenched your *jivatma*."

I squinted thoughtfully. "Not—exactly. Killed *something*, yes, but not what you might expect. And not in the way you told me."

Del, frowning, was very intent. "What have you done, Tiger?"

"Killed something," I repeated. "Cat. White, dappled silver." For some reason I said nothing about the pelt, which I'd tucked away into saddle-pouches. "But I didn't sing."

"Snow lion," Del said. "You didn't sing at all?"

"I'm a *sword-dancer*, Del. Not a sword-singer, or whatever it is you claim. I kill people with my sword. I don't sing to it."

Del shook her head thoughtfully. "It doesn't really matter if you didn't sing aloud. Even a mute can earn a *jivatma*. Even a mute can sing a song."

I scowled. "How?"

She smiled. "A song can be sung in silence. A song can be of the soul, whether anyone hears it or not. Only the sword counts, and it only requires the soul and all the feelings in it."

I thought of the song I'd heard on the overlook by the lakeshore. The song I'd heard in my head ever since I'd named the blade. Thanks to the Cantéada, I'd been unable to forget it.

And now it was my sword.

"I don't need it," I declared. "I don't *want* it, Del."

"No. But it wants you." She pointed to my sword. "To find you, I used my *jivatma*, I painted the sky with my sword—you saw all the colors. You saw all the lights. All from a song, Tiger—and you could do the same."

The questions boiled up. "Why *did* you do it? And how did you find me so fast? *Especially* with that wound . . . it should have put you down longer than my own did." A sudden chill touched a fingertip to my spine. "You didn't do anything—*odd*—did you? Make any promises? Any pacts? I know how you are about those things."

"What I do is my business."

"Del—what did you do?" I looked harder at the strain etched into her face. "What *exactly* did you do?"

Her mouth was flat and hard. "I have a *jivatma*."

An answer, of sorts. It told me more than enough. "So, you sang to it, did you? Begged more magic of it? Offered up even more of your humanity in exchange for arcane strength?"

"What I do—"

"—is your own business; yes, Del, I know, I know . . . you've always been at such pains to make certain I understood that." It was all I could do to keep my tone even. "How did you manage it? Magic?" I lifted eyebrows. "Is that how you caught up so fast?"

Her face was pensive. "There is no magic about that, Tiger. They told me you were bound for Ysaa-den. I know the North well—I took a shortcut."

I waited. She offered nothing further. So I asked. "Why did you paint the sky?"

After a moment, she shrugged. "I thought it might bring you in."

It was something. From her, it was everything. "But you came to me," I said. "After I left you in the clearing. You came to *me*."

She touched the hilt of her sword. Very gently. "I realized, after I did it, and you came, that you wouldn't stay. That I'd have to go to you." Del smiled sadly. "A man's pride is a powerful thing."

I scowled balefully, disliking the twinge of guilt. "I've got no use for painting the sky."

She laughed a little. "Maybe not. But there are other things. Other magics available; you've seen my *jivatma*."

"Hunh."

Del shrugged. "You swore to me you'd never use it. You'd never kill, never blood it. But you *have* killed, Tiger, and you made your blade a song." She looked again at my sword. "Whether you like it or not, there's magic in your blade. There's *power* in your blade. And if you don't learn to control it, it will control you."

I looked at Boreal, so quiescent in her sheath. I knew what she could do. But only at Del's bidding. If left to her own devices—

No. Don't think about that. Think about something else.

"You," I said, "are sandsick. So now it's your turn to watch."

And as Del, disgruntled, glared, I bundled myself in bedding.

Chapter 8

*I*t's very easy to fall into old patterns. Del and I had been together long enough to develop certain rhythms in our day-to-
day existence. Simple things, mostly: one of us built and tended the
fire, another laid a meal; each of us tended our horses. We knew
when to rest them, knew when we needed rest, knew the best
times and places to stop for the night. Much of what we did required no conversation, for most was a reflection of things we'd
done before.

It was easy to forget. Easy to recall only that we were together.
And then something, some little thing, would crop up and remind
me that for the space of six weeks we *hadn't* been together—and I'd
remember the reason why.

We rode toward Ysaa-den, following hound spoor. Saying little
to one another because we didn't know what to say. At least *I*
didn't. What Del thought—or knew, or didn't know—was, as always, her own business, and always exceedingly private, unless she
chose to share. For the moment, she didn't.

She rode ahead of me. The stud didn't like it, but I was pacing
him. I didn't want him to overextend himself. So I made him stay
behind the blue roan and content himself with second place. Trouble was, he wasn't.

Del's back was straight. She rides very erect anyway, but I knew
some of her exceptional posture had to do with the wound. No

matter what she said, or didn't—or how much magic she had used—I knew it was hurting her. And I knew what an effort it took for her to keep on going.

Boreal cut her back in half from left shoulder to right hip, as Samiel did my own. I glared at Boreal, thinking bad things about it. Thinking also about my own sword; what did it want me to do? What would it *force* me to do?

And then I forgot about Samiel, looking again at Boreal. Noting how quietly she rode in the leather sheath. How meekly the weapon rested, hiding deadly blade. Hiding alien, gods-blessed steel that sang a song of its own, just as Delilah did.

And in cold, abrupt clarity, I wondered just how much of Del's obsession was born of blade instead of brain.

I knew little of *jivatmas* other than what Del and Kem had told me. And even then, I hadn't put much stock in what they said. It wasn't until my own new-made sword had made his bloodthirst known that I'd realized just how independent a *jivatma* could be. Which meant it was entirely possible Del wasn't fully responsible for her own actions. Hadn't she begged, on more than one occasion, for Boreal's aid? For *power?*

I glared at the hilt riding so high on her left shoulder. Had Del somehow willingly subjugated her own personality to the demands of a magicked sword? Did she need revenge so badly?

She had sworn oaths. I swear a lot myself, but generally not oaths. At least, not the binding kind; the kind that make you do something you'd really rather not do. But Del was different. Del took vows and oaths and swearing much more seriously. It was what had driven her to become a sword-dancer. To give up a child. It was what had driven her south, alone, to search for a kidnapped brother.

It was what had driven her to seek out a sword-dancer called the Sandtiger, who knew people she didn't, and how to find them.

A man makes of himself many things, depending on his needs and the shaping of his life. Me, I'd been a slave. And then a free man seeking power to make a real life for himself. A life of his own choosing without demands from other people.

Well, yes, there *were* demands. If I hired on to a tanzeer, I was his to command. But only if what he wanted agreed well enough with my willingness to do it. And there were things I was unwilling to do. Killing people who deserved it, or who gave me no other choice, was something I'd come to terms with many years before. For a long time, killing was almost enjoyable; because it released some of my anger. After a while, having grown up a little, hostility was no longer so evident. I was free. No one could ever make me a slave again. I no longer had to kill.

Except it was the only thing I was good at.

Sword-dancing was my life. I'd freely chosen it. I had apprenticed formally and become a seventh-level sword-dancer, which made me very good. It made me what I was. A dangerous, deadly man.

Who hired out his sword to anyone with coin.

By nature, we are solitary souls. After all, it's hard for a hired killer to have a normal life. Whores don't mind sleeping with us so long as we pay them and they can brag about it—and sometimes our fame is payment enough—but decent women don't generally marry us. Because a man who sells his sword for a living always walks the edge of the blade, and a woman who wants to grow old with her man doesn't like to lose him young.

There are exceptions, of course. Sword-dancers do marry, or take a woman as their own without benefit of rites. But most of us don't. Most of us ride alone. Most of us die alone, leaving no woman or children to grieve.

There was a reason for it. Domestic responsibility can ruin a sword-dancer's soul.

And now here was Del. No longer the same Del. Forever a different Del. Not because of the girl she'd borne, though it did make me think of her differently. Not because we'd shared a bed so many times in the past. But because of what she had done and what *I* had done; because of what we'd become.

Loyalty is a sacred thing. A thing to be admired. A thing to be treasured. It isn't something two people in our profession, where loyalty is so often purchased, experience very often. Loyalty within a circle is very rare indeed, because too often someone dies, or sacrifices pride, which can destroy a relationship. But for a while we'd known it. For a while we had lived it.

But we'd both of us forsworn the virtue in the circle on Staal-Ysta.

Oh, hoolies, bascha, what I'd give for the old days.

But *which* old days? The ones with her, or without her?

Without was easier. Because with I'd nearly killed her.

Del turned in the saddle a moment, hooking hair behind an ear. It bared her face. A fine-drawn face of magnificent planes, and too many of them visible. Pain, oaths, and obsession had reshaped youthful flesh into a mask of brittle beauty. A cold, hard-edged beauty that made me think of glass.

Glass too often breaks. I wondered when she would.

Just after dawn I awoke, looking for Del. It was something I'd found myself doing each morning since we'd joined up together, and it irritated me. But each morning I did it anyway. For reassurance.

And each morning I said to myself: Yes, Del is alive. Yes, Del is here.

It isn't a dream after all.

Grunting, I sat up. Tried to stretch muscles and pop joints without waking her, because no man likes a woman to see how he's growing older, how the years are taking their toll. And then I stood up, slowly, and walked, equally slowly, over to the stud. I checked him every morning, just to be sure. The claw slashes were healing well, but the hair would come in white. Like me, he'd carry the scars to his death.

Still, he seemed in much better spirits—or maybe it was just that the gelding's presence made him take more of an interest in life. Whatever it was, he was more like his old self. His old, unpleasant self.

I ran my hand down the stud's shoulder, peeling winter hair. It *was* nearly spring; he was beginning to shed his fur.

"Tiger."

I glanced back and saw Del standing beside the fire. She had shed all her wrappings and faced me in white woolens, pale hair braided back from her face and laced with white cord. She took the sheath and harness into her hands and slid Boreal into dawn. Rune-worked steel gleamed. "Will you dance with me, Sandtiger?"

I turned from the stud to face her squarely. "You're in no shape to dance, Del. Not yet."

"I have to start sometime. It's been much too long."

For some strange reason it made me very angry. "Hoolies, woman, you're sandsick! I doubt you could hold a stance for more than a single eyeblink, and certainly not against any offense I might show you. Do you think I'm blind?"

"I think you're afraid."

Something deep inside twisted. "That again, then."

"And again, and again." She lifted the deadly *jivatma*. "Dance with me, Sandtiger. Honor the deal we made."

Pride made me take a step toward my sword. But only a single step. I shook my head at her. "Not this time, bascha. I'm older, a little wiser. You can't tease me into the circle. Not any more. I know your tricks too well."

The tip of her sword wavered minutely. And then flashed as she shifted her grip and drove the blade straight down, deep into the earth. "Tease you?" she asked. "Oh, no." And before I could stop her, Del knelt before her sword. She tucked heels beneath buttocks and crossed wrists against her chest. The braid fell over her shoulder to dangle above the ground. "Honored *kaidin*," she said, "will you share with me some of your skill?"

I stared at the Northern woman offering obeisance to me, and all I felt was anger. A deep and abiding anger so strong it made me sick.

"Get up," I rasped.

All she did was bow her head.

"Get up from there, Delilah."

The full name made her twitch, but it did not force her up.

In the end, knowing from experience the strength of her determination, I crossed the clearing to her. She knew I was there; short of being deaf, she could not miss my string of muttered oaths. But she didn't rise. She didn't so much as lift her head.

I reached out a rigid hand. What I grabbed was Boreal.

"*No—*" Suppressing a cry, Del fell back. Illness and pain had taken her strength, stealing away her quickness. In my hands I held the proof.

"Yes," I said clearly. "We made a deal, bascha, and I will honor it. But not yet. Not yet. Neither of us is ready." I shook my head wearily. "Maybe it's just that I'm older. Maybe it's that I'm wiser. Or maybe it's just the blind pride of youth that makes you risk yourself." I scrubbed a hand across my brow, thrusting fallen hair aside. "Hoolies, I don't know—maybe it's just sword-dancers. I used to do the same."

Del said nothing. She half-knelt on the ground, pressing herself upright with one hand while the other clutched her ribs. Color stood high in her face. Flags of brilliant crimson against pearl-white flesh.

I sighed. Set Boreal's tip against the ground and pressed her down, slowly, so she stood freely upright. Then I gingerly lowered myself to Del's level, kneeling carefully, and unbuckled my heavy belt.

Del's eyes widened. "What are you doing?"

"Showing you something." I dropped the belt, pulled up layers of wool. Exposed my rib cage. "There," I said. "See? Your handi-work, Del. A clean, perfect sword thrust. And it hurts. It hurts like hoolies. It will for some time to come, Del—maybe even forever. Because I'm not as young as I used to be. I heal slower. I hurt longer. I learn from my mistakes, because my mistakes are around to remind me."

Del's face now was dirty gray. She stared transfixed at the ugly scar. It was more vivid than it might be because, coming north, I'd lost much of my color. Livid purple against pale brown is not an at-tractive mix.

"I hurt, bascha. And I'm tired. I want nothing more than to go home, to go south, where I can bake myself in the sun and forget about Northern snow. But I can't until I'm finished with the job I said I'd do. And in order to finish the job, I have to stick around."

Del swallowed hard. "I only want to dance."

I tugged my tunic down. "I won't ask you to show me yours, since I've got a good idea what it looks like. It was me who did it, bascha—I know what the thrust was. I know what it did to you. If you went into a circle now, you wouldn't survive the dance." I picked up my own sword, still on the ground between us. "I almost killed you once. I won't risk it again."

"Too much time," she whispered.

With a grunt, I stood up. "You've got all the time in the world, my Northern bascha. You're young. You'll heal. You'll recover your strength. You'll dance again, Delilah—that I promise you."

"How old are you?" she asked abruptly.

I frowned down at her. "I thought I already told you."

"No. All you ever said was you were older than me." Surprising me, Del smiled. "That I already knew."

"Yes, well . . . I imagine so." Irritated, I scratched my sandtiger scars. "I don't know. Old enough. Why? Does it matter? After all this time?"

"*You're* the one making age an issue, Tiger. I only wanted to know how old the old man is."

"How old are *you?*" I countered, knowing perfectly well. But it's a question women hate.

Del didn't flinch. Nor did she hesitate. "In three more days, I will have twenty-one years."

"Hoolies," I said in disgust, "I *could* be your father."

Del's face was serious. "He was forty when he was killed. How close are you to that?"

"Too close," I muttered sourly, and went off to appease my bladder.

Chapter 9

el and I rode steadily northeast for two more days. We took it pretty easy on several counts: one, the stud; two, me; and three, Del herself. Neither of us is the kind of person who enjoys poor health. Neither of us is the kind of person who likes to talk about it, either, which meant we mostly kept our mouths shut regarding respective wounds.

But we did notice, of course. I noticed Del, she noticed me. But we each of us said nothing, because to say something meant admitting to discomfort, which neither of us was prepared to do. Call it pride, arrogance, stupidity; only the stud was completely honest, and he made no bones about it. He hurt. And he told us.

I patted his neck, avoiding healing claw scores. "I know, old man—but it'll get better, I promise."

Del, who rode in front of me amid bare-branched trees, twisted her head to mutter over a shoulder: "How do you know? You don't even know where we're going."

"We're going to Ysaa-den."

"And if you find no answers there?"

That again. It had briefly been a topic of discussion the day we'd set out. She was unconvinced I had made the right decision to follow the hounds to their origins. But since all of *her* decisions were governed by an insatiable need for revenge, I'd told her I wasn't so certain she could be trusted to give me an unbiased opinion regarding much of anything; she had retreated into haughty silence, as women so often do when the man catches them out, and had said nothing of it again.

Until now.

I adjusted my posture to the motion of the stud, trying to find a position that didn't pull at healing scar tissue. "Del," I said patiently, "you didn't know where *you* were going when you went south to find your brother. I don't notice that it stopped you, since before we met up we'd never heard of one another—well, maybe you'd heard of *me*—and here we are now, riding together in the North. All of which means you didn't much care that you didn't know where you were going. You just went."

"That was different."

I nodded wryly to myself; isn't it always different?

Del peered at me over her shoulder, setting her jaw against the pain of twisting her torso. "How will you know when you've found whoever—or *what*ever—you're looking for?"

"I just will."

"Tiger—"

"Del, will you just stop trying to grind me into the ground in hopes I'll give in to you? I've made up my mind, and I intend to carry out my promise." I paused. "With you or without you."

Silence. Del rode on. And then, mostly muffled, "Those beasts were never after *you*."

It was half challenge, half boast. Also truth; it had become fairly clear months before the hounds wanted Del's sword, or Del, or both.

But that was then. Things had changed. "They are now."

Del stopped her gelding. Turned more squarely in the saddle, which hurt her, but didn't stop her from staring back at me intently. "What?"

"I said, 'They are now.' Why do you think the one stole the ward-whistle?"

Del shrugged. "That was Cantéada-made. Magicked. Lure enough, I think, without thinking it was you."

The stud reached out to sample the gelding's bluish rump. I pulled him back, chastised him a bit, turned him off diagonally in hopes of interesting him in something else, like maybe a tree. "They came once before into my camp. All of them. And they tried to take my sword."

"*Take* it!"

"Steal it," I confirmed. "They weren't much interested in me, just in the sword."

Del's frown deepened. "I don't understand."

"What's to understand?" I wrestled with the stud, who was showing signs of reacquainting his teeth with the roan's rump. "Originally all they wanted was *your* sword, remember? And then mine . . . once I'd blooded it. Once I'd killed that cat." Memory was a spasming in my belly. "Even once—" But I cut it off.

Del's brows shot up. " 'Even once' *what?*"

Memory blossomed more fully. I stood on the overlook by the lakeshore, staring down at Staal-Kithra, Place of Spirits, where Northern dead lay entombed in Northern earth, honored by barrows and stone dolmens.

I stood by the overlook by the lakeshore, staring down at Staal-Ysta, Place of Swords, the island floating in water dyed black by winter's embrace. And I had thrust a naked blade into the earth.

Naked when it went in. Rune-scribed when it came out.

A chill pinched my spine. "They've known since I named it."

Del waited.

"The must have," I mused. "They were one large group originally—I followed the spoor for days . . . and then the group split up. Some tracks went on. Others circled back . . ." I frowned. "Those hounds must have known."

After a moment, she nodded. "Names are powerful things. With *jivatmas,* one must be careful. Names must be closely guarded." And then her expression softened. "But you know that. You would never tell anyone the name of your blooding-blade."

"I told *you.*"

Del was astonished. "Told *me!* When? You have said nothing of it to me. Nothing of its name."

I scowled at the stud's ears. "There on the overlook, above the island. After I pulled it free. I just saw the runes, read the name— and told you." I squirmed slightly, knowing how foolish it sounded.

"I didn't really expect you to hear. I mean, I wasn't even sure you were still alive—" I cut that off abruptly. "I just—said it. There on the overlook . . . for you." I paused, needing to explain. "You'd told me the name of *your* sword. I thought I should do the same. So we'd be even." I exhaled heavily. "That's all. That's why. So we'd be even."

Del didn't say a word.

The memory was so clear. "There it was," I told her. "Spelled out. His name . . . in the runes. Just as you and Kem had promised."

"Runes," Del echoed. "Runes you don't know how to read."

I opened my mouth. Shut it.

It had not occurred to me. The runes had looked so familiar I hadn't even thought about it. Not ever. I had just looked at them— and *known*. The way a man knows the shape and texture of his jaw when he shaves every morning. The way his body knows the fit of a woman's without requiring lessons.

Oh, hoolies.

Abruptly I unsheathed. Balanced the blade across the pommel of my saddle and stared at alien runes.

Stared *hard*. Until my eyes blurred and the shapes ran together. The shapes that had not existed in the blade originally. Not when Kem had given it to me. Not when I had dipped it in the water, asking, very cynically, the blessings of Northern gods.

Not when I had sheathed it in Northern earth, at the brink of the overlook.

Only after I had drawn it out.

Del sat next to me on her blue roan. Like me, she stared at the blade. But she was smiling, if only a little; all I did was glare.

"So," she said, "once again the Sandtiger walks his own path. *Makes* his own path, as you have made that sword."

My tone was curt. "What?"

"Do you recall when Kem nicked your hand and had you bathe the blade in blood?"

I nodded sourly; I hadn't liked it much.

"It is part of the Naming ceremony. Ordinarily the runes show themselves then. Mine did; all *jivatmas* do." She paused. "Except, of course, for yours."

I recalled Kem saying something of the sort. I also recalled him saying something about belief being a requisite; that until I fully believed in the magic of a *jivatma*, its true name could not be known. Which was why, at that specific moment, there had been no runes.

But there on the overlook, so frightened Del was dead, I had believed. Because it had been the sword, not me, that had tried so hard to kill her.

And so, in that moment of belief, the sword had revealed its true name. In runes I couldn't read.

I said something very rude. Very violent. It had to do with things I would like to do with the sword. Do *to* it; things that would give me great pleasure, great relief; things that would resolve all potential future problems because if I did them—one, or even all of them—there would *be* no future for the sword.

"Yes," Del agreed. "It is difficult to accept the second soul—especially when that soul was once cat, not man. But you will." She smiled; a bit smugly, I thought, which was altogether unnecessary as well as unappreciated. "It knows you, now. It has told you what it must be. What it wants most of all."

"To kill," I muttered.

Del's tone was even. "Isn't that what you do? Isn't that what you are?"

I stared at the blade. The runes remained. Familiar shapes. But nothing I could read.

I looked away from the sword into Del's face. "Samiel," I told her.

Del drew in a startled breath.

"Samiel," I repeated. "You couldn't hear me the first time. Now you can. Now you know what it is."

I saw her mouth the name. I saw her look at my sword. I saw her think of her own; of what the "honor" entailed.

She turned her horse and rode on.

At sundown, Del watched pensively as I tended the stud, feeding him handfuls of grain and talking to him quietly. I didn't think anything of it; people riding alone often talk to their horses. And she'd seen me do it before, though admittedly not as much. She had talked to her silly speckledy gelding during the ride north; now she had the blue roan, but I doubted she'd change her ways.

She handed me the bota when I returned to the cairn and arranged myself on my bedding, wrapping myself in cloak and pelts. Quietly, she said, "You care for him very much."

I sucked *amnit*, swallowed, shrugged. "He's a horse. Good as any other, better than most. He'll do in a pinch."

"Why have you never named him?"

I tossed the bota back. "Waste of time, names."

"You named your sword. *Both* of them; your Southron sword, Singlestroke, and then your Northern sword." But she didn't say the name. "And you have a name yourself, honorably won. After years of having none."

I shrugged. "Just never got around to it. It seemed sort of silly, somehow. Sort of—womanish." I grinned at her expression. "He doesn't really need one. He knows what I mean."

"Or is it a reminder?"

She asked it mildly enough, implying nothing by it other than genuine curiosity; Del isn't one to purposely ask for hostilities, in words or with weapons. But it seemed an odd question.

I frowned. "No. I have a couple of good reminders: these scars and my necklet." I pulled the leather cord from beneath the woolen tunic and rattled curving claws. "Besides, I got him years later, long after I was free."

Del looked at her gelding, tied a prudent distance from the stud. "They gave him to me," she said, "to encourage a swifter departure."

Her tone was even enough, but I've learned how to read the nuances. More than the wound hadn't healed, and wouldn't for a while.

I let my necklet drop. "You did the right thing."

"Did I?" Now bitterness was plain. "I deserted my daughter, Tiger."

I saw no sense in diplomacy. "You did that five years ago."

It snapped her head around. She stared at me angrily. "What right have you—"

"The one you gave me," I told her evenly, "when you pledged me to Staal-Ysta—without my permission, remember?—to buy time with Kalle. Even though you'd given her up five years before."

I didn't intend to criticize her for it; it had been her decision. But by now she was so defensive she considered any comment at all a questioning of her motives. Which meant, as before, she was questioning them herself.

It is not something Del likes to do.

"I had no choice." Her tone was implacable. "I had made oaths. Blood oaths. All oaths should be honored."

"Maybe so," I agreed patiently, "and you're doing a fine job . . . but losing Kalle was the price. It was the choice you made."

Del turned her head and looked at me. "Another thing," she said quietly, "worth killing Ajani for."

I think there is no way a man can fully share or understand a woman's feelings for her child; we are too different. Not being a father—at least, not as far as I know—I couldn't even imagine what she felt. But I had been a child without kin of any kind, trapped in namelessness and slavery, feeling myself unwhole. Del's daughter had a family, even if not of her blood, and I thought that relationship justified the price.

Even if the mother did not.

"It's done," I said quietly. "You've been exiled from Staal-Ysta. But at least you're alive."

Del stared hard into darkness. "I lost Jamail," she said, "when he chose to stay with the Vashni. And now I have lost Kalle. Now I have no one at all."

"You have you. That ought to be enough."

Del's look was deadly. "You are ignorant."

I arched eyebrows. "*Am* I?"

"Yes. You know nothing of Northern kin customs. Nothing at all of family. Yet so quickly you undervalue things I hold very dear."

"Now, Del—"

Del's impatience was manifest. "I will tell you once. A last time. I will tell you so you know, and then perhaps you will understand."

"I think—"

"*I* think you should be quiet and listen to my words."

I shut my mouth. Sometimes you have to let women talk.

Del drew in a steadying breath. "In the North kin circles are very close. They are *sacred* . . . every bit as sacred as a circle is to a sword-dancer. Generations live within a single lodge, sometimes as many as four if the gods are generous in portioning out our lives." Briefly she nodded. "When a man marries, the woman comes into his lodge—unless he has no kin, and then he goes into hers—and so the circle widens. Children are born, and still the circle widens. And when sickness comes and the old ones die, or even the new-born babies, the circle grows small again, so we may support one another. So we may share in the pain and the grief and the anguish, and not try to withstand it alone."

I waited, saying nothing.

"Brothers and sisters and cousins, aunts and uncles and grand-folk. Sometimes the lodges are huge. But always filled with laughter. Always filled with song. Even when people die, so the soul departs in peace."

I thought back to the lodges on Staal-Ysta. Big wooden lodges overflowing with people. So different from what I knew. So alien in customs.

Del spoke very softly. "When anything of substance happens, kinfolk always share. Courtships, weddings, birthings. *And* deaths. The songs are always sung."

She paused, swallowing, frowning, then continued. "A father begins one for the lost child, and the mother takes it up, and then the brothers, the sisters, the aunts, the uncles, the cousins, the grandfolk . . . until the child is sung to sleep forever. If it is a hus-band, the wife begins. A wife, and the husband begins, and so on. The song is always sung, so the newly passed know a life beyond the world. So that there is no darkness, but only light. The light of a day, the light of a fire . . . the light of a star in the night, or the glint from a *jivatma*. Light, Tiger, and song, so there is no need for fear." She drew in an unsteady breath. "But now, for me, there will be no song. There is no one to sing it for me." She controlled her voice with effort. "No one for whom *I* may sing it; Jamail and Kalle are gone."

It called for something. Something of compassion. Something of understanding. But I found myself lacking the words, the tact, the necessary understanding, because I had known the need for revenge. The need for spilling blood.

And so I blurted the first words I stumbled upon because they were easiest. Because they required no compassion—only quiet, deadly passion. "Then let's rid the world of these hounds, bascha . . . let's rid it of Ajani."

Del blinked heavily. But her tone was very steady. "Will you dance with me, Tiger? Will you step into the circle?"

I looked at my sword, lying quietly in its sheath. I thought of its power. I thought of a man named Ajani, and the woman once called Delilah. "Any time you like."

Lips parted. I knew what she wanted. To say here, now, this moment. The temptation was incredibly strong, but she denied it. And made herself all the stronger.

"Not now," she said quietly. "Not even tomorrow. Perhaps the day after."

She knew as well as I even the day after was too soon. But by the time that day arrived, we could put it off again.

Or not.

I rolled forward onto my knees, pulled one of my pouches close, dug down into its depths and pulled from it the ash-dappled pelt. I tossed it gently at her.

Del caught it. Let it unfurl, exhibiting all its glory. And looked to me for an explanation.

"Your birthday," I told her. Then, feeling awkward, "*I've* got no use for it."

Del's hands caressed it. Much of her face was hidden behind loose hair. "A fine pelt," she said softly. "The kind used for a newborn's cradle."

Something pinched my belly. I sat up straighter. "You trying to tell me something?"

Del frowned. "No. No, of course—" And then she understood

exactly what I meant. She tossed back pale hair and looked me straight in the eye. "No, Tiger. Not ever."

"What do you mean, not ever?" And then I thought about how some women couldn't have children, and regretted asking the question. "I mean—no, never mind. I don't know what I mean."

"Yes, you do." Del smiled, if only faintly. "*I* mean, not ever. Only Kalle. I made it so."

"What do you mean, you *made* it—" And, hastily, "No, never mind."

"A pact," she explained simply. "I asked it of the gods. So I could be certain of fulfilling my oath. Kalle had delayed me enough already."

I blinked. "That sort of thing isn't *binding*." I paused. "Is it?"

Del shrugged. "I have not bled since Kalle's birth. Whether it was that, or the gods answering my petition, I cannot say. Only that you need have no fear I will make you something you have no wish to be."

So. Yet another piece of the puzzle named Delilah clicking into place.

Only Kalle, forever, who was no longer hers. And never could be, now.

Thanks to me.

Thanks to my sword.

Oh, hoolies, bascha . . . what's to become of you?

What's to become of *us?*

After a moment I reached out and touched her arm. "I'm sorry, bascha."

Del stared at me blindly, clutching the moon-silvered pelt. And, eventually, smiled. "Giving up on the wager already?"

It took me a moment because I'd nearly forgotten. "No," I retorted sourly, "I'm not giving up on the wager. But I'll make you wish I had."

She slanted me a glance. "I don't sleep with my father."

Hoolies, she knows how to hurt.

Chapter 10

"Here," Del announced. "It is as good as anywhere else, and we may as well see if either of us is capable."

Having been lulled halfway to sleep by the rhythm of the stud and the warmth of the midday sun—well, maybe not *warmth*, exactly; at least, not the sort I was used to, but it was warmer—I had no idea what she was talking about. So I opened my eyes, discovered Del dismounting, and hastily reined in the stud.

"Good as anywhere else for *what?*—and what is it we're supposed to be capable of?" I paused. "Or not?"

"Probably not," she observed, "but that had better change."

I scowled. "Del—"

"It's been long enough, Tiger. Ysaa-den is a day away—and we have yet to dance."

Oh. That. I was hoping she hadn't noticed. "We could wait a bit longer."

"We *could* wait until we've ridden out of the North completely . . . but that wouldn't fulfill your promise." Del squinted up at me, shielding her eyes with the edge of a flattened hand pressed against her forehead. "I need it, Tiger. And so do you."

Yes, well . . . I sighed. "All right. Draw a circle. I've got to limber up a bit, first."

What I had to do was remind aching joints and stiffened muscles what it was to *move*, let alone to dance. We had ridden northeasterly for six days, and I was beginning to think tracking the hounds to their creator was not such a good idea after all. It hurt too much. I'd rather be holed up in some smoky little cantina with *aqivi* in my cup and a cantina girl on my knee—no, that would probably hurt too much, too. Certainly it would hurt too much if I did anything more strenuous than hold her on my knee, which meant why should I bother to hold her on my knee at all?

Hoolies, I hate getting old!

Del tied her gelding to a tree, found a long bough and proceeded to dig a circle into the earth, thrusting through deadfall, damp leaves, mud. Pensively, I watched her, noting how stiffly she held her torso. There was no flexibility in her movements, no fluid grace. Like me, she hurt. And, like me, she healed.

On the outside, if not on the inside.

Del stopped drawing, threw the limb aside, straightened and looked at me. "Are you coming? Or do you want a formal, ritualized invitation?"

I grunted, unhooked foot from stirrup, slowly swung a leg over and stepped down. The stud suggested we go over to the gelding so he could get in a few nips and kicks, but I ignored his comments and tied him some distance from the blue roan, who had done his best to make friends. It was the stud who was having none of it.

Slowly I unhooked cloak brooches, peeled off wool, draped the weight across the saddle. It felt good to be free of it; soon, I hoped, I could pack it away for good. I wouldn't feel truly free until we were across the border and I could replace wool and fur with gauze and silk, but ridding myself of the cloak was something. It allowed me to breathe again.

My hand drifted to the harness worn over the tunic. Fingers tangled briefly in beads and fringe, then found their way to leather straps, supple and soft, snugged tautly against soft wool. Across my back, slanting, hung the sheath with its weight of sword. My hungry, angry sword.

"Tiger."

I shut my eyes. Opened them again, turning, and saw Del in the circle, all in white, glowing in the sun. It was a trick of clear, unblemished light unscreened by a lattice of limbs, but nonetheless it shook me. It reminded me of the night not so long before when she had stood in fire of her own making and all the colors of the world. Then I had thought, however briefly, she was spirit in place of woman. Looking at her now, blazing so brightly, I wondered if maybe I *had* killed her—

No. No.

You fool.

"Tiger," she said again. Unrelenting, as always.

You sandsick, loki-brained fool.

Del unsheathed. Light took life from Boreal.

She wouldn't sing. She wouldn't. And neither, I swore, would I.

Oh, hoolies, bascha . . . I don't want to do this.

Del's face was composed. Her tone divulged nothing. "Step into the circle."

A tremor ran through my limbs. Something pinched my belly.

Bascha, please don't make me.

Del began to smile. Bladeglow caressed her face. It was kind, too kind; she was older, harder, colder. The light gave her youth again. Boreal made her Del again. The one before exile. And Kalle.

Something tickled the back of my neck. Not an insect. Not a stray piece of hair, falling against bared flesh. Something *more*.

Something that spoke of magic, whispering a warning to me.

Or was it merely fear, setting my flesh to rising?

Fear of my sword? Or of Del?

Oh, hoolies. Bascha.

"Tiger," Del said. "Have you gone to sleep standing up?"

Maybe. And maybe I am dreaming.

I slipped out of my harness. Closed my hand around the hilt and drew the blade from its sheath. Hooked the harness over my saddle and walked toward the circle.

Del nodded, waiting. "It will be good for us both."

My throat tightened. Breathing was difficult. Something stirred in the pit of my belly. I bit into my lip and tasted blood. Tasted fear also.

Oh, bascha—don't make me.

"Gently, at first," she suggested. "We both have healing left to do."

I swallowed tightly. Nodded. Made myself step over the limb-carved line.

Del frowned slightly. "Are you all right?"

"Do it," I rasped. "Just—do it."

She opened her mouth. To comment. Question. Chastise. But she did none of those things. She simply shut her mouth and moved away, closing both hands on Boreal's hilt. Slipping smoothly into her stance. That it hurt showed plainly in the soft flesh around her eyes and the brief tensing of her jaw, but she banished pain. Spread her feet. Balanced. Cocked the blade up. And waited.

In a true dance we would put our swords on the ground in the very center of the circle, and take up our positions directly across from one another. It was a race to the swords, and then a fight. A dance. Combat to name a winner. Sometimes it was to the death. Other times only to yield. And occasionally only to show what dancing was all about.

But this was not a true dance. This was sparring only, a chance to test one another's mettle. To learn how fit we were. Or how much we needed to practice.

I needed it for the beasts. Del for Ajani.

One and the same, perhaps?

She waited quietly. I have seen her wait so before, always prepared, never wavering; completely at ease with her sword. It no longer struck me as odd, as alien, that a woman could be a sword-dancer. That a woman could be so good. Del had made herself both; I had seen—and felt—the results.

Sweat ran down the sides of my face. Tension made me itch. I wished myself elsewhere, *anywhere,* other than where I was.

Del dipped her sword. Briefly. Slightly. Barely. A salute to her opponent. In blue eyes I saw concentration. And no indication of fear.

Did it mean nothing at all to Del that she had nearly killed me?

Did it mean nothing at all to Del that I had nearly killed *her?*

"*Kaidin,*" she said softly, giving me Northern rank. Giving me Northern honor.

I lifted my sword. Shifted into my stance. Felt the familiarity of it, the settling of muscles and flesh into accustomed places. Felt the protest of scar tissue twisted into new positions.

Sweat ran into my eyes. Desperation took precedence over other intentions.

I lowered the sword. Swung around. Stepped out of the circle completely. And cursed as my belly cramped.

"Tiger?" Del's tone was bewildered. "Tiger—what is it?"

"—can't," I rasped.

"Can't?" She was a white-swathed wraith walking out of the circle, carrying Boreal. "What do you mean, 'can't'? Are you sick? Is it your wound?"

"I just—can't." I straightened, clutching at abdomen, and turned toward her. "Don't you understand? The last time we did this I nearly killed you."

"But—this isn't a real dance. This is only *sparring*—"

"Do you think it matters?" Sweat dripped onto my tunic. "Do you have any idea what it's like stepping into the circle with you again, two months after the last disastrous dance? Do you have any idea what it feels like to face you across the circle with this butcher's blade in my hands?" I displayed Samiel to her. "Last time it—*he*—did everything he could to blood himself in you . . . and now he's even stronger because I *did* finally blood him." I paused. "Do you want to take that chance? Do you want to trust your life to my ability to control him?"

"Yes," she answered evenly, without hesitation. "Because I know you, Tiger. I know your strengths, your power. Your *own* share of power, from deep inside . . . do you think I would ever doubt you?"

She should. *I* would.

I flung damp hair out of my eyes. "Del, I can't dance with you. Not now. Maybe never. Because each time I try, I'll see it all over again. You, on the ground . . . with blood all over the circle. With blood all over my sword."

Del looked at my blade. Then at her own. Recalling, perhaps, that Boreal had been bloodied also? That someone other than herself had left his share of blood in the circle?

She drew in a deep breath. Shut her eyes briefly, as if she fought some inner battle; then opened them and looked at me. "I'm sorry," she said softly. "I am—different. For a purpose. I put behind me what may be disturbing to others. Again, for a purpose; memories can turn you from your path. But—you should know it was not *easy* for me to cut you." She frowned a little, as if the words hadn't come out the way she meant them. "You should know that I was afraid, too . . . that *you* were dead. That I had killed *you*."

"I can't," I said again. "Not now. Not yet. Maybe never. I know I promised. I know you need someone to dance with, so you can face Ajani. But—well . . ." I sighed. "Maybe what you should do is head south. Go on to the border. Harquhal, maybe—you should find someone there who will dance with you. Sword-dancers will do anything for coin." I shrugged. "Even dance against a woman."

"It will pass," she told me. "Perhaps—if I made you angry?"

I grinned. "You make me angry a lot, bascha—it doesn't mean I want to settle it with swords."

"It will pass," she said again.

"Maybe. Maybe not. Maybe what—" I stopped.

Del frowned. "What is it?"

My belly rolled. All the hairs on my arms stood up. A grue rippled through flesh and muscle. "Magic," I said curtly. "Can't you smell it?"

Del sniffed. "I smell smoke." She frowned, assessing, identifying. "Smoke—and something else. Something *more*." She glanced around, brow creased. "It is gone now—"

"Magic," I repeated. "And no, it's not gone. It's there. It's there, bascha—I promise." It was all I could do not to shudder again. Instead I contented myself with rubbing fingers through wool to flesh, scrubbing a prickling arm. "Not the hounds—not *quite* the hounds . . . something different. Something more."

Del stared northeast. "We are but a day away from Ysaa-den—"

"—and in clear, cold air like this, smells travel; I know. But this is *more*."

"Smoke," she said again, musingly, and then moved away from the circle. Away from me. Like a hunting hound tracking prey, Del sifted through trees and shadows until she found a clearing open to the sky, unscreened by trees. "There," she said as I came up beside her. "Do you see?"

I looked beyond her pointing hand. There was not much to see other than the jagged escarpments of a mountainside, and the blade-sharp spine of the highest peak, all tumbled upon itself into bumps and lumps and crevices, some dark, some shining white in the sunlight.

"Clouds," I said.

"Smoke," Del corrected. "Much too dark for clouds."

I stared harder at the peak. She was right. It wasn't a cloud I saw, rolling down from the heights to swath the peak, but smoke rising from the mountainside itself. Ash-gray, gray-black; it trailed against the sky like a damp cookfire in the wind.

"Ysaa-den," she murmured.

I frowned. "Then that little mountain village is a lot bigger than *I* was told. That's enough smoke for a city half the size of the Punja—"

Del interrupted. "No, not the village. The name. *Ysaa-den.*"

I sighed. "Bascha—"

"Dragon's Lair," she said. "That's what the words mean."

I scowled up at the mountain. "Oh, I see—now I'm supposed to believe in dragons?"

Del pointed. "You should. There it is."

"That's a *mountain*, Del—"

"Yes," she agreed patiently. "Look at the shape, Tiger. Look at the *smoke*."

I looked. At the smoke. At the mountain. And saw what she meant: the shape of the mountain peak, so harsh and jagged and shadowed, did form something like the head of a lizardlike beast. You could see the ridged dome of the skull, the overhanging brows, the undulating wrinkles of dragon-flesh peeled back from bared teeth. Only the teeth were spires of stone, as was the rest of the monstrous beast.

A *mythical* monstrous beast.

"There's the mouth," she mused, "and the nostrils—see the smoke? It's coming out of both."

Well, sort of. There was smoke, yes, and it kind of *appeared* to be coming out of odd rock formations that did, in a vague sort of way, slightly resemble mouth and nostrils—if you looked *real* hard.

"Dragon," I said in disgust.

"Ysaa-den," she repeated.

I grunted.

Del glanced at me. Tendrils of hair lifted from her face. "Don't you hear it, Tiger?"

"I hear wind in the trees."

She smiled. "Have you no imagination? It's the dragon, Tiger—the dragon in his lair, hissing down the wind."

It was *wind*, nothing more, sweeping through the trees. It keened softly, stripping hair out of our faces, rippling woolen folds, blowing smoke across the sky. And the smell of something—*something*—just a little more than woodsmoke.

The back of my neck tingled. "Magic," I muttered.

Del made a noise in her throat that sounded very much like doubt and derision all rolled into one. And then she turned and walked past me, heading back toward the circle she had drawn in the damp, hard soil of a land I could not trust.

No more than my own sword.

Chapter 11

With a name as dramatic as Dragon's Lair, you might expect Ysaa-den to be an impressive place to live. But it wasn't. It wasn't much more than a ramshackle little village spilling halfway down the mountainside. There were clustered lodges like those on Staal-Ysta, but smaller, poorer. Not as well-tended. There was an aura of disrepair about the whole place; but then the villager who'd come to the island had said something about the inhabitants losing heart because of the trouble with the hounds.

I sniffed carefully as Del and I rode into the little mountain village. There was plenty to smell, all right, and not all of it good, but the stench had less to do with hounds than with sickness, despair, desperation. Also the odd tang I'd noticed back by the circle Del had drawn. Smoke—and something more.

It was midday. Warm enough to shed our cloaks, even this high in the mountains. And so we had shed them earlier, tying them onto our saddles, which left harnesses and hilts in plain sight. And that is what brought so many people out to watch us ride into the village: Northern swords in Northern harness. It meant maybe, just *maybe*, we were the sword-dancers sent from Staal-Ysta. The saviors Ysaa-den awaited.

I am accustomed to being stared at. Down south, people do it because, generally, they know who I am. Maybe they want to hire me, buy me aqivi, hear my stories. Maybe they want to challenge me, to prove they are better. Or maybe they don't know me at all, but want to meet me; it happens, sometimes, with women. Or maybe they'd stare at any man who is taller than everyone else, with sandtiger scars on his face. All I know is, they stare.

Here in the North, my size is not so unusual, because Northern men are very nearly always as tall, or taller. But here in the North I am many shades darker in hair and skin. And still scarred. So they stare.

In Ysaa-den also, they stared. But I doubt they noticed size, color, nationality. Here they stared because someone had loosed magic on the land, and it was killing them. And maybe, just maybe, we could do something to stop it.

By the time we reached the center of the village, the lodges had emptied themselves, disgorging men, women, children, dogs, chickens, cats, pigs, sheep, goats, and assorted other livestock. Del and I were awash in Ysaa-den's inhabitants. The human ones formed a sea of blue eyes and blond hair; the others—the four-legged kind—serenaded us with various songs, all of which formed a dreadful racket. Maybe Del could have found something attractive in the music, since she was so big on singing, but to me all it was was noise. Just as it always is.

We stopped, because we could ride no farther. The people pressed close, trampling slushy snow into mud and muck; then, as if sensing the stud's uneasiness and their lack of courtesy, they fell back, shooing animals away, giving us room. But only a little room. Clearly they were afraid that if given the opportunity to leave, we'd take it.

Del reined in the roan to keep him from jostling a child. The mother caught the little girl and jerked her back, murmuring something to her. Del told the woman quietly it was all right, the girl was only curious; no harm was done.

I looked at her sharply as she spoke, hearing nuances in her tone. She was thinking, I knew, of Kalle, of her daughter on Staal-Ysta. And would, probably, for a long time. Maybe even every time she looked at a blonde, blue-eyed girl of about five years.

But Del would learn to live with this just as she'd learned with everything else. It is one of her particular strengths.

She glanced at me. "It was your promise." In other words, she was leaving the introductions and explanations to me.

Uncomfortable, I shifted in the saddle, redistributing weight. Down south I'm happy enough to talk with villagers *or* tanzeers, to strike bargins, suggest deals, invent solutions to problems—but that's down south, where I know the language. And also where they pay me for such things. Coin is a tremendous motivator.

The thing was, I wasn't south. I didn't know the people, didn't know the language—at least, not very well—didn't know the customs. And that sort of ignorance can make for a world of trouble.

"They're waiting," Del said quietly.

So they were. All of them. Staring back at me.

Well, nothing for it but to do the best I could. I sucked in a deep breath. "I'm hunting hounds," I began in Southron-accented Northern—and the whole village broke into cheering.

It was noise enough to wake the dead. Before all I'd heard was the racket of animals; now there was human noise to contend with, too. And it was just as bad.

Hands patted my legs, which was all anyone could reach. I couldn't help it: I stiffened and reached up for my sword; realized, belatedly, all the hands did was pat. It was a form of welcome, of joy; of tremendous gratitude.

Del's roan was surrounded. She, too, was undergoing the joyful welcome. I wondered what it felt like for her, since she hadn't come to Ysaa-den to help anyone. She'd come for her own requirements, which had nothing to do with hounds. Only with Ajani.

If anyone noticed I wasn't Northern, which seemed fairly likely, it wasn't brought up. Apparently all that mattered was that Staal-Ysta had heard of their plight, answered their pleas, sent us to settle things. No one cared who we were. To them, we were salvation with steel redemption in our sheaths.

I looked out across the throng. Since they expected us to save them, I saw no point in wasting time. So I got right to the point. "Where are these beasts coming from?"

As one they turned to the mountain. To the dragon atop their world. And one by one, they pointed. Even the little children.

"Ysaa," someone murmured. And then all the others joined in. The world rolled through the village.

Ysaa. I didn't need a translation: dragon. Which didn't make any sense. There *were* no dragons. Not even in the North, a place of cold, harsh judgments. Dragons were mythical creatures. And they had nothing to do with hounds.

"Ysaa," everyone whispered, until the word was a hiss. As much as the dragon's breath, creeping down from the gaping stone mouth.

Then, having named it, they all turned once more to me. Bright blue eyes were expectant; clearly, they wanted something. Something to do with the dragon.

I glanced at Del. "This is ridiculous." In Southron, not Northern; I have *some* diplomacy. "I came here to find whoever was sending out the hounds, not discuss bedtime stories."

"Well," she said lightly, "if it *is* ridiculous, your task will be that much simpler."

"Why?" I asked suspiciously.

"Why do you think?" she retorted. "They want you to kill the dragon."

I peered up at the dragon-shaped mountain. It was a pile of stone, nothing more. "If that's true," I told her, "this job will be very easy."

All right, it was a stupid thing to say. If I have learned anything in this business, it is never to underestimate your opponent. But the idea of a *mountain* being an enemy was enough to irritate even me, even-tempered as I am; people who allow religion or mythology to control their lives are begging for trouble. It just doesn't happen that way. We're born, we live, we die—gods don't have anything to do with it any more than *dragons* do.

And I'd come hunting hounds.

Now, inside a lodge, Del shook her head. "It doesn't matter," she said. "No other sword-dancers from Staal-Ysta ever reached them. Only you. And so now you can fulfill your promise, as you said." She paused. "Isn't that what you told me? That you took on the task of aiding Ysaa-den in the name of your new-won rank?"

Well, yes. Sort of. I mean, I *had*, but all I'd been after was a chance to track down the hounds. At the time, it had provided a means of escape. A means of putting behind me what I'd done to Del. Because the only way I could deal with her death was to hide from it in a job.

Trouble was—well, no, not trouble—Del wasn't dead. Which meant I no longer needed the job, because there was nothing to hide *from*.

The people of Ysaa-den—with all their animals—had escorted us en masse to the headman's lodge. It was the biggest, but also the emptiest; he'd lost half of his family to, he told us, the dragon.

I sighed, hung onto my patience, went about my business. Del and I settled our horses in the guest pen behind the lodge—the stud didn't like it much, threatening the sapling fence with iron-shod hind hooves until I told him to mind his manners—then joined the headman inside, where I tried to bring up the hounds. But he waved them off like so much unnecessary baggage. What *he* wanted to talk about was the dragon.

I listened for a moment or two, knowing better than to cut him off too soon—you always have to humor people impressed by their own authority—then mentioned something about a long journey. He took the hint; he bowed himself out of the lodge, leaving us alone. To rest and refresh ourselves.

At least the empty lodge was quiet. The thought of living with multitudinous people and animals was not something I cared to consider.

The headman's dwelling, like the lodges on Staal-Ysta, was built of wood with mud, twigs, and cloth stuffed into the cracks between the logs. It provided shelter from the worst of the cold and wind, but nonetheless remained a bit chilly on the inside despite the fire laid at one end of the lodge, beneath the open smoke hole, which let air *in* as well as letting smoke out. An open corridor ran the length of the rectangle, lined on either side by wooden roof supports evenly spaced about ten feet apart. Beyond the supports were the compartments the inhabitants called their own; small, cramped spaces more like stalls than rooms. It was a place of enforced closeness. Del had spoken of kin ties and blood loyalties strengthened by living customs; I could see why. If they didn't learn to live *with* one another, they'd end up killing each other.

Del went into the first empty compartment she came to. No doubt the headman expected us to use another—his own well-appointed one, I'm sure, down at the far end—but Del has never been one for unnecessary ceremony. She untied her bedding, spread pelts over hard-packed earth, sat down. And took out her *ji-vatma*.

It was a ritual I had witnessed many times. For anyone who lives by the sword, the care of a blade is an important part of survival. Del and I had spent many an evening beneath the moon, cleaning, honing and oiling our swords, tending the little nicks, or inspecting and repairing harness and sheaths. But now, here, in this place, it seemed odd to watch her yet again tending her sword. I don't know why. It just did.

In the distance, beasts bayed. I heard the mournful howls, echoing in rocky canyons; the eerie keening of magic-made hounds drifting down from the dragon to thread its way throughout Ysaa-den, sliding through chinks in the lodges and ghosting down the smoke hole. I shivered.

"Hoolies," I blurted irritably. "How can you people live in a place this cold? I have yet to see a truly warm day, or a piece of ground without some kind of snow on it. How can you stand it, Del? All this cold and snow and drab, gray-white days? There's no *color* here!"

Her head was bent over her work. The laced braid swung, back and forth, gently, as she tended the blade. With abrupt discomfort, I recalled the wager we'd made regarding solitary nights in different beds.

And then recalled other things. Behavior I couldn't condone. Explanations I couldn't accept.

Del didn't even look up. "There is color," she said at last. "Even in winter. There are the subtle colors of snow—white, gray, blue, pink, all dependent upon sun and shade and time of day—and the richness of the mountains, the lakes, the trees. Even the clothing of the children." She flicked a glance at me. "There is color, Tiger. You have only to look for it."

I grunted. "I prefer the South. The deserts. Even the Punja. At least there I know what's what."

"Because there are no dragons?" Del didn't smile, just ran her whetstone the length of the blade. "But there are cumfa, and danjacs, and sandtigers . . . not to mention lustful tanzeers, murderous borjuni, and warrior tribes like the Vashni."

Standing wasn't accomplishing much except sore knees and tired back; I dropped my roll of bedding and perched my rump upon it, addressing her final comment. "They gave your brother a home."

"The remains of him," she said. The whetstone rang out more loudly than usual. "You saw what he was to that old man."

So I had. I am a man for women, having no desire for men in my bed, but I'd seen clearly what there was between Del's brother and the old Vashni chieftain who'd taken him in.

And had thought, at the time, that at least the boy had found someone to love after being stripped of manhood and tongue. Someone to love *him*.

"But you would have brought him back anyway," I said. "Isn't that what you intended, to get him out of the South?"

"Of course. And I would have. But—he chose otherwise."

"I don't think he had a choice, Del. I think he knew it was best for him to remain with the Vashni, where he was accepted for himself."

"Accepted because he *belonged* to the old man."

I knew what she meant by the emphasized word. In the South, where women are little more than brood mares or ornaments, men often seek more stimulating companionship with their own sex. In bed as well as anywhere else. And then, of course, there was the slave trade—

I broke off the thought. "Maybe so," I agreed. "And maybe, by then, it was what he wanted."

Del stopped honing. "But what happens?" she asked. "What happens when the old man is dead? Does Jamail become the slave of a new chieftain? Does he then serve the new man as he served the old?"

"I don't know," I told her. "Short of going back down there to find out, we never can know."

"No," she said sharply. Then, more quietly, "No. You are right: he made his choice. Just as I made mine with Kalle."

I expected something more. But she gave me nothing save the muted ring of whetstone on steel. Another kind of song.

One I understood.

We had privacy until sundown. And then the headman and several other villagers came into the lodge and very politely invited us to dinner. Since Del and I had nothing better to do—and both of us were hungry—we accepted.

Given a choice, I'd have preferred the meal inside a lodge; as a matter of fact, it was sort of what I'd expected. But apparently the Northerners took the first breath of spring as a promise of temperate nights as well as days; when dinner proved to be a village-wide gathering under the naked sky, seated on pelt-covered ground, I wrapped myself so close in my cloak it was next to impossible to move, though I left enough room for my eating arm to do its work.

One thing I'm good at is eating. And you never spit on a gift meal unless it's served by an enemy.

The headman, whose name was Halvar, was very aware of the honor our presence did Ysaa-den; he was also very aware of his own responsibilities in hosting us properly. While Del and I chewed roast pork, bread, tubers, and swallowed mugs of ale, Halvar entertained us with the history of the village. I didn't pay much attention, since I had trouble following his accent, *and* since I kept hearing references to the dragon, which told me mythology ran rampant in Ysaa-den. And I've never cared much for mythology. Just give me a clean sword made of true-honed steel—

"Tiger."

It was Del; no surprise. I glanced over, picking a string of pork rind from between my teeth. "What?"

Briefly, she frowned. Then made a graceful one-handed gesture that somehow managed to indicate the entire gathering. "Because we go tomorrow to face the dragon, the village of Ysaa-den would like to make a song in our honor."

"I don't sing," I answered promptly.

"They don't want to hear *you* sing, Tiger. They want to sing for us."

I swallowed the freed bit of pork and washed it down with ale. Shrugged a single shoulder. "If they want to. You know I'm not big on music."

Del changed languages adroitly, switching to accented Southron and smiling insincerely for Halvar's benefit. "It's considered an honor. And if you have any manners at all—*or* good sense—you will tell them how honored we are."

"They can sing us to sleep, for all I care." I swallowed more ale.

Del's smile fell away. "Why are you being so rude? These people believe in you, Tiger . . . these people are trying to tell you how much it means to them that you've come to save the village. You are the *Sandtiger*—someone out of Southron legends. Now perhaps you can become the man of Northern legends as well. Someone who cares for the troubles of others, who tends the helpless and weak—"

I had to interrupt before she got in any deeper. "Appealing to my pride won't work."

"It has before."

I ignored that. "Maybe because I just can't understand why a village full of adults persists in telling stories instead of discussing things rationally." I gestured with my head toward the looming mountain. "It's a heap of stone, Del; nothing more. If the hounds are up there, I'll go—but why keep telling me there's a dragon?"

Del sighed and set down her own mug. All around us the people stared; we spoke in Southron, not Northern, but undoubtedly the tenor of our discussion was obvious, even if the words weren't.

"Tiger, weren't you listening to anything Halvar told us about how Ysaa-den came to be?"

"I *heard* it, yes . . . but I didn't catch one word in ten, bascha. His uplander is all twisty, and I don't speak it that well anyway."

Del frowned a little. "Mountain dialect; yes, it might be difficult for you. But that doesn't excuse your rudeness—"

"—in not taking his story literally?" I shook my head. "I'm not here to waste my time on a storyteller's fancy, Del. They're all a bunch of liars anyway, if you ask me—spinning tales for coin when they should be spending their time doing real work. I mean, how hard is it to make up stories? And then to be *paid* for it—"

"Tiger." Del's tone cut me short. "We are not discussing *skjalds*, who hold high honor in the North—and how would you know if being a *skjald* is difficult or easy? What does a man who kills other men know of telling stories?"

I slanted her a glance. "Last time I looked, you carried your own share of death-dealing, Delilah."

It shut her up for a moment. And then she looked at Halvar, who waited patiently, and managed a weak smile. But there was nothing weak about her tone of voice. "This man and his village have offered to pay us high honor, Sandtiger. You will listen to the song, and you will wait quietly for its conclusion, and then you will thank Halvar and everyone of Ysaa-den for their kindness and graciousness. Do you hear?"

"Of *course*," I said, affronted, "What do you think I am, anyway? Some fool who fell off the goat wagon this morning?"

"No," Del said coolly. "Some fool who fell off one thirty-eight or thirty-nine years ago and landed on his head."

"Thirty-*six!*" I retorted, stung. And swore as she smiled sweetly and informed Halvar we would be very honored by the song.

At least, I think that's what she said. You never can be too sure with uplander. It's hilly as the North itself. But whatever it was she said pleased Halvar mightily; he called out something unintelligible—to me—and people scattered to lodges, returning moments later with skin drums, pipes, tambors, finger-bells, wooden sticks, and other things I didn't recognize.

Musicians, obviously. The rest, who had only their voices, gathered children into laps or lovers into arms and prepared to make us a song.

The sun was gone, swallowed by the mountains. The dragon smoked sullenly in the dusk, emitting a faint red glow from deep in its "throat." I scowled up at it, noting that darkness did not entirely alter its shape into a more sanguine beast, as expected—if anything, it looked more dragonlike than ever—and realized the odd smell remained. Much of it was covered by other aromas—roast pork, sour ale, unwashed bodies, babies who needed clean wrappings, animals too closely confined—but it remained underneath it all, drifting down from the dragon-shaped mountain to shroud Ysaa-den in a musty, malodorous pall.

Not woodsmoke. Woodsmoke has a clean, sweet scent, depending on the wood. And not dung smoke, either, goat, cow or otherwise—I have reason to know, having gathered dung in my days as a slave—which has a pungency all its own. This was different.

"Hounds," I said sharply.

Halvar broke off his introduction to the song. Del looked at me crossly.

"Hounds," I repeated, before she could say anything, or call me names again. "That's what it smells like. Or, better yet, that's what *they* smell like." I lifted my chin in the mountain's direction. "The smoke."

Del frowned. "Eggs gone bad?" she suggested.

I considered it. "A little," I agreed. Then, upon further reflection, "but more like rotting bodies."

I said it quietly, so only Del could hear. It made her curt with me anyway. And then she turned from me to Halvar again. Pointedly, and told him to begin the long-delayed song.

He was more than ready. Trouble was, he needed one more thing from each of us. And asked it.

Del's face changed. I saw the color go out of it, very slowly; how her eyes, equally slowly, dilated. She shook it off quickly enough, but the damage had been done. When she spoke to the headman it was in her clipped, sword-dancer's tone of voice, all business, with little personality in it. I have heard her use it before. I had not expected her to use it with Halvar, whom she seemed to like.

I stirred within the folds of my cloak. "What?"

Del waved a hand at me, as if it would be enough.

"What?" I repeated, with a bit more emphasis. "There are two of us here, bascha—what did he ask?"

She shot me a deadly glance. "Names," she answered curtly. "The names of living kin, so that should we fail tomorrow, and die, our kinfolk can be told. So funeral songs may be sung."

It was unexpected. Equally discomfiting. "Well," I said finally, "I guess that means less work for Halvar, then, if anything *does* happen. Since there's no one to tell for either of us."

Del didn't answer at once. And then when she did it was very quietly, with an odd lack of emotion. She spoke uplander to Halvar, explaining the truth of things. I didn't catch all of the words, but I did catch his expression.

He looked at Del. At me. Then drew in a breath and addressed the gathered villagers, adult and child alike.

I heard Del's hiss of shock. And then she was trying to override Halvar's little speech, telling him no repeatedly. But he was adamant; I heard the word for honor.

Trust him to hit on the right word. It shut her up immediately. "What?" I asked irritably.

Del was tight as wire. "I told him." Her teeth were gritted. "I told him. That there are no names. There are no kin. Only the Sandtiger and Delilah, with blooding-blades for kinfolk and the circle for our lodge.'

I waited a moment. "And?"

Del sucked in a deep breath, held it, released it. Slowly. Silently. "So," she said, "they will sing. They will make a song for all our lost ones, a song of farewell, because they had no kin to sing it to for them when they died, to guide them into the light." She swallowed visibly. "As you and I have no kinfolk to sing the songs for us."

I heard the first voice. Halvar's: the headman's privilege. And then a woman's voice: his wife's. And another and another, until all the village was singing. Voices only; no pipes, no drums, no sticks, no tambors, no chiming finger-bells. Only voices.

Voices were enough.

Wrapped tightly in my cloak, I sat beneath a star-blotched Northern sky and thought only of the South. Of the desert. Of the Punja.

Where a woman had borne a boy—a strong, healthy boy—and left him to die in burning sands beneath a blazing sun.

Chapter 12

The stench was worsening. Halvar, riding a little ahead of Del, who rode ahead of me, seemed not to notice, which told me either he had no sense of smell, or he'd grown so accustomed to the stink he no longer noticed it. To me, it seemed impossible, in view of the magnitude of the odor. Hoolies, I could *taste* it. It made me want to spit.

I leaned over in my saddle, making sure I didn't threaten the stud, and spat. Twice. He waggled an ear, shook his head, walked on.

We climbed relentlessly toward the dragon, which was making its presence known through smell *and* smoke. Both filled up nose and mouth, lingering unpleasantly in lungs, causing a tight, dull headache that made me irritable as well as impatient. There had been no sign of hounds since Del and I reached Ysaa-den, though we'd heard them. And no sign of any dragon; as we climbed, our closeness to the rock formations and crumbling spires caused them to lose their eerie shapes and became nothing more than stone and earth, which is what I'd said the thing was all along. I felt suitably vindicated; unfortunately, no one wanted to share in my victory.

As we climbed, Halvar entertained us with stories about the dragon and Ysaa-den. Trouble was, I was too far behind the headman and Del to hear everything over the noise of hoof on stone; moreover, his mountain dialect rendered his uplander mostly unintelligible. Which didn't particularly bother me, if you want the truth; I was content to match the rhythm of the stud's steady climbing and spent my time looking around watchfully. Part of me waited for hounds. Now that I no longer wore the Cantéada ward-whistle, the stakes were a bit different. But I still had a sword, and so did Del.

So did Halvar, but it was an old, ill-tended bronze sword, of no use to anyone, let alone a headman untrained in fighting. I had the feeling Halvar would be more hindrance than help, if it came to making a stand. But you can't just pat the village leader on the head when trouble arises and send him off to mother and father; the hounds had eaten Halvar's, and anyway he was too nice a person to dismiss so easily. There would have to be some show of dignity and honor in the name of the headman's pride.

From the heights came a mournful wailing howl that changed, midway, to a vicious growling snarl. Halvar halted his mount.

"Far enough," he said, so emphatically even I understood it. "I am headman, not hero; such things are for sword-dancers and sword-singers trained on Staal-Ysta."

Which meant Halvar was more than a nice person; he was also pretty smart.

We were two-thirds of the way up the mountain. The track had changed to trail some time back; now it began to resemble little more than a trough formed by melting snow. I asked Halvar why, if they so feared the dragon and its hounds, the villagers even bothered to climb far enough to *make* a trail.

Halvar stared back at me blankly a moment. Then he looked at Del.

She sighed. "He explained all that, Tiger. As we climbed."

I didn't like being made to feel guilty. "I told you I don't understood his lingo very well. And besides, *one* of us had to keep an eye out for hounds."

Del didn't answer right away. She looked up the mountain toward the "mouth," which still spewed fitful drifts of smoke. "The hounds weren't always here," she said finally. "Halvar says the first one appeared about six months ago, maybe seven. Apparently it killed one of the villagers; no one is certain, because the man was

never found. But after that, more and more of the beasts appeared . . . and more and more villagers disappeared. There is a
track here because the village holy man suggested the dragon
might be appeased with gifts, and so the villagers began to climb up
to the dragon to make offerings. Unfortunately, the dragon was not
appeased; more people disappeared. So they sent to Staal-Ysta and
begged for help." She paused. "You are what they got."

I wanted to respond to her overly bland tone of voice, which is
infuriating at times, but Halvar pointed up the mountain and said
something to Del I couldn't understand. It sounded like a warning
to me. Whatever it was, Del didn't much like it; she snapped out
something to Halvar that made him redden. But he tapped the hilt
of his useless bronze sword and repeated what he'd said before.
This time I caught part of it. Something about *jivatmas*.

"What?" I asked, as usual.

Del looked at Halvar. "He says we would be wise to leave our
swords sheathed. That the village holy man has decreed magic a
danger to Ysaa-den because the dragon feeds on it."

"Oh?" It sounded suspicious to me. "And how does he know
that?"

"He set wards when the hounds first appeared," she explained.
"Or so Halvar says. And the wards, instead of protecting the village,
drew the hounds. Who stole them."

"Stole what, the *wards*? Is he sandsick? What would hounds
want with wards?"

Del didn't smile. "Maybe the same thing they wanted with the
whistle."

And my sword? My newly-quenched *jivatma*? They hadn't
been even remotely interested in the thing until I'd blooded it; only
in Boreal, who reeked of blood and power.

I looked at Halvar with a bit more respect. "Tell him we appreciate the warning."

Del stared. "Tiger—"

"And ask him if he will send someone each day to feed and
water the horses; we're leaving them here and going the rest of the
way on foot. I'd send them back down with him, but I don't like
the idea of being completely horseless; at least this way they're in

range, if we need them." I looked again at the smoking "mouth," easily an hour's hike from where we were. "Sort of."

"Each day?" Del echoed. "How many do you plan to spend tromping around the mountains?"

"Two," I answered succinctly. "If I can't beat a mountain by then, hounds or no hounds, I'm not worth the coin they're paying me."

"They're not."

I frowned. "Not what?"

"Paying you."

I frowned harder. "What do you mean, not paying me? This is what I do for a living, bascha. Remember?"

"But you took on this task as a duty to your rank as a *kaidin*." Her expression also was bland, but I know that look in her eye. "They didn't hire the Sandtiger, nor did Staal-Ysta send him. A new-made *kaidin* answered the plea of a village in need, and swore to help in any way he could." She raised pale brows. "Isn't that what you told me?"

"Hoolies, Del, you *know* I'm a sword-dancer. I don't do anything for free." I paused. "At least, not anything *dangerous*."

"Then perhaps you should explain that to Halvar, who is head-man of a village which probably has no coin at all—oh, perhaps one or two coppers, if you insist on counting—but survives against all odds because people make a living out of the ground and from the livestock, in coin of wool and milk and pork . . . except you would not consider that a living, would you? If it isn't gold or silver or copper, it's not worth the effort."

I sat the stud and stared at her, taken aback by the vehemence of her contempt. This wasn't the Del I knew . . . well, yes, I guess it was. It was the *old* Del, the one who'd used words as well as a weapon as we'd crossed the Punja on the way to Julah.

Was this the Del I'd wanted back, just so we could reestablish some of the old relationship?

Was I sandsick?

Del reined back the blue roan, who showed signs of wanting to nose the stud. "So, do we turn back now? Do you explain to Halvar that this was all a big misunderstanding, so that he will be forced into offering what little coin Ysàa-den has? Will you hold a village for ransom, Tiger, in the name of your avarice?"

The dragon snorted smoke. One of the beasts bayed.

"Nice little speech," I remarked finally. "You really know how to manipulate a person, don't you? Too bad you're not willing to consider that I had no intention of asking for money in the first place—you just jumped to the conclusion that I'm a no-good, low-down sword-for-hire with no sense at all of humanity, only a well-developed sense of greed." I smiled at her with eloquent insincerety. "Well, I won't give you the satisfaction of thinking you convinced me . . . I'm going to do what I please, regardless of what you think, and let you try to figure out the truth of my intentions. I'm also going to suggest you take your own advice: never assume anything. It can get you into trouble."

I climbed down from the stud and led him off the remains of the track to a stout young tree, where I tied him and explained I'd be back in two days, if not before.

He nosed me, then banged his head against my ribs, which hurt, and which left me less regretful about leaving him. As a matter of fact, it left me downright displeased; I thumped him on the nose and told him he'd just lost his ration of grain for the day.

Of course, I didn't tell Halvar that, which meant the stud would get his share from whoever came to tend him, but *he* didn't have to know that. It would do him good to suffer until nightfall.

I glanced at Del, who still sat her roan. "Well? You coming?"

She tipped back her head and stared up at the crown of the mountain, frowning faintly. Her hair, still laced and braided, dangled against her spine. The line of her jaw cut the air like a blade. I saw her lips part; she said something to herself, mouthing it in silence, and I wondered what was in her mind. Ajani? Delay?

Or maybe a Southron sword-dancer who taxed her dwindling supply of patience.

Hoolies, she didn't have to stay. I wasn't forcing her to. She could turn around with Halvar and ride back down the mountain to Ysaa-den. Or ride clear to the South. To Harquhal and beyond, maybe even to Julah; or to the Vashni, who had her brother;

hoolies, there was no place in the world Del couldn't go if she put her mind to it.

Except Staal-Ysta.

Del slid a leg over her saddle and stepped down carefully, sparing her midriff as much as she could. It would be days, possibly even weeks, before either of us could move freely again, without awareness of stiffness and pain. It was possible neither of us would ever fully recover fluidity of motion, since respective sword blades had cut muscle as well as flesh.

Then again, it was possible only *I* wouldn't; Del was twenty-one. The young heal faster, neater, better.

And maybe she needed it more.

I unpinned my cloak, rolled it, fastened it onto my saddle. No doubt come night I would regret leaving it behind, but its weight and muffling folds would hinder me during the climb. Hopefully the task could be accomplished before it got cold enough for me to need the warmth of its weight.

Hopefully.

Well, one can *always* hope.

Del tied off the roan—outside of the stud's reach—and chatted briefly with Halvar. Like me, she shed her cloak and put it away. Sunlight glinted off the hilt of her *jivatma;* I saw Halvar stare at it in something akin to reverence. No doubt any village full of people who believed in dragons also told bedtime stories about Northern blooding-blades and the men who bore them. Now they could add a whole new raft of tales about the pale-haired woman who summoned a banshee-storm with only a name and a song.

"Let's go," I said irritably. "We're burning daylight."

"So is the dragon," Del observed, as smoke issued from "mouth" and "nostrils." This time sound came with it: a low-pitched, hissing rumble, as if the dragon belched.

"Beware the fire," Halvar said, clearly enough for me.

I looked up the mountain. "If there's fire," I pointed out, "someone has to tend it. Which means there's more up there than rock and hounds . . . likely a man as well."

Halvar looked at me strangely.

"It makes sense," I said defensively; I hate it when I'm doubted.

"Do you really think there's a *dragon* up there, fire-breathing and all?"

Still Halvar stared. And then he looked at Del as if hoping she could explain.

"No," Del said quietly, "he thinks no such thing . . . Tiger, I am sorry you have been so left out of the conversation—I didn't realize it was so hard for you to understand. No one in Ysaa-den believes there's a *real* dragon up there—no one is so foolish as to believe in a mythical creature—but a sorcerer. A specific one, in fact: Chosa Dei."

"*Who?*"

"Chosa Dei," she repeated. "He is a legendary sorcerer, Tiger; surely you must have heard of him, even in the South."

"No." Emphatically. "Del—"

"He has not been seen for hundreds of years, ever since a fight with his brother, Shaka Obre—who is also a sorcerer—but Halvar tells me Ysaa-den has lain in his shadow for nearly ninety years. They believe it is Chosa Dei who troubles them now, awakening; *he* is the 'dragon,' not this pile of stone."

"Have *you* heard of this sorcerer?"

"Of course." Del was dead serious. "He was one of my favorite stories when I was a child. I know all about Chosa Dei . . . and all his fights with his brother, and how they spent all their magic trying to kill one another—"

"Are you *completely* sandsick?" I gaped at her inelegantly. "You're standing here telling me you believe a man out of childhood stories is living in that mountain, blowing smoke out stone tunnels just to pass the time?"

Del smiled. "No," she said in Southron. "But it would be rude to tell Halvar so, and ruin the history of his village."

I blinked. "Then why *are* we here?"

She slipped a thumb beneath a harness strap and resettled her sword. "Because a newly named *kaidin* made a promise he's sworn to keep."

I opened my mouth to respond. Rudely, of course; she was throwing things I'd said back in my own face. But before I could say a word something interrupted.

A keening, rising howl, echoing eerily. And a gout of malodorous smoke, fanned by heated wind.

No matter *who* it was, someone—*something*—was killing people. And I was here to stop it.

"Come on," I said curtly.

Del fell in behind me.

Conditioning is important to a sword-dancer. Because if you lack stamina, speed and wind, you risk losing the dance. And, much of the time, if you risk losing the dance, you also risk losing your life.

Which means a sword-dancer worth his salt always stays in condition.

Unless he's been recently wounded, which changes things altogether.

I suppose two months isn't recent. But it felt like it. It felt like yesterday every step I took—no, let's make it today. Like maybe a moment ago. All I know is, it hurt to climb the mountain.

I knew I was a fool to go charging up a rockpile where there wasn't any air to breathe and I had no lungs to breathe it. I knew I was a fool to even *consider* taking on anything with my sword, be it human or animal. And certainly I was a fool to be doing it with Del, who was in no better shape than I. It's nice to have backup— it's *great* to have backup—but only if they're healthy.

We huffed and puffed and coughed and swore and muttered all the way up the mountain. We also slid, staggered, fell down, gagged on the stink of the dragon's breath. And wished we were somewhere else, *doing* something else; Del no doubt thought of Ajani, while I dreamed of a cantina. A cantina in the *South*, where the days are warm and bright. And there are no mountains to climb.

The dragon snorted smoke. A rumble accompanied it. And then a relentless hiss spitting wind into our faces. It ripped the hair from my eyes and inserted hot fingers into the weave of my heavy wool tunic.

I slipped, slid, climbed. Threw a question over my shoulder toward the woman who climbed behind me. "*Who* is this man again?"

"What man?—oh." Del was breathing hard. She spoke in brief,

clipped sentences, sparing no breath for more. "Chosa Dei. Sorcerer. Supposed to be very powerful—till he lost an argument."

"With his brother."

"Shaka Obre." Del sucked in a breath. "There are stories about both of them . . . tales of great and powerful magic . . . also ambition. Chosa Dei is the example parents put up before greedy children. *'Look, oh look, beware of wanting too much, or you will become like Chosa Dei, who dwells in Dragon Mountain.'*" It faded into a cough.

"So now everyone in Ysaa-den thinks *their* mountain is Dragon Mountain, and that Chosa Dei dwells in it."

"Yes."

"Sounds like they're taking after the old man and his taste for ambition. I mean, saying their village lies in the dragon's shadow is an attempt to claim some fame, isn't it? Just like Bellin the Cat."

It was Del's turn. *"Who?"*

"Bellin the Cat," I repeated. "You know, that silly boy back in Harquhal who wants to be a panjandrum. Who wants to make a name." I sucked more air. "The kid with all the axes."

That, Del remembered. "Oh. Him."

"So, it seems to me Ysaa-den's a little like him—" I bit off a curse as a foot slipped and nearly deposited me on my face. "I mean, isn't it a little silly to adopt a story as truth just to gain a little fame?" I brushed dirt from my clothes and went on.

"If you lived in Ysaa-den, what would *you* do?"

I thought it over. "True."

Del slid, caught at rock, climbed upward again. "After all, what does it hurt? No one really knows where Dragon Mountain lies— there are countless maps with countless mountains called after Chosa Dei's prison—and no one really knows if Chosa Dei ever existed. He's a legend, Tiger. Some believe it, some don't."

"Which are you, Delilah?"

Del laughed once. "I told you, stories about Chosa Dei and his battles with Shaka Obre were favorites when I was young. Of course I want to believe. But it doesn't mean I do."

I wondered, not for the first time, what childhood for Del had been like. I knew bits and pieces only, because that was all she'd shared, but it wasn't hard to put a few of them together.

I imagined a pretty but strong-minded girl who preferred boys' doings to girls'. And who, as the only daughter, was allowed the freedom to *be* a boy, even symbolically, because it was probably easier for father and uncles and brothers. Easier for a mother who knew she was outnumbered. No skirts and dolls for Del; she'd been handed a sword in place of a cooking spoon.

I'd asked her once what she would be if she hadn't become a sword-dancer. And she had said probably married. Probably bearing babies. But it was impossible for me to think of Del in those terms, to even *imagine* her tending a lodge, a man, a child; not because I didn't think she could, but because I'd never seen it. All I had ever seen was a woman with a sword, tending to men in the circle.

For six long years, it was all Delilah had been. But I wondered. Even if she didn't, I did. I couldn't help myself.

What would become of Del once Ajani was dead?

Yet more importantly: what would Del *become* once Ajani was dead?

"Tiger—look."

I looked. Was too out of breath to speak.

"Almost there," Del gasped, nearly as winded as I. "Can't you feel the heat?"

Heat, yes, if you're a Northerner. To a Southroner, it was merely a gentle warming, like the breeze of a spring day. What *I* noticed was, it stank.

"Hoolies," I muttered, "if this man's that powerful a sorcerer, why can't he live in a place that *smells* better?"

"No choice," Del croaked. "It was a spell put on him by Shaka Obre."

"Ah. Of course. I forgot." I topped off the last bit of mountain and arrived at the dragon's lip. Heat and stench rolled out to bathe me in dragonish breath. "Hoolies, this place *stinks!*"

Del came over the edge and paused to catch her breath. I saw her expression of distaste as the odor engulfed her as well. It's hard enough trying to suck wind back into laboring lungs, but when it smells this bad the task is that much harder.

Smoke rolled out of the "mouth." I steeled myself and went over for a closer look.

From below, it *looked* like a dragon. The shape of earth and rock, the arrangement of the same—from below, it looked drago-n*ish*. But from up top, from the opening in the rock, it was only a large odoriferous cave extending back into the mountain. The spires of rock forming "teeth" were nothing more than stone columns shaped by ancient rain and the wind moaning incessantly through the cavern's entrance, bearing the stench of rotting bodies and a trace of something more.

Does magic have a smell?

"No hounds," Del observed.

No hounds. No dragon. No Chosa Dei.

"Wait a moment," I muttered, frowning down at the ground. I bent, squatted, looked more closely at turfy ground and the tracks pressed into it. "Pawprints," I said, "going straight into the cave."

Del took an involuntary step back, one hand drifting up toward the hilt riding above her left shoulder. "It couldn't be their *den*—" But she let it trail off.

"Leave her sheathed," I suggested, thinking of Halvar's warning, "and yes, I think it could be . . . if I believed they were really hounds. It's what I've called them—the Hounds of Hoolies—for lack of a better name, but I never believed they were. And I don't think beasts live in dens." I shrugged. "Although I suppose they *could*."

We stared at one another, not liking the idea. Not liking the vision I'd painted. I thought it pretty disgusting; Del didn't say anything.

She edged closer to the entrance. She didn't draw Boreal, but her right hand hooked in her harness as if to stay close just in case. And I didn't really blame her.

"Tiger, do you think—"

But I didn't hear her finish. A blast of malodorous wind came roaring out of the cavern; with it came an overwhelming presentiment of power.

I itched, because all my hairs stood up on my arms, my thighs, the back of my neck. Even my bones tingled; my belly climbed up my throat. It was all I could do not to vomit. "Del—oh, hoolies—*Del*—"

"What is it? Tiger, what *is* it?"

I staggered back from the opening, trying not to retch. I also tried to wave Del off, but she followed anyway. "Don't, bascha—wait—can't you *feel* it?"

Maybe. Maybe not. But Del unsheathed Boreal.

It drove me to my knees. "I said *wait*—oh, hoolies, bascha—I think I'm going to be *sick*."

But I wasn't. I couldn't be. There wasn't time for it.

I got up, staggered a step or two, swung back around toward the cavern. "In there," I gasped. "I swear, it's in *there*—"

"*What* is, Tiger?"

"The thing we've been chasing. Sorcerer. Demon. *Thing;* I don't know! I just know it's *in* there. It's *got* to be—and that's where we have to go."

Del looked at the cavern. Looked back at me.

"I *know*," I said testily. "Do you think I like the idea?"

Del's *jivatma* gleamed: pale salmon-silver. In answer, the dragon roared.

At least, it *sounded* that way; it was wind keening through the cavern, whining in cracks and crannies, then whooshing out of the opening to splatter our faces with stink.

"Come on," I said unhappily, stepping into the cave. "Let's get this over with."

The weight of rock was oppressive. I stopped dead on the threshold.

"What?" Del asked; it fell away into dimness.

I waited, saying nothing. The feeling did not go away.

Del opened her mouth, then shut it.

Behind me yawned the sky. I wanted nothing more than to spin away from the cave and go out into the sky. To take myself from the dark. To walk on the dragon's spine in the cold, clear air with the sun on my face. Even the Northern sun.

Still Del waited. Somewhere, so did the hounds.

I sweated. Shoved hair out of my eyes. Sucked a breath and spat, cursing myself for the weakness.

"Do you need light?" Del asked.

I looked at her sharply, saw comprehension in her eyes. She

knew. She remembered, even though she hadn't been there. She recalled the result too well.

"No," I rasped.

"All I'd have to do is sing. My *jivatma* will give us light."

I glanced at Boreal: thin silver promise in dimness. Light spilled into the mouth of the cavern from the day beyond, but it died too quickly to gloom. It lent the cavern an eerie insubstantiality, a sense of things unseen. The walls were pocked with shadows.

Light would alter everything. But we couldn't afford it now. "No," I told her curtly. "Let's not offer any more magic to the hounds."

She waited a moment. "Do you really think—"

"I haven't the faintest idea." I was snappish in discomfort. "I just figure it won't hurt anything not to take any chances."

Breath boomed in the dragon's throat. The sound was deafening as air rushed by us toward the entrance. The roar sounded almost real, though both of us knew it wasn't. It was nothing more than wind and smoke being blown or sucked out of the cave into the vast freedom beyond.

"Will you be all right?" Del asked.

"Leave it alone," I snapped. I took a step toward the darkness, then came to an abrupt halt. "It's *gone*."

"Gone?"

"That *feeling* . . . it's faded. A moment ago I could almost taste it, and now it's faded away." I frowned turning in a slow revolution. "It was here . . . it was *here*—" I stabbed a finger downward, "—filling up this place . . . it was like a cistern choked with sand, spilling through all the cracks—only what I felt was *magic*—" I shook my head, frowning. "Now it's all gone."

Wind whined through the cavern. With it came the stink, and the wail of a distant hound.

I shut my hand on my sword hilt and slid the blade into freedom. "To hoolies with those hounds." And led the way into darkness.

Chapter 13

Down the dragon's gullet—or so Halvar might have said. The ceiling dropped, the walls closed in, the darkness was nearly complete. Except for a sickly red glow that crept out of the depths of the dragon to illuminate our way.

A lurid carnelian light that reminded me of new blood.

The fear, for the moment, was gone. Movement provided the opportunity to set it aside, to think about something else. But I couldn't quite forget it. It waited for me to remember so it could creep out again.

The throat fell away into belly; we left behind the gullet and entered a larger chamber. Del and I stopped short, then tightened grips on hilts.

"What in hoolies is *that?*"

Del shook her head.

I scowled blackly. "I thought you knew Northern magic."

"I know *about* Northern magic . . . but I don't know what that is."

"That" was a curtain of flame. A lurid carnelian flame that stretched from floor to ceiling across the width of the cavern. It resembled nothing so much as a curtain hung for privacy, dividing room from room. Opaque, yet oddly vibrant, it shimmered against the blackness. Sparks burned bright, then died, pulsing against a net.

But it wasn't hot. It was cold.

Suspicion bloomed. "You know," I said lightly, "what that re-minds me of—what that reminds me of a *lot*—is the light from Bor—from your sword." I caught myself in time.

Del flicked me a narrowed glance; I was not forgiven. "I don't think it's the same thing."

"How do you know? You yourself said you don't know what that is. For all *you* know, it could be exactly the same."

"But not from the same source." Del edged closer. Red light shirred off her blade, altering its color. Salmon-silver was dyed amber-bronze.

I looked at my own sword. It had not, up till now, shown any inclination to take on a particular color. The phenomenon was fa-miliar—I'd seen numerous *jivatmas* keyed, and all displayed a sig-nature color, but mine never had. It was bright and shining silver, but so was every other sword save those born of Northern magic.

Which left me wondering suddenly if perhaps mine *wasn't* blooded. Wasn't really quenched.

And yet it had to be. It showed too many symptoms. Displayed too much of its power. Even the hounds knew it.

Del frowned at the curtain. "Maybe some kind of ward? Some-thing to keep people out?"

"But why? What is there to hide? Why would wards be *here?*"

Del abruptly smiled. "Chosa Dei," she answered. "It's Chosa Dei's prison."

"Oh, right. Of course; I was forgetting." I squinted against the brilliance of the curtain, looking around, searching for some clue. "I don't suppose there's some way around this thing . . . some tun-nel or passageway."

Del shrugged, saying nothing. Like me, she examined the chamber.

I heard the dragon rumble. Swung and stared as the curtain rippled. The glow intensified, and then the curtain parted. Hot smoke belched out.

Del and I, of course, ducked; flame—or whatever—licked to-ward us both. The curtain wavered in the wind, then shredded on a roar as the smoke was sucked out of the chamber into the tunnel beyond.

The stench drove me to my knees. I forgot all about flaming curtains or passageways and concentrated on holding my breath so I wouldn't lose my belly. Del, half-shrouded by smoke, sounded no better off; she hacked and gagged and swore, though only briefly, in her twisty Northern tongue. I helped out with Southron, with a dash of Desert thrown in.

Then wished I hadn't; swearing made me suck air.

"Agh, *gods*—" I spat. "This is enough to make a man sick."

"Coal," Del said intently. "I know it now: *coal* . . . and something else. Something more. Something that smells—"

"—like rotting bodies; I told you before." The curtain sealed itself as smoke died away. For the moment the dragon slept, or else merely held its breath. I stood up, wished for aqivi to wash away the foul aftertaste, yanked my now-filthy tunics back into place. And clutched my sword in one hand. "What's this 'coal' you mentioned?"

Del got up, brushed gritty dark dust from her no-longer-pristine white clothing, scowled at the curtain. "Coal," she repeated. "It's a fuel. It's sort of like rock, but it burns. We lived in the downlands, where wood is plentiful; I saw coal only once. It comes from high in the mountains, in the uplands above the timberline."

"Well, if it smells this bad, I don't see how *anyone* uses it."

"I told you, there's something more—"

The curtain flowed briefly aside and emitted another belch. Smoky wind rushed through the chamber in its way to the dragon's throat. I swore, waving madly, and tried to peer through the rent in flame.

In shock, I sucked a breath. "Hoolies, I saw *people!*"

Del looked at me sharply; no need for her to ask.

"I did," I declared. "Through the curtain—I swear, I saw people. Men, I think, doing something around a fire. A *real* fire, bascha— not this magical curtain." I strode to the "flame," tried to peer through it again. "When the smoke comes through, it thins. You can see right through it. All we have to do is wait—"

"—then walk right in?" Del's brows arched. "Are you so sure that's wise?"

"Of course I'm not sure. I can't foretell the future, bascha; how in hoolies am I supposed to know what is and isn't wise? But Halvar said there was no other way into the dragon; here we are with nothing better to do, and two magical swords. So we may as well get this thing finished before the place smells any worse."

"I'm not so sure—"

I thrust up a silencing hand. "Hear it? That's the rumble—any moment the curtain will part . . . just use your *jivatma*, Del. Isn't that what it's for?"

"This isn't a circle, Tiger . . . you don't know—"

"Shut up and use your sword . . . Del—*now*—"

I thrust a swordtip into the curtain of cold flame as it thinned and blew apart, and prodded gently, none too sure what sort of response I might get. The tip sliced through easily enough, as if the curtain was made of air. Colored, cold air, shaped to look like a flame.

I slid the sword a bit farther, risking myself carefully. Felt a prickling in fingers and hands; then it spread to encompass forearms. I took a single step forward, closed nose and mouth against stench, felt the curtain snap shut against flesh.

The sensation was odd, but not threatening. I moved forward carefully, aware of a dampening of sound, a dying of the light. Everything was red.

"You coming?" I asked it thickly around the breath I held.

Her tone sounded no better. "Yes, Tiger, I'm coming." She sounded exasperated. Like maybe she didn't think we were doing the right thing. Like maybe she thought I was being foolish.

As if she were humoring me; never her strong point.

I wanted to retort, but I was much too busy.

Almost through—almost—

Something knew I was there.

"Tiger—*wait*—"

—oh—hoolies—

"Del!"

The dragon swallowed me whole.

Chapter 14

They had been beating me again. I could feel it clear to the bone.

I lay facedown on the stone, legs and arms asprawl. Cold, hard stone, biting into flesh. Bruising cheekbone and brow. Cutting into one hip.

They had been beating me again, just as the Salset had.

I twitched. Sucked air. Gagged. Tried not to throw up. Lay very, very still, to soothe my unhappy belly. To give it no reason to protest.

Hoolies, but I hurt.

Listened to the silence. Heard nothing in the darkness. Nothing save ragged breathing; I held it: the sound stopped. Began to breathe again and took comfort in the sound.

Awakening muscles spasmed. A leg jerked, then a hand. Beneath me, metal grated. The sound of iron fetters.

They had *chained* me again.

I surged up frantically, smashed my head against the low ceiling, sprawled on hands and knees. Then lunged backward against the wall and slid down it to land limply in a pile of flesh and bones. Squeezed my eyes tight-shut. Sat there breathing raggedly while I tried to find the Sandtiger and whatever will he had left.

Some, after all. It allowed me to deal with the fear. To push it back again, if only for a moment. It allowed me to open my eyes.

Saw the sword against the stone: dim glint in dimmer light.

Sword?

Astonished, I stared. Then scrambled for it, found it, dragged it chiming across the stone. Sat down awkwardly on uneven rock and held the sword in both hands.

Not Singlestroke.

Not Singlestroke?

And why do I have a sword if I'm in Aladar's mine?

The blade was ice in my hands. Vision blurred; I shook it off, then wished I hadn't tried. The motion jarred my head.

Hoolies, but I hurt.

I leaned against the wall and wiped the sweat from my eyes, shoving damp hair aside. Beard stubble caught on wool; on *wool*, not on flesh. Not on the nakedness of a slave.

All around me the rock waited with a vast complacency. Dim carnelian light washed the walls with illumination. It bathed the blade with blood.

I shifted, caught my breath, eased myself more carefully into another position. Even my ears hurt, filled with a stuffy ringing. I smelled something remarkably foul; also my own aroma, fear and exertion combined. What I needed was a bath. What I *wanted* was out of here.

Down the tunnel something whined.

I'm not in Aladar's mine.

Then where *am*—ah, hoolies.

I know where I am.

Claws scratched stone. Panting crept down the tunnel.

I think I don't want to be here.

Whining echoed in emptiness.

Hoolies—*where is Del?*

With Aladar, of course—no, no, you're not *in* Aladar's mine. You're not even in the South. Where you are is in the dragon with hounds hard on your trail.

Panting crept through the dimness. A snapping growl accompanied it.

Pick a direction and *go*.

I couldn't stand up straight because of the low tunnel ceiling.

All I could do was scuttle, hunched halfway over, clutching a Northern sword and trying not to trip on steel too long for use in the confines of the tunnel. The tip scraped from time to time, screeching against stone; pulling it back from the wall usually resulted in a banged elbow, unless I was very careful.

It's hard to be very careful when you're running for your life. Careful can get you killed.

Oh, Delilah. Where are you?

Don't let her be dead again.

A howl pierced the dimness. I couldn't tell from which direction.

I smacked my head, bit my lip, spat out blood, and cursed. Felt the prickling on my neck; the pinch of fear in my belly. And lurched to a dead stop, having reached the end of the tunnel.

Hoolies, get me out of here. It's too much like Aladar's mine—

I broke it off abruptly. Smelled the stink of hounds.

—end of the tunnel—

But it wasn't the end of the world. The tunnel swelled into a hollow bulb large enough to stand up in. Wide enough for my sword. I straightened and struck a stance, cursing the tautness of scar tissue that pulled against my midriff.

I hadn't been in a circle since the one where I'd faced Del. I hadn't even *sparred* since the fight I'd danced with Del. Conditioning was a word that no longer applied to me.

But I'd been worse off before.

Of course, I'd also been *younger*—

A hound entered the bulb through the narrow neck.

At least, the hound *tried* to; I took its head with one blow.

There is something to be said for standing in an enclosed space while fighting vicious beasts. Because while I'd sooner be out of the mountain, in bright, clean sunlight again, I discovered there were advantages to fighting just as I was. Because each time I killed a hound, the body dropped to the floor. The pile was forming a plug against the beasts still in the tunnel. And it gave me a chance to breathe. To hoard my dwindling strength.

To wet my thirsty *jivatma*.

Eventually, they stopped. When they did, so did I. And I realized there were no more; at least, no more in the tunnel. The rest were somewhere else.

Winded, I stood sucking air, trying to clear my head. Sparks danced at the edges of vision, bursting like tiny flamelets. I leaned over, bracing forearms across bent knees, and tried to catch my breath. While beast-blood flowed over my boots.

When I could, I straightened, arched carefully backward, tried to unknot the kinks. Tried to stretch knurled scar tissue that threatened to crack with the strain.

Something echoed in the tunnel.

I snapped back into position, wincing, with *jivatma* at the ready. Before me was a piled blockade of bleeding bodies. Through the gaps I heard a voice, distorted by rock and distance; by the twists and turns of the dragon.

"*—long I have waited?*"

And Del's voice, softly: "*Six hundred and forty-two years.*"

A pause, and surprise. "*How can you know that?*"

"*They tell stories about you, Chosa.*"

Chosa. Chosa *Dei*? But he was only legend. A man made out of stories.

"*What else do they say about me?*"

"*That you are an ambitious, vengeful man.*"

Uh-oh, bascha. Not the best thing to say.

"*And what do they say about you?*"

"*That I am very like you.*"

I heard a hint of laughter. "*But I am not a woman, and you are not a man; yes?*"

"Sword-dancer," she answered quietly. "*Sword-singer, as well. Staal-Ysta trained, Chosa . . . you do know of Staal-Ysta?*"

"*Oh, I know; yes, of course I know; I know many things, yes? I know Staal-Ysta—I know of jivatmas—I know many things, yes? As I know what you are, yes? Exactly what you are. It's you I've been waiting for. I need you very badly, you and your jivatma—I've needed you for years—*"

My cue, I thought. But my way was blocked by beasts.

Hastily I cleaned the blade on my dirty tunic and set the sword aside by the entrance. Without regard for the slime and putrid blood, I caught and dragged bodies aside, dumping them one on the other. Not all were in one piece; I kicked the bits aside. As soon as I cleared an exit, I caught up the sword and ran.

Trouble was, the moment I moved the voices faded, stolen away by tunnels and crannies. I stopped short, crouching to save my head, and listened. Heard nothing but my own breathing. No more Del. No more Chosa Dei.

It *couldn't* be Chosa Dei.

I swore and went on awkwardly, hating the size of the tunnel. Hating myself for my height. Wishing I had the kind of power that could blast the mountain apart, taking Chosa with it. Chosa and his hounds.

"—so I had to have the whistle, yes? I had to have the wards. I have to have all the magic. It's what I do: collect. And I have to have it all; of course, all, what else? There's no point to it, otherwise; the purpose is defeated, yes? There is no value to any magic if everyone has a little."

I stopped short, breathing hard, but Del made no answer. Or else I couldn't hear it in the maze of the dragon's entrails. I sucked breath and ran on again, bootsteps echoing in the tunnel.

"—were a means, nothing more. I have no particular liking for beasts; I'm not a man for pets. But I had to start somewhere, so I fashioned myself a—hound, I think you said, yes? Well, then, a hound. A good and loyal dog ready to die at my command. Of course, then I needed more; harvesting jivatmas is difficult. A single beast wasn't up to the task, so I had it bring me another human. Who in turn could bring me another. Villagers all, yes? Until I had enough, and sent them after jivatmas."

I took the left branch. Its ceiling was higher; I ran.

Hoolies, hoolies, bascha—what have you gotten yourself into?

The voice boomed by my side. *"—no, no, not 'make'—I do better than that. Making is very simple; I unmake, yes? That is my personal gift; the magic of Chosa Dei. I take what has been wrought and drain it of its power. I unmake it most carefully, then reshape it to personal needs."*

I stopped short as the voice died out, fading behind me gently like a candle carried away. I spun in place, sword tip scraping the wall. Nothing lay behind me. Nothing but emptiness.

Oh, bascha. Bascha.

The voice echoed far down the tunnel. *"—know what you are? Do you know what you are?"*

I listened as I ran, but heard nothing of Del's answer.

"—*think you have denied yourself the awareness, afraid to admit the truth, yes? I can smell that sword; I can* taste *it—I have tasted it all along. There is no hiding it from me, in sheath or in a song. Nor can you hide it now; I can unsing what you sing, unmake what you make.*"

This time I heard Del's voice: "*Why?*"

The sorcerer's tone was gentle. "*So I may unmake the wards. So I may unmake my prison.* The tone abruptly altered; Chosa Dei was angry. "*So I may unmake my brother, who* put *me in this place!*"

The tunnel branched yet again. I started through it; stopped. It branched yet again. The dragon was full of tunnels, and Chosa was in them all.

Oh bascha, bascha. How in hoolies do I find you?

Chapter 15

Rock bit into my knees. Blade clanged down. I realized I had fallen.

Behind me, the beast growled.

I lurched up, caught weapon, whirled. Spitted him as he leaped, then jerked the blade free and struck again as a second hound appeared, lunging out of ruddy shadows. Behind him was a third.

Blood sprayed freely as I scythed through rib cage and spine, shearing the third hound in half. I felt a flicker of pleasure; the jolt of victory.

And then I recalled Chosa's words: that the beasts had once been human. Villagers from Ysaa-den. Sword-dancers from Staal-Ysta.

Bile rose. Briefly, only briefly, the hilt slipped in my hand. And then I smelled the stink. Felt the blood crusting on my face. And knew if I had hesitated the unmade men would have killed me.

Chosa Dei had Del. He no longer needed me. He no longer needed my sword; he had the one he wanted. Had the one he *required* to set himself free of his prison so he could find his brother and unmake Shaka Obre, who had had the abiding good sense to put Chosa away in a mountain where he could harm nothing and no one.

For six hundred and forty-two years.

Six hundred and forty-*one;* for the last six months or so, Chosa Dei had been busy.

And where, I wondered fleetingly, is Shaka Obre *now?*

Chosa Dei's voice slipped through cracks. *"—and a woman is stronger, yes? A woman has greater needs. A woman has greater will. A woman, when she decides to be, is much more dedicated. Much more determined, yes? More* focused *on her need."*

Del's voice echoed oddly. *"Some might say, more obsessed."*

"But yes—yes, of course! *Obsession is necessary. Obsession is required. Obsession is the master when compassion undermines."* I heard Chosa laugh. *"Now I understand. Now I comprehend. More than a jivatma. More than a blooding-blade. More than a sword-dancer's weapon; it is your second soul. It is a second you—"*

"No!" Del snapped. *"I'm more than just a sword. More than just a weapon.* More *than a need for vengeance—"*

Chosa sounded startled. *"What is greater than vengeance when it has brought you so far? It has shaped you; it has* made *you—"*

"I made me! I made this jivatma. *It didn't make* me."

"It unmade you," Chosa answered, *"to make you something else, yes? To make you what you required; vengeance is powerful."* The sorcerer's voice altered subtly. *"Tell me the sword's name."*

One thing she's not, is stupid.

"Chosa Dei," Del answered promptly. *"Now go* unmake *yourself—"*

The voices faded again. Del and Chosa were gone.

Oh, hoolies, bascha—can't you sing out again? Just to give me a little clue?

Chosa's voice boomed loud; a trick of the tunnels again. *"You will tell me the name, yes? While you still have both feet, both hands? While you still have both your breasts?"*

I called him every name I could think of. But I did it silently.

Except for raspy breathing and echoing bootsteps as I ran.

Branch upon branch upon branch. But the light was growing brighter. The stench even more offensive. And Chosa Dei's threats were imperative; I heard the whine and snarl of gathering hounds. The wheezing of a bellows.

Bellows?

Light slashed briefly through a crack in the tunnel wall, glinting off my blade. I stopped short, muttered a curse as sore muscles complained, put out my hand toward the crack. Warm air and smoke wisped through; that, and ruddy light.

I pressed myself against the wall, jamming my face into the crack. I saw light and fire and smoke; all three made my eye water. Tears ran down my face.

I swore, changed eyes, tried to see specifics.

Saw men tending a fire. Men tending a *forge;* Chosa Dei was playing at smith.

Rock bit into my forehead as I slumped against the wall. I couldn't believe what I'd seen. Couldn't trust my eyes. But a second look confirmed it: Chosa Dei had a forge. Men were tending a bellows. He had been stealing *jivatmas,* and now he wanted Del's. So he could break free of the wards set by Shaka Obre.

Chosa Dei had more than a forge. He had a crucible. He was melting down *jivatmas.* Unmaking them, for their magic; to use for his own designs.

And now he wanted Boreal. Now he needed a banshee-storm and all the wild magic of the North in order to burst his bonds. To bring the mountain down so the dragon could fly again.

The voice came through the crack. *"—was powerful, once. I can be again. But I need the wild magic. I have to restore myself; to banish diminishment, yes? To make myself whole again, so I can unmake my brother."*

Del's answer was lost in the roar of newborn flame fanned into life by the bellows. I saw it sucked up, then out; saw it pass through the curtain that Del and I had faced. And at last I had my bearings.

Now all I had to do was find a way out of the tunnels and into the second chamber on the far side of the curtain.

Where I would do—what?

Hoolies, I don't know. Cut Chosa's *gehetties* off—if sorcerers have *gehetties*—and give them to Del as a trophy.

If she was alive to receive them.

If she was in one piece.

Hang on, Delilah. The Sandtiger's on his w—

The hounds began to chorus.

Chosa Dei's voice rose above it. *"—can unsing any song. I can unmake any sword. Shall we try it, yes?"*

—don't let her die again—

Running. Stumbling. Swearing. Coughing in the smoke. Squinting against the light—*light* . . . hoolies, the tunnel floor was broken. The cracks were open fissures leading straight down into the chamber behind Shaka Obre's wards.

I threw myself to the tunnel floor and stuck my head into one of the fissures. Held my breath against odor and smoke as tears sprang into my eyes. Blinked my vision clear; saw, in the instant before tears returned, the glint of Del's *jivatma*. Saw the circle of beasts pressing close.

And Chosa Dei below me.

If I could drop my sword straight down, I could split his head like a melon.

Then again, I might miss. And give him another *jivatma*.

You can't tell much about a man when all you can see of him is the top of his head and shoulders. Eyes will tell you a lot; so will expression and posture. I could see none of those things. Only dark hair and dark-swathed shoulders.

But I could see Del clearly.

She was completely ringed by beasts. Within the circle, she stood umoving; carefully, utterly still. In her arms was Boreal: diagonal slash from left to right, cutting across her breasts. Forgeglow lighted the steel. Wardglow turned it red.

Del could change the color. She only had to sing.

But Chosa Dei could unsing her songs. Del had no weapon to use.

Leaving me with mine.

Hoolies, what do I do?

Chosa Dei spoke again. "Shall I show you how I unmake a man? How I *re*make him into a beast?"

Del said nothing.

"Yes, I think I shall."

Transfixed, I stared in disbelief. Del stood imprisoned by hounds, helpless to stop the sorcerer. Thus free to do as he wanted, Chosa Dei called over one of the men who tended the forge and dismissed the other three. The fourth one knelt, and Chosa put hands on his head.

Part of me screamed at the man to escape, to pull away, to get free of Chosa Dei. But he did none of those things. He just knelt in silence, staring blankly, as Chosa put hands on him.

"No," Del said quietly.

Chosa's voice was as quiet. "Oh, I think yes."

He unmade the man. Don't ask me how. All I know is the shape of the man altered somehow, *was* altered somehow, slowly and subtly, until the nose was thrust outward, the jaw pushed backward, the shoulders folded inward, hips rebent into haunches—the man was no more a man but a *thing* in bestial form.

Eyes shone whitely. A tail was pulled out of buttocks. He—it—the thing—bent upon the rock floor with the joints and hair of a hound, and nothing at all of humanity.

"No," Del repeated, but the tone was shaped by horror.

"Unmade," Chosa said. "Now he will join the others. And perhaps *he* will take your throat."

Oh, hoolies. Oh, *gods*—

I shut my eyes a moment, then forced myself to look.

Smoke gushed up from the forge. Most of it was sucked through the curtain as the wards allowed it to go. The rest dispersed in the chamber, escaping through cracks, fissures, and holes.

Cracks, fissures, and *holes;* mouthing obscenities, I pressed my face more tightly against the fissure and looked for the proper sign. Saw it almost immediately; lunged up and ran down the tunnel all of twelve paces farther, where the hole greeted me. My entrance into the chamber.

It was the largest of them all; I knew from watching the smoke. The greatest amount had been sucked through here, but it wasn't saying much. Del couldn't get through, *maybe*, but I doubted I could. Unless I was stark naked and painted with alla salve.

Flesh quailed; so did spirit. The idea of dropping down unannounced—and bare-butted—to face a sorcerer was not a pretty thought. A lot of me didn't like it.

Especially my *gehetties.*

So, I'd compromise. *Half* of my clothes would come off.

I knelt by the hole and set the sword aside, then unhooked the wide leather belt with its weight of ornamental bosses, which could catch and scrape and grate. Then off came the harness itself, stripped over arms and head without undoing the buckles. And finally both tunics, which I dropped aside without thought. Cool tunnel air chafed bare chest and arms and set the flesh to rising.

First to test briefly: I eased boots and legs down into the hole punched through the rock, then braced forearms and elbows on either side and channeled my weight through shoulders. I lowered myself carefully. Felt hips catch briefly; a twist eased them through. But above them the spread of my rib cage and shoulder sockets promised to wedge me painfully if I didn't take steps to avoid it.

Hoolies, but it hurt—I pulled myself up again, blowing noisy breath between gritted teeth, and clambered out of the hole once more.

Chosa's voice drifted up: *"My beasts are growing hungry. Tell me the name of your sword."*

Come on, Del; hang on . . . I'm doing what I can.

A quick glance showed me jagged protrusions in the rock wall. I knew I'd have to jump when it came right down to it, but I wanted to shorten the distance. The easiest way was to use belt and harness to lower myself through the hole as far as I could go, then drop the rest of the way.

I'd risk breaking a leg. But I was risking so much anyway it didn't really matter.

I snugged the belt around the most promising stone protrusion, then buckled it firmly. I cut the sheath free of the harness, which left me with a crisscross affair of leather straps, and quickly severed the thong stitching. Then looped everything through the belt and dangled it down the hole.

Not very much. But something.

Meanwhile, there was the sword. I couldn't very well carry it down with me as I worked my way through the hole; the extra bulk would end the attempt. And I didn't dare tie it to my body with shredded bits of tunic; if I lost it by accident, Chosa would have a new *jivatma*. And I sort of wanted to keep it until I could stick it in him.

So I very carefully placed it beside the hole opposite my planned entry, and began to ease myself down.

In the tunnel, a beast bayed.

I froze. I didn't particularly relish the thought of being attacked while wedged in the hole; I prefer a fair fight. So I pulled myself up again, grabbed the sword, and made it as far as my knees as the hound leaped out of shadow.

I was getting tired of this. I'd just as soon not have to do it.

On knees, I battled the hound. My balance was off, and my leverage, but clean steel still parts beast flesh. The spray of blood slicked my chest and dribbled down my belly to the drawstring of my trews.

Which gave me an idea.

In the dimness, I saw eyes. The shine of white hound eyes. But this beast turned tail and ran, which was a welcome change.

Again I set the blade carefully beside the jagged hole. Then scooped up dripping handfuls of beast blood and slapped it all over my chest and sides, paying particular attention to the rib cage beneath my armpits, where the spread of bone and muscle was greatest, and to the shoulder joints themselves where they met my upper arms.

Hoolies, but I stink.

No more time to waste—

I slid boots over the lip, took an extra wrap in the harness straps around my left wrist, and lowered myself down.

Hips slid through again, though fabric snagged a little. And my waist, all slick with blood even though it didn't need it. And then my lower ribs. The upper ones stuck fast.

It is a particularly vulnerable sensation to be stuck like a cork in a bottle. From the waist down I was completely accessible, but I couldn't see past my rib cage.

There was still slack in the harness straps. I braced my right arm against the lip of the hole and pushed, trying to twist myself free. Layers of skin peeled away, stinging in protest. And finally I slipped free, leaving bits of me on stone teeth. My shoulder joints lost flesh also, then obligingly added my own blood to the slime already present.

It was enough to loosen the cork; I dropped, felt the straps tauten, winced as the loop snugged around my left wrist. All of my weight hung from it; I wished I weighed a bit less.

My head was level with the bottom of the hole. I peered down past my body and tried to judge the distance. It was still dangerously far from the floor—about seven of me hooked together—and the landing would be on rock. If I didn't break a leg, I'd probably break my head.

The sword still lay in the tunnel. Carefully I began pulling myself back up one-armed, sliding my right arm up through the hole. All I needed was a little lift; then I'd snatch the sword, hold it vertically, and drop straight down to the floor.

To get my bearings, I glanced down. And saw Chosa Dei with a hound.

Hoolies, he was *eating* it!—no, no he wasn't . . . he was—hoolies, I don't *know* . . . something, something disgusting . . . he knelt down before it and put his hands on its head . . . he said something to it, *did* something to it—and the hound began to change.

It melted. I have no better word for it. The beast melted from this known shape into something else. Something vaguely human, but without humanity.

He was *un*making the beast. Making the man again.

Hanging from my harness, I was very nearly sick. I had not, until that moment, realized the full implication of Chosa Dei's powers. If he was free, if he *got* free . . . once he unmade his brother, what would he do to others? By "collecting" all the magic, would he then remake the world?

Chosa Dei rose, leaving the half-made thing on the floor where it twitched and spasmed and died. "Someone is here," he said. "Someone *else* is here . . . hiding in the tunnels. Hiding in my mountain." He swept the chamber with a glance. "And he has a second *jivatma,* fully quenched and blooded."

Hoolies. Oh, *hoolies*—

"There!" Chosa cried, and pointed directly at me.

I saw Del's upturned face. I saw the mass of hounds. Knew what I had to do.

Unmake Chosa Dei.

Straining upward, I thrust my right hand up through the hole and scrabbled at the lip. Touched the blade, traced it back to the hilt, lurched up to lock fingers around it. Began to think of a song as I dropped back through the hole to dangle on my harness.

Beneath me swarmed the hounds, waiting for me to fall.

A song. Think of a song. Of something personal. Of something *powerful.* Of something no one but the Sandtiger fully comprehends.

I thought of the South. I thought of the desert. And then I thought of the Punja with its deadly simooms and sciroccos, the scouring wind-blast of sand that could strip a man bare of flesh, polishing his bones. I thought of the sun and the sand and the heat and the power of a storm blowing the Punja here and there, feckless as a goat kid, going where it was told. Because there is a greater power than merely heat and sand. There is also the desert wind. A hot dry wind. A wind composed of a violence equal to Chosa Dei's.

Scorching desert windstorm stripping everything down to the bone. Scirocco and simoom. But also called *samiel.*

Inside, I sang a song. Of blooding, of quenching, of keying. Of unmaking a sorcerer who thought only Del's *jivatma* was capable of great power.

Your mistake, Chosa. Now come grapple with *me*—

I sliced through the harness and dropped.

Chapter 16

I landed in squirming bodies full of teeth and claws and foul breath. Thanked them for breaking my fall. Then disengaged myself, though my body remained where it was.

Heat—sand—sun . . . the blast of a samiel—

The blast of Samiel, loosed to cleanse the mountain of beasts and sorcerer.

Scorching, scouring sun—blistered, weeping flesh—cracked and bleeding lips—

Del and I had lived it. But Chosa wouldn't survive.

The chanting of the Salset, gathered to celebrate the changing of the year . . . the high-pitched whining of the shukar praying to his gods . . . the hoots and shrieks of desert borjuni, riding down a caravan . . . the clash and clatter of Hanjii with gold rings in nose and ears . . .

Music; all of it music; the song of desert life. The music of the Punja; the music of *my* life.

—dull chiming of the chains binding me into the mine—

—chink of chisel on rock; the crumble of falling reef thick with the promise of gold—

—squealing and snorting and stomping as the stud protests my wishes—

A personal, powerful song no one else can sing.

—the sobbing of a boy with a back afire from the lash, trying to hide his pain; trying to hide humiliation—

No one else knew these things.

—*the song of a blued-steel blade; the song of Singlestroke, gifting me with freedom; with life and pride and strength*—

And the scream of an angry cat flowing down from a pile of stones.

Only I knew these things.

Only I could sing my life.

Only I could unmake Chosa Dei—

Scirocco. Simoom. Samiel.

Try your best, Chosa Dei—you can't unsing *this* song.

Dimly I heard the hounds. The whine of Boreal. The snatch of Delilah's song as she hewed through flesh and bone.

Dimly I heard Chosa Dei, but I couldn't make out his words. Everything in my head was part of my personal song.

Everything in my song was part of Samiel.

Take him. Take him. Take him.

Dimly, Del shouted.

Take him—take him—take him—

Del was shouting at me.

—take him—take him—

—*unmake him*—

"Tiger—Tiger, *no* . . . you don't know what you're doing—"

—*sing him into your song*—

"Tiger, it's *forbidden*—"

Samiel splintered ribs.

Flesh, blood, muscle and bone; Samiel wanted it all.

"Tiger—Tiger *no*—"

Samiel sang his song.

All I could do was listen.

Muscles spasmed. Arms and legs jerked; so did my head. I smacked it against the chamber floor.

Why is my head on the floor?

Why is *any* of me on the floor?

Opened eyes: saw chamber ceiling. Saw *several* chamber ceilings, until I could focus again.

Hoolies, what's wrong with me?

I sat up, wished I hadn't, lay back down again.

Hoolies. Oh, *hoolies.*

What have I been doing?

Much as I'm a man for keeping my aches to myself, I emitted a raspy groan. As well as a favorite obscenity, followed by a string of lesser favorites, until I ran out of breath.

By then Del was back.

"So," she said, "you survived."

I waited a beat. "Did I?"

Del's face was blood-spattered. Hair hung in ruddy ribbons. "I had my doubts at first when I saw you weren't breathing. But I punched you in the chest and you started right up again."

Thoughtfully, I rubbed a sore spot. It was right over my heart. "Why did you punch me?"

"I told you: you weren't breathing. It was your own fault, and I was angry." She shrugged. "It seems a valuable trick, this punching in the chest."

I explored my blood-crusted chest which seemed to be sore in more than one place. There were bite wounds and claw welts in addition to stinging scrapes. "Why wasn't I breathing?"

"Because you were a stupid, senseless, deaf, dumb and blind fool . . . a man so full of himself he has no time for others, and gives no *heed* to others when they're trying to save his life, since he seemed bent on losing it. And you nearly *did;* Tiger, you are a fool! What did you think to accomplish? Sacrificing yourself *or* your sanity is not a useful thing. *Not* a useful thing; did you spare no thought for me? Did you think I *wanted* you dead just to pay you back for nearly killing me?"

From the floor, I stared up at her. Her anger was truly awesome. "What did I do?" I asked.

"What did you do? What did you *do?*"

I nodded. "What did I do?"

Del pointed. "That."

It was hard to see from the floor. So I very slowly and very carefully levered myself up and leaned on one elbow. Looked at where she was pointing.

Someone—*something*—was dead. The remains were sprawled on the floor.

"I did *that?*"

Del lowered her arm. "You have no idea, have you? You truly don't know what you did."

"Apparently I killed someone. Or something; what *is* that?"

"Chosa Dei," she answered. Then, ominously: "Chosa Dei's *body.* His spirit is somewhere else."

"Hoolies, not here, I hope. I'd just as soon not tangle with him again any time soon." I sat up all the way. Glanced around the chamber. "I see you did in the hounds."

"I did. You did. What is important is that they are dead. I think all of them are dead." She shrugged. "Not that it matters now, since Chosa Dei is—gone."

I rolled shoulders gently, rubbed at tension in my neck. "Well, it's what we came to do. Now Ysaa-den is safe, and so are all the *jivatmas.*"

"Oh?" Del asked. "Are you so certain of that?"

"He's *dead,* isn't he? Isn't that Chosa Dei?"

"His body," she repeated. "His soul is in your sword."

I stopped breathing again. "His soul is *where?*"

"In your sword," she answered. "What do you think you did?"

"Killed him." I paused. "Didn't I? I took him through the ribs. It *should* have killed him."

"Not that. I don't mean that. I mean what you did when you sang."

A chill washed across flesh. "What?"

Del's eyes sharpened. "You sang. Don't you remember? You dropped down from the roof of the chamber into a mass of hounds, and all the way you sang. You didn't stop once." She shrugged. "It wasn't very *good*—you have a truly terrible voice—but that doesn't matter. What matters is that you meant it. What matters is that it worked. You unmade Chosa Dei, but you also *remade* your sword."

"What?"

Del spelled it out. "You requenched, Tiger. Just like Theron did."

Theron. I thought back months and months and recalled the Northern sword-dancer who had come south hunting Del. He had a *jivatma,* as she did; a true-made, true-quenched *jivatma.* But he had addressed a new need and requenched his Northern blade in the body of a magician. It had given him an edge. It had nearly defeated Del. Nearly defeated me.

"Well," I said finally. "I didn't do it on purpose."

Del turned on her heel and walked away. I think she was still angry, though I didn't really know why. I had just saved her life. I had just saved the world.

I smiled wryly at that. Then worked my way to my feet and went over to the body.

Well, it was sort of a body. It was charred and shrunken and crisped, collapsed upon itself. It was half the size of me. It was smaller even than Del.

Does a soul take up that much room?

It was odd looking down on the remains of a man I'd never seen, but killed. There were no recognizable features, no normal hair, nothing that spoke of a man. He was a shape, nothing more; it left a bad taste in my mouth.

From the pile of loose cloth and crisped flesh gleamed the hilt of my requenched *jivatma*. Chosa Dei's new prison.

"I'll break it," I said. "I'll melt it." I glanced at the crucible. "I'll melt it into slag, then get me a Southron sword."

Del spun. "You *can't!*"

"Why not? I don't want to lug around a sword with *him* in it."

Del's face was white. "You have to lug it around. You have to carry it forever, until we find a way to discharge it. Don't you understand? Chosa Dei is *in* there. If you destroy the sword, you'll destroy his prison. You're his ward now. His own personal ward. Only you can keep him imprisoned."

I very nearly laughed. "Del, this is ridiculous. Are you really going to stand there and tell me that Chosa Dei is *in* my sword, and that if *I personally* don't guard him, he might get out again?"

Under the blood, she was white. "Always," she said, "always. Always you must doubt."

"You've got to admit it sounds pretty farfetched," I told her. "I mean, *you* were the one who told me Chosa Dei was only a legend, something someone made up for stories."

"I was wrong," she declared.

I stared at her. Here I'd been trying to get her to admit such a thing for the last two weeks with regard to her behavior on Staal-Ysta, and she still hadn't done it. But she was more than willing to say the three magical words when it came to Chosa Dei—or *whoever* he was.

I itched all over from sweat and crusted, smelly blood. Thoughtfully, I scratched through my beard to complaining flesh beneath. "Let me see," I said. "You expect me to spend the rest of my life making sure Chosa Dei stays put."

"No, not your whole life. Only until the sword can be discharged."

I frowned. "How do we do that? And what exactly *is* it?"

Del lifted her own sword, still clasped in her right hand. "There is power in here," she said. "Wild magic, and controlled magic—the control comes from a proper blooding and keying, as well as strength of will. But there is a way of discharging the power, of channeling it elsewhere, so the sword is a sword again." She shrugged. "Magic is magic, Tiger—it has a life of its own. That's why, when Theron died, you could use his *jivatma*. The magic had been discharged."

That, I didn't much like. "So, you're saying if I died, my sword would discharge *its* magic—along with Chosa Dei."

Del's brows arched. "That is one way, yes. But then you would be dead; what sense is there in discharging a sword if you won't be alive to use it?"

I didn't even bother to reply to that. "Is there another way?"

"Yes. But it was not a thing taught on Staal-Ysta."

"Where *is* it taught?"

Del shook his head. "I think it would take someone who understood the magic of *jivatmas*. Someone also who understood Chosa Dei, and the threat he represents. Because Chosa Dei himself is powerful; if the discharging were not done properly, he might free himself."

"He'd have no body," I pointed out. "This one is sort of a mess."

Del shrugged. "He'd find another. It might even be yours, since by then he'll know you so well."

Flesh froze. "What?"

Del sighed, frowning, as if frustrated by my ignorance. "Chosa Dei is no longer *alive*, no more than Baldur is in *my* sword. But his spirit is there, and his soul; the things he most believes in. You will feel it, Tiger. You will feel *him*. After a while you will know him—you will *have* to—and he will know you."

I scowled. "Does he know he's in this sword?"

Del shrugged. "But even if he doesn't, it doesn't really matter. Chosa Dei unmakes things to reshape them to his desires. He will try the same with your sword."

"What if I gave it to someone else?"

Del smiled crookedly. "What blooded, named *jivatma* allows anyone else to touch it?"

"If I told him Samiel's name, he could."

One of her shoulders twitched. "Yes. You could. And then he could touch your sword. But not being you, he could hardly control the magic. Nor control Chosa Dei."

I said something brief and very explicit.

Del ignored it. "I wonder . . ." she murmured.

"Wonder? Wonder what? What are you nattering about now?"

Her face was pensive. "Shaka Obre."

"Chosa's brother? Why?"

"Because maybe, just maybe, he might be able to help."

"He's a *story*, bascha."

"So was Chosa Dei."

I scowled. Considered it. "I don't need any help from a wizard."

"Tiger—"

"I can handle this on my own."

Pale brows arched. "Oh?"

"Just give me a little time. I'll work something out. Meanwhile, let's get out of here."

I made it three steps. "Tiger."

I swung back. "What?"

Del pointed at my sword, still mostly buried in Chosa's remains.

"Oh." I went over, bent down, didn't quite touch the hilt. "What's supposed to happen?"

"I don't know."

"That's helpful," I told her. "I thought you knew all this stuff."

"I know *some* 'stuff,' " she agreed. "But you've done something no one else has ever done."

"No one?"

"No one. *An-ishtoyas* seeking the blooding-journey always take sponsors with them to prevent disasters like this."

"So what you're saying is, I'm on my own."

Mute, Del nodded.

Being best at something is often entertaining. But being *first* is a little different; it can be dangerous. And I've never been quite cocky enough to risk myself like that.

I sucked in a deep breath, stretched out my hand—

"May I suggest something?" Del inquired.

My hand jerked back. *"What?"*

"Make certain you are stronger. Now. This moment. If Chosa senses any weakness, he will use it for himself."

I cast her a baleful glance. Then straightened and *kicked* the sword out of the crispy, shrunken pile of cloth, bones, and flesh.

Steel clanged across the stone floor. Nothing happened. The sword just lay there.

Except the blade was dull.

Frowning, I stepped across the remains and stared down at the sword. The hilt was the same as always—bright, brilliant steel—but the blade was smudgy dull gray, almost black. The tip itself *was* black, as if it had been burned.

"All right," I said. "Why?"

Del stood next to me, sword in hand. She looked down at her own blade, which was a pale salmon-silver. When keyed, it burned richer and brighter. Nothing approaching black. No *jivatma* I'd ever seen had ever been this color.

"I don't know," she said. "No one knows what the color will be until the *jivatma* shows it."

"But you think this is it."

Del sighed a little. "I think so. It comes on the heels of quenching and keying."

"I don't like black or gray. I'd prefer something brighter. Something more desertlike."

Del stared at me in amazement.

Defensively, I shrugged. "Well, we all have our preferences. Mine isn't gray and black."

"Maybe it's what happens when you requench."

I stood staring down at the dull-bladed sword, hands on hips, chewing a bloody lip. Then, with an impatient twitch of shoulders, I bent and picked it up.

Nothing happened. Nothing at all. The sword felt cold and dead.

I frowned. "What's it supposed—"

"Tiger!"

This time I landed flat on my rump on the floor with my knees bent up, feet flat, bracing myself upright, and stared in astonishment at the sword lying but three feet away.

Still gray and black. But the black was a little higher.

Del's hand was over her mouth. After a moment, she spoke through her fingers. "Are you all right?"

"Did you have to punch me again in the chest?"

"No."

"Then I guess I'm all right." It hurt more this time to stand up, but I managed it with a minimum of fuss. And then I stood there for a moment or two, trying to banish disorientation, and scowled at the sword. "He's angry."

"Who?"

"Samiel. Chosa Dei is just shocked. He didn't realize he was dead—or whatever it is he is."

Del took a step forward. "Does *he* know?"

"Know what?"

"Where Shaka Obre is?"

"Oh, for hoolies—" I glared. "I said I'd handle this, bascha— *without* Shaka Obre's help."

"It was a thought," Del commented.

I walked to the sword. "Right now all I want to think about is leaving."

"How?" Del asked. "Don't you remember what happened the last time we tried to go through the wards?"

I remember very well. You don't often forget waking up in the middle of a tunnel in a mountain shaped like a dragon. "But now

Chosa Dei is dead, so the wards are out of a job. Besides, I think if we used a piece of this Northern magic you're always talking about, we ought to be able to figure out a way."

"Only if you can figure out how to pick up your sword."

Basically, it was easy. All I had to do was show Chosa Dei who's boss.

Del and I crossed to the "curtain." Further study told us nothing more than we already knew: the thing was a ward set by Shaka Obre, intended to keep Chosa Dei imprisoned. It let out the smoke, let people in—though where they wound up was not quite certain, as I could testify—and prevented Chosa's escape.

Prevented *our* escape.

Sweat ran down my temples. "Now," I suggested, gripping the hilt with both hands.

Del frowned at me. "You don't look—"

The blade shook; *I* shook. "Now. Not tomorrow."

Del turned, raised her sword, glanced across at me. I mimicked her posture; together we sliced through the curtain as if it were nothing but silk.

Wards wisped into smoke. The prison was breached at last.

After six hundred and forty-two years, Chosa Dei was free of his mountain.

But until we found Shaka Obre, I'd never be free of Chosa.

Chapter 17

We sat in the headman's lodge in Ysaa-den, repairing what we could of battered flesh and spirits. We were alone, as always, being honored with solitude. With one another's help we had washed blood and grime and stink off, replacing missing or ruined clothing with articles given us by Halvar and his wife. Now I sat on a warm pelt with eyes scrunched closed, legs crossed, gritting teeth as Del tended puncture wounds and tooth tears with herbal paste.

"Sit still," she commanded as my eyes snapped open.

"It *hurts*."

"I know it hurts. It will hurt worse if you let these bites get infected. Especially this one *here*."

She did it on purpose. I flinched, swore at her; swore at her harder as she merely smiled and smeared more salve into a bite very low on my belly. Del had peeled the loosened waistband of my trews away, baring scraped and bitten skin, and now took pleasure in poking and prodding.

"I can do it," I said. "For that matter, Halvar's *wife* can do it; she offered."

"Everyone in Ysaa-den offered, Tiger; you're a hero. They will give you anything you ask, if they can." Del sat back on her heels. "Am I to suppose you want their two copper pennies, now?"

She wore blue in place of filthy white, a cool soft blue that heightened the color of her eyes. Pale lashes, pale hair, paler skin; she was, no doubt, feeling every bit as tired and battered as me. But somehow she didn't look it.

"No," I answered testily. "All I want is to be rid of this sword, so I can live in peace. Or, more immediately, a warm bed and a bota of aqivi; since this is the North, I'll take *amnit*."

"You'll get your *amnit*. You'll even get your bed. As to the warmth of it, that will depend on how many women you put in it."

I grunted. I was so full of bruises, bites, scrapes, scratches and claw scores I doubted I could provide much pleasure for a bedpartner. Especially since what I most wanted to do was sleep.

"The meal first," Del reminded, as my eyes drooped closed. "It's a celebration."

"Can't they celebrate without me?"

"No. Then they would have no one for whom to sing their song of salvation and gratitude."

I grunted again. "There's you."

"But *I* didn't kill Chosa Dei."

"You killed half the hounds."

"Who once were villagers." Del's tone was serious. "I think we need not tell that part of the story. Let them think the hounds simply killed their kinfolk, instead of being remade into beasts who killed more people, including kin and friends." She stroked hair from her eyes. "It would be a kindness."

It would also be a lie, but one I understood. "Give me the tunics, then, so we can go get some food. My belly's screaming at me."

Del handed me first the undertunic of soft-combed undyed wool; then, as I dragged it on, she presented the green overtunic. It rattled with intricate beadwork: bronze, copper, and amber.

"This is too much," I muttered. "He's giving away his best."

"A measure of his respect and gratitude." Del's tone, as it can be, was bland.

Frustrated, I glared at her. "I would have come anyway. It had nothing to do with Ysaa-den or their troubles; it had to do with the hounds. If they'd gone somewhere else, *I'd* have gone somewhere else."

"But they didn't, and neither did you." Del got up slowly, suppressing a wince of discomfort. She wore her sword as usual, hanging in harness across her back. "They're waiting for us, Tiger. We're the guests of honor."

I frowned, rising carefully. Little by little I was losing my links with the South. First Singlestroke, broken fighting Theron. Then my Southron silks and gauzes, traded for Northern leather and fur. And lastly my harness, discarded in Chosa Dei's mountain. Bit by bit by bit, scattered along the way.

I gathered up my *jivatma*, lacking sheath as well as harness, and followed Del out of the lodge. There was nothing, *nothing* about her even remotely Southron. Northern bascha to the bone, no matter where she was. I was being altered, while Del remained the same.

Time to go home, I said.

But I said it to myself.

Hot food, fiery *amnit*, and warm wishes all conspired to make it extremely difficult for me to stay awake during the celebratory meal. The evening air was growing chilly, but in addition to new wool clothing I also wore two pelts. I sat like a furry lump on yet a third pelt, managing to keep my eyes open a slit as Halvar regaled—in uplander—the village with my exploits.

Well, *our* exploits; Del was not left out.

"Stay awake," she hissed, sitting on the pelt next to mine.

"I'm trying. Hoolies, bascha—what do you expect? Aren't *you* tired after everything we did?"

"No," she answered cruelly. "I'm too young for it."

I chose to ignore that, since I knew very well she was lying. Maybe she wasn't yet *sleepy,* but certainly she was sore. It showed in all her movements. It showed when she sat very still. "How much longer do we have to sit out here?"

"Until the celebration is finished." Del watched Halvar, half-following his words even as she spoke to me. "We've eaten, and now Halvar's retelling the story. Once that's done, they'll all sing a song of deliverance. Then everyone will sit around retelling the story, marveling at the accomplishment, and drink to your health." She paused, observing me. "But since, from the look of you, I doubt you can manage that, you'll probably be able to slip away."

I nodded, stifling a yawn. It took all the strength I had.

Halvar said something to Del, glanced past her to me—Del had wound up beside the headman to translate—and repeated to me whatever it was he'd said to Del, just to be polite. I caught one word out of twenty: *song*.

I nodded. "Sing, then. I'm listening."

Del slanted me a disapproving glance, then spoke briefly to Halvar. In response the headman grinned, turned to the gathered villagers all wrapped in warmest furs, and announced something. Yet again I saw musical instruments brought out.

I sat there with a polite smile pasted onto my face and tried to look interested as Ysaa-den launched into song. My own bout with singing in order to defeat Chosa Dei had not resulted in improved comprehension or appreciation; it all sounded like noise to me, though admittedly with a pattern. I suppose it was even pretty, if you like that kind of thing.

Del apparently did. She sat all wrapped in white fur with her eyes fixed on distances, losing herself in the music. I wondered if it took her back to her childhood, when her kinfolk had gathered to sing. And I wondered, suddenly, if *she* had ever sung to anything or anyone other than her sword.

At the end of the song Halvar turned yet again to us and said something. This time Del looked surprised.

"What?" I asked, rousing.

"He's bringing the holy man out to throw oracle bones."

"So, the old man likes to gamble."

Del waved a hand. "No, no—to *really* throw the bones, as they were meant to be thrown. Before people began using them for wagering."

I wanted to say something more, but the old holy man had appeared. He stopped before us, bowed to us both, then sat down on the spotted pelt Halvar carefully spread. He was a *very* old man, as holy men often are, having stuffed so much ritual into a single life. With the Salset there'd been the shukar, sort of a holy man/magician; I wondered if Northern customs were the same.

The old man—white-haired, blue-eyed and palsied—seemed to be waiting for something. And then one of the younger men brought a low tripod and set it carefully before him. Onto the triple prongs was placed a platter of polished gold. Its rim, curving upward gently, was worked in Northern runes.

I blinked. "I thought you said Ysaa-den had only two copper pennies."

"In coin," Del agreed. "That's an oracle stand and platter. Each village has one . . . unless it's stolen, or traded away." She shrugged. "Some of the old ways die when the need to survive is greater."

The old man took a leather pouch from beneath his furs and carefully untied the drawstring. He poured the contents into one palm: a handful of polished stones. They were opaque but oddly translucent; pale, pearlescent white showing green and red and blue as the old man spread them in his hand. One was fiery black, but alive with so many colors I couldn't name them all.

I frowned. "Those aren't really bones. Those are stones. Oracle bones are *bones.*"

"Bones of the earth," Del said. "They've been carefully carved and polished."

I grunted. "Maybe so, but they're not the sort of oracle bones *I'm* used to."

"These work," she agreed.

I opened my mouth to protest—yet *another* story—but didn't say anything. Even though I didn't believe in foretelling, I knew perfectly well what Del would throw in my face if I said anything rude about the old man and his stones. She'd mention Chosa Dei, whom even *she* thought was a story until he'd nearly killed her.

So I didn't give her the chance.

The old man threw his stones onto the golden platter. They rattled and slid, as expected, falling into random patterns. Only to the man who uses them to foretell, the patterns are never random. That much even I knew.

He threw seven times before he spoke. And then he said a single word.

This time Del frowned.

"Jhihadi," the old man repeated.

Del glanced at Halvar, ignoring me entirely. "I don't understand."

Halvar shook his head, mystified as Del.

"Jhihadi," the old man said, and swept the stones into his hand.

A great silence lay over the gathering. No doubt everyone had expected profound words of wisdom, or a promise of good health. Instead, the holy man of Ysaa-den had given them a word none of them knew.

"Jhihadi," I said quietly, "is a Southron word."

"Southron?" Del frowned. "Why? What has a Southron word to do with us?"

"Actually, it's Desert, not pure Southron . . . and it might have something to do with the fact that *I* am, after all, Southron." I smiled benignly. "Although, knowing the word, I doubt it indicates me personally." I grinned at her, then shrugged. "He must mean something else, or *someone* else; he is old, after all, and those are just pretty stones."

"Why?" she asked suspiciously. "What does 'jhihadi' mean?"

"Messiah," I said plainly.

Braids whipped as she turned instantly and faced the holy man. She asked him something courteously, but I heard the underlying doubt. The need for an explanation.

Obligingly, the old man threw the stones again. And again they fetched up into varied patterns, none of which I could read.

He studied them, then nodded. "Jhihadi," he repeated. And then added something in uplander, ending in yet another Desert word.

"Iskandar?" I said sharply. "What's Iskandar got to do with this?"

Del looked at me blankly. "I don't know what that *is*."

"An old story," I said dismissively. "Iskandar is a place, named after a man who was supposedly a messiah. I don't know how much truth there is to the tale—you know how stories can get all twisted up." We stared frowning at one another, thinking about Chosa Dei. "Anyway, Iskandar was where this supposed messiah met his death."

Del's eyes were intent. "Was he murdered? Executed?"

I grinned. "Nothing so romantic. His horse kicked him in the head; he died ten days later. Which is why there are questions about his identity, since a true messiah shouldn't be physically vulnerable." I shrugged. "I don't know much about it, really, since it's not the sort of thing I pay much attention to . . . I just know that on his deathbed he promised to come back. But since that was hundreds of years ago and Iskandar lies in ruins, I have my doubts about this jhihadi the old man's talking about."

Del still frowned, locking brows together. "He says we're going there."

"Iskandar?" I didn't bother to hide my amusement. "Then the old man must be sandsick."

Del chewed her lip. "If Ajani's there—"

"He won't be. I promise, bascha . . . Iskandar is a ruin; no one goes there. Not even Ajani would, unless he likes to talk with ghosts."

"Then why would the holy man say so?"

After a judicious glance around at the gathered villagers, I couched my words politely. "Shall we just say that sometimes people try to protect pronouncements by insisting they're true when they're not?"

"He isn't lying," Del declared.

I winced. Here I'd been so careful to speak diplomatically, and now Del was being too blunt.

"No," I agreed. "Did I say he was?"

"You said—"

"I said perhaps he was mistaken. Now, are we done yet? Can we go to bed?"

Del turned back to the holy man and asked something in uplander. Accordingly, he threw the stones once again. Then told her what he read.

"Well?" I prodded, when she didn't translate for me.

"Oracle," she said. "There is an Oracle."

"Those are oracle *bones*—"

"No, not bones—*oracle*. A man is foretelling the coming of the jhihadi." Del's expression was blank as she stared at me. "A man who is not a man, but neither is he a woman." Now she frowned. "I don't understand."

"You're not supposed to, bascha. That's what these people trade on; they make coin off interpretation." I smiled at the holy man, inclined my head respectfully, then did the same to Halvar. "*Now* can we go to bed?"

Plainly, Del was irritated. "Oh, Tiger, I swear—you have become an old man. What happened to the days when you would sit up all night swilling *amnit* or aqivi, trading lies in cantinas?"

"I met you," I retorted. "I joined up with you and got the hoolies beat out of me more times than I can count." I stood up slowly and rewrapped pelts around my shoulders. "Is that answer enough for you?"

Del, taken aback, said nothing in return. I went off to bed.

Some time later I sat bolt upright in the darkness. Beside me, the sheathless sword was glowing. It was red as wind-whipped coals; hot as a smithy's forge. Hot as Chosa Dei's fire in the entrails of the dragon.

"No," I said clearly, and wrapped hands around the grip.

Shock jerked me rigid. Then I began to shake. It wasn't the heat of the sword, but the power surging through it. Raw, angry power, totally uncontrolled.

"No," I said again, moving onto my knees. Pelts fell away until I knelt half naked, wearing nothing but borrowed trews. I'd learned it was warmer sleeping naked under fur, but while in Ysaaden I'd altered the habit a little. It seemed the courteous thing, although only Del shared the lodge.

Power ran through my hands, then crept the length of my arms until elbows and shoulders ached. "Hoolies take you," I gritted. "I already beat you once. I can do it again."

It hurt. Hoolies, it *hurt* . . . but I wouldn't give in to it. I can be stubborn that way.

Chosa Dei wasn't pleased. I sensed him in the sword, testing the confines of his prison. I wondered if he knew what had happened, if he understood his plight; if he realized he was dead. For a man such as he, accustomed to stealing lives as well as magic, it would be a horrific discovery to learn *his* life had been stolen, along with his remade magic.

He tested the blade again. I exerted my own strength of will. Felt rising curiosity; felt a need to understand.

And also felt Samiel trying to reabsorb the magic the sorcerer had borrowed.

How long? I wondered wearily. How long will this go on?

Power hesitated, then abruptly ran out again, leaving my arms numb. Slowly I unlocked my hands from around the grip and set the sword down again. I trembled with reaction; sweat bathed face and ribs.

Chill came rushing in, the kind that eats at bones. Shakily I crawled beneath pelts again, seeking leftover warmth. I snugged fur around my chin, then tried to relax arms and hands. When the shaking wouldn't stop, I thrust my hands between drawn-up knees and held them tightly in place. Waiting for the reaction to diminish.

A hand touched my rigid left shoulder, though I could only just feel it through the pelts. "Tiger—are you all right?"

I sucked in a gut-deep breath, then blew it out again. Trying to steady my voice. "I thought you were still out with Halvar and all the others."

"It's very late. Nearly dawn. I've been in bed for hours."

Hours. Then she'd seen what had happened.

"Are you all right?" she repeated.

"Just leave me alone," I told her. "Let me go back to sleep."

"You're shaking. Are you cold?"

"Go back to bed, Del. You're keeping me awake."

Shock reverberated. The hand went away. In a moment so did Del, crawling back beneath her pelts all of three feet away from my own.

I lay there sweating, shaking, trying to still my hands while my arms threatened to cramp. I felt the strain in shoulder blades, traveling down to tie up my back. I didn't want to cramp; *hoolies,* don't let me cramp . . . I'd almost rather be knifed. At least the pain is cleaner.

Concentrate—*concentrate* . . . slowly, the trembling subsided. I took my hands from between my knees and felt the tendons slacken. The ghost pain of threatened cramp flowed slowly out of back and shoulders; at last I could fully relax. The relief was overwhelming.

I let out a rushing breath of gratitude. Then rolled over onto my left side, resettling pelts, and saw Del watching me.

She sat cross-legged on her bedding, one pelt wrapped around her body. There was not much light in the lodge, only a little from the coals. But pale hair and paler face caught the light and magnified it; I could see her face fairly well. I could see the expression on it.

"What?" I croaked.

She didn't answer at first, as if caught in some faraway place. She just stared at me fixedly, focused solely on my face.

With more emphasis: *"What?"*

Something glistened in her eyes. "I was wrong," she said.

I stared back, speechless.

"I was *wrong*," she repeated.

I watched the tears spill over.

"Wrong," she said huskily. "All the reasons: wrong. All the excuses: wrong. For nothing other than selfishness, I betrayed your trust."

Finally I could force something past my tight throat. "There was Kalle—"

"Wrong," Del declared. "A daughter is a daughter, and worth many sacrifices, but to *use* you as I did—to make you coin with which to barter—" Her voice failed her abruptly. She swallowed painfully. "What I did was no different, in its own way, than what Ajani did to me. He took away my freedom . . . I tried to take away yours."

Any number of responses jumped into my mouth. Each and every one of them was meant to diminish the truth of what she said, to somehow dismiss what she had done. So she would feel better. So she wouldn't cry any more. So I wouldn't feel guilty, even though I wasn't to blame.

I choked all of them back. To give in to the impulse was to dilute the power of her admission.

I took a deep breath. "Yes," I agreed. "What you did was wrong."

Del's tone was oddly empty. "I have done nothing I am ashamed of, save that. I have killed men. Many men. Men who got in my way, in the circle and out. I excuse none of those deaths; all were necessary. But what I offered Staal-Ysta, even for only a year, was not necessary. It was not my right to offer. It was not my life to give."

"No," I said softly.

Del drew in a noisy breath. "If you want me to go, I will. You have finished the task you set out to do. You have fulfilled your promise. It is left to me to finish mine; to end my song. Ajani is not your responsibility."

No. He never had been. But I know I hated the man at least half as much as Del, for what he'd done to her.

I thought about riding alone again. Just the stud and me. No female complications. No mission of vengeance. No obsession. Just riding through the South trying to scare up work. Trying to make a living. Growing older by the day, with nothing to show for it.

And no Northern bascha with whom to pass the time, in argument or in the circle.

I cleared my throat. "I've got nothing to do."

"After what I have done—"

"I'll get over it."

It was abrupt. Off-handed. Casual. It was also enough. We're neither of us good at putting feelings into words.

Del pulled furs into place and lay down on her bedding again. Her back was toward me, right shoulder jutting toward the roof. "I would like that," she said.

I lay there thinking about it, overwhelmed with new feelings. But I was exhausted from the sword, and it took too much effort to think about emotions. Del had made her admission. Del had fulfilled the task I required of her. So now all I had to do was just shut my eyes and let it go, sliding away. Tumbling into darkness. The pain was gone for good, and the lure of sleep beckoned. Beckoned. *Beckoned*—

It was pleasant drifting there, just at the edge of the eddy . . . at the point of dropping off—

"You're not old," Del said. Very low, but distinct.

Sleep retreated a moment. I smiled and yanked it back.

Going home, I thought, and slid off the edge of the world.

Part II

Chapter 1

T iger," she said, "you're whistling."

"No, I'm not."

"Not now, no—but you were."

"I don't whistle, bascha—too much like music."

"Whistling *is* music," she pointed out, "and you were doing it."

"Look," I said patiently, "I don't sing, I don't hum, I don't whistle. I don't do anything even remotely connected with music."

"Because you're tone-deaf. But that doesn't mean you *can't* do any of those things. It just means you do all of them badly." She paused. "And you do."

"Why *would* I whistle? I've never done it before."

"Because, thanks to the Cantéada and your *jivatma*, you have a better understanding of what power music holds . . . and maybe because you're happy."

Well, I *was* happy. I'd been happy ever since Del had made her admission. Happier ever since we'd traded uplands for downlands and then downlands for border country; before an hour was up we'd be out of the North for good.

But I don't know that it made me *whistle*.

I drew in a deep breath, then exhaled in satisfaction. "Smell that? That's air, bascha . . . good, clean air. And *warm* air, too . . . no more frozen lungs."

"No," she agreed, "no more frozen lungs . . . now we can breathe Southron air and have our lungs *scorched*."

I just grinned, nodded, rode on. It felt good to be aboard the stud again, riding down out of hills and plateaus into the scrubby borderlands between the North and Harquhal. It felt so good I didn't even mind Del's steadfast silences, or the dry irony of her tone when she *did* speak. All I knew was that with each stride closer to the border, I was closer to home. To warmth and sun and sand. To cantinas and aqivi. To all the things I'd known so well for the last twenty-some-odd years of my life, once I was free to know them.

"Hah!" I said. "See? There's the marker now." Without waiting for an answer, I booted the stud into a startled, lunging run and galloped the distance remaining between me and the South. I sent him past the stone cairn, then rolled him back, held him in check, watched Del negotiate the same distance at a much more decorous pace.

Or was it reluctance in place of decorum?

"Come on, Del," I called. "The footing's good enough. Let that blue horse run!"

Instead she let him walk. All the way to the cairn. And then she reined in, slid off, looped his reins around the pile of stones. Saying nothing, Del walked a short distance away and turned her back to me staring steadfastly toward the north.

Oh. That again.

Impatiently I watched as she unsheathed, balanced blade and hilt across both hands, then thrust the sword above her head as if she offered it to her gods. It brought back the night she'd called colors out of the sky and painted the night with rainbows. It brought back the night I'd realized she wasn't dead; that I realized I hadn't killed her.

Impatience faded. Del was saying good-bye to her past and her present. No more Staal-Ysta. No more Kalle. No more familiar life. As much as I was pleased to see the South again, it wasn't the same for her. It never could be, either, regardless of circumstances.

The stud stomped, protesting inaction. I stilled him with a twitch of the reins and a single word of admonishment; for a change, he paid attention. Then he swung his head around as far as he could swing it, staring toward still-invisible Harquhal, and snorted. With feeling.

"I know," I told him. "Just a moment or two more . . . you can wait that long, even if you don't like it."

He shook his head, clattered bit shanks, slashed his tail audibly. It needed cutting badly; I knew almost instantly because the ends of coarse horsehair stung me across one thigh.

"Keep it up," I suggested. "I'll cut your *gehetties* off, too, and *then* where would you be?"

Del came back down to the blue roan and pulled reins free of the rock, leading him toward me. She still carried a naked blade, and showed no signs of putting it away.

I frowned. Reined in the stud as he seriously considered greeting the roan with a nip. Tried to ask a question, but was overridden by Del.

"It's time," she said simply.

Eyebrows rose. "Time?"

Sunlight glinted off Boreal. "Time," Del agreed, "to face one another in a circle."

It had been three weeks since the last time the subject had come up, just before reaching Ysaa-den. Del said nothing about sparring, and I'd been content to let the matter rest. I'd hoped it could rest forever.

I glanced down at the hilt of my own *jivatma*, riding quietly next to my left knee in a borrowed sheath buckled onto my saddle. Halvar had been generous enough to give me the sheath he'd used for his old bronze sword; it didn't really suit me, since it was only a scabbard and not the sheath-and-harness as I preferred, but I'd needed something to carry the weapon in. I couldn't lug it around bare-bladed.

"I don't think so," I told her.

Del's brow furrowed. "Are you still afr—"

"You don't know this sword."

She looked at the hilt. Considered what I'd said. Sighed a little and tried valiantly to hang onto waning patience. "I need to practice, Tiger. So do you. If we're to earn a living while we try to track down Ajani, we've got to get fit again. We've got to spar against one another to recover timing, strength, stamina—"

"I know all that," I said, "and you're absolutely right. But I'm not stepping into a circle against you so long as Chosa Dei's in this sword."

"But you can control it. You can control *him;* I've seen you. Not just that night in Halvar's lodge, but all the other times on the way here—"

"—and it's all those other times that make me refuse now," I told her plainly. "This sword wasn't exactly easy to control *before* I requenched it in Chosa Dei . . . do you think I really want to risk losing whatever control I've learned while you and I spar?" I shook my head. "Chosa Dei wanted your sword. He wanted to drain the magic, to reshape it—*remake* it—for his own specific needs. As far as I can tell, I think he still does."

Del was plainly startled. "How can he still—?" She shook her head, breaking it off. "He's in a *sword,* Tiger."

"And do you, not knowing what he's capable of, really want to risk letting him make contact with Boreal?"

"I don't think—" She stopped. Frowned. Stared pensively at Samiel's hilt poking up beside my knee. Then made a gesture of acknowledgment. "Maybe you're right. Maybe if your sword and mine ever met he'd steal my *jivatma's* magic. And then—" She broke off again, staring at me in realization. "If he bound your magic and mine together, what would that make him? What kind of man would he be?"

I shook my head. "There's no way of knowing what could happen. Your *jivatma* is different from others, bascha. You've known that all along, though you say little about it. But it's become obvious even to me, now that I've seen a few others. Now that I know how they're made, and what goes into them." I shrugged. "You blooded her in Baldur and completed your rituals, sealing all your pacts with those gods you revere so much, and then you sang your own personal song of need and revenge." I looked down at her steadily. "I think it gave your *jivatma* a more intense kind of power."

Del said nothing; silence was eloquent.

I spread both hands, reins threaded through fingers. "When I requenched—when I keyed the way you're supposed to, *finally*—I sang of specific, personal things, just like you did. And my sword, like yours, is different, only it's because of Chosa Dei, not any special pacts." I shook my head. "I don't understand it yet. Maybe I never will. But I do know that heat and cold don't mix. One always has to win. And I think it's the same with our swords."

Del was clearly troubled. "It was a mistake . . . it never should have happened . . . in Staal-Ysta, we are taught never to requench—"

"I didn't have a whole lot of choice, now, did I?"

"No, no—I am not blaming you." But still she frowned. "I am thinking of the reason why requenching is forbidden. I am thinking about a sword-dancer who, whenever he desires, requenches his *jivatma*. And how he himself can 'collect' the enemy's personal power, just as Chosa Dei collected magic by unmaking things." Del looked at my sword. "I am thinking about a man—or a woman—who forgets honor and promises and becomes addicted to power. Addicted to requenching."

"Are you saying nothing stronger than *custom* keeps sword-dancers with *jivatmas* from requenching each time they kill?"

"Custom," she answered, "and honor."

I made a sound of derision. "*That's* some kind of control! What you're telling me is a sword-dancer sick and tired of all these customs and honor codes could become a renegade. Ride all over the North and South, requenching as he goes."

"No one would do—"

"Why not?" I interrupted. "What's to keep him from it? What's *really* to keep him from it, if habit isn't enough?"

"A sword-dancer who did such a thing would be formally denounced by the *voca* and declared outlaw," she said. "A blade without a name. He would owe *swordgild* to Staal-Ysta and be subject to discipline by any sword-dancer who challenged him."

I triple-clucked my tongue at her in mock sorrow. "Such a frightening prospect, bascha. Enough to make me go to bed and pull the covers over my head."

Color bloomed in her face. "Just because no one in the South has an honor at all, or assumes responsibility—"

"That's not it," I told her. "That's not my point. What I'm saying is, these swords are dangerous. Whatever magic turns a normal sword into a thing laden with the power to suck a soul from a person is nothing to take lightly. In the wrong hands a *jivatma* could become a devastating weapon." I smiled sardonically. "And yet the *an-kaidin* on Staal-Ysta continue to hand them out." I shifted in the saddle. "Don't know as how that's very wise, Delilah."

"No one except a *kaidin* is gifted with a *jivatma*. Or the one who chooses instead to be a sword-dancer." She shrugged, spreading a hand. "By the time of choice the *an-ishtoya* has proven his or her honor; that's what rank is for. It is a selection process, a way of enforcing the honor codes of Staal-Ysta. It isn't undertaken lightly, Tiger; they don't give a blooding-blade to anyone unless it's quite certain he—or she—knows how to invoke the magic properly, and that he is fully committed to upholding the honor systems."

"Del," I said patiently, "*I* have a *jivatma*."

It sank in. Del stared at me wide-eyed. And then waved a dismissive hand. "Yes, of course, but it's because you were worthy of one."

"Was I? Haven't I requenched?"

She opened her mouth to reply, then closed it slowly. Frowned more deeply, pulling smooth, creamy forehead into lines of tension and concern. It's never easy to come face-to-face with the weakness in lifelong beliefs. I know; I used to disbelieve in magic altogether.

"Del," I said quietly, "I'm not intending to requench again, if that's what you're worried about. I'd just as soon never key this thing again—I'm *sword-dancer,* not sorcerer. All I'm saying is, it seems kind of odd that this kind of power is given away freely with very few restraints. Honor is one thing, bascha—and I don't doubt it counts for something on Staal-Ysta—but not everyone in the world understands the value in such a thing. Certainly most people— everyone *I* know—would be more than willing to use any advantage at hand, if it meant the difference between living and dying."

Del stared up at me from the ground. "Are you telling me you believe I will cast off my honor and defeat Ajani unfairly?"

I grinned. "I believe you will do whatever it takes to kill him.

Because what you're doing is in the *name* of honor, which sort of balances out the effort."

She shrugged one shoulder slightly. "Perhaps. Perhaps not. But how I kill Ajani has nothing to do with your unwillingness to meet me in a circle."

I sighed. "It does, but I guess you can't see it right now. So let's just say that I, being a Southroner and entirely lacking in honor *or* scruples, don't have the slightest understanding of what this sword is capable of. And that's why, in addition to other things, I don't want to dance with you."

"Chosa Dei," she murmured.

I tapped the pommel knot. "Right here, bascha . . . and growing angrier by the moment."

Del looked down at the sword in her hand. "I have to dance," she said. "It's why I went looking for you."

It cut deep. Right through flesh, muscle, belly wall, into the hidden places. For four weeks I had mostly put aside thoughts of personal things because we were busy hunting hounds, but now it was fresh again. Now it hurt again.

It was especially painful in view of the things she'd told me in Halvar's lodge.

"Well, then," I said finally, "why don't you head on down the road to Harquhal, all of twenty miles south or so, where I'm sure you'll find someone there who can give you a proper match."

Del stared up at me for a long moment. Her expression was unreadable. For a woman with only twenty-one years to her name—and that just barely—she was very good at hiding what she felt.

Abruptly she resheathed, turned to her roan, stepped up into the stirrup. Swung a leg over and settled, gathering loose rein.

Hoolies, I thought, she's going. After all this—after settling things at last, she's really going to go—

Del walked her horse to mine. "I lied," she said plainly.

Oh, hoolies, bascha . . . now you've got me confused.

"From the beginning, I lied."

"About what?" I asked warily.

"About the dancing. About why I came looking for you."

"Oh?"

Del nodded. "You are the kind of man—or were—who would take lightly a woman's devotion. A woman's admission of admiration. A woman's need for you. You would take it lightly, and hurt her, because she would have offered something of value—the truth of what she felt—and you would see nothing of value in it."

"*I* would?"

"Men," she said. "You, once, certainly; I recall what you were like."

"But I wouldn't any more?"

Her face was oddly expressionless. "Not around me. Not in reach of my sword."

I grinned, then hid it away behind an arch expression. "So, you're saying—I think—you didn't come looking for me just because of my dancing."

"No."

It brought me up short. I frowned. "No, you didn't come looking for me just because of my dancing; or no, that's not right?"

Del smiled. She *smiled.* "I came looking for you because of your dancing, yes—you are the Sandtiger—but also because of you. Just you, Tiger; now, I have said it aloud. I hope you treat it kindly."

It meant something. It meant a *lot*—but I couldn't show anything of it. Some things are just too private. "So, am I to take this to mean you're devoted to me? That you *need* me?"

Del turned her horse southerly. "Don't assume anything, Tiger. It can get you into trouble."

Chapter 2

It was warm in Harquhal. A faint afternoon breeze blew sand at our faces, lodging grit in our teeth. For once I didn't mind the crunching; it meant I was home again.

Del, however, did. She rode her roan in through the gates and blew her lips free of dust, brushing at blue woolen tunic and muttering in uplander. Something to do with dust and sand. Something to do with dislike. And something, I think, with a bath.

But a bath would have to wait. "Harness," I said briefly, and headed off down the street.

Harquhal is the kind of place that attracts sword dancers. It's a border town, which means two culture come together, and not always peaceably. *This* mean there is often work for those of us who hire on to protect, retrieve, or bestow, depending on circumstances, and depending on the employer. Which means where there are sword-dancers, there are also swordsmiths and craftsmen dedicated to the art.

The man I went to see had been recommended by three different sword-dancers in three different cantinas. There is nothing at all accomplished by being hasty about accoutrements that can possibly save a life. I took my time, asked around, downed a few cups of aqivi just to reacquaint my tongue. Del made no complaint, but I could feel her growing impatience. She wanted to ask about Ajani, but I'd talked her out of it. First I wanted a proper harness and sheath, so that if we ran into trouble I'd be better prepared.

Although she did comment, eventually, that with all the aqivi in me I'd be lucky to remain standing, let alone dance.

"I don't want to dance," I told her. "I'd just as soon avoid dancing altogether, if I can; there's no need to be hostile."

"We want to kill a man. I don't think we can avoid it."

"*You* want to kill him. Ajani's not my problem. My problem, right now, is finding a man who can give me exactly what I want in the way of a proper harness."

Which had led me to ask yet a third sword-dancer, who gave me the same name. So we went to see him.

He was a typical Southroner: brown-haired, brown-eyed, burned dark by the sun. He wore the plain clothing of the tradesman—gauzy tunic, baggy trews, robe—and no ornamentation. Which meant he didn't take an inordinate amount of pride in his appearance, unlike some gifted men, but, more likely, in his craftsmanship.

He stood behind a table. The shop was small, jammed with flats of skins, racks of wood, trays full of wire, thong, tools. He watched Del and me come in through the curtained doorway and nodded greeting. It was very brief to Del, intended mostly for me; the man, the Southroner. Nothing much had changed while I'd been North.

I stopped at the table and looked the man dead in the eye. "It's a very special sword."

Juba smiled. Undoubtedly he had heard the exact same words before, uttered by countless sword-dancers intent upon the blade that earned them a living. Only in this case, what I said was understatement.

"Very special," I repeated, "and in need of precise attention." I set the sheathed sword on the table in front of Juba. "Don't touch," I said.

Again, Juba smiled. It was not a condescending smile, or one of disbelief—he was too professional to let his thoughts show so plainly—but it was a smile of subtle acknowledgement: *Let the customer say what he will. Juba will be the judge.*

Only the hilt was visible above the lip of Halvar's sheath. It was bright, twisted-silk steel devoid of excess ornamentation. The sword was simply a sword.

"*Jivatma*," I said, and Juba's brown eyes widened. "What I want," I continued, "is a true sword-dancer's harness, cut to my size, and a diagonal scabbard as well. Split sheath, of course—six-inch cut at the lip—so when I hook it out of the scabbard the blade rides free. While sheathed I want it snug—I can't abide rattling—but I need it to come to hand easy. No snags or awkward motion."

Juba nodded slightly. "Cadda wood," he said. "It's light, but very strong. And suede lining inside. Outside I will encase it in danjac hide, then lace and wrap it with thong, with a bit of wire for strength." He paused. "Do you want ornamentation?"

Some sword-dancers like to hang coin or rings or bits of jewelry from their sheaths, to prove they've been successful. Some even like to take something from the loser—dead or alive—as a kind of trophy. Me, I've always kind of thought that sort of thing was asking for trouble. While it's true not too many thieves want to tangle with a man who earns his living with a sword, I've never known a bandit yet who wouldn't do whatever he could to separate a man from his wealth. Which meant that a sword-dancer who got drunk, or fell in with a scheming cantina girl, or who simply lost track of his wits, was asking to be robbed.

I started to shake my head.

"Yes," Del said. "Can you copy this?"

She had waited so quietly behind me, saying nothing to Juba or me, that I'd nearly forgotten she was there. But now she came forward, asking Juba for clay slate and stylus. He set the slate out on the table, passed her the stylus, watched in pensive silence as she scraped out the design.

"There," she said at last. "Can you work those into the leather? From top to bottom, like so—twisting around and around and around . . . can you do this?"

Juba and I stared at the slate. Del had painstakingly carved elaborate runes into the unbaked clay, then blown the dust away. The shapes were intricate and precise, and like nothing I'd ever seen.

Except on Samiel's blade.

Juba frowned, then looked at me. "Do you want those?"

His tone expressed doubt; he was, after all, a Southroner, and Del a Northern woman . . . but his job was to please the customer. He'd let me decide.

I glanced sidelong at Del. She offered nothing save silence again, but I felt the tension in her body. She wouldn't ask me to say yes, because it had to be my choice. But clearly she wanted me to let Juba put in the runes.

What the hoolies . . . "Put them on."

Juba shrugged and nodded. "I must measure you," he said, "and also measure the sword. But if you won't allow me to touch it—"

"I'll help," I told him. "Measure me first, then we'll get to the sword."

He worked quickly and competently, wrapping thong this way and that way around me, then tying knots on it to mark his place. When he was done, all I saw was a leather thong full of knots, but Juba knew the language.

Then he looked at the sword.

I slid it clear of Halvar's sheath, dropping the scabbard aside. Now the blade was naked. It was black at the tip, a smudgy dull black extending three fingers up the blade, as if it had been dipped. Runes caught light like water.

Juba sucked in a breath. Desire darkened his eyes. I saw his fingers twitch.

"*Jivatma,*" I repeated. "Did you think the Sandtiger lies?"

I did it on purpose. Not to brag, although there's always a little of that; but to make certain he understood who he was making the harness for. If a sword-dancer like the Sandtiger was pleased by Juba's work, it could improve his reputation and increase business one hundredfold. If he *didn't* like the workmanship, Juba might be finished.

But I did it also because I knew there was a chance that Juba, left alone, might yet touch the sword. Might try to pick it up. And I recalled much too well the pain of Boreal before Del had told me her name.

"Measure it," I said. "If you need it moved, I'll do it."

Swiftly Juba drew out yet another leather thong and measured the sword, tying knots here and there. I moved it as instructed, holding the thong for him when he needed to make contact. When he was done, he nodded. "It will fit. I promise. It will be as you have said."

"And the runes," Del said intently.

Juba looked at her for the second time. This time he *looked* at her, and saw what she was. Saw past the Northern beauty. Saw past the independence. Saw beyond the cool demeanor to the woman who lived inside.

And looked away again, being a Southron fool. "How soon?" he asked.

I shrugged. "As soon as you can. I don't like carrying my sword by hand, and I can't abide a belt or baldric."

No, of course not; no true sword-dancer carried his weapon in anything but harness-and-sheath. I wasn't about to change the custom and risk looking like a fool.

Juba thought about it. He might ask for better payment if I wanted it so quickly; then again, my name ought to be enough. "Two days," he offered.

"Tomorrow evening," I said.

Juba considered it. "Not enough time," he explained. "There is much work for me, with so many going to Iskandar. I would be honored to make by best harness and sheath for the Sandtiger, but—"

"Tomorrow evening," I said. "What's this about Iskandar?"

He shrugged, already digging through piles of leather. "They say the jhihadi is coming."

I grunted. "They say the same thing every ten years or so." I sheathed my sword and picked it up. With Del on my heels, I went out the curtained doorway.

"You heard him," she said as soon as we were outside. "He mentioned Iskandar and the jhihadi . . . are you going to pretend it's nonsense when a *Southroner* brings it up."

"Iskandar is a ruin," I said yet again. "There's no reason for anyone to go there."

"Except maybe if the messiah is coming."

"All sorts of rumors get started, bascha. Are we supposed to believe them all?"

Del didn't answer, but her mouth was set firmly.

"And now," I began, "suppose you tell me what these runes are all about."

She shrugged. "Just runes. Decoration."

"I don't think so, bascha. I know you better than that. You were too precise, which makes me nervous. I want to know what *kind* of runes—what do they say?—and what they're supposed to do."

Del didn't offer an answer. We were just outside Juba's shop; I stopped dead, swung to face her, very nearly stepped on her toes. She looked into my face and probably saw how serious I was; she took a step back and sighed.

"A warning," she told me. "Wards against tampering. Also your name, and who you are . . . and your Northern rank."

"I'm a Southroner."

She took it in stride. "Southron rank, as well," she continued evenly. "Seventh-level, as you have said; I have forgotten nothing."

"You forgot to ask me if I wanted such things on my scabbard."

Del was plainly troubled. "You yourself told me how dangerous a *jivatma* can be in the wrong hands. You pointed out that even a Northerner, if he felt strongly enough, might reject the teachings of Staal-Ysta to gain additional power."

"But what has that to do with *my* sword?"

"Protection," she said quietly. "If an unscrupulous sword-dancer wanted power for himself, he could not do better than to steal your *jivatma*."

"You mean—" I stopped. "Do you mean the runes are to protect *me*?"

"Yes."

"No one can even touch my sword without knowing his name, Del. Isn't that protection enough?"

She didn't avoid my gaze. "You drink," she said. "You have begun to drink already, and you will drink more before the night is through, to celebrate your homecoming. I have seen you do it before." She shrugged. "A man who drinks often does and says foolish things."

"And you think I might tell someone the name of this sword, thereby allowing him—or her—to touch it. To use it. Possibly even to requench it, *if* he or she knew the proper way."

Del's eyes were bleak. "Chosa Dei is no longer a story," she said. "He is a truth, and others will come to know it. You yourself have said you don't know what the sword is capable of; would you have an enemy gain your sword *and* Chosa Dei all at once? Do you know what that would mean?"

"It would free Chosa Dei," I said grimly.

"And more." Creases marred her brow. "A man wanting skill and strength could do worse than to quench a blade in *you*."

I hadn't thought about it, to tell the truth. But now I did. I thought about it hard, scowling down at the scabbarded *jivatma*.

Me, at risk. Me, a source of skill and strength. The kind of "honored enemy" others might find attractive. Hoolies, I was *the Sandtiger* . . . whatever anyone really thought of me no longer mattered. I had a reputation for being very good—well, I am—and anyone who wanted to improve a blooding-blade might indeed seek me out.

"But by putting on these runes, aren't we telling everyone who might be interested that I'm a good target?"

Del shook her head. "They say your name and who you are, yes; they also serve as wards. A man would be a fool to tamper with your sword."

I wasn't convinced.

Del tried again. "Chosa Dei will do everything he can to free himself. Anyone who tried to use this sword would be asking for death . . . or worse. Asking for possession."

"Like the loki. Isn't it?" I shook my head. "I thought we were free of that sort of thing forever, since the Cantéada entrapped them in the circle . . . and now there's *this* to face."

Del stroked a strand of fair hair behind her left ear. "It is well that only Northerners trained on Staal-Ysta understand the power of the *jivatmas* and how they can be used . . . a Southroner has no knowledge of such things. It is therefore unlikely a Southroner will try to steal your sword."

True. It made me feel like a little better. "So—you think Northern runes will warn away unscrupulous Northerners." I grinned. "I thought you once told me all Northerners are *honorable* people."

Del didn't see the humor. "Ajani is Northern," she said.

"But he isn't a sword-dancer."

"Nor is he an honorable man." Del's tone was intensely bitter. "Do you think he has become what he has become through ignorance and stupidity? Do you think he has no way of learning things he considers important? And wouldn't you consider the habits and training of a sword-dancer important, if you knew your life could be threatened by such?"

"Del—"

"Do you think he would be so foolish as to *ignore* a story of how a named blade is blooded? Or to ignore the chance to steal one from someone like the Sandtiger, who is a seventh-level sword-dancer in addition to a *kaidin?* Do you think—"

"*Del.*"

She shut her mouth.

"All right," I said soothingly, "all right; yes, I understand; no, I don't disagree. He's not stupid and he's not ignorant. All right? Can we go on now?" I plucked at heavy wool. "Can we go see someone about trading all this weight in on dhoti and burnous?"

"You don't know him," she said steadfastly. "You don't know Ajani at all."

No, I didn't. And I couldn't. Until Delilah found him.

I sighed, closed a big hand on her shoulder, aimed her down the street. "Come on, bascha. Let's shed this wool. *Then* we can set about finding people who might know where Ajani's been keeping himself."

"No more delays," she said. "*No more* delays."

It had taken six years. Del was, finally, at the end of her patience. And I couldn't really blame her.

"I promise," I told her. "We'll find him."

Del looked me in the face. Her eyes were something to behold. Bluest blue, and beautiful, but also incredibly deadly.

And I recalled, looking at her, something Chosa Dei had said to her in the chamber. Something even Del had agreed with, speaking of herself; thinking of her oath.

Obsession is necessary. Obsession is required. Obsession is the master when compassion undermines.

Chapter 3

She sat herself down on my knee and traced out the scars on my cheek. "Soooo," she purred, "you came."

I opened one eye. "Was I supposed to?"

"Oh, yes. Everyone said you would. And now you are here."

I opened the other eye. It didn't change the view: black-haired, brown-eyed woman, perching her rump on my thigh. Leaning up against me to show off abundant charms, hardly hidden by loose, gauzy blouse.

"Kima," she told me, smiling. "And you are the Sandtiger."

I cleared my throat. "So I am." I shifted a little, trying to find a more comfortable position. Kima was no lightweight, and I was still a bit sore from my travail in Chosa's mountain. "*Who* said I would come?"

Kima waved a hand. "Everyone," she said. "All the other girls and I had a wager as to which of us would get you."

Cantina girls are notorious for wagering, and for vulgarity. But then, when you're a man in dire need of a woman after too long alone in the Punja, you don't really care. It used to be I'd just nod at whatever they said, not being particularly interested in anything other than physical charms; now I frowned at Kima.

"*Why* was I coming?"

"Because all the sword-dancers are." She snuggled up next to my chest, butting the top of her head against my chin. "I know your kind, Sandtiger . . . the lure of coin is powerful. It brings you all out of the desert."

Yes, well, occasionally. Actually, *more* than occasionally; it's sort of part of our lifestyle. Hard to live without coin.

I reached past Kima, managed to snag my cup carried it carefully to my mouth. Downed three swallows, then lost the cup to Kima. "How much did you win because you managed to 'get' me?"

Her giggle was low and throaty. "Haven't won yet. Have to take you to bed."

I sat—and Kima sat—in a corner of the cantina, snugged into a little alcove. I've never been one for sitting plop out in the middle of the place, since it's hard to keep an eye on everyone in the cantina. But give me a corner table, or one pushed into an alcove, and I'm a happy man.

I was not unhappy now, although I've been happier. I couldn't help thinking of Del, gone off to reserve a room at an inn up the street. What would she think of Kima?

Kima traced scars again, sliding fingernails through my beard. The other hand slid lower, then lower still; I sat upright so suddenly I nearly dumped her on the floor. "Sorry," I murmured as she spilled aqivi down her blouse.

She considered being affronted. Then took note of the fact the wet blouse displayed still more of half-hidden charms in a rather unique way. She leaned against me again. "First the son, and now the father. He might be younger, but you're bigger."

I grunted inattentively, trying to reach around her so I could pour more aqivi into the recovered cup. And then her words sank in. *"What?"*

She smiled, applied tongue tip to scars, pouted prettily as I pulled away. "Your son," Kima said. "He was here, too."

"I don't have a son."

Kima shrugged. "He said he was your son."

"I don't have a son." I tipped her off my knee. "Are you sure he said *my* name?"

She stood over me, hands on hips. Breasts strained against wet gauze. "Do you mean to take me to bed or not?"

Del's cool voice intruded. "Don't keep her waiting, Tiger. She might get out of the mood." She paused. "Then again, probably not; do cantina girls *have* moods?"

Kima swung around and came face to face—well, no, not *exactly* face to face; Del was a head taller—with the cold, hard truth: when Del is in the room, no other female exists. It's height, coloring, sword. It's also grace and danger. Plus a lot of their things.

Clearly, Kima knew it at once. She decided to fight *her* way, since she couldn't compete with Del. "He's taking *me* to bed! *I'm* going to win the wager!"

Del smiled coolly. "By all means."

"Wait a minute," I said, scenting trouble. "Right now I don't much care about who's taking who to bed—that can wait till later . . . what *I* want to know—"

Del interrupted. "You never could wait before."

I smacked down the brimming cup. Aqivi ran over my hand. "Look, bascha—"

Kima looked Del up and down. "You don't belong in here. What are you doing here? There's no room for another girl. And you *can't have him*."

Del's smile widened. "I already have."

Women can be *nasty* . . . I stood up, scraping my stool so hard it fell over against the wall, and looked Del dead in the eye, which isn't a problem for me. "Can you just wait a minute? I'm trying to find out something."

Del assessed Kima. "Five coppers, perhaps."

"No, *no*—" I began, but Kima was swearing in outrage.

By this time the turmoil was of interest to the rest of the cantina. I overheard wagers being laid on which of the women would win. Or if either would be worth it.

Which made me want to swing Del around bodily so all could see what she was; the wager would be ended before it was properly begun. Then again, putting Del on display was not a thing I wanted to do, since it was hardly a compliment to treat a woman as an ornament.

Besides, she'd probably kill me.

I turned back to Kima. "You said—"

"Go with her!" Kima cried. "Do you think I care? Do you think you're worth it? I've had sword-dancers better than you. I've had sword-dancers *bigger* than you—"

"How do you know?" Del asked.

I swore. "Will you just—? Del, wait . . . *Kima!*" But she was gone, flouncing across the cantina. It gave me leave to turn back to Del. "Do you have any idea what you just did?"

"If you want her that—"

"That's not *it!*" I scraped a hand through my hair, attempting to control my tone. "What I was *trying* to find out was what she meant about a man claiming to be my son."

"Your son?" Del's brows rose as she hooked a stool with a boot and pulled it out from under the table. "I didn't know you had a son."

"I *don't*—oh, hoolies, bascha, let's just forget about it. Let's just sit here and drink."

Del eyed my mug. "You've been doing that already."

I righted my stool and sat down. "Did you get us a room?"

"Two rooms; yes."

I blinked. "Two rooms? Why?"

"To make it easier for you. So you can win your wager."

"To hoolies with the wager." I was a bit put out. I was feeling a bit kindlier toward Del of late, since she'd finally admitted she was wrong, and wasn't of a mind to make the wager stick. It really was a silly sort of thing, anyway, and I didn't see the sense in continuing the farce. After all, we were both healthy people with normal appetites, and it had been quite some time since we'd shared a bed.

Del smiled. "Giving up so easily?"

"I figure we've taken that wager about as far as we can go with it."

Del's tone was very solemn. "It was undertaken properly."

"I don't care. I don't *care*. Let's forget the wager."

Now her face matched her tone. "We can't. I think two rooms would be best. And not just for the wager . . . I need the time alone. I need the time to focus."

"Focus?" I frowned. "I don't quite understand."

"For the kill." Del's attitude was matter-of-fact.

"So? You'll just kill him. It's what you've come to do. It's what you've been meaning to do for six whole years."

Del frowned. "Before, it would have been easy. But now . . ." Her voice trailed off. She looked at the table, picked at knife and sword scars, flicked bits of wood away with a grimace of distaste. "I'm different now. The task is the same, but I'm a different person." She didn't look at me. "I've *been* changed."

"Del—"

Pale-lashed lids lifted. Blue eyes stared at me. "There was a time when it would have taken no effort at all, my task. When it was my whole world. When it was all I thought of. And the doing would have been sweet, because it was all I wanted."

I waited in silence, transfixed by her intensity.

"But you have changed me, Tiger. You have blundered into my life and changed the way I think. Changed the way I feel." Her mouth tightened slightly. "It's not what I wanted. It was *never* what I wanted. But now you are here, and I find myself confused. I find myself *distracted*—and distraction can be dangerous."

Distraction could be lethal.

"And so I will ask the gods and my sword to aid me in this. To help me focus myself, so I can complete my task without additional confusion. Without the distraction."

I stared at her intently. "Didn't you try that before? The night we met up again?"

Color came and went in her face. "You *saw?*"

"I saw." I wasn't proud of it. "Del, I didn't know what to think. I didn't know what you were doing, out there in the trees with that magicked sword. So I went to see for myself."

She wasn't pleased. "And I will ask it again. Again and again, if need be. I must regain my focus."

"If you mean to strip all the humanity away just to make yourself capable of killing Ajani, maybe it's not worth it."

Blue eyes flickered minutely. The mouth went hard and flat. "I have sworn oaths."

I sighed. "All right. I give up. Do what you have to do." I eyed her askance, assessing her commitment. "But if distance is what you want, don't play games with me. I hate women who play games."

"I never play games."

She never *had;* that was true. It didn't mean she couldn't.

I shoved the jug across the table. "Drink."

Del appropriated my cup. "Do you really have a son?"

"I told you before, bascha: not as far as I know."

"Yes, I remember . . . it's not something you think about."

"And I don't plan to *talk* about it—at least, not with you." I recaptured the jug and drank straight out of it, gulping aqivi down.

Del sipped her share. "But you *could,*" she observed.

I scowled. "I could, yes. I could have several sons. I could have *many* sons; why? Do you want to go find them all?"

"No. But they—or even just he—might want to find you." She glanced across at Kima, now sitting on another man's knee. "He obviously knows who you are, if he's bragging about you in cantinas."

I thought about it. Maybe if I had a famous father I'd brag about him, too—but I wasn't so sure I liked being the subject. It's one thing to be bragged about; it's another thing having a total stranger claim himself close kin. The *closest* of kin.

Del sipped delicately. "The innkeeper asked a fortune. When I threatened to take our business elsewhere, he gave me leave to go, saying the inn was nearly full, and it was the same all over Harquhal because of the Oracle. That everyone's coming here."

Still thinking of my "son," I shifted attention with effort. "What?"

"The Oracle," she repeated. "Do you recall what the holy man in Ysaa-den foretold?"

"Oh. That." I waved a dismissive hand. "There's no reason for us—or anyone else—to go to Iskandar. Oracle or no."

Del studied her cup. "People are going," she said.

"I thought you just said people are coming *here.*"

"First," she agreed. "Do you know where Iskandar is?"

"Someplace off over there." I waved my hand again: northeasterly.

"A little more *that* way." Del mimicked my gesture, but indicated a slight shift in direction to north-northeast. "The innkeeper said Harquhal is the last true settlement before Iskandar, so people are stopping here to buy supplies."

"Iskandar is a *ruin*."

"That's why they're buying supplies."

I upended the jug and drank more aqivi. Then thumped the jug back down. "And I suppose this chatty innkeeper believes in this Oracle. Believes in this messiah."

Del shrugged. "I don't know what he believes. I know only what he told me, which is that people are going to Iskandar."

I couldn't hide my disgust. "Because the jhihadi is coming again."

She turned her cup in circles, watching her fingers move. "People need things, Tiger. For some it is religion, for others it is the dreams born of huva weed. I say nothing about what is good and bad, or right and wrong—only that people *need* in order to survive." Her voice was very quiet. "For me, after Ajani's attack, I needed revenge. That need helped me to live." Now her gaze left the cup and came up to meet my own. "You have needed, too. It's how you survived your enslavement. It's how you survived Aladar's mine."

I didn't answer for a long moment. And then when I did, I said nothing about myself or the months spent in the mine. "So, you're saying that people need this Oracle to be right. Because they need a jhihadi."

Del lifted a shoulder. "A messiah is a very special kind of sorcerer, is he not? Can he not do magical things? Can he not heal the sick and cure the lame and make rain to replenish a land sucked dry by years of drout?"

I grunted. "Is that what he's supposed to do?"

Del shifted on her stool. "When I walked to the inn, I heard talk on the street of the Oracle. When I came back the same way, I heard talk of the jhihadi." She shrugged. "The Oracle has foretold the coming of a man who can change sand to grass."

"Sand to grass? Sand to *grass?*" I frowned. "What for, bascha?"

"So people can live in the desert."

"People *do* live in the desert. *I* live in the desert."

Del sighed a little. "Tiger, I am only telling you what I heard. Have I said I believed any of it? Have I said I believed in Oracles or jhihadis?"

Not exactly. But she sounded halfway convinced.

I shrugged, started to say something, was interrupted by an arrival. A man stood by our table. Southroner, by the look of him; dark-haired, dark-eyed, tanned skin. About forty or so, and showing all his teeth. Some of them were missing.

"Sandtiger?" he asked.

I nodded wearily; I wasn't in the mood.

The smile widened. "Ah, so I thought! He described you very well." He bowed briefly, flicked a glance at Del, looked immediately back to me. "May I have more aqivi sent over? It would be an honor to buy you a jug."

"Wait," I suggested. "*Who* described me so well?"

"Your son, of course. And he was quite complimentary—" He frowned minutely. "Although he said nothing of a beard."

I wasn't concerned about the beard. Only about my "son." Evenly, I asked. "What was his name? Did my 'son' give you a name?"

The man frowned briefly, considered it, then shook his head. "No. No, he didn't. He said merely he was the Sandtiger's cub, and told us stories about your adventures."

"Adventures," I echoed. "I'm beginning to wonder about them myself." I pushed back my stool and rose. "Thanks for the offer, but I have an appointment. Perhaps tomorrow night."

The man was clearly disappointed, but made no protest. He bowed himself out of my way and went back to his friends at another table.

Del, still seated, smiled. "Does the girl win her wager, then?"

"What girl—oh. No." I scowled. "I'm going to the inn. Do you want to come?"

"Tired already? But you've only had *one* jug of aqivi." Del rose smoothly. "It was like this in Ysaa-den, too . . . perhaps age has slowed you down." She shoved her stool back under the table. "Or is it knowing you have a son?"

"No," I said testily, "it's carrying this sword."

Del went out of the cantina ahead of me and stepped into the dark street. "Why should carrying that sword make you feel tired?"

"Because Chosa Dei wants out."

Del gestured. "This way." Then, as we walked, "It's getting worse, then."

I shrugged. "Let's just say, Chosa has finally realized what sort of prison he's in."

"You have to be stronger, Tiger. You have to be vigilant."

"What I have to be, bascha, is rid of Chosa Dei." I sidestepped a puddle of urine. "Where is this inn with the chatty innkeeper?"

"Right here," Del answered, turning away from the street. "I told him you would pay."

"*I'd* pay! Why? Don't you have any coin?"

Del shook her head. "I paid *swordgild* to Staal-Ysta. I have nothing at all."

It silenced me. I'd forgotten about *swordgild*, the blood-money owed Staal-Ysta if a life were ended unfairly. The *voca* had taken everything from Del: money, daughter, lifestyle. I'd nearly taken her life.

We went inside the inn and called for the innkeeper, who came out from behind a curtained divider. He took my coin, nodded his thanks, then welcomed me warmly. "It is an honor having the Sandtiger as a guest."

I muttered appropriate things, then added an extra coin. "I want a bath in the morning. And I want the water hot."

"I will see to it myself." Then, as I turned toward the curtain, "I have given you the same room I gave your son. I thought it might please you. And he liked hot water, too."

I stopped dead in my tracks.

"Never mind," Del said.

"I don't have—"

"*Never mind*, Tiger." And pushed me through the curtain.

Chapter 4

With knees doubled up nearly to chin, I sat gingerly in hot water. It wasn't particularly comfortable—the innkeeper's cask was too small—but at least I could get wet. Part of me, anyway; the rest would have to be hand-washed instead of soaking clean.

Del came in without knocking, carrying a bundle. "A pretty sight," she observed. And then, half-hiding a smile—but only half-heartedly—she suggested a larger cask. "You don't really fit in this one."

I scowled at her blackly. "I'd like a bigger cask. I'd *love* a bigger cask. This is all there is."

She perched herself on the edge of my fragile bed, observing my cramped position. "If you had to get out of that quickly, I don't think you could."

"I'm not going anywhere quickly. What I'm doing is taking a bath." I scratched an itching ear. "What are you doing here? I mean, didn't you rent two rooms for the express purpose of being apart?"

Del ignored the gibe. "I brought you some clothes," she said, and dumped out the bundle she carried.

I tried to straighten; couldn't. "What clothes?" I asked suspiciously, envisioning more wool. "What have you done, Del?"

"I bought supplies," she answered. "Including Southron garb. Dhoti—here—and burnous. See?"

I saw. Suede dhoti, as mentioned, a russet-colored robe with leather belt, and a dull orange silk burnous to wear over it all. Also a pair of soft leather riding boots. "How do you know my size?"

"I know you snore, I know you drink, I know you like cantina girls . . . I know many things about you." Del allowed the silk to slide out of her hand. "You're going to shave, aren't you?"

"I'd planned on it, yes. Why? Do you want me to *keep* all this hair?"

She tipped her head to one side. "You've worn a beard for so long I've forgotten what you look like without one."

"Too long," I muttered. "Too much time, too much hair, too much wool." I tried to reposition myself in the cask, barked my shin on sharp wood. "I thought you said you had no money. How did you buy all this stuff?"

"I told them you would pay." Del shrugged elegantly as I sputtered a protest. "The shopkeepers know you, Tiger. They are honored by your business. They said they would be most happy to wait for you to pay them—so long as it was later today."

"I don't exactly have a whole lot of money, bascha . . . and less, now, than before." I crammed buttocks against wood, hissed as a splinter bit. "You can't go all over Harquhal promising people coin in my name. I might not have any."

Del shrugged. "I'm sure you can win more. Other sword-dancers are arriving daily . . . I think most if not all of them would be happy to meet the Sandtiger in a circle."

"I'm in no shape to meet anyone in a—*ouch*." I swore, worked a splinter free, shifted position. Eventually pulled my legs out and draped them over the rim. Cooling water sloshed across my belly.

Del surveyed my posture. "You're dripping water on the floor."

"I can't help it—my knees were cramping up." More comfortable now, I ran a string of brown soap across my chest, loosening wool-bound hair. "So, you think we can win some coin, do you? Even though we're both out of condition?"

"We wouldn't be out of condition if you'd get *in* a circle." Del smiled blandly. "I've asked you how many times?"

"No." I scrubbed more vigorously and snagged a hair beneath a fingernail, snapping it right out of my chest. "Ouch—Del, do you mind? Can I have my bath in private?"

She stood up, slid out of her harness, set Boreal on the bed. "If you're going to shave," she said, "let me do it. You'll cut your own throat."

"Never have before . . . and I've been shaving this face longer than you've been alive."

Del lifted one shoulder. "I used to shave my father. He wasn't much older than you." Without my permission—and ignoring my muttered oath—she came over to the stool beside the cask and picked up my knife, freshly honed to scrape a jaw clean of beard. "Soap your face," she suggested.

Hoolies, it's not worth arguing . . . I dutifully lathered up, then tipped my head back as ordered. Tried not to screw up my face as Del set blade to flesh.

"Hold still, Tiger." Then, as I held still, "Do these scars hurt any more?"

"The sandtiger scars? No, not any more. Not for a long time." I paused. "But if you cut them, I think they might."

"I'm not going to cut them." Del sounded absent-minded as she concentrated on shaving between the claw welts, which didn't go far toward making me feel any safer. "They're getting whiter and thinner with age," she observed. "But they must have hurt badly when the cat first striped you."

"Like hoolies," I agreed. "Then again, I was in no shape to really notice. He got me other places, too, and his claws weren't budded. The poison made me pretty sick for a couple of weeks. I was lucky to survive."

"Which you did because of Sula."

Yes, because of Sula. Because of the Salset woman who wouldn't let me die. She had gone against the suggestion of the shukar and the rest of the tribe that the troublesome chula be allowed to die. Because they all knew that in killing the sandtiger, I'd also gained my freedom.

I stirred. Sula brought back memories I preferred to forget. "Are you done?"

"Not even half begun."

Her laced braid hung forward over one shoulder, swinging as she worked. The ends of it brushed my chest.

It was, rather suddenly, intensely difficult to breathe. I shifted, sat a bit more upright, shoved myself down again. "Del, do you think—"

"Just hold still."

She had no idea how difficult that was, in view of the circumstances. "You said you wouldn't play games."

She blinked blue eyes. "What?"

"Games," I said in frustration. "What do you think *this* is?"

"I'm *shaving* you!"

"Give me back my knife." I leaned forward, caught her wrist, stripped the knife free with my left hand. "If you think I haven't lived thirty-five or thirty-six—or however many years it is!—without learning a few female tricks, you're younger than I thought."

Which, once said, didn't make me much happier. I sat in cool water and glared, holding a wet knife dripping soap and bits of beard.

Del stood with hands on hips. "And if *you* think I would tell you I wanted two rooms, and then tease you like this—"

Frustration made me testy. "Women do that sort of thing all the time."

"Some women, perhaps. Not all of them. Certainly not *me*."

I scratched violently at my scalp. "Maybe not. Maybe not on *purpose*, but it doesn't disguise the fact—"

"—that you have no self-control?"

I glared. "You *could* take it as a compliment."

She thought about it. "I could."

"So? Can I shave my own face?"

Someone knocked on the door.

"Go *away*," I muttered, but Del turned her back on me and went to open the door.

A stranger stood there. A Southroner. He wore a sword in harness. "Sandtiger?" he asked.

Warily, I nodded. Wishing I had my sword in hand instead of on the stool; feeling foolish for wishing it. But a naked man *often* feels foolish. Or at least vulnerable.

He grinned, showing white teeth in a swarthy face. "I am Nabir," he said. "I'd like to dance with you."

Nabir was young. Very young. Maybe all of eighteen. And I'll wager his knees didn't ache.

"Ask me tomorrow," I growled.

A frown creased his brow. "I won't be here tomorrow. In the morning I leave for Iskandar."

"Iskandar. Iskandar! *What's in Iskandar?*"

Nabir appeared somewhat taken aback by my outburst. "The Oracle says the jhihadi—"

"—is coming to Iskandar; that I know. I think *everybody* knows." I scowled at the boy. "But why do *you* care? You don't look religious."

"Oh, I am not." He made a quick, dismissive gesture. "I am a sword-dancer. That's why I'm going."

I scratched idly at my scars, now bare of beard. "Why is a young, admittedly nonreligious sword-dancer going to Iskandar? There's nothing to *do* there."

"Everyone's going," he said. "Even the tanzeers."

I gazed blankly at Del. "Tanzeers," I echoed.

"Ajani," she said intently.

Frowning, I looked back at Nabir, waiting so patiently. "You said everyone is going . . . sword-dancers, tanzeers—who else?"

He shrugged. "The sects are going, of course, even the Hamidaa and *khemi*. And they're saying some of the tribes as well: the Hanjii, the Tularain; also others, I think. They want to see the Oracle foretell in the flesh."

"Power shift," I murmured. "The tanzeers'll never let him survive, unless he works for them." I straightened in the cask and waved a hand at Nabir. "Go down to the nearest cantina—I forget its name—and have a drink on me." I arched a brow. "And tell Kima I sent you."

"Will you meet me?" Nabir persisted. "It would be an honor to dance with the Sandtiger in the circle."

I looked harder at his face—his young, still-forming face—and also at his harness. His new, stiff harness, squeaking as he moved.

"In a year," I told him. "Now go have that drink."

Del closed the door behind him, then turned to me. "He's young. New. Untried. He might have been worth it for the practice. And at least you wouldn't hurt him; some other sword-dancer might, just to initiate him."

"I can't take the risk, bascha. If I step into a circle, it will be against someone good. Someone up to the challenge of dancing against Chosa Dei."

Del's unspoken comment was loud in the little room.

I shook my head. "Someone who isn't *you*."

"There *will* have to be someone," she said. "*Several* someones, in fact. You are badly out of condition. If you had to dance to the death—"

"I'm not stupid enough to hire myself out to kill anyone at the moment. And besides—"

"Sometimes you have no choice."

"—*and besides*—" I smiled "—you're out of condition, too."

"Yes," Del agreed. "But I intend to dance just as soon as I find an opponent."

I watched her move toward my bed. "What—right *now*?"

"It makes no sense to waste time." Del retrieved harness and sword and slipped it on as she headed to the door. "Perhaps Nabir will do . . . no, don't get up—you've still got half your face to shave."

"He's a *boy!*" I shouted, sloshing awkwardly in my cask.

Del's tone was bland. "Not so much younger than me."

Chapter 5

el was right: she knew me very well. The suede dhoti fit in all the right places without chafing, as did the soft horseman's boots—I've always been partial to sandals, but these were very comfortable—and the dull orange burnous poured into place like water over the belted desert robe. I was a Southroner again.

But I didn't waste much time admiring the clothing. I grabbed up my sword in its borrowed sheath and left the inn quickly, calling back over my shoulder to the innkeeper that someone else could have the water now. By the time he started to answer, I was out of the door.

It's not hard to find a sword-dance, especially in a border town like Harquhal that thrives on competition. All you have to do is look for the largest gathering of people—particularly men in harness—and you will find what you're looking for.

I found Del very easily, since she's the kind of woman who draws attention. She waited quietly within the human circle, the gathering of men and women waiting to see the dance. Someone was carefully drawing a circle in the dirt, taking pains to make the line uniformly deep. It didn't really matter—in a sword-dance, the true circle is in your mind since lines are quickly obscured by displaced dust and dirt—but it was all part of the ritual.

Her expression was unaggressive, as was her posture. But Del is very tall for a woman—tall even for Southron men—and her posture is very erect. Even standing quietly by the circle she invited shrewd assessment from everyone waiting to watch. Especially with a Northern sword riding in harness across her back.

I looked for Nabir and found him waiting across the circle from Del. All his hopes were in his face as was his Southron arrogance. He had no doubt he would beat the Northern woman; I was only surprised she'd gotten him to agree.

Then again, when you're young and proud and new, any dance is welcome. No doubt Nabir thought it worth the trouble to dance against a woman since he was assured of a victory before so many watching sword-dancers, some of them his heroes.

I almost felt sorry for him.

I did a rapid, precise assessment. He was shorter than Del by four fingers, which probably didn't please him, and he lacked the hard fitness that would come with maturity and experience. He wasn't soft, but neither was he mature. He still had some growing to do. He was, I judged, seventeen, eighteen, maybe nineteen. Which meant many things, all of them important to a sword-dancer, particularly one with a vested interest in the opponent.

I am a seventh-level sword-dancer, which translates, in my case, to seven years worth of apprenticeship. But the seven years—with accompanying rank—is never a sure thing. Only those apprentices showing a certain amount of promise are even passed to the fourth level, let alone the seventh; Nabir, by age alone, couldn't be much more than a second-year apprentice, possibly a third. Because the rank, though denoted by the term *year*, has little to do with time as measured by the seasons. An apprentice's "year" is completed only when particular skills are learned, and that can take much longer than twelve months.

I had finished seventh-level in seven years. It was very symmetrical. A source of pride. Something for the stories, for the legend. But now, looking at Nabir, I wondered what *his* reasons were for becoming a sword-dancer. Unlike mine, I thought, fueled by hatred and a powerful need for freedom. That need had been more than physical. It had also been emotional. Mental. And it had been enough to make me the Sandtiger.

Whom Nabir had wanted to meet.

Not for the first time I wished for a true harness-and-sheath. I stood there holding a scabbarded sword in the midst of other sword-dancers properly accoutered, feeling oddly out of place. Lacking, somehow. But it wasn't just the style, which was a badge of our profession. It was also *convenience;* I'd rather carry a blade across my back than have to lug it around by hand.

The circle was finished. I considered stepping up beside Del to tell her she was being a silly, sandsick fool; decided against it when I realized it might throw off her concentration and contribute to her loss, if she lost. And she might. No matter how much she crowed—albeit quietly—about youth being an advantage in the healing process, she still wasn't completely recovered from the wound I'd dealt her. Hoolies, her conditioning was terrible! She'd be fortunate if she lasted long enough to put on a decent showing.

Then again, she wasn't precisely on her own. She did have Boreal.

Someone moved close beside me. Male. In harness: sword-dancer. Smelling of huva weed and aqivi; also a satisfactory visit to Kima's bed, or to another very like hers.

"So, Sandtiger," he said, "have you come to see the debacle?"

I knew him by his voice. Low, raspy, half-throttled, catching at odd times and on odd consonants. It wasn't affectation. Abbu Ben-sir had no choice in the matter of his voice, since a sword-shaped piece of wood had nearly crushed his throat twenty-some-odd years before. He had lived only because his shodo—sword-master—had cut open flesh and windpipe to let air into his lungs.

While that same shodo's newest apprentice looked on in horror at what he'd done to a sixth-level sword-dancer.

"Which debacle?" I asked. "The one about to begin in the circle, or the dance you'll ask of me?"

Abbu grinned. "Are you so certain I will ask you?"

"Eventually," I answered. "Your throat may have recovered—mostly—but your pride never will. It was your own fault I nearly killed you—the shodo warned you I was awkward—but you ignored him. All you wanted to do was knock the former chula on his buttocks so he'd remember what he'd been."

"What he *was*," Abbu said plainly. "You were a chula still, Sandtiger . . . why deny it? It took you all of your seven years to rid yourself of the shame—if you've managed it yet." He pursed weed-stained lips. "I hear you got caught by slavers last year and thrown into a tanzeer's mine . . . has that worn off yet?"

I kept my tone even. "Did you come to watch this dance, or simply to breathe huva stink in my face?"

"Oh, to watch the dance . . . to see the boy humiliate the woman who has no place in a Southron circle." He shrugged, folding arms across a black-swathed chest. "She is magnificent to look at—she would fill a man's bed—but to pick up a man's weapon and enter a man's circle is sheerest folly. The Northern bascha will lose—not too badly, I hope; I would not want to see her cut—and then I will commiserate with her." He grinned at me, dark brows arching suggestively. "I will show her a few tricks with the sword— in bed *and* out."

I had been in the North four, maybe five months. I'd also spent a year or so with Del. Enough time to discover I'd learned a thing or two about myself. Enough time to realize I didn't much like the ignorance of Southron men. More than enough time to feel my own share of disbelief at Abbu's bland certainty that a woman good enough for bedding wasn't good enough for the circle.

Then again, not every woman was Del. *No* other woman was Del. She'd chosen the circle and the sword for things other than equality.

Which didn't make her wrong.

I looked out at Del. She wasn't fit. Wasn't ready. But she was still distinctly *Del.*

I glanced sidelong at Abbu Bensir. "Care to make a little wager?"

"On *this?*" He stared at me in unfeigned disbelief then narrowed pale brown eyes. "What do you know about the boy? Is he that good?—or that bad?"

No question regarding the woman. Good enough for the wager.

I lifted a single shoulder. "He came to me this morning and begged a dance. I refused; he accepted the woman instead. That's all I know."

Abbu frowned. "A woman in place of the Sandtiger . . ." Then he shook his head. "It makes no difference. Yes, I will wager on this. What do you offer?"

"Everything in this." I tapped the coin-pouch dangling from my belt. "But you've caught me between jobs, Abbu. There isn't much left."

"Enough to equal a Hanjii nose-ring?" Abbu reached into his own pouch and drew forth a ring of pure Southron gold, hammered flat into a circular plate.

It brought back memories: Del and I, in a circle, but only to the win. We'd danced in front of the Hanjii, a tribe who believed in eating the flesh of enemies. Also a tribe which placed great emphasis on male pride and honor; Del's subsequent defeat of me—thanks to a well-placed knee in a very vulnerable area—had resulted in the two of us becoming guests of honor in a religious ritual called the Sun Sacrifice. Left in the Punja without food, water or mounts, we'd very nearly died.

But did I have anything in my pouch equal to a Hanjii nose-ring? "No," I answered truthfully; I never lie about money. People can get hostile.

Abbu pursed his lips, then shrugged. "Ah, well, another time— unless you still have that bay stud—?"

"The stud?" I echoed. "I still have him, yes—but he's not part of the stakes."

Light brown eyes assessed me. "Growing sentimental in your old age, Sandtiger?"

"He's not part of the stakes," I repeated quietly. "But I will offer you something of value . . . something you've been wanting for more than twenty years." I smiled as color crept into his swarthy face. "Yes, Abbu, I'll meet you in a circle—*if* the woman loses."

"If the woman *loses*—" He very nearly gaped. "Are you sand-sick? Do you want to *give* the wager away?" Eyes narrowed in suspicion. "Why do you bet on the woman?"

I nodded toward the circle, where Del and Nabir were bending in the center to place blades on the ground. "Why don't you watch and find out?"

Abbu followed my own gaze. As I had, he assessed Nabir as a

potential opponent. But he didn't assess Del as anything but a potential bedmate.

All to the good for me.

Abbu flashed me a glance. "We are not friends, you and I, but I have never thought you a fool. Yet you wager on a woman?"

I smiled blandly. "Someone has to, or there would be no bet."

Abbu shrugged. "You must want to meet me very badly."

I didn't answer. Nabir and Del had stripped out of footwear and harness, positioning themselves outside the circle directly opposite one another. It was to be a true dance, a dance of exhibition; a dance of bladeskills matched for the joy of competition. There was no need for anyone to die, which is the true nature of the dance. Shodos taught no one to go out in the world and kill. They taught only the grace and skill necessary to master a Southron sword; that most of us later hired ourselves out was a perversion of the true dance. It was also one of the few ways of earning a living in a land comprised of hundreds of tiny domains ruled by hundreds of desert princes. When power is absolute, you find your freedom—and a living—any way you can.

Abbu Bensir was right: we had never been friends. When I had been accepted as an apprentice, he was a sixth-level sword-dancer already hiring himself out. He had agreed to spar with wooden swords as a favor to the shodo, but he had been stupid enough to be careless, believing too implicitly in skills learned years before. He was older than I and complacent; he had nearly died of it.

Since then we had met from time to time, as sword-dancers do in the South. We had behaved very much like two dogs who recognize strength and determination in one another; we had circled each other warily, repeatedly, judging and testing by word and attitude. But we had never entered the circle. He was an acknowledged master, if unimaginative; I had, after seven years of apprenticeship and more than twelve of professional sword-dancing, established a reputation as a formidable, unbeatable opponent. Bigger, stronger, faster in a land of quick, medium-sized men. And I hadn't yet lost a dance that required someone to die.

Of course, neither had he.

Which meant he wanted me badly. Now I was worth the effort.

"She is magnificent," Abbu murmured.

Yes, so she is.

"But much too tall."

Not for me.

"And hard where she should be soft."

Strong instead of weak.

"She is made for bedding, not for the circle."

I slanted him a glance. "Preferably *your* bed?"

"Better mine than yours." Abbu Bensir grinned. "I'll tell you if she was worth it."

"Big of you," I murmured. "*In* a manner of speaking."

He might have replied, but the dance had begun. He, like me, watched attentively, assessing posture, patterns, styles. It's something you can't avoid when you watch others dance. You put yourself in the circle and judge how *you* would have done it, criticizing the others. Nodding or shaking your head, swearing under your breath, muttering derisively. Occasionally bestowing praise. Always predicting the victor and how badly the other will lose.

My belly clenched as I watched. There was no doubt in my mind whatsoever that Del was the superior sword-dancer—*far* superior— but she was, to me, all too obviously out of condition. She was slow, stiff, awkward, employing none of her remarkable finesse. Her blade patterns were open and sweeping, which is alien to the woman whose true gift is subtlety. Her stance lacked the lithe, eloquent power so often overlooked by men accustomed to brute strength in opponents. She gave Nabir none of the Del I knew, and yet she would beat him badly. It was obvious from the start.

Which gave me grounds for relief.

Abbu was glowering. "The boy is a fool."

"For dancing with a woman?"

"No. For giving in too easily. See how he defers to her? See how he allowed her to direct the dance?" Abbu shook his head. "He's afraid to hurt her, and so he has given her the circle. He has given her the dance. And all because she's a woman."

"You wouldn't?" I asked as blades clanged in the circle. "Are you telling me you could ignore her sex and simply fight her, dancer to dancer?"

Abbu glowered more darkly.

I nodded. "So I thought."

"And you?" he challenged. "What would the Sandtiger do? He was a woman himself for half his life—"

I closed my hand on his wrist. "If you are not very careful," I began, "our dance will be right now. And this time I will open your throat with steel instead of wood."

A roar went up from the crowd. It had nothing to do with Abbu and me, but with the outcome of the dance. Which meant Del had won. They'd have cheered for Nabir; for her, they'd award only silence once they were over their shock.

Abbu, swearing, jerked his wrist free. "You are soft," he accused. "Do you think I can't see it? Your color is bad, your bones too sharp, the look in your eye is dull. You are not the Sandtiger I saw dance eighteen months ago. Which means you are old, sick, or injured. Which is it, Sandtiger?" He paused. "Or is it all of them?"

I showed him all my teeth. "If I am sick, I'll get better; injured, I will heal. But if I am old, you are older; look in a mirror, Abbu. Your life is in your face."

I didn't exaggerate. His swarthy face was sharply graven at mouth and eyes, and there was gray in his dark brown hair. The nose had been broken at least once, retaining a notch across the bridge that had, in my apprenticeship, boasted a Punja-bred hook. He was, I knew, past forty; in our profession, old. And he looked every year of it.

But then, so do I. The desert is never kind.

Del, in the circle, said something to Nabir. Knowing her, it was something diplomatic. Something to do with victory in the future; she is not a woman to grind a man's pride in the dirt unless he demands it. And Nabir hadn't, not really. Oh, he'd been certain of his victory, but then I'd known a certain other young sword-dancer who'd felt much the same upon receiving his blued-steel, shodo-blessed sword. And who'd lost his first dance to an experienced sword-dancer who had no time to humor the whims and pride of an arrogant young man; I'd deserved to lose. And I had.

Now, so had Nabir.

He took it badly, of course. So had I. It remained to be seen if

Nabir would learn from the loss or let it fester in his spirit. Admittedly he had more to flagellate himself with—he'd lost his first dance to a *woman*—but if he was smart he'd think twice about underestimating his opponent. Too many variables entered into a dance, certainly more than sex. And if Nabir didn't learn how to deal with them, how to adapt, he'd be killed the first time he entered a circle to dance to the death.

When the boy refused to answer Del, she turned away and walked out of the circle. She still wore blue wool tunic and trews, now stained with sweat; she needed to switch to Southron clothing. A lifted arm scrubbed dampness from her face and stripped it free of loosened hair. Her movements were stiff, lacking grace. She bent, scooped up harness and boots, let the crowd fall back from her. She was flushed, a little shaky, obviously tired. But she hid the magnitude of it from everyone save me.

I was so glad to have the dance over I didn't think about anything else.

"The boy was a fool," Abbu declared.

"Yes."

"And I a fool for risking so much on him."

I smiled. "Yes."

Abbu pulled the Hanjii nose-ring from his pouch. "I pay my debts, Sandtiger. I won't have it said I don't."

"Now I don't need to, Abbu."

He glared at me sourly as he handed over the nose-ring, then stared past at Del's retreating back. "There is much she could learn, if a man took the time to teach her."

A man had. *Men* had, Northerners all, *an-kaidin* from Staal-Ysta. And a bandit named Ajani. But I said nothing of it to Abbu Bensir, who wouldn't understand.

"Oh, I don't know, Abbu—seems to me she's already learned a lot."

"She could be better. Faster, smoother . . ." He flicked an expressive hand. "She is a woman, of course, with a woman's failings, but there *is* talent in her. Promise. And she is tall enough and strong enough . . ." Then he shook his head. "But it would be folly to teach a woman. To *attempt* to teach a woman."

"Why?"

He was very sure of himself. "She would cry the first time her shodo spoke to her harshly. She would give up the first time she was cut. Or she would meet a man and lose all interest. She would cook his food, keep his hyort, bear his children. And she would set aside the sword."

I raised eyebrows in nonchalant challenge. "Isn't that what a woman's for? Cooking food, keeping a hyort, having a man's children?"

Still frowning, Abbu glanced at me impatiently. "Yes, of course, all of those things—but have you no eye, Sandtiger? Or do you see nothing but the woman, instead of the woman's skill?" His gaze was very level. "When I saw you dance the first time—your first *real* dance, not when you nearly killed me—I knew what you would be. Even though you lost. And I knew there would be two names spoken in the Punja, instead of just mine." He hitched one shoulder. "I was willing to share, and so I do. Because I am not a blind fool. Because I acknowledge talent when I see it, even in a woman. So should you."

This was not the Abbu Bensir I remembered. He had always been supremely certain of his talent, technique, presence. But then, he *was* an excellent sword-dancer. He *did* have superb technique. And certainly he had presence, ruined nose and all; shorter than I, and slighter, with more distinctly Southron features, Abbu Bensir nonetheless still claimed the unspoken ability to dominate those around him.

But he'd never been known for his humility or fair-mindedness. Certainly not when it came to his dealings with women. He was, after all, Southron, and the women he knew were cantina girls, or silly-headed serving-girls in the employ of various tanzeers or merchants.

He certainly didn't know any woman worth the time to instruct in the ways of handling a sword. I doubt the idea had ever occurred to him, any more than it had to me—prior to meeting Del. But I had met Del, and I'd changed. Would Abbu Bensir do the same?

Not if I had anything to say about it. Better to let him remain the arrogant Southron male.

"I recognize talent when I see it," I told him. "I acknowledge it. Are you forgetting I wagered on *her?*"

"You did it to provoke me," Abbu declared. "We are oil and water, Sandtiger . . . it will always be so between us." He stared past me, watching the crowd slowly disperse. Then his eyes flickered back to me. "You have the nose-ring, Sandtiger. Now I will have the woman."

He brushed by me easily as he turned, black gauze underrobe rippling. He wore a harness and blade, Southron blade, glinting in the sunlight. An old, honorable sword, attended by many legends.

I watched him go, striding away in the fluid gait of a man well-content with his life. A man who, I was certain, entertained no doubts of himself.

Or of the woman he followed.

Chapter 6

By the time I reached the cantina, Abbu Bensir had already cornered Del. Well, not cornered *exactly;* she was sitting in a corner, and he was sitting with her.

She sat with her back to the wall, just as I always did. This allowed her to see me as I approached, although she gave no indication of it. It also allowed me to approach without Abbu knowing, since his back was to me. So I took advantage of it, pausing just behind him. Listening to *his* approach.

"—you could become much better," he said confidently. "With my help, of course."

Del didn't answer.

"You must admit," he went on, "it's unusual to find a woman with your potential and dedication. Here in the South—"

"—women are treated as slaves." Del didn't smile. "Why should I be yours?"

"Not my slave, my student."

"I've already been an *ishtoya*. I've already been *an-ishtoya*."

Now he was confused. "I am Abbu Bensir. Any Southron sword-dancer can tell you who I am, and what I am capable of. *Any* Southron sword-dancer . . . all of them know me."

For the first time since my arrival, Del looked at me. "Do you know him?"

Abbu sat upright, then twisted his head around. Saw me,

scowled, sent me a silent message to leave, then turned back to Del. "Ask anyone but him."

I grinned. "But I *do* know you. And what you're capable of."

"Which is?" Del asked coolly.

Abbu shook his head. "He will not give you a fair answer. He and I are old rivals in the circle. He will not bespeak me well."

"And you're a liar," I said pleasantly. "I'd tell her the truth, Abbu: that you're a superb sword-dancer with much to teach anyone." I paused. "But I'm more superb than you."

Del very nearly smiled. Abbu merely glared. "This is a private table."

"The lady was here first. Why don't we ask *her?*"

Del made an impatient gesture; she has no tolerance for such things.

I hooked a stool over, sat down, smiled disarmingly at Abbu. "Have you told her your scheme yet?"

"Scheme?" he echoed blankly.

I glanced at Del. "He plans on flattering your skill, since women are gullible creatures . . . he'll tell you what he thinks you want to hear, even if he doesn't agree . . . and then he'll take you into the circle, just to keep you interested—" I grinned, "—and then take you straight to bed."

Abbu's pale eyes glittered.

"It won't work," I told him. "I already tried."

"*And* failed," Del declared.

Abbu, who is not stupid, frowned. He looked at Del. At me. Then demanded his nose-ring back.

"Why?" I asked.

"Because it was won under false pretenses. You and the woman know one another."

I shrugged. "I never said we didn't. It didn't come up, Abbu. I offered a wager. You accepted a wager. The nose-ring was fairly won." I smiled. "And I need it to pay *my* debts."

Del was staring at me. "You bet on the dance?"

"I bet on you."

"To win."

"Of *course* to win; do you think I'm a fool?"

Abbu swore under his breath. "*I* am the fool."

"For wanting to teach a woman?" Del's tone was cool again. "Or for betting on the wrong person?"

Kima arrived with a jug. "Aqivi," she announced, and smacked it down on the table.

Abbu Bensir stared across the lip of the jug at Del in obvious challenge. I have seen it before—Abbu, much as I hate to admit it, has success with women—but I didn't consider it much of a risk. He wasn't the type of man who would interest Del. He was too arrogant, too abrupt, too certain of superiority based solely on his gender.

He was, most of all, too *Southron.*

"What can you teach me?" Del asked.

I kicked her under the table.

Abbu considered it. "You are tall," he said, "and strong. You have as good a reach as any Southroner—except perhaps the Sandtiger. But you would do better to make your patterns smaller. More subtle." He reached across the table, tapped Del's left wrist. "You have the necessary strength here—I saw it—to support the smaller patterns, but you don't use it. You were much too open earlier. It slowed your response time and left opportunities to defeat you. That you won had less to do with your better skill than with the boy's inexperience." He smiled briefly. "I would not do the same."

It was an accurate summation of Del's dance. That he also suggested smaller blade patterns did not please me, because it showed me he'd judged her very well. Del usually *does* employ smaller, tighter patterns, but she was out of condition and hadn't employed her usual techniques.

And if anything would impress Del, it was a man judging her on her merits instead of by her gender.

"Here," I said abruptly, "no need to let good aqivi go to waste." I grabbed the jug, started splashing liquor into the cups Kima put down.

Abbu watched me sidelong. In profile, his nose was a travesty—but it lent him the cachet of hard-edged experience. Unlike Nabir, he was not a boy on the threshold of manhood; Abbu Bensir had stepped across many years before. He had the lean, lethal look of a borjuni, though he was sword-dancer instead of bandit.

What he thought of me, I couldn't say. I was considerably taller and heavier, also younger—but Abbu Bensir was right. I hadn't quite recovered strength, stamina, or health from the wound Del had given me, and it showed. Certainly it showed to an experienced sword-dancer who knew very well how to judge what counted.

He eased himself back on his stool and tipped aqivi down his throat. "So," he said idly to Del, "has this big desert cat told you of our adventures?"

"Adventures?" I echoed blankly; Abbu and I had not, to my knowledge, ever shared much more than a cantina.

Predictably, Del said no.

Of course it was what he wanted. With an adroit flick of fingers, Abbu slipped the neck of his underrobe and let it fall open. His throat was now bared, showing the pale scar left by the shodo's knife. "My badge of honor," he said. "Bestowed on me by none other than the Sandtiger."

Del's brows rose.

Abbu's tone was expansive. "It was quite early in his career, but it was a dramatic signal to the South that a new sword-dancer was about to be born."

"There was nothing 'about to be' about it," I said sourly. "It took me seven more years."

"Yes, but it served notice to those of us able to judge such things as talent and potential." He paused. "To those *few* of us."

"Did it?" Del asked coolly.

"Oh, yes," Abbu said. "He was a clumsy seventeen-year-old boy with hands and feet too big for his body—and his brain—but the potential was there. I knew what he would become . . . so long as his inborn submissiveness and all his years as a chula didn't destroy him before he truly began."

Del's lids didn't flicker. "Abbu Bensir," she said softly, "be careful where you walk."

He is not a stupid man; he changed tactics instantly. "But I am not here to talk about the Sandtiger, whom you undoubtedly know much better than I do." There was a glint in his eyes. "I came to offer my services as a shodo, even briefly. I think you could benefit."

"Perhaps I could," Del said. And then looked me dead in the eye. "If you kick me one more time—"

I overrode her by raising my voice and talking to Abbu. "Won't you be going to Iskandar like everyone else?"

"Eventually. Although I think it is nonsense, this talk of a jhihadi." Abbu shrugged, swallowed aqivi. "Iskandar himself, the stories say, promised he would return to bring prosperity to the South, to turn the sand to grass. I see no signs of that." He shook his head. "I think it is nothing more than a foolish man who fancies himself an oracle . . . a zealot who requires attention before he dies. He will rouse the tribes, undoubtedly—that, I hear, is begun—but no one with any sense will pay mind to it."

"Except the tanzeers." I shrugged as Abbu frowned over his tankard. "They won't believe the Oracle's foretellings, but if they have any intelligence at all they'll recognize that this Oracle—and the proclaimed jhihadi, if one ever appears—could siphon off some of their power."

"An uprising," Abbu said thoughtfully, "couched in the name of religion."

"People will do amazing things in the name of faith," I remarked. "Wrap it in the trappings of holy edict, and even assassination is revered."

"I don't understand," Del interjected. "What you say of religion, yes—that I have seen myself—but how would it affect the South?"

I shrugged. "The South is made up of hundreds of desert domains ruled by any man strong enough to hold it. He comes in, establishes his dominance, names himself tanzeer to gain a little glitter—and rules."

She blinked. "So easily?"

"So easily," Abbu confirmed in his broken voice. "Of course, any man who decided to do it would require a large force of loyal men . . . or a large force of *hired* men loyal to his coin." He grinned. "I myself have engaged in establishing several such new reigns."

Del's tone was bland. "But you yourself have never attempted to set up your *own* domain."

He shrugged. "Easier to take the money and leave, then move on to the next desert bandit who has notions of naming himself tanzeer."

Del glanced at me. "Have you done it as well?"

"Never from the beginning," I told her. "I have hired on to protect the tanzeer already in place, but I've never gone in and set up a brand-new domain."

She nodded thoughtfully. "So a tanzeer is not born . . . he becomes a prince only through force of arms."

I shook my head. "A tanzeer is born if his family has held the domain long enough. And some of these desert 'princedoms' have been in existence for centuries, handed down to each heir—"

"—who must himself be strong enough to hold it," Del finished.

"Of course," Abbu rasped. "There have been many newly proclaimed tanzeers, inheriting at an untimely age, who simply could not muster the forces needed to defend against usurpers." He smiled. "That is the easiest way of enlarging a domain."

"Stealing from someone else," she said.

"*All* of the domains were stolen," Abbu countered. "Once, surely, the South belonged to no one, it simply *was*—and then men strong enough to do so selected for themselves the domains they wanted . . . and so on and so on until the land was sectioned off from the sea to the Northern border, and to the east and west as well."

"Sectioned off," she echoed. "Is there no free land left at all?"

Abbu shrugged. "Domains exist where the land is worth having. There is water, or a city, or an oasis, or mountains—a place worth having becomes a domain. What no one wants is free."

"The Punja," I said. "No one rules the Punja. Except the tribes, maybe . . . but they have more respect for the land. They don't divide it up and sit on it. Nor do they give in to the rule of any man proclaiming himself a tanzeer. They just go with the wind, blowing here and there."

"Much like a sword-dancer." Del turned her cup on the table. "So, the Oracle—who gains disciples among the tribes—offers threat to the tanzeers."

"By rousing the tribes, yes," Abbu agreed.

"But the Oracle is only a mouthpiece," I said. "It's the jhihadi who offers the true threat. Because if the stories were to come true—that sand will be turned to grass—it means *all* of the South would be worth having. Each man would be a tanzeer unto himself, and the authority of those petty princes holding the present domains would collapse."

"So they will try to kill him." Del's tone was matter-of-fact. "No matter who he is, no matter why he's come; even if it's all a lie—the tanzeers will have him killed. Just in case."

"Probably," I agreed.

Abbu smiled a little. "First they would have to find him."

"Iskandar," Del said. "Isn't that where he's supposed to appear?"

Abbu shrugged. "That's what the Oracle says."

"*You're* going," she pointed out.

Abbu Bensir laughed. "Not for the Oracle. Not for the jhihadi. I'm going for the dancing. I'm going for the coin."

Del frowned. "Coin?"

Abbu nodded. "Where there are people gathering, there will be wagering. Where there are *tanzeers*, there will be employment. Easier to find both in one place rather than scattered across the South."

"In uplander, a *kymri*," I explained. "We don't have many here in the South . . . but Abbu is right. If this Oracle rouses enough people, they will all go to Iskandar. So will the tanzeers. And so will sword-dancers."

"And bandits?" she asked.

"Borjuni, yes," Abbu agreed. "Even whores like Kima."

"I want to go," Del said.

I sighed. "Seems as good a place as any to learn something of Ajani's whereabouts."

But Del wasn't looking at me. She was looking at Abbu. "And I want you to teach me."

I nearly choked on aqivi. "*Del*—"

"Tomorrow," she declared.

Abbu Bensir merely smiled.

Chapter 7

"Why?" I asked, standing in the doorway. "What are you trying to prove?"

Del, inside her tiny room at the inn, barely glanced at me as she sat down on the edge of her slatted cot to pull off boot and fur gaiter. "Nothing," she answered, unwrapping leather garters.

"Nothing? *Nothing?*" I glared. "You know as well as I do you don't need Abbu Bensir to teach you anything."

"No," she agreed, peeling gaiter from boot.

"Then why—"

"I need the practice."

I stood braced in the doorway, watching her tug off the boot. She dropped it to the floor, then turned to the other boot. Once again, she started with the gaiter. Her bare right foot was chafed at the edges; the rest of it was white.

"So," I said, "you're using him for a sparring partner."

Del unlaced the garter. "Is he as good as he says he is?"

"Yes."

"Better than you?"

"Different."

"And *was* it you who put that scar on him?"

"No."

She tilted her head slightly. "So, he is a liar."

"Yes and no. I didn't give him the scar itself, but I did provide the reason for making it necessary."

Del looked up at me. "He doesn't hate you for it. He could—another man might—but he doesn't."

I shrugged. "We've never been enemies. Just rivals."

"I think he respects you. I think he knows you have your place in the South—in the pecking order of sword-dancers—and he has his."

"He is an acknowledged master of the blade," I said. "Abbu Bensir is a byword among sword-dancers. No one would be foolish enough to deny him that to his face."

"Not even you?"

"I've never considered myself a fool." I paused. "You're really going to spar with him?"

"Yes."

"You could have asked—"

"—you?" Del shook her head. "I did ask you. Several times."

"I'll spar," I said defensively. "Just not with my *jivatma.* We'll go find some wooden practice swords—"

"Steel," Del said succinctly.

"Bascha, you know why I don't want—"

"So you don't have to." She stripped gaiter free of boot. "So I'll use Abbu Bensir instead."

"But he thinks he's *teaching* you."

"He may think whatever he likes." Del tugged at her boot. "When a man won't do what you want him to in the *way* you want him to, you find new names for the same thing. If it satisfies Abbu Bensir's pride to believe he is teaching the gullible Northern bascha, let him. I will still get my practice. I will still improve my fitness." She looked at me squarely. "Which is something *you* need, too."

I ignored that; we both knew it was true. "How long is this to go on?"

"Until I am fit."

Frustration boiled up. "He only wants to get you into his bed."

Del rose, began to unhook her harness. "I am having a bath

brought for me. If you truly believe I would be the kind to tease you, you would do well to leave."

On cue, one of the innkeeper's sons rolled the cask from out of my room. It was empty, of course, which meant Del had paid extra for clean water. But she had no money.

Frustration rose another notch. "Am I paying for this, too?"

Del nodded.

I glared. "Seems like I'm paying for an awful lot, yet getting nothing for it."

"Oh?" Pale brows rose. "Is courtesy and generosity dependent upon how soon and how many times I will go to bed with you?"

I moved aside as the boy rolled the cask through the doorway. I waited impatiently for him to drop the cask flat and depart; once he had, I turned back to Del.

I stood directly in front of her now, halting as she turned from the cot to match me stare for stare. Barefoot, she gave up an extra finger's-worth of height to the five additional I always claimed. But it didn't diminish her.

I drew in a steadying breath. "You're not making this any easier."

Del shut her teeth. "I'm not trying to *make* it anything. I'm trying to end my song."

I tried to keep my tone even. "How many men have you killed?"

Del's eyes narrowed. "I don't know."

"Ten? Twenty?"

"I don't know."

"Guess," I suggested.

She opened her mouth. Shut it. Then gritted between her teeth: "Perhaps twenty or so."

"How many in a circle?"

"In a circle? None. All have been in defense of myself." She paused. "Or in defense of others. Even you."

"And some for plain revenge. Ajani's men; you've killed some of them, haven't you? A few months ago?"

"Yes."

"And did each of those deaths require such intense focus?"

Del's mouth flattened. "I know what you are saying. You are

saying I am wrong to require such behavior, such *focus;* that if I have already killed, one more death will be no less difficult."

I shook my head. "I'm saying I think you might be punishing yourself. That by demanding such rigorous behavior of yourself, you think you can make up for the deaths of your kinfolk."

The innkeeper's son banged the bucket of water as he brought it through the door, slopping water over the rim. Whatever Del might have said died before it was born, and I knew nothing would come of it now. The moment was gone.

"Soak well," I suggested flatly. "I have to go pay all your debts."

Mutely, Del watched the boy pour water into the cask. If she looked after me, it was too late. I was out of the room. Out of the inn. And very much out of temper.

It took me three cantinas to find him. Maybe he was embarrassed. Maybe he was shy. Or maybe he just wanted to do his drinking in a quieter, smaller place, lacking the huva stink and clamor of the cantina Kima worked.

But I did find him. And, having found him, I stood in the dimness of dusk inside the door and watched him from afar.

Nabir was, I decided, a handsome, well-set-up boy. In time he would grow into his potential and offer decent skills to anyone in the circle. Probably decent company, too, although at the moment he was plainly black of mood. More out of sorts than I'd been, if caused by the same woman.

He slouched on his stool at a table in the back of the common room, hitched up against the wall. His head was thrown back indolently, but there was nothing indolent about him. He was scowling. Black hair framed a good if unremarkable face; thick black brows met in a self-derisive scowl over the bridge of his nose. It was a straight, narrow nose, with only the suggestion of a hook. More like mine, in fact, than Abbu's, which displayed—or had once—the characteristic hook of a bird of prey. In some desert tribes, the hook of a man's nose denotes greater prowess as a warrior; don't ask me why. One of those fashions, I guess, like the Hanjii with their disfiguring nose-rings, or the Vashni with their necklets of human finger bones.

Before him on the table lay the harness and sword. It was at that he scowled so fiercely. Next to it sat a jug of liquor and a cup, but he drank nothing. Just sat and scowled and sulked and considered giving up his new profession.

I made my way through the tables and paused as he glanced up. I saw the recognition, the acknowledgement, the dilation of dark brown eyes. He sat up so hastily he nearly overset his stool, which would have damaged his pride even more.

I waved him down when he would have risen, and sat down on another stool. "So," I said, "quitting already?"

Anger flared, died; was replaced by humiliation. He couldn't meet my eyes.

I kept my tone conversational. "It's difficult, getting started. You don't know if anyone will dance with you, so you don't ask. And then when you summon up enough courage to ask an acknowledged master, a seventh-level sword-dancer—because, you think, losing to him will be expected, and therefore easier—he refuses. You leave wondering if anyone will *ever* dance with you—anyone other than another former apprentice only just getting started—and then a woman comes to you and says *she* will dance with you." I shifted on the stool. "At first you are insulted—a *woman!*—and then you recall that she was the woman with the Sandtiger; a woman who carries a sword and goes in harness, just as you do. You see she is tall and strong and foreign, and you think she should be in a hyort somewhere cooking food and nursing a baby; and you think you will put her in her place. In the name of your hard-won sword and your prickly Southron pride, you accept the woman's invitation." I paused. "And you lose."

"I am ashamed," he whispered.

"You lost for one reason, Nabir. One." I leaned forward and poured liquor into his cup: aqivi. "You lost because she won."

Lids flickered. He stared briefly at me, then looked back at his rejected sword and harness.

I drank. "You lost because you could not divide yourself from the arrogance of your sex, and from the knowledge of *hers.*"

He frowned.

I put it more plainly yet. "She won because she was better."

Color swept in to stain his swarthy desert face. "How can a woman be better—"

"—than a man?" I shrugged. "It might have something to do with her training, which began before yours. *Formal* training, that is; but she, like you, played with wooden swords when she was a child."

His jaw clenched. "I am a second-level sword-dancer."

I sipped. Nodded. "Something to be proud of. But I ask you this: why did you leave before you accomplished the other levels? There are seven, you know."

Dark eyes glittered. "I was ready to leave."

"Ah. You wearied of the discipline." I nodded. "*And* you kept hearing the song of coins going to other sword-dancers instead of yourself."

Black brows dove between his eyes. "There is no dishonor in leaving when I did. There are those who leave after a *single* year."

I nodded. "And most of them are dead."

His chin came up. "Because they accepted an invitation to dance to the death."

"So will you."

He shook his head. Black hair caught on the dropped hood of his indigo burnous. "I am not so foolish as to think I am good enough for that."

"But that's where the real money is." I shrugged as he stared intently. "Tanzeers always pay handsomely when they want someone killed."

"I'd rather—"

"—avoid it; I know. But what happens when a sword-dancer is hired to kill *you?*"

Eyes widened. *"Me?"*

"Of course. If you serve this tanzeer—" I flicked my left hand, "—then *that* tanzeer—" my right hand, "—will eventually desire you to be put out of his way. And so someone like me, or someone like Abbu Bensir—or someone like Del—will be hired to invite you into a circle where the dance will end in death."

"I can refuse." But his certainty was fading.

"You can refuse. Several times, in fact. But then you will get the reputation of a coward, and no tanzeer will hire you for anything." I shrugged. "Kill or be killed."

Nabir frowned. "Why are you telling me this?"

"Oh, maybe because I'd hate to see you quit a profession you might be suited for." I sipped again. "All you need is a little practice."

He blinked. "With—you?"

"With me."

"But—I'm not good enough for you."

At the moment, he probably was. But I didn't tell him that. "You were good enough to ask me to dance, weren't you?"

"But I knew I would lose. I just thought—" He sighed. "I just thought that if I was seen in a circle with the Sandtiger, it might help my name a little. I knew I would lose, of course, but I'd lose to the *Sandtiger*. Everyone loses to you."

"And you'll lose in practice, too," I pointed out. "But at least you'll learn a little something." And I'd get my conditioning back. "So, shall we begin tomorrow?"

Slowly, Nabir nodded. "What about—" He broke it off, thought about it, began again. "What about the woman? Is she truly a sword-dancer?"

I grinned. "If you're concerned your reputation—and pride—has been dealt too harsh a blow to survive, I wouldn't worry about it. Del's beaten me."

"*You?*"

"Only in practice, of course." I rose, put down his cup. "Thanks for the aqivi. I'll see you first thing in the morning."

He pushed himself to his feet. "Sandtiger—"

"Oh, yes—you won't be needing that." I pointed to his blade. "We'll be using wooden swords."

He blinked. "Wooden? But I haven't sparred with wooden blades since my first year."

"I know; me neither—and it's a considerably longer time for me than for you." I shrugged. "I'd hate to get carried away and cut your belly open. At least with a wooden sword, all I can do is break a few ribs." I grinned at his stricken expression. "Now go find yourself a woman—maybe that pretty little cantina girl across the way who's been eyeing you so much—and forget about Northern baschas."

"She's beautiful," he blurted.

I didn't need to ask which woman he meant; I've seen that expression before. "First lesson," I said. "Forget about such things. When you're in the circle, even against a woman—" I paused, "—even a woman like Del—you have to think about the dance. And *only* about the dance."

"It isn't a woman's place to be in a circle."

"Maybe not." I didn't feel like giving him any of Del's arguments against that line of reasoning; it would take too long. "But if you meet one there, are you willing to die just because she has breasts instead of *gehetties?*"

"*Gehett—*" He figured it out. It was enough to startle him into thinking about it. After a moment he nodded. "I will try not to think of the woman. I will try not to *see* the woman. I will try to do as you."

Hoolies, I wish when I was in the circle with Del I *could* only see the woman. Like Abbu Bensir. Like Nabir. Like all the other men who'd seen—or met—her in a circle.

Because then I'd forget the blood.

Chapter 8

We met out in the open, away from the center of town. I wanted privacy for the boy's sake, and for my own; one needn't tell the competition one isn't what one should be.

"Draw the circle," I told him.

Nabir's dark eyes widened. "Me?"

I nodded solemnly. "The privilege of rank," I said, "is that you can have others do tedious things like digging in the dirt."

He waved a hand. "No, no—I only meant . . . I thought you would do it to make certain it was right."

"It's not too terribly difficult to draw a circle," I said dryly. "I think a second-level sword-dancer can manage it."

Which reminded him, as I meant it to, that he had some status of his own; as a matter of fact, if there was a first-level apprentice here, Nabir could assign the task to *him*.

But there wasn't. So Nabir took wooden sword in hand and asked me what size circle I wanted.

"Practice," I answered. "No sense in dancing our legs off yet." Especially since even a practice circle seven paces in diameter would test me. "We'll move to a sparring circle next, and then a full-fledged dancing circle once I think you're ready."

He opened his mouth. "But—" And broke it off. So, his discipline wasn't completely eroded.

"I know," I said. "You were going to tell me you danced in a dancing circle yesterday. So? You lost. We'll do it my way."

Nabir flushed, nodded and proceeded to draw a meticulous circle in the dirt. He knew the dimensions as well as I—seven long paces in diameter for a practice circle, ten for sparring, fifteen for a full-fledged dancing circle—and had a steady hand, which meant his line didn't waver very much. It's one of the things a first-year apprentice learns: how to draw a clean circle. It helps to fix the confines in the mind, which is where the true circle must exist if an apprentice is to succeed. It sounds easy. It isn't.

Nabir finished and looked at me expectantly, dusty blade in hand.

"Sandals," I suggested. "Or were you going to give me yet another advantage?"

Again he colored. I knew what he felt—couldn't he remember *anything* in front of the Sandtiger?—but holding him by the hand wouldn't help him one bit. He had to get over being too impressed by me, or it would hurt his concentration.

Although, I'll admit, the boy's regard made me feel good. It's always nice to know *someone* is impressed by what you've accomplished.

Even if Del wasn't.

Nabir stripped out of his sandals and dropped them outside the circle, along with his indigo burnous, cream colored underrobe, belt. In leather dhoti he was suddenly mostly naked, showing a lean Southron frame beneath dark Southron flesh. Tendons flexed visibly as he moved, since every bit of skin was stretched taut. Lean as he was, there was still an undulating section of muscle between shortribs and the top of his dhoti.

I frowned thoughtfully. "What tribe are you?"

He stiffened visibly. Color moved through his face, staining cheekbones, setting dark eyes aflame. "Does it matter?"

There was belligerence in his tone. I shrugged. "Not really. I was only curious . . . you just don't fit any of the tribes I know. And yet there is tribal blood in you—"

"Yes." He cut me off. "I have no tribe, Sandtiger . . . none that will have me." Jaws clenched tautly. "I am a bastard."

"Ah, well, some of the best people I know are bastards." I grinned. "Myself included—maybe. Hoolies, at least you know."

Nabir stared at me across the circle he'd drawn so carefully. "You don't *know* if you're true-born or bastard?"

"It happens," I said dryly. "Now, shall we get about our business?"

Nabir nodded. "What's first?"

"Footwork."

"Footwork! But I learned footwork nearly two *years* ago!"

"Didn't learn much, did you?" Then, more kindly, "Or maybe you've just forgotten."

It did exactly as I expected. It shut the boy up.

Practicing something as rudimentary as footwork was good for us both. It's one of the basics in sword-dancing, part of the foundation that must be laid down if you're to learn anything, or progress. Clumsiness makes for a sloppy sword-dancer and little future; it also makes for a dead one, and no future at all. There just isn't any sense in skimping on the essentials when a few extra hours a day spent practicing footwork can mean the difference between survival and death.

But it had nonetheless been a long time since I had broken the practice routine down far enough to include footwork techniques. Del and I, prior to the dance on Staal-Ysta, had sparred together every day, or very nearly; footwork was not one of the things we practiced because, for us, it came naturally after so many years. It was all part of the sparring. But Nabir required a new attitude, and one way of developing one is to start all over again.

Well, in a manner of speaking. I couldn't spend *that* much time with him. I'm a sword-dancer, not a shodo; I didn't have the years to invest. Hoolies, I didn't even have the *days*. Del would be pushing to move on to Iskandar as soon as she felt sparring with Abbu no longer necessary.

Which meant I needed to get as much out of the practice sessions with Nabir as I could. And *that* meant working a lot harder than I was used to, even in good health.

By the time I called a halt, both of us were dripping. Harquhal is a border town, not a desert town; it was only just spring, even in the South, and the temperature was still mild. But we sweated, and we stank; I'd need another bath.

He stood in the center of the circle, nodding weary satisfaction. Hair was pasted to his scalp, except where it curled damply against his neck. "Good," he gasped. "Good."

Well, maybe for him. I hurt.

"I am remembering some little things the shodo taught very early. The sort of things he said could mean the difference between a thrust through the ribs or a cut on the side."

Good for him, I thought ironically. I'd had both nearly three months before. And from the same sword.

Speechless, I nodded. I stood hands on hips, wooden sword doubled up in one fist, trying not to pant.

"So Sandtiger, is this the new—*ishtoya?*"

Broken male voice, not Del's. I turned abruptly and wished I hadn't. Saw Abbu Bensir standing outside the circle. Next to my clothes, and the Northern *jivatma* sheathed in cadda wood, leather, and runes.

So, he'd learned a Northern word between yesterday and today. No doubt he expected me to react. So I took great care not to.

"New sword, new harness," I said lightly.

"Poor old Singlestroke . . ." Abbu shook his head. "It must have been a great blow. After all, it isn't often a chula wins his freedom, let alone a shodo-blessed sword. And then to have it *broken* . . ." Again he shook his head.

From the corner of my eye, I saw Nabir stiffen as he heard the word chula. I lifted a single eloquent shoulder. "The new sword's better."

"Is it?" Abbu glanced down at the hilt, exposed above the lip of the danjac hide sheath. "Northern, from the look of it. And here I thought a desert-bred Punja-mite like yourself would never carry a foreign sword."

"We all change," I said offhandedly. "We get older, a little wiser . . . we learn not to judge people and things by homelands, language, gender."

"Do we?" Abbu grinned. "So we do. Yes, Sandtiger, the woman is much better than I expected. But there is still much I can teach her."

"Wait till she warms up." I showed him my teeth. "Better yet, wait until she sings."

Abbu wasn't listening. He was staring thoughtfully at my midriff, bared by the shedding of underrobe and burnous. Like Nabir, I wore only a dhoti. It hid nothing at all of the knurls, nicks, and scars gained from nineteen years of dancing. Nothing of the lash marks from sixteen years of slavery. And nothing at all of the stripes earned from a dying sandtiger who had, in that dying, given me my freedom.

But Abbu Bensir had seen all of it before, since a sword-dancer wears only a dhoti in the circle. My story was no secret, nor was the evidence hidden, since I wore it in my skin.

No, he'd seen all that before. What he looked at now was something he *hadn't* seen: the ugly, livid scar tissue left behind by Boreal.

He flicked a quick glance at my face. "I see," he remarked thoughtfully.

"Let me guess," I said dryly. "Now you plan to invite me into a circle."

Abbu shook his gray-dusted head. "No. When you and I meet, you will be the man I saw eighteen months ago. I want no unfair advantage because you are recovering from—*that*." He frowned, locking black brows together. "I've seen men dead of less."

I arched brows. "Big of you."

It was Abbu's turn to display teeth. "Yes." Then the frown came back. He looked again at the healing wound. "You went north," he said. "I heard you went north."

"To *the* North; yes." I shrugged. "Why? I don't know a sword-dancer yet who stays put in one place."

Abbu flipped a dismissive hand. "No, no, of course not. But I have heard stories about Northern magic . . . about Northern swords . . ." He scowled at me in consideration. "Steel *cuts*," he said quietly. "It doesn't burn. It doesn't blister. It doesn't eat skin away."

It hadn't burned. It had frozen. In a way I'd been very lucky.

Boreal's banshee-bite had eaten away enough outer flesh to leave a depressed knot the size of a man's fist, but the icy steel had also frozen blood and inner tissue, preventing significant blood loss. The *jivatma* had missed anything vital, thank valhail. But had Del cut into me with a Southron blade, even missing the vitals, I'd have bled to death in the circle.

"Does it matter?" I asked. "It's healing."

"Don't you understand?" Abbu persisted. "If a sword could do that in the *circle*—"

"No." I said it flatly, leaving no room for doubt. "It's best if the circle is left as we learned it."

"A sword-dancer with a blade capable of doing that would be worth his weight in gold, gems, silks . . ." Abbu shrugged. "He could name his price."

"Maybe found a domain of his own?" I grinned. "Believe me, Abbu, you don't want to pay the price of lugging around a Northern *jivatma*."

He looked down at my belongings once more: at the visible hilt of a foreign sword. At the alien runes looping the sheath from split lip to brass-footed tip.

"*Jivatma*," he breathed, pronouncing the syllables oddly. "I heard her say that word. Only once. But once said, it was loud." Abbu looked away from the sword and back at me with effort. "As one sword-dancer to another—as a student who shared the teachings of your shodo—I ask permission to make the acquaintance of your sword."

It was stilted, formal phraseology. It was also a ritual performed by every sword-dancer who wanted to touch another sword-dancer's weapon. Killers we may be, more often than not, but the true dance is founded in elaborate courtesy. A few of us remember.

Nabir, who had, out of his own sense of courtesy, remained in the circle and left the two experienced sword-dancers to their conversation, now came closer. He had, after all, met the bared steel of Del's blade. I figured he had as much right to ask me about it as Abbu.

"Did you and Del spar with steel? With your own blades?"

Abbu frowned. "Of course."

"Then you saw her *jivatma*."

"Saw. Didn't touch." His smile was twisted. "Something about her—forbade it."

I glanced sidelong at Nabir. His eyes were fixed on the hilt glinting brightly in the sunlight. The blade itself was hidden in rune-warded sheath.

Sighing, I walked the rest of the distance and dropped the wooden practice blade beside the puddle of silk and gauze. Scooped up the harness, beckoned Nabir closer, slid Northern steel out into Southron moonlight. Shed harness and sheath, then displayed the sword in its entirety, resting blade in left hand while the other balanced the hilt at the quillons.

Sunlight poured across runes like water. The pristine brilliance was blinding.

Except for one thing.

"What's the matter with it?" Nabir asked. "Why is the tip all charred?"

Charred. I hadn't put it like that. But it was true: the blade looked like about five inches of it had been thrust into a conflagration.

Well, in a way it had. Only the fire had been Chosa Dei.

"It's like hers," Abbu said intently. Then nodded slowly. "So, it's true. There *is* magic in Northern swords."

"Only some of them. Del's, yes; trust me. But this one—well, this one isn't quite sure what it wants to be yet. Trust me on that, too."

"May I?" Abbu put out a hand.

I grinned. "He wouldn't like it."

Abbu frowned. "He who? *Who* wouldn't like it?"

"Him. The sword."

Abbu glared. "Are you telling me your sword has *feelings?*"

"Sort of." I pulled the hilt away as Abbu's hand threatened imminent capture. "Unh-*unh*—I didn't give you permission." Quickly I bent, scooped up the harness, resheathed the sword. Tucked it into the crook of my left arm. "Take my word for it, Abbu—you don't want to know."

He was red-faced. Pale brown eyes turned black as pupils dilated. "You offend me with this idiocy—"

"No offense intended," I countered swiftly. "Believe me, Abbu, you *don't* want to know."

"I know too much," he snapped. "I know you went to the North and got the sense frozen out of your head, along with the guts removed from your belly." He flicked a disdainful glance at my still-naked midriff with its sword-born scar. "And I have better things to do than stand here listening to your babble."

"So don't," I suggested mildly, which didn't please him any more.

Abbu said something beneath his breath in Desert, which I understood—and spoke—as well as he, then turned on his heel and marched away, black underrobe flapping.

I sighed. "Ah, well, no harm done. We're no *less* fond of each other than we were before."

Nabir's expression was unreadable as I reached down to gather up wooden blade, boots, underrobe, and belt. He waited until I was finished tucking things here and there.

"Is it true?" he asked.

"Is what true?"

"That." He nodded toward my sword. "Is it alive?"

I didn't laugh, because it would offend his dignity. And I tried very hard not to smile. "There's a wizard in here," I said solemnly.

After a long moment, he nodded. "I thought there might be."

I opened my mouth. Shut it. Swallowed the hoot of laughter trying very hard to escape. Not because there *wasn't* a wizard in my sword, but because of Nabir's reaction.

Finally I managed an inoffensive smile as I turned away from the circle. Away from Nabir. "Don't believe everything you hear."

"I don't have to," he said. "I *saw* it."

It stopped me dead in my tracks. Slowly I turned back. "Saw it?"

Nabir nodded. "You were making Abbu Bensir think you lied. You knew he would disbelieve you. And he did. He went away thinking you a fool, or sandsick . . . a man who says his sword is *alive*." He shrugged. "I heard the words, too—but I saw what you did." His youthful mouth twisted. "Or what you *didn't* do."

Now he had *me* intrigued. "What didn't I do?"

Nabir's tone was calm. "Let him touch the sword."

I passed it off with a shrug. "I just don't like others touching my sword."

"May I?"

"No—and for the same reason."

Nabir's dark eyes were steady. "Student to shodo, I respectfully request—"

"No," I said again, knowing I was trapped. "We're not *really* student and shodo, so the forms don't apply."

His young features were almost harsh. There are tribes in the South very feral in nature, and it shows in the flesh. Bastard-born, maybe, but Nabir had more than a splash of Punja-bred fierceness. It altered him significantly.

"If the forms do not apply," he said quietly, "I have no desire to dance with you."

"No?"

"No. And you *need* me to dance with you." Nabir smiled in beguiling innocence. "You aren't helping me, Sandtiger. You're helping yourself. You are slow and stiff and awkward from that wound, and you're afraid you won't get your fitness back so you can dance against men like Abbu Bensir. And if you *can't*—"

"All right," I said, "all right. Yes, I'm out of condition. I'm slow and stiff and awkward, *and* I hurt like hoolies. But I *earned* the pain, Nabir . . . I earned the slowness, the stiffness, the clumsiness. Yours may be inbred."

It wasn't nice. But he'd cut too close to the bone in shedding his awe of me.

"So," he said softly, "you put the dull blade against the newborn whetstone and fashion an edge again."

"Does it matter?" I asked. "You'll be better for it yourself."

Nabir nodded. "Yes. But you might have asked me."

I sighed wearily. "I might have. But you'll learn when you get to my age that pride can make you do and say strange things."

"You are the Sandtiger." He said it with an eloquent simplicity that made me ashamed.

"I was a slave," I said flatly. "You heard the word when Abbu said it: chula. And I was very nearly your age before I gained my freedom. Believe me, Nabir, all those years of the past don't make for an easy future, even when you're free."

"No," he agreed, very softly.

I sighed heavily and scrubbed at my forehead beneath still-damp, itchy hair. "Look," I said, "I can't tell you his name. So you can't touch him. I'm sorry, Nabir—but like I told Abbu, you're better off not knowing."

"That is the answer, then? His name?"

"Part of it," I agreed. "The rest is better left unexplained." I started to turn away. "Are you coming? I'm for a jug of aqivi."

Solemnly, he came. And then, "Am I really slow and stiff and clumsy?"

I considered lying. Discarded the idea; he was worth the truth. "Yes. But that will change." I grinned. "A few more circles with me, and you'll be the Sandtiger's heir-apparent."

Nabir smile was slow, but warm. "Not so bad a thing."

"Only sometimes." I slapped him on his back. "How was the little cantina girl?"

Nabir forebore to answer. Which meant either he liked the girl too much to say, or he hadn't had the courage.

Ah, well, give it time . . . young manhood can be awkward.

Chapter 9

Across our wooden blades, Nabir's face was stiff. "She won't marry me."

As interruptions go, it was terrific. I straightened out of my crouched stance and lowered my sword, frowning. "Who won't—" I blinked. "The little *cantina girl?*"

Nabir, nodding, lowered his own blade-shaped piece of wood. His eyes were very fierce.

It was, I thought, an interesting time to bring it up. We were in the middle of a sparring session, having progressed from the practice circle after two days. "Why do you *want* her to?" I asked.

Nabir drew himself up. Sweat ran down his temples. "Because I love her."

I opened my mouth. Closed it. Thought over how best to discuss the situation with the boy, whose prickly tribal pride—bastard-born or not—sometimes required diplomacy. Not that he could have harmed me, if it went so far; but I had no desire to hurt his feelings.

I scrubbed a forearm across my brow, smearing hair out of my eyes. "Don't take offense, Nabir—but is she your first girl?"

His entire body went stiff. "No," he declared. "Of course not; I have been a man for many years."

I waited patiently. Eventually his gaze shifted.

"Yes." The word was muffled.

So. Now I understood.

"Water break," I suggested.

He followed me out of the circle, took the bota as I slapped it into his hands, sucked down several swallows as I folded myself onto my gauze and silks, nestling buttocks into sand. I set aside the wooden blade and hooked elbows around crooked-up knees.

"So," I said lightly, "you slept with the girl. And you liked it. You like it very much."

Nabir, still standing, nodded. He clutched the bota tightly.

"Nothing wrong with that." I squinted up at him. "But you don't have to *marry* her."

"I want to."

"You can't marry every girl you sleep with."

Obviously, it had not occurred to him that other women might enter into it. He had discovered the magic in a woman's body—and in his own—and thought it was supposed to be that way—with *this* woman—for the rest of his life.

Poor boy.

"She won't have me," he said tightly.

A blessing, undoubtedly. But I asked, since he expected it. "Why not?"

Muscles twitched in his jaw. "Because I am a bastard. Because I have no tribe."

Better yet, because he had little coin and fewer prospects. But I didn't say it. "Look at it this way, then," I said. "It's her loss, not yours."

"If I could rejoin the tribe—" Abruptly, he altered his sentence. "If I could prove myself worthy, they would overlook my birth."

"Who would?"

Nabir scowled, handed down the bota. "The elders."

"Which tribe?"

Nabir shook his head. "I shouldn't speak of it. I have said too much."

I didn't really want to spend too much time trying to decipher Nabir's past, or foretell his possible future. I scratched at sandtiger scars. "Well," I said finally, "it's their loss, too. Meanwhile, we have a lesson to finish."

"If I could be worthy of the tribe, I'd be worthy of her," he persisted. "She said so."

More likely she'd said anything she could think of, just to put him off. It also might be true; a cantina girl hoping for a better life would fix her dreams on someone of greater stature, not a bastard-born halfbreed with nothing to offer but himself. For a girl who sold herself nightly to men of all ilk, Nabir's regard—and his presence in her bed—would not be enough. She'd have to know there was more.

Right now, there wasn't.

I sucked water, replugged the bota. "A sword-dancer really shouldn't think about marriage, Nabir. It dulls the edge."

"We have no edge at all." He grinned, lifting his blade. "See? Only wooden."

I smiled. "Still after me to use real swords, are you?"

"My shodo told me wood was useful for only so long. That to develop a true understanding of the dance, a true sword is required. Because without the risk, nothing is learned."

Yes, well . . . Nabir's shodo had never known my *jivatma*. "Maybe so," I agreed, "but right now I prefer wood."

Nabir looked beyond me. "It's her," he said obscurely.

The cantina girl? I turned. No. Del.

She had, at last, traded Northern wool for Southron silks. Rich blue burnous rippled as she walked, hood puddled on her shoulders. Already the sun had bleached her hair a trifle blonder, and her skin was pinker than normal. In time, it would turn creamy gold. The hair would pale almost to white.

Del crossed the sand smoothly, hilt shining behind her left shoulder. Her sessions with Abbu Bensir had removed some of the tension from her body, as if she understood she was doing something definite toward reaching her goal, since she needed to be fit to meet Ajani. I was glad to see her moving better, feeling better, but I wasn't pleased by the source. If she'd been willing to meet me with wooden blades, like Nabir, I could have done the same. Hoolies, I could have done more.

Del stopped beside the circle. "Tiger is the only sword-dancer I know who practices his dancing by sitting on the ground."

Nabir's eyes widened; how could I stand for this?

"Not true," I replied equably. "Nabir can tell you I've thwacked him upside the head more times than you can count—I'm giving him a breather."

Nabir frowned; it wasn't true. Del, who saw it, smiled crookedly, interpreting it easily. But she said nothing, looking critically at the wooden blade the boy held. "Do you *ever* plan to use steel?"

Nabir opened his mouth.

"No need," I answered for him. "You know as well as I the fundamentals are better taught with wood than with steel."

"He doesn't *need* the fundamentals . . . at least, not independent of steel. There is no risk with a wooden blade, and nothing is learned without risk."

I glared at her sourly as Nabir snapped his head around to stare at me. "I told you why," I said. "As long as we're speaking of risk, what about the kind of risk the boy would face if I *did* use my sword?"

"What of it?" Del returned. "It's as much for you to learn control as for him to learn technique."

Nabir cleared his throat. "I would like to face steel."

"Then face me." Del slipped the burnous easily and left it lying in a puddle at her feet. Beneath it she wore a soft cream-colored leather tunic, cap-sleeved and belted, that hit her mid-thigh. She'd worn something similar the first time I'd seen her. Though there was nothing indecent about the tunic—it was completely unrevealing—it was still considerably less than Southron women wore. Even in bed.

Nabir, who had seen her in Northern tunic and trews and boots, stared. There was a lot of limb showing, since she is long of legs and arms, and therefore a lot of flesh. A *lot* of creamy Northern flesh stretched over exquisite Northern bones.

I, who also had seen her in nothing less than tunic and trews and boots for longer than I cared to recall, stared, too. But with less shock than Nabir; she is very impressive, yes, but also exceedingly frustrating.

Nabir swallowed heavily. "I've already danced against you."

"And lost," she said. "Shall we see what Tiger has taught you?"

I watched her unhook her harness, preparing to add it to her pile once she'd unsheathed. I got up. "I don't think so, Del."

She was unsmiling. "His choice."

"Yes," Nabir said instantly.

I ignored the boy, staring instead at Del. "You're doing this to force my hand. To *make* me use my sword."

"You can't spend your life being afraid of it," she said. "I don't deny it's worth your concern, but you have to learn to control it. Best to do it now rather than in a dance to the death, or in a dangerous situation where hesitation might kill you."

Nabir frowned. "I don't understand."

"You shouldn't," I said curtly. "This has nothing to do with you."

"Then what *does* it—"

"This." I bent, scooped up harness, stripped the sheath from my sword. "This is what it has to do with, Nabir: Blooding-blade. Named blade. *Jivatma*. And one more thing: Chosa Dei. Whose soul is in this blade."

"So is yours," Del said steadily. "Do you think only Chosa Dei went into that sword when you requenched? You sang yourself into it, Tiger, as much as Chosa Dei. That, coupled with your determination and strength, will overcome any attempt he might make to steal the power from you."

"Chosa Dei," Nabir echoed.

I looked at him sharply. "Do you know Chosa Dei?"

"Of course." He shrugged. "In stories about how the South became the South."

My turn to frown. "What?"

Again he shrugged. "I heard as a child that once the North and the South were the same. That there was no desert, only grasslands and mountains. And then Chosa Dei grew jealous of his brother— I forget his name—and tried to steal what his brother had."

"Shaka Obre," I muttered.

Nabir, cut off, blinked. "What?"

"His brother." I flapped a hand. "Go on."

"Chosa Dei grew jealous. He wanted what his brother—Shaka

Obre?—had. And when his brother would not give it up, Chosa tried to steal it."

"*What* did he try to steal?"

Nabir shrugged. "The South. Chosa already held the North, but he wanted the South, too, because he always wanted whatever his brother had. He tried many magics, but none of them worked. Until he learned how to collect the power in things, and how to re-shape it." Nabir frowned. "It was a true threat. So Shaka Obre set wasting wards around the land, knowing Chosa wouldn't dare de-stroy what he wanted so badly—only he was wrong. Chosa *was* willing to risk destroying the land. He thought if he couldn't have it, his brother shouldn't, either."

"But it didn't work." Del, sounding reflective; did she know the ending, too?

I decided to forestall them both. "Oh," I said, "I see. Chosa tried to take the South, and Shaka Obre's wasting wards kicked in. Which laid waste to the land and turned it into a barren desert— most of it, anyway." I didn't believe a word of it. "But if that's all true, why didn't Shaka Obre transform the ruined South back into what it was?"

Nabir took up the tale again. "He wanted to. But Chosa was so angry that he put a spell on his brother and locked him away some-where."

"*Chosa* was the one locked away," I declared, as if it refuted the story.

"I don't know," Nabir said testily. "I only know what I heard, which is that Chosa Dei's brother built wards to imprison his brother inside a dragon. But that by the time the spell was tripped, Chosa's magic finally succeeded. Shaka Obre was also imprisoned."

I looked from him to Del. They wore identical expressions. "Why is it," I began again, "that everyone knows these stories but me? Northerner, Southroner—it doesn't seem to matter. Who *told* you these tales?"

"Everyone," Del answered. "Mother, father, uncles, broth-ers . . . everyone just knew."

I looked at Nabir. "What about you?"

"My mother," he answered promptly. "Before—" But he cut it off abruptly.

I let it go. "No one ever told *me*."

Del's voice was soft. "No one tells stories to slaves."

No. So they don't.

Another thing I'd lost.

I pushed by Nabir and walked into the circle. "All right," I said, "all right. If you want true steel so much, I'll give you true steel. But you're putting your life at stake."

Nabir hesitated only a moment. Then he reached down, traded wooden blade for steel, straightened erect again. And walked into the circle.

His quiet faith was implicit. "You're the Sandtiger."

I'm a fool, I thought. An aging, sandsick fool.

Who doesn't know any stories except the ones he makes up himself.

Chapter 10

*T*he sword knocked me to my knees. Not Nabir's; mine.

"*See?*" I shouted at Del, who waited quietly by the circle.

Nabir, who had backed away instantly the moment my blade had delivered its somewhat dramatic message, stood at the very inner edge of the circle. That he wanted to step out was obvious; that he wouldn't, equally so. Habits die too hard.

"I see," Del observed. "I see also that you *let* it do that."

"Let it! Let it? Are you sandsick?" I rose awkwardly, off-balance, muttering curses about sore knees, and stared at her belligerently. "I didn't *let* it do anything, Del. One moment I was sparring with Nabir, the next I'm in the sand. I didn't have a whole lot of choice."

"Look at it," she said.

I looked. It was a sword. The same old sword it had always been; at least, since I'd requenched it inside the mountain.

Then looked more closely. The sword *was* different. The black discoloration had moved up the blade. Nearly half of it was swallowed.

I didn't want a black sword.

I shut hands more tightly around the grip. "No," I said flatly, and sent every bit of strength I could muster flowing through arms, hands and fingers into the sword itself. I would *make* the sword change by forcing my will upon it.

I felt like a fool. What good would it do to *envision* myself over-coming a Southron sorcerer imprisoned in my sword? What kind of power was that? I couldn't summon demons or create runes; couldn't collect magic from men and things. All I could do was sword-dance.

"Sing," Del said quietly.

"Sing," I blurted in derision.

"Singing is the key. It's always been the key. It's how you de-feated him."

I had also thrust a blade into him. But things were different, now. I couldn't very well stab a sword.

In my head, I muttered. But I also made up a little song; a *stu-pid* little song. Don't ask me what it was. I can't even remember. Just some silly little thing about a Southron sandtiger being fiercer than a Northern sorcerer . . . at any rate, it worked. The black re-ceded a little. Now only the tip was charred.

"It's something," Del said, as I swayed on my feet. "For now, it should be enough."

I squinted, rubbed at my eyes, tried to focus clearly. "I'm dizzy."

"You invoked power." Her tone was matter-of-fact. "You can't just *do* it without expecting to pay some price. Do you come out of a circle as fresh as when you went in?"

Not hardly. I could smell myself. "Dizzy," I repeated. *"And* thirsty, and hungry."

Nabir still stood at the very edge of the circle. He was staring at the sword. "Can it do anything? Anything at all?"

I looked down at the blade. "One thing it *can* do is make you feel pretty sick. Hoolies, I need a drink!"

Del tossed me my harness. "You *always* need a drink."

I sheathed, scowling at her, and hooked arms through the loops. The new leather was still stiff. I'd have to spend some time working oil into the straps. "Put some clothes on," I told her crossly. "Let's go get some food."

Del looked past me to Nabir. "Are you coming?"

He shook his head. "I want to go see Xenobia."

"His light o' love," I told her quietly, as Del looked blank.

She watched Nabir gathering his things as I gathered mine. "I didn't know he had one."

"Since two days ago. Cantina girl. He wants to marry her."

"*Marry* her!"

"That's what I said." I stuffed silk, gauze, bota, and practice sword beneath arms and turned toward Harquhal. "But she's his first girl, and he fancies himself in love." I grinned as Nabir departed at a trot. "Why is it so many boys and girls fall in love with the first one who takes them to bed?"

Del's tone was deadly. "I didn't."

No. Not with Ajani.

"Come on, bascha," I sighed. "You need a drink, too."

The cantina was crowded and noisy. Greenish-gray huva smoke eddied in the beamwork, trailing malodorous tails. The place also stank of sour wine, pungent aqivi, mutton stew, and spiced kheshi, all bound together with the acrid tang of Southron sand, dusty bodies; a trace of cheap perfume. The place was packed with men, making the cantina girls happy. Also overworked—in both modes of employment.

Every table was filled shoulder-to-shoulder by burnous-clad men. I saw swords hanging from belts, swords hanging from baldrics, swords strapped on by harness. If a tanzeer desired an army, he need go no farther than here.

"No room," Del murmured.

"There's room. Just no tables." I pushed through a knot of men next to the door, aiming for a deep-cut window. They ignored me mostly, moving apart only slightly, but when Del started through I heard silence abruptly descend. Not over the entire room—it was too packed for that—but the group by the door most decidedly stopped talking.

I shot a glance over my shoulder. Sure enough, five mouths hung open inelegantly. And then closed, smiling broadly, as Del slid through the stirring knot.

You'd have thought they'd step aside. Southroners have *some* manners—only apparently this bunch didn't. As Del arrived in their midst, on the way to me, they closed ranks around her.

Oh, hoolies, bascha, can't you go *anywhere?*

I doubt they intended much. Maybe a pinch here, a tweak

there; a stroke or a fondle or two. But whatever it was they expected to receive in return, Del didn't offer. She had something else in mind.

I heard, in the blink of an eye, several curses, a blurt or two of pain, a breathy hiss of shock. And then Del was through. She joined me at the window.

I noted the merest glint of steel as she returned her knife to its sheath. Beyond her, two of the men bent to rub shins. One inspected sandal-bared toes; Del was wearing boots. All of them glared at her.

"Here?" Del asked at the window.

"Deep ledge." I stuffed clothing, bota, and wooden sword back into the space. "We can use it for a table."

We could. The adobe walls of the cantina were nearly a man-length thick, with the windows cut into the slabs. As deep as the ledge was, a man could sit on it.

Del glanced around at the crowd. "We should have gotten food and drink up front. Now we have to fight our way through again."

"No, we don't. This little girl will be glad to help us out." I caught the elbow of a cantina girl perching on someone's knee, dragged her up, pulled her over. "Aqivi," I said succinctly. "Also kheshi and mutton stew." I glanced at Del. "And wine for the lady; she has refined tastes." Before the girl could protest, I slapped her on the rump and sent her off through the crowd.

Del's expression was curiously bland. "If you ever do that again, I'll send you to stand with the others."

"What others?"

"The men by the door."

I glanced over, saw she meant the men who'd accosted her, scowled. "What did *I* do?"

"You treated her like dirt."

I nearly gaped. "All I did was send her to do her job. *One* of them, anyway."

Del's mouth was hard. "There are ways of doing the same without degrading the girl."

"Oh, Del, come on—"

"Perhaps this will make more sense: you treated her like a slave."

It got my back up; after all, I'd been a slave. "I did no such—"

"Yes, you did," she said. "And if you can't see it, you're blind."

"All I did was—" But I never got to finish. Someone came up behind me and slapped me on the back.

"Sandtiger!" he cried. "When did you get in?"

Hoolies, that hurt. I turned to scowl at him, then blinked in astonishment. "I thought you were *dead*."

"Hoolies, no," he said, "though it felt like it, even to me." He grinned, glanced past me at Del, elbowed me in the ribs. "I'd show you the scar, Sandtiger, but the bascha might be offended."

"I'd probably even swoon." Del's tone was perfectly bland.

Belatedly, I recalled introductions. "Del, this is Rhashad. Old friend of mine. Rhashad, this is Del. New friend of mine."

"I can see why." He bestowed his best smile on her, displaying big, very white teeth framed by heavy red mustaches drooping just past his jaw. "Northern-born, are you? I'm half Northern myself."

And it showed. Rhashad was a Borderer, born in the foothills near the ruins of Iskandar. His hair was reddish blond, his eyes dark blue. To go with the hair his skin was tanned an odd yellowish red, with a generous sprinkling of sunspots. He was big; his height nearly matched mine. Del was only a finger's-width shorter. He packed more weight than me, though, especially through the shoulders.

"So," I said dryly, "I suppose you're heading home, since home is near Iskandar. No doubt you'll make a side-trip, if only to check out the action."

Rhashad grinned. He has a nice grin. He kept showing it to Del. "It's in my blood, Tiger. And I don't dare go home poor. My mother would throw me out of the hut."

Rhashad's mother was a long-standing joke among sword-dancers who knew him. She was, he claimed, a giantess, able to knock him silly with only the flick of a finger. But someone who'd met her once said she was a little bit of a thing, hardly reaching her son's elbow. Rhashad is known to exaggerate, but it's all part of the package. So far it hasn't killed him, though he came close some time before."

I glanced at Del. "His mother's the Northern half. That's where he gets his color."

Del arched her brows. "That's where he gets his *charm.*"

Which promptly set Rhashad to braying for a cantina girl to reward Del's prescience. I told him a girl was on the way; he settled back into the window, hooking elbows on the sill.

"I'm up from Julah," he said. "New tanzeer down there, now that Aladar's dead. I picked up a little work, then the Vashni got too active and I decided to head back home. No sense in giving up my life just to let their black-eyed women make jewelry out of my bones."

I knew all about Aladar; I'd been present when Del killed him. "What's stirred up the Vashni?"

Rhashad shrugged. "This Oracle fellow. He keeps telling everyone the jhihadi is coming to reclaim the South for the tribes. The Vashni have always been superstitious. So now they're beginning to think maybe they ought to help out the foretelling by making it come true. They've been killing a few people here and there; nothing serious yet, but it's always been the obvious foreigner. You know—anyone blond, red-haired, blue- or green-eyed . . . whoever they *think* looks non-Southron. I guess they feel that if they're to reclaim the South, they've got to rid it of foreigners." He shrugged, stroking one half of his mustache. "I look too Northern, I'm thinking, so I made my way back up here."

"Jamail," Del said blankly.

Rhashad frowned. "Who?"

"Her brother," I explained. Del's face was white. "He's living with the Vashni."

The frown deepened: two lines met between his eyes. "What's a Northerner doing with Vashni?"

"Never mind," Del said grimly. "Are you certain they're killing all foreigners?"

"That's what they've *been* doing. Whether they still are, I can't say. All I know is, this Oracle fellow's got them all stirred up." His blue eyes were solemn. "I'll be frank, bascha—if your brother's with the Vashni, his chances aren't worth much. They take matters of religion seriously."

"They'll kill him," she said bitterly, "because this loki-brained Oracle tells them to."

Rhashad lifted a negligent shoulder. "Take it up with *him*, then; he's heading to Iskandar."

"The Oracle?" I frowned. "How do you know that?"

"Rumor. Makes sense, though. This Oracle fellow's been predicting the jhihadi will show his face at Iskandar; don't you think he might want to be there? Sort of to prove his point?"

I didn't answer. The cantina girl arrived, at last, carrying bowls of stew and kheshi, also a jug each of wine and aqivi. She balanced all with great care and concentration, gritting out Southron "excuse me's" as she fought her way through the throng. Del saw it and reached out at once to relieve her of the jugs and cups.

"Pay her extra," Del commanded as I reached for my pouch.

I scowled as I dug deep. "*You're* awfully free with my money."

"Women are," Rhashad observed cheerfully. "You should see how quickly my mother spends the coin I send home."

Del thanked the girl, then arched an eyebrow at Rhashad. "You send money home to your mother?"

"If I didn't, she'd have my ears. Or worse: my mustaches." Rhashad grinned. "You should come meet my mother. She'd like a bold bascha like you."

"Or not," I said hastily, seeing interest in Del's eyes. It might have been for the mother; I wouldn't risk it being for Rhashad. "Here, have some aqivi. Del prefers wine."

Del preferred not drinking. "Do you know a man named Ajani? He's Northern, not a Borderer, but he rides both sides."

"Ajani, Ajani," Rhashad muttered. "The name sounds familiar . . . Northerner, you say?"

"Very much so," she said flatly, "in everything but his habits. He is blond, blue-eyed, very tall . . . and he likes to kill people. If he doesn't sell them to slavers."

Rhashad's eyes sharpened. He looked at her more closely. This time he really saw her. Saw her *and* the sword.

The note in his voice was odd. "Have you ever been to Julah?"

Say no, I warned her mutely.

Del said yes.

Hoolies, he'll put it together.

Rhashad nodded slowly. His look on me was shrewd, "Eighteen months—or so—ago, Aladar ruled in Julah. Rich man, Aladar: he traded in gold and slaves. And would be to this day, if a slave hadn't killed him." He didn't look at Del. "Nobody knows any names. Only that one was a Northern woman, the other a Southron man. A man with scars on his face, who was a slave in Aladar's mine."

I hunched one shoulder. "Lots of men are scarred."

Rhashad spread four fingers and scraped them down one cheek. "Lots of men are scarred. Not all of them quite like this."

"Does it matter?" Del asked roughly.

Rhashad dropped his hand. "Not to me," he said evenly. "I don't betray my friends. But other people might."

A coldness touched my spine. "Why? If Aladar's gone, what does the new tanzeer care about how it happened?"

"The new tanzeer is Aladar's daughter."

"Aladar's *daughter?*" I gaped. "How did a *woman* inherit the domain?"

"Thank you," Del said dryly.

I waved it off. "Not now; this is important."

Rhashad nodded. "Indeed, it is. And the reason she holds the domain is because she was rich enough to buy men, and strong enough to hold them." He smiled a little. "Too much woman for me."

"A woman," I mused. "Hoolies, things are changing."

"For the better," Del remarked, then sipped her sour wine.

"Maybe not, bascha." I scowled into my bowl of rapidly cooling kheshi. Then I shrugged. "Ah, well, it won't last. They may be taking her money now, but it'll wear off. They won't put up with taking orders from a woman for long. Rhashad didn't, did he? And he's a Borderer. A man afraid of his mother."

"I *respect* my mother. And you should, too; she's a better man than you."

"They'll overthrow her," I said thoughtfully. "They'll change loyalties. They'll sell it to a man, or else one will steal it for himself.

And then another will try to steal it from *him*." I shook my head. "Julah will run with blood."

"See why I left?" Rhashad asked. "First the Vashni begin killing, and now there will be war for control of Julah. I'd rather go see my mother."

"With Jamail in the middle, if he's not already dead." Del sighed and scrubbed at her brow. "Oh, Tiger, how much longer? First there is Ajani to think about, and now Jamail as well. What am I to do?"

"Go to Iskandar," I said. "It's the only logical choice."

Del's mouth was twisted. "There is no logic to feelings."

Which was, I thought, about the truest thing she'd ever said. Especially when applied to *her*.

Chapter 11

Something landed on my head. "Come on," the voice said. "We're going to Iskandar."

I lay belly-down on my precarious cot, mashing my face into the lump of cloth pretending to be a pillow. My left arm was under the lump. *I* was under a gauzy sheet, trying to recapture sleep.

The thing on my head did not go away. Without opening my eyes I reached up, felt the saddle-pouches, dragged them off my head and over the side of the bed. "Who's keeping you?" I mumbled.

Del was not amused. "I have no time for this. Ajani could be at Iskandar."

"Ajani could be anywhere. Ajani could be in hoolies." I freed my left arm. "I *hope* Ajani's in hoolies; then we can forget about him."

Del scooped up the pouches. "Fine," she declared. "I'll go there with Abbu."

Del never threatens. Del does. She was about to do now.

"Wait—" I levered myself up, squinted through too-bright daylight at her, tried to remember my name. My mouth tasted like an old dhoti. "Give me a moment, bascha."

She didn't give a moment. "Meet me at the stables." And thumped the door behind her.

Oh, hoolies.

Hoolies.

Why does she always do this on the morning after the night before?

I swear, the woman plans it. She plans it, and she waits. She knows what it does to me.

With effort I turned all the way over and sat up. Sure enough, the door was still shut. Del was still gone.

I sat on the edge of the bed and buried my face in my hands, scrubbing at sleep-creased flesh. I needed food and a taste of aqivi; Del would give me neither. Nor would she give me time.

"You could always catch up," I suggested.

Yes. I could. I knew where she was going.

And I knew who'd be going with her.

Hoolies, hoolies, *hoolies.*

I hate men like Abbu.

I used the nightpot. Then, in an effort to wake up as much as wash myself, I splashed water all over my face and soaked most of my hair. Wet tendrils straggled down my neck. Droplets broke free and rolled, tickling shoulders, chest, belly.

I didn't feel any better. Just wetter.

I glowered at the door as I reached for underrobe, harness, burnous. "What do you expect? I sat up with Rhashad all night."

Del, being gone, didn't answer. Which was just as well with me. She'd say something back. Then *I* would be required to respond. And we would waste too much time bickering over nothing in an attempt to prove dominance.

Which struck me as pretty stupid.

I bent over to pull on the boots Del had found me. "You *are* stupid," I muttered. "You could be sitting in a cantina right about now with a warm and willing little Southron beauty in your lap and a jug of aqivi at your elbow. Or you could be hiring on with some rich tanzeer to protect his dewy-eyed daughter—some cushy job like that. Or sitting over the oracle bones with Rhashad, stealing all his money. *Or* you could be sleeping." One boot was on. I turned to the other. "Instead, what are you doing? Getting ready to ride to Iskandar on a mission of revenge with a cold-hearted, hot-tongued bascha—"

—whom I very badly wanted back in my bed.

I glared at the door. "Message for you, Ajani: if *she* doesn't kill you, I will."

Del was waiting at the stables. With the blue roan. Out in front. In the street. Which told me a little something.

"It'll be there," I told her. "It's been there for hundreds of years."

She frowned.

"Iskandar," I clarified.

Del's frown deepened. But she spoke about something else. "I'd have had him waiting for you, but no one can get near him."

Him. She could only mean one thing. "That's because they don't have the proper technique." I went by her into the lathwork stable, gathered up bridle, went over to the stall. At least, it was sort of a stall; there wasn't much left of it. "All right," I said, "what have you been up to?"

The stud, who was tied to a thick piece of timber sunk in the ground, answered by pawing violently. More bits of stall came down. The ground around him was littered.

"Ah," I said, "I see."

So did the stableman. He came running when he realized the stud's owner was back. I listened to his diatribe for much longer than I liked, but since I had to bridle, saddle and load the stud anyway, I didn't lose any time. Only my waning patience.

"How much?" I asked.

The stableman took the question as an invitation to start all over again with complaints. I cut him off in mid-stride by drawing my knife.

He went white. Gaped. Then changed from white to red as I bent over the stud's left forehoof to check for stones or caked dirt, cleaning the frog of the hoof with my knifetip.

"How much?" I repeated.

The stableman named a price.

"Too much," I told him. "That would buy you a second stable; he didn't do *that* much damage."

He named another price.

I let the stud have his left hoof back and moved to work on the right. "I could *leave* him here . . ."

A third—and better—price. I nodded and gave him money.

Del was mounted and waiting as I led the stud out of doors into daylight. Her roan snorted. The stud curled back his upper lip and trumpeted his dominance, meanwhile stomping on my heels as he raised his tail and danced. A stallion dancing around on the end of an all-too-human arm is rather disconcerting. So between being momentarily deafened by his noise and having my bootheels tromped on, I was not in a good mood.

But then, neither was Del. "Nice technique," she observed as I bashed his nose with a fist.

"Have to get his attention."

"You did," Del said. "Now he's trying to bite you."

Well, he was. But horses have bad moods, too.

I put my left foot in the stirrup and started to pull myself up. The stud bent his head around and missed getting a hunk of me only because I saw it coming and slapped him in the mouth. He tried twice more; I slapped him twice more. Then I gave up on the leisurely mount and swung up all at once, coming down into the saddle with toes hooking stirrups.

"*Now* try," I suggested.

He might have. He has. This time he didn't. For which I was very grateful, since I had the feeling he'd win.

"Are you done?" Del asked.

Before I could answer—though nothing was expected—the stableman stepped forward. "I couldn't help noticing your scars—are you the Sandtiger?"

I nodded, gathering rein.

The man showed me a gap-toothed grin, "I sold a horse to your son."

"My *son*—" I scowled down at him. "What kind of horse, where was he going, and what does he look like?"

Del's tone was dry. "One at a time, Tiger. You'll confuse the poor man."

The stableman knew horses best. "Old gray mare," he said. "Splash of white down her nose, and three white legs. Very gentle. A lady's mare, but he said that's what he wanted."

"Where was he going?"

"Iskandar."

Where else? "What does he look like?"

The man shrugged. "Not tall, not short. Eighteen or nineteen. Brown-haired, blue-eyed. Spoke Southron with an accent."

"What *kind* of accent?"

He shrugged, shaking his head.

"But he told you he was my son."

"Son of the Sandtiger; yes." He grinned. "Hasn't got the scars, but he wears a necklet of claws."

"And a sword?" I asked grimly.

He frowned. Thought back. Shook his head. "A knife. No sword."

"A necklet, but no sword. And riding an old gray mare." I glanced at Del. "If he's really going to Iskandar, at least we know what to look for."

She was startled. "You'll *look*?"

"Shouldn't be hard to find him. He's obviously not shy of boasting about his parentage—even though it's a lie."

Her tone was a little odd. "How do you know it's a lie?"

"He's too old," I told her. "If I'm thirty-six, and he's eighteen—or even *nineteen*—it means I was all of—" I stopped.

"Eighteen," Del supplied. "Or maybe seventeen."

Not too old after all. "Let's go," I said curtly. "No sense in staying here."

By the time we were out of Harquhal, most of my bad temper was gone. It was too hard staying out of sorts when the Southron sun was shining on my face, warming the place where the beard had been. It felt odd to be clean-shaven. It felt odd to wear gauze and silk. It felt odd to be so carefree.

But it felt *good* to feel so odd.

"You know," I remarked, "you might have warned me last night you wanted to leave. I could have said good-bye to Rhashad, told Nabir there'd be no more lessons—"

"Nabir knows. *I* told him."

"Oh? When?"

"Last night. You and Rhashad were full of aqivi and too busy trying to win one another's money . . . Nabir came in, and I told him." She shrugged. "He said he would come, too, if he could convince Xenobia to quit her job and go with him."

"Xenobia," I murmured.

"And I told Abbu, who also came in last night."

I looked at her. "He did? I didn't see him. When did he come in? Last night? In our cantina?"

"I said you were full of aqivi." Del waved a fly away. "Not long before I left."

"Left," I echoed. "You *left?* When? Why?" I frowned. "With him?"

"Aren't *you* full of questions today."

"I think I have a right."

"Oh? Why?"

"I just do." I scowled, disliking her tone. "Who knows what kind of trouble you might have gotten yourself into, going off with Abbu like that. You don't know what kind of man he is, bascha."

"One very much like you." She raised a hand to forestall my protest. "No—like you *were.* I'll admit, you've changed. You're not the arrogant fool you once were."

"So comforting," I said dryly. "And was he like me in bed, too?"

"You have no right to ask that."

"Hoolies, you mean you *did?*" I jerked the stud up short. "I was only joking, after all your natter about needing focus . . . do you mean to tell me you went off with Abbu last night?"

Del's tone was deadly. "I did not lie to you about requiring a focus. And if I have told you plainly I desire solitude, would I then go to bed with Abbu?"

It slowed me down only a moment. "Maybe. I'm not sure any more."

"No."

I felt a little better—I felt a *lot* better about Abbu's lack of success—but was still a trifle disgruntled about her accompanying him. "You've got to admit, I've got a right to be concerned."

"No," Del retorted. "It's not your place."

That got my back up. "Why is it not my place? We've spent the last—what, eighteen months?—together, *in* bed and out, and you say it's not my place?"

"It's not your place to ask whom I choose to sleep with," Del declared, "any more than it's *my* place to ask the same of you."

"But you *can* ask," I said. "You've been the only woman in my bed since—since—" I frowned. "Hoolies, see what you've done? I can't even remember."

"Elamain," she said dryly.

Elamain. Elamain—oh, *Elamain*.

Del saw my expression. "Yes," she said, "Elamain. *That* Elamain."

How could I forget? How could *any* man forget? Her appetite was insatiable, her skill beyond belief, her stamina unbelievable, her imagination unparalleled—

"Of course," Del remarked, "she did nearly get you killed."

The dream evaporated. "Worse," I said—with feeling.

"What could be worse than—oh. Oh. Yes, I remember. She almost got you gelded."

I shifted in the saddle. "Let's not talk about that. Besides, what did you expect? *You* weren't giving me anything. Why shouldn't I sleep with Elamain—"

"—especially since she didn't give you much choice." Del smiled. "Tiger, you may think other women don't know, but we do. I know very well what kind of woman Elamain is—or was; Hashi probably had her killed—and how she worked her magic on you. Women like that have power. Men can never withstand it." She tossed loose hair behind her shoulders. "You can be sidetracked so easily . . . you can lose sight of what you intended just because a woman—"

"—tells me a story about how a Northern borjuni killed her family and sold her brother into slavery." I smiled. "Sound familiar, bascha?"

"That's not what I meant, Tiger."

"No. You meant women like Elamain luring poor fools into their beds. I know. I won't even deny it hasn't worked on me other times, either." I shrugged. "You used a different method, but the end result was the same."

Del didn't say anything right away. She'd turned her blue roan to face me, and now she had to rein him back to keep him from nosing the stud. Once she had him settled, she met my gaze stare for stare. Then tilted her head a little.

"What would you have done?" she asked. "What would you have done with your life if I hadn't found you in that cantina?"

"Done?"

"Done," she repeated. "You said I'd sidetracked you as much as Elamain might have—sidetracked you from what? Made you lose sight of—what?"

"Well, if you *hadn't* found me in that cantina, I wouldn't have been left as a Sun Sacrifice by the Hanjii. I wouldn't have been thrown into Aladar's mine. I wouldn't have lost Singlestroke and gotten stuck with this Northern sword, or sucked up Chosa Dei."

"That's not what I asked."

"Those things *wouldn't* have happened."

"Tiger, you're avoiding my question."

"No, I'm not." I shrugged. "Hoolies, I don't know. I'm a sword-dancer. I hire on to do things. I'd probably be *doing* things; does that answer your question?"

"Yes," she said, "it does." She waved away another fly. Or maybe the same one. "You asked me once what I'd do when Ajani was dead. Once I'd ended my song."

"Yes, I asked. As I recall, you didn't have an answer."

"Because I refuse to look past that. To look beyond Ajani's death is to lose focus. To dilute the vision. And I can't afford that." Del flicked a hand in the air. "So, I don't look. But you don't have the same restrictions. You *can* look. What I ask now is, have you?"

"No sword-dancer wastes much time thinking about next year, next month, next week. Hoolies, sometimes not even next *day.* Only the next dance. He looks to the dance, bascha. Because that's what he lives for."

Del's eyes were steady. "When will your dance be ended?"

"I can't answer that," I said crossly. "I don't even know what it means."

"You do. Oh, you do. You're not a stupid man. You're not a foolish man. You only pretend to be when you don't want to deal with truths."

I didn't say a word.

Del smiled a little. "It's all right, Tiger. I do the same thing."

"You don't pretend to be stupid. And you never pretend you're a fool."

"No." Her mouth was oddly warped. "Instead, I make myself cold and hard. I make myself dead inside, so I don't have to face those truths."

There are times when I hate this woman.

This was not one of them.

Part III

Chapter 1

Del's voice was distant. "Tiger—what's wrong?"

It didn't make any sense. Just a jumble of words. No, not words; *sounds.*

"Tiger? Are you all right?"

I felt—odd.

"Tiger!"

Oh, hoolies, bascha . . . something's wrong—something's wrong with *me*—something's *wrong* with—

I stopped the stud. Got off. Dragged the sword from its sheath. Then walked across the trail to a tumbled pile of rocks. Found a fissure. Wedged the sword into it.

Wedged the *hilt* into it, leaving the blade stuck up into air.

"Tiger—?" And then she sent her roan plunging between the blade and my body.

It knocked me backward. It knocked me flat on my rump. I sat there on the ground trying to figure out what had happened.

Del reined the roan around. Her expression was profoundly frightened. "Have you gone loki?" she cried.

I didn't think so. What I was, somehow, was sitting on the ground instead of in the saddle.

Silence: Del said nothing. Her gelding pawed, digging pebbles and dust. I heard the clack of rock on rock, the scraping of hoof in hard ground, the clink of bit and bridle.

Saw the sword sticking up from the fissure.

"Hoolies," I muttered hoarsely.

Del said nothing. She watched me get up, watched me slap dust from my burnous, watched me take a step toward the sword. Then put the gelding between.

Brought up short, I stuck out a hand to ward off the roan. "What are you trying to—"

"Keep you from killing yourself," she said flatly, "do you think I couldn't tell?"

"I'd *never*—"

"You just did. Or would have."

I stared up at her in astonishment. Then across the roan's bluish rump to the waiting sword jutting patiently into the air.

I couldn't have. I *couldn't* have. It's not something I would do. I've survived too much travail in my life to end it willingly, let alone by my own hand.

"Let me go," I said.

Del didn't move the gelding.

"Let me go," I repeated. "I'm all right now, bascha."

Her expression was unreadable. Then she moved the gelding out of my way. I heard the hiss of a blade unsheathed. I was visited by an odd thought: would Del try to kill me to keep me from killing myself?

Somehow, I didn't laugh. Not looking at my sword.

I approached it carefully. Felt nothing. No fear, no apprehension, no desire to do myself injury. Just a mild curiosity as to what the thing had wanted.

It didn't say a word.

I bent. Closed one hand around the exposed portion of the hilt, avoiding the blade itself. Worked the sword from the fissure and turned it right side up.

Black crept up the blade. This time it touched the runes.

"It doesn't want to go," I blurted.

Del's voice: *"What?"*

"It—*he*—doesn't want to go." I frowned down at the sword, then wrenched my gaze away to meet hers. "Chosa Dei wants to go south."

Del's mouth flattened. "Tell him we're going north."

"Northeast," I corrected. "And he knows exactly which way we're going—it's why he pulled this stunt." I paused. "One of the reasons, anyway; he also wants out of the sword. Killing me is a way of succeeding."

Del sheathed Boreal and edged the gelding closer. "It's black again."

"Some of it." I turned the blade from edge to edge to show both sides. "What do you suppose would happen if the whole thing went black?"

Del's tone was odd. "Do you really want to find out?"

I glanced at her sharply. "Do you know?"

"No. But *I* wouldn't run the risk."

"Neither will I," I muttered. "Time to show him who's boss again."

As before, I shut both hands around the grip, locking fingers in place. It had taken a song last time, a snatch of a little song sung to put Chosa Dei in his place. I summoned it again and let it fill my head. Thought briefly of nothing else other than proving my dominance. Like the stud with Del's blue roan.

I was sweating when I opened my eyes. The song in my head died away. The runes were free of charring, but not the entire blade. "Only a little," I rasped. "Each time, more of the black remains."

"You must be vigilant," Del declared.

"Vigilant," I muttered. "*You* be vigilant."

Her face wavered before me. "Are you all right?" she asked.

I staggered toward the stud, who, bored, lipped idly at dirt. His muzzle was crusted with it. "Am I all right, she asks. I don't know; *should* I be all right? Every time I have this little argument with my sword, I feel like I've aged ten years." I stopped short of the stud and swung around. "I haven't, have I?"

"What?"

"Aged ten—or *twenty*—years."

Del appraised me critically. "I don't think so. You look the same as before—about sixty, I would say."

"That's not funny," I snapped, and then realized how I

sounded. "All right, all right—but do you blame me? Who knows what Chosa Dei can do, even in a sword!"

"True," Del conceded. "No, Tiger, you do not look like you have aged ten or twenty years. In fact, you look better than a week ago; sparring agrees with you. You should do it more often."

"I would if I could," I muttered. "Maybe at Iskandar."

I turned back to the stud, who greeted me with a bump of his muzzle against my face, followed by a snort. His snorts are bad enough any time; this time it included dirt. Dirt and mucus make mud.

I swore, wiped slime from face and neck, called him a dozen unflattering names. He'd heard them all before and didn't even flick an ear. So I caught reins, dug a foot into the left stirrup, dragged myself up with effort, plopped rump into saddle. Peered over at Del.

"All right," I said, "all right. I give up. The sooner I get Chosa Dei out of this sword, the happier I'll be . . . and if that means finding this Shaka Obre, then that's what we'll do."

Del's expression was odd. "It could take months. Maybe years."

I gritted teeth. "I know that," I told her. "What in hoolies *else* am I supposed to do? Fight this thing for the rest of my life?"

Del's tone was quiet. "I just think you should realize what sort of commitment you're making."

I glared at her. "This sword just tried to make me kill myself. Now it's *personal*."

Her smooth brow creased. "Shaka Obre is little more than a name, Tiger . . . he will be difficult to find."

I sighed. "We found Chosa Dei. We'll find Shaka Obre, no matter what it takes."

Del's smile was oddly abrupt.

"What?" I asked warily.

"Only that you sound very like me."

I thought about it. About Del's quest to find Ajani, and the sacrifices she'd made.

Now it was my turn.

She brought her roan up beside me. "How much farther to Iskandar?"

"According to what Rhashad told me, another day's ride. We should make it by tomorrow evening." I peered down the track winding through scrub trees and webby grass. "You know, maybe it wouldn't be so bad if there *is* a jhihadi due. Maybe he can cure my sword."

Del sounded cross. "There's nothing wrong with your sword that you can't cure yourself. All it takes is control. And the willingness to *try.*"

I looked at her a long moment. Then shifted in my saddle. "You know," I said lightly, "I'll be glad when Ajani's dead."

It caught her off guard. "Why?"

"Because maybe then you'll remember what it's like to be human again."

Her mouth opened. "I *am*—"

"Sometimes," I agreed. "Then again, other times you're a cold-hearted, judgmental bitch."

I turned the stud and went on. After a moment, she followed.

Silence is sometimes noisy.

Iskandar, I knew, had been very old even before Harquhal was born. Which meant the track between them was very new, beaten into the ground only in answer to the Oracle. In time the track would fade, washed away by wind and rain, and the land would be true again, lacking the scars put on it by pilgrims gone to see the new jhihadi. Until then, however, the track would become a lifeline.

Rhashad had been explicit in his instructions, but it wasn't necessary. It was easy to see the way. Easy to see the people leaving Harquhal behind on the way to Iskandar. Harder to avoid them.

We avoided them eventually by riding off the track. It was dusk, growing chilly, and my belly was complaining. Del and I went over a hill and found a private place for a campsite, not desirous of company. On the road you can never be sure.

"No fire," I suggested as I climbed down from the stud.

Del, saying nothing, nodded. She pulled off saddle, pad, pouches, the roll of pelt and blankets. Dumped everything in one spot and went back to tend the roan.

It took no time at all. We settled mounts, spread bedrolls, ate a journey-meal out of our pouches and drank water out of botas. By the time the sun was down there was nothing left but bed. But neither of us sought it.

In the white light of a full moon I sat on my pelt, blankets draped around my knees, working oil into my harness. The leather was stiff from newness and needed softening. In time the oil, my sweat, and the shape of my body would coerce the harness to fit. Until then, I'd tend it every night. It was ritual.

Del performed her own even as I completed mine. But it was not her harness she tended. It was Boreal's blade. Whetstone, oil, cloth. And exquisitely tender care.

She had braided back her hair. It left most of her face bare. In the moonlight, the angles were harsh. The planes were cut from glass.

Down the blade and back again: seductive sibilance. Then the whisper of silk on steel.

Her head was bent, and tilted, as she looked down the length of blade. White-lashed lids were lowered, hiding the eyes from me. Thick, pale braid fell over a silk-clad shoulder, swinging with her motion. Down the blade, then back again: slow, subtle seduction.

Abruptly I had to know. "What are you thinking about?"

Del twitched minutely. She had been very far away.

Quietly I repeated it: "What are you thinking, bascha?"

The mouth warped briefly. Then regained its shape. "Jamail," she said softly. "Remembering what he was like."

I'd only seen him once. Never as she had.

"He was—a boy," she said. "No different from any other. He was the youngest of us all, at ten—five years younger than me. Trying so hard to be a man when we wanted to keep him a boy."

I smiled, seeing it. "Nothing wrong with that."

"He thought so. He would look at my father, my uncles, my brothers, then look at me. And swear he was as brave . . . swear he was as strong . . . swear he was as capable as any man full-grown."

I had not had a normal boyhood. I couldn't say how it should have been. Couldn't feel what Jamail had felt. Couldn't say the words I might have said if I had been Jamail, wanting to soothe my sister.

"They took us together," she said. "We hid beneath the wagon, trying to make ourselves small, but the borjuni fired the wagon. There was no place left to hide. We ran—Jamail's clothing caught fire—" She broke off a moment, face twisted oddly. "They caught fire, but he wouldn't scream. He just stuffed his fists in his mouth and bit them until they bled. I had to throw him down. I had to trip him and throw him down so I could smother the flames . . . and that was when they caught us."

My hands stilled on the harness. Del's continued to work her blade. I doubt she even knew it.

"He was burned," she said. "They didn't care. He was alive, he would mend; he would still bring a pretty price. That was all they thought of: what the Southron slavers would pay."

No, it was not all they thought of. There was Delilah as well—fifteen-year-old Northern beauty—but Del wasn't speaking of her. Jamail was the topic. Jamail was all that counted, and the fate of her family.

Del didn't count herself worthy enough to warrant the obsession.

Oh, bascha. Bascha. If only you knew.

"But he survived it," she said. "More than I, surely: slavery, castration, losing a tongue. He survived all of that only to fall to the Vashni." Del drew in a breath. "So now I am left to sit here, wondering if he's dead."

"You don't know that he is."

"No. No, I don't. Not knowing is what hurts."

Her hand continued its task, never faltering in its stroke. Boreal sang a song, a song of promises.

"Don't borrow grief," I told her. "Jamail could be perfectly safe with the Vashni."

"They're killing foreigners. He's all too obviously Northern."

"Is he? Was he?" I shrugged as she glanced up. "By the time we found him, he'd spent five years in the South. Two years with the Vashni. For all we know, they might consider him one of their own. The old man loved him; that should carry some weight."

"*Old* men," she said quietly, "often lose their power."

"And sometimes they don't."

"But all old men die."

I shook my head. "I can't make it any easier for you, Del. Yes, he could be dead. But you don't *know* that."

"And I wonder: will I ever? Or spend the rest of my life not knowing if there is anyone left of my blood."

"Believe me," I said roughly, "you can learn to live with that."

Del's hand closed over the blade. "And do you say *that* because I am a coldhearted, judgmental bitch?"

I looked at her sharply, startled by the question. More startled by the raw tone. "No," I answered honestly. "I say that because it's what *I've* done."

"You," she said blankly.

"Me," I agreed. "Are you forgetting the circumstances? No mother, no father for me . . . no brothers or sisters, either. I haven't the vaguest idea if there is anyone left of *my* blood, since I don't know what blood it is."

"Borderer," she said. "Borderer, or foreign."

I straightened. "That's what you think?"

Del shrugged. "You have the size of a Northerner, but your color is mostly Southron. Not as dark, of course, and your features are not as harsh. You are a little of both, I think, which might make you a Borderer." She smiled a little, assessing. "*Or* a foreigner. Have you never imagined it?"

That, and more. Everything. Every day of my enslavement. Every night in my bed of dung. Admitting it to no one. Not even to Sula, or Del. Because the admitting could make me weak. The weak do not survive.

"No," I said aloud, driving the weakness away.

"Tiger." Del set the sword aside. "Did it never occur to you that the Salset might have lied?"

"Lied?" I frowned. "I don't understand."

She sat cross-legged. Fingers curved around her knees. "You have spent your life believing you were left in the desert to die. Abandoned by mother, by father . . . that's what you have said."

"That's what I was told."

"Who told you?" she asked gently.

I frowned. "The Salset. You know that. What is this all about?"

"About lies. About deception. About pain inflicted on purpose, to make the foreign boy suffer."

Something pinched my belly. "Del—"

"*Who* told you, Tiger? It wasn't Sula, was it?"

My answer was instant. "No. Sula was never cruel. Sula was my—" I stopped.

Del nodded. "Yes. Sula was your salvation."

In my hands I clutched the harness. "What of it?" I asked. "What has Sula to do with this?"

"When were you first made aware you weren't Salset?"

I had no real answer. "I just always knew."

"Because they told you."

"Yes."

"*Who* told you? Who told you first? Who told you so young that you would never think otherwise?"

"Del—"

"Was it the adults?"

"No," I said crossly. "The adults completely ignored me until I was old enough to be useful. It was the children, always the children . . ." I let it trail off. Recalling all too well the painful days of my past; the nightmare of childhood.

Recalling and *wondering*.

Could it have been a lie?

I sat very still. Everything was suddenly, oddly, clear, the way it is just before a sword-dance. When you walk the edge of the blade, knowing an instant can make the difference.

All my senses sharpened. I knew who and where I was, and what I had become. And I knew it was hard to breathe.

In perfect stillness, Del waited.

"The children," I repeated, feeling the abyss crack open below.

Del's face was taut. "Children can be cruel."

"They said—" I broke it off, not daring to say it aloud.

After a moment she took it up. "They said you'd been left for dead in the desert by parents who didn't want you."

"They all said it," I murmured vaguely. "First one, then all the others."

"And you never questioned it."

I couldn't sit there anymore. I couldn't sit at all. How could I just *sit*—?

I thrust the harness aside and stood up stiffly, then walked away four paces. Stopped. Stared blindly into darkness.

Swung back numbly to challenge. "There was no one *to* question. Who was I to ask? What was I to say? I was a chula . . . chulas don't *ask* questions . . . chulas don't talk at all, because to talk invites a beating."

"There was Sula," she said gently.

Something stirred sluggishly. Anger. Desperation. A kind of pain I'd never felt because I'd never cared before. Not the way she made me care. "I was *fifteen*." I didn't know how to explain it; not so she could see, could understand, could comprehend. "Fifteen when I met Sula. By then I knew better than to ask. By then I didn't care. By then there was nothing in me to even wonder who I was."

"That's a lie," she said.

Despair cuts like a blade. "Oh, hoolies . . . oh, bascha, you just don't know . . ." I scraped stiff fingers through my hair. "There's no way you *can* know."

"No," she agreed.

I stared at her in the moonlight. It hurt to look at her. To think about what she'd said. To wonder if she was right.

"You were wrong to do this," I said. "You shouldn't have done it, bascha. You should have left it alone—should have left *me* alone . . . don't you see what you've done?"

"No."

"*Before,* I knew what I was. I knew what had happened. It didn't make me happy—who would be happy knowing he was abandoned?—but at least I had an idea. At least there was something to hate. At least I didn't wonder if it was falsehood or truth."

"Tiger—"

"You took it away," I said. "And now there's nothing at *all*."

Del's face was stricken. She stared at me blindly a moment, then drew in a noisy breath. "Wouldn't you rather know you *weren't* abandoned?"

"Do you mean would I *rather* know my parents were murdered

by borjuni? Or maybe murdered by the Salset, who then took me for a keepsake?"

She flinched. "That's not what I—"

I turned my back on her again. Stared very hard into darkness, trying to sort things out. She had changed everything. Altered the stakes. I had to regain my footing. Had to find a new way of playing.

My turn to suck a breath. "What do I do now? What do I do, Del? Drive myself sandsick wondering about the truth?"

"No," she answered harshly. "What kind of life is that?"

I swung around. "Your kind," I told her. "You punish yourself with *your* life. Shall I punish myself with mine?"

Del recoiled. Then swallowed visibly. "I only meant to give you a little peace."

All the anger died out of me. With it went the bitterness, leaving emptiness in its place. "I know," I said. "I know. And maybe you have, bascha. I just don't know it yet."

"Tiger," she whispered, "I'm sorry."

The moonlight was on her face. It hurt me to look at her.

"Go to bed," I said abruptly. "I've got to check on the stud."

The stud was tied all of four paces away. He was fine. He was asleep. He needed nothing from me.

But Del didn't say a word.

Chapter 2

*I*skandar was a child's toy: a pile of unfired clay blocks left too long in the sun and rain. There were no corners left on the buildings, only rounded, slump-shouldered shells being transformed slowly to dust. Into the dirt and clay and piles of shale from which the city had come.

"This is stupid," I said. "All these people, on the word of an unknown zealot, are leaving behind their homes to come to a ruined city. And for all anyone knows, there isn't even any water."

Del shook her head. "There's water; too much green. And don't you think the jhihadi will provide if this is where he plans to return?"

Her tone was dry, ironic. A reflection of my own. Del believes in religion more than I do—at least, in the worth of faith—and she had not, up to now, shown any intolerance for the predicted return. If anything, she had admonished me for my cynicism, saying I should respect the beliefs of others even if they didn't match my own.

But now, faced with Iskandar, Del wasn't thinking of faith. Nor even of religion. She was thinking of Ajani. She was thinking of killing a man.

And of the oaths to her own gods, far from Iskandar.

"Where's the border?" I asked. "You know all these things."

Which she did, better than I. Part of Del's training on Staal-Ysta was something she called *geography*, the study of where places were. I knew the South well enough, particularly the Punja, but Del knew all sorts of different places, even those she'd never been to.

"The border?" she echoed.

"Yes. The border. You know: the thing that divides North from South."

She slanted me a glance that said precisely nothing. Which meant it said a lot. "The border," she said coolly, "is indiscernible."

"It's what?"

"Indiscernible. I can't tell where it is. The land is too—odd."

The stud stumbled. I dragged his head up, steadied him, let him walk on again. "What do you mean: odd?"

Del waved an encompassing hand. "Look around you, Tiger. One moment we are in desert sand, the next in Northern grassland. Then another step into borderland scrub; a fourth into wind-scoured stone."

"So?"

"So. It is one thing to ride from Julah to Staal-Ysta and see how the land changes . . . it is entirely another to see the same changes in the space of ten paces."

I hadn't really thought about it. But now that she mentioned it, the land did change a lot. So did the temperature. One moment it was hot, the next a tad bit frosty. But one melted into the other and made it mostly warm.

We skirted, as did the track, the edge of a broad plateau. On our left rose the foothills of the North; to our right, beyond the plateau, stretched scrubby borderlands that, if the eye could see so far, would flatten into desert. Below us, directly northeast, was another, smaller plateau. In the center, on the top, stood the city of Iskandar.

It could not be characterized as a hilltop fortress, or even a desert city. There were no walls, only buildings, with dozens of alleys and entrances. Most were cluttered with fallen adobe blocks, crumbling away into dust, but shale walls marked foundations, mortared together with dried, grassy mud.

Once, the ruins might have been majestic, markers of human pride. But humans had returned, and the majesty was destroyed.

Iskandar was a warren overrun by desert vermin. There were carts, wagons, horses, danjacs, and countless human beasts brought to carry in the burdens. Most had moved into the city, filling in all the chinks, but many had staked out hyorts around the edges, creating little pocket encampments of desert dwellers unwilling to mix with city rabble.

We halted our mounts at the edge of the plateau. The trail wound down, but we didn't look down. We looked across at the city.

"Tribes," I said succinctly.

Del frowned. "How can you tell? They look like everyone else."

"Not when you get up close; do I look much like a Hanjii?" I nodded toward Iskandar. "The tribes don't build cities. They won't live in them. Most of them travel in carts and wagons, staking out hyorts when they stop a while. See? That's what all those tents are, skirting the edges of the city."

"But they've just made their *own* city by all settling in one spot."

"Special circumstances." I shrugged as she glanced at me. "You don't find this many tribes gathered together ever—at least, not without bloodshed. But if this Oracle's got all of them stirred up, it will change things. They'll suffer one another until the jhihadi question is settled."

Del looked down at the ruined city. "Do you think the Salset are there?"

Something tickled inside my belly. "I suppose it's possible."

"Would they come for the jhihadi?"

I thought about the shukar. The old man's magic had been failing, or *he'd* have killed the cat and left me with no escape. Among the Salset, magic is religion-based; when magic doesn't work, the gods are looking away. They'd looked away from the shukar. Otherwise how could a mere chula kill the cat in the shukar's place?

I thought about Del's question. Would he bring them to Iskandar? If he thought he needed to. If he thought it would bring him honor. If the old man was still alive.

He had been a year before.

"Maybe," I said. "Maybe not. Depends on how things are going."

"You could see Sula again."

I gathered up my reins. "Let's go. There's no sense in staying here just to gaze across the landscape."

Well, there wasn't. But I might have put it better.

Del turned the roan and headed down the trail winding off the plateau rim. Down, across, then up. And we'd be in Iskandar.

Where she might find Ajani at last.

The stud topped the final rise and took me onto the plateau where Iskandar jutted skyward. The trail, instead of narrow, was wide and well-rutted, showing signs of carts and wagons. It wound around trees and close-knit bushes, then split into five fingers. Five smaller tracks leading toward five different parts of the city, where they fractured yet again. Most didn't enter Iskandar. Most stopped at clusters of hyorts, at knots made of wooden wagons.

Which told me a thing or two.

"What is it?" Del asked as she put her roan next to me.

I frowned bemusedly at the hyorts. There were tens and twenties of them staked between the plateau's edge and the city. It changed the look of the place. Softened Iskandar's perimeter. Altered the lay of the land in more ways than one.

"Tribes," I said at last. "Too many, and too different."

"They have as much right here as anyone."

"I'm not questioning that. I'm wondering where it will lead."

"If there really is a jhihadi—"

"—he could be dangerous." I reined the stud around a goat standing in the middle of the track. "Too much power held by a single man."

Del also passed the goat. "And if he used it for good?"

I make a noise of derision. "Do you know anyone who holds that much power and uses it for *good?*" I shook my head. "I don't think it's possible."

"Just because you haven't seen it doesn't mean it can't exist. Maybe that's why he's coming."

"*If* he's coming," I muttered.

Hyorts lined either side of the track. I smelled the pungent aroma of danjac urine. The tang of goat's milk and cheese. The al-

most overwhelming stench of too many people—of too many customs—living too close to one another.

And this was outside of the city.

Del and I were hardly noticed. I didn't know how long some of
the tribes had been camped here, but obviously long enough so
that the sight of two strangers was no longer worth comment. In
the Punja, half a dozen of the tribes gathered would have killed us
on the spot, or taken us prisoner. But no one bothered us. They
looked, then looked away.

Looked away from *Del.*

I frowned. "There must be Northerners here."

"Why do you—oh. Oh, I see." Del glanced around. "If any *are*
here, they must be inside the city."

"It's where we're going," I said. "We'll know sooner or later,
bascha; sooner—we're almost in."

And so we were. We passed through the last cluster of hyorts
and wagons and entered Iskandar proper. No walls, no gates, no
watch. Only open roads, and the city.

The city and her new people.

Southroners, most of them. Fewer Borderers. A handful of
towheaded Northerners, head and shoulder above the rest. And
goats and sheep and dogs and pig running loose through the streets
of Iskandar.

I couldn't help grinning. "Doesn't much look the kind of place
a long-awaited jhihadi might come back to."

"It smells," Del observed.

"That's because no one actually lives here. They don't care.
They're only *borrowing* it for a while . . . they'll leave with the jhihadi."

"If the jhihadi leaves."

I guided the stud through a narrow alley. "Wouldn't make
sense for him to stay. Iskandar's a ruin. He might prefer a livable
city."

"It could be *made* livable . . . Tiger, where are we going?"

"Information," I answered. "Only one place to get it."

Del's tone was dry. "I don't think there is a cantina."

"There probably *is*," I remarked, "but that's not where we're
going. You'll see."

So she did, once we got there. And it wasn't a cantina, either. It wasn't one thing at all, but two: the well, and the bazaar.

In every settlement, the well is the center of town. It is where everyone goes, because it is a necessity. Also an equalizer, especially in Iskandar where no tanzeer reigned. It was the only place in the city where all paths would cross.

Thus it becomes the bazaar. Where people go, they buy. Others had things to sell. Even in Iskandar.

"So *many,*" Del exclaimed.

More than I expected. Stalls filled much of the central square and spilled into adjoining alleys. There were vendors of all kinds, shouting at passersby. The whine of dij-pipes filled the air, keening in ornate Southron style, while street dancers jangled finger bells and beat taut leather heads of tambor-drums. They wound their way through the crowds, trying to scare up a coin or two, or lead customers back to the stalls of the merchants who'd hired them.

"It is," Del said. "It's just like a *kymri.*"

But this was the South, not the North. We don't have *kymri.*

I reined in the stud. Before us lay the choked square. "No sense in riding through there," I said. "We'd do better to walk—*hey!*" The shout was to stop a boy trying to squeeze by the stud. "You," I said more quietly. "Have you been here long?"

"A six-day," he answered, in Desert.

I nodded. "Long enough to know a little something about the place, then."

The boy smiled tentatively. Black-haired, dark-skinned, light-eyed. Half-breed, I thought. But I couldn't name the halves,

"How do we go about finding a place to sleep?" I asked.

The boy's eyes widened. "All around," he answered. "There are many, many rooms. Many more rooms than people. Stay where you want." His eyes were on my sword hilt. "Sword-dancer?" he asked.

I nodded confirmation.

"Then you will want the circles." He waved a hand. "On the other side of the city. It's where all the sword-dancers are."

"All?"

"All," he repeated. "They come every day. That's where they all stay, to challenge one another so they can impress the tanzeers."

"And where are the tanzeers?"

The boy's quick smile flashed. "In the rooms that still have roofs."

Ah. Of course. In a ruin as old as Iskandar, timber would have rotted. Dwellings would be roofless, except for those with more than one story. Which was where the tanzeers would go.

So. The division of power began.

Boys often learn things other people don't. "How many?" I asked. "How many tanzeers?"

He shrugged. "A few. Not many yet. But they have brought sword-dancers with them . . . the rest they are hiring." His eyes were very bright. "You'll have no trouble finding work."

It didn't ring quite true. "And do you know *why* they're hiring so many of us?"

The boy shrugged. "Protection against the tribes."

It made sense. The tribes and tanzeers didn't mix much; didn't see eye to eye when they did. And if the promised messiah was appealing primarily to the tribes, which is what it sounded like, the tanzeers would want to know.

I dug a copper out of my pouch and flipped it at the boy. He caught it, grinned again, glanced past me toward Del. Said something quickly in Desert, then turned and ran into the square.

Grinning, I kneed the stud out. We'd cut straight across the bazaar to the outskirts directly beyond. Where the boy had said there were circles.

"What did he say?" Del asked. "And you know which part I mean."

I laughed, then twisted my head to glance back. "He complimented me on my taste in baschas."

"That boy must have been no more than twelve!"

I shrugged. "In the South, you start young."

It wasn't easy cutting directly across the square. There was no organization to the tangled walkway between stalls. Some turned, some stopped, some doubled back. Twice I got turned around, then finally found the way. Through the cheek-by-jowl crumbling buildings, then out onto the plateau.

We were, I judged, directly opposite the hyorts with Iskandar in between. But here there were no hyorts. Here there were no wagons. Only horses, bedding, and circles.

"Looks more like a war," I observed, "than a gathering for the jhihadi."

Del halted her gelding beside me, gazing upon the scene. "Many wars," she agreed. "Are there not many tanzeers?"

Slowly I shook my head. "It doesn't feel right."

"What doesn't?"

"The tanzeers *are* hiring an army . . . an army of sword-dancers. They only do that on an individual basis—feuding tanzeers hire men to fight one another, so they can destroy one another—never as a group. The *nature* of desert domains is each man for himself . . . it just doesn't seem right that so many are here together, and all are hiring men."

Del shrugged. "Does it matter?"

"Maybe," I said uneasily. "Maybe it does."

And then I thought about what Abbu Bensir had said concerning going to a single place to win coin and find a job. It wasn't the Southron way, but I saw certain advantages. No doubt so did the others; it was why so many were here.

"We could get rich," I said thoughtfully. "If we hired on with the right tanzeer, we could get *very* rich."

"I didn't come to get rich. I came to kill a man."

"*If* you find him," I said, "what do you plan to do? Challenge him to a dance?"

"He's not worth the honor."

"Oh. So, are you just going to walk up to him and gut him?"

Del's expression didn't change. "I don't know."

"You think you might want to consider it?"

Now she looked at me. "I have considered it for six years. Now is the time for doing."

"But you can't *do* without thinking it through." I shifted in the saddle, taking weight on locked arms braced against the pommel. "He's not a popular man. Others will want to kill him. I doubt he walks alone. And if he's done all the things you say, I doubt he *pisses* alone."

Del's tone was steady. "I will find a way."

I sat back down in the saddle. "Can we at least get a meal first? And maybe a place to stay?"

Del extended a hand, indicating the plateau. "*There* is a place to stay."

"I kind of thought we might go find a room. It might not have a roof, but then neither of us is a tanzeer. And it doesn't look like rain."

Automatically, Del glanced up at the sky. It was a clear, brilliant blue, without a cloud apparent. But this was border country. This was *odd* country; it just didn't feel right. Too many bits mixed together: vegetation, temperature, people.

"Sandtiger! Tiger! *Del!*"

I glanced around. Frowned. Peered at the circles, but saw no one I knew. Only men in the circles with swords in their hands.

"There." Del pointed in the other direction. "Isn't that—Alric?"

Alric? "Oh—*Alric.*" The Northerner who'd helped us in Rusali, the domain just before Julah. I squinted. "Yes, I think it is."

Alric approached, waving. With him walked a short, fat woman. Two little girls preceded them; in one arm he carried a third. At least, I think it was a girl; sometimes it's hard to tell.

Del slid out of her saddle. "Lena had her baby."

I stayed in mine. "And, from the look of it, is expecting yet another."

The little girls, upon arrival, hurled themselves at Del, who bent down to receive them. I was privately astonished they even remembered her; they were all of three and four—or maybe four and five; at this age, who can tell?—and they'd only spent a week or so around us when Alric had taken us into his home after I'd gotten myself wounded. But Del is very good with children, and the girls had adored her. Obviously their opinions hadn't changed.

I watched her as the girls competed for her hugs. She was smiling, laughing with them, exchanging Southron greetings. I almost expected pain, expecting Del to see Kalle in their faces, but there was only happiness. I saw no trace of anguish.

About then Alric arrived with his heavily pregnant wife. The last time I'd seen her she'd also been heavily pregnant. And since the older girls were but a year apart, I began to suspect Lena and Alric enjoyed active nights together.

Lena was Southron, and looked it; he was clearly Northern. The girls were a little of both. They had their mother's black hair and dark skin, but their father's bright blue eyes and high-arched cheekbones. They'd be beauties when they were grown.

Alric was grinning. "I thought so!" he said. "I told Lena it was you, but she said no. She said by now Del would have come to her senses and looked for a Northern man instead of a Southron danjac."

"Oh?" I looked down at Lena, who showed white teeth at me. "I suppose you think she'd be better off with another Alric."

Lena patted her swollen belly. "A strong, lusty Northerner is good for a woman's soul." Black eyes glinted. "And other things as well."

Alric laughed aloud. "Although so far all this lusty Northerner makes is girls." *He* patted Lena's belly. "Maybe this one will be a boy."

"And if not?" I asked.

Alric's grin widened. "We'll keep trying until we get one."

I waited for Del's comment; surely she had one. But the girls were chattering at her and she had no chance to speak.

Lena waved welcoming hands. "Come, come . . . we have a house in the city not far from here. You will come and stay with us; there are plenty of rooms. We can wait for the jhihadi together."

I glanced at Alric. "Is that why you came?"

He shifted the baby in his arms. "Everyone else was coming to Iskandar. Even the tanzeers. I thought it might be worthwhile to come up myself and see how the dancing was." He gestured with his head in the direction of the circles. "And, as you can see, there are sword-dancers aplenty. There will be coin as well. Or a tanzeer who'll hire me. With all these little mouths to feed, extra coin would be welcome."

Three little mouths to feed, and a fourth on the way. No wonder he'd come to Iskandar, but I thought it odd for Lena. She couldn't be far from delivering.

Lena sensed my thought. "A child born in the presence of a jhi-hadi will be blessed throughout his life."

"Or hers," Alric said affably; the possibility of yet another daughter did not appear to trouble him.

He hadn't changed much. Still big. Still Northern. Still a sword-dancer. But it seemed odd to look at him now—smiling, cheerful, openly friendly—and recall how I had felt when I'd first met him. How I'd thought he was after Del. I hadn't trusted him at all until we'd sparred in an alley circle. You learn a man that way. Learn what he is made of.

"Alric," I said suddenly, "how is your dancing these days?"

His brow creased. "Well enough. Why?"

"How'd you feel about going a few matches? For old time's sake."

He grinned, displaying big teeth. Alric was big all over. "You always beat me," he said. "But I've been practicing. Now maybe I can beat you."

I glanced across at the circles. "Shall we go find out?"

"Not *now*," Lena said. "First you will come to our house. You will eat. Rest. Give us the news you have. And we will give you ours." She slanted a glance at Alric. "Time for dancing and drinking later."

Del came forward with a girl on either arm. The roan trailed behind them. "We are grateful for your offer. Your news will be welcome."

I was a little surprised. I expected Del to want to go haring off after news of Ajani, trying to track him down in Iskandar, or find out if he was expected. But apparently she'd thought about what I'd said. If she was to kill the man, it would have to be carefully planned.

"Come," Lena said. She turned and waddled away.

Alric looked at Del over the black-fuzzed head of the baby. He smiled, said something in Northern dialect, slanted an oblique glance at me.

Del's chin came up. She answered briefly in the same dialect, then told the girls to show her the way to their quarters. Tugging on her arms, they led her toward the city. The roan trotted behind.

"And what was that?" I asked Alric.

He grinned. "I asked her if a Southroner was enough man for a free-hearted uplander woman." Blue eyes glinted. "Speaking as an older brother looking out for a sister's welfare."

"Of course," I agreed dryly. "And what did the sister *tell* the older brother?"

"There is no Southron translation. It was a Northern obscenity." Alric's grin stretched wide. "Which says something all on its own."

Well, I suppose it does. But he didn't tell me what.

"Let's go eat," I said sourly.

Alric's eyes were guileless. "Would you like to hold the baby?"

Which gave me an opportunity to use an untranslatable *Southron* obscenity.

The toothy grin widened. "And here I heard you were a father."

The stud walked onto my heels. Since I'd stopped moving, it wasn't surprising. "A father—? Oh. That." In disgust, I elbowed the stud in the nose and pushed him back a step. "Have you seen him?"

Alric hitched the baby higher on a big shoulder and headed for the city. "Your son? No. Just heard there was a boy here—young man, really—who says he's the Sandtiger's son."

"He isn't," I muttered, matching my pace to his. "At least, not as far as I know."

"Does it matter if he is?"

I thought about it. "Maybe."

"Maybe? *Maybe?* What an odd thing to say." The baby caught a handful of blond hair and tugged; Alric freed it gently. "Don't you want to have a son to carry on your blood?"

What blood? And whose? For all I knew, it could be the blood of borjuni killers. "I figure I'm doing a good enough job carrying it all on my own."

Alric scoffed, but gently. "A man should have a son. A man should have a family. A man should have kinfolk to sing the songs of him."

"Northerner," I muttered.

"And if you meet him in the circle?"

I stopped short. "He's a sword-dancer? My s—this young man?"

Alric shrugged, frowning a little. "I heard of him at the circles. I assumed he was a sword-dancer, but perhaps he isn't. Perhaps he's a tanzeer."

My son, a tanzeer. Which meant he could hire me.

"No," I said, "I don't think so."

"Well, it doesn't matter. He is whatever he is." Alric lengthened his stride and led me into the city.

Chapter 3

The building Alric had claimed for Lena and the girls was large—four rooms—but lacked a roof and half of a wall on one side. Into the room lacking most of one wall he put the carthorse and his own mount, a bald-faced bay gelding. It left two rooms vacant: he offered one to Del and me.

I've never been one for sharing close confinement, preferring privacy, but in some situations it's good to have folk around. I thought it possible this might become one of them. As the city filled with strangers, trouble would inevitably break out. There would be thieves, certainly, come to prey upon worshipers, and feuds between hostile races. And if the promised jhihadi never arrived—which I believed was likely—frustration would drive impatient people to do things they might not otherwise think about. Like starting fights, and killing. All things considered, I thought Alric's offer generous. Del and I agreed.

Lena sent the two little girls—Felka and Fabiola; don't ask me which was which—off to help Del with settling our belongings in one of the other rooms. I briefly considered lending a hand, then decided against it; Del looked pleased to spend time with the girls, even though they'd be little help, and I felt more like sitting with Alric by the fire, sharing a bota of aquivi. Lena prepared food.

Alric wiped his mouth. "Did you ever find Del's brother?"

I accepted the bota. "We found him. We left him."

"Dead?"

"No. With the Vashni."

Alric grimaced. "Good as dead, then. They're not a hospitable tribe."

I cocked an eyebrow in his direction. "It was a Vashni you got your sword off of, wasn't it? The blade with human thighbone hilt?"

Alric nodded. "But I put it away and got a Southron sword. I decided it was a bit too grisly to use a sword with a hilt made out of the bone of a man I never knew—or maybe a man I *did* know."

"New swords," I reflected. "A lot of that going around."

"I noticed." Alric's eyes were on the harness next to my leg. "No more Singlestroke?"

I accepted a flat, hot loaf from Lena, blew on it to cool it. "Got broken in a sword-dance after we left Julah." I blew some more, then bit. The steaming loaf was nutty, flaky, delicious. "Like you, I've got another."

"But yours is a *jivatma*."

Alric's tone was odd. I glanced at him, glanced at the sheathed sword, then looked back at him. Recalled it was Alric who'd first told me about *jivatmas*. About Northern blooding-blades, and how rank in the North was reckoned.

"*Jivatma*," I agreed. "Del took me to Staal-Ysta."

Blond brows swooped up. Then down. "Since you have a blooding-blade, I'm assuming you are a *kaidin*."

"I'm Southron," I said. "I'm a seventh-level sword-dancer. I don't need a fancy name."

"But you carry a *jivatma*."

Irritably, I swallowed hot bread, then washed it down with aqivi. "Believe me, Alric, I'd give it to you if I could. But the thrice-cursed thing won't let me."

Alric smiled. "If you enter a circle with a blooding-blade at your beck, no one will defeat you." He paused thoughtfully. "Except maybe Del."

"No," I blurted.

"But she has a *jivatma*, too—"

I shook my head. "That's not what I meant. I meant, Del and I have done it once. We'll never do it again."

Alric grinned. "You lost."

It stung, but only a little. "Nobody lost. Nobody won. Both of us nearly died." I drank, then continued before he could ask any questions. "And as for taking my sword into a circle—no. Not *here* at any rate—this is exhibition. I just don't think it's fair."

Alric shrugged. "Then don't sing. An unkeyed *jivatma* isn't much more than a sword."

"It isn't like that." I accepted a second loaf. "You don't understand. This sword wasn't quenched properly, the first *or* second time."

"Second!" Alric's eyes widened. "You requenched your blade?"

"No choice," I muttered, biting into the second loaf. "The thing's a pain in the rump, and I plan to replace it. I'll put this one away and use a Southron sword."

"There's a swordsmith here," he said. "With so many sword-dancers present, a smith would be a fool to ignore such a windfall. His name is Sarad, and he's set up a smithy out by the circles."

"I'll see him tomorrow," I said, as Del came back with the girls.

A faint frown puckered her brow, though she gave nothing away in behavior. The girls joined their mother in preparing the meal, and Del came over to sit near Alric and me.

"What's up?" I asked.

The puckered brow didn't smooth. "Can't you feel it? The weather is changing. It doesn't feel right."

Alric and I both glanced around, assessing daylight and temperature. The way the day *tasted*, odd as it sounds.

"Cooler," Alric remarked. "Well, I won't complain. After living so long in the South, I could use some Northern weather."

"This is the border." I shrugged. "Sometimes it's cool, sometimes hot."

"It *was* hot," Del said, "all of an hour ago. But now it's cooler. Significantly cooler; it just doesn't feel right."

I glanced up at the roof, which wasn't really a roof. A few spindly timber rafters remained, but most had rotted and fallen in, supplying wood for Lena's cookfire. All four rooms were in similar shape, which left them mostly open to the elements. No proper shade, but no cover, either. Alric had strung up a couple of blankets to provide a makeshift roof, but it wouldn't do much if the weather did turn chancy.

Del just shook her head. "I feel something in my bones."

I arched unsubtle brows. "Getting along in years?"

She slanted me a glance. "One of us certainly is."

"Here." Lena handed clay bowls around with bread and mutton stew. "With the tribes coming in, we should have mutton enough to spare. And all the merchants, too; we could live here for months."

I thought it unlikely they'd have to.

"I could set snares," Del offered, and instantly Felka and Fabiola wanted to accompany her.

It reminded me of something. For a moment I was swept away somewhere familiar, and yet unknown; abruptly the feeling died, and I realized what I remembered. Del offering to set snares while a tow-headed Borderer boy asked to help her. Massou, Adara's son, who had hosted a Northern demon and nearly destroyed us all.

Loki. It was enough to make me shiver. Thank the gods for the Cantéada, who had sung them into a trap-circle and freed the Borderers.

"Later," Del promised the girls. "We'll see first if it's going to storm."

Lena cuddled the baby against her breasts. "At least this little one need not concern herself with where her meals are coming from."

Alric's eyes glinted. "Nor I, if it comes to it."

A gust of wind blew into the room, scattering handfuls of dust. A cool, damp-tasting wind, hinting at coming change. After months spent in the North, I knew the promise well.

Del looked at me. "Rain."

Well, it *was* the border. A day's ride south of here and rain was almost an unknown thing.

"Maybe." I drank *amnit.*

"Rain," she said again, mostly to herself.

Alric looked overhead. Two blankets tied to rotting timbers, and the weather tasted of rain.

Lena shifted uneasily. Southron-born and bred, rain was not to be trusted, or understood very well. "Maybe we should look for a house with a roof."

Alric's blond hair swung against shoulder blades as he shook his head, still staring into the sky. "No roofs for people like us . . . the tanzeers have claimed them all."

"All?" I asked. "There aren't *that* many people here—and there can't be that many tanzeers. Not yet."

Alric shrugged. "I looked. All the decent dwellings were claimed. We took the best we could find."

I set the bota aside. "Tell you what . . . I want to take a little walk anyway, just to check things out. I'll see what I can find in the way of better shelter. If there *is* to be a storm, we might as well be prepared."

Alric rose. "I'll go to the merchants and buy more blankets, some skins . . . we can put up a makeshift roof."

Del shook her head as I glanced her way. "I'll stay and help Lena."

It surprised me a little. Del is not a woman for women's things, as she has so often been at such pains to tell me. But neither is she a woman to ignore the needs of others; Lena had her hands—and belly—full with four children. Del never shirks assistance if she can offer any.

Well, it was fine with me. I didn't think Del would approve of me talking to a swordsmith about another blade.

I left them all behind and headed out toward the circles. More wind kicked up as I walked, gusting down through narrow alley-ways and curling around corners to snatch at my burnous. Grit stung my face; I blinked to clear my eyes.

"Sandtiger? *Tiger!*"

I stopped, squinting, and turned. From out of a broken door-way stepped a Northerner, blond braids hanging to his waist. And a scar across his top lip.

"Garrod," I said, on a note of disbelief.

He grinned as he approached, blue eyes bright. "I never thought to see you again, once you and Del left the Cantéada and went north." He sobered, recalling the reasons. "Did Del settle her trouble?"

"Yes and no," I answered. "What are you doing here? Iskandar isn't exactly Kisiri."

He shrugged, hooking thumbs into a wide belt. His braids swung; dangling colored beads rattled in the wind. "We started for Kisiri. Got about halfway there—but then we heard about Iskandar; that people were coming here. I didn't know anything about any Oracle, or this promised messiah—at least, not right away—but I'd picked up a string of horses along the way. Since trading is my business, I wanted to go where I could buy or sell. Only a fool would ignore such an opportunity, and I've never been a fool."

Not lately, maybe. I hadn't been so sure before, when we'd briefly ridden together. Garrod was a horse-speaker, a man who had a knack with horses. He called it a kind of magic. He claimed he could *talk* to them, understand them, the way a man understands a man. I wasn't so certain that was true, but he did have a way with them. I'd seen it in the stud.

"So, you didn't go on with Adara and her children after all." It surprised me a little. Garrod had sworn he'd take them to Kisiri, but a man can change his mind.

Garrod grinned. "Oh, I went with them . . . by then I had no choice. The girl didn't give me any." And he shouted for Cipriana.

She came. So did Adara, her mother. And so did her brother, Massou.

I blinked in dull surprise, surrounded on the instant. They were clearly as startled, and certainly more pleased. I felt a little awkward: the last time I'd spent any time with them, they'd been hosting hostile demons.

Bronze-haired, green-eyed Adara was flushed with color, which didn't quite agree with her hair, but set her eyes aglint. She was oddly reserved, almost shy; I recalled, with a twinge of discomfort, she had hoped for affection from me. But it was Del who had it all; Adara had surrendered the field, but obviously recalled it.

Massou, blond and blue-eyed like his sister, was taller than I remembered. Now eleven, in place of ten; Cipriana was sixteen.

Cipriana was also *pregnant*.

Now I knew what Garrod meant about not having any choice. Women can do that to you.

Like her mother, she was red-faced, but for a different reason. It didn't take much to figure it out, either; she stepped up next to Garrod and twined fingers into his belt. Pale hair was tied back from a face delicately rounded from pregancy. I saw again the Northern features that had reminded me of Del. A younger, softer Del. The Del before Ajani.

Garrod dropped an arm around her shoulder. "We're kinfolk now."

"So I can see," I said dryly.

"Is Del here?" Massou demanded.

"Del's here," I agreed. "We're a couple of streets over."

The boy's eyes lighted. "You could come *here*," he asserted.

Adara nodded. "You could. We have enough room. See?" She gestured toward the building.

"We're with friends," I explained.

Garrod shrugged. "Bring them."

"They have three small girls, and another on the way."

The horse-speaker grinned again. "*We* have one on the way." Which made Cipriana blush.

"There is room," Adara said quietly. "I understand if you have no wish to share, but there is room for you all."

Her manner was a mixture of emotions. Clearly she recalled how I had proved uninterested in her availability: a widow whose husband had been unable because of bad health. It had taken courage for her to speak at all; I'd let her down gently, but no doubt it had been difficult. And then the loki had invaded her body, and her children, forcing them all into bizarre behavior.

She recalled it all, was embarrassed, and yet wanted my company, which embarrassed her yet again.

I looked past her at the building, thinking of the others. "Do you have a roof?"

Garrod shook his head. "The tanzeers have all the buildings with proper roofs."

"So I keep hearing." I glanced up at the graying sky. "I think there's a storm brewing."

"But it's warm," Cipriana protested.

Massou disagreed. "Cool."

Garrod sniffed the wind, and frowned. "It smells almost like snow."

"Snow!" Adara was astonished. "Are you forgetting we come from a place not far from here? We know the weather. It never snows on the border."

"It smells like *something*," I said. But nothing like the hounds.

Garrod still frowned. "I think I will see to the horses."

Cipriana lingered. "Do you still have the stud?"

"Of course."

"Oh." Her expression changed. The stud hadn't liked her much. Hadn't liked any of them, once the loki had climbed inside.

"He'd be different, now," I told her.

"He bit me," Massou said.

"Yes, well, he had his reasons. He's bitten me, too, and I was never a loki."

Adara's color deepened. "I wish we could forget that."

"It wasn't you," I told her. "I know that, and so does Del. We don't blame you for any of it."

"We could have *killed* you."

Or worse. But I didn't say it. "Let it go," I said quietly. "Don't let it eat at you."

"Can I see Del?" Massou asked.

As always, I looked to Adara. There had been a time when she'd wanted her children to avoid us.

Adara, comprehending my hesitation, nodded at once, as if to dispell any hint of her former reluctance. "Of course you may go, but only if invited."

"Del won't mind," I said. "I'm sure she'll be glad to see him."

"I want to go," the boy declared.

I gestured. "Two streets over, third house on the left."

Massou darted away.

Cipriana murmured something about finding Garrod and went away. Adara smiled at me and stripped wind-teased hair out of eyes. "You look a little tired. Would you care for something to drink? Eat?"

"Just ate." I was oddly ill at ease. "How long will you be staying?"

"Until Garrod is ready to leave." She shrugged a little, hearing how dependent it sounded. "He is a good man and treats Cipriana well. They care for one another. And it's easier for Massou and me to stay with them. I can help with the baby."

I smiled. "First grandchild."

Her eyes glowed. "Yes. Kesar's blood will be carried on."

She had buried her husband on the road from the border to Kisiri. A strong woman, Adara; as strong, in her own way, as Del. Borderers have to be.

Wind blew grit in our faces. It gave me an excuse. "Best go inside," I said.

Adara nodded absently, looking into my face intently. As if she sought an answer. I don't know what she saw. I don't know what she wanted. All I could do was wait.

She smiled a little eventually, sensing my unease. She put a hand on my forearm. A callused, toughened hand. But its touch was somehow tender. "A good man," she said gently. "We will never forget you."

I watched her turn toward the house. Watched her walk through the door. Saw the quiet swing of hips; the flicker of wind-blown skirts; a glint of bronze-colored hair. Heard the lilt of a woman's voice lifted in soft song.

Don't ask me why. I've never been one for music. But it touched something inside me, and I followed it anyway.

Adara turned, startled, as I stepped into the doorway. The song broke off in her throat; one hand was spread across it.

She was suddenly vulnerable. And something in me answered. "Are you all right?" I asked. "Do you need anything?"

Adara swallowed heavily. "Don't ask that," she said. "You might not get the answer you want."

I glanced at a broken wall.

"They're somewhere else," she said, interpreting the glance.

"No, I just meant—" I broke it off. "It could be awkward, if they misunderstood."

Adara smiled a little. "Yes."

Shadows crept into the room, softening her face. Snow or no snow, a storm was brewing. The light had changed.

"I wanted to say something," I told her.

Adara's color altered.

It was harder than I'd thought. I've never been a man for really talking to a woman of things that have substance, of things to do with feelings, except for Del. And even that is sometimes uncomfortable, because we think so differently. But something about Adara made me want to help.

I drew in a deep breath. "It's none of my business. But I'll say it anyway."

"Yes," she said faintly.

"A woman like you needs a husband. You've been alone too long. Del might disagree . . . she'd probably say a woman is often better without a man—maybe, for some, she's right—but I don't think you're one of them."

"No." It was a whisper.

"You shouldn't be alone. I know there's Garrod to help, but that's not what you need. You need a man of your own. Someone you can tend; someone who can tend you."

Adara said nothing.

I shifted a little. "All I mean is, there might be a chance for you. Here, in Iskandar. There will be plenty of men."

A brief, eloquent gesture indicating herself. "I'm no longer a young woman, and I have two children."

"Cipriana has her own life now. Massou will be a man soon enough; for now he needs a father. He's quick-witted. A man could do much worse than to take you and the boy."

She stared at me a long moment. Her eyes were full of thoughts. Of possibilities.

She shut them a moment. Then looked straight back at me and carefully wet her lips. "I think you'd better go."

It took me aback. "What?"

Her mouth trembled a little. "This is not what I want to hear, this talk of other men. Not from you. Not from *you*."

It wasn't what I had intended. Somehow I'd made it worse. And for both of us; after too many weeks without Del in my bed, I was very aware of Adara. I'm not made for abstinence. I didn't *want* Adara . . . but part of me wanted a woman.

Most of me wanted Del so bad it confused the rest of me.

Adara's smile was bittersweet. "I didn't think I could say this: I won't be a substitute."

It was cold water. The wind blew through the room, rippling the gauze of her skirts. Stripping the hair from her face, so I could see her pride.

I wanted to touch her, but couldn't. It would only make things worse.

"For someone else, you won't be." I turned and went out of the house.

Chapter 4

Sarad the swordsmith was one-eyed. The blind eye was puckered closed behind a shrunken lid. The good eye was black. Matching hair was twisted into a single braid and bound in dyed orange leather at the back of his neck. He wore an ocher-colored burnous and a leather belt plated with enameled copper disks. The colors were bright and varied.

Sarad showed me his smile. He sat cross-legged on a blanket with swords set out before him. Steel glowed sullenly in the dying light of the day. "These are my best," he said. "I can *make* better, of course . . . but that would take time. Have you the time to spare?"

Well, yes and no. I could spare the time for him to make a blade to order, but only if I was willing to use my *jivatma* in the meantime.

Squatting across from Sarad, I thought about Kem, the swordsmith on Staal-Ysta. It had taken days to fashion Samiel, and with my help. But mostly because of rituals; Kem rushed nothing. And while Sarad probably wouldn't hurry either—not if he wanted to forge a good sword—he had no elaborate rituals to eat away extra hours.

The swords all looked fine. They felt fine, too; I'd already handled six, trying them out on simple and intricate patterns. Two had a balance I found to my liking, but they were only halfway measures. I'd spent more than half of my life using a sword made specifically for *me*. I didn't like the idea of dancing with a ready-made blade created for anyone with the coin to buy it.

But I liked even less the idea of dancing with Chosa Dei lying in wait in my steel.

Sarad gestured, indicating a sword. "I would be pleased to offer the Sandtiger my best at a very good price."

I shook my head. "Your best isn't here. Your best is still in your hands."

Something glittered in his eye. "Of course. A sword-dancer such as yourself appreciates true skill and creativity; I can make you a perfect sword. All I require is time."

I picked up one of the two swords I thought would do. The steel was clean and smooth, with keen, bright edges. It had the proper weight, the proper flex, the proper grip, the proper promise.

"This one," I said finally.

Sarad named his price.

I shook my head. "Too much."

"It comes with a scabbard—see? And I am a master, Sandtiger—"

"But this isn't the best you can do. Do you expect me to pay full price?"

He thought it over. Considered what it might do for business if the Sandtiger carried his sword. Named a lower price.

I counted out the coin.

Sarad pocketed it. "Have you a tanzeer yet?"

"Not yet. Why?"

The swordsmith gestured casually. "I have heard tanzeers are looking for sword-dancers."

"I heard that, too." I frowned a little. "Do you know *why* the tanzeers are hiring so many all at once?"

Sarad shrugged. "I hear things . . . things about the tribes, and the jhihadi." He glanced around, then looked back at me. "I think the tanzeers are afraid. So they unite in the face of a powerful enemy and hire men to fight."

I looked at Sarad gravely. "If this rumor is true, it would indicate the tanzeers believe this jhihadi exists—or *will* exist. And I've never known tanzeers to believe in much of anything except their own greed."

Sarad shrugged. "It's what I have heard." He eyed me thoughtfully. "I thought surely a man such as the Sandtiger would be sought by many, and hired immediately."

I sheathed the new-bought sword and thought about how best to attach it to my harness, specifically made for another sword. "I only got here at midday."

"Then you are slow." Sarad smiled. "Your son arrived a week ago."

I stiffened. "Where *is* this person?"

He shrugged. "I've seen him here and there. He visits the circles, lingers, then goes to the cantinas."

"Which ones?"

A flick of his hand. "That one. And that one. And the other one street over. There are many cantinas here. Sword-dancers like to drink."

I rose. "I think it's about time I paid 'my son' a visit."

"He will like that," Sarad said. "He's very proud of you."

I grunted and walked away.

He had, I'd been told, an old gray mare with a white splash on her face and three white legs. He was dark-haired and blue-eyed. Young; maybe eighteen or nineteen. No sword. A necklet of claws at his throat. And a tongue busy with my name. All of which meant it shouldn't be hard to find him.

Except I couldn't find him.

Oh, people knew of him. I went to each of the three cantinas Sarad had mentioned, plus two more. None of them were *real* cantinas, being little more than broken buildings where a Southroner with liquor had set up hasty shop, selling cups of aqivi and *amnit* at premium prices. But no one seemed to mind. It was a place—or places—to gather, swapping tales and seeking work.

Yes, men said, they knew him. And they described him in the fashion I'd grown accustomed to hearing. But none of them had a name. Everyone knew him only as the Sandtiger's cub.

I found it disconcerting. *Anyone* could claim the same, since no one knew any different, and do all sorts of nefarious deeds, thereby harming my reputation, which I'd been at some pains to establish. It had taken years. And then some boy fancying himself my son appropriates it without my knowledge.

I didn't like it much.

Even if he *was* my son.

After a while, I gave up. But I cautioned everybody to point him out to me if he ever showed his face where I could see it.

Which gave them all something to laugh at: a grown man—the *Sandtiger*—had mislaid his own son.

I went "home" with my new-bought sword and thought bad things about the man who claimed my blood; by inference, also my name. I didn't like it at all. My name was *mine*, won at a very high cost. I didn't want to share it. Not even with a son.

I woke up because of the stud. It was very late and very dark, and everyone else was asleep, bundled up in blankets because of the temperature. Alric, in the other room, snored gently in Lena's arms.

Del, in our room, slept alone in her personal bedding. As I did in my own.

The stud continued to stomp, paw, snort. If I let him go much longer, he'd wake up everyone else. And since I didn't much feel like making excuses for a horse, who wouldn't have any, I decided to shut him up.

I sighed, peeled back blankets, crawled to my feet. Alric's makeshift roof dipped down from rotting rafters, but it cut out some of the wind. It also cut out the light. I had to strain to see.

It was cold outside of my blankets. Here I'd been saying how nice it was to be back home again where it was warm, and it had to go and get cold. But I shut it out of my mind—glad I'd slept in my clothes—and went out to see to the stud.

Del's blue gelding was tied in one of the corners of the room Alric had deemed the stable. He'd been roused by the stud's noise, but stood quietly enough. The stud, however, did not; tied out of reach of the roan, he nonetheless warned him away.

Alric's blanket-and-skin roof did not extend to the "stable," but the light was little better. There was no moon, no stars. It was all I could do to see through the damp gloom. Wind brushed my face, crept down the neck of my tunic. I put my hand on the stud's warm rump, then moved around to his head. Promised to remove his *gehetties* if he didn't quiet down; meanwhile, I tried to interpret his signs of unease.

It wasn't just the gelding. The stud didn't like him, but he tolerated him well enough. He'd learned to over the weeks. And I doubted it was the packhorse belonging to Alric, an old, quiet mare. He'd already proved uninterested in her, which meant it was something else entirely. Something I couldn't see.

Wind scraped through the broken wall, spitting dust and bits of grit. The stud laid back his ears.

I put a soothing hand on his neck. "Take it easy, old son. It's just a little wind. And the wall's breaking most of it; let's hear no complaints out of you."

There was, in the dimness, the faint shine of a single eye. Ears remained pinned.

I thought briefly of Garrod. He'd tell me he knew what it was just by "talking" with the stud.

Who wasn't talking to me.

Then again, he was. He stomped a foreleg smartly and came very close to my toes.

"Hey. Watch yourself, old man, or I *will* cut off—"

A quick sideways twist of his head and he shut teeth upon my finger.

I swore. Punched him in the eye to make sure I had his attention; he'd ignore me otherwise, and I might lose the finger. Then, when he paid attention, I retrieved my hand from his mouth.

And began to swear in earnest.

I backed up a prudent step, out of the stud's reach, and squinted at the finger. It was ugly.

I swore some more, gritting the words in my teeth, and then proceeded to hold the entire hand out—torn finger included—and tell myself, repeatedly, it didn't hurt at all.

I wrung the hand a little. The finger didn't like it.

I walked around in a jerky circle, thinking mean thoughts about the stud. Wished briefly I was a woman so tears wouldn't be disapproved of; I didn't cry, of course, but thought it might be nice to have that kind of release. But a man, with others near, doesn't show that much of himself.

"Let me see," she said.

I jerked around, swore some more, told her I was fine.

"Stop lying," she said. "And stop trying to be such a *man*. Admit the finger hurts."

"It hurts," I gritted promptly. "And now it *still* hurts; admitting it didn't help."

"Is it broken?"

"I can't tell."

"Did you look?"

"Not very long."

Del came closer. "Then let me see."

The hand was shaking. It didn't want to be touched.

"I'll be gentle," she promised.

"That's what they all say."

"Here, let me see." She took my wrist into one hand.

"Don't touch it," I said sharply.

"I'll *look*, I won't touch. Of course if it *is* broken, the bone will have to be set."

"I don't think it's broken. He didn't bite that hard."

Del inspected the finger as best she could in poor light. "Hard enough to shred the skin. You're bleeding."

"Blood washes off—*ouch*—"

"Sorry," she murmured.

Her head was bent. Pale hair obscured her face; fell softly over her shoulders; lingered on her breasts. I couldn't see her expression. Only hear her voice. Smell her familiar scent. Feel her hands on mine.

Arousal was abrupt.

Oh, hoolies, bascha—how long can this go on—?

"It's raining." Del glanced up, peering at the sky through the place where the roof had been. Lips parted. Hair fell away from her face. A sculpted, flawless face made brittle by years of obsession. By months of determined *focus*.

I thought suddenly of Adara, who'd be more than pleased to have me. But wasn't a substitute; for Del, what woman could be?

"So it is," I said tightly.

Raindrops crawled through her hair, running with pinkish blood, the blood from my bitten finger resting, like my hand, unquietly on her shoulder. Wanting to cup her jaw; wanting to touch her face; demanding to lock itself tightly in slick pale hair——

Del swallowed visibly. "We should get under cover."

I didn't even blink as water ran down my face. "Yes, we probably should."

Del looked at me. Neither of us moved.

Rain fell harder yet. Neither of us moved.

My voice was unsteady. "I can think of better places."

Del didn't say anything.

"I can think of *dryer* places."

Del didn't say anything.

Tension exploded between us. "You'd better go back," I said harshly. "I don't know how much longer I can respect your precious focus."

Del touched my face. Her sword hand trembled.

Oh, Delilah—*don't*—

In the darkness, her eyes were black. *"To hoolies with my focus."*

Chapter 5

By dawn, we were back in bedrolls. This time we shared one, spreading blankets and pelts in the chill of a too-damp morning, trying to hide from the breeze curling down through dripping blankets.

"Too long," I murmured weakly. "Can we forget your focus more often?"

Del, pulling hair from beneath my shoulder, twisted her mouth a little. "Sidetracked already; I told you men can't keep their minds on anything if a woman is at issue."

It didn't sting at all, because she didn't mean it to. I found it a welcome respite. "Have I destroyed your concentration?"

"Last night, certainly. But not today."

"No?"

"No," she answered lightly. "I'll ask my sword for it back."

For some strange reason, it disturbed me. "Bascha—you don't mean it."

"Of course I mean it."

I twisted sideways, putting room between us, so I could look at her clearly. "Do you mean to tell me you plan to shed all the humanity you just regained?"

Del's brows arched. "And do *you* mean to tell me I should forget who I am in the name of a single night's bedding?"

I scraped at a stubbled cheek. "Well, I sort of thought it might lead to *more* than a single night's bedding. Like maybe *lots* of single nights' bedding all strung together, until we can't tell them apart any more."

Del thought about it. "Possibly," she conceded.

I was moved to protest, but didn't. Couldn't. I saw the glint in her eyes. "Hoolies, I think she's thawed!"

But the amusement faded away. "Tiger, I dismiss nothing about last night. But neither can I dismiss what I came here to do."

I sighed, stretched out again, scratched at an eyebrow. "I know. I wish I could ask you to forget about Ajani, but I don't suppose it would be fair."

"I'd never ask it of you."

No, maybe not that. "But you *did* try to sell my soul to Staal-Ysta for a year."

Del stiffened beside me. "And how many years will you remind me?"

I lay there not breathing. Not because of her tone, which was a combination of shame, distress, irritation. And not because of her posture, which bespoke the deep-seated pain. But because of the words themselves.

"Years," I echoed softly.

"Yes." She *was* irritated. "Will you bring it up once a year? Twice? Even once a week?"

I swallowed heavily. "Once a year, I think."

"Why?" The cry was instinctive. "Haven't I said I was wrong?"

"Once a year," I repeated, "because it means we *have* that year."

Del lay very still. She didn't breathe, either. "Oh," was all she said, after a time of consideration. Of self-interpretation.

The prospect was frightening. But also strangely pleasing.

I'm not alone anymore.

You could argue I hadn't been, not really; not since Del and I had first joined up, except for a couple of enforced separations. But we had not, until this moment, explored anything past the moment. Sword-dancers never do.

Men and women must.

Which led me to other things. "I wonder if he *is* . . ." I let it trail off.

Del shifted beneath blankets. "Wonder what? About who?"

"If he really is my son."

She smiled. "Would it please you if he is?"

I thought about it. "I don't know."

"Tiger! A *son*."

"But what good is it to discover you have a grown son you never knew existed? And that if he *does* exist, it's only because of a bedding you can't even remember.'

Del's tone was dry. "Have you had so many as that?"

"Yes."

She eyed me askance a moment, then rolled her head straight again and stared up at the lightening sky. "Well, a son is a son. It shouldn't matter how he was gotten, just that he was."

"How Kalle was gotten matters."

I thought she might snap at me, as she can. I thought she might swear at me, as she can; I taught her most of the terms. I thought she might even withdraw all together; she's very good at that, if she's of no mind to share. Del hides herself very well.

But this time she didn't try.

Del sighed heavily. "Kalle was never Kalle. Kalle was a cause. Kalle was an excuse. She justified the pain. She made it easier to hate."

"So you could give her up."

"Yes. So I could fulfill my oaths."

"Which were made *before* you even knew you were pregnant."

Del frowned. "Yes. I made them even as my kinfolk died; even as Jamail burned; even as Ajani broke my maidenhead. Does it matter when? They were made. Well worth the doing. The honor is worth the strife."

Like Del, I stared at the sky. "You gave up a child. Why should I acknowledge mine?"

After a lengthy, painful silence, Del turned her head away. "I have no answer for you."

"There isn't one," I told her, and rolled over to pull her close.

I had fully expected, when Del discovered it, she would say something about the new sword. But not that it was broken.

I turned from arranging bedding to dry in the sun. Except there wasn't any; clouds still choked the sky. *"What?"*

"It's broken," she repeated.

"It *can't* be!" I stepped across bedding and stopped dead by the new scabbard. It lay precisely where I had left it: on a blanket by Samiel.

The sword was spilled out of the scabbard. The blade was broken in half.

"Bad steel," she said.

I shook my head. "It wasn't. I'm sure of it. I examined it carefully."

Del shrugged; the weapon, being plain, unmagicked sword, held no interest for her. "When pressed too hard, it can break. Who did you dance against? Alric?"

"Del, I didn't dance. Not against anyone. All I did was buy this sword. I've never even *sparred* with it."

"Bad forging, then."

"I'd never buy a bad sword. You know that." Now I was irritated. It shouldn't matter that it wasn't a Northern *jivatma*, only that it was a sword I was entrusting my life to. Or would have, had it been whole. I inspected the sword closely. "The hilt and this half look perfectly normal. Let's see the rest of it."

I picked up the scabbard, turned it upside down, shook the rest of the blade out. It landed on the hilt half with a dull, ugly clank.

Del's indrawn breath was loud.

"Black," I said blankly.

"Just like your *jivatma*."

We locked eyes for only an instant. And then I was grabbing harness, grabbing scabbard, closing a hand on the hilt. And jerking it from the sheath.

Samiel was whole. Samiel was unchanged. Steel shone bright and unblemished—except for black charring stretching fully a third of the blade.

"There's more," I said. "More discoloration."

Del didn't say a word.

I looked at the broken blade. "He unmade it," I said plainly.

She knelt down beside me, looking more closely at the *jivatma*. "He's trapped in your sword."

"He *unmakes* things," I declared. "Don't you understand? The new sword was a threat. He wants me on his own terms, not risking a loss by default."

Del's tone was carefully modulated. "Tiger, I think you're—"

"—sandsick? No." Somehow, I was certain. Don't ask me how. I just *knew,* deep in my gut, deep in my heart, deep in the part of me no one else could share. "I'm beginning to understand. I think I'm beginning to know him."

"Tiger—"

My look cut her off. "You said he'd come to know me. Why can't I come to know him?"

Alric stepped into the doorway. "Do you want to spar?" He asked. "They're betting on matches at the circles . . . there are wagers to be won."

Del and I looked at him. Then we looked at the sword.

Thinking of Chosa Dei.

"When?" I asked aloud, of anyone who might know. "When is this jhihadi supposed to arrive?"

Del and Alric were equally uncertain of the question, and why *I* would ask it. They exchanged glances then looked at me, shrugging.

"I know as much as you," Del said.

I shot a glance at Alric, still plugging the doorway between our two rooms. "You've been here longer."

"The Oracle's coming," he answered. "I imagine he's supposed to get here first. Since he's the one foretelling the coming of the jhihadi, I'd think he'd want to do it from Iskandar instead of just tribal gatherings."

Something sounded odd. "Tribes," I said intently. "Are you saying this Oracle is aiming his foretelling *only* at the tribes?"

Alric shrugged. "I imagine his foretelling includes everyone; wouldn't it have to, since he's talking about the South? But all anyone knows for certain is he's moving among the tribes." He paused. "Or else they're coming to him."

I thought back to the discussion Abbu Bensir and I had had with Del regarding tanzeers, jhihadi, tribes. "I don't know how much of this is real, or how much of this is some ambitious man's attempt to gain himself a name," I said slowly. "You'd think if he wanted the obvious kind of power, he'd go straight to the tanzeers. They rule the South . . . parts of it, anyway."

"But they're corrupt," Alric remarked. "Tanzeers are bought and sold all the time. Domains fall overnight."

"There are people who aren't corrupt," I said evenly. Southron people whose only interest is in surviving, in keeping alive their own way of life. They owe nothing at all to tanzeers, and they ignore the petty pacts and power struggles. All they do is live, drawing strength from their homeland."

"The tribes," he agreed.

"I should know," I said. "I grew up with one."

Del shook her head. "I don't understand."

I frowned, trying to put it into words that meant something. "The tribes are all little pieces of the South. Different races, different customs, different religious beliefs. It's why no one can really rule the Punja . . . the tribes are too fragmented, too difficult to control. And so the tanzeers content themselves with the pieces they *can* control, and the people . . . the tribes are left alone."

Del nodded. "You said something like this before, with Abbu."

"*Now* I'm wondering if this jhihadi nonsense has nothing whatsoever to do with the tanzeers—at least, directly—but is aimed instead at the tribes." I chewed my bottom lip. "The tribes, put together, outnumber the rest of us. No one really knows how many there are—they live in all parts of the South, and almost none of them stay put. Which makes it impossible for anyone to deal with them, even if they wanted to."

Del nodded. "So?"

"So, if you were a man who wanted absolute power, what is the surest way of getting it once and for all *without* involving tanzeers?"

She didn't waste any time. "By uniting the tribes."

I nodded. "Which might explain why so many tanzeers are leaving their domains to come to Iskandar. Not because of the jhihadi. Because of the *tribes.* They're hiring sword-dancers to mount a defense of the South."

Alric shook his head. "Impossible," he said. "I'm a Northerner, yes, but I've lived in the South for years. I don't think anyone *could* unite all the tribes, for all the reasons you've given."

My turn to shake my head. "It's a matter of language," I said. "All you have to do is find the sort of message that appeals to every individual tribe, and then use the proper language."

"Religion," Del said flatly.

Now I nodded. "Religion, stripped of faith, of belief, is nothing more than a means to enforce the will of a few upon the many. Don't you see? Tell a man to do something, and he may not like the idea. He refuses. But tell him his *god* requires it, and he'll rush to do the task."

"*If* he believes," Alric cautioned.

"I don't know about you," I said, "but I'm not a religious man. I don't think there's much use in worshiping a god or gods when we're responsible for our own lives; relying on something—or *someone*—you don't know is a fool's game. But a lot of people disagree. A lot of people arrange their lives around their gods. They talk to them. Make offerings. Ask them for aid." I looked at Del. "They make oaths in the names of those gods, then live their lives by those oaths."

Color flared in her face. "What I do is my own concern."

"Yes," I agreed. "I'm not arguing that. What I'm saying is, the tribes are full of superstitions. If a nanny bears twin kids, the year is supposed to be generous. And when it isn't, *if* it isn't, something else is blamed." I sighed and scratched at scars. "If a man discovered a way of uniting the tribes in a common goal, he could claim the South for himself. That's what I'm saying."

Alric was frowning, considering implications. Thinking about tanzeers, who would want the jhihadi dead. Who would want the Oracle dead. And all the sword-dancers they could hire in order to win a holy war.

Del shook her head. "Would it matter? How do you know it wouldn't be better for the South if one man *did* rule it, instead of all these tanzeers?"

"Because who's to say what this one man will do?" I countered. "For one, if he's got the tribes on his side he wouldn't need to hire sword-dancers. We'd be out of a job." Del's expression was sardonic. "All right," I conceded, "aside from that, what if the tribes decided the rest of us didn't deserve to live? That we profaned the South? What if this jhihadi declared holy war and made the rest of us his enemies, fit only for execution?"

"He wouldn't," Del declared. "An entire people? An entire land?"

Alric's tone was odd. "The Vashni are killing foreigners."

Del's color faded.

"If the sand is changed to grass," I said, "the South becomes worth having."

Del frowned, thinking. "But if the South is changed so drastically, it alters the way the tribes live. Would they want that? You yourself said they're trying to protect their way of life."

"There is that," I agreed. "But there's also the knowledge that, for his god—or gods—a man will do many strange things."

Alric nodded slowly. "The *khemi,* for instance. How many men do *you* know would willingly give up women?"

Del's tone was disgusted. "I know about *khemi,*" she said. "Giving up women is one thing . . . claiming we are excrescence and not worthy of speech, of touching, of *anything* is carrying things too far."

"They interpret the Hamidaa'n a bit too literally," I agreed. "Those scrolls don't really say women are completely worthless, just inferior to men. If you talk to anyone of the true Hamidaa faith—not the *khemi* zealots—they'll tell you how things are."

Del's brows rose. "And that makes the opinion right?"

"No. What it does is prove what I've been saying: religion is a method of control."

Del tilted her head. "If you allow it to be. It can also offer security, a focus for your life. It can make your life worth living."

I looked at her harness, lying next to mine. At the intricate, twisted hilt of a dangerous, spell-bound sword. "You worship *that.* Does it make your life worth living?"

Del didn't even blink. "What it promises does."

Alric dismissed our argument. "If what you've said is true, something should be done."

Del overrode me before I could get started. "What if what the *Oracle* has said is true? Do you mean to argue with a messiah?"

"Right now," I said, "I need to go buy another sword."

Alric shook his head. "I have the Vashni sword. I would be pleased to loan it."

Del waited until he went in the other room. "You are a fool," she said. "You're avoiding your *jivatma* when you should be learning to control it."

"That's *right*," I said sharply, and bent to pick up the sword. "Here. You won the wager. The sword is now forfeit."

"Tiger, *no*—"

"You won, bascha. You said I couldn't last." I put the sword in her hands. I knew she was safe; Del knew his name.

She closed fingers over the blade. Knuckles shone white.

I frowned. "You know better, bascha. You'll cut your fingers like that."

Del said nothing. Her eyes were wide, and black; color drained out of her face.

"Bascha—?" I thought again of how Sarad's sword had been broken. "Here, let me have—"

"It wants me—"

My hands were on the sword. "Let go, Del . . . let *go*—"

"It *wants* me—"

"*Let go*—"

"Boreal," Del whispered.

It shocked me. It turned me to stone.

"He wants us *both*—"

I took one hand off the sword and stiff-armed her in the chest.

Del fell away, releasing my sword, hands springing open. She tripped over the bedding, landed sprawled on her back, gazed up at me in horror.

Not because I'd hit her. She understood that. But because of what she'd learned. Because of what she'd *felt*.

"You have to kill it," she said.

"How can I—"

"Kill it," she repeated. "You have to discharge it. You have to strip it of Chosa Dei. You have to—"

"I know," I said. "I know. Haven't I been saying that?"

Del gathered herself, rearranged herself, remained sitting on the damp dirt. "He wants me," she said. "Do you understand? He is a man; he is a *sword* . . . do you realize what that means?"

It was a hideous thing to consider. Bile moved in my belly.

"Kill it," she said again. "Before it does worse to me."

Chapter 6

el didn't like the idea. "It should be watched," she declared. "It should never be left alone."

Quietly I continued wrapping the *jivatma* in a blanket, wincing
as I jarred my swollen little finger. We had determined it wasn't
broken, but it hurt like hoolies. Tight wrapping protected torn
flesh, but didn't do much for the pain.

I set the bundle aside, next to the wall, and rose. "I'm not taking it with me. I've got the Vashni sword to use; this one can stay
here."

"You saw what it did."

"When you touched it. If no one knows it's here, it can't do
anything."

"The girls—"

"Lena has them well trained. They won't come in here because
they've been told not to, and they respect privacy."

Del was unconvinced. "It should be attended to."

I sighed. "Yes. Why do you think I asked about the jhihadi?"

Eyes widened. "But you don't *believe*—"

"Right about now, I'll try anything. I think this messiah is probably nothing more than an opportunist, but why not give it a try?
The tanzeers will demand proof of his divinity . . . they'll ask for
specific signs, give him specific tasks. Why not ask him to 'cure' my
sword."

"Because maybe he can't."

"Maybe he can't. Maybe he can." I shrugged. "I figure it's worth a try."

Del frowned at me. "This isn't like you, Tiger."

"What isn't? My unwillingness to agree with you, or my willingness to let the jhihadi try?"

"You're almost *never* willing to agree with me; that's not what I mean. I mean the latter. You're the one who claims religion is nonsense."

"I used to say the same about magic, too, and look where it got me." I hooked arms through my harness, settled my borrowed Vashni sword. "Look, bascha, I'm not saying I believe in religion—I really don't think I could—but who's to say this jhihadi, if he's real, isn't something more than a messiah?"

"More?"

"If he's supposed to change sand to grass, I'd say he's got something more than divine charm going for him." I grinned. "Maybe he's a sorcerer. Maybe he's Shaka Obre."

It startled her. "The *jhihadi?*"

"Well? Isn't Shaka Obre the one who once held the South? Who made it green and lush? Doesn't it make sense that if he really did create the South, he might want to restore it to what it once was?"

"Chosa Dei imprisoned him."

"And he imprisoned Chosa. But Chosa's out now—sort of—and maybe Shaka is, too. *He* could be the jhihadi. *He* could be the man the Oracle's spouting about."

Del considered it. "If he is—"

"—then he owes me."

She raised a skeptical brow. "And you think he'd be so grateful he'd do you a special favor."

"Chosa Dei was on the verge of destroying the wards. He had who knows how many *jivatmas* he was collecting magic from, as well as a few other tricks. Given a bit more time—or your sword—he'd have broken through. I may have sucked him into *my* sword but at least he's not roaming free. If I were Shaka Obre, I'd be grateful to me."

Del sighed wearily. "It makes as much sense as anything else."

"And if this jhihadi *isn't* Shaka Obre, what does it matter? He might still have the ability to discharge my *jivatma*."

She glanced at the tightly rolled bundle. The sword was completely hidden. "It deserves to die," she said flatly.

"I sort of thought you'd agree . . . once you saw my point." I resettled the harness and turned toward the door. "Do you have plans for today?"

"Seeking out word of Ajani."

Something pinched my belly. "But not the man himself."

Del shook her head. "I need to learn about him. I need to learn who he *is;* what makes him think. It's been six years, and I never really knew him. Just what he'd done." She shrugged. "I need to see him without him seeing me. Then I will talk to my sword."

"You don't mean—ask for your focus again? *Now?*"

Del smiled. "You had last night, didn't you?"

"*We* had last night. And I'd like for it to continue."

The smile went away. She was calm, controlled, commited. "It will . . . if I win."

I left the stud behind because trying to pick my way on horseback through the increasing throngs of people would try my patience, and might even result in a fight if the stud decided to protest. And besides, you can overhear gossip better if you're on foot with everyone else; if I wanted to learn the latest about the Oracle or the jhihadi, I'd do better to mix with the others.

By the time I'd fought my way through the alleys, streets and bazaar, I knew a little more. The Oracle, it was said, was busily foretelling the jhihadi's arrival soon. Of course, soon is relative; by oracular reckoning, it still might take a year. And I sincerely doubted anyone would wait that long.

But the Oracle was also foretelling a few other things. He was mentioning specifics, things about the messiah. Things like *power:* a power newly gained. A revelation of *identity:* a man of many parts. And an unwavering commitment to make the South what it was.

No wonder the tanzeers were worried.

I approached the tribe side of the city with a twinge of foreboding. Generally an individual tribe, on its own, can be dealt with one way or another, through trades, gifts, agreements. Some tribes, like the Hanjii and the Vashni, tend to be a bit more hostile, and are generally avoided. Except when you're riding through the Punja—where the tribes, being nomads, go wherever they feel—sometimes it's hard to avoid them. But it was very unusual to have so many different tribes all clustered together. It changed the rules of the game.

I wasn't certain my visit would do any good. For one thing, the Salset might not be present. For another—even if they were—they might simply ignore me. The adults all knew very well what I'd been. And none of them let me forget it.

Certainly not the shukar, who had his reasons for hating me. But maybe he was dead. If the old man was dead, I might have an easier time.

But the old man wasn't dead.

I found the Salset mostly by accident. After picking my way through goats, sheep, danjacs, children, dogs, and chickens, winding through the clusters of hyorts and wagons, I came to the end of the hyort settlement beside the city. I wavered uncertainly a moment, thinking about approaching another tribe, then swung around to go back. And saw a familiar red hyort staked out beside a wagon.

The Salset had settled behind a cluster of blue-green Tularain hyorts. Since there were more of the Tularain, it wasn't surprising the Salset were hard to see. So I wound my way through the Tularain cluster, then stopped at the shukar's hyort.

He was sitting on a blanket in front of his open doorflap. His white hair was thinning; his teeth were mostly gone; his eyes were filmed and blind. Not much life left in the old man. But he knew me anyway, the moment I said a word.

"We gave you horses," he snapped. "We tended your ailing woman. We gave you food and water. You have no more claim on us."

"I can claim courtesy. You owe that to anyone. It's a Salset custom."

"Don't tell *me* what Salset custom is!" The quaver of his voice came from age and anger, not fear. "It was you who revoked custom and sought aid from an unmarried woman."

My anger rose to meet his. "You know as well as I do that was Sula's decision. She was free, bound to no man; Salset women take who they will, until they accept a husband. You're just jealous, old man—she took a chula, not the shukar."

"You forced her to say *you'd* killed the beast—"

"I did kill it," I said flatly. "You know it, too . . . you just don't want to admit a chula succeeded where you'd failed." A glance at the shabbiness of clothing and hyort told me times were no longer easy. Once he'd been a rich man. "Is your magic all used up? Have the gods turned their eyes from you?"

He was old, and probably would not last a year. A part of me suggested I not be so bitter, so harsh, but the greater portion of me remembered what life with the Salset had been like. I owed him no courtesy. I owed him nothing but honesty; I hated the old man.

"You should have died from the poison," he said. "Another day, and you would have."

"Thanks to Sula, I didn't." My patience was at an end. "Where is her hyort, shukar? Direct me to Sula, as you are required to do in the name of Salset courtesy."

He peeled back wrinkled lips and showed me his remaining teeth, stained brown by beza nut. Then spat at my feet. "When the jhihadi comes, you and others like you will be stripped from the South forever."

It confirmed my foreboding, but I said nothing of it to him. "Where's Sula, old man? I have no time for games."

"I have no time for *you*. Find Sula yourself." Filmed eyes narrowed. "And I hope you *like* what you find, since you are the cause of it!"

I didn't waste my time asking futile questions, or trying to decipher his purposely vague pronouncements. I just went to find Sula.

And when I found her, I knew she was dying. Clearly, so did she.

"Sit," she said weakly, as I lingered in the doorflap.

I sat. I nearly fell. I couldn't say a word.

Sula's smile was her own. She hadn't been robbed of it yet. "I wondered if the gods would grant me the chance to see you again."

The day was dull and sullen. Fitful light painted a harsh sienna patina against the ocher-orange of her hyort. It washed the interior with sallowness, like aging ivory. To Sula, it was unkind.

This was my third Sula. The first had been in her early twenties, a slim, lovely young woman of classic Salset features: wide, mobile face; dipped bridge of nose; black hair so thick and sunkissed it glowed ruddy in the daylight. At night it was black silk.

The second had been over forty, run to fat; lacking former beauty, but none of her generosity, the kindness I'd come to crave. She had saved Del and me from the ravages of the Punja. And now I'd see her die.

The third Sula was not much older, but the plumpness had melted away. There was nothing of Sula left except hide stretched over bones. The hair was lank and lifeless. The eyes dulled with pain. Lines graven in flaccid flesh bespoke a constant battle. The hyort smelled of death.

All I could manage was her name.

I don't know what she saw in my face. But it moved her. It made her cry.

I took her hand in mine, then closed the other over it. Brittle, delicate bones beneath too-dry, fragile flesh. The woman of my manhood was a corpse in Salset gauze.

I swallowed heavily. "What sickness is it?"

Sula smiled again. "The old shukar says it's not. He says it's a demon put inside to punish me. It lives here, in my breast—eating away my flesh." She was propped against cushions. With one hand, she touched her left breast.

"Why?" I asked harshly. "What have you ever done?"

Sula raised a finger. "Many years ago, I took in a young chula who was no more a boy, but a man. And when he killed the sandtiger—when he won his freedom—I made certain he was given it. For that, I am being punished. For that, I host a demon."

"You don't *believe* that—"

"Of course not. The old shukar is jealous. He has always

wanted me. And he has never forgiven me." She made a weak gesture. "This is his punishment: he tells people about the demon, so none will give me aid."

"*No* one—"

"None," she said raggedly. "Oh, I am given food and water—no one will starve me to death—but none will aid me, either. Not where the demon can see."

"He's a dangerous old fool. And he's a *liar*—"

"And he's been shukar forever." Sula sighed and shifted against her cushions. "But now he has lost even that."

"*Lost* it . . ." It stunned me. "How?"

"His magic was bad. Ever since you left, his magic has been weak. And so when the summons was made—when the Oracle called our names—the old shukar was replaced with a younger, stronger man." Black eyes were sad. "The old man sits in the sun. The young man speaks of power."

"Gained from the jhihadi."

Sula nodded weakly. "The Oracle says the South will be given back to the tribes. There will be no more need for lengthy journeys from this oasis to that one; from this place to another. The sand will be changed to grass and water will run on the land."

I cradled her hand in mine. "Is that kind of change what you want?"

She was very tired. Her voice was a travesty. "All I have known is the desert . . . the heat, the sand, the sun. Is it wrong to long for grass? To ask the gods for water in plenty?"

"If war is the cost, yes." I paused. "Let me get you a drink."

Sula lifted a hand. I sank back down at her side. "You see only one side," she said. "You, of all people."

"I don't understand."

She smiled, but very sadly. "Why did you stay with us?"

"Stay—?" I frowned. "I had to. I didn't have any choice."

"Why not run away?"

"Water," I said at once. "I couldn't carry enough water to get me far enough. The Punja would have killed me. At least with the tribe, I was alive."

Stiff fingers curled in my hand. "If the land were lush and cool, no one could keep any slaves. It would be easy to run away, to survive a day unsheltered, with water in abundance."

I had run away once. I had been caught. As punishment, I was tied to a stake in the sand and left for a second full day with no water to slake my thirst. Left there, and ignored, all of ten paces away from the camp so I would know what it was to realize the Salset were my deliverance; that I owed my life to them.

I had been nine years old.

I drew in a painful breath. "I came for information. You've already given me some . . . but I need to know about the jhihadi. About what the tribes are planning."

Sula held onto my hand. "They are planning a holy war."

"But no one worships the same gods!"

"It doesn't matter. We are to have the jhihadi."

"And *this* is what he wants? To destroy the South completely?"

"To make it new again. To make it what it was, before the land was laid to waste." She rolled her head against her cushions. "I am only a woman . . . I don't sit in councils. All I am told is the jhihadi will unite all the tribes. The Oracle promises this."

"So, this man is just supposed to *arrive* one day, wave his hands and declare everyone friends, then send them out to kill?" I shook my head. "Not a peaceful kind of messiah."

"The young men don't want peace." Sula closed her eyes. "They have listened to the Oracle, but have heard what they want to hear. When he foretells the ascendancy of the tribes, they think it can only come at the cost of other lives. They think nothing of living in peace with the tanzeers. They forget how our lives will change . . . how crops will grow on the land, how water will come to the tribes instead of the tribes following it." She dragged in a laboring breath. "He says nothing of a war, but that is what they hear."

"You've heard him? The Oracle?"

"He has gone to a few of the tribes. Word is being carried."

"And they accept him without question, believing what he says."

Sula rolled her head. "They believe what they choose to believe. The Oracle speaks of a jhihadi who can change the sand to grass. A man need only walk out into the Punja to know what that could mean."

I knew. I'd lived there. Hoolies, I'd been *born* there.

Which reminded me of something.

"Sula." I shifted closer. "Sula, there's something I have to know . . . something I have to ask. It has to do with how I came to be with the Salset—"

Sula's eyes were glazed. "—histories say the South and the North were one . . . divided between two brothers—"

I hung on to my patience. I owed this woman too much. "Chosa Dei," I said. "His brother was Shaka Obre."

"—and that after a final battle one half would be laid to waste—"

"Shaka Obre's wards. Chosa Dei tripped them."

"—and after hundreds of years the brothers would be freed to contest for the land again . . . to make whole the broken halves—"

"Sula," I said sharply, "is the jhihadi Shaka Obre?"

Her lips were barely moving. "—only a small favor—a single small favor . . ."

"Sula—"

"Let me die free of pain."

"*Sula*—" I bent over her. "Sula, please—tell me the truth . . . did the Salset find me? Or did they *steal* me?"

Pain-graved brow creased. "Steal you?"

"I was told—they always said—" I stopped short and tried again. "It would mean something to me to know how I came to the Salset."

Tears rolled free of her eyes. "I heard what they told you. The children. How they taunted you."

"Sula, was it true? Was I abandoned in the Punja? Exposed and left to die?"

Her hand closed on mine. The voice was but a thread. "Oh, Tiger . . . I wish I knew . . ."

It was all she had left to give. Having given it, she died.

I sat there and held her hand.

Mother. Sister. Bedmate. Wife.

All and none of those things.

Chapter 7

The man stepped out in front of me. I checked, moved aside; he blocked me yet again.

Not a man: a Vashni.

"Not now," I said clearly, couching it in Desert.

Dark eyes glittered. He didn't move a muscle, didn't say a word, made no indication he intended to step aside.

Three others came up behind me; this wasn't coincidence.

The day was gray. Dull, sullen sunlight gave way to heavy clouds. Rain stained the ground.

Vashni wear very little. Brief leather kilts with belts. No boots, no sandals. Jewelry made out of bone, claimed from enemies' skeletons. In the rain, bare torsos were slick, smooth as oiled bronze. Black hair was plaited back from fierce desert faces in a single long braid, hanging clear to belted waists in sheaths of gartered fur.

Bone pectoral plates chinked and tinkled as they breathed.

I wore a knife and a sword. I touched neither of them.

Oddly, I felt tired. Too weary to deal with this on the heels of Sula's death. "If it's foreigners you're killing, why start with me? There's a whole city full of them all of ten paces from here."

The warrior facing me smiled, if a Vashni can do such a thing. Mostly he bared his teeth, very white in a dark face. His Desert was quick and fluent. "Your time will come, Southron . . . for now your life is spared."

"Generous," I applauded. "So what is it you're after?"

"The sword," he answered calmly. Behind me, the others breathed.

Hoolies, how had word of Samiel gotten around already? I hadn't killed anyone. Hadn't displayed his magic. Only Del and I knew of the broken sword and its blackened, discolored half. And the Vashni, as far as I knew, weren't partial to any weapon other than their own, with its wicked, curving blade and human thighbone hilt.

Slowly I shook my head. "The sword is mine."

Color stained his face and set black eyes aglitter. "No one but a Vashni carries a Vashni sword."

A Vashni—oh, a *Vashni* sword . . . like the one hanging from my harness.

Vashni aren't quite like anyone else, and they don't judge outsiders by anything but their own customs. They don't engage in socially unacceptable behavior like the Hanjii, who eat people, and they don't condone outright murder. But they do have a habit of provoking hostilities so the death meted out to an enemy is considered an honorable one.

And then they strip away flesh, muscle, viscera and distribute the still-damp skeleton in a lengthy celebration.

Right about now an engagement of hostilities might be what I needed, but I was angry. Too angry to think straight: this Vashni had no right to interfere with my life out of a perverse tribal whim, regardless of the cause.

Not right after Sula—

I cut it off. Knew better than to protest, or to say anything he might interpret as rude. I had no intention of becoming anyone's pectoral. "Take it," I said flatly.

He flicked a finger. I stood very still. I felt the touch of a hand on the hilt, the snap of a blade sliding free. Weight lessened across my back; all I wore now was the harness.

The Vashni's black eyes showed only the slightest hint of contempt. "A Vashni warrior also never gives up his weapon."

I clenched teeth together. "We've already established I'm not Vashni. And I don't see the point in trying to protect—or in dying over—a sword that was only borrowed."

Eyes narrowed. "Borrowed."

"My own sword broke. This was loaned to me."

"A Vashni never *loans* his sword."

"He does if he's dead," I snapped. "Call it a permanent loan."

Clearly the warrior had not expected such a response. Vashni are accustomed to cowing frightened people into instant acquiescence, and I wasn't cooperating. He glared at me through the rain, then glanced past me to the others. One hand was near his knife; was the insult enough to repay? Or would he have to work harder?

Deep inside, anger rose. Instinctively I called to memory my recollection of our immediate surroundings and situation: tribal hyorts clustered but a pace or two away—rain-slick ground—poor footing—no sword—four Vashni—no support—the city entrance ten paces away—chickens and dogs and goats—

And then something occurred to me. It made me forget about fighting. "What part of the South are you from?"

The arched nose rose. "Vashni are from everywhere. The South is ours to hold."

"So the Oracle says." I smiled insincerely. "But it isn't yours quite yet, so why don't you answer my question?"

He contemplated my attitude. "Answer mine," he countered. "Why does it matter to you?"

"Because the mountain Vashni down near Julah have been 'hosting' someone I know. I just wondered if you knew him."

He spat into the mud. "I know no foreigners."

I continued anyway. "He's a Northerner—blond, blue-eyed, fair . . . he's also castrate and mute, thanks to Julah's former tanzeer." I shrugged offhandedly so my real concern wouldn't show, which might give them a weapon. "His Northern name was Jamail. He's sixteen now."

He assessed me. Black eyes didn't blink. "Is this boy kin to you?"

I could have said no, and been truthful. But lying has its uses; in this case, I'd get my answer. "I'm blood-bonded to his sister."

Kinship. Such a simple, obvious key to unlock Vashni secrets. To force the warrior's hand.

He looked past me again to the others. But I knew he'd have to tell me what he knew, no matter how he felt. They are a fierce, ferocious tribe, but the Vashni have their weaknesses just like anyone else. In this case, it was kinship. They won't tolerate bastards or half-bloods, but full-birth kinship or blood-bond takes precedence over pride.

His eyes were not kind. "There was such a boy."

"A Northern boy—sixteen?"

"He was as you describe."

I kept my voice even. "You said 'was'?"

The Vashni didn't play diplomat to try to soften the blow. "The Northern boy is dead. This is a holy war, Southron—we must purge our people of impurities to prepare for the jhihadi."

I tried not to think of Jamail—or Del—as my own contempt flowered. "Is that what the Oracle said?"

I expected offense to be taken. I expected to have to fight. But the Vashni warrior smiled.

It was open, unaffected, and utterly genuine. Then he turned and went into the rain.

How do I tell Del? How in hoolies do I tell her?

Sula's gone, chula. Salvation no longer exists.

How am I to tell her she's the only one left of her blood?

How do you thank Sula for all that she was and did?

I can't just walk into our borrowed bedroom and say: "Your brother's dead, bascha."

You can't go to the gods of valhail and ask to have Sula back.

It would kill her. Or *get* her killed; she'd immediately go after Ajani.

How do you tell a childless woman that she still gave birth to a son?

She's only just now coming to realize there's more to life than revenge.

How do you tell a dead woman she's the one who gave you life?

Is her freedom worth the price?

Is my freedom worth the price?

Something was wrong. I knew it immediately as I got closer to the house Del and I shared with Alric and his brood. There is a feeling, a *sound* . . . when a crowd gathers to witness death, everybody knows.

Too much dying, I thought. First Sula, then Jamail—who was dying now?

The death-watch was on. It took all I had to break through, trying to reach the house. And then all I had to stop.

Oh, gods—oh—*hoolies*—

All the hairs stood up on my body. My belly began to churn. The street stank of magic.

Oh, hoolies—no—

Someone had my *jivatma.*

No—my *jivatma* had him.

But I put it away. I wrapped it up, set it aside, put it away—

And someone had stolen it.

Now it was stealing him.

He dug in mud with his feet. Sprawled on his back, he dug. Because the blade had gone in at his belly and threaded its way through his ribs to peek out at the top of a shoulder.

Showing a blackened tip only slightly tainted by blood.

No one kills that way. A clean thrust through ribs, through belly; a slash across abdomen. But no one threads a sword through ribs like a woman weaving cloth.

Except for Chosa Dei.

He lay on his back in the rain, digging mud with his feet. Trying to shred the cloth of his flesh so he could unstitch the hideous needle.

How can he be alive?

Because Chosa Dei wants the body.

I thrust my way through the gathered crowd and knelt down at his side. His eyes saw me, knew me; begged for me to help.

Slowly I shook my head: he'd known what the sword was. He'd told me about Chosa Dei.

"Why?" was all I asked.

His voice was wracked by pain. "She wouldn't have me—have me . . . Xenobia wouldn't have me . . ."

"Is she worth dying for?"

"They wouldn't have me—have me . . . they said I was a bastard . . ."

From whom I had come, I knew. "Vashni," I said grimly. "That's your tribal half."

Nabir didn't nod. Black eyes were wide and fixed. *"My brother,"* he said. *"My brother; yes? I must unmake my brother."*

"Nabir!" I shut my hand on his arm. "Give him up, Chosa."

"I must unmake my brother."

"But I'm here, Chosa. How do you plan to win?"

Nabir dug mud with his feet. "I knew what it was—I knew . . . with this sword, they might have me . . . with this sword, *she* might have me . . . the sword of the Sandtiger—"

There was very little blood. Chosa Dei was taking it all.

"Nabir—"

"I tripped . . . he made me *trip* . . . he took my feet away—"

Immediately, I looked. Nabir still dug mud, but there were no feet to do it. Only mud-coated stumps.

"—and I fell . . . and it turned . . . without a hand on it, it turned—"

"Nabir—"

"CHOSA DEI—don't you know who I am?"

I put a hand on the hilt. Felt the virulence of his rage.

"Don't you know WHAT I am?"

Only too well.

"I'm sorry," I said. "I'm sorry . . . I've got no choice, Nabir."

"I'll give him back his feet—"

"No, Chosa . . . too late.'

"I'll unmake YOU—"

"Not while *I* hold this sword.'

"You don't want this sword—"

Two hands on the hilt. "And you can't have this body."

Nabir's body arced. *"SAMIEL!"* it shouted. *"The sword is Samiel—"*

Chapter 8

He wasn't quite dead. But I knew I'd have to kill him.

"Nabir," I said, "I'm *sorry*—"

—unthreaded the deadly needle—

Nabir was mostly gone. Chosa used what was left. "Sam—Sam—Sami*el*—"

"No good, Chosa. Now it's just me."

—blood and breath rushed out.

Unfettered rage exploded.

Hoolies, but this *hurts*—

I was aware, if only dimly, of the crowd gathered around. For the moment, what they saw was a dead man on the ground and another man by his side, holding on to the sword that killed him. What they *heard* was a low, keening wail like the moan of a stalking cat. They didn't know it was steel. They didn't know it was Chosa. They only knew the boy was dead in messy, spectacular fashion.

Faces: Alric. Lena briefly, with the girls; she hustled them back inside. Garrod, braids and all, working his way out of the crowd to the inside perimeter. And Adara, staring mutely, trying unsuccessfully to send Massou away. And many, many strangers.

No Del. Where's De—

Chosa Dei was angry. Chosa Dei was *very* angry—and he took no pains to hide it.

It wasn't unexpected. But the power was overwhelming.

I knelt in bloody mud while the rain ran down my back, wishing I knew what to do. Wishing I had the strength. Wishing I had the ability to unmake my perverted *jivatma*.

Heat coursed down the sword. In cold rain, steel steamed.

I shook. I *shook* with it, trying to suppress the raw power that strained to burst free of the sword. Chosa Dei was testing all the bonds, attempting to shatter the magic that bound him inside the steel. I knew better than to wonder what could happen if I just let him go, let him free—if he left the sword entirely, he'd be nothing but an *essence*, lacking face or form. In order to be what he wanted to be he'd have to have a body. He'd tried to take Nabir's. He'd take mine if I let him.

In rain, the blood washed away, leaving the blade free of taint . . . except for the discoloration reaching nearly to the hilt.

If Chosa ever touched it—

No.

My bones ached. They *itched*. Blood ran hot and fast, *too* hot and too *fast*, surging toward my head. I thought my skull would burst.

Samiel was shrieking. The sword was protesting Chosa.

If we could work *together*—

Light flashed inside my head.

Go to hoolies, Chosa . . . you're not beating me.

The blade began to smoke.

You're not beating *me*—

Rain stopped falling. Mud began to dry. The ground beneath me steamed.

If it's a song you want, I'll sing it . . . I can't sing, but I will . . . I'll do what I have to, Chosa . . . whatever it takes, Chosa . . . you're not going to beat me, Chosa . . . you're not going to have my sword . . . you're not going to have *me*—

Parched mud began to crack.

I got off my knees and stood. Clutching the hilt in my hands. Watching the black creep forward, licking at the hilt.

I'm a Southroner, Chosa—you're in *my* land, now.

A wind began to blow.

Do you really think you can *win*—?
The wind began to wail.
This is *my land*—
A hot, dry wind.
—you're not welcome here—
A wind from off the Punja.
—*I don't want you here*—
Blasting down through the alleyways, the streets, shredding silk burnouses, stripping makeshift roofs, drying eyes and mouths.
Go away, Chosa. Go back into into your prison.
Dried mud broke and crumbled, blown northward out of the city.
Go back to sleep, Chosa. I'm too strong for you.
The sun ate into flesh.
Don't be stupid, Chosa . . . you're no match for *me*—
Black flowed down the sword and lodged again in the tip.
No, Chosa—away—
Chosa Dei refused.
No, Chosa—*away*—
Chosa withdrew a little . . . and then the firestorm engulfed me.

I came around to voices.
"Keep him covered," someone said.
"But he looks so hot," another protested.
"He's sunburned. What he feels is cold."
Sunburned? How could I be sunburned? The last I recall, the day had been full of rain.
I shivered beneath the blanket.
"I wish we could get him to let go of that sword."
"Do *you* want to touch it?"
"After what it did? No."
"Neither do I."
Nothing was very important. I let it all drift away.
And then came back again, trying to make sense of the words.
"—what they're saying about the Oracle . . . do you think it's true?"

Alric's voice now; I was beginning to tell them apart. "It's why most of the people came here . . . to see the Oracle and the jhihadi."

"But they're saying he's coming *now*." That was Adara.

Garrod's tone was dry. "Right this very moment?"

"No. But any day. Maybe even tomorrow."

Lena's quieter voice: "I heard he's already here, but being hidden by the tribes."

"Why would they hide him?" Garrod asked. "He's what the people want."

Alric's tone was crisp. "There are those who'd like to kill him—or *have* him killed. And besides, would you show off your holy oracle before things were ready?"

Adara sounded puzzled. "What do you mean: things?"

Garrod understood. "If there really is a jhihadi, it would be more dramatic to have the Oracle appear not long before the messiah. If he arrived too soon, everyone would get bored."

"People are already bored," Alric observed. "The tanzeers—who are perhaps the most bored of all, and yet have the most at stake—have already taken to challenging one another. They're pitting sword-dancer against sword-dancer, wagering on the outcome . . . I was at the circles earlier, trying to earn a wage. They're talking about the Oracle there, as well—wagering on him, of course, and what kind of person he is. Rumor says he's neither man nor woman." Alric's tone changed. "I'll go back as soon as I know Tiger is all right."

"Is he?" Adara asked.

Something I wanted to ask myself.

And then Del's voice, raised, from a little distance away, responding to Massou's treble comment in the other room. "What do you mean, he's sick?"

I peeled open an eye. Saw Lena, Alric, Garrod, Adara—and Del, pushing through. The eye closed again.

"It's the sword," Alric told her. "It's done something to him."

She knelt down next to me. I realized, somewhat vaguely, I was lying on my own bedding in the room Del and I shared.

She stripped away blankets. "Done *what* to him?"

Alric shook his head. "I can't tell you exactly what happened . . . I don't think anyone really knows. But it was the sword. The *jivatma*—and Tiger. In the middle of some kind of battle."

I cracked the eye again.

"Chosa Dei," Del said softly, creases marring her brow. Fingers were gentle and deft, then she stopped examining me. "Tiger, can you hear me?"

I opened the other eye. "Of course I can hear you," I answered. "I can hear *all* of you—now."

"What happened?"

"I don't know."

She pressed the back of her hand against my cheek. "You're sunburned," she said. "And the day is blazing hot."

I blinked. "It was raining."

Del lifted her hand and pointed straight up.

I followed the direction of her finger. Realized Alric's makeshift blanket-and-skin roof had come down—or been torn down, since shreds were left to dangle—and saw the sky clearly. The blue, burning sky, full of Southron sun. No rain. No clouds. No wind. It was still, very still; my skin quailed from the sun.

I moved a little. Felt weight in my right hand. Realized it held a hilt, with the blade still attached. "What in hoolies—?" I frowned at Del.

Alric answered instead. "You wouldn't let go. And no one dared to touch it."

Well, no; it was, after all, a *jivatma*—

I stiffened. Then wrenched myself off the bedding into a sitting position. "Hoolies, that was *Nabir!*"

"It was." Garrod's face was solemn. "Whoever he was, he's dead."

I stared at the sword. Slowly, very slowly, I unlocked stiffened fingers and set it down beside me. "He unmade Nabir's *feet*—" swallowed heavily, realizing I was dizzy; that my belly was none too content. "Then put himself into the boy. First the sword, then himself . . . he nearly got what he wanted."

Adara's voice was puzzled. "I don't understand."

Del barely glanced over a shoulder, watching me instead. "Do you remember the loki, Adara?"

"*Yes.*"

"Something very like one is trapped in Tiger's sword."

"Not a loki," I said. "Something far worse."

Adara shuddered. "Nothing could be worse."

Garrod's brows rose. "You saw what Tiger did . . . and what it did to Tiger."

Something began to concern me. "What *did* it do to Tiger?"

Garrod was very succinct. "Tried to burn you up. Except you wouldn't let it do it . . . you stopped it cold—in a manner of speaking." He grinned. "The rain went away, the mud dried up, the sun came out for good."

Lena's voice was hushed. "It was a simoom."

Simoom—or samiel.

I looked at Del. Neither of us said a word.

Lena's face was troubled. "The young man came after Alric was gone to the circles, saying he wanted the Sandtiger. When I explained you weren't here, that you'd left for a while, he asked what sword you wore." She lifted wide shoulders. "I told him: Alric's Vashni sword. And then he went away."

"Only to come back later when Lena and the girls were gone." Alric's voice was heavy. "Who would steal a *jivatma?*"

"A young, proud man trying to impress his first woman. An outcast Vashni half blood trying to buy his way into the tribe." I rubbed at my cheek, then wished I hadn't. Del was right: I was sunburned. "He probably got word to the warriors that I had the Vashni sword, knowing it would create a diversion so he could steal the *jivatma.*" I sighed. "I'm sorry Nabir's dead, but I can't say he wasn't warned."

Del looked at the sword lying naked beside the bedding. "Tiger—the black is higher."

So it was: discoloration reached nearly halfway up the blade. "Less than there was," I told her. "It almost touched the hilt." I glanced around, saw the harness, stretched out an arm to reach it. Del dragged it closer, then put it into my hand. I sheathed the discolored sword, then set it back on the ground. "Do you think—" But whatever it was started to ask slid off my flaccid tongue.

Del's voice was startled. "Tiger—? *Tiger—*"

"What is it?" Adara cried.

Cramps wracked me the length of my body. Toes, calves, thighs, then through abdomen and chest, until it reached my back. Pectoral muscles knotted, stretching the flesh of my shoulders. Pain crawled up into my neck, then reached out and snared my jaw.

Hoolies, but I *hurt.*

"What *is* it?" Adara repeated.

"Reaction," Del explained crisply. "It's because of the magic—it's happened before . . . it will pass, in time; Lena, have you any huva weed? If not, could you send Alric to fetch some? I can brew a tea that will help."

"I have some," Garrod said, and took Adara and Massou with him.

I found it somewhat discomfiting to be discussed as if I were not present, but since basically I wasn't—only my spasming body—I didn't bother to protest. I just lay there tied up in knots, trying to breathe in and out through the cramping of midriff and back.

Alric, catching Del's twitch of the head, herded Lena and the girls back into the other room.

"Bascha—I can't—*breathe*—"

Del moved the sheathed sword aside, out of the way. "I know. Try to relax. Try to think about something else."

"*You* try it."

Her tone softened. "I know," she said again.

It took effort to speak an entire sentence. "Has this—happened to you?"

Del was busy trying to knead out the worst of the cramps. Trouble was, I was cramping all over, and she only had two hands. "Not like this," she answered. "A bit, yes, the first time I invoked my *jivatma.* But never again, and nothing like this . . . this is the worst I've ever seen."

Trust it to happen to me. "If these swords are supposed to be so *helpful*—" I broke it off and ground my teeth. "Oh, hoolies . . . this hurts."

"I know," she said yet again. "It must be because of Chosa Dei . . . if it were only the *jivatma,* it wouldn't be so painful. I don't know what you did, but it roused too much of the wild magic. And now you're paying the price."

"I don't know what I did, either." Oh, hoolies, it hurt. Sweat ran off my body, stinging sunburned skin. "I just—I just tried to stop Chosa Dei from taking Nabir's body—from trying to take *mine*."

Del dug into my neck, trying to loosen a locking jaw. The pain was exquisite. "You changed the weather, Tiger. You called up a storm."

She sounded so certain. "How do *you* know?" I demanded through locked teeth. "You weren't even here."

"Because with mine I call up a banshee-storm, which is known only in the North. Your storm is a samiel . . . a hot desert wind blasting straight out of the Punja." She paused. "Don't you understand? You have the strength of the South in your sword. The strength, the power, the magic . . . your sword *is* the South, just as mine is the North."

It took some thinking about. "Since when—*ouch*—has this been so clear to you?"

"Since you used the sword against Chosa in the mountain."

"So why wait until now—*ouch!* . . . hoolies, bascha be gentle . . . you sent Garrod for huva?"

"Yes."

"Huva weed is a narcotic."

"Yes."

"It will muddle up my head."

"No more muddled up than it is when you drink too much aqivi . . . ah—here is Garrod now. Lena will brew some tea."

Lena brewed tea. Del kneaded. I sweated and cramped. By the time the tea was ready, *I* was read for anything if it meant the pain would go.

"Here." Del held the cup. "It will be bitter because it hasn't been properly brewed or steeped as long as it should be, but drink. It will help."

It was worse than bitter. It was *horrible*. "How long does it take?"

"This concentrated, not long. Try to relax, Tiger."

"I think I've forgotten how."

She worked the rigidity of my shoulders. "Give it a little time."

I gave it time. I gave it a lot of time. And then when I wasn't looking, the tea snuck up on me.

"Bascha—?"

"I'm here, Tiger."

"The room is upside down."

"I know."

"And you're floating in midair."

"I know."

"And *I'm* floating in midair."

"I know."

Pain diminished a step. Relief tapped at my consciousness, but I wouldn't let it in. I was *afraid* to let it in. If I let it in, and it didn't stay, I'd never be able to bear it.

Drowsily, I said: "He unmade Nabir's feet."

"And tried to unmake *you*."

"He wanted Nabir's body . . ."

Her hands still worked sore flesh. "Do you see now, Tiger, why you must be vigilant? Why you can never set it aside, or sell it, or hide it, or give it to anybody? Why the sword is yours to ward?"

I didn't answer.

"You are right to seek out Shaka Obre. He may be the only one who can aid you . . . the only one who understands Chosa Dei well enough to defeat him."

I slurred everything together. "If things keep going the way they've been going, Chosa may get to know *me* well enough . . . he wants my body, you said?"

"You are strong enough for Chosa Dei. You are his match, or better . . . he cannot defeat you."

The words were getting harder to say. "You don't know that, bascha . . . he nearly beat me today . . ."

"But he didn't. You stopped him. You fought him, and you beat him. You have every time, and you *will* every time."

More pain flowed away. With it went much of my sense. "I have—to get rid of . . . it . . ."

"Then have it discharged properly."

"Shaka Obre," I mumbled. "Maybe the jhihadi . . . may *be* the jhihadi . . ."

Del smiled a little. Through the veil of my lashes, the tense Northern features softened. "If the jhihadi has time for such."

"Hoolies . . . tea . . . *strong* . . ."

Cramps began to untie. I let the relief wash in, denying it nothing now. It could take me, it could *have* me . . . and its gift was akin to bliss. "Oh, better . . . *better* . . ." I drifted drowsily, letting the huva take me. And then words fell out of my mouth. "I asked Sula," I slurred. "I asked her about the truth."

Del's fingers slowed, then resumed their steady kneading. "What did she say?"

It was hard to stay awake. "She didn't know the truth . . . she said she didn't know . . ."

The fingers now were gentle. "I'm sorry, Tiger."

My tongue was thick in my mouth. "And then—she died. She *died*."

The hands stopped altogether.

My eyes were too heavy to open. "I'm sorry—bascha . . ."

"Don't be sorry for *me*."

"No . . . because—because of Jamail." The world was sliding away.

"Jamail! What *about*—" She broke off.

It was harder to make the effort. "I didn't—I'm sorry—I meant . . ." Vision was slowly fraying.

Del said nothing.

I walked the edge of the blade. *One—more—step—*

"That's not—that's not how—" I licked dry lips. "—I meant it to be different—"

Del sat like a rock.

One more tiny *step—*

I was nearly incoherent. "I'm . . . sorry . . . bascha—"

The rock moved at last. Del lay down beside me, one hip jutting toward the sky. I felt the angle of her cheekbone against the loosening flesh of my shoulder.

So—close—now—

She rested her arm on my chest and put the flat of her hand over my heart, as if to feel its beating.

"—*Del*—"

She locked her feet around mine. "I'm sorry, too," she whispered. "I'm sorry for us both."

—over the edge—

—and *off*—

Chapter 9

Del's face was white. "This is *serious*."

After a moment, I nodded. "That's why I brought it up."

"If the name is freely known—"

"It wasn't my fault, bascha. Nabir said the name."

"But—how did he know?" She waved the question away before she finished the intonation. "No. He knew because Chosa Dei told him. Chosa Dei was *in* him . . . the *jivatma* had no secrets."

"You're saying if my blade ever cuts into someone, he'll know all about the power?"

Del's tone went dry. "While he's dying, yes. But I don't think it will do him much good."

Alric came into the doorway. "I couldn't help overhearing . . . and anyway, I heard the boy scream it out yesterday." He shrugged. "If you're worried about the blooding-blade's name being known, I don't think it's as serious as all that."

Del scowled at him. "You're Northern. You know better—"

"*Because* I'm Northern, yes." Alric shook his head. "Named blades aren't known down here, Del. Not by very many. And the people I saw in the crowd yesterday were Southron, most of them; the name won't mean a thing. Certainly they won't realize that to know the name means they can freely touch Tiger's sword—and even if they did know it, I doubt they'd do anything about it." His expression was grim. "You weren't here yesterday. You didn't see what happened."

"No, but I know the results." Del still looked concerned. "Southroners may be no threat, but if there were Northerners present—"

"—then they know it, too." Again, Alric nodded. "But even in the North *jivatmas* are mostly legend. Unless you've trained to be a sword-dancer, you don't hear so much about blooding-blades."

"Hoolies," I said wearily, "what I'd give for a Southron sword."

Del's tone was implacable. "That, you can never have. Not while Chosa lives."

It irritated me. "What do you mean? What if I went out and bought *another* sword?"

"Like the one from Sarad the swordsmith?" Del's contempt was delicate. "Like the one you borrowed from Alric?"

I didn't say anything.

She sighed. "Don't you understand? He won't *let* you have another. He'll break it, like the first one."

Alric nodded. "Or see that it's taken away, like the Vashni sword I loaned you."

"That was probably Nabir . . . I think he went to the Vashni and told them, hoping it might buy him goodwill." I peeled dead skin off a forearm. For some odd reason the sunburn was already fading, sloughing off dead skin two days quicker than usual. I stared at the curl of skin; at the pattern of flesh and hair. "I can't risk another Nabir. I can't risk another—fight."

"Another storm, you mean." Alric's mouth twisted. "I don't know, Tiger—you controlled that one well enough. And if *I* had the ability to call up a simoom any time I wanted—"

"I *don't* want," I stated clearly. "All I want is to go back to the kind of life I had before, when I hired on with local tanzeers, or made money on circle wagers.'

"You can't have it," Del said. "That is over for you."

Alric's brows rose. "Maybe not. I mentioned to the others earlier . . . there is wagering at the circles. Tanzeers are hiring, so the sword-dancers are showing off. Some of the tanzeers are pitting their sword-dancers against one another for the hoolies of it. Some are settling scores. Those dances are real."

I shook my head. "I'm in no shape for dancing. Everything hurts too much."

Alric shrugged lightly. "That will pass soon enough."

"Will it?" Glumly I picked at dead skin. "I'm not as young as I once was."

"In the name of *hoolies!*" Del cried. "You're only thirty-six!"

Only. She said *"only."*

How generous of her.

Alric slouched against the door jamb. "*I'd* bet money on you."

"On me, or on my sword?"

He grinned a Northern grin. "A little of both, I think."

I shook my head slowly. "I don't know, Alric . . . I'm not so sure anyone around here will ever risk a coin on a dance with me involved. If as many people as you say saw what happened yesterday . . ." I let it trail off.

"You're sandsick," he answered pleasantly. "Do you know how many people will pay just in case you *might* key that sword again?"

I twisted my mouth briefly. "Maybe. People *are* bloodthirsty—they might like that sort of thing. But how many sword-dancers would be willing to risk their lives against a possessed sword? I'll have no opponents."

Alric straightened hastily and moved aside as Lena thrust immense belly between man and doorjamb. "Tiger," she said, "someone is here to see you."

"See me?"

She nodded. "He asked for you."

I glanced thoughtfully at Del a moment, then gathered aching muscles and harness and made myself get up. The huva disorientation was gone, but not the aftermath of the cramping. I hurt all over.

"Shall I send him through?" Lena asked.

"No, I'll go outside. It's time I got some sun." With a glance at the blatant sky, uncluttered by blanket or skin.

Outside, the day was as bright. So was the man waiting for me, swathed in blinding silks. Baubles flashed on his fingers.

"Lord Sandtiger," he said, and grinned at me happily.

Dumbfounded, I stared. And then reached out to slap a plump shoulder. "Sabo. *Sabo!* What are you doing here?"

The eunuch's grin was undiminished. "I've been sent to fetch you."

My answering grin died. "Fetch me? Fetch *me?* I don't know, Sabo—the last time you were sent to fetch me it was to play me right into Hashi's palsied hands . . . and nearly under the gelding knife!"

Some of his gaiety faded. "That is over," he told me. "My lord Hashi, may the sun shine on his head, died two months ago. You need have no fear of his retribution now."

I hoped not. Sabo's master, tanzeer of Sasqaat, had proved a very inhospitable host. Of course, he claimed retribution because his intended bride's virginity was missing, so I suppose he had a right . . . except no one else had ever accused Elamain of being a virgin—*ever*—so the so-called retribution had been little more than an old man's jealous spite. But it nonetheless nearly got me gelded. Only Sabo's help had freed Del and me.

The round-faced eunuch still smiled. "I have a new master, now."

"Oh? Who?"

"Hashi's son. Esnat."

"Esnat?"

"Esnat. *Lord* Esnat."

I nodded deferentially. "And is Lord Esnat anything like his father?"

"Lord Esnat is a fool."

"So was Hashi—excuse me: *Lord* Hashi. Was a fool."

"My lord Hashi, may the sun shine on his head, was an old, bitter man. Lord Esnat is a fool."

"Then why are you serving him? *You've* never been a fool."

Sabo's tone was bland. "Because the lady asked me to."

Deep in my belly, something twitched. "The lady," I echoed ominously. "You don't mean—"

"—Elamain," he finished. "May the sun shine on her head."

"And other parts of her anatomy." I chewed at my bottom lip. "Then am I right in assuming it's Elamain who's sent for me?"

"No. Lord Esnat sent for you."

"Why?"

"Elamain asked him to."

I decided to say it straight out. "I'm still with Del, Sabo."

The eunuch smiled. "Then you have retained your good sense . . . and your taste."

"But—don't you see? I can't go to Elamain."

"Elamain won't care."

"About Del? She certainly will. I'm not *that* stupid, Sabo."

"The lady wants to *see* you."

"She'll want to see *all* of me."

Sabo's pale brown eyes were guileless. "That didn't stop you before."

I shifted uncomfortably. "Yes, well . . . maybe not—"

"Come tell her yourself," he suggested. And then his face brightened. "Ah, the Northern bascha . . . may the sun shine on your head!"

Del, in the doorway, glanced skyward. "I think it already is."

I stared at her. Thought back on the topic Sabo and I had discussed; on my invitation from Elamain. Found I had nothing to say.

Del's smile was slow. "Don't keep the—*lady*—waiting."

I wet my lips. "I don't suppose you'd want to come."

Her smile stretched wider. "You sound almost hopeful, Tiger."

Yes, well . . . maybe so. But I wouldn't tell Del that.

I shrugged. "Just a thought," I mentioned. "I thought maybe you'd want to gossip. Two women, after all—"

Gravely, Del shook her head. "I'd sooner step into a circle . . . at least *there* I know the rules."

I started to answer, then remembered something. "Wait. You went to find out what you could about Ajani."

Del was expressionless. "So I did."

"And did you?"

She shrugged. "It can wait."

"Maybe it can, but will it?" I shook my head. "I know you, bascha . . . you'll tell me nothing, then go off all by yourself."

She smiled. "Go off to Elamain."

"Del—"

"Go," she said plainly.

Irresolute, I offered a promise: "I'll come straight back."

Her tone was perfectly bland. "And perhaps I shall be here."

Hoolies, she can be difficult.

I looked at Sabo. Saw the gleam of amusement in his eyes. Knew I couldn't delay any longer without giving myself away.

You're a grown man, I told myself. And Elamain's only a *woman*.

Hoolies, what a fool.

Esnat wasn't alone.

Chapter 10

Elamain *was* alone. "Hello, Tiger," she purred.

Oh, hoolies. Del.

And then wondered what I was thinking. I mean, I was a grown man. One who makes his own decisions, needing no woman to do it for him. Needing no guidance, no suggestions, no commands. I could make my own way in the world, with or without a woman, and therefore didn't even need to *think* of Del right at this very moment.

Elamain shed her burnous. "Remember how it was?"

Hoolies, hoolies, *hoolies* . . . where's Del when I need her?

"Which time?" I asked. "In your wagon? Or in Hashi's cell?"

Elamain pouted. Elamain pouting is enough to move all the sand out of the Punja.

Except I didn't want to.

Elamain had set up housekeeping in one of the buildings that still had a roof; Esnat was, after all, a tanzeer, and Elamain the widow of one. The room she inhabited had been much improved by rugs and silks and gauzes, draped and piled here and there. She reclined on fat cushions tumbled invitingly on thick rugs.

Her golden eyes were sorrowful. "Do you blame me for that?"

Golden eyes; black-silk hair; smooth, dusky skin. The woman was made for bedding.

The woman *enjoyed* her bedding.

With studious care, I kept my eyes above the artful droop in the silk of her underrobe, falling away from her breasts. "You *did* have something to do with it. Wasn't it you who offered Del as a wedding present to Hashi, so he'd give me to you?"

Lids lowered minutely. Black lashes veiled her eyes. "I didn't want to lose you."

"Maybe not. But that's a pretty nasty way of trying to *keep* me, wouldn't you say? It nearly got me castrated."

She sat upright stiffly. "*That* wasn't my fault! How was I to know Hashi would be so annoyed?"

Annoyed. Interesting word: annoyed. I'd have put it more strongly, considering the penalty Hashi demanded in retribution for me sleeping with a woman who slept with whomever she liked—and was widely known for it. Hashi *himself* had known.

I lifted eyebrows. "Are you sleeping with Esnat?"

"Of course I am." Elamain's tone was matter-of fact. "Hashi's *dead* . . . I had to retain my position somehow."

"Sons don't often marry their father's wives."

"I don't have to marry him, Tiger. I only have to sleep with him. Esnat is—" She paused.

"A fool?" I supplied.

She made a gesture of casual acknowledgment with one graceful hand. Then stretched the hand toward me. "I was hoping you were in Iskandar. Come to me, Tiger. Let us rekindle what we once shared."

So much for Sabo's assurances. "I can't, Elamain."

Silk slid lower. "Why not? Have I gotten old and fat?"

She knew better. Elamain was no fatter than she'd been a year and a half before, when I'd helped rescue her caravan from borjuni. And though she was that much older, it didn't show anywhere. She was a lovely, alluring woman.

And I'm not made of stone.

I cleared my throat hastily. "Sabo said *Esnat* sent for me."

Elamain pouted again. "Because I told him to."

"Sabo said that, too. So, now I'm here. Was it business you wanted, Elamain . . . or something else entirely?"

Elamain stopped pouting. Her eyes lost their seductive cast and took on another expression. Elamain was thinking.

A woman like Elamain—*thinking*—can often be dangerous.

"There is someone else," she said.

"Maybe," I agreed warily. "Maybe it's just that I don't *feel* like—"

Elamain didn't let me finish. "No man has ever not *felt* like it," she snapped. "Not with me."

The situation took on an entirely new complexion. Now I was curious; women are often baffling creatures. "Are you serious?" I asked. "No one? Ever? No matter the circumstances?"

"Of course I'm serious." Elamain wasn't amused. "No man—not a single man—has ever said no to me."

"And that means something to you."

Color bloomed in her cheeks. Lovely, dusky cheeks. "How would you feel if you ever lost a sword-dance?"

"We're not talking about a sword-dance, Elamain . . . we're talking about you sleeping with men. One has nothing to do with the other."

"One is very *like* the other," she retorted, "and not in the obviously vulgar sense, either."

"Elamain—"

She rose. Straightened flowing silks. Crossed the carpeted floor to me. "There's someone else," she declared. "A man like you would never say no otherwise."

It intrigued me. "A man like me? What is a man like me like?"

"A man like you is *all* man; why should he say no?"

Elamain had a point, although it didn't please me. "Are we all so predictable?"

"Most of you," she agreed. "Not a single man I've ever met—except Sabo, and other eunuchs—has been blind to the bedding, and what it might be like. *You* certainly weren't."

No.

"And no man," she went on, "whom I have invited into my bed has ever refused the chance. Even men with sworn women, or men with wives at home."

No, I imagine not. She's that kind of woman.

Elamain frowned. "Except you."

"I'm not blind," I told her. "I'm not even deaf. And I'm *certainly* not a eunuch."

"But you won't go to bed with me."

I sighed. "Elamain—"

"Because there is someone else."

I said it clearly: "Yes."

A faint crease marred her brow. Then, abruptly, it cleared. "When you rescued my caravan, there was a woman with you . . . a Northerner. You don't mean *her*, do you? That woman who thinks she's a man?"

I cleared my throat. "First of all, Del doesn't think she's a man. She doesn't *want* to be a man; why should she? She's more than adequate as a woman . . ." I paused. "*More* than adequate."

Elamain was shocked. "She's nearly as tall as you! *Much* taller than me!"

"I like tall women." I thought about where I was, and whom Elamain could call on: a tanzeer with authority. "But I like shorter women, too."

"She's *white-haired*. She looks old."

"She's not white-haired, she's blonde. It bleaches out, down here. And she certainly isn't old; she's several years younger than you."

Uh-oh. Shouldn't have said that.

Elamain glared. "I've *seen* her, Tiger. She looks like a man with breasts."

Unfortunately, I laughed.

Hands went to hips. "She does. She's huge. *And* she carries a sword . . . do you know what that means?"

It took effort not to laugh more. "No, Elamain. Why don't you tell me?"

"It means she hates men. It means she wants to kill them. She probably wants to kill *you*."

"Sometimes," I agreed. "She nearly did, once."

Golden eyes narrowed. "You are teasing me."

I grinned. "A little. And you deserve it. Haven't you learned by now not all men appreciate hearing a woman yowl?"

Elamain lifted an eyebrow. "I'd rather hear the Sandtiger *growl.*"

I smiled. "Not this time."

"You did before."

"That was before."

The crease in her brow came back. "Is she really that good?"

Patiently, I explained, "There's more to it than that."

"Oh?"

"But you wouldn't understand."

Elamain considered it lengthily. And then smiled—as only Elamain can smile—shook back her silky, sooty curtain of unbound hair, took a single smooth step forward to merge her body with mine. And Elamain knows how to merge.

"Then," she said huskily, "I will have to *apply* myself."

Hoolies, she's making it hard.

I was four steps away from the doorway when a man came out of an alley and stepped into my path. A slender, youngish man with dust-colored hair straying out from beneath a wilted turban. He wore plain white gauze, now smudged and soiled. There were spots on his chin, which tried to bury itself in his neck. His eyes were a medium brown. His manner hesitant.

"Sandtiger?" he asked. When I nodded, he looked relieved. "I'm Esnat," he said.

Esnat. *Esnat.* Guilt made me hot. Or maybe it was the sunburn.

"Esnat," I answered; a stupid sort of answer.

He didn't seem to mind. "Esnat," he agreed. "I'm tanzeer of Sasqaat."

Elamain's sleeping with *this?*

Well, Elamain would.

I cleared my throat. "So Sabo said."

"Yes. I told him to."

Esnat was not the sort of man I expected Hashi to sire. He was diffident, polite, altogether too unassuming for a man in his position. Which meant, I thought resignedly, Elamain had free rein. He only *thought* he ruled.

I thought about Elamain. "So," I said, "can I help you?"

Esnat glanced pointedly past me to the doorway which made me feel even hotter. Then gestured for me to follow.

I did not, at first, intend to. After all, I'd just come from Elamain, and who knows what Esnat might do? He *was* Hashi's son; appearances don't always count.

But his manner remained much the same: hesitant, polite, almost too unassuming. He was a very humble man—or else a clever one.

I stayed where I was. "What is it?" I asked clearly.

Esnat stopped, came back a few steps, looked worriedly past me again. "Will you *come?*" he hissed "I don't want her to hear."

I didn't move. "Why not?"

He fixed medium brown eyes on me and glared. It was the first expression of any passion I'd seen on his face. "Because, you lumbering fool, how am I supposed to plot in secret if I'm not *in* secret?"

Lumbering fool, was I? Well, at least it sounded more like a man who really was tanzeer. Or believed he was.

I remembered I had my *jivatma*. I went with Esnat.

Not far. Only around the corner, where he sheltered in a deep doorway. It left me out in the street, but since I wasn't yet part of the secret I decided it didn't really matter.

Esnat cast quick glances around the street behind me. "All right," he said finally, "I sent for you because—"

"*Elamain* sent for me."

He only nodded, clearly impatient. "Yes, yes, of course she did . . . *I* wanted you, too, but I've learned it's easier to let her think she runs things." His manner was matter-of-fact, very like Elamain's when speaking of Esnat's status. "And I know what she wanted, too . . . but you don't know what *I* want."

I shifted stance a little.

Esnat saw it; smiled. "That's what I want," he said.

I froze. "You want *what?*"

"You," he said plainly. "I want to hire you."

I relaxed a little. For a moment . . . hoolies, the moment wasn't yet gone. "Why do you want to hire me?" And delicately: "What for?"

"Your sword," Esnat said.

I wasn't born yesterday. "Excuse me," I said. "What sword are we talking about?"

Esnat scowled at me blankly. And then understood, and gaped. "Not *that*, you fool . . . I want to hire a sword-dancer to do sword-dancerly things."

I wished he'd stop calling me a fool. Particularly since it was what everyone called *him*—and I didn't think Esnat and I were anything alike.

"Sword-dancerly things," I echoed. "What sort of things are those?"

Esnat blinked at me. "Don't you know?"

We were, I began to think, talking at cross-purposes. Time for plain speech. "What do you want me to do?"

"Help me win a woman."

"I thought you were already sleeping with Elamain."

"Not *that* woman . . . a woman I can marry."

I grinned. "Then send Elamain away."

Esnat laughed. "No, not quite yet—Elamain serves a purpose. For now. And besides, how else would a man like me get a woman like that in my bed?"

He wasn't *that* bad . . . well, maybe he was. But still—"You're a tanzeer, Esnat . . . you can have any woman." I amended it quickly, thinking of Del. "Almost any woman."

"Any I bought, yes . . . even *Elamain* is bought." His smile wasn't amused. "The issue isn't Elamain. The issue is Sabra."

I nodded slowly. "And I'm supposed to help you win her. How?"

"By dancing, of course."

With effort, I retained my patience. "Esnat, my dancing isn't going to help you marry this woman."

"Of course it will," he assured me. "She'll know I'm serious about courting her." He paused, observing my frown. "Don't you see? It used to be when a man wanted to impress a woman, he fought her other suitors. Whoever won, won the woman. Well, I'm a tanzeer, and we don't do those things. It's stupid to risk ourselves when there are sword-dancers to do it for us."

I ignored the implication. "You said something like that before."

"And I meant it. This will be a proxy dance. A way of getting her attention, of making her see my point. So she'll accept me as a suitor."

Maybe this was the way tanzeers got married. At any rate, it wasn't really my business. Something else was. "How much are you offering?"

Esnat told me.

"You're sandsick!" I exploded.

"No. I'm serious."

I stared at him. "That much for a woman?"

Esnat looked right back. "Isn't a woman worth it?"

He was as bad as Del. "You're putting a lot at stake," I told him. "What if I lose? Will you want my *gehetties*, then?"

"Your *gehett*—oh." He laughed out loud, which didn't amuse me much. "No, no—that was my father's style. I'd just as soon you kept your *gehetties*, Sandtiger . . . I don't need any more eunuchs."

"What if I lose?" I repeated. "You're offering a lot if I win. What happens if I lose?"

Esnat's smile died. "You won't lose," he said. "I saw that sword."

I began to understand. "You're not such a fool after all."

Esnat's eyes glinted. "I let them think I am. It makes it easier. If they have no expectations, I don't have to waste my time trying to live up to them. I can do what I want. What I want is Sabra." He shrugged. "I am not the sort of man women notice. You know that by looking at me; *I* know that by looking at me."

"Oh, I don't know—"

"Don't try to be kind, Sandtiger." He shrugged a little, tucking hands inside wide sleeves. "A woman like Sabra will not notice me, either, unless I find a way to make her look. She's wealthy herself; coin will not impress her. I need help. I need an advantage. I need a way of making her *see* me, to see what I can offer." He looked a little above my left shoulder. "That sword," he said plainly, "can give me my advantage. News of it is all over Iskandar. Every tanzeer will want it, and you. But if *I* hire the man who carries that sword . . ." Esnat smiled happily. "I can win Sabra's regard."

Men have done more for less. "You knew," I said. "You knew if you baited the hook with Elamain, I'd come at once. And you would buy my service before anyone else could offer."

"I have learned," Esnat said, "to strike before anyone else. To do the unexpected. To *anticipate* certain things . . . things like magical swords."

"You couldn't have anticipated this sword."

"Well, no, not exactly," he agreed judiciously, "but I have made it a practice to be *aware* . . ." Brown eyes were shrewd. "Will you hire yourself to me?"

It would be easy enough, I thought, even with a possessed *jivatma* I didn't want to use. I am good, very good; if I wasted no time at all, fighting to win instead of dance, it could be over immediately. And I wouldn't risk hurting anyone, meanwhile making a huge profit.

But I *liked* Esnat. Slowly, I shook my head. "I admire your intentions, but you're offering too much."

Esnat's eyes took on anxious appeal. "Don't you think you're worth it?"

I shrugged. "What I'm worth doesn't really matter. I just think this is too much. I don't want to beggar you. There'd be nothing left over for Sabra."

Esnat grinned. "If you want to *win* the game, you have to be willing to lose it."

Hoolies, this was ridiculous. But if that's the way he felt . . . "All right," I agreed at last, "I'll accept your terms. You make it hard not to."

Esnat smiled happily. "I'll see to sending the challenge. The dance will be in two days."

There was nothing left to say. I turned to walk away.

Esnat's voice stopped me. "Did you find the bait to your liking?"

I didn't bother to look around. "Ask Elamain."

Chapter 11

The walk back through Iskandar's teeming bazaar was odd. There were still hundreds of people, all jammed together in the alleyways and streets, but the feel of it was different. The *smell* of it was different.

At first, elbowing my way through clusters of people gathered here and there at stalls, or talking together in groups, I thought it was simply that there were more of them. And then I realized, as I worked my way more deeply into the center of the city, it had nothing to do with numbers. It had to do with emotions. I could actually *taste* them: anticipation, impatience, a tense expectancy.

Puzzled, I glanced around. And knew almost at once what part of the feeling was.

The city was empty of tribes. It hadn't been so the day before. People of the desert had walked freely throughout the city, doing much the same as the others: looking, talking, buying. But now the tribes were gone. Only the others remained.

Also tanzeers, and their guards, filling narrow streets.

"This isn't right," I muttered, pushing my way through the crowd.

Nearby, someone spoke of the Oracle, discussing divinity. A listener disagreed; an argument ensued. I don't know who won.

Nearby, someone spoke of the jhihadi and the changes promised the South. That a man with a newborn power could unite the Southron tribes, then change the sand to grass.

I shook my head as I walked. It was impossible.

At last I made my way through and went to find Del, to tell her about Esnat and the dance I'd accepted. But discovered she was gone.

Lena looked up from cooking. "Some men came by earlier, looking for you."

"Oh?"

"They said they represented a tanzeer named Hadjib, who wanted to hire you."

I shook my head. "Don't know him."

Lena's expression was odd. "They said their employer had heard about your sword."

So it began. Everyone wanted the power. "Where's Del?"

"She went to the circles, with Alric. She said she had a sword-dance."

Foreboding was swift and painful. "She said she'd wait here for me."

"No, she didn't." Lena grinned. "She said she *might* be here."

I glared down at her. "It isn't fair," I complained. "You women always protect one another."

Lena's brows rose. "Is that what Elamain does?"

I blinked. "She *told* you about Elamain?"

"A little." Lena's smile didn't waver. "I've known her kind before."

I had no more time for Elamain or her kind. "Never mind, it doesn't matter—" And then I broke it off as something occurred to me. "Hoolies—she wouldn't. Would she? *Would* she?" I stared at Alric's wife. "She wouldn't challenge Ajani without telling me."

Lena looked right back. "Why don't you go and see?"

But I was already gone.

He was big. He was blond. I'd never seen him before.

Oh, hoolies, bascha . . . you said you wouldn't . . . not with *him*—he wasn't worth a circle . . . you said he wasn't worth it . . . you said you wouldn't do it—

Maybe it isn't Ajani.

Don't let this be Ajani.

As always, she'd drawn a crowd. Most were sword-dancers, which was to be expected; many were tanzeers; the rest were simply people. Southroners mostly, with a Northerner here and there.

Don't tease him, bascha . . . just get it over with.

My belly knotted up. My hands itched for a sword. My eyes wanted to shut; I wouldn't let them do it. I made myself watch.

He was not particularly good, but neither was he bad. His patterns were open and loose, lacking proper focus, but he was big enough to do damage if he ever got a stroke through. I doubted that would happen; Del's defense is too good.

Hurry up, bascha.

I wet dry lips. Bit into a cheek. Felt the tickle of new sweat under arms and dribbling down temples.

Oh, bascha, please.

I thought again of Staal-Ysta. Of the circle. Of the dance we'd had to dance, before the watching *voca*. Before the eyes of her daughter. No one was there for me. No one thought of me.

Except for the woman I faced.

Then, I hadn't felt helpless. Used, yes; tricked, certainly. But not helpless. I knew Del would never go for the kill, any more than I would. And we hadn't; not really. That had taken the sword. A thirsty, nameless *jivatma* demanding to be blooded.

Now, I felt helpless. I stood on the rim of the crowd watching Del dance and was conscious only of fear. Not of her skill, not of her grace, not of her flawless patterns. Only of my fear.

Would it always be like this?

Someone moved next to me. "I taught the bascha well."

I didn't look. I didn't have to. I knew the broken voice; the familiar arrogance. "She taught herself, Abbu. With help from Staal-Ysta."

"And some from you, I think." Abbu Bensir smiled as I chanced a quick glance at him. "I won't deny your skill, or sully my own in the doing. We learned from the same shodo."

I watched Del again. She had recovered quickness, timing, finesse. Her strokes were firm and sure, her patterns artlessly smooth. But she wasn't trying to kill him.

I frowned. "Then this can't be Ajani."

Abbu, startled, looked at the man in the circle. "Ajani? No, that's not. I don't know who that is."

I turned sharply. "You *know* him?"

"Ajani? Yes. He rides both sides of the border." He shrugged. "A man of many parts."

The phrase stopped me a moment. *"A man of many parts."* I knew I'd heard it before. It had to do with the jhihadi; something the Oracle had said—

No time for that now. "Is he here? Ajani?"

Abbu shrugged. "Possibly."

The sound of the forgotten sword-dance faded. "Abbu—is he *here in Iskandar?"*

Abbu Bensir looked straight at me. Saw how intent I was. "Possibly," he repeated. "I haven't seen him yet, but that doesn't mean he's not here. No more than it means he *is.*"

"But you'd know him if you saw him."

Abbu frowned. "Yes. I told you; I know the man."

"What does he look like?"

"He's a Northerner. Blond, blue-eyed, fair . . . taller even than you and heavier in bone. A little older, I think. And a little younger than me." Abbu grinned. "Do you want to ask him to dance? He's not a sword-dancer."

"I know what he is," I retorted, staring grimly out at Del.

Abbu looked also. "If I see him, I'll tell him you want him . . . *ah*—there, she's won. And no disgrace in the doing."

Blades clashed a final time. The Northerner, patterns destroyed, reeled out of the circle, which meant the dance was forfeit. He stood on the ruined perimeter and stared in shock at Del.

Who was, as always, contained, not glorying in her win.

Relief was a tangible thing. "I don't want him," I said. "And don't tell him anything."

Abbu studied me. "Is this an old hatred?"

Now I could give him my full attention. "I said: it isn't anything."

He rubbed thoughtfully at the notch in the ruined arch of his nose. "We are not friends," he said, "this Northerner and I. I *know* him; that is all."

It didn't really matter. Even if Abbu was lying and he and Ajani *were* friends, advance warning would do very little. One way or another, Del and I would find him.

I looked out at Del, who was tending to her sword. "What would you call a man," I began, "who raids the unguarded caravans of families, killing everyone he finds except those he can sell as slaves. Those who are only children, because they offer less trouble. Those who are *Northern* children, because they fetch a higher price on the slaveblock in the South."

Abbu looked also, and for a long time. Dark eyes were fathomless, masking what he thought. When he did speak, his voice held no emotion. "What I would call *him* doesn't matter; what matters is what I call her."

Something moved deep in my belly. "And what is that, Abbu?"

"Sword-dancer," he said huskily, then shouldered his way through the crowd.

I turned back, intending to go to Del; was stopped by a hand on my shoulder. "Sandtiger!" the hand's owner cried. "I didn't know you had a son. Why didn't you tell me? And such a fine speaker, too—the boy was born to be a *skjald*."

Red hair, blue eyes, flowing mustaches. "Rhashad," I said blankly. Then, with exceptional clarity, "Where—is—he?"

He jerked a thumb. "Over in that cantina. He's right in the middle of a story about his father, the South's greatest sworddancer . . . I didn't offer to argue, since the boy's proud of you, but he might recall there is *me*, after all, and Abbu Bensir—"

I cut him off. "—and your mother, no doubt." I scowled briefly out at Del, who was taking her own sweet time. "Over in that cantina, you say . . . ? Well, I think it's time I met this son." I sucked air. *"Del!"*

She heard me. Saw me. Made her way across the circle. Her face was a trifle flushed and pale hair was damp at the temples, but she appeared no worse for wear. "What is it?" she asked quietly, as if to reprove me for noise.

I had no time for it. "Come on. Rhashad says this fool who's been going around telling everyone he's my son is over in that cantina." I waved a hand in the proper direction.

Del looked over at it. "Go ahead," she suggested. "I have to claim my winnings."

"Can't they wait?"

"Yours never do."

Rhashad beamed at Del. "Won the dance, did you? A delicate girl like you?"

Del, who is not precisely delicate, knew the manner for what it was. And since she liked Rhashad—don't ask me why—she was less inclined to argue. "I won," she agreed. "Do you want to dance with me next?"

Blue eyes widened. "Against you? Never! I'd hate to crack those fragile bones."

Del showed him her teeth. "My bones are very hardy."

"Talk about your bones some other time," I suggested. "Are you coming with me?"

"No," Del said. "I told you that already. Go ahead; I'll catch up."

Rhashad made a grand gesture. "I'll show her the way."

Hoolies, it wasn't worth it. I went off to see my son.

The cantina was small. It was, after all, culled from the rest of the ruined city, which meant it offered little in the way of amenities. There was a makeshift blanket roof, which gave its customers shade in which to drink, but that was about it.

I lingered in the doorway, looking for my son.

Dark-haired, blue-eyed, nineteen or twenty. Who couldn't ride very well, judging by his mount. Who didn't carry a sword, having a tongue instead, and liking to use it more than was good for him.

Not much to go on. But I thought it would do, under the circumstances.

There were men gathered in the cantina. No chairs, but hastily-cobbled stools and benches were scattered about the room. In the center, on a stool, sat a man with his back to the door; never a good thing. But plainly he wasn't concerned about who might come through. He had an audience.

The voice was young and accented. He obviously reveled in the attention his story gained; everyone was enthralled. "—and so I, too, found myself the destroyer of a great cat, just as my father was, the Sandtiger—you all know of *him*—and so I marked my victory by taking the cat's claws and making myself this necklace." A hand went to his neck, rattled something briefly. "It was, I thought, a most opportune and appropriate meeting between this great cat and the Sandtiger's cub—such is in the blood—and when at last I meet my father I will be most pleased to show him the claws and tell him what I've done. Surely he will be proud."

The listeners nodded as one: surely the Sandtiger would be.

Except I wasn't. Not *proud*. What I was, was—hoolies, I don't know what I was. I felt very odd.

"Of course," the boy added, "I kept my face pretty."

The men in the cantina laughed.

Is this my son? I wondered. Could I have sired this mouth?

I left the door and moved quietly into the room, saying nothing, pausing behind the young man. There wasn't much to see: dark brown hair brushing his shoulders; a vivid green-striped burnous; eloquent, graceful hands of a different color than mine. He was tanned, yes, but the sun marked him differently. Darker than a Northerner. Lighter than a Southroner; lighter even than me. And there was the foreign accent, coloring his Southron.

Why wait any longer?

I drew a steadying breath. "Where I come from," I said quietly, "a man doesn't name a father unless he's certain of the truth."

He started to turn on his stool, swinging around easily. His face was young, open; a bit, as he'd said, on the pretty side. "Oh, but I *am* certain . . . I am the *Sandtiger's* son—" Dark blue eyes abruptly widened in belated recognition.

"Oh?" I asked softly.

The young man rose in a single smooth movement. I didn't even see it coming.

"Do you *know*," the boy cried, "how long I've been waiting for this?"

I am big enough and strong enough to withstand most single punches, especially when they come from a smaller, slighter man. But there was a stool behind me, and as the blow connected with my jaw I spread both feet for balance and promptly fell over the thing.

It wasn't a graceful fall. It was an *embarrassing* fall.

And Del was there to see it.

I sat up, dragged my sheathed, harnessed blade into a more comfortable position, sat there swearing. Ignored the staring audience and looked around for the boy, who'd headed for the doorway. He was gone, but she wasn't.

Del drifted into the cantina. Her arrival did have one advantage: now they gaped at her instead of gaping at me.

"Fatherhood," she commented, "can be a painful thing."

I got up, untangling my legs from the stool and kicking the thing aside. "That lying Punja-mite isn't my son . . . what he is, is a charlatan!" I scowled at her. "*You* saw who he was!"

"Yes," Del agreed.

"I'll kill him," I promised.

One of the men spoke up. "You'd kill your own son?"

I glared at him. "He isn't my own son. He isn't even Southron."

The man shrugged a little. "*You* don't look Southron, either." And then reconsidered it. "Maybe a half, or a quarter. But you're not a full Southroner. There are other things in the stewpot."

For some reason, it offended me. Usually I don't much care what I look like, or what people think of me. In my business it doesn't matter where I was born, or to how many races. Just that I can dance. And win; I'm paid to win.

I glared. "At least I was *raised* here. The Punja is my home; *that* boy's from somewhere else. He's a lying, scheming foreigner, using my name to gain *him* one."

The Southroner shrugged. "No harm in that."

No harm. No *harm*. I'd give him "no harm."

"Tiger," Del said quietly. "Is it worth fighting over?"

No. Not here. And not *him;* who I wanted was Bellin the Cat.

"Panjandrum," I muttered disgustedly, and stalked out of the cantina.

Del's tone was quiet. "Are you angry because he lied? Or because it isn't true?"

We sat in one of the broken rooms in one of the broken buildings doubling as a cantina. Because there was no proper roof the full moon had free rein, painting the room silver. Dripping candles and smoky lanterns added illumination. There were no proper tables, either, and nothing resembling chairs; merely bits and pieces of odds and ends appropriated for things on which to sit, or on which to put the liquor. It was very much like the cantina in which I'd discovered Bellin.

Masquerading as my son.

I had known all along there was nothing to it. While it wasn't *impossible* I'd sired a son of his age, it was a bit unlikely. At least, unlikely that the boy would know enough to tell everyone the Sandtiger had sired him. It seemed more likely that if there *was* a sandtiger cub wandering about the South, he wouldn't know who he was.

He wouldn't know who *I* was.

I sighed. "I don't know."

Del smiled a little. "It bothers you now, doesn't it? You had begun to think what it might be like to have a son . . . begun to think how you'd feel, seeing your own immortality; it's what a child is." She hunched a shoulder, looking at liquor instead of at me. "I know what it was for me, seeing Kalle, but I *knew* I had a daughter. For you, it was different."

Different. One might say so.

I sighed again, sipped slowly, let aqivi slide down my throat. The familiar fire was muted; I was thinking of something else. "He shouldn't have done it, bascha. That kind of lie is wrong. If he wants so badly to become a man of repute—a *panjandrum*—he might look for a better way than borrowing someone's name."

"Or someone's other than yours."

Dull anger stirred. "It took me too long to get it . . . I won't share it with anyone, certainly not with a liar."

"He must have had a reason."

"That foreign-born Punja-mite doesn't need a reason for anything, remember?" I said testily. "All he wants is fame. So he decided to borrow mine."

Del's tone was dry. "You have more than enough to share."

"That's not the point. The point is he's been riding around the South for hoolies knows *how* long telling hoolies knows *how many* people he's my son." I heard the passion in my voice and purposely damped it. "I just don't like it."

Del sipped her wine. "If you find him, you can tell him."

"*I'll* find him," I promised. "He can't hide from me."

Her mouth twitched slightly. "He seems to have done a good job of it for the last several weeks. I doubt you'll find him again unless he wants you to."

"I'll find him," I repeated.

A body arrived at our low "table." "Well, Sandtiger," he said, "I hear you've been hired to dance the day after tomorrow."

I glanced up: Rhashad. "The word's gone around already?" Thinking Esnat hadn't wasted much time bragging about his suit.

The red-haired Borderer grinned. "All over Iskandar. Doesn't take long when the Sandtiger is involved." He sat down on the floor, not bothering with a "stool," and leaned against the crumbling wall. A sun-spotted hand, waving, signaled for more aqivi. "I plan to put money on it."

I shrugged. "Nothing to bet on, yet . . . I don't have an opponent."

Rhashad displayed big teeth in the shadow of ruddy mustaches. "Could even be me."

I didn't even blink. "Your mother wouldn't like it."

"Why not?"

"She wouldn't want you to lose."

"Hah!" Rhashad had played this game before. "I wouldn't be so certain of winning, Sandtiger . . . word is also making the rounds that you're not the dancer you once were."

I drank sparingly. "Oh?"

Rhashad waited until the recently summoned aqivi jug arrived, then splashed a measure into a cup. "Oh, yes. It's quite well known. The Sandtiger, rumor says, hasn't danced in months. He's lost his speed, his edge . . . lost a lot of his fire. Because of a wound, I hear . . . a cut not fully healed."

I smiled insincerely. "You've been talking to Abbu. Or *listening* to him; that's worse."

Rhashad shrugged. "You know Abbu Bensir. Part of the reason he's who he is, is because of the dance up here." The Borderer tapped his head. "You've never been a victim; you don't know what it's like."

"Abbu says whatever he likes." I drank more aqivi. "You know rumor as well as I, Rhashad. How many times have we heard how old and slow someone is—or how young and undisciplined—and discovered how wrong we were?" I grinned, showing teeth white as his own. "Sounds to me like someone—Abbu, maybe?—is try-ing to force better odds."

The Borderer nodded. "Not a bad attempt, since you *don't* look as healthy as I've seen you look." He grinned back pointedly. "And yes, I know rumor . . . like the ones about this Oracle fellow and the jhihadi."

I sighed. "What now?"

He shrugged. "Just that this Oracle fellow is supposed to show up here in the next couple of days. Tomorrow, maybe the next day. Maybe the day after that."

"They've been saying that for days."

"This time the rumors are a bit more specific." Rhashad sucked down aqivi. "I figure it doesn't matter. Except, of course, it'll have some effect on our coin-pouches."

"Why?" Del asked. "What has the Oracle—or the jhihadi—have to do with money?"

"There's likely to be a war." He sat against the wall with legs splayed, combing mustaches with his fingers. "Haven't you seen the change? The tribes have all but disappeared—the warriors, that is . . . word is all the tribesmen have gathered in the foothills to welcome this Oracle fellow. And then they're supposed to bring him down into Iskandar, so he can name the jhihadi."

I nodded thoughtfully. "I noticed things felt different. The tanzeers are hiring armed men."

"And a few assassins." Rhashad's teeth showed briefly. "That's never been my style, but it didn't stop him from asking."

I frowned. "Who asked what?"

"A tanzeer asked me to help assassinate the Oracle." Rhashad gestured. "Not in so many words, of course, but that was the gist of the talk."

I rubbed at gritty eyes. "I thought it might come to that. They can't afford to let him live . . . *especially* if he's rousing the warriors like this. They'll try to kill him before he does any more harm."

Del shook her head. "That will *cause* a war."

Rhashad pursed his lips. "A small one, yes . . . but without the Oracle to rouse them, the tribes will never remain united. They'll end up fighting themselves."

"And the tanzeers will win." I nodded. "So, they're hiring sword-dancers to fill out their guard, planning to send them against the tribes."

"Seems likely." Rhashad drank. "I'm not an assassin. I told the tanzeer's man I'd hire on to dance, but not to murder a holy prophet. He wasn't interested in that, so I still don't have a job."

Del looked at me. "You have a job."

"I hired on to *dance*," I emphasized. "Believe me bascha, the last thing I'd do is get myself tangled up in a holy war, *or* an assassination. I don't mind risking myself in a circle—since it really isn't a risk—" that for Rhashad's benefit, "—but I won't hire on to assassinate anyone. Let alone this Oracle."

Rhashad's blue eyes glinted. " 'A man of many parts.' "

Del frowned. "What?"

"Oh, that's one of the things they're saying about the jhihadi. That, and his special 'power.' Since nobody knows who—or what—he is, they're making up anything."

I looked at Del. "That's how Abbu described Ajani."

"*Abbu* described him . . ." Del let it go, interpreting other things. "So, Abbu knows Ajani. And does he ride with him, too? Both sides of the border?"

"I don't think so, bascha."

"How do you know? *I* danced with him; I have learned a little about him. Abbu could be—"

"—many things, but he's not a borjuni. He's not a murderer, or a man who sells children." I kept my tone even. "He said he knew Ajani. He also said they were not friends. Do *you* claim everyone you meet as a friend? Or are they all enemies?"

Rhashad, not much of a diplomat, didn't sense the danger. "*I'm* not an enemy, bascha . . . I'd much rather be a friend."

Del's tone cut through his laughter. "Do you know Ajani?"

Rhashad stared at her. Amusement died away, "I don't know him. I know *of* him. What's he to you?'

Del was very succinct. "A man I plan to kill."

Ruddy brows arched up. "Oh, now, bascha—"

"Don't," I said clearly.

He is slow, but he gets there. "Oh," he said at last. And then went off in another direction. "You danced with Abbu Bensir?"

"Sparred," she answered briefly.

I grinned. "That's what *she* calls it. Ask Abbu about it: he'll tell you he was teaching her."

"Abbu wouldn't teach a woman." Rhashad eyed her thoughtfully. "*I* would, though. Do you still need a shodo?"

Del's tone was cold. "What I need is Ajani."

I set down the jug of aqivi. "What *I* think you need—"

But I didn't finish it. Something intruded.

It was, at first, unidentifiable. It was noise, nothing more; an odd, alien noise. I thought immediately of hounds, then dismissed it impatiently. It didn't sound like that; besides, there *were* no hounds any more.

Rhashad stirred uneasily, leaning forward from the wall to alter posture and balance. He did it without thinking; ingrained habits die hard. "What the hoolies is *that?*"

I shook my head. Del didn't move.

The noise renewed itself in the silence of the cantina. No one spoke. No one moved. All anyone did was listen.

It was a high-pitched, keening wail. It echoed in the foothills, then crept onto the plateau and into the city itself.

"Tribes," I said intently, as the noise abruptly changed.

The keening wail altered pitch. Hundreds of voices joined in exultant ululation.

Rhashad's eyes were fixed. "Hoolies," he breathed in awe.

Del looked at me. "You know the tribes."

It was an invitation to explain. But there was little I could say. "If I had to guess," I murmured finally, "I'd say it's the Oracle. They're paying tribute to him . . . or else preparing for an attack."

"Foolhardy," Rhashad muttered. "They'd have to come up the rim trail. The plateau is too easy to defend."

I flicked a glance at him. "Who's camped at the head of that trail?"

"Tribes," Del murmured. "But still, I think they're outnumbered."

"We don't even know their numbers. Some of the warriors may have come through here every day, but most have camped elsewhere. The *families* have been here . . . with a few men to protect them."

Rhashad nodded. "To make things look normal."

I rose and kicked back my stool. "I think we should go back. Alric's probably with Lena and the girls, but you never know."

Even as we moved, the ululation died. The absence was eerie and strangely unsettling. Then everyone in the cantina was heading out the door.

"Come on, bascha," I said. "I don't like the way this feels—like something's going to happen."

Del followed me into the street.

* * *

Something did happen. It waited until we were a most all the way back to the house we shared with Alric, giving us time to breathe, but then it grew impatient. The time for waiting was done.

Del and I heard it before we saw it. Hoofbeats, then frenzied shouting. About four streets over.

"The bazaar," Del said, unsheathing Boreal. In the moonlight, the blade was white.

I unsheathed my own, hating it all the while.

In the bazaar, people gathered. They hugged the shadows of empty stalls and dwellings uneasily, disliking uncertainty, but not knowing what else to do. In the middle of the bazaar, in the city's precise center, tribesmen had gathered. Not many; I counted six, all mounted and ready to ride. We outnumbered them vastly.

A seventh horse was mounted, but not in the usual way. The man who rode it was dead.

"What are they?" Del asked.

"A couple of Vashni. A Hanjii. A Tularain. Even two Salset."

"Do you know the Salset?"

"I knew *them*. They didn't know a chula."

A stirring ran through the crowd. One of the tribesmen—a Vashni—continued his harangue, pointing at the body, then gesticulated sharply. Clearly, he was unhappy.

"What is he saying?" Del asked, since he spoke pure Desert in the dialect of the Punja.

I released a noisy breath. "He's giving us a warning—no, not *us;* he's warning the tanzeers. The man—the dead man—crept up to their gathering and tried to murder the Oracle, just as Rhashad predicted. Now he's telling the tanzeers they're all fools; that the Oracle will live to present the jhihadi to us, just as he has promised." I paused, listening. "He says they don't want war. They only want what's rightfully theirs."

"The South," Del said grimly.

"And the sand changed to grass."

The warrior stopped shouting. He gestured, and one of the others cut the ropes binding the body on the horse. The body fell facedown; it was turned over roughly, then stripped of its wrappings to display the bloody nakedness and its blatant mutilation.

I must have made a sound. Del looked at me sharply. "Do you know him?"

"Sword-dancer," I answered tightly. "Not a very good one—and *not* a very smart one—but someone I knew nonetheless." I drew in a deep breath. "He didn't deserve that."

"He tried to kill the Oracle."

"Stupid, stupid Morab." I touched her on the arm. "Let's go, bascha. The message has been delivered."

"Will the tanzeers listen?"

"No. This just means they'll have to look to their own men to find another assassin. No sword-dancer will take the job; I'm surprised Morab did."

"Maybe he wanted the money."

I slanted her a disgusted glance. "It'll be hard to spend it now."

Even as Del and I went back into the shadows, the hoofbeats sounded again. I knew without having to look: the warriors were riding out. And Morab was dead and gone, lost to greed and stupidity. Someone would bury him; already the gawkers gathered.

The darkness was thick and deep in the caverns of recessed doors. Del and I knew better; we avoided those we could without exposing ourselves too much by using too much of the street. A compromise was best. Compromise—and a sword.

And yet the sword didn't help much when the *thing* slashed across my vision and thunked home in the wood of a door jamb but two feet from my face.

"Sorry," a voice said. "I just wanted a little practice.'

He should have known better. Not only did the voice tell me who he was, it told me *where* he was. And I went there quickly to find him.

He grinned, stepping smoothly out of a doorway directly across the street. In each of his hands was an ax; the third was stuck in the wood.

"Ax," Del said quietly, inspecting the planted weapon as I moved to cut off its thrower.

"Oh, I know," I answered lightly, and teased his chin with my blade.

"Wait," Bellin said.

"*You* wait," I suggested. "What in hoolies do you think you're doing?"

Bellin's tone was disingenuous. "Practicing," he declared.

"Not any more." A flick this way and that; axes spilled out of his hands. "No," I said plainly, as he made a motion to scoop them up.

In the moonlight, his face was young. Almost too young, and too pretty. The grin bled away from his mouth. "I knew what I was doing."

"I want to know: *why?*"

He stared back at me unflinchingly, ignoring stinging hands. "Because I could," he told me. "And because you're *you*."

Del jerked the ax from the doorjamb and brought it over to me. "He might have sheared off your nose."

Bellin the Cat smiled. "I just wanted your attention."

I eyed him assessively, disliking his attitude. Then reached out my left hand and caught a wad of cloth at his throat, jamming him back against the wall. "You," I said, "are a fool. A lying, conniving fool who's lucky to be alive. I should give you a spanking—with three feet of Northern steel."

With my fist tucked up beneath his chin, Beilin's face was less than happy. But he didn't sound repentant. "I hit you in the cantina because I had to."

"Oh? Why is that?"

"If I *hadn't*, they might have begun to suspect me."

"Who is that?" I asked.

"The men I'm riding with."

"The men you're riding with would have required you to hit me? I find that hard to believe."

"You don't know them." He swallowed awkwardly. "If you'd remove your hand from my throat, I might be able to breathe . . . and then I could explain."

I let go all at once. "Explain," I said harshly, as Bellin staggered his way to regained balance.

He rubbed gingerly at his throat, then set his green-striped robe into order. "The story would sound better over a jug of aqivi."

I lifted my blade slightly. "Or over three feet of steel."

Bellin looked past me to Del. Smiled weakly, eyeing the ax in her hand, then glanced back at me. "It was your idea."

"*My* idea—" Abruptly I stepped close, forcing him to back up. The doorway behind him was open; Bellin fell in, then through. I followed silently with Del on my heels. "My idea, panjandrum?"

"Yes." He stopped and stood his ground. "My axes," he said plaintively.

Del and I didn't move.

Bellin, seeing it, sighed. Rubbed vigorously at his head, which hurt his cut hand and mussed his hair, then glared back at me. "You said I could ride with you if I found Ajani for you."

Now it was Del's turn. "Have you?" she asked. "Or is this another trick?"

"No trick," he assured us. "Do you know how many months it took me to find him?"

"Less than me," she snapped. "What about Ajani?"

Bellin sighed. He was, I realized all over again, no older than nineteen, maybe twenty, and a stranger to the South. I didn't know much about him except he was seeking fame, and he had a smooth way with his tongue. I was surprised he was still alive, that no one had killed him yet.

And then I remembered the axes.

"We're waiting," I said grimly.

Bellin nodded. "Not long after meeting you, I set out to find Ajani. It was the condition, you said; I decided to fulfill it."

The ax in Del's hand flashed. "Don't waste time, panjandrum."

He eyed her. Eyed the ax. Considered what it might be like to die by his own weapon; at least, I *think* he did. But it got him talking again.

"You can't just walk into countless towns and settlements asking for Ajani," he explained, even though Del, so straightforward, had. "It takes more than that. Cleverness, guile, a hint of ingenuity." Briefly, he smiled. "What it takes is a man who knows how to fit a story to suit his needs."

"The Sandtiger's son," I murmured.

Bellin nodded. "Who was I, but a stranger? A foreigner, to boot.

No one would tell me the truth if I said what I really wanted. So I fed them a story. The best one I could think of." He touched a shadow at his neck; strung claws rattled. "I said I was your son. People talked to me."

"Why?" Del asked harshly. "Why go to so much trouble? You must know we want no part of you."

It was blunt, but true. Bellin only shrugged. "But if I told you what you wanted to know, you'd think more kindly of me. Stories would make the rounds. My name might be mentioned in them."

"Oh, *your* name is known," I said, "except you stole it from me."

He grinned. "Besides, I might grow on you. I grow on a lot of people. Once they get to know me, they're rather fond of me."

Pointedly, Del and I said nothing.

Bellin cleared his throat. "Using your name made me known, with some claim to fame, so I could get some attention. It bought me into places, gave me a card to play when—*if*—Ajani became aware of me, or was *made* aware of me." Bellin shrugged. "It got me what I wanted: hired by Ajani. And it got *you* what you wanted . . . but more than you ever expected."

Del's tone was curt. "What is that, panjandrum?"

"Ajani is the jhihadi."

Chapter 13

"*What?*" I blurted.

Del managed more. "If you think for one moment we will believe such nonsense—"

Bellin merely smiled. "It doesn't matter what either of *you* believe, only what everyone else does."

That silenced us a moment; it was too true to ignore.

Then Del got angry. "I don't care what he calls himself. I know what he is—I know what he's *done*."

Bellin interrupted. "But it matters. Can't you see? Ajani is setting himself up as the jhihadi. He will make people believe he is; if they believe hard enough, he *will* be the jhihadi, because they'll make him so."

"Do you mean . . ." I trailed off a moment, thinking about everything that had happened since we'd first heard about the jhihadi. "You're telling us this entire charade was Ajani's idea? The Oracle and everything?"

"Impossible," Del said curtly. "Not with the tribes involved. Not with so many people ready to name him messiah."

Bellin shrugged. "I don't know anything about Oracles and jhihadis—I'm a foreigner, remember? All I know is, Ajani's manipulating the city for his own benefit."

I shook my head. "Not the whole city. Not everyone who's

here. Not all the tribes, the tanzeers, the people who need a god. He *can't* do all that . . . it just isn't possible."

Bellin sighed. "He's hired men to spread the rumors. I'm one of them. We've been going out among all the people dropping hints here and there, making them think about it. It was Ajani's idea to say the Oracle would arrive in two days. Because then he can point out the jhihadi—"

Del took it up, nodding. "—who really will be Ajani."

Slowly I shook my head. "There's too much to it. Too many people involved . . . a man can't just decide one day he wants to be a messiah, and then proclaim himself one. It doesn't happen that way."

"Of course it does." Bellin laughed. "Religion is an odd thing. A *very* odd thing—and Ajani understands that. He understands that if one very strong man surrounds himself with equally ambitious men, he can create his own religion, or set himself up as a king. All he requires is a core of loyal followers willing to do as he asks, *no matter* what he asks, and then have them spread the word." He gestured. "He has that already. And we've all been working the crowds."

"Sula," I said intently. "She spoke of the histories . . . of a promised jhihadi supposed to change the land to grass."

Bellin merely shrugged. "If you want to make something seem real, you borrow from real things."

It was utterly impossible. Not the idea, which I could understand very well, but that he could manage to rouse so *many* people willing to name him messiah. "He's only a borjuni—a Northern-born renegade. He kills people. Kidnaps children and sells them into slavery. Are you telling us Ajani has the wherewithal to create a new religion and make himself a *messiah?*"

Bellin's expression was odd. "Have you met Ajani?"

"I have," Del said coldly.

He spread his hands. "Then you know."

"Know *what?*" she snapped. "How much he enjoys his job?"

Bellin didn't flinch. "If you met him, you know."

"Tell *me*," I suggested. "I don't know anything."

The young man gestured fluidly with eloquent hands. "In islander-talk we'd call him a *musarreia*, a man who shines very brightly, like the biggest star in the sky. I am a sailor also; he could be called the polestar, by which we navigate." He frowned, seeing our faces. "Do you understand? He shines more brightly than anyone else. He is the flame, we are the moths . . . Ajani attracts us all. And for those who are not wary, the flame will burn us to death."

I couldn't say anything. Del, however, could.

"He's a *murderer*," she declared. "He killed all of my kinfolk and sold my brother to slavers. I was *there*; I know."

Bellin looked at her. His voice was very quiet, but no less convincing for it. "No one else knows that. And by the time he's proclaimed jhihadi, no one will believe it."

Del's expression was odd, almost painful to see. It was obvious she wanted to call Bellin a liar, to refute everything he'd said, because to admit he might be right gave Ajani additional power. She had spent six years of her life building a prison for him, some place to keep him whole, until she could deal with him. There, he was simply Ajani, the man who'd destroyed her life.

Now he was someone else. Someone no longer in prison. Someone she had to deal with in terms other than her own.

It hurt me to see her. It hurt me to see the pain, the struggle to comprehend. To confront Ajani again before she ever saw him.

I slid my sword back home, deep into the sheath. "I'll get the axes." And went out to retrieve them.

By the time I was back, Bellin was seated on the ground, leaning up against a crumbling brick wall. Del paced in silence: palehaired, black-eyed cat, protesting imprisonment.

I gave Bellin his axes. He already had the other. "Are you sure?" I asked quietly. "Are you very sure?"

In the moonlight, he looked younger. "I don't know everything. Only what he's told us." Axes clinked together as he handled them nimbly. They weren't heavy chopping axes, but smaller, more balanced weapons. Deadly all the same. "I am a pirate," Bellin said quietly, "a fortuitous mariner. I know how to spot good fortune, and I know how to steal it. I've made my way in the world on quick wits and a quicker tongue; you've seen the result." His boyish smile was lopsided. "I've learned to judge men under their skin. Ajani's is thicker than most."

I squatted down nearby. "Go on."

Bellin sighed. "I don't *know* this—now I'm only guessing. But I've been here for a while, and I think I understand a little about how the South works." He glanced briefly at Del, who stood listening cloaked in shadows four paces away. "To have power in the South, a man must be a tanzeer."

"That's obvious," I said. "Everyone knows that."

"Could a Northerner claim a domain?"

"Probably not," I replied. "Even if he had enough men to win himself a small domain, the people would never accept him. Someone else would come along—someone *Southron*, and with more men—and depose him forcibly. He'd lose his domain, and probably his life."

Del moved into the light. "He's a borjuni," she said. "He has been for years. Why would he change now?"

Bellin shrugged. "Ajani is forty years old."

It hit home. I rubbed a scar thoughtfully. "Time for a change," I said. "Time for something more permanent." Scowling, I rose and began to pace myself, walking out speculation. "All right. Let's say Ajani is ambitious; we know he is. Let's say he's greedy; we know that, too. And let's say he's gifted in the ways of inspiring—and controlling—men; *you* say he is." I shrugged. "Then let's also say he wants more than a simple domain. Maybe he wants them all—or at least a large portion."

" 'Let's say,' " Bellin echoed, by way of agreement.

I went on, still pacing. "But how does he go about it? By killing the enemy; in this case, enem*ies*." I thought it over. "We know killing is an obvious means for Ajani—he's done it often enough—but he also needs a weapon. A particular kind of weapon no one else can oppose. And I don't mean a sword."

"People," Del declared, understanding too well.

"People," I agreed. "So many people the tanzeers are forced to give in."

She came farther into the light, leaving the shadows behind. "He wants the tribes. But he knows nothing can unite them. Nothing can make them willing to stand together to defeat the Southron tanzeers. You've said that often enough."

I nodded. "So he uses religion. The tribes are incredibly super-stitious . . . he makes himself a messiah, whom the tribes will re-vere utterly, because he tells them the things they most want to hear: he can change the sand to grass." I stopped pacing abruptly. "If he is as compelling as Bellin suggests, they'll do anything Ajani asks, even start a holy war."

Del's protest was desperate. "He's only *one man*."

Bellin's tone was soft. "His burning is very bright."

Silence was loud. Then I stated the obvious: "This changes things."

Del shook her head. "I still intend to kill him."

Dryly, I suggested, "Then you'd better do it in secret."

It stung. "I am not an assassin, Tiger. What I do, I do in the day-light, where everyone can see."

"Fine," I agreed. "Go ahead, bascha, but you'll start a holy war."

Del made a sharp gesture. "But there *is* no messiah! There *is* no jhihadi. All of it is a lie!"

"Didn't you listen to Bellin? Didn't you hear what he said?" I jabbed a thumb in his direction. "It doesn't matter what we know or what we think . . . only what *they* believe. If you kill the jhihadi, they'll be after your blood. They'll be after *everyone's* blood."

"Tiger—"

"Do you want that on your head?"

"Do you want me *not* to kill him?"

"After swearing all those oaths?" I shook my head. "I only want you to think."

"I've thought." She looked at Bellin. "Where *is* Ajani?"

The boy didn't hesitate. "Somewhere in the foothills. I don't know where."

Her eyes narrowed. "And yet you are working for him."

Bellin shrugged. "All I was hired to do was ride into Iskandar and help spread rumors. He met with us near Harquhal and told us what to do. Then he went to ground to prepare for his divine ar-rival."

"Can you find out where he is?"

"He'll be *here* in a day or two."

"You heard Tiger," she said. "For once he's making sense."

How nice of her to say so.

Bellin stood up, tucking axes underneath his robe. He snugged them into a belt at the small of his back, where they didn't show at all beneath the billowy fabric. "I can try," he said. "But Ajani went to ground on purpose. He doesn't want to be found. He wants to remain hidden until the jhihadi can appear."

I thought about the warriors, gathered in the foothills. Likely they knew where he was; possibly he was *with* them.

Then I thought about dead Morab, lacking so much of his skin and all of his genitals.

Not worth the risk.

"We'll think of something," I muttered.

Bellin grinned at me. "So will the Sandtiger's son."

Chapter 14

Del was silent all the way back to the dwelling we shared with Alric. There wasn't much I could think of to say, to shake her out of the silence; and anyway, I was too busy thinking myself.

Ajani. The *jhihadi?* It just wasn't possible.

And yet Bellin's explanation made perfect sense. Made too much sense; if all of it were true, Del's oaths were in serious trouble.

Clearly, she knew it.

We did not go into the dwelling because Del stopped short of the door. Then twisted aside and half collapsed against the crumbling wall, arms folded tightly beneath her breasts as she leaned.

"Six years," she said tightly. "Six years they've been dead—six years *I've* been dead. . . ." She rolled her head against the wall in futile, painful denial. "A messiah—a *messiah* . . . how can he do such a thing?"

"Del—"

"He's *mine*. Always mine. It's what I stayed alive for. It's *how* I stayed alive. It's why I didn't give up."

"I know. Del—"

She wasn't listening. "All the way to Staal-Ysta, I fed myself on hatred . . . on revenge promised to me in the name of Northern gods. When I had no food, I had no hunger, because there was the hate . . . when I had no water, I had no thirst, because there was always the *hate*—" She broke it off sharply, as if hearing herself and the lack of control; Del dreads loss of control.

More quietly, she went on. "And when I knew there would be a child, I feasted on the hatred . . . it gave me a means to live. It wouldn't let me die. I wasn't *allowed* to die, because I had sworn my oaths. The child would bear witness, even inside my womb."

I said nothing.

Del looked at me. "You understand hatred. You lived on it, as I did . . . you ate and drank and slept it . . . but you didn't let it consume you. You didn't let it *become* you." She put both hands to her face. "I am—warped. I am *wrong*. I am not a woman, not a person, not even a sword-dancer. I am only hatred—with nothing left to eat."

The echo of Chosa Dei: *"Obsession is necessary when compassion undermines."*

Del raked splayed fingers through her hair, stripping it from her brow. The moonlight bared her despair in the travesty of her face. "If Ajani is taken from me, there is no more 'me' left."

It hurt too much. I made my tone hard. "So, you're going to let him win after all. After six years. After all those oaths."

"You don't underst—"

"I understand very well, Delilah. As you yourself said, I lived on hatred, too. I know its taste, I know its *smell*—I know how it is in bed. And I know how seductive it is, how completely all-consuming . . . how *satisfying* it is in place of a human partner."

Del's face was bone-white. "All of the things I have done were done in the name of that hatred. I bore a daughter and gave her up . . . I apprenticed myself to Staal-Ysta . . . I killed many men—" she swallowed jerkily. "—I tried to usurp the freedom of a man I care about—and then I nearly killed *him*."

It took me a moment. "Well," I said, "he survived."

Del's gaze didn't waver. "If he had not, I would have allowed myself no time to grieve. I would have set aside the pain and gone on, seeking Ajani . . . alone, as before: a woman fed on hatred, sleeping with obsession—" The voice cut off abruptly. And as abruptly, came back. "Why are you here, Tiger? Why do you stay with me?"

I wanted to touch her, but didn't. I wanted to tell her, but couldn't. I have no skill with words. This particular sword-dance required more than what we both knew. Much more than what we had learned, in the circle with our swords.

When I could, I shrugged. "I kind of thought you were staying with *me*."

Del didn't smile. "You have sworn no oaths. Ajani is not your duty."

Idly, I kicked at a stone, rolling it aside. And then moved against the wall, next to Del, letting it hold me up. "I think there are times when no oaths *have* to be sworn. Some things just—happen."

Del stared at me. Then drew in an unsteady breath. "You make it too hard."

I stared steadfastly across the alley. "You're afraid, aren't you?"

"Of Ajani? No. I've hated too much for fear."

"No. You're afraid of what comes after."

Del shut her eyes. "I am afraid," she said, "that I won't feel the things I know I should feel."

"What are those, bascha?"

"Pleasure. Satisfaction. Elation. Relief. Fulfillment." Her eyes opened; the tone was edged with bitterness. "The things that should come with bedding unencumbered or colored by hatred."

I frowned down at the ground. "When I was young," I told her, "I swore to kill a man. And I meant it utterly; there was no room in my soul for anything but hatred, for anything but this oath. Like you, I lived on it. I drank it. I went to bed with it each night, whispering to the stars the oath I swore to keep: that I would kill this man. I was a boy; boys swear things, and never keep them. But I *meant* it . . . and that oath helped me survive until the time a sandtiger came into camp and killed some of the children. That oath made me take my crude spear and go out into the Punja by myself to kill that sandtiger. Because I knew that if I succeeded, if I killed the sandtiger, I could ask for a boon, and then I would get the one thing I most wanted."

"Freedom," Del murmured.

Slowly I shook my head. "A chance to kill the shukar."

She stiffened. "That old man?"

"That old man did more to destroy what was left of my life than anyone else in the tribe. And he was what made me survive."

"But you didn't kill him."

"No. I was sick for three days from the poison. Sula spoke for me, saying I was owed my freedom." I shrugged. "I thought killing the shukar would give me a freedom—of mind, if not of body. It was the only kind I knew."

"But they sent you away, instead."

"They gave me physical freedom. No more was I a chula."

"What are you saying, Tiger?"

"That in the end I won. That what the old man most wanted was me *dead*, not free . . . and I cheated him."

"Tiger—"

I kept my voice quiet. "Sometimes what we want is not what's best for us. No matter how much we want it."

Del made no answer. She leaned against the wall, as I did, staring into darkness. And at last spoke. "Do you think I am wrong?"

I smiled wryly. "It doesn't matter what I think."

Del looked at me. "It matters," she said. "I have always cared what you thought."

"Always?"

"Well, perhaps not at first . . . not when we first met. You were insufferable then, so cocksure and Southron and *male*." Del smiled a little. "I thought what you needed was a kick in the head, to knock some sense into you . . . or maybe castration, so you wouldn't think with your manhood instead of with your brain."

"You have no idea what you can do to a man, Delilah, when he first sets eyes on you. Believe me, no man—no *whole* man—can think with anything else."

Del grimaced. "I never asked for that. It is a burden, not a gift."

"Funny," I said idly, "*I've* never found it a burden."

She slanted me a glance. "Vanity doesn't become you."

"Everything becomes me."

"Even Chosa Dei?"

I scowled; the game was over. "As far as I'm concerned, he has no stake in this. He's not part of me. He's not even part of the sword; he's merely a parasite.'

"But deadly. And now that we know Shaka Obre is in no way linked to this jhihadi . . ." She let it trail off. "I still can't believe it. Ajani—a messiah?"

I shrugged. "He's an opportunist. Maybe there really is something to this jhihadi business—after all, it was the old holy man in Ysaa-den who first mentioned the Oracle and jhihadi—and Ajani concocted a plan based on what he'd heard."

Slowly, Del shook her head. "I can't reconcile the man I knew with the man Bellin knows."

I gave it a moment, then spoke carefully. "Are you so sure you can reconcile him with anything? Who you remember is brutality and murder . . . you saw Ajani and his men kill your entire family. You saw Jamail on fire. You suffered Ajani's—*attentions*. At fifteen years of age—and under those circumstances—you could never judge a man. Never see his potential for anything as complex as this. All you could do was *feel* . . . and emotions—or the lack of them—don't allow for much objectivity."

Del's tone was flat. "What they allow for is the ability—and the desire—to kill a murderer."

"And so we are back where we began." I straightened. "But maybe not."

"Maybe not? Tiger, what are you—"

"Come on," I said intently, "there's someone I have to talk to."

"Now? It's late."

"Come on, bascha. This won't wait."

Elamain, of course, thought I'd come to see her. Until she saw Del.

"Esnat," I said succinctly.

Sabo, who had greeted us at the door, went at once to fetch his master. This left Elamain standing in the room swathed in the silk of her hair as it poured down the front of her nightrobe. Delicate feet were bare. I found it oddly erotic; then recalled that to Southroners, any part of a woman was, since she hid it under so much.

"Esnat?" she echoed.

"Business," I said briefly. "You may as well go back to bed."

Elamain flicked a glance at Del, then looked back to me. "Only if you're in it."

"Don't waste your time," Del suggested. "He is a man, Elamain, not a tame cat . . . and I, unlike you, believe he has more sense and integrity than you give him credit for. Teasing and tricking a man is no way to win him."

Elamain's eyes widened. "Who is teasing? Who is tricking? I hide nothing of what I want. No more than you do what *you* want, wearing a man's weapon—"

But she didn't get to finish, because Esnat came into the room.

He'd been asleep and was not yet fully awake. He blinked as he saw us, pulled his robes into order, raised brows at Elamain's presence. Thin dust-colored hair, now unencumbered by a turban, hung lankly to narrow shoulders. The spots on his chin were worse. I realized all over again I was supposed to dance for this man, so he could impress a woman.

Except his courtship might have to wait.

"I want honesty," I said. "Why are you here?"

Sabo, Elamain, and Esnat stared. It was not what they'd expected.

"Why?" I asked again. "Sasqaat is clear across the Punja. It's a small domain. Why would you come all the way to Iskandar? Why, for that matter, would *any* tanzeers come? What's in it for them?"

Something flickered in Esnat's eyes. Now I knew I had him.

"Don't waste my time," I said. "You're a tanzeer, and not a stupid one, no matter what you've led Elamain and others to believe. The masquerade is over, Esnat. I want the truth. Then I'll give you mine."

Esnat glanced around. Then gestured at cushions and rugs. He sank down on the nearest one even as Del and I found seats. "The Oracle," he said.

Elamain, who had opened her mouth to protest the situation, now closed it. A crease marred her brow. Clearly Esnat's answer was unexpected and baffling; she'd believed they'd come to Iskandar for another reason entirely.

Esnat gestured irritably, "Oh, Elamain, sit *down*. It would do no good to send you to bed—you'd only listen at the doorway. So sit down and keep your mouth closed; maybe you'll learn something."

He glanced now at Sabo. "You, too, Sabo. You know this man better than I."

Elamain sat. Sabo sat. Esnat looked back to me.

"You view him as a threat," I said. "All his foretelling of a jhihadi has every tanzeer frightened he might be telling the truth."

Esnat nodded. "There is no doubt the Oracle has roused the tribes. When word came he was foretelling the coming of the jhihadi here in Iskandar, no one could believe it. But the tribes did, and they left the Punja en masse. That made us nervous."

"So you came up here to kill him before this jhihadi can appear."

Esnat shook his head. "*I* don't want to kill him. I think that would touch things off. There are other tanzeers who believe as I do, and we want to avoid a holy war, not start one by killing the Oracle. We came to Iskandar hoping to convince the others."

"The other tanzeers want war?"

He shrugged. "Hadjib and his followers consider it unavoidable. They believe nothing will calm the tribes now, unless the Oracle is killed. Without a leader to unify them, the tribes will fracture again." Esnat scratched his chin, leaving red streaks. "They have brought as many men as they can hire, and are hiring more. They fully believe they can smash this rebellion before it occurs—or else consume the tribes in war." He grimaced. "These men are accustomed to absolute power. They have no conception of religion, or what it can do to unify men . . . even desert tribes."

Hadjib. *Hadjib.* Somehow I knew the name . . . and then I recalled how. Lena had told me about a tanzeer who'd come looking for me. Now I knew why.

"But you *do* understand it," I said. "You understand, you and a few others, what could happen."

Esnat didn't hesitate. "It would be a bloodbath."

"And you don't want that."

"No. Such a thing would be harmful." Esnat frowned, glancing briefly at Sabo, Elamain, Del. "The tribes are no threat to us if they remain as they have been for decades: insular, independent races with no specific home, simply traveling about the South. But if they unite in a common goal motivated by faith, they become the greatest enemy we could know. They will gladly die in the name of their jhihadi, believing what they do is for divine favor . . . that sort of fanaticism can destroy the South. For us—for everyone—it is better left the way it is."

"The tribes might not agree."

Esnat shrugged. "They have been content with their lives, as you well know . . . had the Oracle not appeared, they would not now be here."

"They believe," I said quietly, "this jhihadi will change the sand to grass."

"It doesn't matter," Esnat said. "You and I know such a thing cannot occur."

"Magic," Del said quietly.

Esnat glanced at her. He assessed her quickly, then smiled. "You have your own share of magic, bascha, and so does the Sandtiger. But surely you must see what it would take to alter the South. I don't think such magic exists any more, if it ever did."

"Never mind the magic," I said. "There's something else we have to think about." I shifted on my cushion. "Esnat, what would you and the others say if I told you there was no jhihadi?"

He smiled wryly. "That we are all of a like mind. But what good will it do? Hadjib and his followers don't care if the jhihadi is real or not."

I leaned forward slightly. "What if I told you a man *was* behind this holy war, but not a true jhihadi? Merely a man, like you and me, but a very clever one. A man who has very carefully manipulated the tribes into believing he is the jhihadi, so he can gain power."

Esnat's eyes widened. "A single man?"

"A single Northerner with a gift for inspiring others."

He sat stunned, thinking about it. Thinking of what it could mean. "But the *magnitude* of it . . ." He let it trail off. "It's impossible."

"Is it? Think about it. A man hires another and calls him an 'Oracle.' He sends him out to a few of the tribes well-primed with the kind of words that would appeal to nomadic peoples. This jhihadi, the Oracle says, can change the sand to grass, so that the tribes will know comfort again. The tribes will know *power* again."

Esnat said nothing.

"After a while, the tribes themselves carry word throughout the Punja; eventually throughout the South. Bit by bit by bit this 'Oracle' seeds his ground, and eventually it takes root. Eventually it bears fruit."

"One man," Esnat murmured.

"Ajani," I said. "A Northern borjuni—a man who burns very brightly."

Frowning, Esnat rubbed his chin. "Hadjib wouldn't listen," he murmured. "We have tried, all of us; they ignore the wisdom we offer. They are angry, powerful men unwilling to think of compromise when war is another way." He stared blankly at me. "They want this war, Sandtiger. They want it contained in Iskandar so no domains are threatened."

"More than domains are threatened," I declared. "Things are bad enough in the Punja for caravans, what with borjuni and a few hostile tribes. If the tribes went into full revolt, they could cut off all the caravan routes. *That* would destroy the domains as well as anything else." I shook my head. "Some would survive, yes, but not the small ones so dependent on trade. What about Sasqaat? You supplement your people with outside trade, don't you?"

"Of course. Sasqaat would die without trade."

"Well, then?"

"Well, then," he echoed. "What is there to do when the other tanzeers won't listen? We can't just send them home, though it would be the best thing."

"Challenge them," Del suggested.

Esnat blinked at her. "What do you mean: 'challenge'?"

Her voice was very quiet. "This is the South, is it not? Where things in the lives of tanzeers are often decided by a sword-dance. Two men hired for a single purpose: to settle differences. To make a ruling by the sword. To declare a single winner."

"Southron tradition," I said, "can be a very powerful thing."

Esnat stared at us. "They have already tried to assassinate the Oracle."

"*If* there's an Oracle," I agreed. "Ajani may have already relieved him of his duties. And I have no doubts that if he's shown himself as the jhihadi to the tribes—or is planning to—he's surrounded himself with guards." I shook my head. "Already tonight we've seen what the tribes will do to protect their Oracle. For the jhihadi, they will do worse. I don't think the tanzeers will find another man willing to risk that."

"But there are other ways. And they will look for that way."

I shook my head. "Not if a ruling based on the outcome of a traditional sword-dance won your side the chance to defy them openly, to declare the Oracle and jhihadi safe. If all the tanzeers attended—from both sides—and agreed to abide by the outcome, you could end the war before it began."

"*If* we won," he said.

"That's always a risk," I agreed. "If Hadjib's faction won, you'd have to let them do whatever they wanted. You'd have no say in their plans, even if it included assassination."

His tone was thoughtful. "But if they *lost*, we could send them home."

"And probably prevent more violence."

Esnat frowned. "But the *tribes*. No one can be certain what they'll do."

"No. But if Ajani's behind this thing, and all the tanzeers go home, he'll lose some of his power. If they left, I doubt Ajani could keep the tribes reconciled long enough to march all over the South capturing domains for himself. Eventually, the tribes would fall to quarreling." I shook my head. "For all we know, it was Ajani's idea to lure as many tanzeers as possible here to Iskandar. Contained, tanzeers are controllable; scattered, they are not. Much like the tribes."

Esnat studied me intently. "He is playing one against the other."

"The trick is to dilute Ajani's plan. Forcing the other tanzeers to withdraw would do it. If your side won the dance and all the other tanzeers went home, half the battle would be won without a sword being drawn, except for those in the circle." I shrugged. "Maybe the whole war."

Esnat considered it. "If I talked with the others who feel as I do and they agreed . . . we'd have to find the proper words, the kind of words that will cause the other tanzeers to accept such a challenge . . ."

I interrupted. "Make it a formal challenge to Hadjib. If he feels he's in control of the pro-war faction, his pride will require that he answer the challenge personally. I can give you the ritual phrases that will demand an acceptance."

Esnat continued, easily incorporating my suggestion into his plan. "—then hire a sword-dancer worthy of the dance, one worthy of the risk, because it wouldn't *be* a risk, if we were certain he could win—" Brown eyes sharpened. "Will you do it, Sandtiger?"

I smiled. I've never been the kind of man to ignore an opportunity as golden as this one. "You already hired me to dance in hopes of impressing a woman. For that, you offered a very generous—"

Esnat didn't bother to hear me out. "Coin," he said dismissively. "For this, you will have a domain."

Elamain gasped. "You can do such a thing?"

Esnat smiled at her. "I can do many things."

"But—an entire *domain?*"

He raised a dust-colored eyebrow. "I think stopping a war might be worth the cost."

Elamain looked at me. Then she looked at Esnat.

Sabo merely grinned.

May the sun shine on his head.

Later—actually, *late*—I sat contemplating my future, scratching idly at a kneecap. I guess the scratching was loud, because Del rolled over.

"Tiger, can't you sleep?"

"No. I'm sitting here thinking about what it will be like to be a tanzeer."

" 'Will'?" she asked ironically. "*You're* sure of yourself."

"Why shouldn't I be? I'm the best sword-dancer in the South."

"Who hasn't danced for months."

"I danced against Nabir."

"You *sparred* against Nabir."

"Besides, I've got this sword."

"Which you swore not to use in a dance."

I decided not to answer. Seemed like every time I said anything, Del had a retort.

Which meant we were back to normal.

I sat against the crumbling wall in our private room. Del was snugged up in blankets next to me, nothing much visible except a little hair, pale luminescence in the light of the moon. Next door, Alric snored. I'd tried to sleep, but couldn't; too many thoughts in my head.

Me: a tanzeer. A sword-dancer-turned-tanzeer. It seemed impossible to consider, in light of my origins. A baby, left to die in the desert, born of people no one knew. And then a slave, in bondage to the Salset. And finally, a killer. A man who lived by the sword.

Me: a tanzeer. It made me want to laugh.

I stretched out legs and carefully adjusted the arrangement of my knees from the inside, shifting tendons and cartilage through interior muscle control. I heard the dull chatter, the snaps; felt the catch, the pop into place. I'd need my knees to dance. I wished they were a bit younger.

Del, whose head was close to my legs, peeled a blanket back. "That sounds terrible."

"You should hear the rest of me."

"*I* don't sound like that."

"You're not old enough to." Not an encouraging thought; except, maybe, for Del. "Be silent as long as you can."

"I have a finger that cracks." Del demonstrated. "I broke it on Staal-Ysta."

"Hoolies, I've broken fingers and toes so many times I don't even remember which ones." I looked at the still-wrapped little finger the stud had tried to eat. "Except for this one. This one I remember."

"That one's not even broken." Del shifted and rolled over onto her back. "Maybe it will be a good thing, this domain. Maybe it's time you settled down. No more traveling, no more dancing—no more broken bits."

Settled down. Me. I hadn't thought of it that way. I'd just been thinking about the things that came with the title. Coin. A place of my own. A stable for the stud. People to cook and clean. Aqivi whenever I wanted it. Maybe even a harem.

I slanted a glance at Del.

Maybe not a harem.

I scooched down the wall and stretched out on my bedroll again, pulling a blanket over me. Del lay very close; her hair caught on my stubble. I picked it away, then moved a little closer. Thought about how it had been for so many years, sharing nothing with no one.

The question occurred again. "Bascha, what are you going to do once Ajani's dead?"

"Ask me when he's dead."

"Del—"

"I'm hunting him tomorrow. Ask me tomorrow night."

Her tone of voice was definitive; she wanted no more questions, especially about Ajani. I watched her shut her eyes.

"Bascha—"

"Go to sleep, Tiger. You're older than me; you need it."

I lay there in aggrieved silence for long moments, trying to think of an appropriately cutting retort. But by the time I did, Del was sound asleep.

So then I lay there wide awake and wide-eyed, glaring into darkness, thinking uncharitable thoughts about the woman by my side, and snoring Alric, and sleeping Lena and the girls.

Why do people who have no trouble falling asleep think it's easy for everyone else?

It just isn't fair.

If I were tanzeer, I'd make everyone stay awake until *I* was asleep.

If I were a tanzeer?

Hoolies . . . I just might be.

If I managed to win the dance.

Chapter 15

I went out to inspect the circle, and that was where he found me.

His words were mostly ritual. "I'm sent to tell you my lord Hadjib accepts Lord Esnat's formal challenge. His personal sword-dancer will meet you in the circle when the sun is directly overhead."

Which didn't give us much time; it was already mid-morning. "Does your lord Hadjib understand the challenge fully? That should I win the dance, he and his followers must leave Iskandar at once and return to their domains?"

"He understands the challenge fully. My lord Hadjib swears not a drop of blood shall be spilled, should he and his fellow tanzeers be required to leave Iskandar. And he asks in return if your lord Esnat understands his part in the challenge should *you* lose the dance."

"Lord Esnat understands the challenge fully. Should I lose the dance, Esnat and his followers will join battle as Hadjib commands."

Simple terms, spelled out. It wasn't a dance to the death, simply to victory.

The ritual was finished. No more need for formality.

"So," I said expansively, "care for a jug of aqivi?"

He smiled. "I don't think so."

I looked at the dark eyes; at the lines carved deep in his face; at the notched arch of his nose. Remembered what I'd felt when I nearly crushed his throat.

"Too bad," I said lightly. "You might have enjoyed the time spent retelling our tall tales."

Abbu Bensir's smile widened. "Oh, I think we'll have a new and better tale to tell when this day is over. And so will the rest of the South."

I shook my head a little. "This isn't your sort of dance. What did they promise you?"

"Any dance is my sort of dance; you know better, Sandtiger." He grinned. "As for what they promised me? A domain all for myself."

I blinked. "You, too?"

A silver-flecked eyebrow arched. "A popular gift, this domain. I wonder if it's the same one."

"They wouldn't."

"They might. Do you trust your tanzeer?"

"Do you trust yours? He tried to hire me."

"Not for this."

"No. He wanted an assassin."

"Ah. I see." Abbu rubbed his nose. "I think we've gone beyond that, judging by this dance. Was it your idea?"

I frowned. "What makes you say that?"

"You lived with the Salset. You know what the tribes are like. I'd be willing to wager you'd want to avoid a holy war, since you have a very good idea how messy one would be."

"Messy," I echoed. "A good way of putting it."

"I, on the other hand, don't really care. As far as I'm concerned, the tribes are nothing but parasites stealing water out of our mouths. It's better left to us what little there is of it."

"So, you'd just as soon *win* this dance so you can kill a few warriors."

"I'd just as soon win *any* dance, Sandtiger. But I must admit meeting you will make it all the sweeter.'

"Finally," I said.

"Finally," he agreed.

Which left us with nothing much else to say; both of us went away.

I sat outside in the shade, leaning against the wall. The sun climbed the sky; everyone watched it closely. Once it was overhead, we'd all adjourn to the circle.

Massou watched me. "Are you going to die?"

Adara, of course, was aghast. I waved her into silence.

"It's an honest question," I told her, "and I don't blame him for asking it. He's only curious."

Adara's green eyes were transfixed by the motion of hand and arm as I carefully honed my sword. "He has no *business*—"

"At his age, I'd have asked the same thing." If I'd been allowed to ask anything. "No, Massou, I'm not going to die. It's not a dance to the death. Only to victory."

He thought about it. "Good. But I'd rather see Del dance."

It stung a little. "Why?"

"Because she's better."

Del, who leaned against the wall not so far away, smiled, then tried to hide it behind a mask of cool neutrality.

I shot her a scowl, then looked back at the boy. "That's only because when you saw me spar, I wasn't at my best."

Del's tone was dry. "You're not at your best *now*."

"Sound enough for Abbu."

Alric stood in the doorway. "Are you?" he asked seriously. "Abbu Bensir is good."

"I'm not exactly *bad*."

Del's voice again: "But not as good as you were."

"And besides, it's not like I've never danced against him before. I'm the one who gave him that throat."

Del, once more: "With a wooden sword."

I stopped honing the blade. "All right, what is it? Do you *want* me to lose? Is that why you're being so pointed about doubting my confidence?"

Del smiled. "I have *no* doubts about your confidence. What I have doubts about is your willingness to recognize that you are not in proper condition."

"I'm fine."

"Fine is not fit." Del straightened from the wall. "I don't want you to walk into that circle thinking Abbu stands no chance. He is good, Tiger—I have sparred with him myself. You are good, also—I have *danced* with you myself. But if you refuse to acknowledge the truth of the matter, you've lost before you've begun.'

"I have no intention of stepping into the circle without being careful, if that's what you're afraid of. Hoolies bascha, you'd think I'd never danced before!"

Del looked directly at me. "How many times have you been wounded in the circle?"

"More times than I can count."

"How many times have you been *seriously* wounded in the circle?"

I shrugged. "Two or three times, I guess. It happens to all of us."

"And how many times have you come very close to death in the circle?"

"All right," I said, "once. You know that as well as I."

"And you have not danced a proper dance since then."

The defensiveness was abrupt. "I'm not afraid, if that's what you mean."

Del didn't smile. "Of course you're afraid."

"Del—"

"I saw it, Tiger. I was in the circle, remember? The last time you tried to dance, the fear drove you out."

I forgot all about Massou and Adara and Alric. "That was fear for *you!* It had nothing to do with me." Angrily, I glared. "You have no idea what it was like for me seeing you sprawled on the ground with steel in your ribs. You don't know what I felt. You don't know what I thought. When I stepped into that circle on our way to Ysaa-den, I was on Staal-Ysta again. All I could think about was that dance, and I was afraid it might happen again."

Del drew Boreal. "Then dance with me now."

"*Now?* Are you sandsick? Besides, you're supposed to go meet with Bellin, remember? He'll have information about Ajani."

"Now," she said coolly. "A warm-up will do you good. It will loosen all your muscles . . . quiet your noisy knees."

"Oh, *good*," came from Massou, before Adara could hush him.

Hoolies, hoolies, hoolies. I don't want to do this.

So tell the bascha no.

Not so easy to do.

Especially when she's right.

I wiped the blade clean. Glanced up at the sun. Knew we had the time. "Alric?"

He nodded. "I'll play arbiter."

Adara, muttering, forcibly dragged Massou to the end of the alley. He protested, of course, but she didn't let him go. Eventually he subsided, since she threatened to take him away entirely if he didn't shut his mouth.

There was no need for a circle, so we didn't bother to draw one. We just faced one another in silence, took the measure of each other, thought our private thoughts.

Mine were not happy ones. I don't know *what* hers were.

"Dance," Alric said.

Hoolies, but I don't want—

Too late, Tiger. Nothing to do but dance.

Nothing to do but *sing*—

No—don't sing—

Don't give Chosa Dei the chance—

Northern steel clashed. The sound filled up the alley.

Get looser, I thought. Get *looser*—

Del's blade flashed. In and out of shadow, slicing the sun apart. Shattering the daylight with the brilliance of magicked steel.

Gods, but she can dance—

Well, so can I.

Of their own accord, my feet moved. I felt the acknowledgment of muscles too long kept from the circle; the sharpening of eyes. Focus came back quickly, blocking out the alley, the sun, the others gathering. All I saw was Del. All I heard was Del: the sloughing of her feet, the keening of her steel, the breathy exhalations.

This is the true dance, where two perfectly balanced halves come together at last and form a perfect whole. This is a dance of life, of death, of continuity; the world within seven paces. Nothing else exists. Nothing is as important. Nothing can fill the need the way a proper sword-dance can, danced with a proper opponent.

There is no other for me.

Ah, yes, bascha . . . show me how to dance.

And then, abruptly, my sleeping sword awoke. Chosa Dei awoke. I felt him swarm through the blade from wherever it was he lived. Felt him test my strength. Felt him gather himself. Knew what he meant to do.

Confusion diluted the focus, seeping through concentration: But I haven't sung. I haven't even *thought* of singing.

Chosa Dei didn't care. Chosa Dei was awake.

Oh, bascha—*bascha*—

She felt it in the swords. Tasted it in the air, in the acrid stink of magic. And jerked her blade from mine falling back two steps. "Control it!" she cried. "Control it! You have the power; *use* it!"

I could feel it—feel *him*—trying to leave the sword. Trying to creep up the blade to the hilt, where he could make contact with my hands. Once it was made I was lost, because the flesh is much too weak. He'd nearly taken Nabir—he *had* taken Nabir—he'd un-made Nabir's feet—

What would he do to me?

I stood in the center of the alley clutching the blooding-blade, wondering how to fight it. How to *beat* it, before it beat me.

"Control it," Del repeated. "You have the strength; use it!"

Power, she'd said. Strength.

The blade was turning black.

Use it, she'd said. *Use* it.

Do I know how to do that?

Hoolies, of course I do. I'm *the Sandtiger*.

No one defeats me.

Not even Chosa Dei.

"Yes!" Del shouted. *"Yes!"*

I must be doing it right.

Samiel, I whispered. But only inside my head. Nabir had said it aloud. Nabir had put me at risk.

Or was it Chosa Dei?

Samiel, I repeated. But only inside my head.

Del's face swam into my vision. A sweat-glossed, laughing face. "I *told* you you could do it—but you never want to believe me!"

I was panting. Breathing like a bellows. I felt the twinge in my midriff: knurled scar tissue had been pulled. Hands still clenched the sword, clamped around the grip. Knuckles shone white.

"It's—done?" I looked down at the sword in my hands. "Did I do it?"

She nodded, still grinning. "You drove him back down, Tiger. This time without the simoom. This time without the heat. This time with just yourself. With the strength from inside here." She put a hand to my heart. "And you have it in abundance."

I frowned, looking at the blade. "But it's still black. The tip. Chosa Dei's still in there."

She nodded, withdrawing her hand. "He's not banished. Only beaten. Banishment will take time. We have to discharge it properly."

And for that, we needed more magic. We needed Shaka Obre.

"Tiger?" Alric's voice. "Tiger—can you come? Something's upset your stud. He's trying to tear down the house."

Now I could hear it. He was stomping and pawing and kicking, squealing his displeasure.

"It's the magic," I muttered resignedly. "He hates it as much as I do."

I sheathed my defeated sword and went in to see the stud. He was indeed trying to tear down the house; he pawed chunks of crumbling brick and ancient mortar out of the wall, grinding it into the dirt.

"All right." I said, "you can stop now. I've put the sword away." I stepped in through the door, entering the "stable." "You're not going anywhere, so you may as well be qu—"

He let loose with both hind hooves. One of them caught my head.

Voices.

"Alric—get him *out*—"

"I can't, Del—the stud's broken his tie-rope . . . he won't let me near him—"

A spate of unintelligible words in a language I didn't know, or else I had forgotten.

The same male voice. "I know, Del—I *know* . . . but how can I drag him out if the stud won't let me near him?"

A woman's voice answering: frightened, angry, impatient. "—need a horse-speaker—" Then, abruptly, "Get *Garrod*—"

A boy's voice: "*I* will!"

"Then hurry, Massou—hurry!"

I was flat on my back in the dirt.

Why am I in the dirt?

Tried to sit up. Couldn't. All I could do was twitch.

The woman's voice again. "Tiger—stay still! Don't try to move."

Eyes won't open.

Everything sounds distorted.

"Tiger—don't *move* . . . don't give him a second chance."

Give who *what* second chance?

"Is he bleeding?"

"I can't tell."

Why would I be bleeding?

Sharply: "Don't try it, Del. I don't need two of you down."

"I can't leave him there, Alric. The stud's liable to stomp his head in."

Someone was moving around me. No—*something*. It breathed heavily. Pawed. Moved around me again.

Now a new voice. "Where is—oh. Here, give me room."

"Tiger, don't *move*."

Don't worry, I don't think I can.

"Talk to him, Garrod. Tell him to let us in so we can get Tiger out."

Silence, except for nearby scraping. I tasted dust. Felt it. It feathered across my face. I tried to lift an arm to brush the dust away, but nothing did what I wanted. All I did was twitch.

The scraping stopped. I smelled the tang of sweat and fear. Something was afraid.

"Now," said a quiet voice.

Hands. They touched me, grasped me, dragged me.

Hoolies, don't *drag* me—my head will fall off my neck—

"Here," someone said, and they put me down again.

"Is he alive?"

Hoolies, yes. I wouldn't be anything else.

Something pressed my chest. "Yes." Relief. *"Yes."*

I tried to open my eyes. This time I succeeded.

Not that it did much good. What I saw wouldn't stay still.

"Bascha?" My voice was weak. "Del—what happened?"

"The stud tried to kick your head off."

"He wouldn't—"

"He almost *did.*"

Memory snapped back. "Hoolies—" I blurted. "The dance—"

"Tiger—Tiger *no*—"

I lurched into a sitting position, thrusting away the hands. "I have to go—the dance—" And then clutched my head.

Del sounded exasperated. "You're not going anywhere."

Through the pain, I gritted it out. "Abbu will be waiting. *All* of them will be waiting—"

"You can't even stand up."

It even hurt to blink. "Too much depends on the dance . . . they *agreed*, all the tanzeers . . . if I don't dance, Hadjib and his followers win—there'll be *war*—oh, hoolies . . ."

Everything went gray around me. I lingered on the edges, wondering which way I would fall.

"Tiger?"

I yanked my senses back. "—have to get up," I mumbled. "Someone help me up."

"Postpone the dance," Del said. "Do you want me to see to it?"

"They won't—there's no—I don't think—" Hoolies, it was hard to think. Harder yet to talk. "I won't forfeit this dance."

Del's face was tight. "They won't expect you to dance when you're in this kind of shape."

"Doesn't matter . . . Abbu will claim victory, and there'll be no chance for peace—"

She took her hand from my arm. Her tone was very cold. "Then if you *must* do this, get up and walk out of here. Now. Waste no more time on weakness."

I rocked forward, slopped over onto an elbow, tried to gather legs. It took me two tries. Then I staggered to my feet.

Only to fall again. This time to my knees. And eventually to a hip, levered up on an elbow. I shut my eyes, shut my teeth, tried to wait it out. Begging the pain and sickness to wane.

"I'll postpone it," she said.

I was sweating. "You can't . . . bascha, you *can't* . . . they'll claim forfeit—they have the right . . . Abbu would win, and Hadjib would win . . . we can't afford to lose—"

"We can't afford to lose *you*."

"—sick—" I muttered tightly.

"You've been kicked in the head," she said curtly. "What do you expect?"

Maybe a bit more sympathy—no, not from Del. Too much to hope for.

And then another voice intruded. A husky, male voice, asking after me. Mentioning the dance.

He came through the doorway. I blinked up at him dazedly, trying not to vomit. It was very hard to think clearly.

"Ah," Abbu remarked, "one way of avoiding the truth." He glanced at the others, then looked back at me. "I came over to see what was keeping you. Everyone is gathered. Everyone is waiting." He smiled. "Your lord Esnat came close to forfeiting, but I said I would come here myself. It's very irregular, of course . . . but I want this dance too badly. I've waited too many years."

It was all I could do to lift my head high enough to see the sun without spewing my belly across the floor. "I'll be there," I mumbled; the sun glared balefully down from directly overhead.

Abbu Bensir laughed.

Del's tone was deadly. "Will you accept another dancer in his place?"

"Oh, bascha—"

Del ignored me. "Will you?"

"—South," I slurred. "Do you think Abbu or anyone else will accept a woman in my place?"

Del only looked at Abbu.

He was, above all, a Southroner: old habits die very hard. But every man can change, given reason enough to do so.

Abbu Bensir smiled. "It's the Sandtiger I want—but that can wait a little. You are no disgrace to the circle."

Del nodded once.

Abbu glanced at me. "Another time, Sandtiger . . . first I will beat your bascha."

"Go," Del said coolly.

Abbu Bensir went.

Time to protest again. "—can't—Del . . . *Del*—" I sucked in a breath. "You have to go look for Ajani." The world was graying out. "You have to go meet Bellin, to find out where Ajani is . . . bascha, you have to go . . . you've waited too long already—"

Del knelt down by me. She put a hand to my temple and drew away bloody fingers. The look in her eyes was odd.

I squinted through the fog. "You have to find Ajani."

Her tone was very fierce. *"To hoolies with Ajani."*

"Dell—*wait*—come back—"

But Del didn't wait.

And Del didn't come back.

Chapter 16

He knelt next to me. I looked him in the eye. "Am I dying?" I asked. "Is there something I should know?"

Alric smiled. "No. You only feel like it. Here." He gave me a bota. "Drink a little of this. It'll make you feel better."

I drank. "Hoolies, that's aqivi!"

"It'll help settle you. I got hit over the ear once . . . it takes away your balance."

"Is that why I keep falling down?"

"That, or clumsiness."

Gingerly, I touched the tender place. It was, as Alric said, right over my ear. It was swollen, matted, a little crusty; no new blood. It also hurt like hoolies.

It was too quiet. "Where is everyone?" I asked. "Where did everyone go?"

"To the dance. They wanted to wager on Del."

"Oh, hoolies . . . it's *my* dance—"

"You're in no shape for dancing."

"Maybe this will help." I drank more aqivi. Tried to uncross my eyes. "I have to go," I said. "Do you think I can sit here while she's out there dancing?"

"I don't expect you to, no. But I also don't expect you want me to carry you."

I drank yet again, then hitched myself to my feet. Stood there wavering, trying to maintain balance. "Why are there two of you?"

Alric stood up. "Two of *me?*"

"Yes."

He took the bota away. "I think you should go to bed."

"After I see about Del."

"Tiger—"

"I have to see about Del."

Alric sighed. Put away the bota. Took me under one arm. "We'll never make it to the circle."

It took great effort to speak. "Certainly we will."

"Then why don't you show me the way?"

"First just show me the door."

Alric steered me toward it.

By the time we made it through the alleys and out to the circles, I was more than ready to lie down and pass out. But I didn't dare do either, in any particular order, after what I'd said.

"Hoolies," I mumbled, "the *people*—"

They thronged around the circle. Behind us lay the city, broken walls and rubble now serving as steps and platforms from which to watch the dance. People hung out of the windows of crumbling second stories and lined the fallen rooftops. Others rimmed the circle itself, forming a human perimeter. Someone had drawn a second circle around the first as a line of demarcation. The three paces between the true circle and the second one was meant to serve as a buffer zone, to keep the people back.

I swayed. Alric's hand tightened. "What did you expect? This is a dance between two of the best sword-dancers in the South—even with you out of it—and a lot depends on it."

I squinted against the sunlight. "I wonder where Esnat is. He ought to be here. He *better* be here . . . him and all his friends . . . and Hadjib, too."

"They're probably watching from the city."

Someone jostled me. Unbalanced, I nearly fell. Only Alric kept me upright.

"Everything's moving," I muttered.

I shouldn't have had the aqivi. Or maybe it was just that I

shouldn't have been kicked in the head. Nothing fit together. I saw faces, heard talk, felt the press of the crowd. But everything seemed to exist at a very great distance from me.

I squinted through the rising thumping in my head. "Where's Del? Can you see her?"

"Not through all the people."

"Then let's get closer. I have to see Del."

"Tiger—wait—"

But I wasn't waiting for anyone. Not when I had to see Del.

It's not easy trying to *walk* when your balance isn't right, let alone push your way through a crowd. I stumbled, staggered, nearly fell, ignored oaths and insults, shouldered my way through the throng as Alric brought up the rear. A few people tried to stop us, but Alric and I are big. They didn't try for long.

We broke through at last and nearly fell over the line. People protested, complaining about my pushiness, but a few were sword-dancers who recognized me. The word went around quickly: I was given room. It gave me a chance to breathe.

All right, I'll admit it. I had thoughts of forcing Del out of the circle by claiming the dance mine; after all, it was. But just as I broke through, nearly falling flat on my face, someone told them to dance.

"Wait—" I blurted.

Too late.

It was a true dance. Both swords lay in the precise center of the circle. Abbu's back was closest to me; Del stood across from him. He blocked her view of me, but it didn't really matter. Now that the dance had begun, Del would see nothing at all except the man who danced against her.

At the word, they ran. Scooped. Came up. Swords flashed, clashed; screeched away to clash again.

All around us the people hummed.

Hoolies, my head hurts.

"Are you all right?" Alric asked. "You're looking kind of gray."

I didn't bother to look. I knew where he was: on my right.

"Tiger, are you—"

"Fine," I snapped. "*Fine* . . . just let me watch the dance.

The dance was mostly a blur. Abbu's back was still to me. He wore only a suede dhoti, as is customary, bare of legs, arms, torso.

The crowd muttered and hummed. Talking about the man. Talking about the woman. Discussing who would win.

To a man, they said Abbu.

I squinted, spreading feet in an attempt to maintain balance. "Watch his patterns," I muttered. "Bascha—watch his patterns."

Alric's voice was calm. "She's doing all right, Tiger."

"She's letting him tie her up."

"Del knows what she's doing."

Abbu blurred into two people. I scrubbed a hand across my eyes. "She has to take the offensive."

Blades clanged and scraped.

"Bascha—drive him back. Bring him across to me."

When he moved, I could see her. She wore only the ivory tunic and a relentless ferocity. She didn't want to kill him; she most certainly wanted to beat him beyond the hope of redemption. It was what she'd have to do in order to force his hand. Abbu wouldn't yield unless he knew she could kill him.

Unless he knew she *might.*

Del's patterns were flawless. His better still.

"Come on, bascha, watch him . . . don't let him draw you in—"

She drove him across the circle. Behind me, the spectators moved, fearing a broken circle. I knew better. They'd neither of them break it.

"Yes, bascha—*yes*—" The dance blurred again. I tried to squint it away. "Hoolies, not *now*—"

Abbu Bensir's turn to move. I nearly moved with him.

Alric's hand clamped around my right arm. "This isn't your dance."

Someone bumped my left elbow. He'd come in close, moving across the outer circle, usurping the little space left to me and Alric. I reeled, nearly fell. Scrubbed my eyes again. "Two of everything . . ."

"Aqivi," Alric remarked. "I should have given you water."

I felt drunk. I felt *distant.* Noise increased, then receded. The clamoring hurt my head. Around me, the world squirmed. Even Alric squirmed.

"Stay in one place," I suggested, as he moved closer on my left. "Come on, bascha—*dance*—"

Everything was gray. The steelsong hurt my ears.

"What's that?" Alric asked.

I chanced a glance to my right. Waited for vision to still. "Will you stop switching sides?"

"What's that sound?" he asked.

All I could hear was the steel. It cut my head right open.

Del broke through Abbu's guard and stung him in the elbow. Abbu skipped back, but the trick was a telling one. The woman had drawn first blood.

"Better, bascha . . . better—"

"What's that *noise?*" Alric asked.

I heard the clang of steel, the screech and scrape of blades. What did he think it was?

"Come on, bascha—*beat* him—"

"Tiger—look at that."

All I saw was the dance. Two moving bodies: one male, one female. Both perfectly matched. Both moving easily to a rhythm no one else heard. A desire no one else felt.

Come on, bascha—

"Tiger!"

Alric's voice got through. It stole my wits from the dance, from Del; it made me look beyond.

Across the circle from us, behind Del's back, the crowd abruptly parted. Lines of spectators peeled away like bark from a willow tree.

Leaving Vashni in their place.

Vashni. *Vashni?*

"Tiger," Alric repeated.

In the circle, the dance went on. Steel rang on the air.

The ululation began.

Softly, first; then rising. It swallowed. It swallowed the song of the swords. It swallowed the murmuring. It swallowed the whole world.

I rubbed at aching eyes. "Too much noise," I complained.

Alric, having moved again, now stood on my left. He smiled down at me. And odd, triumphant smile.

Smiled *down* at me; but we are the same size. "Wait—" I began, but the world grayed out again.

"Tiger. Tiger?"

Now from my right. "Two of you," I muttered "trading places with one another."

In the circle, Del danced. But no one watched any more.

"Oracle!" someone shouted. "Show us the Oracle!"

The ululations stopped. Vashni divided and flowed aside, leaving the middle open.

"Oracle," someone murmured. The word threaded its way through the crowd until all I could hear was the whisper. The sound of the syllables.

I squinted across the circle. Saw the hair, the eyes, the skin. "Alric," I said in disgust, "how did you get over *there?*"

He sounded startled. "What?"

"There." I tried to point. "One minute you're over there—the next you're here on my right—the next you're on my *left*. There aren't three of you, are there?"

Alric didn't answer. "He's a *Northerner,*" he blurted.

Northerner? Northerner?

What is he talking about?

Del and Abbu danced. I heard the steelsong threading through the humming, the shouts from everyone else.

Not shouting for the dance. Shouting for the jhihadi.

So many Northerners. So many Alrics.

I looked right: Alric.

I looked left: Alric.

Across the circle: Alric.

Hoolies, I must be sandsick.

"Aqivi," I muttered. "It's muddled up my head."

My muddled head swam.

I squinted again across the circle. "Alric—is that you?" I swung my muddled head and stared at the man on my left. "Or is *that* you . . . no, neither one . . . then who's *that* man?"

The Alric on my left looked at me out of piercingly bright blue eyes. No, not Alric—Alric's smile is different. Alric's *eyes* are different. He doesn't cut you with them.

These eyes were cold. These eyes were icy. These eyes waited for something.

"The Oracle," repeated Alric—the Alric on my right, mimicking everyone else.

I stared across the circle. Blond, blue-eyed Northerner: Alric was right in that. He looked a lot like Alric. He looked a lot like Del. Maybe it's just that Northerners all look alike to me—

My mouth dropped open. "Hoolies, that's *Jamail*—"

Alric's voice: "Who?"

"Del's brother—but the Vashni said he was dead!"

"He doesn't look dead to me. He looks like an Oracle."

Oracle. Oracle?

In the circle, in the dance, swords scraped and clashed and screeched.

"Wait—" I said, "*wait* . . . I don't—this isn't—*he* can't be the Oracle . . . Jamail doesn't have a tongue!"

Jamail opened his mouth and began to prophesy.

Now *my* mouth dropped open. "Am I awake?" I asked numbly, "or did the stud really kill me?"

Alric didn't answer.

"Del!" I shouted. *"Del!"*

But Del was busy dancing. Her back was to her brother.

"Hoolies, bascha—can't you hear? That's your brother talking!"

That's her brother—*talking?*

A flash of salmon-silver blade; the cry of magicked steel.

"He has no tongue," I protested.

Hoolies, everything fit. A mute who wasn't a man, but wasn't a woman, either.

Oh, bascha, *look.*

Steelsong filled the air, punctuating the Oracle's words as he lifted an arm to point.

"Jhihadi!" someone shouted. "He's naming the jhihadi!"

The crowd behind me surged forward. Jostled, I nearly fell. A hand on my left arm steadied me, another hooked into my harness; Alric was on my right.

Alric was on my *right.*

"Jhihadi!" the crowd roared, as the Oracle made it clear.

The man on my left laughed. It was a wild, exultant laugh filled with surprise and gratification, and an odd sort of power. "All that money spent on a false Oracle, and now the real one picks me anyway . . ." He tightened his grip on my harness. "Now all I need is this."

I knew as I turned to look. By then it was too late.

Ajani wasted no time. He locked one hand around the hilt and jerked my *jivatma* free, shoving me back as he moved. I very nearly fell.

He watched me out of pale, icy eyes. Saw me stagger. Saw me struggle. Saw me gather flagging wits. Saw me open my mouth to protest.

And smiled. "Samiel," he whispered. The blade flared to life.

Oh—hoolies—*Ajani*—

Ajani with Samiel.

Ajani with Chosa Dei.

Who now was pointed at me.

I heard Alric's curse. Saw Ajani's eyes. How could I have confused them?

"Thank you," Ajani said. "You made it easy for me."

I sucked in a breath, trying to hold off disorientation. "You don't know what you have. You don't know what that sword *is*."

Ajani's voice was smooth. Incongruously soft. "Oh, I think I do. People are talking about it . . . even my own men, who saw what you did with it and remembered what the boy said." The smile was brief, but warm. "I know what a *jivatma* is. I knew what to do with the name. It will be very useful for a man just named jhihadi."

I kept my tone steady. "If your men were there, you know. You know what else it can do. What it can do to *you*."

All around us the people fled.

Ajani lifted the sword. I thought about what it would be like for Chosa Dei to have me at last. And what it would be like when he—in my skin—tore Ajani to pieces.

It might be interesting. But I'd rather just be *me*.

Beyond me, Alric shouted. Said something about men: borjuni.

I looked only at Ajani, who held my *jivatma*.

And then heard Delilah's song, cutting through the circle.

Oh, bascha, bascha. Here is your chance at last.

The song rose in pitch. The circle was filled with Northern light so bright even Ajani squinted.

I pointed a courteous finger toward the woman who approached. Politely, I told Ajani, "Someone wants to see you."

By the time he turned, she was on him.

Chapter 17

I knew she should be tired, after dancing with Abbu. But this was Ajani at last; I knew it didn't matter. Del could be on her deathbed and Ajani would get her off it.

So she could put him on his.

She drove him back, back, into the crowd; the crowd scrambled away. And then surged close again, surrounding Alric and me, murmuring about the jhihadi and the woman who tried to kill him.

Hoolies, they believed it! They thought he was the jhihadi!

Which meant if Del killed him, the crowd would tear her apart.

"Don't kill him," I said. "Oh, bascha, be careful—think about what you're doing."

I didn't expect an answer. Del didn't give me one.

They'd kill her. They'd shred her to little pieces.

Bascha, don't kill him.

Unless I could get to Jamail. But I knew better than to try. I could barely stand, jostled this way and that. And even if I could, the Vashni would kill me outright for daring to approach their Oracle, no matter what the reason. Already things had gone wrong; the Oracle had spoken, and a woman was trying to thwart him.

The Oracle's own sister.

Jamail, remember me?

No. He'd only seen me once.

Jamail, remember your sister?

But between Jamail and his sister were hundreds of Southerners: tanzeers, sword-dancers, tribesmen. Even the Oracle might have trouble getting through the crowd, now the jhihadi was named.

Jamail no longer mattered. His part in the game was done.

The crowd closed up tight. Hoolies, Del, where are you?

The crowd abruptly parted.

"Tiger—*down*—"

Alric's hand on my harness jerked me to the ground. Then his sword was out and slicing through someone's guts.

What?

What?

Ajani's fellow borjuni. Now become holy bodyguards warding the jhihadi.

Oh, hoolies—not *now*. My head hurts too much and my eyes won't focus.

I rolled through screening legs, scrabbling away, cursing as fingers got stepped on. Wished I had a sword.

Above me, battle commenced. Alric was all alone.

Hoolies, where's Del?

And then I saw the light. Heard the whistle of the storm. Felt the sting of flying dust. With the power of *jivatmas*, they built a private circle. They created a fence of magic made of light and heat and cold.

"I need a sword," I muttered, staggering to my feet.

In the circle, the wind howled. Ajani had my sword.

"Tiger! Tiger—*here!*"

I turned; caught the weapon. An old, well-known blade. I stared in muddled surprise.

Through the brief gap, Abbu Bensir grinned. "You're mine," he called, "not theirs." And was swallowed by the crowd.

More of the new jhihadi's borjuni friends arrived with weapons drawn. Alric and I didn't count them; we knew they outnumbered us. But we also knew how to dance. All they knew was how to kill.

Time. Too much, and the tribes would reach the circle Del shared with Ajani. They couldn't break through until the dance was done and the magic muted, but in the end they'd reach her. In the end they'd kill her.

If she was still alive.

Too much time, and Ajani's borjuni bodyguards would wear down Alric and me. Too little, however, and we might be able to get away, if we had a bit of luck.

Luck decided to call.

"Duck," a voice suggested. I didn't wait; I ducked. The thrown ax divided a head.

Bellin laughed aloud. "Practicing," he said.

Now we were there. The fourth was still in the circle.

Come on, Delilah, *beat* him.

Fire flared in the circle. People began to scream.

At first I assumed it was in the natural course of fighting, since by now others had joined in as well. And then I realized it had nothing to do with fighting, and everything to do with magic.

Chosa Dei wanted his freedom. Others would pay the price.

Even Del might.

Not again, bascha. You already paid it once.

Ajani was shouting something. I couldn't understand him; my head pounded unmercifully and my vision still was muddled. But I heard Ajani shouting.

He said something about Shaka Obre.

Ajani didn't know Shaka Obre.

I cut down a borjuni. "Hold him, bascha—*hold him*—"

Boreal keened. A cold wind burst out of the circle, shredding silk and gauze. It frosted hair and eyebrows. Those who still could, fled.

I sucked in a breath and jerked my borrowed blade from a body. "Sing up a storm, bascha . . ."

In a mad dash to escape, people fell over one another. I saw their breath on the air.

Winter came into the circle. Summer drove it back. The blast of heat baked us all; I blocked my eyes with an arm.

Samiel burned white-hot. The air was sucked out of lungs.

The hostility around us turned abruptly to fear. Even Ajani's borjuni exuded a different stench.

Ajani. Ajani in the circle.

With Del.

Hoolies, bascha, where are you—?

Shouting died away. Light corruscated. All the rainbows danced, though there was no rain to form them. No moisture in the air. Only scorching heat.

Ajani was shouting still. Del stalked him in the circle. Back, back, back; Boreal teased Samiel, salmon-silver on black.

"Dance," Del invited. "Dance with me, Ajani."

Back. Back. Back. He tried to parry, couldn't.

I saw the bared teeth, the strained face. Saw the fear in piercing eyes. It wasn't fear of Del, but of what he felt in the sword.

He was a very large man, a man of immense strength as well as strength of will. But he didn't know Samiel. He didn't know Chosa Dei.

"Too much for you," I muttered.

Ajani shouted something. Tendons stood up in his neck.

Heat exploded from the circle. Nearby, a blanket roof caught on fire. Then another. People began to scream. People began to run. Iskandar was on fire.

Wind ripped through the streets, spreading flame in its wake. Now burnouses caught fire, and people began to burn.

"No," Del declared.

Boreal's song-summoned banshee-storm howled out of the sword, shredding Samiel's flame. Winter came at Del's call. Fire doesn't burn in sleet.

It was abrupt and unpleasant. It doused Iskandar completely, then wisped into nothingness. I was wet, cold, sweaty. But so was everyone else, even Ajani's borjuni.

With renewed vigor, they attacked. With renewed vigor, I repulsed. Next to me, Alric fought; behind me Bellin counted Ajani's supporters they moved in to surround us. He called out greetings to each, naming them to their faces, which served to startle them. For Alric and me, it was an infallible way of knowing which man meant us harm.

Bascha, I said, I'm coming.

Something stung a rib. I smashed the sword away, then buried my own in a belly. Ripped it free again to turn on another man, but a misstep sent me by him. I staggered, tried to catch my balance, was swallowed by heat and cold and light and all the colors of the world.

Bascha, bascha, I'm coming—whether I want to or not.

I broke through, swearing, and fell into the circle, landing hard on a shoulder. Abbu's sword spilled free.

Hoolies, my head hurts . . . and the world's gone gray again.

Inside, the storm was raging. A hot rain fell. Steam rose from the ground. The breath of winter blew, whistling in my ears. Numbing nose and earlobes.

Boreal was ablaze with all the colors of the North, all the rich, vivid colors. Samiel was black.

A new thought occurred: If Chosa Dei takes Ajani, Del can take Chosa Dei.

But Del didn't wait that long.

Sprawled on the ground, I saw it. Hatred. Rage. Obsession. The memory of what he'd done; of what had shaped her life. Of *who* had shaped her life, bringing her to this moment; bringing her to the edge, where balance is so precarious, so incredibly easy to lose. She teetered there, on the edge, looking just beyond. Acknowledging the price, because she'd paid it so many times.

Paying once more would change nothing. And also change everything.

Delilah's long song would end.

Wind screamed through the circle. It caught on blades and tore, shrieking an angry protest. Ajani's face was stripped bare. An unforgettable face; an assemblage of perfect bones placed in impressive arrangement. A Northerner in his prime: taller than I, and broader, with a lion's mane of hair equally thick and blond as Del's, flowing back from high brow. The magnificence of a woman made masculine for a man.

Bellin had summed it up: his burning was very bright.

His burning was *too* bright—Chosa Dei looked out of his eyes.

Pale, piercing eyes alight with unholy fire. With the knowledge of promised power.

Time to extinguish him, bascha—before he extinguishes us.

Del stopped singing. Del lowered her sword. And stood there waiting for him.

Waiting? Waiting for *what?*

Was she blinded by his burning?

No, not Delilah. This was the man who had made her, the way I made my sword. In blood and fear and hatred.

Ajani bared his teeth. *"We meet again,"* he said. *"This time to end it, yes?"*

Del, like me, stared. His features were softening. The perfect nose, the set of his mobile mouth; the upswept angle of Northern cheekbones, slanting down his face. Ajani was being *unmade.*

Hoolies, bascha, *kill* him!

She slashed the blade from his hands. Her own was at his throat. "Kneel," she said hoarsely. "You made my father kneel."

Bascha, that isn't Ajani—

My sword lay on the ground. My clean, silver sword made of unblemished Northern steel.

My *empty,* unblemished sword.

Oh, bascha—wait—

"Del—" I croaked.

Ajani bared teeth at her. Chosa Dei stared out of his eyes. *"Do you know what I am?"*

"I know what you are."

Ajani shook back his hair. The shape of his jaw was changing. He was wax, softening. Light a candle; he would melt.

Del's voice was deadly. "I said: *kneel.*"

Around us, beyond the circle, hundreds waited and watched, too frightened to attempt escape. I lay on the ground and panted, trying to clear my head. Thinking: If I can get to the sword—

But Ajani was too close. He had only to pick it up. He *would* pick it up—

"Del—" I croaked again. It was all I could manage.

Ajani did not kneel. Chosa Dei wouldn't let him.

"I am power," he said. *"Do you think you can defeat me? Do you think I will do* your *bidding, after waiting so long to do mine?"*

Hoolies, he didn't need a *sword.* All he needed was himself.

Bascha—bascha, *kill him*—don't play games with this man—not even in the name of your pride—

Ajani spread his arms. There was no wasted flesh on him, nor a pound out of place. He was taut, fit, *big*. He made me look puny. His magnificence rivaled Del's.

"Do you know what I am?"

And I wondered, as I watched him, which man asked the question.

Del shifted her grip. The sword scythed down from above. She sliced a hamstring in two.

He fell, as she meant him to. It wasn't a proper posture, but no longer did he stand upright to tower over her. To tower over *me* as I staggered to my feet.

His burning was very bright.

"Now," I whispered intently.

Del began to sing.

Chosa Dei was in him, but some of Ajani was left. Northern-born, he knew. I saw it in his eyes; in Ajani's still-human eyes, as the flesh of his face loosened. I saw it in his posture as he slumped before the sword, wearing a bloody necklace. Boreal was thirsty. She tasted him already.

Del sang a song of the kinfolk she had lost. Father, mother, grand-folk, brothers, aunts, uncles, cousins. So many kinfolk murdered. Only two of them spared: Jamail and Delilah, the last of the line. The man could never sire a son; the woman could never bear one.

She would kill Ajani. But in the end, he would win.

Delilah ended her song. Stood there looking at him. Did she feel cheated, I wondered, that Ajani wasn't alone? That when the moment came, she would kill more than the Northerner?

Chosa wasn't stupid. He reached out. Touched the sword. Closed slack fingers on the grip. Dragged it up from the ground. Black flowed into the blade; better a sword than useless meat.

Pale hair tumbled around his face. His magnificent Northern face, with no hint of softness about it. Chosa Dei was gone.

Ajani shook back his hair, holding the blackened *jivatma*. But he didn't try to use it, with Boreal kissing his throat. All he did was stare at the woman who held Boreal, progenitor of storms.

"Who are you?" he asked.

Del didn't bother to tell him. "You have a daughter," she said.

And then she took his head.

Chapter 18

The body slumped to the ground. Del, set free at last, staggered back and fell.

Oh, hoolies, bascha . . . don't pass out *now*.

She tried to get up, and couldn't. Exhaustion and reaction stripped her of her strength. All she could do was gasp, clinging to her sword.

Hoolies, Tiger, *move*—

The private circle was gone, banished by banished magic. Anyone who reached us now would find us easy to touch.

Del had killed Ajani. To the rest, he was the jhihadi.

I heard the ululations, the shouts of angry tanzeers. The clash of Southron steel.

"Sorry, Esnat," I mumbled. "I think Hadjib will get his war."

Samiel, I knew, was the answer . . . before they got to Del.

Bellin got there first. "Don't touch it!" I shouted.

He dove, thrust out with his axes, scooped up the blade. As I took an unsteady stride—Del and I were a pair—the sword came flying to me. I plucked it out of the air.

Southroners stirred, shouted. They saw the headless jhihadi; the woman with the sword; the Sandtiger with another. And a foreign boy with axes.

Bellin grinned at me. "Do something," he called. "You're supposed to be good with that thing."

Do something?

Fine.

How about a song?

The crowd surged forward en masse. But I cut the air with a re-blackened sword and the crowd lurched back again. Across from me stood Alric, teasing the air with his swordtip. Promising violence.

Alric. Bellin. Me. And Del, but she was down. For now we had stopped the crowd, but that wouldn't last long. We needed more help.

Samiel might give it. All I had to do was sing.

Sing. I hate singing. But how else do you call the magic?

Bellin juggled axes. It was an impressive feat; also a useful one. They'd all seen how he used them. Everyone hung back as Bellin moved easily around Del and me, building a fence of flying axes.

"Just curious," he mentioned, "but why are you singing *now?* Especially when you do it so badly?"

I just kept on singing. Or whatever you want to call it.

"Jivatma," Alric said briefly, as if it answered the question. For some, it might; for Bellin, it answered nothing.

"Get Del," I said, and went right back to my song. Samiel seemed to like it.

Behind us, far behind us, the ululation increased. The tribes were coming in.

We edged toward the city. Hoolies, if they got through they'd cut us down in a minute. Samiel would take a few, but eventually we'd lose just because of sheer numbers.

Bellin, being helpful, started to sing along. He had a better voice, but he didn't know my song.

Samiel didn't seem to mind.

"Alric—have you got Del?"

"I've got her, Tiger . . . come on, we've got to go."

"Tiger?" It was Del. "Tiger—that was *Jamail.*"

The keening wail increased. Moving this slowly wouldn't gain us any time. We needed something special.

All right, I said to my sword, let's see what you can do.

I thrust it into the air over my head, balanced flat across both palms, as I'd seen Del do. And I sang my heart out—loudly, and very badly—until the firestorm came.

It licked out from the blade, flowed down my body, spilled across the ground. I sent it in all directions, teasing at feet and robes. It drove everyone back: tanzeers, tribesmen, borjuni.

Magic, I thought, can be useful.

I called up a blast of wind, a hot, dry wind born of the Punja itself. It tasted at sand and sucked it up, then spat it at the people.

The tribes, if no one else, would know what it was. Would call it samiel, and give way to its strength. You can't fight the desert when it rises up to rebel.

"Go home!" I shouted. "He was a false jhihadi! He was a *Northerner*—is that what you want?"

In the sandblast, they staggered back. Tribesmen, borjuni, tanzeers; the samiel knows no rank.

"Go home!" I shouted. "It's not the proper time!"

The wail of the storm increased.

"Now," I said to the others, as the crowd, shouting, scattered.

I peeled the storm apart, forming a narrow channel. With alacrity, we departed.

Garrod met us with horses: the stud, and Del's blue roan, "Go," he said succintly. "They're watered and provisioned; don't waste any time."

The thought of riding just now did not appeal to me. My head was not very happy. "He'll dump me, or kick me again."

"No, I've spoken to him. He understands the need."

It was, I thought in passing, a supremely ridiculous statement. He was *horse*, not human.

Ah, hoolies, who cares? If Garrod said he would . . . I pushed away a damp muzzle come questing for reassurance.

Del sheathed her sword. "Jamail," was all she said.

That decided me. "Don't be sandsick," I snapped. "Jamail's the Oracle; do you think anyone will hurt him?"

"I thought he was dead, and he's not."

"So be happy about it. Let's go."

Garrod handed her reins. "Waste no time," he repeated. "I can hold the other horses, but not for very long. There are far too many of them . . . the sandstorm will only delay them, not stop them—once they've recovered their courage they'll come after you again. If you want a head start, *go.*"

Del swung up on the roan and gathered in her reins, staring down at me. "Are *you* coming, then?"

I took the pointed hint. Sheathed my sword. Dragged myself up on the stud, who stomped and pawed and snorted. I clung muzzily to the saddle. "Which way is out?"

"This way," Del said, pointing, as Alric slapped the stud's rump.

"What about me?" Bellin called. "Aren't I supposed to come? I found Ajani for you!"

I held the stud up a moment. "I can think of better ways of becoming famous than riding with the woman who killed the new jhihadi. Certainly *safer* ones; it's no good being a panjandrum if you're not alive to enjoy it."

"True," Bellin agreed. "So I guess I can still be your son. You look old enough."

I called him a foul name and sent the stud after Del.

We clattered through the ruined city with no respect for its inhabitants. Garrod was absolutely right: now that I'd banished the sandstorm and Del and I were gone, there was nothing to prevent the crowd from solidifying its deadly intention. No matter what I'd shouted about Ajani being a false jhihadi, he was still the only one they knew, thanks to planted rumors and Jamail's misinterpreted gesture. The crowd, fired by bloodlust, wouldn't listen to the truth no matter who gave it to them. Not even the Oracle.

Through the city and out, then bursting through colored hyorts huddled together on the plateau. And over the rim and off, swarming down the trail. Behind us, as we fled, the shouting slowly died, shredded by canyons and distance. And Iskandar was gone.

We rode as long and hard as we could, knowing we needed the distance. Del eventually called halt as we traded border canyons for border foothills, and scrubby, tree-clad ridges carved out of Southron soil. I wasn't so certain it was a good idea to stop yet, but she said I looked like I'd fall off if the stud so much as sneezed.

I held my head very still. "If he so much as *blinks*."

"Can you follow me?" she asked.

"As long as you don't go fast."

Del took us off the trail and over a snaky line of ridges and foothills closer to Harquhal than Iskandar. Trees were low and twisted and scrubby, but plentiful, providing decent cover. Behind a sloping, tree-screened hillside well off the new-beaten trail, Del dismounted her roan.

She reached out to catch the stud. "Do you need help?"

With great care, I dismounted, clinging to the stirrup. "Help doing what?"

She just shook her head. "Go sit down somewhere. I'll tend the horses.

I did. She did. And eventually came back, carrying saddle-pouches, bedrolls, botas.

In the hollow of the hill, we ate, drank, stretched out. Thought about what had happened. Thought about what we'd done.

Del was close beside me. I could hear her breathing "Well," I said, "it's done."

She didn't say anything.

"You sang the song for your kinfolk, the one you swore to sing, and collected the blood-debt he owed for murdering everyone."

She still didn't say anything.

"Your song is over, bascha. You sang it very well."

She drew in a lengthy, noisy breath.

"You said I should ask you after Ajani was dead." I waited a moment. "What will you do now?"

Del's smile was sad. "Ask me in the morning."

"Bascha—"

"Ask," she said softly. "And then ask me the next morning, and the next . . ." She rubbed at eyes undoubtedly as tired and gritty as mine. "If you ask me enough times, maybe one of these days I'll know. And by then it won't matter, because years will have passed, and I'll have forgotten why I never knew what I would do once Ajani was dead. I will have simply *done* it."

It was, I thought, convoluted reasoning. But at that particular moment it didn't rea"y matter.

I released a sigh. It felt so good just to *stop*. "Busy day," I observed.

Del only grunted.

The sun dipped low in the west. "Who won the dance?"

Next to me, Del shifted. "Nobody won the dance. The dance was never finished."

I attempted to summon outrage. "Do you mean to tell me you threw away my chance at a domain? My chance to be a tanzeer?"

Unimpressed, Del shrugged. "You'd be a bad tanzeer."

"How do *you* know?"

"I just do."

My turn to grunt. "You're probably right."

"*I'd* make a better tanzeer."

"You're a woman, bascha."

"So?"

"So we're South, remember?"

"Aladar's daughter is a tanzeer."

"That will never last."

She sighed. "You're probably right. The South is still too backward."

The sun dipped lower still. "I think instead of a sword, I'm going to get a new horse."

Del grinned briefly. "The old one might protest."

"The old one can protest himself right into the stewpot, for all I care. I'm not about to put up with him taking pieces out of my head just because he hates magic."

"You hated magic, once."

"I still hate magic. It doesn't mean I'm going to kick somebody's head off if they use it."

"You used to *bite* mine off."

I grunted. "Long time ago, bascha."

"Hours ago, maybe."

I sighed. "Why are we arguing?"

"We're not arguing. We're delaying."

"What are we delaying?"

"Discussing what we're going to do."

"What *are* we going to do?"

"Go north?"

"No."

"Go south?"

"We have to. There's Shaka Obre to find."

Del didn't answer at once. When she did, her tone was odd. "You're certain you want to do that?"

"I have to. How else am I going to discharge this sword?"

"You've already learned to control it better."

I frowned. Rolled my head to look at her. "You sound like you don't think it's such a good idea to go hunting Shaka Obre."

She chose her words carefully. "I just think it will be very difficult to find him. His name is shrouded in myth—he's part of children's stories."

"So was Chosa Dei, but that didn't make him any less real. *I* can attest to that."

Del sighed, picking at the thin blanket she'd thrown over her long, bare legs. "It isn't easy, Tiger."

"Nothing much is, but what do *you* mean?"

"Looking for a man very difficult to find. I had reason, I had *need* . . . but the task was no easier."

"You're saying you don't think I'll stick with it."

"I'm saying it will be a very difficult quest."

"I don't have a lot of choice. Chosa Dei's presence will provide a good enough reason, I think."

Del sighed. "It will be complicated. We are wanted now, more so than anyone in the South—we killed the jhihadi. They will track us without respite. We killed the *jhihadi*, the man who intended to change the sand to grass."

"The man they *think* was the jhihadi."

Del considered it, then laughed a little. "Jamail was very clever, doing what he did. I wouldn't have thought of it."

"What did Jamail do?"

"Pointed at Ajani. He must have known someone would try to kill him . . . if not me, then the tanzeers. He got his revenge after all."

I grunted. "He wasn't pointing at Ajani. And it wasn't Alric, either; I know: I was there."

"Who *else* was he pointing at? I saw him do it, Tiger."

"So did I, bascha."

"Well, if it wasn't at Ajani—" Then, lurching up out of blankets: "You're *sandsick!*"

"Oh, I don't think so."

Loud silence.

"He wouldn't," she said at last. "He *didn't*—you know he didn't. Why would he do such a thing?"

I didn't offer an answer, thinking it obvious.

Del stared at me. "That horse kicked you harder than I thought."

I yawned. "I might make a bad tanzeer, but I think I can handle messiah."

Louder silence.

Then, in pointed challenge, "Can you change the sand to grass?"

Another yawn. "Tomorrow."

Del's tone was peculiar. "He didn't *really* point at you. You were right there, yes, but it was *Ajani* he pointed at. I saw him. I saw him point. It was Ajani, Tiger."

I just lay there and smiled, blinking drowsily.

"Swear by your sword," she ordered.

I grinned. "Which one?"

"The *steel* sword, Tiger; don't be so vulgar."

I put out a hand and caught the twisted-silk hilt. "I swear by Samiel: Jamail pointed at me."

I knew she wanted to admonish me not to speak the name aloud. But she understood what it meant. She understood the oath.

Del thought about it deeply. Then made a careful observation. "You know better than to swear false oath on your *jivatma*." As if she wasn't certain; maybe, with me, she wasn't.

Through yet another yawn, "Yes, bascha. You've made it very clear that's a bad thing to do." I paused. "Would you like me to swear on *your* sword?"

Very firmly, "No."

I drifted off toward sleep. The edge was so very close. All I needed to do was take that final step and slide myself off the horizon, in concert with the sun—

Del lay down again. Said nothing for several long moments.

I just drifted, aware of her nearness in an abstract, pleasing way. Legs and elbows touched. My temple brushed her shoulder.

Drowsily, I thought: A good way to fall asleep—

Then she turned a hip, shifting closer to me. Her breath in my ear was soft. "Do sword-dancers-turned-messiahs have bedmates? Or are they celibate?"

I cracked open a gritty eye. "Not tonight, bascha. I have a headache."

The sun fell over the edge. Laughing, so did I.

Sword-Breaker

*This book is dedicated to the memory of Jan Carpenter,
to her beloved Tootsie and Kizzy,
and to all the friends who miss her.*

Acknowledgments

Appreciation and gratitude to the following, for a variety of reasons: Russ Galen, agent extraordinaire; Alan Dean Foster and Raymond E. Feist, wise men both, for advice most sound in all respects; Betsy Wollheim and Sheila Gilbert, the Future of Fantasy (but next time let's stay in the suite and send out for pizza and beer!); Debby Burnett, for Kismet Cheysuli Wld Blu Yond'r, AKA "Pilot"; and Mark for everything.

Lastly, to the men and women who understand sexism is a sword that cuts both ways and are working diligently to break it.

Prologue

There are things in life you just *know*, without having to think much about them.

Like *now*, for example.

I lurched to my feet in the darkness, staggered two steps through rocks, landed painfully on my knees. "Oh, hoolies," I muttered.

And promptly discarded my supper.

Supper such as it *was;* Del and I hadn't really had much chance to eat a proper meal the night before, being too tired, too twitchy, too tense. And, in my case, too dizzy.

Around me, insects fell silent. The only sounds I heard were the scraping of shod hooves in dirt—my bay stud, Del's blue roan, hobbled a few steps away—and my own rather undignified bleat that was half hiccup, half belch, and all disgruntlement.

From behind me, a sleep-blurred voice, and the scratch of pebbles and gritty dust displaced by a moving body. "Tiger?"

I hunched there on my knees, sweaty and cold and miserable. My head hurt too much to attempt a verbal answer, so I waved a limp, dismissive hand, swiping the air between us, and hoped it was enough.

Naturally, it wasn't. With her, it never is.

Blurriness evaporated. She wastes little time waking up. "Are you all right?"

My posture was unmistakable. "I'm praying," I mumbled sourly, wiping my mouth on a burnous sleeve; it was already filthy dirty. "Can't you tell?"

Sand gritted again. From behind she slung a bota, which landed next to me. The sloshing thwack of leather on stone was loud in the pallor of first light. The stud snorted a protest. "Here," Del said. "Water. I'll warm the kheshi."

Belly rebelled at the thought. My turn for a protest. "Hoolies, bascha—kheshi's the last thing I need!"

"You need *something* in your stomach, or you'll be spewing your guts up all day."

Nice way to start the morning. Glumly, carefully, I reached down and hooked the bota thong, shifting weight to ease aching knees. I was stiff and sore inside and out from the exertions of the sword-dance.

Well, no, not really a sword-dance; more like a sword-fight, which is an entirely different thing with entirely different rules; better yet, a sword-*war*. Del and I had won the battle, with a little help from luck, friends, and magic—not to mention mass confusion—but hostilities were not concluded.

I thought briefly about rising, then considered the state of head and belly and decided staying close to the ground in an attitude of prayer, regardless of true intention, was a posture worth practicing.

Squinting against my reasserted headache, I uncorked the bota, drank a little, discovered tipping my head back did nothing at all to still the hammer and anvil. With great care I leveled my head again and peered out at the pale morning, focusing fixedly on dimming stars to distract me from the discomfort in offended skull and belly.

Realizing, as I did so, something *besides* my belly desired emptying.

Which meant I had to get up anyway, if only to find a bush.

Hoolies, life was much easier before I joined up with a woman.

"Tiger?"

I twitched, then wished I hadn't. Even blinking hurt my head. "What?"

"We can't stay here. We'll have to ride on."

I grunted, thinking instead of ways to rid myself of the

headache. Drinking aqivi might help, except we had none. "Eventually," I agreed. "First things *first*, bascha, like finding out if I can walk."

"You don't have to walk. You have to ride." She paused: elaborate, sarcastic solicitude. "Do you think you can ride, Tiger?"

My back remained to her, so she didn't see the oath I mouthed against the dawn. "I'll manage."

She chose to ignore my irony. "You'll need to manage soon. They'll be coming after us."

Yes, so they would be. Every "they" they could muster. Tens and twenties of them; possibly even hundreds.

The sun began to crawl above the swordblade of the horizon. I squinted against the light. "Maybe I *should* pray," I muttered. "Aren't I the jhihadi?"

Del grunted skepticism. "You are no messiah, no matter what you say about Jamail pointing at you."

Injured innocence: "But I swore by my *sword*."

She said something of succinct, exquisite brevity in Northern, which is her native tongue, and which adapts itself as readily to swearing as my Southron one does.

"Hah," she said, more politely. "You forget, Tiger—I know better. I know *you*. What you are is a man who's been kicked in the head, and drunk on top of it."

Well, she had the first part right: I *had* been kicked in the head, and, of all the indignities, by my own horse. But the second part was wrong. "I'm not drunk."

"You were yesterday. *And* last night."

"That was yesterday—and last night. And most of *that* was the kick in the head . . . besides, I don't notice it kept me from rescuing you."

"You didn't rescue me."

"Oh, no?" With meticulous effort, I got off my knees and onto my feet, turning slowly to face her. Movement hurt like hoolies. Sweetly, I inquired, "And who *was* it who held back an angry mob of people intent on ripping you to pieces for killing the jhihadi?"

Del's tone, surprisingly, was perfectly matter-of-fact. "He wasn't the jhihadi. He was Ajani. Bandit. Murderer. Rapist." She looked through thready smoke seeping upward from the handful of coals masquerading as a fire. Lumpy, bone-gray kheshi dripped from a battered cup as she scooped up a generous serving and held it out to me. "Breakfast is ready."

The stud chose that moment to flood the dirt. Which reminded me of something.

"Wait—" I blurted intently.

And staggered off to the nearest bush to pay tribute to the gods.

Chapter 1

I hooked my foot into the stirrup as I caught reins and pommel—
and stopped moving altogether. Which left me sort of *suspended,* weight distributed unevenly throughout sore legs stretched
painfully between stirrup and ground. Since the stirrup was attached to saddle—which was, in turn, attached to a horse, however
temporarily by dint of a cinch—I realized it was not the most ad-
vantageous of positions if the horse decided to move. But for the
moment, it was the best I could manage.

"Uck," I commented. "Whose idea was this?"

The stud swung his head around and eyed me consideringly
with one dark eye, promising much with nothing discernible. Except I know how to read him.

I exhibited a fist. "Better not, cumfa-bait."

Del, from atop her roan, with some asperity: "Tiger."

"Oh, keep your tunic tied." With an upward heave that did
nothing at all to ease the ache in my head—or the rebellion in my
belly—I swung up. "Of course, in *your* case, I'd just as soon you *untied* the tunic." I cast her a toothy leer that was, I knew in my heart
of hearts, but a shadow of the one I am capable of displaying. But
a battered body and too much liquor—*and* a kick in the head—will
do that for you.

One pale brow arched. "That is not what you said last night."

"Last night I had a headache." I gathered loose rein as I settled my rump in the leather hummock some people call a saddle. "I *still* have a headache."

Del nodded. "It often comes of a man who believes himself a person of repute. The head swells . . ." She gestured idle implication.

"That's a panjandrum. I never claimed I was a panjandrum—although I suppose I am, being the Sandtiger." I ribbed a gritty, sun-dazzled eye. "No, what *I* am is a jhihadi; even the Oracle said so." I displayed teeth again. "Will you call your brother a liar?"

She gazed at me steadily. "Before yesterday, I would have called my brother *dead*. You told me he was."

I opened my mouth to explain all over again that the Vashni had told me Jamail was dead; I'd had no reason not to believe the warrior since the tribe is so meticulous about honor. Telling a false-hood is not a Vashni habit, even though no one in his right mind would even suggest such a thing. I hadn't, certainly. Nor had I thought it.

No, Del's brother wasn't dead, no matter what the Vashni had told me. Because Jamail—supposedly dead, *mute* Jamail—had pointed across a milling throng in the midst of a violent sword fight between his older sister and the man who had murdered his kin—and proclaimed me the messiah.

Me, not Ajani, who had gone to great pains to convince everyone he was the jhihadi. Although no one, including Del (*still*), believed Jamail had pointed at me.

Which had a little something to do with our present predica-ment.

I stared blearily eastward beyond Del, raising a shielding hand to block the brilliance of the sun. "Is that dust?"

She looked. Like me, she squinted, lifting a flattened palm. Against the new day she was a darker silhouette: one-quarter pro-file, mostly fair hair; a shoulder, an elbow, the turn of hip and the line of thigh beneath the drapery of Southron silk.

And the slash of a scabbarded sword, slanting diagonally across her back to thrust an imperious hilt above one taut-muscled shoulder.

"Out of Iskandar," she said quietly of the gauzy haze. "I would not waste a copper on a wager that it could be anything else."

Which made a decision imperative.

"North across the border into your territory," I suggested, "but, under the terms of your exile, that's not exactly an option—"

"—or south," she interposed, "into the Punja again, *your* territory, which will surely kill us both if we give it the opportunity."

"Then again," I continued, "there is Harquhal. Half a day, maybe—"

"—where they will surely come, all of them, knowing it is the only place to buy supplies, and we with little to spare."

Which was true. Our sudden and unanticipated departure—better yet, *flight*—from Iskandar had given us little time to pack our horses. We had a set of saddle-pouches each, thanks to a friend, but food was limited. So was our water, something we *had* to have if we were to cross the Punja. While I knew of many oases, cisterns, and settlements—I'd grown up in the Punja—the desert is a transitory and unforgiving beast. The only certain thing is death, if you don't play the game right.

I spat out a succinct oath along with acrid dust as I lifted eloquent reins, putting the stud on notice. "Doesn't seem to me as if we have much choice. Unless, of course, you can magick us out of here with your sword."

"No more than you with yours." Unsmiling, as always. But the glint in blue eyes was plain.

The weight of the weapon in my harness was suddenly increased tenfold, just by the mention of it. And the implications.

"You sure know how to ruin a perfectly good morning," I muttered, swinging the stud.

"And you a beautiful night." Del turned her roan toward Harquhal, half a day's ride from the border. "Perhaps if you shut your mouth, the snoring would not be so bad."

I didn't bother to answer. The thundering of the stud's hooves drowned out anything I might say.

The thunder in my skull drowned out the desire to even *try*.

We hadn't done much, Del and I. Not when you really think about it. We'd just gone south through the Punja hunting a missing brother, stolen by Southron slavers. To Julah, the city near the sea, where we had, with little choice, killed a tanzeer. That sort of offense is punishable by death, as might be expected when you knock off a powerful desert prince; except Del and I had gotten clean away from Julah and her freshly murdered tanzeer. And gone on into the mountains at the rim of the ocean-sea, where we'd encountered Vashni. The tribe that held her brother.

Except he wasn't really being *held*; not any more. Mute and castrated, he'd nonetheless managed to make a life for himself. Del's plans for rescue were undone by Jamail himself, who clearly had no desire to leave the tribe that had delivered him from a lifetime of slavery. While not precisely a Vashni—they don't take kindly to half-bloods, let alone foreigners—neither was he suitable for sacrifice. He'd made his place.

So we'd left him, and ridden north, across the border to Del's homeland. Where she had taken me to Staal-Ysta, the island in black water, and delivered me as ransom to buy her daughter back.

Well, not *exactly*—but close enough. Close enough that I'd discovered just how single-minded she could be; to the point that nothing else in the world mattered, only the task she'd set herself: to find and kill Ajani, the man who'd murdered her family, raped a fifteen-year-old girl, and sold a ten-year-old boy into Southron slavery.

To find Ajani, she needed to be free of the blood-debt, which she owed to the Place of Swords, high in Northern mountains. Where she'd left her infant daughter to find and kill the daughter's father.

And, eventually, where she'd offered my services, me all unknowing, to pay part of her blood-debt.

My services . . . without even asking me.

Now, I've always known women are capable of doing just about anything they set their minds to, once they've made a decision. Getting *to* that decision isn't always the easiest thing, or the most logical, but eventually they get there. And, when pressed to it, they make promises they have to, no matter what it takes.

For Del, it took me. And very nearly our deaths.

Oh, we'd survived. But not before I wound up with a Northern sword, a magical *jivatma* as dangerous as Del's—only I didn't know how to key it, and it damn near keyed *me*.

And then, of course, there had been that thrice-cursed dragon, which wasn't a dragon at all, and the sorcerer called Chosa Dei.

A man no longer a man. A *spirit*, I guess you'd call him, who now lived in my sword.

Ahead of me, riding hard, Del twisted in the saddle. Horse-born wind snatched at white-blonde locks, tearing them free of burnous. Pale, glorious silk masquerading as hair . . . and the flawless face it framed, now turned in my direction.

I have never failed, not once, to marvel at her beauty.

"Hurry up," she said.

Of course, then there's her *mouth*.

"One of these days," I muttered, "I'm going to pin you down—*sit* on you, if I have to—and pour as much wine as I can buy down that soft, self-righteous gullet, so you'll know what my head feels like."

I didn't say it where she could hear it. But of course she *did*.

"Even a fool knows better than to drink after being kicked in the head," she commented over the noise of our horses. "So what does that make you?"

I shifted on the fly, finding a more comfortable position over the humping spine of my galloping horse. "You left me," I reminded her, raising my voice. "You left me lying there on the ground with my broken, bloodied head. If you'd stayed, I probably wouldn't have drunk anything."

"Oh, so it's *my* fault."

"Instead, you went flouncing off to fight Abbu Bensir—*my* dance, I might add—"

"You were in no shape to dance."

"That's beside the point—"

"That *is* the point." Del reined her roan around a dribble of rocks, then tossed hair out of her face as she twisted to look at me again. "I took your place in the circle because someone had to. You had been hired to dance against Abbu . . . had I not taken your place, you would have forfeited the dance. Do you want to consider the consequences?"

Not really. I knew what they were. The dance was more than merely a sword-dance: it was binding arbitration between two factions of tanzeers, powerful, ruthless despots who, whenever they could, chopped the South into little pieces among themselves and passed out the remains as rewards.

A reward *I* had been promised, if I won.

Except I didn't win, because the stud kicked me in the head, and Alric got me drunk.

My belly was, I thought unhappily, riding somewhere in the vicinity of my breastbone, jounced and bounced and compressed within the cage of my ribs. Knees, bent by shortened stirrups, reminded me whenever they could that I was gaining in age, while losing in flexibility. And then there was my head, which shall go unremarked so as not to give it ideas.

Hoolies, this sort of thing is enough to give a man pause. To remind him, rather emphatically, there are better ways than this of making a living.

Except I don't know of any.

The stud's misstep threatened to rearrange a portion of my body I was rather fond of. I bit out a curse, lifted weight off formed leather, and thought rather wistfully of other fleshly saddles.

"You're falling behind," she said.

"Just wait," I muttered. "There will come a day—"

"I don't think so," Del said, and bent lower over her roan.

Harquhal is . . . well, Harquhal. A border settlement. The kind of town no one *means* to build, really, because if it had been planned from the beginning, everyone contributing would have done the job right.

Oh, it was good *enough*, but not the sort of place I'd want to raise a family.

Then again, I didn't have a family, nor did I intend to start one, which meant the kind of town Harquhal was was good enough for me.

Del and I rode in at a long-trot, having dropped out of a gallop sometime back, then from lope to trot as we approached the wall-girded town. The stud, who has an adequate gallop and a soft, level long-*walk*, does not, most emphatically, know how to trot very well. He just isn't built for it, any more than I am built for low doorways and short beds.

A long-trot, trotted by a horse who does not possess the ability to offer this gait in anything approaching comfort, is nothing short of torture. Particularly if you are male. Particularly if you are male, and your head has been abused by aqivi and the kick of the horse you're riding.

So why trot at all? Because if I dropped to a walk I surrendered the advantage to Del, except I suppose it wasn't really an advantage, since we weren't actually racing. But she can be so cursed patronizing at times . . . especially when she thinks I'm in the wrong, or have done something stupid. And while I suppose there *have* been times I haven't been right, or I've behaved in such a way as to cast doubt upon my intelligence, this wasn't one of them. It hadn't been my fault the stud had kicked me. Nor my decision to suck down so much aqivi. And anyway, I *had* still managed to save her.

No matter what she said.

We reached the first sprawl of adobe wall encircling Harquhal. I eased the stud to a walk, breathing imprecations as he took most of the change of gait on his front legs, instead of distributed through his body. It makes a man sit up and take notice, in more ways than one.

Del cast a glance at me over a shoulder. "We shouldn't stay long. Only to buy supplies—"

"—and get a drink," I appended. "Hoolies, but I need a drink."

She opened her verbal dance pedantically, in the glacial way she has that ages her three decades. "We will not waste time on such things as wine or aqivi—"

I reined the stud next to her roan, hooking a knee just under the inner bend of her own. It is a technique, when fully employed, that can unhorse an enemy. And while Del and I were not precisely *enemies,* we were most distinctly at odds. "If I don't get a drink, I'll never make it through the day. In this case, it's *medicinal* . . . hoolies, bascha, haven't you ever heard of biting the dog back?"

Del disentangled her leg by easing the roan over. Her expression was wondrously blank. "Biting the dog? What dog? You were not bitten. You were *kicked.*"

"No, no, not like that." I scrubbed at a stubbled, grimy face. "It's a Southron saying. It has to do with having too much to drink. If you have a taste of whatever it was that made you sick, it makes you feel better."

Blonde brows knitted. "That makes no sense at all. If something makes you sick, how can it make you feel better?"

A thought occurred to me. I eyed her consideringly. "In all the time I've known you, I've never seen you drunk."

"Of course not."

"But you do drink. I've seen you drink, bascha."

Her tone was eloquent. "It is possible to drink and not get drunk. If one employs *restraint*—"

"Restraint is not always desirable," I pointed out. "Why employ restraint when you *want* to get drunk?"

"But why get drunk at all?"

"Because it makes you feel good."

Lines appeared in her brow. "But you have just now said spirits can make you sick. As you were sick this morning."

"Yes, well . . . that's different." I scowled. "Drinking spirits, as you call them, is not a good idea after you've been kicked in the head."

"It is not a good idea to drink so much at *any* time, Tiger. Especially for a sword-dancer." She tucked a strand of hair back. "It was a thing I learned on Staal-Ysta: never surrender will or skill to strong spirits, or you may defeat yourself."

I scratched my sandtiger scars idly. "I don't lose much, strong spirits or no. Matter of fact, I haven't *ever* lost, not when it counted—"

Del's tone was level as she cut in. "Because you and I have never danced for real."

The riposte was too easy. "Oh, *yes* we did, bascha. And it nearly got us killed."

It shut her up altogether, which is what I'd meant it to. It's how you win a dance: find the weakness, then exploit it. It is a strategy that carries over even to life outside of the circle, in every single respect. Del knew it well. Del knew how to do it. Del knew how to win.

Except this time she didn't.

And this time she knew she couldn't.

Chapter 2

*U*nder the eye of the morning sun, Del and I dismounted in an elbow-bend of a narrow, dust-choked street. She headed in one direction, leading her roan gelding, I in the other with the stud, until we realized what had happened and turned back, each of us, speaking at the same time. Telling one another which way was the proper direction.

I pointed my way. She pointed hers.

I pointed a bit more firmly. "Cantina's down there."

"Supplies are down *here*."

"Bascha, we don't have time to argue—"

"We don't have time to do anything more than reprovision and leave."

"Getting something to drink *is* reprovisioning."

"For *some*, perhaps." Nothing more. She obviously believed it enough. Del is very good at saying much with little. It's a woman's thing, I think: they get more out of a tone of voice than a man out of a knife.

Of course, some men might argue a woman's tongue is sharper.

"Or," I continued, overriding what she would undoubtedly refer to as common good sense, "we could hole up in one of the cantinas. Rent us a room." Which *I* thought was good sense; we'd have plenty of provisions, plus a roof over our heads.

One hand perched itself on a burnous-swathed hip. A jutting

elbow cut the air, eloquent even in silence. "And do what, Tiger? Wait for them to come find us?"

I ground teeth. "They *might* assume we'd ridden on."

"Or they might realize we'd need provisions and rest, and search all the rooms. Each and every one." She paused. "Then again, I think there would be no need for such trouble. Do you truly believe there is a soul alive in Harquhal who would not sell us to them?"

Maybe one or two. Maybe three or four.

But all it took was one.

We glared at one another, neither of us giving an inch. The roan slobbered on Del's left shoulder; with a grimace of distaste, she shook off the glop of greenish grass-slime. Meanwhile the stud dug a hole, raising gritty Southron dust that insinuated itself between my sandaled toes.

Which put me in mind of a bath; I'm as clean as I can be, mostly, though the desert makes it hard. The sun makes you sweat. Dust sticks to sweat. Pretty soon you're caked.

I hadn't had a bath in days. *During* those days I'd gotten real sweaty, drunk, and bloody, not to mention dust-crusty. I needed a bath badly. And if we had a room, I could *have* a bath.

But.

"How many do you think?" I asked finally, ignoring the dispute altogether.

She shrugged, avoiding it also; thinking, as I did, of other considerations. "We killed the jhihadi—at least, the man they *believe* was jhihadi. It is all to pieces, now—the prophecy, the Oracle, the promises of change. Many will not come, but the zealots will not give up."

"Unless your brother has managed to talk some sense into them. Convince them Ajani wasn't their man at all." And that I *was*, but that I doubt they'd believe. To everyone in the South— well, at least to the people who knew me, which wasn't *quite* the whole South (if I do say so myself)—I was the Sandtiger. Sworddancer. Not messiah. Not the person who was supposed to, somehow, change the sand to grass.

Del raised an illustrative finger intended, I knew, to put me in my place by pointing out lapses in logic. She likes to think she can. She likes to think she can *tell.* "If my brother *can* talk. You say he can. You say he *did*—"

"He did. I heard him. So did a lot of others. The only reason *you* missed it was because you were dancing with Ajani."

"It wasn't a dance," she countered instantly. (Trust a woman to change the subject in mid-discussion.) "Dances have honor attached. That was an execution."

"Yes, well . . ." It had been, but I didn't feel like debating it just now, under the circumstances. "Look, I don't know what those religious fools are going to do, and neither do you. They could still be back in Iskandar—"

"Then what was all that dust we saw earlier?"

Sometimes she has a point.

I sighed. "Go get the provisions, bascha. I'll go get us some wine."

"*And* water."

"Yes. Water."

And aqivi as well. But I didn't tell her that.

Eventually, she came looking. I'd known she would, because women always do. They make you wait forever when *you* want to go somewhere, but when *they* want to leave they don't give you even a moment. I'd barely swallowed my aqivi.

My *second* cup, that is, but I wouldn't tell Del that.

The cantina was dim, because cantinas in border towns—in any desert town, for that matter—always lack for light except for what the sun provides. Here in the South, a little sun goes a long way; hence, windows are nearly nonexistent, and usually cut in the eastern wall because the sun's morning eye is coolest. Which means that by midday the sun's altered angle cuts off much of the light that would otherwise slant through a window and illuminate the room. By late afternoon, it starts to get downright gloomy. But at least it's not so hot.

Del pulled aside the door sacking hung to cut the dust, and stepped into the cantina. One swift glance assessed the place easily: tiny, grimy, squalid. A barely breathing body sprawled on the dirt floor in a corner near the door, far gone in huva dreams. A second, more lively body hunched on a stool by one of the eastside windows. As Del entered, it murmured and sat up. I'd gotten used to that. I wondered if Del had.

For just that suspended moment, I saw her as others did; as *I* had, so often, the first few times I'd laid eyes on her. She was—and *is*—spectacular: tall, long-limbed, graceful, with a powerful elegance. Not feminine, but *female,* in all the vast subtleties of the word. Even swathed in a white burnous the body was glorious. The flawless face was better still.

Something flared deep in my guts. Something more than desire: the knowledge and the wonder that what other men might dream about was freely shared with me.

A brief, warm moment. I lifted my cup in tribute. "May the sun shine on your head."

Del eyed me in speculation. "Are you ready yet?"

I grinned fatuously, still oddly touched by the moment. "A swallow, but a swallow . . ." I downed the last of my drink.

Blue eyes narrowed beneath down-slanting, dubious brows. "How many have you had?"

The moment was over. Reality intruded. I sighed. "Only as many as I had time for in the very brief moment of freedom allowed while you purchased provisions." I inspected the interior of the cup, but the aqivi was gone.

"The way *you* gulp wine, you might have had an entire bota." She scowled at the numerous suspect botas hanging over both shoulders. "Can you ride?"

I resettled bota thongs. "I was born on the back of a horse."

"Then I feel sorry for your mother." Del angled a shoulder, reaching toward the sacking. "Are you coming?"

"Already halfway there." I strode past her rapidly, pausing long enough to bestow upon her outstretched arm five sloshing botas.

Del, muttering as she struggled to untangle thongs, followed me out of doors. "I am not carrying your foul-tasting aqivi."

"I have the aqivi. *You* have the water."

She glared up at me as I mounted the stud. "Equitable arrangement. I have more botas than you."

"Extra water," I agreed. "I thought at some point in time you might want to wash your face."

I swung the stud as she mounted, grinning to myself as she rubbed surreptitiously at her face. She is not a woman for vanity, though the gods have blessed her threefold, but I've never yet known a woman not to fall for the implication.

We all have our petty revenge.

Riding. Again. Only this time my head was better. This time I could see straight. Biting the dog back does wonders for the soul.

Del reined her horse in beside me as we left Harquhal behind and took the straightest road. "So," she said, "where?"

I planted a heel into the stud's shoulder as he reached to bite the roan. "Give it a rest, flea-bag. . . . Well, since we're already heading south, I thought it was sort of decided."

"We *discussed* it last night. Nothing was decided."

I vaguely remembered our conversation. Bits and pieces of it. Something to do with finding someone.

Realization pinched my belly. "Shaka Obre," I blurted.

Del unstuck a strand of hair from her bottom lip. "And again, I say it will be difficult. If not impossible."

I shifted in my saddle. The nape of my neck crawled: hairs standing up. Even my forearms tingled. "Hoolies, bascha, now you've brought it all up again."

She slapped aside the stud's questing nose as it lingered near her left knee. "One of us had better."

I worked my shoulders, trying to shake off the crawly feeling. I'd spent all morning mostly concerned with abolishing my headache and the discontent of my belly. While neither was completely cured, both were much improved—which left me with the time to think about something else. Something downright confusing, as well as unsettling.

"I don't like it," I muttered.

"It was your idea to seek out Shaka Obre."

"That's what it was: an *idea*. Not everyone acts on them."

Del nodded sagely. "So, we are merely running, then? Not seeking?"

"It might make things easier. I know enough places in the South. We could find a spot and hole up until all the furor dies down."

Del nodded again. "There is that. Given time, even a holy war will pass."

I didn't think much of her tone of voice: too guileless. "Wait." I dug under my burnous and caught hold of my coin-pouch. Years of experience had taught me to count by weight. "How much coin do you have?"

Del didn't bother to check. "A few coppers, nothing more. I spent most on the provisions."

I tugged the burnous back into place, pulling it free of harness straps. "Well, we'll just have to rustle up a few dances here and there. Fatten the purses a little. Then go into hiding." I sighed. "Hiding always takes coin."

Pale brows arched. "You are suggesting we accept sword-dances to make money?"

I scowled. "It *is* how we make our livings."

"But only when people are willing to pay to see the match, or to hire us to dance for some other reason. Why would they pay us to dance now, in hopes of winning a few wagers, when all they need do is take us prisoner? Surely the price on our heads outweighs any profit in a dance."

"I'm not so sure there's a price on our heads—" The stud tripped over a rock. "Pick your feet up, lop-ear, before you fall on your nose."

"We—*I*—killed the jhihadi. What do you think?"

I leaned down from the saddle and spat grit out of my mouth. "What do I think? I think they'll be like the hounds of hoolies, tracking us to ground. I don't necessarily think there's a price on our heads . . . I think they'll want to kill us just for the doing of it, because we stole their dreams."

"And such folk will pay to find us. Even a rumor of our direction will earn a copper or two."

"Maybe. Maybe not." I sighed and scratched stubbled scars. "All right. I agree it might be best if we didn't go looking for dances. But there are other occupations . . . we could hire on with a caravan.

Holy war or no holy war, there will be caravans trying to cross the Punja through borjuni-infested areas. They'll need us."

"There is that," she agreed. "Except that a holy war disrupts trade, and therefore the caravan traffic may not be quite what it was, for a while. And if you were a caravan-serai, would you hire on the two people who killed the messiah?"

"He wouldn't have to know who we were."

Del perused me intently. Her expression was exquisitely bland, which meant I was in trouble. "How many *other* Southron sword-dancers are there who are a head taller than other men, two shades lighter at least, without being Northerner-pale, who bears sandtiger scars on his face—not to mention the *green* eyes—and who carries a Northern *jivatma*?"

I scowled. "Probably about as many of them as there are six-foot-tall, blonde, blue-eyed, mouthy Northern baschas who *also* carry a sword. And a magical one, at that."

Del's tone was sanguine. "The price a panjandrum must pay."

"Yes, well . . ." I aimed the stud monotonously southerly, suggesting he rediscover his soft-stepping long-walk. "We have to do something. We're running out of money. Life on the run costs."

"There is another option."

"Oh?"

"We could steal."

In shock, I stared at her. *"Steal?"*

Del's Northern accent and word choice colors all her speech, but she managed a decent mimicry of my Southron drawl. "In all your vastly honorable life, have you never heard of such a thing?"

I thought it unworthy of an answer. "But *you*. This is *you* suggesting theft? I mean, isn't it against Staal-Ysta's code of ethics, or something? You're always nattering on about how much emphasis you Northerners place on honor." I stared at her more intently. "Have you ever stolen anything in your whole entire Northern life?"

"Have you?"

"I asked you first. And anyway, I'm not Northern. It doesn't count."

"It does count. Of you I would expect it . . . you yourself have said, time and again, you would do anything for survival."

"A certain amount of ruthlessness does help in my line of work."

"Well, then, as my line of work and yours are the same, regardless of gender, it would seem logical to assume I understood the concept of stealing."

"Understanding and *doing* are two different things," I reminded her. "Have you ever stolen? You, personally? You, the Northern sword-dancer, master of a *jivatma*? Trained in all the ancient and binding honor codes of Staal-Ysta?"

Del's turn to scowl. Except hers is prettier. "Why is it impossible for you to believe I might have stolen? Have I not killed men? Have you not seen me kill men?"

"Only those who wanted to kill you. There's a bit of difference between self-defense and stealing, bascha." I grinned. "And the 'might have stolen' phrase is a dead giveaway."

Del sighed. "No, I have not personally ever stolen. But it does not mean I can't. Before Ajani murdered my family, I had never killed, either. And now it is my trade."

A discomfiting chill touched the base of my spine. "It isn't your trade, bascha. You have killed, yes—but it isn't your *trade*. You're a sword-dancer. Not all of us kill. When some of us do, it's because we have to. When our own lives are in danger."

The line of her jaw was tight. "The last seven years of my life, I have done little *but* kill."

"Ajani's dead," I told her. "That part of your life is over."

"Is it?" Her voice was grim.

"Of course it is. The blood-debt is paid. What is left for you to do?"

"Live," she bit out. "I have nearly twenty-three years. How many are left to me? Twenty more? Thirty? Perhaps even forty—"

"Occasionally," I agreed, trying to lighten the mood.

"And what am I to do with *forty more years?*"

A man my age—thirty-six? Thirty-seven?—would love to have forty more years. Meanwhile, Del made the length of time sound obscene. Which didn't sit real well.

"Hoolies, bascha—*live* them! What else is there to do?"

"I am a sword-dancer," she said tightly. "I have made myself such on purpose. But now you say that purpose is finished, because Ajani is dead."

"Del, in the name of valhail—"

Naturally, she did not allow me to finish. "Think, Tiger. You say that part of my life is over. The killing part; the part where I compromised my humanity in the name of my obsession." Something glittered in her eyes: anger, and frustration. "If that is true, what is left to me? What is left to a woman?"

"Not *that* again—"

"Shall I retire to a tanzeer's harem? Surely I would bring a fair price. I am exiled from the North—should I therefore marry a Southron farmer, or a Southron caravan-serai, or a Southron tavern-keeper?" She lifted an explanatory finger. "Remember, I am now barren. There can never be any children to repopulate the name." The hand slapped down. "Of what use am I, then?"

I grinned wryly, a little amused, a lot self-conscious, because the answer was so easy. The answer was *too* easy; Del had taught me to see it. Nonetheless, it was true. "In your case, some men—a *lot* of men!—might argue children are not necessary in order to maintain interest."

A wave of color washed through her face. Then Del gritted teeth. "If I am beautiful now, enough to 'maintain interest,' of what use will I be when the beauty has all faded? What do I *do*, Tiger? What is left to me?"

"Well, I hadn't really thought in terms of you going off to marry some Southron farmer—"

"Do I become a cantina girl? *You* appear to like them."

"Now, Del—"

"Or do I try to catch the eye of Julah's tanzeer?"

"Julah's tanzeer is a woman."

She shot me a glare. "You know what I mean."

"Julah's tanzeer would also like to kill us, remember? Especially you. You killed her father."

"*Killing,*" Del said vehemently, "is what I do best."

"You don't like it? Then change it," I declared. "You've been spouting off to me for the last—what, almost two years?—about how a woman has to fight to make her way in a man's world.

You've fought, and you've won. But expecting me to give you your answers is devaluing what you've accomplished. You became what you had to be for a specific purpose. That purpose is finished. So now find another one."

Del watched me. What she thought I couldn't tell; she is, even for me, difficult to read. But she had lost the burning intensity of her anger moments before. Her tone was much less strident. "As you have found a purpose?"

I shrugged. "I don't have a purpose. I just *am*."

Del smiled at last. The last trace of tension flowed out of her face. "The Sandtiger," she murmured. "Ah, yes, more than enough. A veritable panjandrum."

"Speaking of which," I said, "we still haven't made a decision."

"About what?"

"Where we're going."

"South."

"I've got that part. *Where* in the South?"

Irritated, she scowled. "How in hoolies should I know?"

Which pretty much summed up the way I felt, too.

Chapter 3

The oasis was little more than a tumble of squarish, yellow-pink boulders stacked haphazardly against the southerly encroachment of wind and sand, and a few sparse palm trees with straggly gray-green fronds. Not much shade to speak of, except the north-side blanket's-width of curving line at the foot of the boulder "wall," but not much is better than none. And besides, we weren't truly into the South by much; the border between the two lands is considerably cooler, and lacking in Punja crystals.

The water itself, captured in a natural stone basin rimmed by hand-mortared stones, was little more than wrist-deep, and therefore suspect as a sufficient supply—except that deep in the earth, buried beneath sand, soil, pebbles, and webby, red-throated grass, there was a natural spring. While it was simple enough to drain the basin within a matter of minutes—a horse could do it faster—it refilled itself rapidly. The resource appeared undiminished, but no one in the South took any chances. The hand-mortared rim of rocks kept the basin from being fouled by wind-blown sand; the crude lettering cut into each stone supposedly protected the oasis from anyone—or any*thing*—that sought to destroy its bounty.

I swung off the stud and gave him rein, letting him suck the basin dry. The sand-colored stone briefly glistened wetly, then hid itself beneath water as the spring refilled the basin. I let the stud drink half again, then pulled him away.

Del, still atop her roan, frowned as I began to undo knots in pouches and cinch. "You don't mean for us to stay here. . . ?"

"It's getting on toward sundown."

"But this is so exposed . . . would we not do better to go elsewhere? Somewhere less obvious?"

"Probably," I agreed. "Except there's water here. You know as well as I that in the South, you don't pass up water."

"No, but we could refill the botas, let the horses cool, and then ride on."

"Ride on where?" I dropped the pouches to the ground. "The next closest water is a good day's ride from here. It would be foolish to leave now with nightfall coming on. There's no moon tonight . . . do you really want to chance getting lost in the darkness?"

Del sighed, absently battling her roan with restraining reins. The gelding snorted wetly. "I thought you told me once you knew the South like the back of your hand."

"I do. Better than most. But that doesn't mean I'm stupid." I undid the saddle, peeled it and the sweaty blanket-pad off, dropped everything atop the pouches. The stud's back was wet and rumpled. "We haven't been through here in some time, bascha. For all I know there've been twenty sandstorms since then. I'd just as soon discover the changes in landscape when I can *see* them."

"I understand," she said patiently. "But if we stay here, it makes it easy for others to find us."

I pointed toward the basin. "See those carvings? In addition to protection for the water, it gives sanctuary to desert travelers."

Her chin rose a notch. "Even to travelers accused of murdering a messiah?"

I gritted teeth. "Yes." I didn't know any such thing, but I wasn't disposed to argue.

She grunted skepticism. "Will they respect it?"

"It all depends on who shows up." I braced and stood my ground as the stud planted his head against my arm and began to rub exuberantly, scratching heat- and dust-born itches. "The tribes have always honored the traveler's truce. They're nomads, bascha . . . such places as this carry meaning. Those are tribal devices carved into the stone, promising protection to water and traveler. I don't think they'd break that custom, even *if* they caught up. And that's not a certainty."

"What if it's someone else? Someone who *doesn't* honor this custom?"

The stud rubbed even harder, nearly upsetting my balance. I pushed the intrusive head away. "Then we'll just have to deal with it. Sooner or later. Tonight, or tomorrow." I squinted up at her. "Don't you think it's time you gave that horse a drink? He's been pulling rein since we got here."

He had. The roan, inhaling water-scent, had been stomping hooves and swishing tail, trying to edge toward the basin. Del had kept him on a taut rein, fighting his head.

She grimaced and unhooked from the stirrups, swinging a long, burnous-swathed leg over as she slid off the roan. She let him water as I had, cursorily attending amount—you don't let a hot horse drink too much right away—but still knitted pale brows in a faint, annoyed frown. But the expression faded as she pulled the roan away and tended to the untacking. Work smoothed her face, banishing the tautness of jaw and the creases between her brows. It made her young again.

And gloriously beautiful, in a deadly, *edged* way, like a sword blade newly honed.

Ordinarily I'd have slipped the stud's bridle and left him haltered and hobbled. But current circumstances called for a bit more care and preparation. We needed the ability to mount and ride instantly; a hobbled, unbridled horse makes for too much delay. So the stud I left bitted with the reins trapped beneath a flat stone, although he was not much for wandering when water was near. Desert-born and bred, he knew better than to leave a known supply.

I stacked saddle and pad against the boulder wall, hair-side up to dry, and made my own arrangements with blankets, botas, pouches. All in all I was feeling pretty cheerful. My head had stopped throbbing, although a whisper of discomfort remained, and my belly no longer rebelled. I was human once again: I cast Del a grin.

She eyed me askance and tended the roan, rock-tying him as I had the stud, and stripped him free of saddle and pouches. He was a good enough horse, if tall—but then I'm used to my short-legged, compact, hard-as-rock stud, not a rangy, hairy Northern gelding with too much fat beneath his hide. Then again, in the North it was cold, and the extra layer of fat undoubtedly kept him warmer, along with the extra coat. As it was, the roan was shedding; Del, grimacing, stripped a few handfuls of damp blue-speckled hair and let them drift down through still air.

With the roan tended to, Del turned to me. "So, we are staying here the night."

I considered her a moment. "I thought we'd settled that."

She nodded once, decisively, then turned her back on me and stalked off through the grass and dirt and pebbles to a spot facing north. There she unsheathed her sword.

"Not again," I murmured.

Del lifted the naked weapon above her head, balancing blade and pommel across the flat of both bare palms, and sang. A small, quiet song. But its quietude had nothing to do with power, or the quality thereof; she summoned so easily, then dealt with what she wrought: a shimmer of salmon-silver, a spark of blinding white, the blue of a deep-winter storm. All ran the length of the blade, then purled down as banshee breath to bathe her lifted arms.

She held the posture. I could not see her face, only the arch of spine beneath burnous, the spill of hair down her back. Still, it was enough; deep inside of me, painfully, Del stirred emotions I could not fully acknowledge. More than simple lust, though there is always that; less than adoration, because she is not perfection. But all the things in between. Good and bad, black and white, male and female. Two halves make a whole. Del was my other half.

She sang. Then she brought the sword down, slicing through the breath of frost, and plunged the blade into the earth.

I sighed. "Yes: again."

Another soft little song. Undoubtedly she meant me not to hear it; then again, maybe she didn't care. She'd made her feelings known. This little ritual, so infinitely *Northern,* was undoubtedly meant as much for me as for the gods she petitioned.

Abruptly, I sniggered. If I really *was* this jhihadi, she might as well pray to me. At least I was Southron.

Then, unexpectedly, a doubt crawled out of darkness to assail me in the daylight. A quiet, unsettling doubt, ancient in its spirit, but wearing newer, younger clothing.

Was I Southron? Or something else entirely?

I hitched a shoulder, scowling, trying to ward away the unsettling doubt. There was no room for it here, no place in my spirit for such things; I was home again after too many months away: warm, whole and contented by life, feeling comfortable again. Familiar.

Home.

Del sang her Northern song, secure in heritage, kinships, customs. I lacked all three.

Irritably, I scowled. Hoolies, what was the use? I *was* "home," no matter how odd it felt once I thought about it. I mean, even if I *weren't* fully Southron, I'd been born here. Raised here.

Enslaved here.

Del jerked the blade from the soil and turned back toward me. Her face was smooth and solemn, hiding thoughts and emotion.

With effort, I hid mine. "All better?" I asked.

She hunched a single silk-swathed shoulder. "It is for them to decide. If they choose to offer protection, we will be doubly blessed."

"*Doubly* blessed?"

Del waved a hand briefly toward the rock-ringed basin. "Southron gods. Northern gods. Nothing is wrong with asking the favor of both."

I managed a grin. "I suppose not. Doubly blessed, eh?" I caught up my sheath and drew my own sword, sliding it free of scabbard. "I'm not much for little songs, as you know, but this ought to be enou—*hoolies!*"

Del frowned. "What?"

Thoroughly disgusted, I inspected the cut on my right hand. "Oh, not much—just a slip . . ." I scowled, sucking the shallow but painful slice in the webbing between thumb and forefinger. "Stings like hoolies, though." I removed the flesh from my mouth and inspected the cut again. "Ah, well, too far from my heart to kill me."

Del, thus reassured, sat down on her own blanket, spread next to mine. "Getting careless in your old age."

I scowled as she, all innocence, turned her attention to cleaning her blade, soiled with gritty dust and sticky grass juices.

As for my own, I'd intended much the same. I'd unpacked oil, whetstone, cloth. Such care was required if the steel was to stay unblemished and strong, and it was nothing I considered a chore. It was as much a part of me as breathing; you *do* it, you don't think about it.

Cross-legged, I settled the sword across both thighs. In dying light it glowed, except for the blackened tip. About a hand's-width of darkness, soiling beautiful steel as it climbed toward the hilt; as always, I swore beneath my breath. Once upon a time the blade had been pure, unblemished silver, clean and sweet and new. But circumstances—and a sorcerer—had conspired to alter things. Had conspired to alter *me*.

"Thrice-cursed son of a goat," I muttered. "Why'd you pick *my* sword?"

It was an old question. No one bothered to answer.

I put one hand around the grip, settling callused flesh against taut leather wrappings knotted tightly around the steel. I felt warmth, welcome, wonder: the sword was a *jivatma*, blessed by Northern gods because I'd troubled to ask them, "made"—in the Northern way—by a Southron-born sword-dancer who wanted no part of it. I'd blooded it improperly by killing a snow lion instead of a man; later, knowing just enough to get myself into serious trouble, I'd requenched the thing in Chosa Dei, a sorcerer out of legend who turned out to be all too real. In requenching I'd finally keyed it. The sword was alive now, and magical—as Northern beliefs had it—only I'd perverted that life and magic by requenching in Chosa Dei.

That I hadn't had much choice didn't seem to matter. My *jivatma*, Samiel, hosted a sorcerer's soul.

An *angry* sorcerer's soul.

"Tell me again," Del said.

Distracted, I barely glanced at her. "What?"

"Tell me again. About Jamail. About how he *spoke*."

Frowning, I stared at blemished steel. "He just did. The crowd separated, leaving him in the open, and I heard him. He prophesied. He was, after all, the Oracle—or so everyone said." I shrugged. "It fits, in an odd sort of way. Rumor had it the Oracle was neither man nor woman . . . don't you remember the old man in Ysaa-den? He said something about—" I frowned, trying to recall. "—'a man who was not a man, but neither was he a woman.' " I nodded. "That's what he said."

Del's tone was troubled. "And you believe he meant Jamail."

"*I* don't know what he meant. All I know is Jamail showed up at the sword-dance and pointed me out as the jhihadi. *After* he spoke."

"But his tongue was *cut out*, Tiger! Aladar did it, remember?" Del's face was pale and taut. Words hissed in her throat. "He made him a mute, and *castrate*—"

"And maybe an Oracle." I shrugged, wiping soft cloth the length of the blade. "I don't know, bascha. I have no answers. All I can tell you is he did point at me."

"Jhihadi," she said. The single word was couched in a welter of emotions: disbelief, bafflement, frustration. And a vast, abiding confusion no weaker than my own.

"I don't know," I said again. "I can't explain any of it. And besides, I don't know that it really matters. I mean, right now all anyone wants to do is *kill* me, not worship me. That doesn't sound much like a true messiah to me."

Del sighed and slid her sword back into its sheath. "I wish—" She broke off, then began again. "I wish I could have spoken to him. *Seen* him. I wish I could have found out the truth."

"We had to leave, bascha. They'd have killed us, otherwise."

"I know." She glanced northward. "I just wish—" Then, more urgently: "*Dust.*"

Hoolies. So there was.

I climbed to my feet even as Del unsheathed her sword. "We could run," I suggested. "The horses are rested."

"So am I," Del said, assuming a ready posture. She made no motion to mount the roan.

Two steps and I was beside her. "After this, I could use some dinner."

Del shrugged. "Your turn to cook."

"*My* turn!"

"I fixed breakfast."

"That glop we ate wasn't my idea of breakfast."

"Does it matter? You were spewing it anyway."

Trust her to remember that.

Trust her to *say* it.

Chapter 4

The dust, dyed orange by the sunset, resolved itself into a single rider. A man, with thick reddish-blond hair and great drooping red mustaches waving below his chin. He was too far yet to see his eye color, but I knew what it was: blue. I even knew *him*: Rhashad, a Borderer, half Southron, half Northern, who made his living as I did.

A rich blue burnous billowed in horse-born wind as he galloped up to the oasis. I saw big teeth bared in a grin half hidden in mustaches, the hand lifted in friendly greeting. He halted the sorrel before us, furrowing dirt and sand and grass, as multiple botas sloshed. Peeping over his shoulder glinted the pommel-knot of his sword, worn in Southron-style harness.

Teeth again: for Del. Blue eyes glinted against sun-creased, sunburned skin. "Hoolies, but you're a woman made for a man like me! I *saw* what you did against Ajani . . ." Rhashad laughed joyously, slewing a sly glance in my direction. "No, Sandtiger, no need to unsheathe your claws—*yet.* I don't steal women from friends."

I grunted. "As if you could."

"Oh, I could—I *have.* Just not from my friends." He arched ruddy, suggestive brows and aimed a bold stare in Del's direction. "What do you say, bascha—once you grow tired of the Sandtiger, shall you come ride with me?"

I recalled that for some strange reason, Rhashad's swaggering manner did not offend or irritate Del. In fact, she seemed to enjoy it, which I found somewhat puzzling. *Other* men, behaving in much the same way, met with a colder reception.

I had, once. A very long time ago.

And sometimes not so long. It all depended on her mood.

Del didn't even flick an eyelash. "Would your mother approve?"

Rhashad's braying laugh rang out. He slapped a thick thigh, then reined in the pawing sorrel. "Oh, I think so. She's a woman much like you . . . how *else* do you think she got me?"

I lowered my sword and stood hip-shot. "Have you come for a *reason,* or just to trade gibes with me?"

"Gibes with you, pleasantries with her." But even as he spoke, some of the gaiety faded. Rhashad unhooked a leg and slung it across a saddle well-hung with plump botas. He jumped down easily, raising dust, which he waved away absently. "Yes, I came for a reason. I thought you might need some help." He led his sorrel to the basin and gave it leave to drink, doling out rein. "Like I said, I saw what she did. Now, *we* all know Ajani was no jhihadi, but all the tribes thought he was; at least, they're all sure that Oracle fellow pointed straight at him. Which means now they all think Del killed the jhihadi when she lopped off Ajani's head."

"Yes," I agreed patiently. "We had that part figured out."

He was unperturbed by my irony. "And *that* means now they all want to kill you." Rhashad shrugged wide shoulders; the Borderer is bigger than I. "For now, at any rate."

Del, who still wore her harness beneath burnous, sheathed her sword easily, making most of it disappear under shelter of slick white silk. As always, it was impressive; I saw the appreciative flicker in Rhashad's eyes. "For now?" she echoed.

"Eventually they'll stop," he declared. "After all, they can't chase you all over the South. Not forever. Even if they *are* nomads. One of these days this little mistake will get all straightened out, and you two will no longer be hunted."

" 'This little mistake,' " I muttered.

"Meanwhile," she said lightly, "they might yet catch us, and kill us."

"Well, yes, they could." Rhashad pulled his sorrel from the basin, dripping water. "If you're stupid enough to be caught."

I nodded. "We'd sort of hoped to avoid that."

"That's why *I'm* here." Rhashad looked past Del and me to the horses. "I rode out before dawn, hoping to catch you. The tribes were still in disarray. After all, they're none of them accustomed to cooperating, being solitary sorts." He shrugged. "But that won't last. By now they'll have banded together for one purpose: to kill the jhihadi's murderer. So, I decided to do what I could to help." He jerked his chin to indicate our horses. "I've come to take one of your mounts."

I blinked. "You've what?"

"Come to take one of your mounts."

"Details," Del suggested, waggling fingers in invitation. "I'm rather fond of details."

"A pretty little thing like you?" Rhashad grinned at her. He was big, bold, uninhibited; not at all Del's type. (I think.) "This is men's business, bascha . . . Tiger and I will attend to details."

In the spirit of the moment, Del offered cool smile and arched brows. "Is that what you tell your mother?"

He laughed. "Hoolies, *no*—I know better. She'd have both my balls." The smile slid into crooked consideration. "Of course, then there'd be no one to carry on the line . . . no, I think she'd settle for an ear instead, which would then destroy my good looks." Blue eyes twinkled beneath heavy brows. "Which do *you* want, bascha? Balls, or an ear?"

If he meant to shock, he failed. Again the cool smile. Only I saw the glint in *her* eye; no one else knew her as I. "And do you think I could take neither?"

Rhashad's grin wavered in the depths of red-blond mustaches. He frowned, thinking about the promise implicit in Del's tone, but only for a moment; the expression cleared quickly. His manner was bluff as he shifted in the sand, but I could tell her implication had gone home. Rhashad liked what he saw. It was easy to think only of that, and forget what she could do. "Well, I think that's a question that will have to be settled another time. Right now we'd best attend to those details." He looked at me. "They'll be tracking *two* horses. Why don't you switch to one?" He glanced again at our mounts. "I'd take the roan. He's bigger, more suited to carrying two, and neither of you is little—"

I shook my head, cutting him off. "He'd never last if we went into the Punja. He's Northerner-bred . . . the stud's smaller, but he's tough. He won't give up."

Rhashad shrugged. "Whatever you like. Give me one of them— I'll ride off in the other direction and lead them a pretty chase."

"If they catch you—" Del began.

"If they do, I'm just a Borderer. My hands—*and* face—are clean." He cast a glance at the scars in my cheek. "I'm not the Sandtiger. I'm not his woman, either. I think they'll let me go."

I spoke up hastily, before Del could light into Rhashad for daring to suggest she was my woman. Even if she was, in Southron parlance; Northerners are like that. (Or maybe just *Del* is like that.) "*Meanwhile*, it's given us time to put some miles between them and us." I nodded. "A good plan, Rhashad."

He lifted a single big shoulder off-handedly. "Even my mother would like it." He inspected our tiny camp, then glanced at the horizon as it swallowed the sun. "No moon tonight. You can get a few hours' sleep, then ride out just before dawn. Meanwhile, I'll take the other horse now. They might as well think you're that far ahead of them; it'll make them all the more willing to overextend their own mounts."

"Why?" Del asked. "Why are you doing this?"

Rhashad smiled, chewing mustache. "Tiger and I are old friends. He's taught me a trick or two for the circle, tricks that saved my life. I just figure I owe him. As for you, well . . ." The Borderer grinned. "My mother wouldn't mind if I brought home a bold bascha like you. But since I can't do that, I'll settle for helping you escape. It would be such a waste if they killed you." Rhashad shot me a glance. "Though not so much of one if they killed *him*."

"Ha-ha," I said dutifully, and turned back to lean my sword against the wind- and sandbreak. "Can you stay for food? Del's just about to cook it."

"Del is just about to do nothing of the sort," she retorted. "Don't try to trick me into it simply because Rhashad is here. I have no skills, remember? No devotion to womanly duty." Del smiled sweetly. "I have no manners at *all*—I'm a sword-dancer, am I not?"

I ignored the implication. "He's a *guest*," I explained.

"No, he's not," she countered. "He's just one of us."

Rhashad, laughing, waved a hand. "No, no, I can't stay. I'm going to ride out now. But—there is one more thing."

The humor was gone from his eyes. Del and I waited.

The Borderer turned to his horse and mounted. "You remember what I told you about how things are in Julah? About how Aladar's daughter succeeded to the tanzeership?"

"Yes," I answered. "And at the time we also discussed the fact she probably won't be tanzeer for long. This is the South. She's a woman. Someone will take it away."

"Maybe," Rhashad said. "And maybe not. She's got the gold mines, remember? She may be a woman, but she's a very *rich* woman. Money buys men. Money also buys loyalty. If she pays them enough, they might not care if she's a woman."

I knew very well she had gold mines. Her father had held them before her; it's where he'd made me a slave.

I suppressed an involuntary shudder. Even now, I dreamed about it. "Anyway, what's this got to do with us? Del and I aren't necessarily heading to Julah."

"Doesn't matter," Rhashad declared. "She's coming after *you*."

Del glanced at me, inspecting my expression. "Does she know, then? Or is it merely convenient to blame the so-called jhihadi's murderers for every drop of blood spilled from this day forward?"

Rhashad shrugged slightly. "Probably. Except Sabra has a very good idea exactly who killed her father. I told you that before: there were rumors about a big Southron sword-dancer with claw-marks on his face, and a magnificent Northern bascha who was living in Aladar's harem."

"Not my choice," Del snapped. "As for his death, he deserved it."

"Undoubtedly," Rhashad nodded, "but his daughter doesn't agree. She's put a price on your head."

"Oh?" I brightened. "How much are we worth?"

Rhashad's expression was solemn. "Enough to buy sword-dancers."

I sighed. "Anything else?"

Rhashad nodded. "Late last night, after you and Del rode out, I had a few drinks with Abbu Bensir."

I shrugged. "So?"

"So, he said Sabra had sent for him."

Del frowned. "But—he would not . . ." She glanced at me. "Would he? He is your friend. Like Rhashad."

"Not like Rhashad," I countered. "And not properly a *friend;* Abbu and I were—and are—rivals." I shook it off with a twitch of shoulders. "It makes no difference. If he hires on, it becomes a matter of money. And a contract."

"Did he not take oaths to honor the code of the dance?" she asked sharply.

"Southron circle oaths have nothing whatsoever to do with not killing specific people," I told her. "We're free to hire on however we will . . . even if it means dancing to the death against someone we know rather well." I exchanged a glance with Rhashad. "Are you sure about all of this?"

He nodded. "Iskandar was full of it, *and* Harquhal, when I stopped for water . . . you were named, and Del, although mostly they just call her the Northern bascha." He grimaced briefly. "And other less flattering things."

"It doesn't matter." Del's brows were puckered. "If she has hired Abbu Bensir—and *other* sword-dancers—the situation changes."

"A little," I agreed. "We've got tribes after us for murdering the jhihadi, and assorted sword-dancers—maybe even Abbu Bensir—hunting us to complete a tanzeer's contract. *If* Abbu hired on; we don't know that."

"If he has, he is dangerous." Del's tone was deadly. "He is very, very good. I danced against him, remember?"

"So did I," I sighed, "a very long time ago."

Rhashad, smiling, touched his throat. "He makes no secret of it. Other men might be ashamed, but not Abbu Bensir. The ruined throat is a battle scar gained while in the circle against an honorable opponent."

I hissed another oath. "I was seventeen," I muttered. "Does he say that, too?"

Rhashad laughed. "No, not that. Your name is more than enough. Let the others think what they will."

Del removed a few things from her saddle-pouches, transferred them to mine, then saddled the roan. Slowly, she led him over to Rhashad. "What will you do with him?"

"Take him southeasterly for a few days, just to throw them off, then head back toward the border. My mother can use a good horse."

She nodded. "He is that." She slapped a blue-speckled rump. "May the sun shine on your head."

Rhashad displayed big teeth. "Not much chance it won't." He swung his sorrel aside and pulled the roan up close as he looked at me. "It may work for a while. The tribes are too worked up right now to think things through, which means they'll make mistakes, and I doubt many of the established sword-dancers will hire on, since you're one of their own—and she's a woman, after all. I'd say it'd mostly be the younger ones trying to make a name. Capturing the Sandtiger would really mean something, in which case they might get careless in the rush to track you down." He chewed one of his mustaches. "But if *Abbu* has hired on . . ." The Borderer shrugged. "You know Abbu. He's not a stupid man."

"It does change things," I agreed. Then, seriously, "I owe *you*, Rhashad."

He shrugged. "One day." And headed out at a lope with the Northern roan at the end of taut reins.

I turned abruptly. "Let's pack."

She was startled. "Now?"

"We'll do as he's doing: ride out now and get a few hours' head start. Hopefully, it'll give us an edge in addition to leaving tracks for only one horse." I bent down to pick up my sword. "It was a good idea. I should have thought of it my—*hoolies*—"

"What now?" Del asked.

I stared down at the fallen sword. I had put out my hand, closed fingers around the grip, lifted—and the thing had pulled free of my grasp. Once free, it had fallen. It now lay across my right foot.

I'm a Southroner: I wear sandals. There's not a whole lot of protection against a falling sword when you wear sandals—but then you don't ordinarily figure you'll drop one, either. Not if you're a sword-dancer, and you know how to handle a sword.

I was. I did. I hadn't dropped the sword. The thing had pulled *free*.

"Hoolies," I murmured, very softly.

Blood began to flow.

"Tiger!" Del stood next to me, staring down at the mess. "Tiger—" She reached for the sword, then drew back. "I can't touch it; you know that. I may know the name, but there is still Chosa Dei."

"I don't expect you to touch it," I muttered, pulling my foot from beneath the blade. I let the weapon lie there.

"You're bleeding . . . here—" She knelt down and began to unlace my sandal. "I'm beginning to think you *are* getting careless . . . first you cut your hand, now this—"

I pulled my foot away. "Leave it alone. You don't have to do that." I rested the ball of my still-sandaled foot against the sandbreak wall and took up where Del had left off, untying leather knots. "Pack up whatever we need and saddle the stud . . . I'll be with you in a moment."

She turned away, gathering gear and saddle-pouches, and said nothing more about carelessness, teasing or otherwise. As for me, I slipped off a sandal no longer worth very much; the blade had cut through leather straps before slicing into flesh.

I used the hem of my burnous to sop up the blood. The cut was not very deep and the blood stopped quickly enough. It wouldn't bother me much, although the sandal required repairing. We didn't have the time; for now I'd simply ride barefoot.

I stripped off the good sandal and toed through pockets of sand and webby grass patches to the stud. I tucked the sandals into one of the pouches, then turned back to stare at the sword. It lay naked in the dirt: four feet of deadly *jivatma*.

Del, making a last inspection sweep of the tiny oasis, glanced at me sidelong. "Do you intend to leave it there?"

"In a minute," I declared. "If I could. But you've convinced me it would not be a wise thing to do. Look what it's doing to me—if someone *else* got a hold of it . . ." I shook my head. "I remember all too clearly what Chosa Dei, in that sword, did to Nabir. How it un-made Nabir's *feet*—" I shook off a sudden chill. "Imagine what it— *he*—might do if he got control of a weaker man."

"You're saying *Chosa*—?" Del let it trail off, staring at the sword. "The tip is still black."

"And will be, I'm beginning to think, until it's fully discharged. And you know what *that* means."

"Shaka Obre," she breathed.

"Shaka Obre," I echoed, "and the strength to destroy Chosa Dei before he destroys me."

Chapter 5

We rode for maybe an hour, heading due south. A straight line would take us into the heart of the Punja. I had no plans at that particular moment to actually *enter* the Punja, but then the beast is often perverse; thanks to frequent sandstorms, called simooms, the Punja is rarely where you expect it to be. Wind-powered, scouring, it moves. Anything in its way, including something so trivial as a boundary—or a city, or a tanzeer's entire domain—is swallowed by acres of sand. Which means sometimes no matter how hard you try to avoid it, the Punja gets in your way.

We stopped riding because I knew if we kept going we'd stand a very good chance of getting lost. Getting lost in the South is ridiculously easy, especially if you're stupid enough to ask for it by riding too far on a night with no moon, and only stars to see by. Stars make it easy to choose a general direction, but they're not so great at providing light enough to ride by.

So we stopped, and Del asked why, and I explained. Somewhat testily, I'll admit; I was not particularly happy about life, and when I am not happy I can be surly. Sometimes downright unpleasant. But not very often; I am, by nature, a particularly good-natured, even-tempered individual.

"Enough already," I growled. "Get off, bascha—you're sitting over his kidneys. And you're not what I'd call light."

Del, who was seated behind me, stiffened. But, for once, did as she was told: she slid backward over the stud's rump and then down his tail.

"Well?" she said after a moment. "You outweigh *me*—are *you* not going to dismount?"

Engaged in untangling my harness straps from bota thongs fastened in front of my knee—not being a fool, I had *not* put the harness back on where the sword might next decide to try for my neck—I did not immediately answer. The stud, for his part, snorted noisily. Then he shook himself. Violently. From head to tail.

"Oh, *hoolies*—" A horse, shaking himself, spares no thought for the rider on his back. He simply shakes, like a big, wet dog, only with much more enthusiasm.

Botas sloshed. Bridle ornaments clashed. Assorted gear rattled. As for me, every joint protested. As did my innards.

"Jug-headed, flea-bitten *goat*—" I climbed down painfully, dragging harness and sword with me, and made sure my head was attached. Just when it had begun to feel better. . . .

"Well?" Del asked.

"Well *what?*"

"What are we doing?"

"What does it look like we're doing?"

She considered it seriously. "Stopping?"

"Good guess!" I said heartily, then stomped off into the darkness.

Del caught the stud before he could follow. "Where are you going?"

Did she have to know everything? "Something I have to do."

"Are you sick again?"

"No."

"Then what—oh. Never mind."

"Not that, either," I muttered. "First things first."

Or last things last, depending on who you are, and what you intend to do.

With a sword.

My sword.

Whose true name was Samiel: hot desert wind, with the strength of storm behind it.

Whose name had been perverted by a man known as Chosa Dei, a sorcerer out of legend whose gift, when he could use it, was to *collect* powerful magic. Duly collected, its original form was unmade, and Chose Dei reshaped it to serve his own purposes.

He had unmade many things, including much of the South. He had unmade human beings.

And now he wanted me.

I stripped out of burnous, clad now only in suede dhoti and the necklet of sandtiger claws. Not even sandals adorned my feet; grit lodged itself beneath toenails. For a long time I just stood there in the desert darkness, holding harnessed sword. The mere *thought* of pulling the blade free of the rune-scribed scabbard and summoning life to it set my bones to itching. Magic does that to me: it eats its way into my bones, making even my teeth ache, and sets up housekeeping. A belly sick on magic is worse than the biting dog who lives in a wine bota.

Futility welled up. My voice was thick with it. "Gods-cursed, hoolies-begotten sword . . . why couldn't those Northerners let me *borrow* a blade, instead of making me take—instead of making me *'make'*—this thrice-cursed thing called a *jivatma*?"

Sweat ran down my temples; down the scarred corrugations of ribs encased in muscle and flesh. Like I said, I hadn't had a bath in too long. I smelled me, I smelled sweat, I smelled fear. And the acrid tang of magic that coated even my teeth.

I jerked Samiel free. In starlight, the steelglow was muted. A flash, a sheen, a shimmer. And the blackness of Chosa Dei climbing a third of the way up the blade.

I leaned. Spat. Wished for wine, aqivi, water. For something to cut the taste. Something to settle my belly. Something to still the itching that ached inside my bones.

A brief shudder wracked me. Hairs writhed on arms and thighs. The back of my neck prickled.

"I know you're there," I whispered tightly. "I know you're in there, Chosa. And you know I'm out *here*."

A rolling drop of sweat threatened one eye. I wiped the salty dampness away impatiently with a brusque, thick forearm, scrubbing wrist against itching eyebrow. And clenched my jaws tightly shut as I let the memories flow in prelude to the dance.

I recalled what I had done, in the depths of the Dragon's gullet. How I had, pushed to the farthest extremes of strength and will and *need,* somehow managed to defeat Chosa Dei within the walls of his prison, deep in Dragon Mountain. By calling on all my reserves and banishing all my beliefs in things other than magic; in powers of the flesh, not of gods or sorcery. I had, because I'd *had* to, set aside skepticism and welcomed the Northern magic deeply seated within the steel. I'd used it, bending it this way and that, *singing* it, in Northern fashion; forcing it to serve *me*—until I was no better than Chosa, unmaking and then *re*making . . . requenching at my need. Keying when I shouldn't, on the brink of the gates of hoolies, and knowing why, how, how much. Knowing exactly what I did, and the woman for whom I did it.

Did I blame her? No. She'd have done the same for me. Months before we'd met in combat to determine her fate, and mine; we'd both of us lost, but neither had surrendered. And when it came down to it, we'd each of us do it again. But at that moment in Chosa's cave, in the heart of Dragon Mountain, I'd called up all the power and remade my Northern *jivatma* into something more than sword. Something more than magic.

And something *less* than good.

I let the harness fall from my left hand. Now I held only the sword, as a sword is always held: firmly, by the grip, fingers wrapped around knotted leather; twenty-year-old palm calluses settling into familiar patterns of flesh and leather and steel. Into patterns of soul and spirit, and the thing that makes a man whatever the man is supposed to be.

Nearly half my sword was black, charred as if by fire. But the flame was cold as death, and lived *inside* the steel. Coexisting unpleasantly with what the sword *should* be: a *jivatma* named Samiel, progenitor of storms much as Del's own Boreal. *Her* storms were Northern-cold. Mine were Southron-hot.

But Chosa lived there, too. Chosa filled every strand of the magic laced throughout the blade. The invisible net pulsed, turgid with poison. If Chosa were not destroyed, if the blade were not discharged, Samiel would die. And Chosa, breaking free, would require the nearest body in order to house himself. The sword-dancer known as Sandtiger would simply cease to exist. In his place would be Chosa Dei, aged six-hundred and forty-two years.

Or was it forty-*three?*

Hoolies, but time flies.

I lifted the sword and plunged it deep into Southron sand, sinking it halfway down. I heard the hiss of grit displaced; the entry of steel through soil. Then I knelt and encased the leather-wrapped grip in a hard, callused prison. Another prison for Chosa.

One he'd already begun to destroy.

Chapter 6

The roar broke free of my throat. For the moment I didn't care; it was enough merely to shout, to scrape my throat hoarse with will and strength expended in an effort to beat Chosa.

But the roar died almost instantly, and so did comprehension. I knew only I held the sword, or it held me, and that was the whole of it.

He was strong, was Chosa Dei. And so very, very angry. He hated being entrapped within a prison of Northern steel. He hated the sword itself, for daring to hold him. And he hated me as well, much deeper and far stronger, with a cold, abiding strength. *I* was the one. *I* was the man. I was the enemy who had stolen away his soul and lodged it in a sword.

The thin slice in the webbing of thumb and forefinger stung. So did the cut across my foot. And I knew, with perfect certainty, that such clumsy "accidents" wouldn't stop. If anything, they'd get worse. Eventually, even deadly. Chosa had learned a little something of Samiel. Now he exerted himself, stretching the boundaries, doing whatever he could to harm me. To make the sword as dangerous to me as to my enemies.

So now it was up to me to show him who was boss.

Easier said than done. In addition to smelling so bad, magic also *hurts*.

I clung to the grip with all my strength, hands locked around steel and leather. I shook, and the sword shook with me, cutting down through Southron sand. I felt the strain envelop wrists, forearms, then shoulders, setting muscles into knots. Tendons, like taut ropes, stood up all over my body. I gritted teeth and hissed violent Salset curses, spewing all the invective the tribe had bestowed upon me as I labored in Southron bondage, too big in body to break, too small in spirit to fight.

Now I fought. The Salset had merely beaten me. Chosa Dei would *unmake* me.

Sweat ran down my face, dripping onto a dusty chest. Unencumbered by sandals, toes dug spasmodically into sand. I itched all over. Bile tickled my throat, leaving behind its acrid taste.

"—not—" I said. "—NOT—"

It was all I could manage.

Starlight flickered. Or was it my eyes? Speckles of white and black, altering vision into a patchwork curtain of pitch-soaked darkness and blinding, frenzied light.

I smelled the stink of magic; of power so raw and wild only a fool would try to control it. Only a fool would summon it.

A fool, or a madman. A man like Chosa Dei.

Or a fool like me?

Hoolies, but I hurt. The dull headache flared anew, pounding behind wide-stretched eyes. I felt the labored repetition of my heart, squirming behind my breastbone; the annoying tickle of fine hair stirring on arms and thighs and groin; the deep, hollow cramping of a belly soured by fear.

A hissing, breathy rasp: in and out, in and out, forcing lungs to work. Trying to clear a befogged head battered by a hoof as well as the presence of alien magic, and the promise of Chosa's power.

If I could just *prove* to him that mine was the stronger soul—

Inwardly, I laughed. Scornful and derisive, clogged with self-contempt. Who in hoolies was *I*? An aimless, aging man with aching knees and much-scarred hide who sold his sword for a living, honoring only the skill sheer desperation had forged, and the need to be someone better—someone *more*—than a nameless Southron slave deserted as an infant by a mother too jaded to care.

Uncertainty flickered briefly. Del had said once there was no proof. That perhaps the Salset had lied. That maybe I *hadn't* been left to die, at least not intentionally.

But I could never know. The only link to my past willing to speak of it had died but days before, ridiculed by her people because a jealous old magician, stripped of fading power, had said she deserved punishment for succoring me. And though no one had actually killed her, the disease had been as much of the spirit as of the flesh.

Sula. Who had, without fail, *always* believed in me.

Self-contempt melted away.

I drew in a guts-deep breath and gave myself over to the power gathering in answer to my summons. In answer to Chosa Dei. Both of us wanted it. Both of us needed it. But only one could wield it. Only one could win.

Into my head came a song. A tiny, quiet song. I snatched at its edges, fraying with every moment, and wove it back together. Tied all the ties, knotted all the knots. Then made it whole again. Made it *mine* again.

A breeze began to blow. Sand kissed my cheek greedily, lodged in my teeth, forced tears to wide-open eyes. But I didn't give up my song.

The world turned white. I stared, blinked, stared again. I could see nothing. Nothing but all the white.

Steel trembled in my hands. It warmed, softening, until I felt it flowing freely, squeezing its way between leather wrappings and the unsealed grasp of rigid fingers. I clutched more tightly, trying to push the steel back in, but it continued to flow. It dripped from fisted hands, spotting the star-washed sand.

If Chosa unmade the sword—

"—*not*—" I said again.

The breeze blew harder, but I could see none of it. Only white, nothing but *white*—

And then, abruptly, red. The red of an enemy's blood; the red of eyes bleeding inside from the strain of staring too hard. Of trying so fiercely to conquer.

The sword trembled. Runes flared brass-bright, then blazed briefly blood-red before fading once again into silver. Where the blade met the sand, I saw an ashy bubble burst. And then the quiet explosion of dust and grit and soil; the silver-gilt bloom of crystals from deep beneath the surface.

Translucent Punja crystals, deadly in Southron sunlight.

Sand bubbled away until most of the blade was naked, baring its charred black stain. It had climbed a finger's-width higher.

"Can't go down," I muttered. "—have to come *up*, to me—"

But of course, I wouldn't let him.

I clung to the song, wrapping myself in its power. Del says I can't sing, that mostly I croak discordantly, not knowing how to shape notes or melody, but that didn't matter to me. Samiel doesn't care about *skill*, only about focus, and the strength to sing the magic before Chosa unmade it all.

Noiselessly, a thin line fractured the pan of sand. I watched it trickle outward from the blade tip, then spread. The silence of it was eerie. A fissure here, a fissure there, until I knelt in the center of a webwork tracery spreading in every direction, black in the light of the stars.

It did not, as you might expect, fold in upon itself, sucking sand this way and that. It held, flat as glass: a complex netting of fracture lines spilling out into the desert.

"Can't unmake it," I gritted. "—can't unmake *me*—"

I clenched my hands more tightly. Sang my song more strongly, if tucked away inside my head. And felt the power wax.

Smoke. A puff at first, a wisp, like warm breath on a cold Northern morning. Expelled from the fracture lines.

Smoke, followed by fire.

But only a little bit.

The air grew warmer. On the horizon, stretching before me, sheet lightning crackled. The air stank with it. Hair rose on my body. The back of my neck prickled. Flesh jerked, then stilled; breathing was harder yet.

The breeze became a wind. It came to visit me, bringing gritty, unwelcome company and throwing it in my face. It hissed as it flung itself against rune-scribed blade. As it scraped against my flesh, finding creases and folds and scars, leaving sand to mark its passing. Stripping hair away from my face so the scouring was surer.

I spat. Squinted. Gripped the sword harder still. No longer did it leak liquefied steel through rigid, cramping fingers. What I held now was whole.

"—hear me, Chosa? *Mine*—"

Wind blew flames out. Carried smoke away.

"Mine," I mouthed again.

Wind died quietly. Sand settled itself. The world was the world again, and I still myself within it.

A thought occurred: Was I? Myself?

What *was* I?

What in hoolies had I just done?

Summoned—and fought—Chosa Dei.

A chill rippled flesh. I knew why, and what I had done. I didn't question the need. Didn't question that it was real.

Just questioned who had done it: Me? Me? *Me?*

A handful of months before I'd have laughed at the possibility. Laughed at the *idea*, that a man could do such a thing. Would have scoured myself with self-contempt, for allowing the thought to occur.

Knowing to think of such things, such victories of the spirit, opens the door to anguish and pain.

With the Salset, I hadn't dared.

But with Chosa Dei, I did. Not only dared, but *did*.

Was I stronger because of the magic? The Northern sword? Or just more willing to take risks with things I didn't understand?

Inside me, the voice was cruel: *You're a fool, chula. You are what you've made yourself—what you can* make *yourself, using whatever tools lie at hand. If you turn your back on magic, you turn your back on yourself.*

I swore. Laughed softly. Called myself names. Put my mind to the task at hand: dealing with what had happened.

Spasmodic breathing slowed. I swallowed and wished I hadn't; grit and harsh breath had scoured my throat. A shudder ran through my body as tension melted away, leaving in its place a twitching, itching body well-caked with dust and powder.

The stink of magic was gone. What rode the air now was the tang of human effort expended.

When at last I could move, I unlocked aching hands. The sword fell away. As it landed, something cracked.

For a moment I could not move. I could only kneel, too stiff to shift my weight, until at last muscles loosened and I climbed awkwardly to my feet. All around me more cracking, and a shower of silvery powder.

Hoolies, but I itched. Sand, grit, and powder clung to sweat-damp skin like a shroud, burrowing into joints and flesh-creases to mimic Punja-mites. I shook myself head to toe, freeing myself from one layer of debris, and heard the tiny chiming.

I glanced down. Like oracle bones, thrown, tiny bits of glass were strewn across my feet. Stretching in all directions was a near-perfect circle, slick and flat and glossy.

Somehow, I had made glass. Conjured of sand, birthed in fire, I'd created a circle of glass.

Glass which broke, I might add, if I even so much as twitched.

And me without my sandals.

I thought of asking how and why, but didn't waste my breath. There wouldn't be an answer.

The sword was whole. The leakage I'd sworn was real was nothing more than illusion. Samiel lay silently in a puddle of shattered glass, birthing fractures in all directions that sparkled and glinted in starglow. I bent and picked him up.

Then turned, and saw Del.

She stood at the perimeter of the glass circle, Boreal unsheathed in her hands. The sword was a slash of star-lighted steel diagonally bisecting her chest. She had shed the white burnous. She wore only the Northern tunic of soft, creamy leather, which bared all of smooth, lithe arms and most of magnificent legs; bared also determination. It sang throughout her body in tensed, defined muscles and the watchful tilt of her head. In the hard readiness of her eyes.

But also something else. Something that shocked me.

Del was afraid.

She is a woman who kills, but not out of whim. Not out of irritation, or a perverse desire to harm. She kills when she must, when circumstances push her to it; if she is a woman who, by her strength of will and dedication, puts herself *into* those circumstances in the name of murdered kin, it does not make the accomplishment less valid, nor the ability less dangerous. She has honed her skills, her talent, her mind, shaping the woman into a weapon. She knows how, and when, to kill. She even knows why.

One of Del's strengths is a remarkable *control:* the ability to do what needs to be done without expending anything more, in strength, breath, and state of mind, than the moment absolutely requires.

Fear destroys that control. In anyone, that is frightening. In Del, it is lethal.

I did not lift Samiel. I did not so much as blink.

Del waited. Lids lowered minutely as she glanced quickly at the tip of the blade, measuring discoloration; then back at me, *weighing* me, until at last the assessment was done.

Almost imperceptibly, the posture relaxed. But not the awareness of what had taken place, or what I had accomplished in my "discussion" with Chosa Dei.

I decided now was not the time to resort to irony. *"Sulhaya,"* I said quietly, using her own tongue. "It's what I'd have wanted, too, had I lost the fight to Chosa."

Still Del waited. Measuring and weighing, if at a quieter intensity. Clearly, the initial danger had passed; she weighed me differently, now.

Eventually, she smiled. "Your accent is atrocious."

Relief was overwhelming; I did not want to deal with Del's fears just yet, because they magnified my own. "Yes, well . . . you don't say thanks very often, so how am I to know?"

Lips twitched. She took down the sword, easing the tilt of the blade. "Are you all right?"

Now I could be the me I knew better. "Stiff. Sore. A little shaky." I shrugged. "More in need of a bath than ever before. . . ." I raked a hand across my belly. "Hoolies, this stuff *itches—*"

Del squatted, picked up a sliver, inspected it. In starlight, it glittered like ice. "Interesting," she murmured.

All of ten feet separated us. Del knelt in sand. Before me

gleamed a fractured sheet of glinting, magicked glass. "Do me a favor," I said. "Go get me my sandals?"

In the desert, at night, it is cool, belying the heat of the day. I lay on spread blankets, wrapped in underrobe and burnous, and tried to go to sleep. We had, at best, three hours before the sun climbed into the sky. Only a fool would waste them.

I shifted minutely, trying not to wake Del, who is a light sleeper, but also trying to settle myself yet again. For a moment the position felt just fine—then the impulse renewed itself, as it had so many times, and I scratched abraded flesh.

A finger poked my spine. "Sit up," she said. Then, "Sit *up*. Do you think I intend to lie here all night while you scratch yourself raw?"

She sounded uncommonly like many mothers I had heard chastising children. Which made me feel worse. "I can't help it. All the dust and grit and glass powder is driving me sandsick."

The finger poked again. "Then sit up, and I'll tend to it."

I rolled and levered myself up on one elbow as Del knelt beside me. "What are you doing?"

She motioned impatiently as she dug a cloth from the pouches and reached for a bota. "Strip out of everything. We should have done this sooner."

"I can't *bathe*, Del . . . we can't waste the water."

"To me, the choice is simple: we wash off as much of the powder as we can, here and now, or spend the rest of the night awake, with you scratching and complaining."

"I haven't said a *word*."

"You say more than most without even opening your mouth." Del pressed folded cloth against the lip of the bota and squeezed. "Strip down, Tiger. You'll thank me when I'm done."

Since once Del has her mind set on a thing there's no arguing with her, I did as ordered and shed everything but the dhoti. A glance at arms and legs, lighted by stars, displayed the powdering of glass and sand adhering to skin and hair.

Del clucked her tongue. "Look at you. You've scratched so much you've got raw patches. And *stripes*—"

"Never mind," I growled. "Just do what you want to do."

Unexpectedly, Del laughed. "Quite an invitation . . ." But she let the comment die and set to work on legs and arms, taking great care with the creases at the backs of knees and elbows. She was right: I was raw. Abraded flesh stung.

So did my pride. "I *could* do this myself."

"What? You? Do you mean you don't like having a woman kneeling at your feet, tending you carefully?" Del grinned briefly, arching eloquent brows. "Not the Sandtiger I met all those months ago in that filthy, stinking cantina."

"*Give* me that." I bent, snatched the damp cloth away, began to swab my ribs. "We all change, bascha. None of us stays the same. It's the way life works."

She stood before me now, one hand resting on the taut-muscled border between narrow waist and curving hip. The starlight was kind to her; but then, it's hard to be cruel when the bones and flesh are so good. "Admit it," she suggested. "You're a better man now than you were when I met you."

I scrubbed at gritty flesh. "And is that supposed to mean you're taking credit for the improvement?"

A slow, languorous shrug of a single sinewy shoulder. Her answer was implicit: had I *not* met her, I'd not be the kind of man she believed me to be now.

Whatever man that *was;* who knows what a woman thinks?

The glint in her eyes faded. Her expression now was pensive. She put out a hand and gently traced the knurled scar cut so deeply along my ribs. The ruined flesh was still livid, requiring more time before purple would alter to pink, and later to silvery-white.

Where she touched, flesh quivered. Tension tightened my belly, and deeper. Del looked at me.

"What do you expect?" I growled. "I've never made a secret of what you do for me."

Del's mouth flattened. "Do for? Or do *to?*" She pulled her hand away from the scar. "I would have done it, Tiger. The killing. Had it been necessary."

"Which one?" I countered. "The one on Staal-Ysta? Or the one earlier tonight?"

"Either. Both." Briefly, her face convulsed. "You don't know what it was like that time . . . that time I touched your sword, and felt Chosa's power. Felt the violence of his *need*." Del, uncharacteristically, shuddered. "Given the chance, he will take me, with a sword made of steel. *Or* a sword made of flesh."

She had been raped by Ajani, and very nearly, later, by demons known as loki. Such violence takes its toll. I could see it in her eyes; most, craving her body, wouldn't even bother to look.

I inhaled deeply, oddly light-headed. "So you really would have killed me earlier, thinking I was Chosa."

Del's face was taut. White. Stark. "There may come a time when you are."

Oddly, it didn't hurt. I'd acknowledged it myself, on the sand with Chosa Dei.

I gave her back the cloth. "And there may come a time when you have to."

Chapter 7

"Hunh," I commented; I thought it was enough.

"*Look* at it," Del urged. "Do you see what you did?"

I shrugged. "Does it matter? I didn't really *mean* to; and anyway, I don't know that it's worth getting into an uproar over. I mean, what can you do with it?"

"Very rich men put it in windows."

"That?"

"It's glass, Tiger."

"I *know* what it is." I scowled at the shattered circle. Dead center was a downward spiraling funnel of pale sand, hemmed by a swollen rim resembling the lip of a bowl. Radiating outward, stretching in all directions, was a complex network of hairline cracks. A brittle, perfect circle, but hazardous to a sword-dancer foolish enough to go barefoot. (Not me; I'd repaired my sandal.) "But every window *I've* ever seen—" (which weren't very many: one) "—had regular *sheets* of glass. Thick glass, maybe, hard to see through—but not little bits and pieces no bigger than my thumb."

"You broke it up last night," she pointed out. "You did a lot of things last night, not the least of which was making the glass in the first place."

I shifted weight irritably, still stiff from the night before. "With the magic I summoned."

"With *some*thing, Tiger—I don't think it was your good looks." Del smiled sweetly.

I eyed her in annoyance. "Are we not happy this morning?"

"Happy?" Pale brows arched. "Happy *enough;* what more is there to be with assassins on our trail?"

I glanced northerly. "Speaking of which, we really ought to be moving."

"Don't you want a keepsake?"

"Of that? No. Why would I? It's just *glass,* bascha!"

Del shrugged almost defensively. "In the sunrise, it's very pretty. All the creams and pinks and silvers. Almost like thousands of jewels."

I grunted, turning. "Come on, Delilah. No sense in burning daylight."

She glared after me as I shuffled through sand and soil toward the waiting stud. "You have *no* imagination at all."

I gathered hanging reins. "Last time I looked, neither did you."

"Me!" Outraged, Del followed.

"Hoolies, woman, all you ever thought about for six whole years of your life was revenging yourself on Ajani. That sort of obsession doesn't require imagination. What it requires is a *lack* of it." I snugged a sandaled foot into the stirrup and pulled myself aboard. "I'm not taking you to task for it, mind—you did what you set out to do. The son of a goat is dead—but now there's us."

Del waited for me to kick free of the stirrup so she could put it to use. "Us?"

"Lots of other people with no imagination are coming after us. Do you really think we have time to gather up bits of pretty glass?"

Del gritted her teeth and mounted. "I only meant you might want a keepsake of the magic you worked last night. I'm sorry I said anything."

I leaned into the right stirrup to counteract her weight, keeping the saddle steady. I waited until she was settled, arranging legs, pouches, and harness, then turned the stud southward. "That's the trouble with women. Too sentimental."

"Imaginative," she muttered. "And a lot of other things."

"I'll drink to *that*." I shook out the reins and kneed him forward. "Let's go, old son . . . we've got a ways to travel."

The "ways to travel" turned out to be farther than anticipated. And in a different direction. But first things first.

Like—swearing.

It was now late midday. Not hot, but hardly cool; not even *close* to cold. It lingered somewhere in between, except the farther south we rode, the hotter it would become. And anticipation always makes it seem worse, even when it's not.

For now, it was warm enough. Beneath burnous and underrobe, sweat stippled my flesh. It stung in the scratchy patches of powder-scoured scrapes.

Del brushed a damp upper lip with the edge of her hand. Fair braid hung listlessly, flopping across one shoulder. "It was cooler back home."

I didn't bother to answer such an inane, if true, comment; Del generally knows better, but I suppose everyone can have lapses. I *could* have pointed out that "home" wasn't home to me, because I, after all, was Southron; then again, "home" wasn't home to *her* anymore, either, since she'd been formally exiled from it. Which she knew as well as I, but wasn't thinking about; probably because she was hot, and the truth hadn't quite sunk in all the way yet.

I wasn't about to remind her. Instead, what I did was swear. Which probably wasn't of any more use than Del's unnecessary comment, but made me feel better.

Briefly.

But only a little.

I stood beside the marker: a mortared pile of nine mottled, gray-green stones chipped to fit snuggly together. The top stone was graven with arrows pointing out directions, and the familiar blessing (or bless*ed*, depending on your botas) sign for water: a crude tear-drop shape often corroded by wind and sand and time, but eloquent nonetheless. Cairns such as this one dotted much of the South to indicate water.

In this case, the marker lied.

"Well?" Del asked.

I blew out a noisy breath of weary, dusty disgust. "The Punja's been here."

She waited a moment. "Meaning?"

"Meaning it's filled in the well. See how flat it is here? How settled?" I scraped a sandal across a hard-packed platform of fine, bone-colored sand, dislodging a feathering of dust, but nothing of any substance. "It's fairly well packed, which means the simoom came through some time back. The sand has had time to form a hardpan . . . it means there's no hope of digging deeply enough to reach the water." I paused. "Even if we had the means."

"But . . ." Del gestured. "Ten paces that way there is dirt and grass and vegetation. Could we not dig there?"

"It's a *well*, bascha, not an underground stream. A well is a hole in the ground." I gestured with a stiffened finger. "Straight down, like a sword blade . . . there's nothing else, bascha. No chance of water here."

"Then why is there a well at all?"

"Tanzeers and caravan-serais used to have them dug for the trade routes. There are wells scattered all over, though some of them have dried up. You just have to know where they are."

She nodded pensively. "But—we are not far enough into the South to reach the Punja. Not yet." She frowned. "Are we?"

"Ordinarily, I'd say no; the Punja *ought* to be days ahead of us yet, holding to this line." I flapped a hand straight ahead. "But that's why it's the Punja. It goes where it will, forsaking all the rules." I shrugged dismissively. "Maps most times aren't worth much here, unless you know the weather patterns. The boundaries always change."

Del stared pensively at the hard layer of packed sand full of glittering Punja crystals. "So we go elsewhere."

I nodded. "We'll have to. For now, we're all right . . . we can last until tonight, but we'll need water before morning. Let's see . . ." Into my head I called the map I'd carried for so many years. If you don't learn the markers, if you don't learn the wells, if you don't learn the oases, you might as well be dead.

And even *if* you learn them, you might die anyway.

"So?" she asked finally.

I squinted toward the east. "That way's closest. *If* it's still there. Sometimes, you can't know . . . you just go, and take your chances."

Del, still mounted, hefted flaccid botas. Dwindling water sloshed. "Most for the stud," she murmured.

"Since he's the one carrying double." I moved toward his head. "Time for walking, bascha. We'll give the old man a rest."

The sunset glowed lurid orange, glinting off horse brasses sewn the length of the stud's headstall. Also off the bits and pieces of metal gear—*and* weapons—still a ways distant, but suddenly too near.

"Uh-oh," I murmured, reining the stud to a halt.

Del, slouched behind, straightened into alertness. "What is it?"

"Company at the oasis."

"Is that where we're going? An oasis?" She leaned to one side to peer around my body. The stud spread his legs to adjust to the redistribution of weight. "Surely you don't think *everyone* in the South is looking for us!"

"Maybe. Maybe not." I scowled over a shoulder. "Sit straight, or get off altogether. The poor old man is tired."

Del slid off, unhooking legs from a tangle of pouch thongs and dangling botas, not to mention other gear. "He isn't an old man, he's a horse. He was bred to do such work. But the way you persist in talking to him—*and* about him—like a person, I'll begin to believe you *are* sentimental."

"He wasn't bred to haul around *two* giants like us. One is more than enough. One is what he's used to." I peered toward the oasis. A thin thread of smoke wafted on the air, swallowed by the sunset. Could be a cookfire; could be something else. "I can't see well enough to count how many there are . . . or to see *who* they are. It could be a caravan, or a tribe—"

"—or sword-dancers hired to kill us?" Del resettled her harness, yanking burnous folds into less binding positions. "And what do you mean, 'giants like us'? In the North, you are not so very tall."

No, I hadn't been. I'd been sort of average, which was quite a change for me, as well as a bit annoying. In the South I *was* a giant, standing a full head taller than most Southron men, while towering over the women. I'd grown used to ducking under low lintels, adept at avoiding drooping lath roofs. I'd also grown accustomed to using the advantage in the circle: I am tall, but well proportioned, with balanced arms and legs. My reach is greater than most, as is my stride. I am big, but I am quick; no lumbering behemoth, I. And many Southron men had learned it to their dismay.

Then, of course, there was Del. Whose fair-haired, blue-eyed beauty set her apart from everyone else in a land of swart-skinned, black-haired peoples; whose lithe, long-limbed grace disguised nothing of her power, or the strength she would not hide no matter the proprieties of the South, which she found an abomination.

Ah, yes: Delilah. Who had absolutely no idea what she could do to—or *for*—a man.

I raked her with a glance. Then turned pointedly away. "If you like, bascha."

Which, of course, prompted the response I expected. "If I like? If I like what? What do you mean?"

"If it pleases you to think of yourself as a delicate, feminine woman . . ." I let it trail off.

"What? You won't disabuse me of the notion?" Del strode past the stud to stand beside me. Flat-footed, in sandals, she was nearly as tall as me; I am a full four inches above six feet. "I have no desire to be a simpering, wilting female—"

I grinned, breaking in. "Just as well, bascha. You don't exactly have the talent."

"Nor do I want it." Del's turn to look me up and down. "But if we were to discuss *softness*—"

I overrode her. "We're here to discuss water, and whether we want to risk ourselves trying to get it."

She stared past me at the distant oasis, sheltered by fan-fronded palms. We could hear the sound of shouting, but could not distinguish words. It could be a celebration. It might be something else.

Del's mouth twisted. "The botas are nearly empty."

"Meaning it's worth the risk."

"Everything's worth the risk." A twitch of shoulders tested the weight of Northern *jivatma* snugged diagonally across her back.

"We are what we are, Tiger. One day we will die. It is my fervent hope a sword will be in my hands when I do."

"Really?" I grinned. "I'd always kind of hoped I'd die in bed with a hot little Southron bascha all a-pant in my arms, in the midst of ambitious physical labor . . ."

"You would," she muttered.

"—or maybe a *Northern* bascha."

Del didn't crack a smile; she's very good at that. "Let's go get the water."

Chapter 8

By the time we reached the oasis, all the shouting had died down. So had all the living.

"Stupid," I muttered tightly. "Stupid, foolish, ignorant *idiots*—"

"Tiger."

"They never learn, these people . . . they just load everything up and go traipsing off into the middle of the desert without even *thinking*—"

"Tiger." Very soft, but steadfast.

"—that valhail only knows awaits them! Don't they ever learn? Don't they ever stop and think—?"

"*Tiger*." Boreal was still unsheathed, though the threat was well past. "Let it go, Tiger. What they need now is a deathsong."

My face twisted. "You and your songs . . ." I waved a rigid hand. "Do what you want, bascha. If it makes you feel better." I turned and strode away, slamming home the Northern *jivatma*. Walking until I stopped and stood stiff-spined with my back to the tiny oasis, hands clenching hips. I leaned, spat grit disgustedly, wanted nothing better than to wash the taste of anger and futility from my mouth. But nothing we had would do it: neither water, wine, nor aqivi. Nothing at all would do it.

"Stupid fools," I muttered. And felt no better for it.

It wasn't the bodies. It wasn't even that one was male, one female, one the remains of an infant whose gender was now undetermined. What it was, was the waste. The incredible senselessness and *stupidity*—

The familiar *Southronness* of it.

Recognition was painful. It washed up out of nowhere and sank a fist into my belly, making me want to spew out anger and frustration and helplessness. What I said was true: they had been senseless and stupid, ignorant and foolish, because they had mistakenly believed they could cross the desert safely. That their homeland offered no threat.

I knew they had been stupid. I could call them idiots and ignorant fools, because I knew why it was so senseless: no one, crossing the desert, was safe from anyone. It was the nature of the South. If the sun doesn't get you; if the Punja doesn't get you; if lack of water doesn't get you; if the tribes don't get you; if greedy tanzeers don't get you; if the *sandtigers* don't get you . . .

Hoolies. *The South.* Harsh and cruel and deadly, and abruptly alien. Even to me.

Especially to me: I began to wonder if I was a true son of the South, in spirit if not in flesh.

It was my home. Known. Familiar. Comforting in its customs, in the cultures, in the harshness, because it was all I knew.

But does knowing a deadly enemy make him easier to like? Harder to destroy?

Behind me I heard the stud snuffling at the rock-rimmed, rune-carved basin, the need for water far greater than the fear of death. And I heard Del, very quietly, singing her Northern song.

My jaws locked. Between my teeth, I muttered, "Stupid, ignorant *fools*—"

Two adults, alone. And one tiny baby. Easy prey for borjuni.

I swung. "If they'd only hired a sword-dancer . . ." But I let it trail off. Del knelt in the sand, sword sheathed, carefully wrapping the remains of the infant in her only spare burnous. Very softly, she sang.

I thought at once of Kalle, the five-year-old girl Del had left on Staal-Ysta. She had borne the girl, then given her up, too obsessed with revenge to make time for a baby. Del was, I had learned, capable of anything in the patterns of her behavior. It was why she had offered me in trade for her daughter's company for the space of one year. She knew it was all she could get. She knew I was all she had to offer in exchange, and counted it worth the cost.

The cost had come high: we'd both nearly died.

But obsession and compulsion didn't strip her of guilt. Nor of a deep and abiding pain; I slept with the woman: I knew. We each, for different reasons, battled our demons in dreams.

Watching her tend the body, I wondered if she, too, thought of Kalle. If she wished the exile ended, her future secure in the North with a blue-eyed, fair-haired daughter very much like the mother who had given her up; who had been *forced* to give her up, to satisfy a compulsion far greater than was normal.

Now Ajani was dead. So was the compulsion, leaving her with—what?

Del looked up at me, cradling the bloody burnous. "Could you dig her a grave, Tiger?"

Her. I wondered how Del could tell.

Futility nearly choked me. I wanted to tell her this wasn't the South, not *really* the South. That it had changed since we'd gone up into the North. That something terrible had happened.

But it wasn't true. It would be a lie. The South hadn't changed. The South was exactly the same.

I stared hard at the bundle Del cradled in her arms. We didn't have a shovel. But hanging from the ends of my arms was a pair of perfectly good, strong hands with nothing else to do, since there were no borjuni present for me to decapitate.

At dawn, they came back. It wasn't typical—borjuni generally strike quickly and ride on after other prey—but who cares about typical when you're outnumbered eight to two?

Del and I heard them come without much trouble just at dawn, since we'd slept very lightly in view of the circumstances, and we had more than enough time to unsheathe blades from harnesses kept close at hand, and move to the ready. Now we stood facing them, perfectly prepared, backs to the screen of palm tree trunks huddling vertically near the rock basin.

"I thought you said something about those runes protecting the traveler," Del murmured. "So much for desert courtesy."

"Against tribes, yes. Not much of anything protects anybody against scavengers like borjuni—unless you want to count on a sword." I stared at the eight gathered men mounted on stocky Punja-bred horses. They were all typically Southron: black-haired, dark-eyed, swart-skinned, robed against the rising sun, aglitter with knives and stickers and swords. "A camp," I muttered thoughtfully. "There must be a camp nearby. . . ."

Del, from beside me, "Do you want to pay a visit?"

I grinned. "Maybe later. *After* we're done with these."

It was said for their benefit in clear, precise Desert, though Del's was accented. Not that it mattered: language skill was the last thing the eight mounted borjuni considered while staring down at the Northern woman so different from their own.

Which really was all right, when you looked at the scheme of things. It meant they didn't notice—or didn't *care*—that a sword was in her hands.

More likely, didn't care. It's hard not to notice Boreal.

Deep inside, I laughed. I had a *jivatma*, too.

"Well?" I invited.

One of the men stirred. His dark face was pocked by childhood disease. Long hair, greased back, glistened with too much oil. The curling ends stained grimy gray-brown the shoulders of his dusty cream-colored burnous. He challenged me with a stare. "Sword-dancer?" he asked.

I altered the tilt of my blade minutely, just enough to catch the newborn sunlight and throw it back into his eyes. Answer enough, I thought; you don't mess around with borjuni, or consider subtleties of feelings. You go straight to the point; in this case, it was *my* point, blackened by Chosa Dei.

The borjuni swore, squinted, thrust up a forearm to ward away the light. Behind him, his men muttered, but a single sibilant word held them in their places. He brought down his arm, settled a hand on his knifehilt, glared down the length of his pocked, bony nose. He didn't look at Del. But then, he didn't need to. He'd seen all he needed to see, to know how much he wanted.

The other hand he took from the reins and waved in a fluid gesture of encompassing possession: seven mounted men, all dangerously ruthless. Their worth was already proven, if you counted the bodies we'd buried.

The hand settled once more. He waited expectantly.

"I'm not impressed," I told him.

Dark eyes narrowed. He flicked a glance at Del, eyed the bared blade a moment, then looked back at me. "The woman," he growled, "and you go free."

A bargain, yet. *Very* unlike a borjuni. Being a sword-dancer has its uses—except in this case I wasn't so sure of things. Eight to two were not good odds, even if the borjuni, in their ignorance, believed it eight to one. I am big, yes, and quick, and I've cultivated a tough appearance, but I'm not *that* big or quick or mean.

Still, I was willing to play up the chance.

I displayed a cheerful, toothy grin. "I go free anyway. Do you think you can take the Sandtiger?"

Del, trained according to the exquisite honor codes of Staal-Ysta, no doubt considered it unnecessary braggadocio, but it's the way things are in the South. With borjuni, you need every edge. If they were at all concerned about me and the dangers of trying my skill, all the better. It could tip the balance in our favor.

Black eyes flickered. The borjuni leader tried a different approach. "Why has the woman a sword?"

"Because she, too, is a sword-dancer." I didn't see the sense in lying; besides, he wouldn't believe me. "And she has magic," I added casually. "Powerful Northern magic."

He squinted, assessing Del. Looking for magic, no doubt. Except he wouldn't see any, not so obviously, other than the magic of a leggy Northern beauty with a thick plait of white-blonde silk falling over one muscled shoulder bared by the almost sleeveless leather tunic. It didn't occur to him to consider the sword seriously, or what it was capable of.

Then again, who would? Boreal is very good at keeping secrets. Almost as good as Del.

A subtle flick of fingers. The seven men behind him began to spread apart. Del and I, without speaking, shifted stance at once, moving to stand back-to-back. I balanced very precisely, feeling familiar tension in thighs and calves, the tightening of abdomen.

Behind me, Del hummed. Prelude to the song. Prologue to the dance.

The leader did not move. "Sandtiger," he said, as if to be very sure.

It occurred to me then, and only then, that even borjuni might find it opportune to listen to the rumors. Maybe I hadn't been so smart in giving him my name. Maybe I'd been downright *stupid*, handing him the truth to lend credence to the tales. If what Rhashad had said were true—and I had no reason to doubt him— gold had been set on our heads.

Very softly, I swore.

Del's song gained in volume just as the borjuni charged.

Chapter 9

One of the easiest—and most violent—ways of taking out a mounted enemy is by cutting down his horse. It isn't clean, it isn't nice; what it is, is quick. It also has the occasional benefit of doing the whole job for you; I have known opponents killed by falling horses, or by the fall alone. It saves time and energy. And while you can't always hope for that, you do hope for the shock alone to drop the mounted man into your path. Then you finish the work.

When I fight, whether within the confines of the circle or outside in the codeless world, I experience an odd sort of slowing in time. While nothing is really still, it *is* nonetheless slowed so that my vision is unobscured by motion too fast to follow.

Once I'd thought it was the way everyone viewed fight or dance, until I'd mentioned it in passing to my shodo. The next day he had kicked me up a training level and handed me over to a well-known, established sword-dancer by the name of Abbu Bensir in order to test my claim. Whom I had not only beaten, but had also marked for life by nearly crushing his throat.

I'd explained to my shodo, once I'd gotten over the shock of actually winning the sparring dance, that Abbu's patterns had been relatively easy to block, because he'd been lazy and complacent, but mostly because I'd seen the path-within-the-path: the angles and sweeps and snaps *before* Abbu carried through. It was simply a matter of seeing the possibilities, probabilities, and alternatives, and selecting the action judged by my opponent as most likely to succeed. It required snap judgments of his technique, a rapid assessment of his style, and an immediate counter move.

I thought everybody did it. How else is the dance won?

Eventually I was told no, that *not* everyone had the ability to see motion before it happened, or to select the likeliest course for the opponent to follow, and then fashion a counter measure before the action occured. Such anticipation and countering ability was, my shodo explained, the truest gift a sword-dancer could ever hope for. And that I, more gifted than most, would reap the reward for a very long time, *years,* even—if I didn't throw the gift away by growing lazy, or too complacent.

Arrogant, always. Robustly confident. But never, ever complacent.

The mounted borjuni came on. Everything dutifully slowed, so I could see all the possibilities, and the path-within-the-path. Patiently I waited, sword at the ready, and watched him come riding at me, keening a promise of death.

Oh, it was promised, all right. But it wasn't *my* death.

I cut the horse out from under him, then spitted him on the way down.

One gone: seven to go. Of course, some of them would be Del's.

I spun in place even as the horse thrashed and screamed, briefly sorry about the waste, but knowing that survival requires many distasteful things. Later, if I lived, I'd dispatch the horse completely, but for now—

Senses thrummed. My ears focused on the sussuration of hooves digging through sand; the clatter of bridle brasses; the thick snort of a horse reined up short. I ducked, darted a false cut at the forelegs, let the borjuni jerk his horse aside as he swooped down with glinting blade. I caught it on my own, steel screeching; hooked, twisted, counter-rotated; snapped free, flowed aside, ducked a second time. Yet again the dart at the forelegs; yet again the sideways jerk: he valued his mount too well. It split his concentration.

I snap-chopped with a leveled blade, cut deeply into his calf-booted leg, heard him scream in shock and rage. The pain would follow quickly enough—except I didn't wait for it. As he slopped sideways in the saddle, clutching impotently at the nearly severed leg, I reached up, caught an arm, jerked him down from the horse. Sliced fragile throat effortlessly.

Two.

The rune-worked blade ran wet with bright new blood. In my head I heard a song, a whispered murmur of song, creeping into my bones. This was what it was for, my gods-blessed *jivatma.* This was its special task, to spill the blood of the enemy. This was its special talent: to part the flesh from bone, sundering even that, and *unmake* the enemy—

Rage and power and need.

Dimly I recognized none was born of me, but of something—some*one*—else.

The song wouldn't go away.

I spun, lunged, sliced. Horses everywhere, crowding the tiny oasis, compressing my personal circle. I heard Del's harsh breathing, the snatches of Northern song, the muttered self-exhortations spilled on choppy, blurted breath. Horses *everywhere*, snorting and stomping and squealing and thrashing—

—teeth snapping, hooves slashing—

—wild, rolling eyes—

—shouted Southron curses and threats of dismemberment—

—the thick hot scent of blood commingling with the sand—

—Del weaving sunlight with a shuttle of magicked steel—

—*rage*—and *power*—and *NEED*—

Chosa Dei wanted free.

The daylight around me exploded.

The enemy was shouting. I couldn't understand, couldn't decipher the words; knew only the enemy was required to be unmade—

"Tiger—Tiger, *no*—"

Trapped at the end of the blade; transfixed by discoloration: all I had to do was cut into the enemy's neck, barely slit the fragile flesh, and the enemy was unmade.

"Tiger—don't make me *do* this—"

It whispered in my head. A tiny, perfect song.

Take her now, it sang. *Take her NOW, and set me free.*

So many horses destroyed. So many enemies—

The swearing, now, was in Northern. For a moment it nonplussed me . . . then the song swelled in my head.

"—unmake—" I muttered aloud.

I had only to touch her throat with the blackened tip of the blade—

"You thrice-cursed son of a goat!" she cried. "What kind of an idiot are you? Do you *want* this dance, you fool? Do you really want us to do to each other what no one else can do?"

No one else?

Rage.

And power.

And *need.*

Blood dripped from the blade. A droplet ran down the sweep of Northern-fair collar bone and beneath the ivory tunic.

Del lifted her weapon. In her eyes I saw frantic appeal replaced by grim determination.

Something occurred to me.

I leapt, even as she snapped the blade aside in preparation of engagement. I leapt, lunged, dropped, and rolled, scraping through blood-soaked sand. Somehow got rid of the sword and came up empty-handed—

—to kiss turgid Northern steel as it lingered on my mouth.

I hung there on my knees, sucking air, trying very hard not to twitch or itch or blink, while Del gazed down at me out of angry banshee-storm eyes.

She looked at me, measuring. Looked at the sword, lying ten feet away. Stared hard at me again.

After a long, tense moment, Del gritted teeth. "How in hoolies am I to know when it's you, and when it's not?"

Because I could, because I knew her name, I put a finger on Boreal's edge and moved her slightly away from my mouth. "You could *ask,*" I suggested mildly.

"Ask! *Ask!* In the midst of hostilities, not knowing if I am to be spitted by a borjuni blade—*or on yours*—I am to *ask* if I can trust the man supposedly my partner?" Blue eyes blazed as she shaped a sarcastic tone. " 'Excuse me, Sandtiger, are you feeling friendly today, or not?' " Del shook her head. "What kind of a fool are you?"

"Bad joke," I murmured. "Either that, or you have no sense of humor."

"I find very little humorous about what just happened." Del scowled blackly. "Do you even *know* what happened?"

"I think I killed some people." I glanced around briefly, absently noting bodies. I counted eight of them. "Do you mind if I stand up?"

"You may piss rocks for all I care, so long as you do not go near that sword."

My, but she *was* perturbed. I sucked in a breath and got myself to my feet, marking aches and pains and twinges and tweaks, all epilogue to the battle.

I took a step. "Del, I'm not—" I broke if off on a throttled oath of discovery. Then sat down awkwardly on the sand.

"What is it?" Del asked suspiciously.

I was too busy swearing to answer. With great care I stretched out my right leg, felt the grinding pop within, then bent over it in supplication to the gods of ruined knees.

"Hoolies—not my knee—*please* not my knee—" I sucked in a ragged breath, sweat stinging scrapes and cuts. "I don't need this— I *really* don't need this . . . oh, hoolies, not my *knee*—"

Del's tone sounded more normal. "Are you all right?"

"*No*, I'm not all right—do I look all right? Do I *sound* all right?" I glared up at her, trying to will away the pain. "If you hadn't made me lunge and roll just now—"

"*My* fault! My fault? You son of a goat—that was *my* throat at the end of your sword!"

"I know—I know—I'm sorry . . ." I was, too, but couldn't deal with it just then; it was too big, too threatening—besides, my knee was killing me, and it was easier to focus on that rather than on what I'd done—or nearly done—to Del. "Oh, hoolies, let it be all right—not something permanent—"

"What have you done?" she asked.

"Twisted it," I blurted. "Oh, hoolies, I hate knees . . . all they do is give out just when you need them most, or keep you awake at night . . ." I scrubbed sweat away from eyes. "I suppose you're just *fine*. You with your twenty-one years."

"Twenty-two," she corrected.

"Twenty-one, twenty-two—who cares? You can do anything you want, ask anything of your body, and it does it without fanfare . . ." I probed gently at the knee, checking for things that shouldn't be there, wincing at the pain. "I wish I were your age again. . . ."

"No, you don't," she said briskly, finally sheathing her sword to squat down beside me, examining my knee. "I don't know a soul who would trade the wisdom he's gained for a younger, more ignorant body." She paused. "Of course, that's if he *has* any wisdom."

I saw blood on arms and legs, staining the ivory tunic. Her braid was sticky with it. "Are *you* all right?"

"One of us has to be, and you are already damaged." Her palm was cool on my knee. "Will you be able to ride?"

"Not if I have a choice."

Del's mouth quirked. "That depends," she said, "on whether you want to wait and see if their fellow borjuni come out to discover what's keeping the rest from the midday meal."

I glanced again at the bodies. Eight of them, as before. Also a handful of dead and dying horses. My stud was where I'd left him, tied to a palm tree. He was not particularly happy, surrounded by so much death.

I frowned. "Four are missing."

"They galloped off. If there *is* a camp, that is where they will go."

"Thereby carrying word." I stretched the leg again, testing the knee. "You're right: there is no choice. Find me something to bind this with, and we'll be on our way. We don't dare stay long enough even to tend the bodies—we'll let the other borjuni do that." And as she walked away, "Don't forget to refill the botas."

Del shot me an eloquent glance that said she knew very well what was to be done before we departed, but she checked it without saying a word. Grimly she went to the nearest body, cut a portion of burnous, came back ripping it. She dropped the pieces down to me. "There. I will see to the botas. You tend your knee—and then you will tend that sword."

That sword.

As she walked away I looked, and saw the suspect sword. Lying quietly in the sand, stained red and black and silver.

The sword with which I had killed a handful of borjuni, who without question deserved it . . . and had also tried to kill Del?

Hoolies, I was *afraid*. But I didn't dare let her see it, because then she would realize how precarious was my control.

I rubbed wearily at my face. Then bound up my aching knee.

Chapter 10

I waited. I watched her unsaddle the stud and stake him out, doing my work for me in deference to my knee, and then I watched her settle us in for the night. It wasn't precisely night *yet*, but close enough; besides, the stud was extra tired because I hadn't been able to do my share of walking in order to rest him.

We had no shelter to speak of, just a scattered cluster of spare, scrubby trees with next to no foliage on knotty branches, and a fringe of sparse, sere desert grass. A few rocks and a little kindling served as a fire cairn. A sad, shabby encampment, but adequate to our needs.

Whatever those needs might be, under the circumstances.

I waited. I watched her spread blankets, build the tiny fire, portion out food and water. She didn't say much. Didn't look at me much. Just did what needed doing, then settled down on her blanket.

Across the fire from me.

Foreboding flickered, but I ignored it, seeking a restoration to normality by falling back on familiar banter. "It's only a knee," I told her. "Not exactly catching."

Del's frown was brief, but significant. There is a look she gets in her eyes no matter how hard she tries to hide it. She masks herself to the world—and still to me, sometimes—but I can read her better now than when we first met. Which is to be expected.

With effort, I maintained a light tone. "Ah," I nodded, "it isn't the knee at all. That must mean it's *me.*"

Del's mouth flattened minutely. She flicked me a glance, chewed briefly and thoughtfully on her bottom lip, then twisted it into a crooked grimace of futility.

"Well?" I prodded. "I know it's been a long time since I had a proper bath, but that goes for you, too. And that never stopped *me.*"

"Because you have no self-control. Most men do not." But the rejoinder was halfhearted; no sting underlay the tone.

I gave up on normality. "All right, bascha—say what you have to say."

Del was clearly unhappy. "Trust," she said softly.

I put my hand upon the sheathed sword lying next to me. "This."

"It is abomination. The soul of the sword is black. Chosa Dei has perverted the *jivatma,* perverted the honor codes—"

"—and you're afraid he's perverted me."

Del didn't answer at once. Color bloomed in her face, then drained away as quickly. "It shames me," she said finally. "To trust, and then not trust. To question the truth of the loyalty . . ." She gestured emptily, as if lacking the proper words. "We have done much, you and I, in the name of honor, and other things. Trust was never questioned, as is proper in the circle, whether drawn or merely believed." Her accent was thicker, twisting the Southron words. "But now, there is question. Now there must be question."

I sighed heavily. My bound knee ached unremittingly, but so did everything else. "I suppose I should ask you what it was I did. Just to understand. I don't remember much after the second borjuni."

"You killed them," Del said simply. "And then you tried to kill me."

"Tried? Or merely *appeared*—" I let the irony go. The shield fashioned of bluster and sarcasm was not required. The imagery was too lurid; the truth too painful. "Bascha—"

"I am sure," she forestalled. "I know it wasn't you, not *really* you—but does that matter? Chosa Dei wants me. Chosa Dei wants *you* . . . and for a time today, he had you." Del picked violently at her blanket, shredding a fraying corner. "The song you sang was—not right. It wasn't a song of your making. It was a song of *his*—"

The first stirrings of comprehension made me itchy, shifting on the blanket. It was easier to dismiss her fears than consider them. "I can control him, Del. It's just a matter of being stronger."

"*He* is growing stronger. Tiger, don't you see? If you give in to violence, it lends the power to him. Once he collects enough, he will use the sword as a bridge to *you*, then use you for his body." Distaste briefly warped her expression. "I saw it today, Tiger. I saw *him* today, as I saw him inside the dragon."

Denial was swift. Was easy. "I don't think—"

She didn't let me finish. "Chosa Dei looked out of your eyes. Chosa Dei was in your soul."

The tiniest flicker of fear lighted itself in my belly. "I beat him," I blurted urgently. "Last night, and again today. I'll *go on* beating him."

The setting sun was gone. Firelight overlay her face. "Until he grows too strong."

Desperation combined with impotent anger. The explosion was potent. "What do you *expect?* I can't get rid of this sword the way any sane man would—you said it's too dangerous to sell, give away, or cast off, because then he'd have his body. And I can't *destroy* the sword—you said it would free his spirit. So what does that leave me? What in hoolies am I to do?"

Del's voice was steady. "Two choices," she said quietly. "One you already know: find a way to discharge the sword. The other is harder yet."

I swore creatively. "What in hoolies is harder than tracking down a sorcerer out of legend—Chosa's *brother*, no less!—who may not even exist?"

"Dying," she answered softly.

It was a punch in the gut, but I didn't let her see it. "Dying's easy," I retorted. "Look at what I do for a living."

Del didn't answer.

"And besides, Chosa—in this sword—already tried to kill me once. Remember? So how would dying serve any purpose?"

Her mouth twisted. "I doubt he wanted to kill you. More like he wanted to *wound* you; seriously, yes, because then you would be weakened. Then he could swallow the sword . . . and eventually swallow you. But if you were to die . . ." She let it trail off. No more was necessary.

Trying not to jar my knee, I flopped spine-down on my blanket and stared up at the darkening sky. As always in the desert, the air at night was cool, counterpoint to the heat of day. "So, as I understand it—" I frowned "—all I have to do is stay alive—and in one piece—long enough to find Shaka Obre, who can help me discharge this thrice-cursed sword . . . or avoid all kinds of violence so as not to give him power . . . or not turn my back on you."

It startled her. "On *me!*"

I rolled my head to look at her. "Sure. So you won't start thinking of ways to defeat Chosa—through me—without benefit of discharging."

Stunned, Del gaped. It was almost comical.

I managed a halfhearted grin. "That's a joke, bascha. But then I keep forgetting: you don't have a sense of humor."

"I would not—I *could* not—I would never . . ." She broke it off angrily, giving up on coherency.

"I *said* it was a joke!" I rolled over onto a hip, easing my sore knee, and leaned upon an elbow. "See what I mean about no sense of humor?"

"There is nothing amusing about loss of honor, of *self*—"

Abruptly very tired, I smeared a palm across my face. "Forget it. Forget I said anything. Forget I'm even here."

"I can't. You *are* here . . . and so is that sword."

"That sword," again. I sighed heavily, aware of a weary depression, and lay down again on my blanket. "Go to sleep," I suggested. "It'll be better in the morning. Everything's better in the morning—it's why they invented it."

"Who?"

"The gods, I guess." I shrugged. "How in hoolies should I know? I'm only a jhihadi."

Del didn't lie down. She sat there on her blanket, staring pensively at me.

"Go to *sleep*," I said.

A dismissive shrug. "I will sit up for a while. To guard."

I also shrugged, accepting it readily enough; it was a common enough occurrence. I snugged down carefully beneath a blanket, swearing softly at the taut bindings that made it hard to settle my knee comfortably, then stopped moving entirely.

Something new occurred. Something I didn't like, but knew was possible. More likely *probable*.

"Guarding, are you?" I growled. "Guarding me against danger—or guarding against *me?*"

Del's voice was even. "Whatever is necessary."

Chapter 11

I woke up surly, which I do sometimes. Not very often, on the whole; like I've said before, I'm generally a good-natured soul. But occasionally, it catches up to the best of us.

Usually it's after a night of too much aqivi (and, once upon a time, too many women, but it seems like everything changes as you get older); in this case, it was after a night of too-active sleep, and a sore knee less than pleased about having to move.

Del, one of those perfectly disgusting people who wakens with relative ease and no disgruntlement that the sun has reappeared, watched me untangle the blanket, muttering beneath my breath as I did so, and then, equally silently, watched me try to lever myself up. Sitting was easy enough. Standing was not. Walking was worse.

I hobbled off, tended my business, hobbled back. I was stiff, itchy from healing sand scrapes, smelly from lack of bath, stubbled on cheeks and chin. My knee hurt like hoolies. So did a few other things: namely, my pride.

"You talked," Del mentioned, neatly folding her blanket aside.

It was, I thought, basically inconsequential. But since she'd brought it up . . . "Talked?"

"Last night. In your sleep." Kneeling, she set about stirring life into the coals of the cairn. "I almost woke you, but—I was . . . well . . ."

"Afraid?" I bit it out between gritted teeth. "Did you think I'd snatch the sword out of my sheath and have at you with it in the middle of the night?"

Del said nothing.

Which hurt most of all: it meant there was a chance my sarcastic question was more accurate than I liked.

Explosively, I challenged her. "Hoolies, bascha, this is going to have to be settled once and for all. If you really are afraid of me—"

"*For* you," she said quietly.

"For me? Why? *For* me?"

She bent, blew on the coals, looked through ash grit and smoke at me. "I am afraid of what he will do to you. What he would make of you, once you were *un*made."

I'll admit it: it was unsettling. "Yes, well . . . I don't think he'd get very far, with me. I'm sort of stubborn about things like sorcerers trying to make me over into some sort of *thing,* like those men-turned-hounds." A grimace of distaste warped my mouth. "Hoolies, what a way to die . . ." I let it go, forcibly thinking about something else as I sat down awkwardly. "What was it I said, in my sleep?"

"Patterns," Del answered, tossing a bota to me. "Lines and patterns and furrows."

I stared. "*That's* what I talked about?"

"Some of it. Some I could not understand. Drawings in the sand, you said." She pointed. "See?"

I looked. Beside my blanket, near to hand, was a "pattern" of four straight lines, with the hint of a curve at the bottom. As if someone had taken a stick and sketched one line after another.

I frowned. "I did that?"

She nodded, digging through saddle-pouches. "You muttered something about patterns and lines. Then you stuck all four fingers in the dirt and drew that." She touched her cheek. "It looks like you."

"You" meant my own cheek, beneath the stubble: four slashed lines, very straight, to the bottom of the jaw. Where the sandtiger had at last been persuaded to take his claws out of my face.

The lines in the dirt *did* look very much like claw marks. A "pattern," I guess you could say.

I grunted, unimpressed. "Who knows? I don't even remember dreaming." I sucked down water, then replugged the bota. "Our best bet is to head toward Quumi. It's a trade settlement on the edge of the Punja—that is, *usually* it's on the edge. Depending on what the Punja feels like."

Del nodded absently, staring beyond me toward the horizon. She squinted, frowning; the expression didn't inspire trust.

I was instantly alert. "What?"

"Dust. I think. In thin light, it's hard . . . no, it is. Dust." She rose, dropping the pouch, and bent swiftly to retrieve the salmon-silver blade from its rune-worked sheath. "If it is borjuni—"

"—then we may as well offer them breakfast," I finished. "I'm not exactly mobile . . ." But I tried anyway, levering myself up and dragging my own sword from its sheath.

Wishing I could trust it.

Wishing I could trust *me*.

Not borjuni. Sword-dancer. A young, Southron male, spare in frame but not arrogance; he stared down at me from atop a sand-colored horse and put his imperious desert-bladed nose into the air.

He wore a pale, bleached yellow burnous, and the hilt of a properly harnessed sword peeked over the set of his shoulder. "Sandtiger?" he asked.

It is not easy to put a considerable amount of contempt into a single word—into a single *name*, for that matter—without overdoing it when you're eighteen or nineteen, but he managed. It takes practice; I wondered if he was as attentive to his dancing. The tone was mostly contempt, and a few other things—namely stupidity; did he really think I would start quivering in my sandals because he knew my name?

"If I said no," I began mildly, "would it convince you to leave us alone and ride straight on into the Punja? With nearly empty botas, no less?"

Dark eyes glittered. His mount fidgeted. He stilled it with an impatient snatch at reins. "My botas are as they are because I chose to ride harder and faster than the others, so as to keep the honor for myself."

The "honor" meant challenging me to a dance, no doubt. The reference to *"others,"* however—that bothered me.

"Pretty stupid, aren't you?" I asked affably. "How will you get back on so little water?"

"You will forfeit your botas to me when I have won." His eyes flicked briefly to Del, then back. "Botas—and your woman."

"And my *woman*," I echoed. "Well, let me give you a hint—you might want to ask her, first. She *prefers* being asked, generally . . . although I doubt you'd get very far. Del sort of does her own choosing when it comes to bedpartners."

Idly, Del tilted her blade. It flashed in new light. He glared down his nose at her, clearly affronted to see a sword in the hands of a woman, *any* woman, but particularly a foreign one; then looked back at me. "My name is Nezbet. By all the honor codes of the Southron sword-dance, I challenge you to step into the circle, where we may settle the contention."

"What *is* the contention?" I asked. "That I killed the jhihadi?" I smiled, shaking my head. "But I didn't. I *am* the jhihadi. And I, most obviously, am not dead, so there is no need to dance at all."

It worked about as well as expected. "I am Nezbet. I am a third-level sword-dancer. I have been hired to bring you back to Iskandar."

"*Third*-level?" I grunted, leaned sideways, deliberately spat. "I'm seventh-level, boy. Haven't they told you that?"

Elegant nostrils flared. "I know who—*and* what—you are. Will you step into the circle?"

I assessed him openly, provocatively, letting him see what I did. Then I lifted one shoulder in a lazy, eloquent shrug. "Not worth it," I answered idly.

Dark color stained his face. "I need not be of your level to challenge you. *Any* level may challenge—that is a tenet contained in the honor codes—"

"I *know* what is and is not contained in the honor codes, boy. I learned them before you were born." I altered my stance slightly, to take some of the weight off my sore knee. "I know many things Nezbet, in his youth, has yet to learn."

Youthful Nezbet was disturbed. "Then, if you know them, you

know also that if you refuse to dance against me after formal challenge has been laid—according to the codes—you can be proscribed."

"*Any* man can refuse a dance," I reminded him. "It's not good for his reputation, and in the long run he'd lose any chance at making a living because people would stop hiring him, but he can still refuse."

"This is *formal* challenge," he stressed, and then uttered one of the long-winded, twisty phrases I'd labored so hard to learn myself, back when I was his age.

I bit out an oath short and sweet and succinct. Del glanced the question, as what the boy had said was in a Southron dialect only rarely spoken. A Northerner would not know it, not even one as well-traveled—and well-taught—as Del. The language of the circle, it was called in Desert; the more formal name is nearly unpronounceable.

"Shodo's Challenge," I told her, explaining the shortened—and comprehensible—idiomatic form. "Seems this boy and I learned from the same school, so to speak . . . my shodo is long dead, but he had apprentices. And one of them apparently trained this Punjamite of a boy." I smiled up at him insincerely, though I still spoke to Del. "It means I *am* required to dance against him, or forfeit my status. Which means I become little more than a borjuni, since no one will hire me." I glanced at her. "Remember how up north they said you were a blade without a name, stripped of honor and rights? Well, it's sort of the same thing."

"But—" she began, and stopped.

"But," I agreed. I looked back at the Southron boy, whose pride in place was so evident. Had I ever been that cocky?

Rephrase that. Had I ever been that cocky so *young?*

"I can't accept," I told him. "Shodo's Challenge or no. A true challenge is predicated on equality in health, if not rank—" another gibe; often, they work, "—and I have a very sore knee. See?" I pointed to the wrapping. "I'd just *love* to open up your guts with this sword, Nezbet, but I'm a bit hampered at the moment. And an injury forfeit is not a true forfeit, since we are not yet in the circle."

His jaw worked. The beardless flesh was stretched tight over distinctly desert bones. He was, as are nearly all Southroners, swarthy of coloring. His age and attitude reminded me a little of Nabir, the Vashni halfling who had wanted my Chosa Dei-ridden sword. And had died for it. Horribly.

"I will wait," he said at last. "I will follow you and wait, until your knee is whole."

"You want me *that* bad?"

"Defeating you and taking you back will earn me another level. Possibly *two*."

So that was it. More important than coin. It touched on pride, on status; on the name that would shape the boy, as mine had shaped me.

I swore. "You stupid little Punja-mite—the only true way of earning a level is by staying with your shodo! For however long it takes! There are no *tasks* to be done, no *quests* assigned and undertaken. It's *work*, Nezbet, nothing more. Years and years of discipline, until the shodo declares you have reached the level for which you are judged the worthiest—" I broke it off, because I was too angry. Why is it so many young sword-dancers want to take shortcuts? Don't they know their lives could depend on the extra training a year or two—or *three*—offers?

No. They don't. Or they just don't care.

Stupid Punja-mite.

Now I wished my knee *was* sound. So I could teach him a lesson.

"There is me," Del offered.

I frowned. Nezbet said nothing, not comprehending what she meant; he wouldn't: she's a woman.

"There is me," she repeated. "I will stand proxy for him."

Nezbet stared at her. Then looked back at me. "I will wait. I will follow."

Del moved forward a step. "And if the Sandtiger *allows* me to stand proxy for him? According to your codes?"

"You are a woman," Nezbet said.

Del's smile was cool. "And this is a sword."

"And if it *matters* so much to you," I interjected, "why are you working for a woman?"

"I am not."

I frowned. "*Why* have you been hired to bring me back to Iskandar?"

"You murdered the tanzeer of Julah."

Del scowled. She was never proud of killing, but undoubtedly she was weary of me getting credit for all of her doings. I didn't really blame her.

"I didn't," I said mildly, "but at the moment it doesn't really matter. Who hired you?"

"The new tanzeer of Julah."

"She's a *woman*, Nezbet! Or are you too young to notice things like that?"

Color stained his face. "I did not speak with the tanzeer himself."

"Ah," I said. "I see. So you're going to persist in believing the tanzeer's a man, because you didn't really *meet* the tanzeer. And it couldn't possibly be a woman."

Dark eyes glittered. "I have laid formal challenge."

"Would you unlay it if you believed the tanzeer was a woman?" I asked curiously.

Del stirred. "You can't prove it," she murmured. "He's never going to believe you."

No. He wasn't. Any more than he'd believe Del was a sword-dancer.

Which brought us once more to the challenge.

"She's my proxy," I said, "formally designated." I grinned cheerfully at Nezbet, leaning upon my planted weapon. "Too bad there aren't enough people to lay a wager on this."

Nezbet glared. "You would allow a *woman*—"

"Try her and find out." I shrugged. "Might as well, you know. Find out what she's like in the circle before you find out what she's like in bed."

Del winced. Indelicate, maybe. But it did the job.

Nezbet's nose went up. "If she is proxy, it is done according to the proper codes. A loss equals a forfeit. If she loses, *you* lose . . . and will become my prisoner."

"If," I agreed, and bent to draw the circle.

Chapter 12

A farce. Pure and simple. The boy was young, strong, nimble, and trained. Del was that, and more. Del was simply herself: exquisite, elegant excellence. A potent, lethal enemy, more skilled than any he knew, regardless of the gender.

It didn't take her long. She didn't even bother to sing, which helps her focus. Del is not arrogant, nor is she interested in the games I like to play, designed to unbalance an opponent. She wastes no time at all, thinking merely of the dance and the ways to force a win. It doesn't matter to her if it is exhibition, or to the death. She takes either equally seriously because, she'd told me once, a woman in any employment considered a man's will be ignored unless she forces the issue, no matter what the game.

It was illuminating. It also taught me a lot about dispensing with entertainment and getting right to business. Wasted effort, she said, was wasted energy; she had no time for either.

Now that I was older, with aches and stiffness becoming a factor, I needed every edge. And Del was not a fool.

Nor was she one now. She caught and trapped Nezbet's blade even as the dance opened, disallowing disengagement, and backed him easily to the thin curving line of the circle. There she stripped him of his sword, tossed it wheeling out of the circle, and pinned him at the perimeter with the faintest of Boreal's kisses.

"How many?" she asked. "Who? And how far away?"

Nezbet's already dark eyes glazed black with shock. Empty hands clutched air; the mouth gaped inelegantly. But he dared not leave the circle for fear Boreal would object. Her touch is never sanguine, nor lacking in promises. He knew as well as I that a single wayward step could result in his death. Del had won the right.

"A day or two," he rasped, answering the last first. "Sword-dancers and warriors. The sword-dancers want the Sandtiger. The warriors want the jhihadi-killer."

"Me," she said tightly. "I killed them both: Aladar and Ajani."

I saw the look in his eyes: masculine disbelief, underscored by a trace of doubt. The beginnings of comprehension, tempered by the overwhelming power of Southron beliefs. She would not convince him, not even here and now. But she had planted the seed of doubt. The seed of *possibility.*

"The jhihadi isn't dead," I told him, knowing the tribes offered more threat. Religion makes fools of people. "That man's name was Ajani. He was a Northerner, and borjuni, riding both sides of the border. He *told* people he was the jhihadi, but none of it was true. The tribes are caught up in prophecy, not in the truth of things . . . they have only to ask the Oracle." Who was Del's brother.

Nezbet shrugged carefully. "They want to execute you. They saw you, in the city . . . they saw you summon fire from the sky with your sword."

"That's magic," I said, having no time to marvel at my matter-of-factness. "Not perverted truth, just magic. Ajani was borjuni. Rapist and murderer. He sold this woman's brother to slavers—he'd have sold her, too, but she got away from him. And became a sword-dancer." I didn't bother to smile; I didn't care if he believed me. "He wasn't the jhihadi. I am the jhihadi."

Nezbet managed to spit. "You were a sword-dancer held up as an example. And now you come to *this:* liar and murderer."

"I have lied," I agreed. "And certainly I have murdered, if you count enemies trying to kill *me.* But in this I am neither." I drew in a breath, changing topics. "As for Aladar's death, all I can say is he deserved it. It was personal. I'll accept challenges as I have to, even if it *was* Del who killed him." I flicked a glance at her, then looked back at Nezbet. "But no matter what you believe, you *are* working for a woman. She used a man to hire you, knowing how you would feel. Which means she hired you on a falsehood. The coin you accepted is tainted."

"There is no payment until you are delivered!" he snapped.

"Really?" I arched brows. "Then you're even stupider than I thought."

"Tiger," Del said; her way of asking a question.

I shrugged. "He's lost. The dance is over. And unless he turns borjuni, sacrificing his status and pride, he won't bother us again." I gestured. "Let him go. Send him back to the others. He can tell them what we've said." As she lowered Boreal, I caught his gaze with my own. "Hear me, Nezbet: one sword-dancer to another. I swear on my shodo's name what they have told you is false. Tell the warriors that."

Nostrils flared. The mouth, suddenly old, was a grim, flat line. "Then you are disgraced," he spat, "and your shodo's name dishonored."

I waved dismissal at him. "Get out of here, Punja-mite. You're too stupid to live, but I won't be the one to kill you. My sword likes the taste of men."

Nezbet scooped up his blade and snapped it back into the diagonal sheath. He cast me a final withering stare, then turned and mounted his sand-colored horse. Dust showered us as he jerked his mount around and rode off at a hard gallop.

I sighed heavily. "Short on water," I said, "and now he runs his horse. He'll be lucky to *reach* the others; we may yet be safe."

"No," Del said.

"No," I agreed. "Time we rode on, too."

"Tiger?"

"What?"

"Why didn't you take his horse? The others are coming, he says . . . they could have picked him up."

I thought about it. Scowled. Looked at Del. "Guess we're just not cut out to be thieves, after all."

Del grinned. "Guess not."

It began imperceptibly, as the worst of them usually do. The tiniest of breezes, lifting a ruffle of sand; a wisp of wind swirling down to ripple silken burnous; the pressure of air against face, stripping hair from brow and eyes. Sand kicked up by the stud was caught, trapped, blown free, stinging ankles and eyes. Del and I, riding double, retreated beneath drawn hoods, until I yanked mine off my head and reined the stud to a halt.

"Samiel," I said; meaning the wind, not my sword.

It took Del a moment. Then she stiffened against me. "Are you sure?"

"I can smell it." I squinted. The sun still blinded the eye, unobscured by rising sand, but if the wind grew much stronger the samiel would transform itself into simoom. A hot wind was bad enough. A sandstorm was worse. "Our best bet would be to find some sort of shelter, like a sandwall at an oasis—" I shook my head, blocking sun and sand with a shielding hand. "We're too far. The best we can do is a sandrill blown against the scrub."

Del shivered. "I recall the simoom. . . ." She let it trail off.

I recalled it, too. We'd barely met, and Del was still most distinctly unobtainable. . . .

I smiled crookedly, recalling those days. And the long, dark nights of frustration.

Del poked me in the spine. "Do we ride on? Or stay here?"

"*One* of us needs to walk. Give the stud a rest."

Delicate irony: "Oh, let me be the one. . . ." She slid off, patting the stud's brown rump, and moved to his head. "There are bushes just ahead."

I shrugged. "Might as well. Much as I hate to stop, with the new hounds of hoolies on our trail . . ." I twisted, squinting back the way we had come. "If they're as close as Nezbet said they were, it won't take long before they catch up. Some of them. We're slowed like this. Much too much."

"What else is there to do? If we stop and wait for them, they will surely outnumber us."

"Eventually," I agreed. "Let's just hope if any more show up soon, it's because they did what Nezbet did: rode ahead of the larger contingent."

Del's face was grim. "I like not the idea that so many sword-dancers have been hired to hunt down two of their own."

I turned back. "Sword-dancers we can handle. We're two of the best, remember? If not *the* best." I gave her the benefit of the doubt by saying "we," figuring she'd earned it. "And besides, they won't converge upon us—that's not the way of the circle. They'd take us one by one. No, I'm more concerned with the tribes."

Del was stuck on the sword-dancers. "And how many can *you* defeat, even in single combat, injured as you are?"

"Me? Hoolies, bascha—I can plead sore knee for a very long time." I grinned. "Maybe until they get tired of waiting and give up."

"Did you ever give up when hired to do a job?"

"Once. The man got real sick . . . he was dying, so I let him go. Didn't pick up the second half of my hire fee, either, which should restore some of your faith in me."

"Some," she agreed. "But you should have returned the first half, since you did not complete your contract."

"Yes, well . . ." I blinked against stinging sand. "Let's get to those bushes. And hope this blows itself out before it becomes a full-fledged simoom."

A little while later, as we huddled amid the bushes, Del stated the obvious: "It's not stopping."

"No."

"If anything, it is worse."

"Yes."

"Then it *will* become a simoom."

"Seems like." I shifted my knee, swearing absently, and sat up judiciously. She was right. It wasn't stopping. It was worse. And it was just on the verge of becoming—

No. It *was*.

"Hoolies," I murmured.

Del, hunkered down against the scrubby bush, twisted. And saw what I saw: ocher-dark cloud of sand and debris rolling across the horizon.

The stud whickered uneasily and pawed, adding to the mess. I got up, hobbled the two steps to him, passed a soothing hand down his neck. "Easy, old son. You know the dance. Lie down for me, shut your eyes . . ." I put my hand on his headstall, intending to urge him down.

A thought blossomed into idea.

Frowning, I scowled out at the roiling mass of sand as it blew across the horizon. At the moment it was still samiel, not simoom, in our location, but in a matter of minutes the true strength and fury of the sandstorm would swallow us. It was not impossible that we could die from it, although unlikely; we had water and blankets and food, so even if the simoom lasted days—

No. Let's not think about that.

Think about something else. Like magic.

Nezbet had said it: I had called fire from the sky with my sword. I had also made glass but a day or two before. Twice I had created something out of nothing, by using the magic in Samiel and enforcing my will upon it. In Iskandar I had created a controllable firestorm to ease our flight. The circle of glass had been unintentional, and only vaguely interesting—to me—but it did indicate I could do strange and wondrous things with Samiel, given the motivation, the need, the wherewithal.

And the control.

The jhihadi, the tribes believed, could do impossible things, like changing the sand to grass. So why didn't they believe *I* was the jhihadi since I called fire out of the sky?

Because the Sandtiger was a only sword-dancer who once had been a chula. Ajani—huge, powerful, clever Ajani, whose burning, as Bellin the Cat had put it, was very bright indeed—had swayed them in his direction. With lengthy, meticulous care.

The only way I could ever prove to them their Oracle had pointed at *me* was to show them what I could do.

In properly jhihadi-ish ways.

Which meant, of course, magic.

The stud nodded unhappiness, then swung his head to plant a forehead against my chest and rub very hard. It destroyed my already precarious balance; I stayed upright only by clutching at the saddle, swearing as my sore knee blared a protest.

The song of the wind altered.

"Tiger—"

I quit swearing and looked. Night was engulfing day.

No more time.

Purposely, I untied the stud from the bush he could easily have uprooted, but didn't, because it hadn't occurred to him that he was considerably stronger—and smarter—than the bush. Horses are like that. I looped the reins up over his neck and hooked them to the saddle. If he needed to run, as I feared, I wanted him unencumbered. A dangling rein usually breaks when stepped upon. But I'd seen a runaway once plunge a foreleg into a loop of loose rein, snug himself tight, and fall. He'd broken his neck on landing.

"Stay down," I told Del. "Lie down, if you like. You might even cover your eyes, or hide under a blanket. I don't really know what might happen."

Del sat bolt upright. "What are you . . . *Tig*er!"

I unsheathed the sword. "Long as I've got the thing, I may as well see what I can do with it."

"And what it can do to *you!*"

"Yes, well . . ." I squinted against the sand, spat grit, shrugged. "Chance I'll have to take. Look at it this way, bascha—it might slow down our hounds."

"It might *kill* you!"

"Nah," I scoffed. "That will be for *you* to do, if Chosa Dei gets too uppity."

It silenced her instantly.

Sort of the way I planned it; I wasn't any happier about what I was about to do than Del.

And a whole lot more at risk.

I think.

Hoolies, but I hate magic.

Chapter 13

I thought of a song. Just a silly little thing; I'm not much good at singing (Del would say I'm not *any* good), and therefore I always feel a trifle stupid standing in the middle of the desert thinking up a song, let alone *singing* it, but it seemed to be required. At least, it had been all the other times.

The Northerners on Staal-Ysta had explained it thoroughly to me, the rite of singing to focus the sword, to focus the dancer, and to summon whatever power there was in the ritual- and rune-bathed *jivatma*. Left to my own devices, singing a focus was about the last thing I'd do. I'd been taught the inner path, the way to summon the soul within a soul, as you prepare to enter the dance. There are mental preparations—

Ah, hoolies, it *all* sounds silly, when you think about it; and even stupider if you say it out loud. So let me make it easy: I look at myself as a weapon, and the sword an extension of me. So that when I think about *me* cutting in a certain direction, or twisting a specific way *just so*, the sword does it, too.

Singlestroke had been perfect for me, before he'd broken in combat against a Northern sword-dancer who'd requenched his *jivatma*. Together we'd carved out a piece of the South as our domain, though unacknowledged by the tanzeers who *really* ruled; but in the way of the sword-dancer, who rules the South by fighting skills and a willingness to kill for pay, Singlestroke and I had been perceived as the best.

Of course, Abbu Bensir might object, claiming *himself* the best, but Abbu and I had only rarely crossed paths. He had his portion of the South, I had mine. We respected one another.

Whether he still respected me, I couldn't say. Probably. That he'd hired on to track us down didn't mean he respected us any less, just that we were worth money. After all, it was Abbu who'd tossed me his sword in the midst of the confusion in Iskandar, when I'd briefly lost mine.

Of course, that was before I was worth money.

Now he wouldn't toss me a sword to replace the one I'd lost. He'd *take* mine, if he could get it . . . which brought me around to Samiel—and Chosa Dei—once again.

Wind and sand buffeted my ears. I heard a low-pitched growling, the complaint of a sandstorm trying to satisfy an insatiable appetite. I'd heard the noise before, and felt the power. If I didn't do something very soon, it might be the last thing I heard—and felt.

I flicked a glance over my shoulder at Del. She was huddled down against the sandrill—a mound of sand created by wind blowing it into a lopsided pile against some kind of obstruction—with burnous hood pulled up and a blanket swaddled around her body. I thought momentarily of that body, recalling long limbs entangled with my own, the scent of white-silk hair, the taste of Northern flesh. I did not want to lose it—or the spirit that went with it—to a simoom.

Nor to untamed magic.

Hoolies.

Nothing for it, then, but to prove I was the master.

"All right," I muttered into the wind, "let's have a little talk, you and I, about the merits of blowing in *this* patch of desert—or in the patch holding all those sword-dancers after our hides . . . and the money that comes with it, of course."

The simoom growled on, whining and hissing and roaring. Even with my eyes squinted nearly closed, sand and grit stung them. My lashes were fouled and crusty, my nostrils halfway obstructed, my mouth stiff and caked. Sand grated in my teeth, scouring gums and throat. But if I turned my back to the wind, I gave precedence to the simoom.

From behind me, the stud made verbal protest. I was faintly surprised he hadn't gone yet. But, then, likely he thought he was still tied . . . I should have whopped him on the rump and sent him off.

Two-handed, I gripped the hilt and lifted the sword into the air. Wind whined against steel, screeching and shrieking as the edge bit in. Around me the world howled. Hair was stripped from my face, blown back almost painfully. I spread and braced both legs as best I could, hampered by my sore right knee, and dug supporting hollows for sandaled feet, ridding myself of precarious underpinning. I raised both hands high above my head, slicing vertically through the storm, until arms—and blade—were outstretched.

It is the classic pose of the conqueror; the barbaric swordsman counting coup, or singing his own praises with posture rather than voice. *"I am master,"* it says. *"I am the lord. You who would have my place must first remove me from it."*

I thought it rather fitting, in light of the situation.

"Mine," I said aloud.

The storm was unabated.

"Mine," I said more forcefully.

The simoom sang on, scouring at wind-bared legs and arms. And then more than legs and arms; it ripped the burnous and underrobe from my body, shredding them like rotted gauze, and left me bare on all counts, save for sandtiger necklet, which rattled; the suede dhoti anchored too firmly around my hips; Southron sandals cross-gartered to my knees; and the Northern harness hugging ribs and spine and shoulders.

Barbarian, indeed.

"MINE," I roared, and the song in my head rose up to deafen me.

Samiel answered simoom. I felt it before I heard it: a thrumming, numbing, gut-deep tingle that rattled the bones of my elbows and threatened to shatter wrists. I clamped down every muscle I owned, locking joints into position. The power I sensed was sweet, seductive, oh so attractive. It knew me. It knew my song. I had quenched it, then requenched. We were doubly bonded, Samiel and I.

And then the power changed. The essence of Samiel winked out, like a spark caught in a maelstrom, and I felt something else burst into flame to take his place. Something very strong. Something very *angry*.

It sheeted down from the sword, corruscating like heat lightning across the Punja's horizon. Black light. *Black* light. Not true illumination, because it wasn't sunlight or moonlight or firelight. It was black. And yet it glowed.

Sweat broke out on my flesh. Sand adhered at once. Every hollow, crease, and furrow began to itch.

Hoolies. Here we go again.

Black light, radiating. It flooded down the blade, tapped tentatively at my hands upon the grip, then flowed downward again, engulfing fingers, hands, wrists.

I swore. I said something very rude. Because I was, abruptly, more frightened than I had ever been before.

The light was *touching* me—

Black, radiant light, coating flesh in darkness.

"Hoolies," I croaked.

Not magic. I knew it. *Not* magic. Something worse. Something more powerful. Something infinitely more dangerous.

The sword had been partly black. The discoloring had waxed and waned, like the moon, dependent upon Chosa Dei. Dependent upon me, and the strength of will I employed to drive the sorcerer down.

The entire blade was black. The hilt. The hands upon it.

Black-braceleted wrists.

He had been waiting for this.

I shouted. Tried to let go. Tried to cast off the blackened sword, to throw it arcing far into the wind, where the simoom would swallow it. But I could not let go of the weapon that imprisoned Chosa Dei.

Who now imprisoned me.

I felt him, then. A feather-touch. Caress. The merest whisper of breath across my soul. Blackness spread.

"Del," I croaked. "Del, do it *now*—"

But Del didn't—or couldn't—hear me.

I thought, *If I turn this on myself*—wondering if my death would indeed destroy Chosa; remembering belatedly that by giving up my life I also gave up my body. Chosa had already proved himself capable of unmaking and remaking things he found suitable to his needs. A dying body would hardly stop him. Even mine.

The simoom howled on. It stopped up eyes, and ears; took residence in my soul. I felt Chosa's fingertip—or *something*—touch my right forearm. Then my left. Blackness welled coyly, flirting, then swallowed another portion of my flesh.

The hairs stood up on my flesh. My belly twisted and cramped, threatening to spew everything I'd eaten.

Oh, hoolies, what have I done?

Blackness.

So much blackness.

Eating me inch by inch.

Deep inside, bones ached.

Was he trying to unmake them?

Fear and sand had scoured my mouth dry. I swallowed painfully, wishing for water; for wine. For the strength and courage I needed so desperately.

I gripped the sword more tightly, squeezing leather wrappings until my knuckles complained. Toes curled against leather soles, cracking noisily. Even my good knee ached; I flexed muscle, reset, locked everything down once again.

One last try.

"Mine," I mouthed soundlessly. "This sword, this body, this *soul*—"

Abruptly my eyes snapped open. Staring sightlessly into the storm, unheeding of sand and grit and wind, I knew. I *knew*.

There were things Chosa didn't understand. About the spirit. He knew magic and flesh and bone; he knew *nothing* about the spirit.

Nothing about the obsessive compulsion of a young Southron chula sentenced to life as a beast of burden . . . and finally being given something no one else knew about. Something secret. Something he could keep. Something he could touch, and stroke, and talk to, speaking of dreams of someday; of spells to destroy his demons, living and dead.

Something of his *own*.

I grinned grittily into simoom.

"*Mine,*" I whispered triumphantly, with a powerful, peculiar virulence born of a chula's childhood; of the man-sized boy branded foreign, and strange, and stupid.

Who believed everything he was told.

"Mine," I said again.

This time Chosa heard me.

Pain.

It drove me to my knees.

Ground me into sand.

Fragmented wits and awareness and sense of self, stripping me of everything but fear and comprehension.

Chosa Dei was no legend. The story of his imprisonment at the hands of his brother-sorcerer, Shaka Obre, was truth, not a tale-spinner's unfounded maundering. Chosa Dei was everything they said he was.

Chosa Dei was *more.*

In my hands, the sword turned. The blackened tip—*no.* Not black. The tip was *silver.* Like steel. Clean, unblemished steel, tempered in Northern fires, cooled in Northern water, blessed by Northern gods.

Samiel?

Black light corruscated. Chosa Dei lashed out, swallowed another piece of me, climbed higher on my forearms. Halfway to my elbows.

The sword was aimed downward, twisting in my grip. Another sliver of Samiel showed his true colors.

And then I understood.

Chosa Dei was leaving. Chosa was deserting. Chosa was trading a Northern-made *jivatma* for a Southron-bred sword-dancer.

Freeing Samiel.

If the sword was empty of Chosa . . .

If.

But emptying Samiel would mean filling me.

With Chosa Dei.

If.

If I took him. If I let him come. If I let him have the body, forsaking the sword, would the sword then be strong enough to defeat him?

But with no one able to wield it.

Hoolies.

Guts cramped. Teeth ground. Eyes bulged and refused to close.

Black up to the elbows.

Muscles contracted. Down through the air, slicing wind and wailing. Black light flashed. Clean steel glittered. Shoulders locked as I thrust the sword tip into the sand. Then deeper. Driving it down, down. Scouring steel flesh.

Kneeling, I clutched the sword. Hung there, transfixed. Powerless before the sword. The sorcerer. Nothing more than the shell he wanted to fill.

"No," I mouthed.

Vision flickered. Went out. Blindly, I stared wide-eyed into the scouring wind.

"Tiger—" I husked. "Wizard's wooden tiger . . ."

The memory was distant. A small wooden sandtiger, shaped to catch the eye. It had been mine. Only mine. And I had petitioned it, begging it for power. For the means to escape.

Sandtiger, I had called it. Sandtiger I had made it.

In flesh: deliverance.

Children and men, eaten. More killed in the attempt. Then *I* had tracked it down. *I* had found its lair. *I* had leveled the spear and plunged it into the belly.

Screaming from shock and pain as the claws raked cheek. As the poison filled the body.

I had killed the sandtiger. He had nearly killed me.

Chosa was killing me.

The flesh would go on living, but the spirit, the soul, would not.

Vision flickered. Died.

Inside me, something laughed.

The inner eye opened. And Saw.

"Del!" I screamed. "Del—*Delilah*—Del— Do it! Do it! Don't let—don't *let*— Del— *Do what you have to do*—"

The inner eye *Saw.*

"Del—" I croaked.

Sandaled feet. Wind-whipped burnous. The glint of a Northern sword.

I couldn't see her expression. Maybe it was best. "Do it, Del— *do* it!"

Wind stripped her face of hair, leaving it stark and bleached and anguished. In her hands, *jivatma* trembled.

"—have to—" I managed. "You said—you could . . . you said . . . like Ajani—"

Del flinched. The wind screamed around us, hiding her face again.

Hoolies, bascha. Do it.

Deep inside, something laughed.

Chosa was *amused.*

"Like Ajani," I husked. "Quick. Clean. No risk to you— *Del*—"

Why was she taking so long?

The Northern sword glinted. It cut through the simoom's howling and sang its own song. Of nightsky curtains of color; of the hue of a banshee-storm, screaming through Northern mountains.

Too cold for me.

I was Southron-born.

My storm was the samiel.

From the sand I ripped the sword. Blackness glistened.

"Too late," I mouthed. "*—left it too late—*"

The wind stripped hair away. I saw her face once more: the architecture of bones framed in precise perfection; the smooth, flawless flesh; the contours of nose, of cheekbones; the symmetry of the jaw.

The warped line of her mouth, parting to open.

Delilah began to sing. Deathsong. Lifesong. The song of a sword-dancer's life. Of a Southron chula's passing from the world of free men he had tried to make his own.

Don't wait, bascha.

A new determination came into Del's expression. She cut off

her song in mid-note and raised the deadly *jivatma,* whose name was Boreal.

Even as I raised mine.

As Chosa made me do it.

"Samiel," she said.

But it was lost in the wail of wind.

Chapter 14

*W*ith his brother upon the pinnacle, staring across the vast expanse of the land they have created; marveling that they could, because they are sorcerers, not gods—

He frowns.

—or is it possible, he wonders, that gods are merely constructs of magic? A magic so deep and abiding and dangerous no one else has dared try it, before now; to summon it, collect it, wield it, shaping something out of nothing—

—unmaking what had been, to make what now exists.

He smiles.

—I have done this

He pauses. Rephrases.

WE have done this. Shaka and I.

He glances at his brother. Chosa Dei and Shaka Obre, twin-born, inseparable, indistinguishable from one another. Matched in will, in strength, in power. In so very many things, offering two halves of a whole; the balance of dark and light.

Matched in everything save ambition.

"What we have done—" Chosa begins.

Shaka smiles, completing it: "—is truly remarkable. A gift for the people."

Chosa frowns, distracted from triumph. "Gift?"

"Surely you do not expect them to PAY for this," Shaka says, laughing. "They did not ask it, did not request—"

"—except in petitions to gods."

Laughter dying, Shaka shrugs. "Men petition for many things."

"But this time WE answered. We gave them what they wanted."

"And now you want payment?" Shaka shakes his head. "How is it we are so alike, but so different? The power we have wielded is compensation enough." Shaka thrusts out an illustrative hand, encompassing the grasslands below. "Don't you see? We've made the land lush. We've made the land fertile. In place of sand there is grass."

Chosa's expression is grim. "We have answered their worthless petitions. Now they must compensate us."

Shaka sighs deeply. "With what? Coin? Goats? Daughters? Useless gems and domains?" He puts his hand upon his brother's stiffened shoulder. "Look again, Chosa. Behold what we have wrought. We have remade the world."

Chosa's face spasms. "I'm not so benevolent."

Shaka removes his hand from his brother's shoulder. "No. You've always been impatient. You've always wanted more."

Chosa stares down across the vast expanse of grass that had once been sand. He speaks a truth no one has ever before considered, but he has long suspected: "We are two different people."

Shaka's eyes widen. "But we want the same thing!"

"No," Chosa says bitterly. "No. You want THAT." And points to the grass.

"Chosa—don't you?"

Chosa shrugs. "I don't know what I want. Just—more. MORE. I am bored . . . look what we've done, Shaka. As YOU said: Look what we have wrought. What is there left to do?"

Shaka laughs. "We will think of something."

His brother scowls blackly. "We are very young, Shaka. There is so much time, so MUCH time. . . ."

"We will find ways to fill it." Shaka gazes at the grasslands below, nodding satisfaction. "We have given a dying people the gift of life, Chosa . . . I think I want to watch how they use it."

Chosa makes a dismissive, contemptuous gesture. "Watch all you like, then. I have better ways to spend my time."

"Oh? How?"

Chosa Dei smiles. "I have acquired a taste for magic."

Shaka's expression alters from indulgence to alert awareness. "We have always had magic, Chosa. What do you mean to do?"

"Collect it," Chosa says. "Find more, and collect it. Because if it was this easy to MAKE this, it will be more entertaining to destroy it." He sees the shock in Shaka's eyes, and shrugs offhandedly. "Oh, not at once. I'll let you play with it a while. I'll even let you keep part of it, if you like; exactly half, as always." Chosa laughs. "After all, everything we've ever had has been divided precisely in two. Why not the land we've just created?"

"No," Shaka says.

Chosa's eyes widen ingenuously. "But it's the way we've ALWAYS done it. Half for you, half for me."

"No," Shaka says. "This involves people."

Chosa leans close to his brother and speaks in a pointed whisper. "If any of them get broken, we'll simply make MORE."

Shaka Obre recoils. "We will do no such thing. They are PEOPLE, Chosa—not things. You are to leave them be."

"Half of them are mine."

"Chosa—"

"It's the way we DO it, Shaka! Half and half. Remember?"

Shaka glares. "Over my dead body."

Chosa considers it. "That might be fun," he says finally. "We've never done that before."

Now Shaka is suspicious. "Done what?"

"Tried to kill one another before. Do you suppose we could? Really die, I mean?" Excitement blossoms in Chosa's face. "We have all those wards and spells . . . do you think we should try to counteract them, just to see if we really could?"

"Go away," Shaka says. "I don't like you like this."

Chosa persists. "But wouldn't it be FUN?"

Shaka shakes his head.

Frustration appears in Chosa's eyes. "Why do you always have to be such a spoilsport, Shaka?"

"Because I have more sense. I understand responsibility." Shaka nods toward the grasslands. "We created this for people in need, Chosa. We sowed the field. Now we ought to tend the crop."

Chosa makes a derisive sound. "YOU tend the crop. I'm going collecting."

Shaka watches him turn away. "Don't you do anything! Don't you
hurt those people, Chosa!"

Chosa pauses. "Not yet. I'll let you play with your toy. For a while.
Until I can't think of anything else to do. By then, centuries will have
passed, and you'll be tired of it, too. Ready for something NEW." *He smiles.*
"Yes?"

Sound. No sight: I can't open my eyes. Sound only, no more; flesh
and bone won't answer my need.

"Curse you," she whispered. "I hate you for this."

It was not what I might have expected.

"I *hate* you for this!" A warped, throttled sound, breaking free
of a too-taut throat. "I hate you for what you have done; for what
you have become, in spite and *because* of this sorcerer—" She broke
it off abruptly, then continued in a more controlled, but no less
telling tone. "What am I to do? Let him have you? What am I to
do? Turn my back? Walk away? Refuse to acknowledge the worth
of the doing, the worth of the man, because it is easier *not* to do?"

I had no answers for her. But then, she didn't want them from
me. Had she known I could hear her, she wouldn't have said a
thing . . . except maybe those words designed to draw blood. Even
now, she tried to do that. All unknowing. Which more than anything underscored the strength of her anguish.

"If you could see what he has done . . ." Despair crept into the
tone. "If I could kill him, I would. If I could cut off his head as I cut
off Ajani's, I would. If I could use magic or whatever else it might
take to free you, *I would*—" Then, on a rush, expelling words and
emotions, "There are things I would say to you, could I do it, could
I say them . . . but we are neither of us the kind to admit weaknesses, or failures, because to admit them opens the door to more.
I know it. I understand it. But now, when I *need* to know who and
what you are . . . you offer me nothing—and I can't ask. I lack the
courage for it."

Deep inside, I struggled. But no words were emitted. Eyelids
did not lift.

"What am I to do?" she rasped. "I am weak. I am *afraid*. I am not the person I need to be to vanquish this enemy. I am not the Sandtiger."

And then a spate of muttered uplander, all sibilant syllables of twisty, foreign words strung together into a litany made to ward off that fear.

Silence. A hard, shattered silence. I wanted to fill it badly.

"You have warped my song," she declared. "You have reshaped all the words, and altered all the music."

Oh, bascha, I'm sorry.

"Please," Del said. "I have been so many things and sung so many songs, to make myself hard enough. To make myself strong enough. I am what I am. I am—not like others. I can't *be* like others, because there is weakness in it. But you gave me something more . . . you *make* me something more. You don't make me less than I am—less than I have had to be and *still* have to be . . . you make me more."

I wanted badly to answer, to tell her I made her nothing at all, but that she made *me* something; something better. Something *more*—

The tone was raw. "What am I to do? Kill you for your own good?"

Not what I had in mind.

Nor Chosa Dei, either.

Who stood once more on the overlook beside Shaka Obre.

Again, sound. The hissing sibilance of edged steel pulled from lined sheath. The sluff and grate of Southron sandals. The subtle beat of a soft-stepping horse approaching across the sand.

"So," she murmured quietly. "He comes to us after all."

Metallic clatter: bridle brasses, bit shanks; the creak of Southron saddle. A horse, protesting vaguely, reined to a halt.

"Come down," she invited. "I give the honor to you: you may draw the circle."

The answering voice was male, catching oddly on broken syllables. "Why do I want a circle?"

"Have you not come to challenge him?"

He didn't answer at once. Then, "He seems a bit indisposed."

"For the moment," she agreed. "But there is always me."

"I didn't come for you. At least—not to meet in the circle. Beds are much softer."

"A circle is the only place we *will* meet."

"Unless I beat you. If bedsport were the prize." Creaking leather again. "But that's not why I came."

"She sent you."

A trace of surprise underlay his tone. "You know about her?"

"More, perhaps, than she would like."

"Well." He cleared his throat, but the huskiness remained. "What has befallen him? Certainly not Nezbet . . . unless the Sandtiger has grown so old and careless even boys may defeat him."

Contempt laced her tone. "Nezbet didn't beat him. This was—" She stopped. "You wouldn't understand."

Bridle brasses clattered as the horse shook its head. "What I understand is that he hasn't been himself for some time. There are rumors in Iskandar, and even in Harquhal . . . tales that make good telling when men gather to drink and dice."

"*You* are undoubtedly the subject of such tales. How often are they truthful?"

He laughed huskily. "Ah, but even I have seen he's not the same. And he *isn't*, Del . . . but then, you never saw him in his prime."

"His *prime*." She was angry. "In his prime he was—*is*—three times the man you are."

"*Three* times." He was amused. "And as for being a man—as a woman judges a man—only you can say. I've never slept with him."

"Three times the man," she said coolly, "in bed—and in the circle."

The broken voice was dangerously mild. "And I've never slept with *you*."

"Nor will you," she retorted.

"Unless I win it from you."

The answering tone turned equally lethal. "Just like a man," she said, "to make a woman's body the issue instead of the woman's skill."

He dismounted, jangling brasses. "I know you have the skill. We danced together, remember? I was, however briefly, shodo to—" he paused. "—the *an-ishtoya?*"

"You served a purpose," she answered, avoiding the question. "That is all, Abbu."

Steps sloughed through sand. Paused beside my head. "Is he dead?"

"Of course not. Do you think I'm keeping vigil?"

The voice was very close. "I don't know what you might be doing. You're Northern, not Southron—*and* you're a woman. Women do odd things."

"He's exhausted. He's resting."

"He's *unconscious*, bascha. Do you think I can't tell?" He paused. "What's wrong with him?"

"Nothing."

"Is that why he looks half dead?"

"He's not."

The tone was speculative. "I was in Iskandar, remember? I was in the middle of the fury just like everyone else. Only I'm not a man for religious ecstasy." He paused. "Does the condition he's in have something to do with magic?"

Reluctantly: "Yes."

"I thought so," he said. "And it begins to make me wonder."

"Wonder what?" she snapped.

"The tribes think Ajani was the jhihadi."

"Yes. Because Ajani took pains to make it appear he was."

"But the Sandtiger took no pains at all, at anything, because it isn't his way. He just *does*." A single step nearer; the body knelt at my side. "What I'm wondering—now—is exactly how *much* he can do."

"Tiger is Tiger," she said. "He isn't the jhihadi, no matter what he says."

"*He* says he's the jhihadi?"

Silence.

Dryly: "Of course, he could be saying it just to try and impress you."

"No." Grudgingly. "He says my brother pointed at him."

"Your brother? What in hoolies does your brother have to do with any of this?"

"He's the Oracle."

Silence. Then, ironically. "Do I seem that gullible to you? Or is this a game you and the Sandtiger have cooked up?" He snorted. "If it is, I don't think it's working. Right now you have dozens of *very* angry warriors on your trail, not to mention ten or so sword-dancers hired by Aladar's daughter."

"Believe what you wish to believe." Sand grated as she shifted her position. "Will you draw the circle?"

"Not now." A husky chuckle. "You've frightened me badly, bascha. I don't dare a dance with you."

She said something in eloquent uplander. I opened my mouth to answer.

Chapter 15

Chosa Dei nods. *"You'll grow tired, Shaka. You'll grow bored, like me. And there won't be anything else to do, except start all over again."*

In counterpoint, Shaka Obre shakes his head. "I won't let you hurt those people."

"Puny, fragile toys."

Shaka, angry, lashes out. "Then go make your own! If you're so good at it, go make your own. Somewhere ELSE, Chosa. Leave my world alone."

"Your world! YOUR world? We made this together, Shaka."

"It doesn't matter. You don't want it anymore. I do."

Contempt warps Chosa's expression. "You don't know what you want."

"Neither do you, Chosa. That's part of your problem."

"I don't HAVE a problem. And if I do, it's you!"

Shaka Obre sighs. "Just go away. You're cluttering up my world."

"You'll miss me, if I do."

Shaka shrugs. "I know how to keep myself busy."

Abbu again. "What exactly did you *do* to him, Del?"

"You wouldn't understand."

"Tell me anyway."

"The story is very long."

"Tell me anyway. We have time."

"The others will come, and then where will we be? I can't dance against them all, and you *won't*."

He was amused. "Of course not. You think I'm one of them, after all."

"Aren't you? Why else would you come?"

"Curiosity."

"Greed, more like. Did she offer you enough?"

"She offered me a very great deal. I am something of a legend, after all."

"Panjandrum," she muttered.

"That, too," he agreed. "Now, as for the Sandtiger—"

Ice descended abruptly. "You would have to dance against me *first*."

"I know that, bascha. You've made that very clear." He shifted. "What did you do to him? And what did *he* do to make you risk his life?"

I struggled to open my eyes. Tried to speak. Tried to do *something* that told them I was alive, awake, aware.

Nothing worked.

—*Chosa Dei on the pinnacle, overlooking the grassy valley cradled by forested hills; sunlight glinting off lakes—*

"*I made this,*" *he says. "I could UNmake this—*"

Back.

"Hoolies," Abbu remarked. "You did all this by taking his *sword* away from him?"

"Not—precisely." Del's tone was a mixture of things: weariness, worry, reticence. "As I have said, there is much more to it. A long story."

"As *I* have said, bascha, we have time."

Del sighed. "I don't understand why you're doing this."

"Healing instead of hindering?" He laughed in his broken, husky voice; I'd given him that. "Because maybe I didn't hire on to catch him. Did you ever think of that? And even if I *did*, it's no challenge to capture a man in his present condition. Does nothing for the reputation. This is the *Sandtiger*, after all . . ." Abbu paused. "At least—it *was*."

"And will be again." A cool hand touched my forehead, smoothing back sweat- and sand-crusted hair. "It begins with his sword," she said finally. "A Northern sword. *Jivatma*."

Abbu grunted. "I know about them. And I've seen yours, remember? When we danced."

The fingers tightened briefly against my brow. I realized my eyes were held forcibly closed with a damp cloth binding. "There is more," Del said quietly. "A sorcerer. Chosa Dei."

Abbu's tone was incredulous. "Chosa Dei? But he's only a *story!*"

"Wards!" Chosa shrieks. "You put wards upon the land!"

"Of course I did," Shaka says quietly. "I didn't want you showing up one day, sick to death of boredom, and deciding—out of spite—to destroy what I made."

"YOU made!" Chosa bares his teeth. "WE made, you mean. It was both of us, Shaka—and you know it!"

"But only one of us wants to destroy it."

"Not destroy. Unmake," Chosa explains. "And if you like, we can RE-make it once we're done." He grins, reaching out to clasp his brother's shoulder. "It would be fun, yes? To unmake what we made, then remake it all over again. Only better—"

"I will not release the wards."

Chosa's fingers tighten rigidly, digging into Shaka's shoulder. "You will. You have to. Because if you don't. . . ."

The implication is clear. But Shaka shakes his head.

They stand again upon the pinnacle, overlooking the lush green grasslands they had, centuries before, made out of barren wasteland. Five generations have labored on the land, knowing fertile soil, water in plenty, abundant crops. Shaka's benevolent blessing has allowed them the freedom to blossom and grow, knowing little hardship.

And now Chosa Dei wants to unmake it. Out of boredom.

"No," Shaka says. "The land stays as it is."

"Divide it," Chosa counters. "Half is mine, after all; you couldn't have done any of it without my portion of the power."

Shaka's expression is distasteful. "I've heard all about you, Chosa. You do destroy. You kill. You—"

"I unmake," Chosa clarified. *"And remake, yes?"* He smiles. *"We learn from our mistakes. Each generation is an improvement upon the last; don't you think we might do better this time?"*

Shaka shakes his head.

Rage contorts Chosa's features. *"Lift the wards, Shaka. Enough of this folly. Lift the wards or I will unmake them, and then I'll unmake YOU."*

Shaka laughs. *"I think you're forgetting something."*

"What am I forgetting?"

"I have magic, too."

"Not like mine," Chosa whispers. *"Oh, not like mine. Trust me, brother. Test me, thwart me, and you will suffer for it."*

Shaka assesses his brother. He shakes his head very sadly. *"You weren't always like this. As a child, you were cheerful and kind and generous. What happened? Where did you go wrong?"*

Chosa Dei laughs. *"I acquired a taste for magic."*

"Then magic will be your bedmate." Shaka no longer smiles nor assesses; his decision is made. *"Try my wards, Chosa, and you will find out how powerful they are. And how powerful I am."*

Chosa scoffed. *"You have been here for two hundred and fifty years, stagnating. While I have been in the world, collecting all the magic."* He pauses. *"Have you any idea AT ALL how powerful I've become?"*

Shaka smiles sadly. *"Yes. I think I do. And that's why I can't let you 'unmake' what I have labored to protect."*

"You must share," Chosa appeals beguilingly. *"The way we've always shared."*

"Not in this."

Rage convulses Chosa's features. *"Then you will see what I am, yes? You will see what I can do!"*

"Probably," Shaka agrees. *"Since I can't change your mind."*

"And you will suffer for it!"

Shaka looks down upon the lush grasslands. *"Someone will,"* he says sadly. *"You. Or I. Or them."*

"THEM!" Contempt is explicit. *"What do I care for them? I can make as many of them as I need."* He bares his teeth. *"But I don't need them, yes?"*

"Yes," Shaka says. *"You do. Though you haven't the wit to see it."*

Chosa Dei raises one hand. *"Then let the testing begin."*

Shaka Obre sighs. "It already has. But you haven't the wit to see THAT, either."

One finger stabs toward the valley below. "I will remake it into hoolies!"

Shaka shrugs. "And I will restore it. One day."

"Not if you're destroyed. Not if YOU'RE unmade!"

"Someone will," Shaka says. "If not me, someone else will. Hoolies can't last forever."

"I'll make it last," Chosa threatens.

Shaka merely smiles. "Do try," he suggests. "You're ruining a perfectly beautiful day with your danjac's braying."

Chosa's expression is malignant. "You'll see," he says. "You'll SEE what I can do."

Shaka Obre strokes a languid hand through dark hair. "I'm still waiting."

Chosa stares. "You mean it," he says finally.

"Yes."

"But you're my brother."

"You're not mine. My brother would never have done this. BECOME this." Shaka's dark-eyed stare is harsh. "You must have unmade your brain when you were playing all your games."

"I'll send you to hoolies!" Chosa shrieks.

Shaka's smile is wintry. "After I send you."

"Shaka!" I screamed. "*Shaka—*"

Hands closed over my wrists, clamped down, forced me back against the blanket.

"Shaka!" I cried. My voice was a mockery.

Another set of hands joined the first. "Hoolies," Abbu breathed.

"Do you see?" Del pressed spread fingers against my chest, speaking quietly. "Lie still, Tiger. Shaka isn't here. Shaka's never been here."

"The wards," I rasped. "Don't you see? Chosa destroyed them. He *did*. Shaka's magic didn't hold—Chosa was too powerful—" A bone-deep shudder wracked my body. "He unmade the *wards*—"

"And thereby imprisoned himself; remember?" Del asked. "That's how the story goes."

Breathing was difficult. My lungs felt constricted. Abdomen contracted as I labored to draw in breath, then expel it. "I don't know the story. I only know the truth. I was *there*—"

"There!" Del's fingers tightened.

"—bascha . . . gods, *Del*—" I tasted blood in my mouth.

"He's delirious," Abbu commented. "Remember how he was when his horse kicked him in the head?"

"—bascha, I can't see."

"You will," she promised. "You're not blind. But too much sand got into your eyes . . . they need to heal, that is all."

"I have to see . . ." I tried to pull my hands from Abbu's grip, and could not. "Let go. Abbu—take your paws off me!"

He did. I dragged the cloth from my eyes and realized what Del meant at once. My eyes were gritty, itchy, and very sore. Sunlight made them water.

But I forgot about my eyes. What I wanted was my hands.

Flat on my back, I thrust them into the air and inspected every inch of them. Then expelled a gusty breath of relief. "He's gone," I murmured dully. And then to myself, bewildered, afraid to say it aloud: *No, he's not. He's IN me. I can feel him.*

I sprang up, hurling myself against their arms; fell back as my knee collapsed. I was weak, trembling, undone. "Hoolies," I choked. "Am I him?"

A thin line of moisture dotted Del's upper lip. She scraped it away with a forearm. "But you said he was gone." She exchanged a glance with Abbu Bensir. "Do you believe me now?"

His face was ashen. "Sandtiger . . ." But he let it trail off, as if not knowing what to say.

"Am I him?" I repeated. And then: "Where's my sword?"

Del pointed. "There."

I looked. "There" was not so far. Unsheathed, it lay in the sand. Sunlight bathed charred steel.

"Black," I blurted in relief. "Half of it, now . . . but that's better than none of it. Better than—" I let it go, slumping back against the blanket, and stared again at my arms and hands, lifting them against the sun. Turned them this way and that. "*Not* black," I murmured.

No. Pallid white. Like they'd been left too long in the snow. But the hair was all burned off, and the flesh was flaky and scaled. From elbows to fingertips. The nails were all discolored, as if they'd been frozen.

Del drew in a deep breath. "You asked me to kill you," she said. "You *begged* me to kill you."

I stared at my hands, working blue-nailed fingers in distracted fascination. "Something tells me you didn't do it."

"No. I did something else. I knew it might kill you, but since that was what you wanted anyway . . ." Wearily, she scrubbed hair back from her face. Tension had drained her of color, of life. "I sang a song, and then I knocked your sword away. Chosa hadn't taken all of you yet, just some. I thought it worth the risk."

I frowned, chewing my lip. "And by separating me from the sword . . ."

Del nodded. "I hoped that because part of Chosa remained in the steel, he would have to let you go."

I avoided the truth by denying it aloud. "It could have gone the other way. Chosa could have jumped to me."

"Yes," she agreed. "And had I judged that accomplished, I'd have done to you what you begged me to do."

Memories were not clear; at least, not *my* memories. They were all jumbled up with Chosa's. "What was it?" I asked warily. "What was it I asked you to do?"

"Cut off your head," she answered. "Like I did with Ajani."

"Hoolies." Abbu again.

Which distracted me. "What are you doing here?" I asked. "Making time with Del?" It hadn't been beneath him before.

Fleetingly, he grinned. "No, but now that you mention it—" He waved it away. "Nezbet appeared at my campfire, mouthing nonsense about a white-haired woman sword-dancer." He shrugged. "I knew right away who he meant. And since I was well ahead of the others, I sent him on his way and came on myself."

"Doesn't Nezbet have any idea who I am?" Del asked. "You'd think Tiger was the only one involved, the way that boy talked."

"That boy" was probably all of two or three years younger than Del.

Which made me feel all the older.

"Nezbet's a fool." Abbu rubbed a hand through gray-frosted black hair. "Like most Southroners, he bears little respect for women—except as bedpartners. Then again, neither do I." He grinned at Del; she'd changed a lot of his opinions, but he wasn't about to admit it. "So if he heard anything about a woman being involved, he dismissed it as unimportant." He shrugged. "So Tiger's taking the blame for Ajani's murder."

"People *saw* me," she declared. "Have they all gone sandsick? Hundreds of them saw me cut off his head!"

"Ah, but there's a story going around that you're a Northern afreet conjured by Tiger to distract the jhihadi's attention long enough for Tiger to kill him." He laughed. "I told you about the stories."

"Afreet!" Del was astounded. "*I'm* not a spirit!"

Abbu leered pointedly. "I know *that*."

It made me irritable. I shifted against the blanket, aware of aches and itches; the protests of a body driven beyond its final reserves. "Bascha—"

But what I'd intended to say wisped into nothingness.

"Tiger?" she asked.

No, bascha.

Chosa.

Chapter 16

Dawn. Three of us gathered as the sun broke over the horizon. Two of them would watch. I would do more than that.

Del's frown was clearly worried, drawing pale brows together. Boreal glinted in her hands, as Abbu's blade in his. Only *I* lacked a weapon; mine lay on the ground.

"You don't—" But she broke it off.

"Yes, I do," I told her.

"Why?" Abbu asked in his half-throttled, broken voice. "If it's that dangerous . . ." His tone was a mixture of disbelief and disgust, that he could give any of it credence. Underscored by reluctant acknowledgment: he, like so many others, had seen me call fire from the sky.

"Because I can't just leave it here," I told him. "Believe me, if I could I would . . . but Del's told me time and time again that it's too much of a risk to take. If someone *else* wound up with this sword . . . someone innocent . . ." I shrugged, suppressing a shiver born of morning chill. I still wore only a dhoti, wishing I'd pulled my other burnous from the saddle-pouches. But there had been other things to concern us.

"Or someone Chosa Dei could unmake, then *re*make for his own uses," Del added. "But—I wish . . ." She sighed, raking loose hair from her eyes. She had yet to confine it in a tightly woven plait. It spilled across her shoulders, tumbled down her spine, lin-

gered at her breasts. Snagged on the rune-broidered leather tunic
that bared so much arm and leg.

Chosa Dei had seen her. Deep in Dragon Mountain, when he'd
asked her for the sword that could break imprisoning wards set by
Shaka Obre. Chosa *remembered* her.

With effort, I shut him out. "You know what to do," I said
harshly. "Don't wait for me to invite you . . . I can't—I don't
think—" I stopped, sucked air, tried to speak more evenly. "I don't
have the strength to hold him off. Not this time." But I couldn't tell
her why.

"Tiger—" But she bit her lip on the rest.

I flicked a glance at Abbu. "If she can't—or won't—you'll have
to be the one."

His dark Southron face, older than mine, was oddly gaunt and
tight. Silently, he nodded.

I bared my teeth in a grin. "Look at it this way, Abbu—you'll finally be able to say you really are the best."

He raised his Southron sword. He managed a ghost of a smile.
"Any way it comes."

I didn't look at Del. I bent and picked up the sword.

—*nothing*—

"Tiger?" she ventured, and I realized I'd been standing there for
gods' knew how long, waiting for something to happen.

I considered things. "My knee hurts," I said. "My eyes itch like
hoolies. I'm still in need of a bath." I arched eyebrows. "Nothing
seems to have changed.

"Is he—in there?"

I looked down at the sword in my hands. Samiel was blackened
to the halfway point of the blade. My hands on the grip were blue-
nailed, pallid white, still cracked and scaly, but not a drop of blackness touched them.

Nothing on the outside. How much was on the *inside*?

"He's in there," I confirmed, offering part of the truth. "But—I
think he's hurt."

"Hurt?" Abbu blurted. "First you expect me to believe there's a
sorcerer *in your sword,* and now you say he's *hurt?*" He snapped his
own back into its sheath, harnessed diagonally. "I think you've

made this up. I think there's no truth in this at all, and you are *using* it to keep from dancing against me. Because you know you will lose."

"Oh, I'd lose," I agreed. "I've only got one knee."

He scowled. "And how long will you use that as a crutch, Sandtiger?"

"It's true," Del said quietly. "What would you have me swear on, that you will believe me?"

Abbu grinned. "Oh, bascha—"

"Never mind *that*," I interjected. "Like I said, I think he's hurt." I scowled down at the sword. "I can't tell you why. It just feels different. Sort of—*bruised*." I glared at both of them, knowing how it sounded. "It feels a lot like I do: a horse ridden hard and put away wet."

"Poetic," Abbu said dryly. He rubbed idly at the scarred flesh of his throat, where my wooden sword had nearly killed him so many years before. "So, is this how we leave it? You on one knee, with a *bruised* magical sword . . ." He let it go, laughing. "I should challenge you anyway."

Del stiffened. We both knew what she intended to say, except Abbu cut her off with a raised hand.

He eyed her thoughtfully as he lowered it. "We never finished the dance we began in Iskandar."

"And you won't," I snapped. "Knee or no knee, *I'll* dance. I'm tired of you taking on Del in my place."

The smile was as expected; his unspoken rejoinder was implicit.

"Well?" Del asked curtly, wise to the ways—and thoughts—of men. "How is this to be settled?"

Abbu and I stared meaningfully at one another for a long moment. Then he ended the contest. "Hoolies," he said affably, "there's nothing in this for me. Not enough coin, anyway." He patted the coin-pouch hanging from his belt. "The shodo always said money couldn't buy friendship—or rivalry. When the Sandtiger and I dance our final dance, it will be for another reason."

"*More* money?" I gibed.

"Undoubtedly," he drawled, turning away toward his horse. "If I were you, either of you, I would not go to Julah."

"Why?" Del asked. "If there is a need—"

He overrode her. "There is a need *not* to." All pretense was dismissed; Abbu was no longer amused. "Yes, I was asked to track both of you, catch you, and bring you back to Iskandar. Because Sabra knows exactly who killed her father. Unlike all the tribes, she doesn't care about the jhihadi. She just wants revenge."

"And you're working for her," I said.

"Me work for a woman?" He grinned. "What do you think, Sandtiger? You were a Southroner, once."

It got to me, as he intended. *"Once?"*

Abbu swung up into the saddle and turned his horse to face us. "Before you crossed the border, so to speak." He gestured negligently, indicating Del and Samiel. "Northern sword. Northern woman." His grin was sly and crooked. "But one might be worth the trouble."

I scowled at him. "Get the hoolies out of here."

"Wait," Del said.

He reined in his horse, eyebrows arched.

"Are you working for her?" Del asked quietly.

"You should know the answer," he told her. He hooked his head in my direction. "Tiger knows. Ask *him.*"

Del waited till he was gone. "Well?"

"No," I answered.

Her eyes narrowed. "How can you be certain? You yourself have said you are not friends, and so has he. How do you know he isn't lying?"

"He isn't working for her. Because if he were, he'd do exactly what he'd hired on to do: invite me into a circle, beat the hoolies out of me, then haul me back to Iskandar."

Del's expression was odd. "Do you think he can beat you?"

"Right now, with this knee, Rhashad's *mother* can beat me." I hefted the sword. "Believe me, if he'd hired on—woman tanzeer or no—he'd finish the job. Abbu Bensir always finishes what he starts."

Del watched me maneuver my knee, extending it to pop it, then bending it back again, testing flexibility. "How are you? How are you *really?*"

It had nothing to do with my knee. The woman knows me well, but not well enough.

I expelled a breathy half grunt, half laugh. "How am I? I don't
know. Sore. Tired. Itchy. Smelly. Beat to death inside and out." I
turned gingerly, hobbling back toward my blanket spread next to
the tiny cairn. "Pretty well bored with the whole situation."

Del followed, offering no assistance as I levered myself awkwardly down to sit. Without thinking I set the sword aside—it was,
at the moment, quiescent—and began to untie knee wrappings.

She had not yet resheathed. "What you said . . . what you
asked. Before." She sounded half ashamed, half concerned. "You
asked if you were him."

I shrugged negligently, unwinding ragged fabric that had once
clothed a borjuni. "Just a little confused." With wrappings gone,
the knee was fully displayed. I prodded it carefully with a forefinger, checking for puffiness and pain. "Not so bad," I observed.
"Should be mostly healed in a day or two. Then Abbu, when he
comes calling, can have the dance he wants."

Del sighed and squatted, finally sheathing her sword. "You
would be foolhardy to undertake it. Better or not, your knee will
not support you in a true dance . . . and why are you so certain he
will come back? He could have challenged you now, and had a better chance. Why do it later, when you are a tougher opponent?"

"Because he will. I would." I cast her a glance, smiling. "This
has nothing to do with woman tanzeers. This has to do with something that's lain unsettled between us for years."

"His throat." She touched her own.

"That's part of it. But so's pride. So's reputation." I smiled. "The
South isn't big enough for *two* sword-dancers like us."

"So one of you will kill the other."

"Only if one of us insists. Myself, I think I could stand it if he
beat the hoolies out of me and made me yield . . . I don't see much
good in dying in the name of pride. *Dancing*, yes; it's been a long
time coming. As for Abbu?" I shrugged. "I don't know. I just know
he'll be back. He only gave up for now because he *wasn't* working
for Sabra, and because he doesn't want anyone to think he won the
dance because I wasn't in proper condition."

"*You* think."

"I know. These things are important, Del . . . Abbu Bensir and

I have spent most of our respective careers hearing stories about one another. And since *he* was here before I was, it grates on him harder. Nobody who's been the premier sword-dancer in the South wants to give up any part of that honor . . . then I came along." I arched my brows. "Of course, he had full warning. When I nearly crushed his throat with a wooden sword."

Del's smile was wry. "Will it be like that for you?"

"You mean, will I be annoyed when someone younger and better comes along?" I shrugged. "By the time that happens, I'll be an old man. It won't matter any more."

Del laughed aloud. "Old man," she jeered, "it has *already* happened."

"Ah, but you'll never be acknowledged," I countered, "not that I'm admitting you're better. *Good*, yes—but better?" I shrugged. "Anyway, you're a woman. No Southron sword-dancer will ever acknowledge you."

"You do. Abbu does." She frowned. "I think. Either that, or he's only saying he does because he thinks sweet words will win my regard and make me want to share his bed." She tucked hair behind one ear. "Men do that."

"Because it works." I grinned as she glared, then began to rewrap my knee. "Too bad he didn't leave us his horse."

It startled her. "Did you think he would?"

"Maybe. If the other sword-dancers are still only a day behind, he could have waited for them, then gone on back to Iskandar."

"They are not a day behind. Sword-dancers *or* tribes. They are perhaps *two* days, because of the simoom." Del frowned. "Don't you remember?"

"Remember what?" I asked warily.

She stroked hair out of an eye. "You turned the simoom. You stopped the wind, stopped the sand . . . then sent it on around us."

"But—I thought . . ." I frowned, trying to remember. I recalled *wanting* to do all of that, but I couldn't remember accomplishing it. There had been too much of Chosa Dei clamoring at my soul. "Well, good," I said finally. "It'll help us get ahead a little, if the simoom has set them back."

"Besides, had Abbu left us his horse, it would have made him a fool."

That caught my attention. "You think Abbu Bensir could never be a fool?"

Del assessed me a moment. Her face was masked, but something—was it amusement?—lurked in her eyes. "I suppose he could be," she said finally, with careful solemnity. "You and he are much alike."

"Now, bascha—"

She expressed overly elaborate surprise. "But you are. He is older, of course—though how much I couldn't say—" Hoolies, she *was* amused! "—and he is undoubtedly wiser, because of experience . . . but there are remarkable similarities." She caught up her hair and began to divide it into three sections. "But probably only because you were trained by the same shodo."

"I'm not anything like Abbu! You heard what he said: 'Me work for a woman?'—as if it might contaminate him." I glared at her wide-eyed expression. "He'd like nothing better than to get you into bed, because that's all he thinks you're good for. Like most Southroners."

Del continued braiding. "Like you were, once."

I scowled. "I'm still a Southroner. Just because I went traipsing off across the border to help you out . . ." I frowned at my knee. "Maybe there are some things different about me now, thanks to you, but I'm still a Southroner. What else would I be?"

Del's tone was soft as she tied off her braid. "You don't know, remember? The Salset never told you."

Vigorously, I knotted the wrapping on my knee. Changing the subject. "Our best bet is to go on to Quumi and buy another horse. Then we can head on down to Julah."

"Julah! But Abbu just said—"

"Abbu doesn't know what I know." I moved off my blanket, began to roll it up. "Nobody knows what we—what *I*—know."

"We?" Del rose, resettling harness straps. "If you mean *me*, enlighten me . . . I don't know what you're talking about."

The "we" hadn't meant Del. But I couldn't tell her that.

"Let's get going," I said. "We're burning daylight again."

Chapter 17

"It isn't much, is it?" Del rode double behind me, which was hot in the warmth of the day. "When you said a trade settlement, I thought you meant something significant."

"It used to be." I aimed the stud toward the lath gate attached precariously to the shattered adobe wall. "Quumi was once one of the largest settlements in the South, bursting at the seams with caravans and merchants. But the Punja came along and swallowed it, and the caravans began going another way. Soon most of the merchants left. Quumi never recovered."

"But this isn't the Punja."

"Close enough." I waved a hand in a southerly direction. "Half a day that way. Anyway, everyone got so used to the alternate route that Quumi was mostly forgotten. It's never been what it was."

It never would be, either. What once had been a thriving settlement was now a shadow. Lath instead of adobe. Powdered dirt in place of brick. The narrow streets were clogged with windblown drifts of sand, and most of the buildings had surrendered to decades of the scouring desert wind. Quumi was tumbled together like ancient oracle bones, spills of brickwork here and there, drifts of powdery dust, slump-shouldered dwellings with all the edges rubbed off. Quumi's profile was round and soft: bone-colored, sun-baked adobe chewed through like a loaf full of weevils.

We approached from the north, paused at the broken city gate to flip the so-called guard a copper, then rode through.

Del was horrified that we had to pay to enter. "The wall is broken," she said. "But five paces down the way anyone can *walk* through . . . why pay to ride through a dilapidated gate?"

"Because you just do." I thought it answer enough. Anyone who knew what Quumi had been ignored its disrepair. It was a game everyone played.

Through the broken gate into the city itself: the stud scuffed across scoured hardpack, rattling pebbles, and into the labyrinth. Quumi was a warren of tumbled buildings, but I knew my way around. I headed straight for Cantina Row.

"It's sort of—gray," Del observed, as we passed into the sand-choked narrow street.

"We're at the edge of the Punja."

"But even the sky is gray."

"That's dust," I told her. "Punja dust mixed with dirt. It's very fine, like powder . . . if you breathe, it blows. See?" I pointed at the powdery dust rising from the stud's hoofprints.

"It looks like ash," she said. "Like a fire cairn gone to ash . . . or a funeral pyre."

The sun-bleached, wind-tattered awnings drooping from flimsy lattices and framing poles above deep-cut windows and doors lent but a trace of tired color to the overall gray-beige of the city. They fluttered faintly in a halfhearted breeze. Sunlight striped pale walls, making blocky, patched patterns against lopsided brickwork. With the hand-smoothed outer coating of adobe scoured away, drifted tufts of long-dead grass were exposed. The stud tried to grab a mouthful on the way by.

"So long as we can find a horse—and a bath—I don't care what it looks like."

"Does this place have water?"

"Yes. But we'll have to pay for it."

"We already paid at the gate."

"That was the entry toll. There's also a water toll in Quumi. It's how the place survives."

"But—to charge for *water!* What if you have no coin?"

The stud tangled a hoof in a fallen awning, stumbling and snorting. Sun-rotted cloth tore, freeing him. I dragged his head up. "You make shift where you can."

"It is abysmal," she declared.

"Undoubtedly," I agreed, looking ahead to my favorite cantina.

Del figured it out as soon as I halted the stud. The building was much like the others: the outer shell of the adobe egg had cracked, baring the yolk of lopsided bricks. A bleached, patched orange-brown awning dangled from the sole remaining pole, obscuring most of the doorway. The aroma of wine, aqivi, and other liquors drifted into the street.

She frowned, reining in. "What are we doing *here?*"

"I know the owner."

"He or she?"

"He, of course. This is the South." I waited. "Are you getting off? Or do I have to climb down the hard way?"

"Once you explain just why we have to stop *first* at a cantina, before buying water or a horse."

"There is a room for rent."

"How long are we staying?"

"Overnight, at least. I want a bath, a good meal, a bed. You may join me, if you like." I thought it only polite to extend an invitation; Del hates to be taken for granted.

She slid off the stud. "I thought you wanted to buy a horse."

"First a drink. And a bath. Then food. Then a bed. In the morning comes the horse." I kicked free of the stirrup and hoisted my fragile knee across the saddle. "What I want most to do is sit quietly for a while in the shade, out of the sun, musing contentedly over aqivi—or wine, if there's no aqivi—and then I'll tend to the rest."

Del smiled as I somewhat gingerly allowed the street to take my weight. Everything I owned ached. "Go in," she said kindly as I bit my lip on an oath. "I will see to the stud."

I wasn't about to remonstrate, even if her behavior was out of the ordinary. Usually she argues against stops at cantinas. "Around there." I flopped a hand in the proper direction. "It isn't much of a stable, but there's shade and water."

Del took the reins. "Will I have to pay for it?"

"I told you: I know the owner." I paused. "He only charges me half."

"Half," Del muttered, and led the stud around the corner.

When she came back, I was sitting on a rickety three-legged stool in the rickety cantina, slumped forward over the rickety table with my chin in blue-nailed hand, elbow planted so as to prop me up. In my other hand was a bone-beige, unglazed clay cup of aqivi, mostly drunk. Altogether I was feeling rather rickety myself, in a numb, groggy, twitchy sort of way.

There was no one else in the cantina. Del, fighting her way through tattered awning, stopped short upon seeing me—and no one else—and stared musingly around the room.

"Well," she said finally, "I knew you needed a bath, but maybe I've just gotten used to you and it's worse than I thought."

"You know," I opined, "you're not particularly good at that."

Pale brows arched. "Good at what?"

"Making up jokes." I hoisted the clay up to my mouth, swallowed more aqivi, set it down again. "But then, that's never been a quality I looked for in a woman."

Pale brows came back down. And knitted. "How much have you had?" She moved carefully through a thicket of rickety stools and tables. "I haven't been gone *that* long."

I considered it. "Long enough," I told her eventually. "Long enough for me to find out Akbar's dead."

She paused at my—our?—table. "Akbar was your friend the owner?"

"Yes." I drank more aqivi.

"I'm sorry," she said inadequately.

"Yes." The cup was empty. I put it down, picked up the ceramic jug—the lip was chipped and cracked—and splashed liquor in the general vicinity of the cup. The pungent tang of very young aqivi filled my nose. "Have some aqivi, bascha."

She glanced around. "Water will be fine . . . is there anyone here?"

"Water costs three coppers a cup. Aqivi's cheaper."

"I don't *like* aqivi." Still she looked around, peering into the gloom. "Are we alone here?"

"Akbar's cousin is somewhere in back." I waved a hand.

"Is he that borjuni who charged me ten coppers to stable the stud, then five more for water?"

"I told you aqivi's cheaper."

"You can hardly give aqivi to a horse." She hooked a stool with a foot and dragged it out. "Of course, with his temperament, you might as well." She eyed my jug. "Are you going to drink all of that?"

"Unless you want to help me."

Del assessed me a moment. "Are you all right?"

"I'm tired," I told her. "Tired of finding out my friends are dying. Wondering if I'm next."

A brief smile curved her mouth, then died away. "I'm sorry your friend is dead. But I think *you're* in no danger."

"Oh? Why not? My line of work is rather risky, upon occasion."

She picked at the splintered table with a fingernail cut short for bladework. "Because you are much like your horse: too stubborn to give up."

"Right now I'm not stubborn. Just a little drunk." I swallowed more aqivi. "You'll say I should have eaten first, and be right. You'll say I should quit now, and be right. You'll say I'll feel better in the morning after a good night's sleep, and be right." I stared balefully at her over the thumb-printed rim of the clay cup. "Is there anything you're ever *wrong* about?"

Del stopped picking splinters. "I was wrong about offering your services to Staal-Ysta."

I brightened. "So you were."

"And wrong about you, period." She eyed the cup darkly, but said nothing about aqivi souring my temper. Of course, she didn't have to. "When we first met, I disliked you intensely. And you deserved it. You *were* everything I thought you were. A typical Southron male." Her mouth quirked. "But you improved with time. You're much more bearable now."

"Thank you."

"Mmm." She glanced around again. "If Akbar's cousin does not arrive very soon, I'm going to help myself to the water. For free."

She wouldn't. She'd leave the money. "Here." I held out the cup. "It'll wet your throat."

"I don't want it."

"Have you ever had it?"

"I tried it once."

"A whole cup? Or just a swallow?"

"One swallow was enough."

"You didn't like me either, at first. You just said so."

Del sighed, scratching wearily at a shoulder. "Sit here and drink, if you like . . . I think I will gather the botas and fill them."

I waved a hand. "There's a big well in the market square. That way. They'll charge you."

"Three coppers a cup?" Del rose, kicking back her stool. "And how much for a bota?"

I thought about it. "Don't know. Prices fluctuate. Depends on how good you are at dickering." I eyed her: tall, lean, lovely. And incredibly lethal. "If you went about it right, you could probably save yourself a few coppers."

"Probably," she said dryly. "But I don't think submerging my dignity for a few coppers' worth of discount is a fair exchange."

I filled my mouth with aqivi as Del walked out of the cantina.

Because I had no answer.

Sundown. And no candles, lamps, or torches because you had to pay for them. At the moment, I saw no need; orange-pink-purple sunset tinged the lath-screened cantina pale violet.

The hand was on my shoulder. "Come on," she said calmly. "Time you were in bed."

I looked blearily up from my plate of inedible mush masquerading as mutton stew. "Can I finish my dinner first?"

"I think it would finish *you*." The hand changed shoulders from left to right. Now each resided in a strong, unfeminine grasp that cut through burnous, underrobe, harness straps, and flesh to the sore muscles beneath. It felt wonderful. "You can eat more in the morning, once you have killed the dog."

A bizarre image. "What dog?"

"The one biting you. Or are you biting *it?*"

Oh. Now I understood. "—gods, bascha—don't stop—"

"This?" She kneaded more firmly. "You are tight as wire."

"—hoolies . . . *that feels good—*"

"I have left our things in the hideously expensive room that will probably fall down on our heads before sunrise. The bedding is ready. Shall we put you in it?"

"Right now I just want to sit here while you do that."

Her right hand moved to my neck. Cool fingers squeezed sore tendons, biting through rigidity. "Up," she said only.

I stood up unsteadily, felt her slip beneath an arm, let her take the weight my knee didn't want to carry. "I'm terribly drunk, bascha. Incredibly, horrifically drunk."

"I know that. Here. This way . . . please don't fall down. Your dead weight would be more substantial than most."

"Dead weight . . ." I echoed. "Like Akbar."

Del didn't say another word. She just walked me into the tiny little, hideously expensive room that probably *would* fall down on our heads before sunrise, and helped lever me down onto bedding. It smelled of horse and sweat and human flesh in dire need of a bath.

I didn't lie down. I hitched myself up against the wall and stared blearily through the violet gloom of sunset to the pale-haired Northern woman who knelt before me. In silence I unhooked awkwardly from harness straps, then set aside the sheathed sword.

"He was a good friend," I told her. "When I left the Salset, Quumi was one of the first places I came. I was sixteen years old, with hands and feet too big for the rest of me. I'd been a chula for all of my life. I didn't know how to be free."

Del said nothing.

"I didn't even know how to talk to people. Oh, I knew the *language*—I mean, I didn't know how to speak to them. I'd been taught to say nothing, and answer only if an answer was required." I grimaced. "I went into four cantinas before this one, hoping to find some kind of work so I could buy a meal . . . in all four I just stood there inside the door, saying nothing, hoping someone would speak to me, because I couldn't speak first. If I did, I'd be beaten . . ." I shifted against the wall. "No one said anything to me. Oh, they talked *about* me—insults, jokes, you know—but no one spoke to me. So I couldn't ask for work. Couldn't ask for food."

Del's face was taut.

"So when I came here to this cantina, the fifth, I expected much the same. Without understanding why. And I got it. Until Akbar spoke to me." I smiled a little, recalling. "He asked me if I wanted a drink. I thought he meant water: I nodded yes. Instead, he gave me aqivi."

Del's eyes were strangely bright.

"I'd never had it before. Only water. But I was thirsty. And free to drink what I wanted. So I drank it *all*. As fast as I could." I rubbed a hand across tired, grit-scored eyes. "I was drunk almost immediately. Akbar saw it, but instead of throwing me out into the street, he took me to a room. He let me sleep it off." I flopped a hand on the bedding. "This room."

Del swallowed tightly.

"Every time I came here, he put me up. At half price. And gave me all the aqivi I wanted." I sighed, peering up at the woven lath roof trailing strips of bark and dried desert grass. Through the cracks and gaps I could see the purpling night. "One time I came, he said he had a horse. A stallion. No one could ride him, he said. He tried to kill everyone who climbed into the saddle. No one wanted to buy him. Akbar didn't want to feed a horse who couldn't be used. So he said if I wanted him, I could have him." I smiled lop-sidedly. "He said I was hard-headed enough to beat the flea-bitten, jug-headed, lop-eared Punja-mite of a horse at his own game."

Silence.

"He threw me off four times. Then he gave in. I guess he decided anyone stupid enough to keep trying wasn't worth the effort."

Del smiled. Her voice was husky. "But he still makes the effort. Occasionally."

"And sometimes he even wins. Except I climb back on again." I sighed and scrubbed muzzily at a stubbled, grimy face. "I'm tired. I'm drunk. I need to sleep . . . but I don't think I can."

"Lie down," she said quietly.

"Bascha—"

"Facedown," she said, cutting off an unnecessary protestation of too much aqivi for bedsport. Which was just as well; who wants to admit such a thing? "You're tight as wire, Tiger. And much too close to snapping. Let's see if I can loosen the tension a little."

Facedown, as ordered. Head resting on interlaced hands. It felt good just to be still.

Even better when she touched me.

Neck. Shoulders. Shoulder blades. The layers of rigid muscle knotted much too tight for comfort. Then up and down the spine, pressing and popping carefully, thumbing the tension away. At the bottom of the spine, deep in the small of the back. Then up again to the neck, tucking just behind the ears.

She laughed as I growled contentment, murmuring incoherent thanks.

But the laughter died. So did the vigor of her efforts. She smoothed the wavy brown hair left too long on the back of my neck. "I'm sorry," she said softly. "It is never easy to lose those who are special to you."

Especially when there are so very few to start with. Sula. Akbar. My shodo, twelve years dead. Even Singlestroke, a sword, who had nonetheless been very special.

All dead. Even the sword.

The only one left was Del.

Chapter 18

I awoke to familiar, repeated noise: the metallic, ringing scrape of whetstone against blade. I smelled oil, stone, steel.

And Del.

I rolled over, cursing tangled bedding, and peered squinty-eyed through morning. Not dawn; beyond it. The sun was well and truly up, striking slatted patterns of mote-fogged light and shadow through the lath roof.

Which reminded me of something. "It's still up," I observed. "The roof."

Del didn't look. "Yes," she agreed tightly, working the whetstone in intense concentration.

Combed damp hair was loose on her shoulders. The creamy tunic beneath was water-marked, but drying. "You bathed," I observed.

"Yes." Scrape. Slide. Ring. Hiss. "Earlier, I went to the bathhouse."

"Akbar would bring—" I broke it off abruptly. Del flicked a glance at me, then returned her attention to her work. "I feel better," I told her, stripping off bedding. "You worked all the kinks out of my neck and shoulders. Of course, there's still my head . . ." I let it go. She wasn't listening. "What's the matter?"

Scrape. Slide. Hiss. "Nothing."

"It's not 'nothing.' What is it?"

She shook her head.

"If it's because I got drunk yesterday—"

"No."

I thought it over. "Something I said? I mean, when I passed out. . . ?"

"You didn't pass out. You just went to sleep. I know the difference. And, no, it's nothing you said; you talked, yes, but I could understand none of it, so I can't accuse you of impropriety."

Progress. I'd gotten more than a shrug or a single sentence. "Then what's bothering you?"

She stopped working the steel. Displayed the blade. "There."

I looked. In morning light, it glinted. Salmon-silver steel, warded by tangled runes indecipherable to anyone but Del. "Bascha—"

"There," she repeated. And put her fingertip on the blade, profaning it with skin oil, but I knew she'd wipe it clean.

I saw it then. A smudge. A blemish. A patch of darkness. "I don't understand—"

"I knocked your sword from your grasp with mine," she said evenly. "I struck aside your infested blade with my *jivatma*. And this is the result."

Infested. Interesting term.

Appropriate, too.

I pursed lips, then chewed one. "It could be something else."

"No." She began to work the steel again. "No, it is not 'something else.' It is Chosa Dei's handiwork. He has tainted my *jivatma*."

"You don't know—"

"I know." Her eyes were icy as she glared at me over the blade. "Do you think I can't tell? Look at your fingernails, Tiger. Look at your hands and arms. Then tell me again it could be 'something else.' "

I looked, as she suggested. My nails had darkened from blue to black. Not Chosa Dei's black, though he had caused it, but the blackening of deep bruising. Of nails peeling up from fingers, readying to fall off. The hairless flesh of hands and forearms was still scaly and flaky. Still an odd corpse-white.

I shivered, then sat up rigidly, throwing aside bedding.

Squinted at the light. The headache was not so bad after all . . . but I needed to bite the dog back. At least on the end of his nose. "I don't know what to tell you. How long have you been working the whetstone?"

"Long enough to know it isn't doing any good." She gazed at me in despair. "Tiger—my *blooding-blade*—"

"I know." I did. More than she believed. "Bascha, I don't know what to tell you. Can a spell take it off? Maybe a song?"

Mutely, she shook her head. Damp hair fell over her shoulders. The fine locks next to her face were mostly dry. Such pale, lustrous silk . . . and so alien to the South.

I cleared my throat. "You can't be certain it won't go of its own accord."

"I have told you. Chosa Dei wants this sword. He has always wanted this sword. It is the key to his power. If he had it—if he tapped into this sword—he would have all the power he needs to overcome you and break free. Do you see?"

I saw. I also felt. I knew very well why Chosa Dei wanted—and needed—Boreal.

"Then we had best be on our way." I got up carefully, favoring my knee, and limped with slightly more steadiness into the common room. "I need a cup to start the day, and a bath—" I stopped and turned back. "Can you wait long enough for me to take a bath and get a shave?"

Del had risen also. She stood in the doorway, one hand holding aside the thin gauze curtain. The other held her sword. "For that," she said gravely, "I will wait through the day and all of the night."

"Thank you very much," I said sourly. "I don't think it will take me *that* long."

"Perhaps not," she agreed politely. "But you are very dirty."

So I was. But I didn't bother to fashion a properly biting retort. If Del could tease me, however lamely, about needing a bath, she wasn't as upset as I feared.

Then again, maybe it was just that I *was* that filthy.

Bath first. Then the aqivi.

The dog would have to wait.

* * *

The price for bath and shave was, of course, exorbitant, like everything else in Quumi. But worth it, which is why they can ask for the moon. Even though it nearly emptied my coin-pouch, I felt very much the new man as I walked out into the street again, stroking freshly shaved jaw approvingly, and resettled the fit of the harness. Now all I needed was a cup, and I'd be ready to go.

Except for one thing.

She sat atop a dark bay mare, holding the stud's reins. She wore a white burnous; pale hair was braided back. In harness. With pouches loaded and attached to respective saddles.

I nearly gaped. "A *mare?*"

Del shrugged. "It was all there was."

"In all of Quumi, there are no geldings for sale?"

"None. I asked. I *looked.*"

"Did you explain about the stud?"

"The stud's behavior is no concern of mine. That is for you to control." She smiled sweetly. "Surely you understand how a male might learn to curb his appetites."

"Hoolies, bascha—"

"She's not in season."

I swore. "Are you sure?"

Del glared. "Do you see him mounting her?"

A point. "But if she comes in, he'll lose his mind."

"Had he one to lose." She shifted in the saddle. "Will you come along?"

I snatched the stud's reins. "Come along *where?* Do you even know where we're going?"

She frowned. "You said something about Julah."

"Yes. Julah. Aladar's daughter's domain."

"But she's in Iskandar. At least, she was. We can stay ahead of her—and out of danger—if we leave *soon.*"

"I thought you said you'd wait all of the day and all of the night so I could have my bath."

"You've had it. I can tell. My *nose* can tell." Del grinned briefly as I scowled. "Shall we go?"

I flipped reins over the stud's neck and climbed aboard. "Why are you in such a hurry?"

"If finding Shaka Obre will rid my sword of Chosa Dei's taint, I would prefer to do it today rather than tomorrow."

"You don't even know where he is."

"Neither do you." She paused. "Do you?"

I aimed the stud toward the southern gate, hidden by slumping, sloppy gray-beige buildings, and flapped a hand. "Somewhere out there."

Del made a sound of derision. "*That's* promising."

"Then suppose you lead."

In grave silence, she reined her bay mare around in front of the stud. Who noticed. As was intended. "Like so?" Del asked innocently.

"Never mind," I muttered.

The stud was less than happy when I made him take the lead once again. I had a brief but firm discussion with him, and convinced him to let *me* be the guide.

I didn't think we could go all the way to Julah walking backward.

Around midday, we stopped. In silence we stared grimly at the expanse of crystal-flecked desert before us. The border was subtle, but clearly defined. This side, we were safe. Cross it, and we were at risk.

But we'd been at risk before.

Del's mare bobbed her head. The stud answered with a rumbling, deep-chested nicker that threatened to rise to a squeal. I kicked him high on the shoulder. "She's not interested," I said.

Del merely smiled. Then lifted her chin toward the Punja. "How many days to Julah?"

"Depends on the Punja."

"I know that. How many did it take us before?"

"I don't know. Who can remember back that far?" I slapped the stud's thick neck and reined him aside. "Besides, we met with a few delays, remember? Like the Hanjii and their Sun Sacrifice . . . that ate up a few days. Recovery even more."

"And Elamain," Del recalled. Naturally, she would. "We rescued Elamain's caravan from borjuni. Then we took her to that tanzeer—"

"Hashi."

"—who wanted to make you into a eunuch." Del glanced side-long at me. "I remember that."

So did certain parts of _me_. "Then we stopped in Rusali—"

"—and met Alric and Lena and the girls." Del paused. "Only two, then. But she was expecting what became the third—"

"—and the last time we saw them—all of four days ago—she was expecting _another_ child."

Del's mouth pulled sideways. "I hope this one's a boy. Maybe then she can rest."

"Seems to me Lena didn't much mind having Alric's babies." I prodded the stud's questing nose with a sandaled toe. "Don't even think about it."

"And there was Theron," Del recalled.

Whom I had killed in the circle.

"And Jamail," I countered.

Del's face tautened. "And Jamail," she echoed. Then she looked at me. "Are you _really_ this jhihadi?"

"How in hoolies should _I_ know?"

She stared at me. "But you said Jamail pointed at you. You swore on your _jivatma._"

"He did. I did. I'm not making it up."

"Then maybe . . ." She frowned. "No. It can't be. It is impossible."

"What? That I might be a messiah?" I grinned. "I can't think of a single man better suited to the job."

Her look was withering.

"All right. I know it all sounds silly. But it's true, Del—he really did point at me."

"So when are you going to change the sand to grass?"

I snickered. "As if I could."

"The jhihadi supposedly can."

"Maybe he can."

"And you _did_—" Del stopped short. Her face went red, then white. She turned to stare wide-eyed at me. Her expression was particularly unnerving.

"What?" I asked sharply. _"What?"_

She swallowed tightly. Her voice was mostly a whisper. "You changed the sand to *glass*."

Del and I spent several moments staring at one another, trying to deal with new thoughts and implications. Then I managed a laugh. It wasn't my usual one, but enough to get by with. "Hoolies, bascha—wouldn't it be funny if it turned out this desert prophet got the word wrong?"

Even her lips were white. "What do you mean?"

"That this jhihadi won't restore the South to lushness, but change it instead to *glass*."

"But . . ." Del frowned. "What good would glass be?"

"It means everyone can afford to put it in their windows." I grinned. "Glass, grass—who can say? I think it's all a bunch of nonsense."

"But—" She chewed a lip, then gave it up, sighing. "I think it would indeed be a foolish thing if you were the man."

It stung. "Why?"

She eyed me thoughtfully. "Because you are a sword-dancer. Why should you be more?"

"You don't think I'm good enough? You don't think I could do it?"

"Be a messiah? No."

"Why not?"

"You lack a certain amount of delicacy. Diplomacy." She smiled. "Your idea of dispensing wisdom is to invite someone into a circle."

"The sword is a very *good* dispenser of wisdom."

"But jhihadis aren't sword-dancers."

"How do you know? You didn't even know what one was until I explained it to you."

"Because—I just know."

"Not good enough." I whopped the stud between the ears. "Not now, flea-brain . . . no, bascha, really—I want an answer."

She shrugged. "You're just—you. You have your good points. A few here and there, tucked in behind all the bluster. But a jhihadi? No. Jhihadis are *special*, Tiger." She watched me pop the stud again as he tried to sidle into the mare. "Jhihadis don't have trouble dealing with horses."

"How do you know? Iskandar himself got kicked in the head, remember?"

"And died ten days later, or so you told me." Del eyed me speculatively. "How many days ago was it that *you* got kicked in the head?"

"See? That's proof—I got kicked, too."

"No," Del countered. "*Real* proof would be if you died because of it."

I scowled. "What kind of jhihadi would I be if I died before I could do anything?"

"Well, if you really were supposed to change the sand to *glass,* rather than grass . . ." Del's expression was guileless. "How many days again?"

I kneed the stud into motion. "Never mind that. Let's just go."

"Four?" Del fell in behind. "That leaves six days to go."

"And I suppose you're going to *count!*"

Her tone was exquisitely tranquil. "I like to be prepared."

Hoolies. What a woman.

Depending on your perspective.

Chapter 19

"*I*t makes my skin hurt," Del said.

Eventually, I roused. "What?"

We rode mostly abreast. She glanced across at me. "Are you asleep?"

"No."

"*Were* you asleep?"

"No. Just thinking."

"Ah." She nodded sagely. "Your version of deep thought resembles sleep in others. Forgive me."

We were still horseback. Still riding south out of Quumi. It was mid- to late afternoon. We'd eaten on the move but an hour or so before, and I'd washed mine down with wine. The motion of the stud, walking monotonously onward, combined with food, wine, and the warmth of the day—not to mention boredom—had proved overwhelming.

Which meant I *had* been asleep, if only briefly; actually, it was more like a momentary nap caught between one blink and the next. When you spend as much time as I do atop the back of a horse, you learn to sleep however—and whenever—you can.

But you don't admit it to Del.

I scowled. "*What* makes your skin hurt?"

"The South. The Sun. The Punja." Del twitched her sword-weighted shoulders. "I remember what it was like, before. When the sun was so bad, and I got so sick." She rubbed a cupped hand down one burnous-sleeved arm. "I remember very clearly."

So did I. Del had nearly died. So, for that matter, had I, but the sun hadn't been quite so ruthless to my copper-hued Southron hide. Oh, it had tried its hardest to burn me to bits, but I'd survived. Del very nearly hadn't.

"Well, we don't have to worry about it this time," I observed comfortably.

She arched one brow. "Why not? We could come across the Hanjii again, could we not? And they could turn us loose once again in the desert with no mounts or water."

Comfort evaporated. I grunted disagreement. "More likely this time we'd wind up in the cookpot."

"Oh. I'd forgotten that." Del, squinting, peered across the sand. "It all looks exactly the same."

"It's hot. Dry. Sandy." I nodded. "Pretty much the same."

"But *we're* not." She glanced sidelong at me. "We're both a little more experienced than the last time."

I knew what that meant. "And older?" I showed her my teeth in an insincere grin. "Believe me, bascha, now that we're back where it's warm, I feel a whole *lot* younger."

Her assessive expression very plainly suggested I didn't *look* younger. The problem was, I couldn't tell how much of it was part of the gibing, and how much was unfeigned.

"Thirty-six is not so old," I growled.

Del's smile was too sanguine, and therefore suspect. "Not if you're thirty-seven."

"To *you*, maybe, it's old—you're not long out of infancy. But to *me*—"

"In sword-dancer years, it is." She had dropped the bantering. "You are of an age now that many never see, if they live their lives in the circle." Her tone was very solemn. "You should seriously consider becoming an *an-kaidin*, a—" she frowned, breaking off. "What is the Southron word?"

"Shodo," I said sourly. "I don't think I'm ready for that."

"You have been a professional for many years. You have learned from the best. Even on Staal-Ysta, they honored your skill—"

"No, they didn't. They just wanted another body." I reined the stud away from the mare. "I'm not made for that, Del. Being a shodo takes a lot more patience than I have."

"I think if you had a student, you would find patience in abundance. If you knew that what you taught the *ishtoya* could mean survival or death, you would come to know how much you had to offer."

"Nothing," I said grimly. "What kind of shodo would I make with Chosa Dei in my sword?"

"After it was discharged—"

"No, bascha. I'm a sword-dancer. I just do it, I don't teach it."

"You have taught *me*," she said. "You have taught me very much."

"I nearly killed you, too. What did you learn from that?"

"That you are a man with immense strength of will."

I stared. "You're serious!"

"Of course I am."

"Bascha, I nearly *killed* you. Once on Staal-Ysta, and once at the oasis, after I slaughtered all the borjuni."

"But each time you held back." She shrugged. "On Staal-Ysta, you denied a newly awakened *jivatma*, freshly keyed and wild for the taste of blood, the chance to make a first kill. At the oasis, you denied Chosa Dei. A weaker man with a lesser will would have lost himself on either count. And I would no longer live."

"Yes, well . . ." I shrugged uncomfortably. "That doesn't make me a shodo."

"I do not insist," she said quietly. "I only point out you have another choice."

Something pinched my belly from the inside. "Or is it that you've accomplished your goal of killing Ajani, and now you're looking ahead to a different way of life?" And different people in it?

Del's mouth tightened. "We spoke of this before. There is nothing else for me. I am exiled from the North, and I could never be a shodo here. Who would come to a woman for teaching?"

I shrugged. "Other women might."

Blue eyes were smoky. "How many Southron men would allow their women that freedom?"

"Maybe it would be women who had no men to placate."

Del made a sound of derision. "There are no women in the South willing to risk losing a man, or the chance of winning a man's interest, by apprenticing to me."

No. Probably not.

"Which leaves us," I said, "right where we started out. Why don't we just accept what we are, and not worry about the future?"

Del stared into the distance.

I waited. "Well?"

"There." She pointed. "Is that something moving?"

I followed her finger and saw what she meant. A dark blotch against the horizon. "I don't—wait. Yes, I think you're right . . ." I stood up in my stirrups, peering over the stud's ears. "It looks like a person."

"On foot," Del declared. "Who in his right mind would *walk* through the Punja?"

"We did," I said. "Of course, you were sandsick, so you weren't *in* your right mind—"

"Never mind that," she snapped. "Let's not waste any more time talking about it. He—or she—might not have any to spare."

Del sent her mare loping across the desert, kicking dust into the air. The stud snorted loudly, then went after her.

There was nothing better to do. So I let him go.

It turned out to be a he, not a she. And Del had been right: he didn't have any time to spare. By the time I reached him, Del was off her mare and kneeling beside the man, helping him suck down water from one of her botas.

She glanced at me over one dusty, burnous-clad shoulder. She said nothing; she didn't have to. Del has a considerable vocabulary in simple body motions, let alone expressions. All in all I thought censure uncalled for—I'd gotten there not long after she had, if without her haste—and scowled back at her to tell her the silent reprimand was unappreciated.

Whether she cared was entirely up to her.

The man wore a plain burnous of tattered, saffron-hued gauze, and a matching underrobe. No sword. He was perhaps in his early twenties, but dust caked his face, so it was hard to tell. Sweat—and maybe tears?—had formed disfiguring runnels.

Now, as he sucked at the bota with eyes closed in the pure physical bliss of a great need fulfilled, water spilled down his chin. It splashed onto his grimy, threadbare burnous, drying quickly; before Del could say a word, he thrust a hand up to cup his chin and catch the runaway water.

A Southroner born and bred in habits as well as color.

The desperate thirst initially slaked, he opened his eyes for the first time and peered over the bota at Del. Brown eyes dilated as he acknowledged several things, among them her gender.

He sat bolt upright. Then saw me beyond her. He stared again at her, disbelievingly. And back again to me. He husked a single word: "Afreet?"

I snickered. Del glanced over her shoulder at me, frowned bafflement at my amusement, then turned back. That she didn't understand the tongue was clear; she'd have said something, otherwise. But then I hadn't expected her to. The language he spoke was an archaic Desert dialect, unknown to anyone outside the Punja. I hadn't heard it for years.

I briefly debated the merits of lying. It would be amusing to tell him she *was* a Southron spirit, but I decided against it. The poor man was dry as bone, nearly delirious; the last thing he needed was me convincing him he was dead—or near death—by agreeing with him.

"No," I told him. "Northerner."

He sat very still, staring at her, drinking in Del as if she were sweeter than bota water.

Which amused me briefly, until I thought about how that amusement could be considered an insult of sorts. Del was worth staring at. Del was worth dreaming about. Del was even worth looking upon as salvation: she *had* given him water.

I grinned. "You've impressed him."

Del hitched a self-conscious shoulder; she's never been one for trading on her looks, or talking much about them. Down South, for the most part, those looks got her in trouble, because too many Southron men wanted a piece of her for themselves.

"More?" she asked briefly, offering the bota again.

He took it by rote, still staring. And drank by rote, since the first thirst had been satisfied; now he drank for pleasure instead of need.

And, I suspected, because her actions suggested it.

The stud bent his neck, trying to reach the mare Del had left groundtied a pace or two away. He snorted gustily, then rumbled deep in his chest. Tail lifted. The upper lip curled, displaying massive teeth—*and* his interest in getting to know the mare better.

The last thing I needed—the last thing *anyone* needed—was the stud developing an attachment to Del's mare. And since a stallion outweighs a man by a considerable amount, it takes firm methods in dissuading him of such interest. Before someone got hurt.

I punched him in the nose.

Bridle brasses clanked as the head shot skyward. I took a tight grip on the reins, managed to retain them, managed to retain *him*— and avoided placing sandaled feet beneath the stomping hooves.

Del, of course, cast me a disapproving glance across one shoulder. But she wasn't on the end of an uncut horse taking decided interest in a mare; *her* mare, I might add. If she'd bought a gelding in Quumi, we'd all be a lot better off.

Meanwhile, the bay mare nickered coy invitation.

Also meanwhile, the young man on the ground was getting up from it. At least, partway: he knelt, then placed one spread-fingered hand over his heart, and bowed. All the while gabbling something in a dialect even *I* didn't know.

And then he stopped gabbling, stopped kneeling; stood up. He pointed westerly. "Caravan," he declared, switching back to deep-Punja Desert.

I squinted. "How far?"

He told me.

I translated for Del, who frowned bafflement. Then I invited him to be more eloquent.

He was. When finished, I scratched at brown hair and muttered a halfhearted curse.

"What?" Del asked.

"They were bound for Iskandar," I told her. "Him and a few

others. They hired a couple of guides to see them across the Punja. These so-called guides brought them out here, and left them."

"Left them," she echoed.

I waved a hand. "Out there a ways. They didn't hurt anyone. Just brought them out here, took all their coin and water, and left." I shrugged. "Why waste time on killing when the Punja will do it for you?"

Del's eyes narrowed. "Had he no mount?"

"Danjac. He was thrown, and the danjac deserted." I grinned. "They do that a lot."

Del looked at the young man. "So, *he* came looking for help."

"He figured out pretty quickly they'd been led a merry dance. Off known tracks, far from any markers . . ." I shrugged. "He just wanted to find some help, someone who knew the way to a settlement, or an oasis. He's hoping to trade for a mount and botas." Again, I shrugged. "Meanwhile, the others are with the wagons."

Del glanced skyward, squinting against the glare. "No water," she murmured thoughtfully. Then glanced assessively back at the young man, scrutinizing him.

I knew what was coming.

I also knew not to protest; she wasn't really wrong. I sighed gustily, putting up a forestalling hand. "I know. *I* know. You want to go out there. You want to take him back to his caravan, then lead them all to Quumi."

"It's the closest settlement."

"So it is." I stared into the west. "Might as well, I suppose. I mean, the Salset picked *us* up out of the desert and saw to it we recovered."

"Don't sound so ungrateful."

"I'm not ungrateful. Just thinking about how much time this will eat up. *And* what we may find once we get back to Quumi."

Del frowned. "What?"

"Sword-dancers," I answered. "And, for all that, religious fools like this one."

Eyes widened. "Why do you call him a religious fool? Just because he believes in something you do not—"

I cut her off, forestalling a lengthy discussion on the merits of religion. "He *is* a fool," I declared, "and I have every right in the world to say so."

She bristled. "Why? *What* gives you the right—"

"Because any man who worships me has *got* to be a fool."

That stopped her in her tracks. "You?" she ventured finally. "Why do you say that?"

"I'm the one he and the others are going to Iskandar to see."

She blinked. "What *for?*"

"Seems they heard the Oracle's stories about the jhihadi." I shrugged. "They packed up their lives and headed north."

Del's mouth opened to protest. But she said nothing. She stared at the religious fool a long moment, weighing what I'd said against the man himself, and eventually sighed, rubbing a hand across her brow.

"See what I mean?" I asked. "You think he's a fool, too."

Her mouth twisted. "I will admit that opinions can be led astray, but that doesn't make him a fool for believing in a man whose coming is supposed to improve his homeland."

"Right," I agreed. "Which means the least I can do is get him and his people to Quumi. It seems like a properly jhihadi-ish thing to do, wouldn't you say?"

"Will you tell him?" she ventured.

I grinned. "What—that I'm a fraud?"

Del's expression was sour. "He would probably figure that out for himself."

"I thought you'd see it my way." I patted the stud's neck. "Well, old son, looks like we'll be carrying double again."

Del hitched a harness strap. "Why not put him with me? Together he and I weigh less than *you* and he."

I looked at the religious fool who gazed at Del raptly. "Yes," I agreed sourly. "He'd probably like that."

Del frowned.

"Never mind," I muttered. "Let's just get going."

Chapter 20

His name was Mehmet. Mehmet was a pain in the rump.

He didn't start out that way. He was what he was: an exhausted, thirsty young man badly in need of help. Trouble was, we'd offered that help, and he'd taken us up on it.

Now, I'm not really as ungracious as I might seem, some of the time. I admit I sound that way upon occasion, but the truth of the matter is, I'm soft-hearted enough to get myself in trouble. So here we were, helping Mehmet, who wanted to help his companions.

Who wanted to help them *now*.

Trouble was, now meant now, the way he looked at things; while Del and I looked on it as an in-the-morning thing, since the sun had disappeared, and we saw no great benefit from riding through the night.

Mehmet, however, did.

Del, busily unrolling a blanket beneath a dusky sky, frowned across at me as I did the same with mine. "What's he saying *now?*"

"What he said a minute ago. That we can't wait till morning while his aketni is in need."

"His what?"

"Aketni. I'm not exactly sure what it means, but I think it has something to do with the people he's traveling with. Sort of like a family, I think . . . or maybe just a group of people who believe in the same thing."

"A religious sect." Del nodded. "Like those ridiculous *khemi* zealots who shun women."

"They carry things a bit far. Mehmet doesn't seem to feel that way." I glanced at him, standing expectantly between us with hands clutching the front of his grimy burnous. "Matter of fact, about the *last* thing Mehmet would shun is women, I think—he's staring at you again."

Del scowled blackly.

We didn't bother with a fire, since there was no wood on the crystal sands, and the charcoal we carried with us was for emergencies. We had plenty of supplies for a trip across the Punja, and while we were not enthusiastic about travelers' tedious fare, we knew it would get us where we were going. So Del and I settled in for the evening. The sun was down, the twilight cool; what we wanted now was to eat and sleep.

Mehmet, seeing this, started in yet again on how we should not stop, but ride on to his aketni. Where, he announced, we would be well recompensed for our services.

"How's that?" I asked dryly. "You said the guides stole all your money."

His chin developed a stubborn set. "You will be paid," he declared, "in something much better than coin."

"I've heard *that* before." I unrolled my blanket the rest of the way, shaking out folds and wrinkles. "Look, Mehmet, I know you're worried about them, but the best thing to do is get some sleep. We'll start out again at first light, and reach them by midday. *If* you remember your distance right." I shot him a baleful glare. "You *do* remember it right, don't you, Mehmet?"

"That way." He pointed. "If we left *right now*, we would be there before morning."

"We're not leaving *right now*," I told him. "*Right now*, I'm going to eat something, digest it in calm, quiet dignity, then go to sleep."

He was offended. "How can you go to sleep when my aketni is in need?"

I sighed and scratched at claw scars. "Because," I said patiently. "I'm not part of your aketni, whatever the hoolies it is."

Mehmet drew himself up. He was a slender, dried out stick of a young man, with very little fat beneath his flesh, which made his desert features sharper than ever. Punja-born, all right—he had the prominent nose that reminded me of a hawk, but his brown eyes lacked the predator's piercing impact.

He stood rigidly between Del and me, glaring down at us both. He was young and full of himself, if in a more subtle way; Mehmet wasn't as obnoxious as a cocky young sword-dancer trying to earn a reputation, such as Nezbet, but he had that mile-wide streak of youthful stubbornness that eclipsed the wisdom of experience and age. To him, Del and I were simply being selfish—well, maybe only me; I don't think he looked on Del as anything other than a wonder, and wonders aren't selfish—and purposely difficult.

Behind him, the night sky unrolled its own version of blanket bedding, spangled with glittering stars. A sliver of new crescent moon glowed overhead.

And Mehmet continued to glare, although I noticed he stared with more virulence at me. Trust Del to escape the wrath of a male firmly smitten by her beauty.

"It is an *aketni!*" he hissed. "A *complete* aketni!"

Del heard his tone, even if she missed the context. "What's he so upset about?"

"Nothing new," I explained. "He's singing the same old song." I sat down on the blanket, automatically settling my knee in the position least likely to stress it, then looked up at Mehmet. "I don't know what a complete aketni *is,* let alone what it means. So why don't you just spread out that spare blanket, settle in for the night, and worry about it in the morning?"

He stood so rigidly I thought he might break. But he didn't. He wavered eventually, then collapsed to his knees, bowed his head as he spread one hand over his heart, and began mumbling in the dialect even I didn't understand.

"That again," I muttered.

Mehmet stopped mumbling. He appeared to be applying tremendous self-control. "Then may I borrow a horse?" he asked quietly. "And water? *I* will go now; you may come in the morning."

It crossed my mind that if we let him take a horse and water, *we* wouldn't need to go. But that gained us nothing we hadn't encountered before: two people on one horse, with less water than ever. "No." I dug through pouches to flat, tough loaves of traveler's bread, and two twisted sticks of dried cumfa meat. "Just bide your time."

Abruptly, Mehmet turned to Del, who, arrested by his fervor, stared warily at him as he spewed out an explanation to her, along with a request for her mare and some water.

"She doesn't understand," I told him. "She doesn't speak your language."

He considered it a moment. Then began again in dialect-riddled Desert.

Del glanced at me. "If I say no, he won't try to steal her, will he?" She as much as I wanted nothing to do with riding double and walking again.

Smiling, I repeated Del's question to Mehmet, who was horrified. He leapt to his feet, then fell down to knees again, clutching his tattered burnous as if he meant to rend it, and gabbled on in something akin to a reproachful dialogue, except parts of it were addressed equally to Del, to me, and the sky.

"I don't know." *Before* Del could ask. "But I'm guessing we've offended him."

"Oh." She sighed and reached into the pouch to dig out her share of the evening meal. "I'm sorry for that, but if he's so horrified, he probably won't try for the mare."

"Better the mare than the stud." I chewed tough bread while Mehmet muttered prayers. "Do you think he'll do that all night?"

Del's expression was perplexed as she stared at him. "If he is *so* worried—"

"No."

"If they are in danger—"

"They aren't. They're probably pretty thirsty, but they'll survive the night. These are deep-Punja people, bascha . . . going without water for a day or two won't kill them. They know how to adapt. Believe me, if you know the tricks—"

"Mehmet is afraid—"

"Mehmet just thinks he'll get in trouble for taking so long." I stuffed too much dried cumfa into my mouth, and chewed for a very long time.

Del clicked her tongue in disgust.

Bulge-mouthed, I grinned.

"Jamail used to do that," she remarked. "Of course, he was considerably younger, and didn't know any better."

"See there?" I glanced at Mehmet, who glumly unrolled the spare blanket. "Just like a woman—always trying to remake a man. The thing *I* can't understand is, if she liked him in the first place, why does she want to change him?"

"I didn't like you," Del answered coolly, as Mehmet stared at me in blank-faced incomprehension; was he really *that* young? Or just slow to assert himself in the way of a man with a woman?

I chewed thoughtfully. "You've done your share of trying to change me, bascha."

"In some things, I've even succeeded." Del bit off a small piece of cumfa from her own dried stick and ate it elegantly.

I indicated her with air-jabs of my stick. "See there?" I said again to Mehmet. "What kind of women do you have in your aketni?"

Mehmet gazed at Del. "Old ones," he answered. "And my mother." Which said quite a lot, I thought.

I hefted a bota. "And I suppose they've done their best to change *you*, too."

He shrugged. "In the aketni, one does as one is told. Whatever is cast in the sands—" He broke it off. "I have said too much."

"Sacred stuff, huh?" I nodded. "Women'll do that to you. They twist things all around, make it ritual, because how else can they convince anyone to do some of the things they want? Old, young— doesn't matter." I slanted a glance at Del. "Even Northern ones."

Del chewed in stolid silence.

I looked back at Mehmet. "About this recompense . . . anything worthwhile?"

Mehmet pulled cumfa from the pouch. "Very valuable."

I arched a skeptical brow. "If it's so valuable, how come the 'guides' didn't relieve you of it?"

"They were blind." Mehmet shrugged. "Their souls have shutters on them."

"And mine doesn't?" I beat Del to it. "Given that I have one, that is?"

Mehmet chewed cumfa. "You are here." Which also said something.

I shifted irritably, rearranging my knee, and sucked down more wine. "Well, we'll see to it you get to Quumi. It won't take long—you're not that far off the track. Maybe your guides didn't really mean for you to die."

Mehmet shrugged again. "It doesn't matter. Their futures have been cast."

I quirked an eyebrow. "Oh?"

But Mehmet was done talking. He ate his cumfa in silence, washed it down with water, lay down on his back on the blanket, and stared up into the sky.

Murmuring again. As if the stars—or gods—could hear.

I kinked my head back and stared up into darkness. Wondering if anyone did.

I roused when the stud squealed and stomped. I was on my feet and moving before I remembered my knee, but by then it was too late. Swearing inventively, I hobbled toward the stud.

Mehmet turned as I arrived. He held the saddle pad. When he saw my expression—and the bared sword—he fell back a step. "I meant only to help," he protested. "Not to steal, to *help*. By readying him for you." He placed a hand across his heart. "First light, you said."

It *was* first light, but just barely. More like false dawn. But I was willing to give him the benefit of the doubt; if he'd really meant to steal a horse and ride out quietly, he'd have taken the mare. He knew that already, having ridden with us the day before.

Del, too, was up, folding her blanket. Pale braid was loose and tousled, flopping against one shoulder. "We can eat on the way."

I scrubbed grit from eyes and face, turning back toward the bedraggled encampment. The blade glinted dull black in the weak light of a new dawn. A little more sleep would have been very welcome; dreams had awakened me on and off all night.

"Come away from him," I told Mehmet. "He's surly in the morning."

Del snickered softly, but forbore to comment.

Mehmet came away with alacrity, glancing over a shoulder at the thoroughly wakened stud, and knelt to refold his blanket. I bent, picked up harness, slid the sword into scabbard. And cursed as a fingernail caught on the leather lip and tore.

It didn't hurt so much as implied it. Blackened nail loosed itself from cuticle and peeled away entirely, vacating my finger. It left behind the knurled bed of pinkish undergrowth.

I wavered on my feet.

Del came over, inspected the "injury," looked into my rigid face. "It's a *fingernail*."

"It's—ugly."

"Ugly?" She stared, then laughed a short, breathy laugh of disbelief. "After all the wounds you've had—not to mention the gutting I nearly gave you on Staal-Ysta—*this* bothers you?"

"It's ugly," I said again, knowing how it sounded.

Del caught my wrist and pushed the back of my hand into my range of vision. "A fingernail," she repeated. "I think you've done worse shaving!"

"You're enjoying this," I accused.

Del let my hand go. A smile stole the sting. "Yes, I think I am. I find it very amusing."

I rubbed the ball of my thumb across the ruined bed of index fingernail, and suppressed a shudder. I don't know why, but it made my bones squirm. Also weak in the knees—and since one was *already* weak, I didn't need the help.

"Let's go," I said crossly. "Mehmet's aketni is waiting."

Del snickered again as I turned away. "*Now* he wants to move swiftly."

"Never mind," I grumbled, and knelt to roll my blanket.

Del went back to her own, laughing quietly to herself.

I hate it when women do that. They take their small revenges in the most frustrating ways.

Chapter 21

By midday, I'd lost the nail off my right thumb and two other fingers, and very nearly my breakfast. But we'd found Mehmet's aketni.

Five small wagons, huddled together against the sun, with domed canopies of once-blue canvas now sunbleached bone-gray, stretched tautly on curving frames. Unhitched danjacs hobbled but paces away in a bedraggled little herd brayed a greeting as we rode up. I wondered if Mehmet's bad-tempered one had come back to join the others.

As expected, everyone was excited to see Mehmet again, but more excited to learn he'd brought water. Del and I handed down botas as Mehmet jumped off the mare and quickly doled them out, answering excited questions with enthusiasm of his own in the deep-Punja dialect I'd yet to decipher. Dark eyes shone with joy and relief and browned hands stroked the botas.

But no one drank. They accepted the botas with fervent thanks, yet stood aside as Mehmet turned to Del and me. We still sat atop our mounts, staring down in bafflement.

"It's yours," I told him in Desert. "We've kept enough back to get us all to Quumi—go ahead and drink."

Mehmet shook his head even as the others murmured. I counted five at a glance, heads wrapped in turbans, dark faces half-hidden by sand-crusted gauze veils. I couldn't see much of anyone beneath voluminous burnouses, just enough to know the five were considerably older than Mehmet, judging by veined, spotted hands and sinewy wrists. But then, he'd told us that.

"What is it?" Del asked.

I shrugged, reining in the stud, who wanted to visit the danjacs to show them who was in charge. Horses hate danjacs; the ill-regard is returned. "Nobody's thirsty."

Mehmet took a single step forward. "We owe you our thanks, sword-bearers. The gratitude of the aketni, for bringing water and aid to us."

I started to shrug it away, but broke it off, stilling, as Mehmet and his companions dropped to knees and bowed heads deeply, then tucked sandaled feet beneath buttocks and rocked forward to press foreheads against knees. Deep, formal obeisance; much more than we warranted. Five of them turbaned, with narrow, gray-black braids dangling beneath the neck-flap meant to shield flesh against the sun. All women? I wondered. Who could tell with so much burnous swaddling and veiling?

Mehmet intoned something in singsong fashion, and was answered instantly by a five-part nasal echo. They all slapped the flat of a hand against the sand, raising dust, then traced a line across their brows beneath turban rims, leaving powdery smudges of crystalline sand to glitter as they raised their heads.

Four women, I decided, and one old man. Six pairs of dark desert eyes locked onto blue and green ones.

I felt abruptly alien. Don't ask me why; I just did. I realized, staring back, there was nothing of me in these people. Nothing of them in me. Whatever blood ran through my veins was not of Mehmet's aketni.

I shifted in the saddle. Del said nothing. I wondered what she was thinking, so far away from home.

"You will come," Mehmet said quietly, "for the bestowing of the water."

"The bestowing—?" I exchanged a puzzled glance with Del.

"You will come," Mehmet repeated, and the others all nodded vehemently and gestured invitation.

They seemed a harmless lot. No weapons were in sight, not

even a cooking knife. Del and I, after another glance exchanged, dropped off respective horses. I led the stud to the nearest wagon and tied him to a wheel. Del took her mare around the other side and tied her to the back.

Mehmet and his aketni gathered around us, but with great deference. We were herded respectfully to the very last wagon and gestured to wait. Then Mehmet and the other male drew back folds of fabric and climbed up into the wagon, murmuring politely to the interior. The wagon eventually disgorged an odd cargo: an ancient, withered man swathed in a gray-blue burnous draped over a gauzy white underrobe.

Mehmet and his fellow very carefully lifted the old man down from the wagon, underscoring his fragility with their attentiveness, even as the others gathered cushions, a palm-frond fan, and makeshift sunshades. The old man was settled on the cushions as the others stretched above his turban the gauzy fabric that cut out much of the sun. Then Mehmet knelt down with one of the botas, murmuring quietly to the old man.

I've met my share of shukars, shodos and priestlings, not to mention aged tanzeers. But never in my life have I seen anyone so old. Nor with such life in his eyes.

The hairs on my neck rose. My bones began to itch.

Mehmet continued murmuring, occasionally gesturing to Del and me. I didn't know the lingo, but it was fairly obvious Mehmet was giving an account of his adventures since leaving the caravan. I thought back on my unwillingness to ride through the night. I'd had my reasons. But now, faced with the bright black eyes of the ancient man, guilt rose up to smite me.

I shifted weight, easing my knee, and exchanged a glance with Del. Neither of us were blind to the old man's acuity as he weighed each of us against the truth of Mehmet's story. If Mehmet had only *said*—

No.

Mehmet *had* said. I'd chosen not to hear.

Like the others, he was turbaned. The facecloth was loosened, looped to dangle beneath a chin and throat nearly as wattled. The dark desert face was quilted like crushed silk, with a sunken look around the mouth that denoted a lack of teeth. He hunched on his cushion, weighing Del and me, and listened to the man so many decades younger than he.

Grandfather? I wondered. Maybe *great*-grandfather.

Mehmet ran down eventually. And then, bowing deeply, offered the old man the bota.

The bestowing of the water. Around us the others knelt. Del and I, noting it, very nearly followed. But we were strangers to the aketni, and both of us knew very well that even well-meant courtesy can be the wrong thing to offer. It can get you in serious trouble.

We waited. And then the old man put a gnarled, palsied hand on the belly of Mehmet's bota and murmured something softly. A blessing, I thought. Or maybe merely thanks.

Mehmet poured a small portion of water into the trembling, cupped hand. The old man cracked his fingers to let the water spill through, watching it splatter, then slapped his palm downward against wet sand, as if he spanked a child.

I don't know what he said. But all the others listened raptly, then sighed as he drew a damp sandy line across an age-runneled brow.

It was nothing. But I stared. At the runnels. The furrows. The lines. Carved deeply into his flesh; now drawn in wet sand.

"Tiger?" Del whispered.

I stared at the old man. Pallid forearms crawled, as if trying to raise the Chair Chosa Dei had burned away. My scalp itched of a sudden. Something cold sheathed my bowels.

I should get out of here—

Lines and runnels and furrows.

Del again: "Tiger?"

I should leave this place, before this old man unmasks me—

I lifted my hand to my face, tracing sandtiger scars. Lines and furrows and runnels. Not to mention deep-seated stripes carving rivulets into my cheek.

The old one smiled. And then he began to laugh.

Dusk. We sat in a circle with the old man atop his cushion. Face-cloths were loosened and looped, displaying at last a collection of very similar blade-nosed, sharp tribal faces leeched of water fat. What I'd told Del was the truth: these Punja-bred people were more accustomed to limited water, and didn't require as much as others. The bodies reflected that.

We'd passed around the bota, each of us taking a swallow, and passed around the cumfa and bread, each of us taking a bite. Ritual duly completed, the others began to talk quietly among themselves.

They were, Mehmet explained, close kin all. Aketni were like that, he said—founded in blood and beliefs. He was the youngest of all, the last born of his aketni, and unless he found a woman to wife there'd be no more kin of the old hustapha.

The hu-*what?* I'd asked.

Mehmet had been patient. The hustapha, he explained, was the tribal elder. The aketni's father. Each aketni had one, but theirs was very special.

Uh-*huh*. They always were.

Their hustapha, he went on, had sired three girls and two boys on a woman who now was dead. They had, in their turn, sired other children, but none remained in the aketni. Two had died in fever season; three others had fallen away.

Del and I looked at each other.

Fallen away, Mehmet repeated. They had deserted their aketni to seek out a tainted life.

Ah, yes. Any life outside of the aketni—or outside of any belief system, for that matter—always had to be tainted. It was easier to explain.

Hoolies, but I hate religion.

The aketni was very small. Seven people, no more, and only one young enough to sire more. Mehmet needed a wife.

I looked at Del. Mehmet looked at Del. Everyone in the circle looked at Del.

The recipient of such rapt attention abruptly tensed like wire. Even without the language, Del knew something had occurred. The air vibrated with it.

"He wants a wife," I told her, enjoying the moment.

Del stared at Mehmet. I have been in warmer banshee-storms.

But Mehmet wasn't stupid. He lifted a limp hand. "O white-haired afreet of the North, I am too humble for you."

It was, I thought, a deft way of escaping her wrath, and of killing off the aketni's instantly burgeoning hopes without being too rude. No doubt it had crossed Mehmet's mind on more than one occasion during the ride back that he'd like Del in his bed— only a dead man wouldn't, and even then she might resurrect him—but he knew better. A woman such as Del was not for the likes of him.

He had to content himself with bringing back help and water. Enough for a start, I thought sourly. He shouldn't be so greedy.

Del settled slowly, like a dog unsure of surroundings. Her hackles barely showed, but I knew how to see them underneath the outward demeanor.

Mehmet went on explaining things, telling us how even they, deep in the Punja, heard word of the jhihadi, and what he was meant to do.

I perked up. That was *me* he was talking about.

Of course, it had long been expected by their hustapha, that such a one would come. It was why their aketni existed.

I frowned. Mehmet saw it. Voluble as he was, he explained it thoroughly.

When he was done, I nodded. But Del didn't. He'd couched most of it in the dialect she didn't understand.

"What?" she prompted.

"An aketni is what we thought it was: a group of people who have developed their own religion. This sort of thing happens a lot in the Punja . . . tribes break up into little pieces whenever the auspices are bad, or when they lose a battle, or when sickness invades, the 'magic' weakens, and so on. Sometimes whole families do it, which is what this one seems to be. They just go off from the tribe and live their own lives, working out their own rules and religion." I shrugged. "I never paid much attention, except when I had to."

"Then *khemi* are an aketni?"

I twisted my mouth. "The *khemi* are different. That group got entrenched early, spreading taproots into the Punja. Then someone dug up some scrolls from a ruined city, and decided to worship them."

"The Hamidaa'n," she said sourly, "that claims women are abomination?"

"Never mind that," I said hastily, before she got carried away. "The thing is, Mehmet's aketni dates way back. This old man—the hustapha—is grandson of the founder. Which means it's been around for awhile, as time exists in the Punja." I shrugged at her frown. "Groups—tribes—die out. Sometimes within a single gener-ation. Borjuni, simooms, drought, disease . . . this one's lasted five. That's a long-lived aketni."

She glanced at the old man. "This—hustapha. What is he?"

"Holy man," I answered. "Seer, if you will. It's what the word basically means, as far as I can tell." I shrugged. "Each aketni de-velops its own language hand-in-hand with a religion. I can only catch half of what Mehmet says, and translations can't be trusted."

"Why are they here?" Del asked. "Why have they come so far?"

"Bound for Iskandar," I explained gravely, "to witness the jhi-hadi's arrival."

Del recoiled. "No."

I lifted a chastening finger. This one still had a nail; for how long, I couldn't say. "Now, now—you're viewing it in terms of what you know about me. *These* people know only what they've heard . . . and what the hustapha's told them."

"You can't tell me they've left their *home*—"

"Others did," I declared. "Alric and Lena, Elamain and Esnat, not to mention all those tanzeers, and the tribes."

She stared at me. "But you say *you're* the jhihadi—"

"*Someone* has to be!" I scowled, switching to Northern in mid-spate so the aketni wouldn't understand. "Look, I don't know what's going on, or why your brother pointed at me—"

"—if he didn't point at Ajani—"

"—and I don't know what's expected of me—" I glared bale-fully, "—but I *do* know one thing: you can't tell them who I am."

Del blinked. "What?"

"You can't tell them I'm the jhihadi. Even if *you* don't think so."

She frowned. "Why not? If they've come to see the jhihadi, shouldn't they be allowed to?"

I glanced at the old hustapha, at Mehmet, at the rest of the aketni. And was glad I could speak Northern, so they couldn't understand.

"Because," I gritted through tight-clenched teeth, "if you'd based your life on a lie, would you want to find out?"

"On a *lie?*"

"These people worship the jhihadi. According to Jamail, that's me; would *you* worship me?" I continued before she could answer, since I knew what she would say. "They also worship that silly prophecy about changing the sand to grass." I scowled, recalling Del's discovery of word similarity. "Grass or glass, whatever; it's what they live by. That's what this gesture is all about—" I slapped sand, then traced a gritty stripe across my brow. "It means the sand will one day be grass again, as it was at the Making. When the jhihadi comes."

"Making," Del murmured. "You mean—like a *jivatma?*"

"They're talking about the *world*, Del—not a magicked sword."

"So," she said finally, having digested that, "they want to get to Iskandar to see the jhihadi." She flicked a glance at the old man. "Are you going to tell him the truth? *Your* version, that is?"

"No. I told you that already."

"You'll just let them go on believing as they have for five generations; that the jhihadi's coming."

"It won't hurt anything."

She arched pale brows consideringly. "It might save old bones a long, wearing journey."

I looked at the hustapha. Saw the glint in eyes so dark pupils were indistinct. Measured the old man's power. I could smell the stink of it. No one, Mehmet or anyone, had to tell me he was special. I could *taste* the truth.

"Tiger?"

Hair rose on the nape of my neck. My belly clenched painfully. "No," I said thickly, knowing it wasn't enough.

Del's mouth tightened. "Do you want your reward so much?"

Without thinking, I answered in Southron. "I don't care about the reward. These people don't have anything."

Mehmet stiffened. "But we *do*," he insisted, "and we intend to reward you."

I waved a hand, sighing. "No, no—it's not necessary—"

Mehmet ignored me, speaking quickly to the old man. The hustapha smiled, fingered his mouth, said something in return. His grandson turned back. "The hustapha agrees."

"Agrees to what?" I asked warily.

"He will cast the sand for you."

Something writhed in my belly. Sweat dampened my brow. Even the words were powerful. "Cast . . ." I let it trail off in dull surprise. Something was pressing me down. A huge, encompassing hand. "You mean—" I thought about something he'd said the day before, about the man who'd stolen food, water, coin. "You said their futures had been cast."

Mehmet nodded. "Of course."

"Then . . ." I looked at the old man. Black eyes wreathed in ancient folds glittered blackly at me.

"What is it?" Del asked. "What is he saying, Tiger?"

Mehmet looked at her. "He is a sandcaster."

"A sandcaster . . ." Blue eyes slewed to me, asking explanation.

My chest felt tight. Breathing was difficult. "Sandcaster," I said dully. "He can foretell the future."

Del's brows arched. "But you don't believe that nonsense—or so you've always said."

Feeling sick, I licked dry lips and gazed across the circle at the old man. "You don't understand."

"He tells the future," she said lightly. "There are many who do that. At *kymri*, at bazaars, even in the streets—"

"This is different," I snapped. Something stirred deep within. "I don't want to know. Not today, not tomorrow—not next month. I just don't want to know."

Del laughed. "Do you think he would tell you a *bad* fortune, after what you have done to help them?"

"He tells the *truth!*" I hissed. "Good or bad doesn't matter. What he shows you is what will happen, no matter what you do."

Del shrugged. She just didn't understand.

Neither did I, really.

But Chosa Dei did.

Chapter 22

The ritual was meticulous. A designated plot of bone-white Punja sand was tended carefully by each aketni member save the old hustapha. He sat on his cushion, overseeing the work being performed directly in front of him.

Each member took turns employing a short-handled wooden rake to rid the plot of impurities. Then a finer rake, combing the selfsame plot. And finally a slender straight-edge to smooth the plot very flat. Both rakes and the straight-edge were of blood-veined, age-dyed wood daubed with ocher squiggles. I assumed the squiggles were runes, but I didn't recognize them.

I shivered. Sweat ran down my temple. I scrubbed it away with a hairless, scaly forearm, then let the limb fall away. The old man was staring at me.

Dusk had faded to night. Mehmet and another had removed two staff-torches from the hustapha's wagon, planted one on either side of the old man, then set the oil-soaked wrappings afire. The torches cast eerie sharp-edged shadows across the tended plot, limning its perfect smoothness.

Mehmet brought seven small pouches to the hustapha, setting three on each side, and the seventh directly in front of the old man's cushion. The pouches were of pale, soft leather, closed with beaded drawstrings. Mehmet carefully opened each one, taking care not to slip a finger inside or spill the sacred contents, then withdrew to join the semicircle of burnous-swathed, veiled aketni hunched behind the turbaned hustapha.

Del and I sat side by side. Between us and the hustapha stretched a flat rectangle of silk-smooth sand, and an acre of reluctance.

On my part, that is.

Sweat dribbled, scribing a runelike squiggle down my right temple, until it was caught in sandtiger welts and channeled to my chin.

Of their own accord, fingertips rose to trace the dampened scars, following the pattern of lines excavated in my face.

Del gathered herself. I knew she meant to rise, to leave me by myself. But I reached out and caught a wrist. "Stay," I hissed.

"But—this is for *you*—"

"*Stay*," I repeated.

Only an instant's hesitation. Then she settled again at my side.

I swallowed painfully, nearly choking on a closed throat. The back of my neck itched. Layers of sinew tautened, threatening to burst crawling flesh.

The hustapha closed his eyes. For a moment I thought crazily he had merely fallen asleep, until I saw the stuttering of wrinkled eyelids and the twitching of his lips. Gnarled hands curled limply over bent knees.

The aketni made no sound.

The torches tore in a breeze that, an instant before, had not existed. Smoke shredded in silence, like sun-rotted, ancient gauze.

The old hustapha murmured. Then the eyes snapped open.

He was blind, I realized. Swallowed by his trance, he saw nothing of the night. Nothing of the sand. Nothing of the unsettled sword-dancer who sat in front of him, with the baby's butt of Punja shining pure and pristine before him.

Blind, he reached unerringly for the first pouch. Poured a measure of sand into one hand. A fine, bronze, burnished sand. He cast it across the tended surface, shaking it from his hand as he chanted unknown things, letting it fall as it would.

Six times he did this. Six measures of sand: bronze, vermilion, ocher, carnelian, sienna, slate-blue. Each cast against the ground.

There was no artistry to it. No attempt to blend hue, or juxtapose color for contrast. He merely cast and let it fall.

One last pouch. He reached into his voluminous burnous, removed an object from it, and held it up to the light. A small wooden spoonlike thing, hollow, with a square of gauze stretched across the bottom, bound on with brass wire. He placed the flat of one palm against the gauze, sealing it against spillage, then poured a measure of sand from the last pouch. Perfectly transparent Punja crystals glittered in the torchlight, like a shower of Northern snow.

He removed the sealing hand from the bottom of the spoonlike object. He began to shake it smoothly, slowly, with methodical precision. Punja crystals sifted through the gauze, powdering the colored drifts. All hue was muted by an almost translucent layer of glittering icelike crystal.

The sifter was hidden away once more. The pouch was closed and set aside. The hustapha, no longer blind, leaned forward over the rectangular window of randomly cast sands.

He blew. A single whuffing exhalation that barely ruffled the crystals, not much more than a baby's breath. Then he drew back and gestured for me to do the same.

I choked on the stench of magic. The contents of my belly crawled halfway up my gullet.

The old hustapha waited.

I gritted teeth. Bent. Blew a single perfunctory breath, getting the silliness over with.

Black eyes glittered. He lifted palsied hands, clapped them together once, then crossed one over the other and flattened palms against thin chest.

Torches whispered of wind.

A breeze only. It caressed eyelids, brushed lips, teased at sweaty flesh. Then settled on the palette of crystal-clothed colored sands.

I watched it. The breeze tugged at Punja crystals, shifted some, stole others, teased away grain by grain. As each gauzy layer was lifted, a new color was born. The random casts of sands began to form a pattern. And a pattern within the pattern.

"Behold," the hustapha invited.

The breeze died, allowing the sands to still. The hustapha waited patiently, letting me look upon the casting. The aketni behind him said nothing, nor made any movement. Beside me, Del was as still.

I was, abruptly, alone. I looked, as I was meant to. Read what was written there, in sand-conjured images still writhing like knots of worms. Bronze, ocher, ash. Others. All the colors of magicked casting, dependent upon the subject.

I stared at the threefold future wind- and breath-scribed in the sands.

What could be. Might be. Would be.

What I did not want to be.

Del's voice was soft in the star-glimmered darkness. "You're not asleep."

Sleep? How could I sleep?

"What's the matter?" she asked. Her breath stirred the sweat-stiffened hair on the back of my neck.

I sat bolt upright, scrubbing frenziedly at my nape. "Don't *do* that!"

She levered herself up on one elbow. We slept apart from the wagons, well-distanced from the aketni, but it was still much too close as far as my comfort was concerned. She brushed hair out of her face. "Why are you so jumpy?"

I stared hard through the darkness. I knew the hustapha and the others had raked the sandcast patterns into nothingness, dispersing the magic, but still I looked for them. Still I smelled the odor. Still I searched for images squirming in the sand, hoping they might change.

I drew in a deep, uneven breath. "I. Hate. Magic."

Del's soft laugh was inoffensive. If anything, it was relieved. "Then you may as well hate yourself. You have your own share of it."

Ice caressed my spine. "Not like that," I blurted. "Not like that old man."

Del said nothing.

I twisted my head, looking at her. Asking it at last. "You saw, didn't you? What the sands foretold?"

A muscle twitched in her jaw.

"You saw," I said.

"No."

It stopped me. "No?"

"No, Tiger. It was a private thing."

I frowned. "Are you saying you *saw* nothing? Or that by saying nothing about it, you create that privacy?"

"I saw nothing." She tucked hair behind an ear. "Nothing but sand, Tiger. Little drifts of wind-blown sand."

"Then—you didn't see. . . ?" But I let it go. As I unclenched my fists, another fingernail peeled off. "Then if no one else saw, maybe it won't happen. Maybe I can make it not happen."

Del's face was pale in starlight. Her voice was a thready whisper. "Was it so very bad?"

I frowned into darkness. "I'm not sure."

She thrust herself upright, sitting atop her blanket. "Then if you're not *sure,* how can it be so bad?"

I stared into the night.

"Tiger?"

I twitched. Traced the sandtiger scars. "I'm not sure," I repeated. Then I looked at her. "We have to go to Julah."

Del frowned. "You said something of that before. You gave no reason, just said we had to go. Why? That is Sabra's domain. She won't remain in Iskandar forever. It is not the destination *I* would choose."

"If you *had* a choice."

Del narrowed blue eyes. "Have you no choice?"

"We."

"We?"

"Have *we* no choice."

Pale brows hooked together. "What are you saying?"

"That of all the futures I saw, yours was the most potent."

"*My* future!" Del's spine snapped straight. "You saw *my* future in the casting?"

I reached out and caught a lock of white-silk hair. Wound it around a callused finger, wishing I could feel it. Then slipped the hand behind her neck and pulled her close, so very close, holding her very tightly against my left shoulder. Losing the threefold future in the curtain of her hair.

Wanting to hold her so hard I cracked all her bones.

Before Chosa Dei did it for me.

Chapter 23

My eyes snapped open. I roused instantly and without fanfare: one moment asleep, the next completely awake, with no residual grogginess, or a desire to curse the inner sense that jerked me out of oblivion.

I lay perfectly still in my blanket, rolled up in a sausage casing of Southron-loomed, nubby weaving dyed gray and bloody and brown. Del slept beside me, pale hair hooded by blanket, except where one stray lock had escaped the others and ribboned across the skyward shoulder.

Something crawled from the pit of my belly. Trembling beset my limbs.

Fear? No. Just—trembling. *Tingling.* A quake of bone and muscle no longer willing to be quiescent.

I gritted teeth. Squeezed shut eyes. Willed myself back to sleep. But the tingling increased.

Feet twitched. A knee jumped. A palsy swallowed my hands, then spat them out again. From head to toe, my skin *itched.* But scratching didn't help.

I peeled back the blanket. Thrust myself up. Gathered scabbarded sword and walked deliberately away from Del, danjacs, wagons, aketni. But not away from the stud. I went straight to him, untied hempen hobbles, threw reins onto his neck. I didn't take time for saddle or pad, just swung up bareback, clamping legs around silk-smooth barrel; hooking bare heels into the hollows behind the border of shoulder and foreleg.

He snorted. Pawed. Stomped twice, raising dust. And then settled, waiting alertly.

"Toward the sun," I told him, doing nothing to give him guidance.

He turned at once, eastward, and walked away from the wagons. No saddle, stirrups, pad. Just the suede dhoti between us, allowing flesh and muscle to speak in the language of horse and rider.

He walked until I stopped him, speaking a single word. I swung a leg across sloping withers, dropped off, walked four steps away. Unsheathed the discolored *jivatma* and let the dawn inspect its taint.

A question occurred: *Why am I here?*

Was washed away in a shudder.

I set the tip into the sand and drew a perfect circle, slicing through the top layer of dust and sand to the lifeblood beneath, glinting with crystallized ice.

Yet another question: *What am I doing?*

A twitch of shoulders dismissed it.

When the circle was finished, I stepped across it, entered, sat down. Set the sword across my lap, resting blade and hilt on crossed legs. Steel was cool and sweet against the Southron (Southron?) flesh too light in color for many tribes, too dark for a Northerner-born.

Something in between. Something not of either. Something that didn't fit. Something—some*one*—different. Shaped by an alien song he didn't know how to hear.

I placed my palms across the blade. Shut my eyes to shut out the day. Shut out *everything* save the bone-deep, irritant itch that set muscles and flesh to twitching.

And a third: *What is happen—*

Unfinished.

The inner eye opened. It Saw far too much.

Would he unmake me? I wondered. Or did he need me too much?

The blade grew warm in my palms.

Eyes snapped open. I lurched up, spilling sword, staggered two steps toward the perimeter of the circle, then fell to my knees. Belly writhed as gorge rose. But there was nothing to spew.

I gagged. Coughed. Poured sweat.

Hoolies, what have I—

Limbs abruptly buckled. I sprawled facedown in the sand, laboring to breathe.

Digging fruitlessly with fingers that had shed each blackened nail. And was now replaced with new.

The urge that had brought me here died away into nothingness. The inner eye closed.

I rolled over onto my back, arms and legs awry. Breathed air unclogged with sand. Stared up at the changing sky as stars were swallowed by light. Heard the stud whicker softly, unsettled by the workings of a power he didn't know, and couldn't understand.

He hates magic as much as I do.

But he doesn't know the need seeping out of the darkened places into the light of day, lapping at a soul. He doesn't know what it can do. He doesn't know what it *is*.

He doesn't know what *I* know: there is bliss in ignorance.

I stared at the sky and laughed, because laughing is better than crying.

Hoolies, but I'm a fool.

Hoolies, but I'm *scared*.

Danjacs were hitched to wagons. The aketni sat on the seats. Del waited quietly atop her bay mare. Her face was taut and pale.

I halted, slid off, bent to gather gear and saddled the stud quickly, arranging botas and pouches. Grabbed one squirt of water, then remounted the stud. The language now was muted; saddle and pad interfered.

"Let's go," I said briefly.

Mehmet, driving the lead wagon, called out the departure order to the dun-colored danjac hitched to his wagon. Then lifted the stick from his lap and tapped the bristled rump. The danjac moved out, jingling harness brasses and gear. The wagon jolted into motion. Others followed suit.

Del brought her mare in close as I tapped heels to the stud, urging him to move, and planted herself in my way. I swore, reeled in rein, jerked the stud's head aside before he could bite Del, or go after the mare. "What in hoolies—"

"Where were you?" she asked curtly, cutting through my irritation.

"Out there." I thought it enough.

"Doing what?"

"Whatever I felt like," I snapped. "Hoolies, bascha—how many times have you gone off by yourself to sing your little songs?"

It opened the door to doubt. Del frowned faintly. "Is that what you were doing?"

"What I was doing is none of your business."

"You took that." "That" was my sword.

"And you take *that*." This "that" meant *her* sword.

More doubt. A deeper frown. A twitch of jaw muscle. "I'm sorry," she said quietly, then turned the mare after the wagons.

I followed. Feeling guilty.

We might have made Quumi in a day and a half. With the wagons, it took two. At sundown on the second day we reached the gray-beige settlement, and Mehmet called me over.

"There is the toll," he said.

I nodded.

The dark face grew darker. "The others took our coin."

Yes. So they had. "Do you want me to find them? Get the money back?" I paused, seeing his startled expression. "They're probably here, Mehmet. Quumi's the only settlement in these parts where a man can buy food, liquor, women . . . where else would they go after stealing all your coin?"

Mehmet glanced toward the last wagon, where Del brought up the rear. The hustapha rode inside. Then doubt turned to decision. "No." He shook his head. "We have no business hiring a sword-dancer to right a wrong done us. It makes us no better."

"But it's *your* money."

He shrugged. "Let them keep it. There will be other coin, once the city knows we have a sandcaster with us."

I twitched. Then shrugged it away. "And how do you know they won't steal your coin again?"

"The hustapha has cast their futures."

Deep in my belly, something clutched. "He doesn't . . ." I let it trail off, intending to dismiss it, but the idea wouldn't die. "I mean, he can't, can he? Shape his casting to suit a whim?"

Dark arched brows knitted themselves above a Punja nose. "Do you mean purposely shape a future? For personal pleasure, or retribution?"

"If he thought it was necessary."

Brows unraveled. Mehmet smiled faintly. "*You* cast your future in the sands last night. The hustapha cast possibilities."

"*I* cast . . ." I glanced back at the last wagon. "You mean, all of that rigamarole we went through—"

"Ritual. Ritual is required."

I waved it away. "Yes, yes, the ritual . . . Mehmet, why is it necessary if *I'm* responsible? Why all the sacred secrecy?"

"He is holy," Mehmet said simply. "Holy men are different. The hustapha is a seer. Father of the aketni, which waits for the jhihadi."

I forbore to consider the jhihadi, even though that more than anything convinced me this was all foolishness. My mind was on the hustapha. "He's a wizard," I snapped. "I could smell the stink of it, with or without the wind and a contrived future-casting."

Mehmet's dark eyes focused on the sword hilt peeking above my left shoulder. "All men with power *are* power: the name doesn't matter."

Obscure, I thought. And out of character for Mehmet. It made me wonder how much *had* been divulged in the casting the night before. Del said she'd seen nothing. But that was *Del*, not the others, who understood better than I what a casting was all about. "Are you trying to say something, Mehmet? Something about me?"

The young man smiled. "A man with a knife has power. A man with a sword has power. A man with knife *and* sword has more power yet."

"I'm not talking about knives and swords."

"Neither was the hustapha."

I gritted teeth. "That's not what—" But I broke it off, disgusted. "Oh, hoolies, I've had enough. . . ." I rode on ahead of the caravan to the broken gates of Quumi, and paid the aketni's toll. Which is all Mehmet had asked in the first place.

It was me who'd wanted more.

It was me who *needed* more, to learn what I could do to avoid the threefold future.

Because it *might* be true.

The threefold future: Could be. Might be. Would be.

Up to me to choose.

Chapter 24

Dust from the caravan drifted, working its way toward the street. Del and I sat on horseback at Quumi's battered gate. Sunset stained gray-beige adobe a sickly, washed out copper, tinged with lavender.

"Why did you come?" she asked.

"Why did I *come?*" I scowled. "I was under the impression I was helping the aketni. Which was *your* suggestion."

My sarcasm had no affect. "You might have stopped once Quumi was in sight. There was no need to come in all the way."

I arched brows. "Little thing called water."

Del raised one shoulder in an eloquent, negligent shrug. "You could have asked Mehmet to bring the water out."

"Could have," I agreed. "But why? Since we're this close, we may as well spend the night under a roof again."

Her gaze was steady. "You said you were concerned about sword-dancers and borjuni. That they could be here by now, to try and catch us both."

"Could be. Might be—" I bit it off abruptly, suppressing the sudden shiver prompted by unexpectedly familiar words. "Let's just go, bascha. We can take care of ourselves."

We made our way to Akbar's cantina as the sun fell behind the horizon. A crescent moon hung in the sky, urging the stars from hiding. They glittered like Punja crystals on a sandcaster's raked rectangle.

Feeling twitchy, surly, grouchy, I took the stud around the back and put him in the stable, in one of the tiny partitioned slots masquerading as a stall. Del wisely put the mare in one at the other end of Akbar's shabby stable, and pulled off gear and supplies. Bridle brasses clattered. I heard her speaking softly in uplander to the mare.

The language was still strange on my own tongue, but I spoke enough of it to survive, and understood a bit more. Yet it wasn't the words that spoke, but the tone underlying them. Del was worried about something.

I tended the stud, stripping him of tack and supplies as Del had stripped the mare, gave him fodder and water, walked back up the way to Del. Both of us carried pouches and botas, not risking them to others.

"Hungry?" I asked brightly, in an attempt to lighten the air.

Del shook her head.

"Thirsty, then."

All I got was a shrug.

"Maybe a bath, in the morning?"

A crooked twist of Northern mouth, indicating nothing.

Patience fled entirely. "Then what *do* you want?"

In the gloom, blue eyes were pale. "*That* discharged."

"That" again. My sword. "Hoolies, bascha—you're making too much of it. I admit it's not comfortable, and I'd as soon dump it here as carry it to Julah, but I don't seem to have much choice." I walked past her and out of the stable. "Let's get rid of this stuff. I want food and aqivi."

Del followed, sighing. "That, at least, is unchanged."

We divested ourselves of burdens in short order, buying ourselves a bed, and retired to the taproom, already full of patrons. Huva weed drifted in beamwork. Spilled wine made the floor sticky. Rancid candles shed sickly light. The place reeked of young liquor, old food, older whores, and unbathed, sweaty bodies.

The way a cantina *should* smell.

If you have no nose, that is.

Del muttered something beneath her breath. I indicated a tiny lopsided table in a corner of the room, headed through the human stockyard, hooked a toe around a stool leg and dragged it from under the table.

"Aqivi!" I called to a plump cantina girl already laden with cups, and a jug of something. "And two bowls of mutton stew, with danjac cheese on the side!"

Del paused at the table, glancing around in silence. Her distaste is never blatant, but I read her easily.

"Sit down," I said curtly. "Do you expect it to be any better?"

Del's head snapped around. She studied me a long moment, then sat down on the other stool. The table was tucked into a tight corner, away from the raucousness; the stool I left to Del would ward her back and two sides. I *had* made an effort. She just chose not to see it.

The cantina girl arrived with the things I had ordered. A jug, two cups, two steaming bowls with spoons. I opened my mouth to ask for water, counting coppers in advance, but Del cut me off. "I will drink aqivi."

I very nearly gaped. But hid it instantly, merely raising an eyebrow. "Heady stuff, bascha."

"It seems to agree with you." She reached for the jug, poured both cups full. The pungent aroma was so thick I thought a sword could cut it in half.

I flipped the cantina girl an extra copper, then waved her on her way. I had other concerns to tend. "Look, bascha, I know I've said in the past that you have no call to chide me for drinking so much of something you don't approve of, but—"

"You are right," she said quietly, and lifted the cup to her mouth.

"You don't *have* to, bascha!"

"Drink your own," she said coolly, and took a decent swig.

I have no subtlety: I laughed into her face. "Oh, gods, Del—if you could see your face!"

She managed to swallow the mouthful with elaborate dignity. Then took another one.

"Bascha—enough! You have nothing to prove."

Blue eyes were steady. She managed this swallow better, and the expression afterward. "One cannot judge a man until one has tried his vices."

I blinked. "Who told you *that?*"

"My *an-kaidin,* on Staal-Ysta."

I grunted. "Northerners. All pompousness and wind."

"Did your shodo not teach you something similar?"

"My shodo taught me seven levels of swordwork. That was all that mattered."

"Ah." A third swallow. "Southroners. All sweat and buttock blossoms."

Always in the middle of a swallow . . . I sputtered, choked, wiped my face. "What's *that* supposed to mean?"

Del considered a moment. "Something you do in your sleep, after too much cheese."

"After—oh. *Oh.*" I scowled. "I can think of better topics."

Del smiled sweetly. Drank more aqivi.

"Be careful," I warned uneasily. "I told you what happened to me. One cup of that too fast, and I was falling-down drunk."

She pulled her braid free of burnous, letting it dangle against one shoulder. "There are things I do better than you. This may be one of them."

"Drinking? I doubt it. I've had years more practice. Besides, I'm a man."

"Ah. That explains it." Del nodded, swallowed. "It is part of a man's pride, then, to drink more than a woman."

I thought back on contests to establish that very thing, though always among men. Women were not included, except as the reward.

Warmth stole up my belly, blossomed at my neck, traced its way into my face. Del, seeing it, smiled; my answer was implicit.

Which made me a bit touchy. "Men do a lot of things better than women. Men do things than other men, too. There's nothing wrong with that. There's nothing wrong with pride. And there's nothing wrong with a competition to see who is best."

"Out-drinking one man is a way of proving yourself?"

"In some cases, yes." I could remember many.

"Pissing contests, too?"

"How do you know about that?"

"I had lots of brothers."

I grunted. "I don't make a habit of it. But I won't deny it's happened."

"What about women?"

"What?"

"Have you competed for a woman?"

I scowled. "What is this about? Are you angry with me about something? What have I done *now?*"

Del smiled, and drank aqivi. "I am merely trying to understand what makes a man a man."

I swore. "There's more to being a man than drinking and pissing—and whoring."

Del rested chin in hand. "And there's more to being a woman than baking bread and having babies."

"Hoolies, don't I know it? Haven't you made it clear?" I splashed more aqivi into my cup. "Do *you* want more?"

Del smiled. "Please."

"Eat your stew," I muttered, digging into my own.

"The cheese is green," she remarked.

So was the mutton, a little. "Eat around it, then. You won't find any better."

She excavated in her stew. "No wonder Quumi faded. How many survive its food?"

I found a chunk of meat-colored meat. "There's cumfa in our pouches."

Del grimaced. I grinned.

"Eat," I advised kindly. "So you'll have something to throw up."

Chapter 25

*S*he drank more than expected. Ate less than I'd hoped. But one thing I've learned is, you can't tell a woman anything. Especially a drunk Delilah.

Except, I wasn't sure she *was*. A little maybe. A bit on the warm side, with a glitter in blue eyes and pale rose blooming in her cheeks. But mostly, she was happy.

Now, you might argue being generally happy is not a bad thing for a man. A happy woman is even better. A happy Del might be best of all—except I didn't know what to do with her.

Well, yes, I did. But she was in no condition.

Or was she?

But it was a bad idea. She'd only argue that I'd taken advantage of her, and I suppose she'd be half right. And saying half is a big concession; we *were* bed partners. How do you take advantage of someone who shares your bed anyway?

By letting her get herself drunk, then taking her off for a coupling she wouldn't remember anyway in the thumping of her head and the upheaval in her belly.

I like to think I leave a woman with a better memory than that.

Left, more like. I hadn't had a woman other than Del for—oh, I can't remember.

Which worried me, a little.

Shouldn't I remember?

Shouldn't I *want* to remember?

Hoolies, it wasn't worth it. I poured more aqivi.

Del saw him before I did, which wasn't really surprising since she sat with her back to the wall, and I sat with mine to the room. Which meant that when the man arrived, Del was already watching every move he made with intent, almost avid eyes.

Hands hung at his sides. Rings glinted in poor light. Gauzy saffron underrobe, embroidered with golden thread; copper-dyed burnous of exquisite cut and fabric; a wide leather belt studded with agate and jade. "I have coin," he said. "How much will you sell her for?"

For only an instant it caught me off-guard. And then I remembered: this was the South. I'd been north for long enough to forget some of the customs, such as buying and selling people whenever the urge struck.

I looked at Del. Saw the illusory blandness that was prelude to attack.

I beat her to it. "Who? Her?" A flick of a newborn fingernail indicated the subject. "You don't want to buy *her*."

"I want her. How much?"

I didn't look up at him. Didn't have to. I knew he had the coin. He wore too much of it. "Not for sale," I said, and drank more aqivi.

"Name your price."

Inwardly, I sighed. "How do you know she's worth it?"

"I buy—differences." The word was oddly inflected. "I judge differently than other men . . . worth is what I make it."

Carefully, I set down the cup. Swiveled slightly on my stool and looked up at the man. Contained my surprise: he was about my age, and very fair of feature. A Southroner, no question, but crossed with something else. The sharp tribal edge was blunted, softening his angles. The aqivi-pale eyes were intelligent, and very, very patient.

This could be trouble.

"No," I said briefly.

"What do you want?" he asked softly. "I have more than merely coin—"

"No." I glanced at Del, expecting a comment. She waited mutely, leaning indolently against the wall, which is not to suggest she was unprepared; then again, she was drunk. "She's not mine to sell."

"Ah." Enlightenment flickered in nearly colorless eyes, and I realized I had demoted myself without intending to. Now he thought me a bodyguard, or some other kind of hireling. "Then whom do I see regarding her purchase?"

"Me," Del answered.

Dark brown eyebrows arched slightly, expressing mild surprise. "You?"

"Me." She smiled her glorious smile; I snapped out of aqivi-induced relaxation into taut wariness. When Del smiles like *that*. . . .

"You?" This time he was amused. "And how would you price yourself?"

White teeth glinted briefly. "More than you would be willing to pay."

Pale eyes were amused. "Ah, but you have no idea how much I have to spend."

"And *you* have no idea how much it would cost you."

"All right," I said, "enough. This serves no purpose. Let's just end it right here, right now, and let all of us go on about our business." I started to rise. "I think it's time—"

"Sit *down*, Tiger," she said.

"Bascha, this has gone too far—"

"He has taken it this far. As I am the reason for it, it will be my decision." Her voice was cool, but color suffused her face. Blue eyes glittered. "I want to find out *exactly* how much he will pay."

I managed not to shout. "And if he pays it? What then?"

"Why, then he will have bought me." Del languidly pulled the leather thong confining her braid, shook loose pale hair, sectioned it again.

"*Enough*," I hissed. "If you think I'm going to sit here and let you bargain yourself into slavery—"

"*Not* a slave," the man interjected. "I don't purchase slaves. I purchase—differences."

"Who cares?" I snapped. "You can't buy her."

Del rebraided her hair. "Don't you trust me, Tiger?"

I stared back at her, grinding teeth. "You're *drunk*," I accused. "Drunk and stupid and foolish—"

"As you have been often enough." The smile was perfectly bland. "Have I ever stopped you from doing exactly as you wished?"

"This is *different*—"

"No, it isn't." She smiled at the man. "You will assume responsibility for paying my price?"

Pupils dilated. He thought she was his already. "I have said I will pay it."

"No matter what it is."

"Yes." Rings glittered as fingers twitched. "Name your price."

Del nodded once, tying off her hair. Pushed her stool back and rose. Unbelted her burnous, unhooked the split seam from her sword hilt, slid soft silk to the floor. The harness bisected breasts, accentuating her body. It snugged her tunic tight.

Bare arms were pale in burnished, malodorous light. Silver hilt glinted pale salmon. "Choose a man," she said.

"A—man—?" For the first time, he was nonplussed.

"For the dance. Choose."

I stirred. "Now, Del—"

"Choose," she repeated. Then blonde brows rose. "Unless you mean to dance yourself?"

"Dance?" He looked at me. "What is she talking about?"

Resignation outweighed annoyance. "Ask her, why don't you? She's the one you want."

"My price," Del said. And drew Boreal, setting tip into tabletop. The sword jutted upright, braced against falling over by a single long-fingered hand wrapped loosely around the grip. Softly, she said, "I *love* to dance."

She's drunk, I told myself. She's drunk, and on the prod—what in hoolies do I do?

Could I do anything?

No one had ever stopped me.

He protested instantly. "I am not a sword-dancer—"

"*I* am." She smiled. "Choose another, then."

"You are not—" He stopped. One had only to look at her. And then he looked at me. "She is not."

"Tell you what," I said lightly, "why don't we wager on it?"

"But—she is a woman—"

"I did sort of think you had that part figured out." I warmed to the verbal skirmish, beginning to feel relieved. Del didn't mean to dance. She was playing games with him. "I don't know a soul who could miss that fact."

"Choose," Del said. "If I lose, you have won."

By now, of course, everyone else in the cantina had discovered our discussion. Silence filled the taproom, along with all the stink.

Which reminded me of something. "What in hoolies are *you* doing here?" I asked him. "You don't seem the type to spend much time in Akbar's place. Another, better cantina, maybe . . ." I shrugged. "You're sadly out of place."

"I have informants. One came with word of a woman worth the trouble of putting myself out of place." He smiled faintly, turning my words back on me. "I will have to give him a bonus."

"She's a Northerner," I declared. "She isn't for sale. They don't *do* that, there."

"Here. There. It makes no difference. Most of the things I own were never for sale. But I bought them anyway." He shrugged delicately. "One way—or another."

A man pushed out of the throng. Young. Southron. Eager. A scabbarded sword hung from his hip, which meant he wasn't a dancer. He just *wanted* to be one. This was probably the closest he would ever come. "*I'll* dance against her."

Del's eyes narrowed. She assessed him carefully.

The rich man smiled. "I will pay you, of course."

"How much?" the young man asked.

"That can be arranged later. I promise, I will be generous; I see no point in shortchanging you, if you win the dance."

Now I did stand. "This has gone far enough—"

"Tiger—*sit down*."

"Del, don't be ridiculous—"

She said a single word in clipped, icy Northern. I reflected silently she knew more of gutter language than I'd given her credit for.

"Fine," I said agreeably.

Then overset the table and walloped her one on the jaw.

Chapter 26

Del folded, dropping her sword. I caught her, missed the sword, dumped her ungently into the corner, then spun to face the others.

Samiel was in my hands.

"My name is the Sandtiger," I said. "Anyone who wants to dance can take it up with me."

A ripple ran through the room. But nobody said a word.

"No?" I flicked the sword, throwing a bi-colored flash across the cantina: silver and black. "No one? No one *at all?*" I glanced at the man who had wanted to buy Del. "How about you?"

His mouth was set tautly, but he said nothing, also.

"No? You're sure?" Another glance around the cantina. "Last chance," I warned. Then I locked gazes with the young man who had offered to dance against Del. "What about *you?* You were awfully eager. Would I satisfy you?"

Nervously, he licked his lips. "I didn't know it was you. I didn't know she was yours."

"Not *mine,*" I said clearly. I looked around the room yet again. "I ought to challenge every one of you to a true dance. I'm bored, and I need the work."

"Sandtiger." The young man again. "No one here would stand a chance against you."

I smiled thinly. "I'm glad you realize that."

Behind me, Del stirred.

"Stay put," I snapped, not even bothering to look. I stuck a toe against Boreal, slid her toward the corner. I doubted anyone would try, but I didn't want to take the chance. He would thank me for it. "So," I said, "why doesn't everybody go back to whatever it was they were doing?" I turned toward Del's "purchaser," lowering my voice. "Because unless *you* want to dance, the entertainment's over."

Aqivi-pale eyes glinted. Rings glittered as fingers stiffened. But he shook his head in silence.

"Then go home," I suggested. "Go back where you belong."

He inclined his head briefly in elegant acknowledgment, then turned and walked out of Akbar's.

That much done. Now for the rest.

"Show's *over*," I declared.

They all agreed hastily.

When I judged the cantina sufficiently settled, though not quite itself again, I sheathed my sword and turned to Del. She had gathered up Boreal and sat against the corner, cradling her sword.

"Here." I reached for Boreal. "Let me put her away before you cut off a leg."

Deftly, Del flipped the grip into both hands and angled the sword upward. I discovered the tip threatening intimate knowledge of my suddenly sucked-in belly. Unexpectedly, the blade was rock steady.

"Back away," she said.

"Bascha—"

"Back *away*, Tiger."

I took a sharper look at her eyes. Then backed. Del watched me every step, judged the distance between us sufficient, pushed herself up the wall as she scooped up dropped burnous. The misleading brightness of eyes and cheeks was banished, betraying the truth I'd missed: Del was not drunk. Del had *never* been drunk.

"What in hoolies—"

"To the room. Now."

I debated arguing it with her. But when a man's at the end of a sword—the sharp end, that is—he usually does as he's told. I did as she suggested.

The room was tiny, a rectangular sliver tucked away on the northern side, with a lopsided window block cut through chipped and flaking adobe letting in muted, lopsided light. The wall between the room and the next was of heat-brittle lath and paste-stiffened, bug-eaten cloth. Not the room I'd rented from Akbar, or the one we'd shared before. It was, I thought somewhat inconsequently, not so much better than the stall housing the stud. Possibly smaller.

Two paces into the sliver, I turned to face Del. "All right, what do you think—"

"A test," she said calmly, jerking closed the fraying curtain to lend us tissue-fine privacy.

"Test? What kind of test? What are you talking about?"

"Sit down, Tiger."

I was getting sick and tired of being told to sit down. I displayed teeth, giving her the full benefit of my green-eyed sandtiger's glare. "Make me."

She blinked. "*Make* you?"

"You heard me."

She thought it over. Then snapped the sword sideways, out of the way; rotated on one hip; caught me flush very high on the right thigh with one well-placed foot.

It wasn't what I was expecting. The day before I'd have gone down. But now I took the foot, the power, let it carry on through as I rolled my hip to the right to channel the blow past, then snapped back into position.

Del's smile died.

I waggled beckoning fingers. "Care to try again?"

She narrowed suddenly wary eyes. "Your knee . . ."

I shrugged. "Good as ever."

"I thought it would buckle . . . I *planned* for it to buckle."

"Dirty trick, bascha."

"No dirtier than the trick you pulled this morning, disappearing for so long." The sword glimmered between us; once more the tip teased my belly. "Why do you think I did this?"

"I have no idea why you did '*this.*' Idiocy, maybe?"

Her turn to show teeth, but she wasn't smiling. "You're different. *Different,* Tiger! First you say little of what the sandcasting told you, as if it doesn't concern me, and then you disappear with nothing but that sword. Why do you *think* I did this?"

"A test, you said. But of what, I don't know—what do you expect from me?"

Del's face was taut and pinched. "I tell myself it is the strain, the constant knowledge of Chosa Dei's presence . . . and that you are as you are because you fight so hard to win. And sometimes I think you *are* winning . . . other times, I don't know."

"So you decided to play drunk to see what I would do?"

"I did not 'play drunk'—I merely let you believe what you wanted to believe: that a woman drinking so much aqivi would *have* to be drunk. And then you would become careless, thinking me fair game." Del's chin rose. "A test, Tiger: if you were Chosa Dei, you would not hesitate to take my sword—*or me.* He wants both of us."

I recalled thinking about hauling her off to bed. Guilt flared briefly, then died away as quickly. What I'd thought wasn't any different from what any man might consider, looking on a softened, relaxed Delilah. It wasn't a sign of possessiveness. Just typical maleness.

Which was not, I thought sourly, adequate grounds for sticking me with a sword.

I pulled myself back to the matter at hand. "But since I didn't try to take your sword—or you—I can't be Chosa Dei. Is that it?"

Del's mouth twisted. "It was a way of getting an answer."

I pointed. "Why not put her away?"

Del looked at the *jivatma.* A crease puckered her brow. Something briefly warped her expression: I recognized despair. "Because—I am afraid."

It hurt. "Of me?"

"Of what you could be."

"But I thought we just settled this!"

Her eyes sought mine, and locked. "Don't you see? You rode out this morning with no word to me. I don't ask you to tell me everything—I understand privacy, even for a song . . . but what was I to think? Last night your future was cast—and you told me *I* was in it."

I managed a small smile, thinking of other women who had grown a little possessive. "Don't you want to be in my future?"

"Not if it's Chosa Dei's." She stabbed a hand toward my knee. "And now—*this*. Your knee is suddenly healed. What am I to think?"

"And my arms." I lifted hands, waggled fingers. "New fingernails, too."

"*Tiger*—"

"Bascha—wait . . . Del . . ." I sighed heavily and put up placating hands. "I understand. I think I know how you feel. And believe me, I'm as confused—"

It cut to the heart of the matter. "Are you Chosa Dei?"

I didn't even hesitate. "Part of me is." I shrugged. "I won't lie, Del—you saw what he did to the sword. He left it—*part* of him did . . . and put a little in me. But I'm not wholly him. That much I promise, bascha."

She was intent. "But part of you *is*."

"Part of me is."

Del's eyes were glazed with something I thought might be tears. But I decided I was mistaken. "Which part of you healed yourself? Which part *remade* yourself?"

I drew in a very deep breath. "I tapped him. I used him."

"*Used* him! Him?"

"I went out there on purpose, summoned him, and used him. I borrowed Chosa's magic."

The sword wavered. "*How* could you do that?"

"Painfully." I grimaced. "I just—*tried*. There's a bit of him in me, bascha. I told you. And it gives me certain—strengths. But there's more of *me* in me."

"You bent him to your will? Chosa?"

"A little." I shrugged. "You once said yourself—and not so long ago—that I am a man of immense strength of will." Del said nothing. Self-conscious, I shrugged defensively. "Well—I thought I'd test *that*. To see if you were right."

Her lips barely moved. "If you had been wrong . . ."

"I addressed that. I drew a binding circle."

"What?"

"A binding circle. To keep Chosa trapped." I shifted weight, uneasy. I thoroughly disliked magic, and using it myself irritated me. It made me what I detested, and I hated admitting it. "Sam—my *jivatma* isn't dead, or empty. There's still *that* power available, if I remember how to key it; work my way past Chosa's taint. And I have the means to use it, if I feel like it. If I can." I scratched a shoulder. "I'm not very good at it. I nearly made myself sick."

"Magic does that to you, remember?" Del's brow puckered: "Then you healed yourself on your own. Remade yourself. Using Chosa's power."

"Some of it. I made it do what *I* wanted." I sighed. "I was getting awfully sick of aches and pains."

"Why didn't you try before? You might have saved yourself some trouble." Eyes glinted briefly. "Saved your knee some pain."

"Might have. But before, I didn't think I could do it. When it first occurred to me . . ." I shook my head. "It's not my way to use or depend on magic. It's a *crutch*, like religion."

Blue eyes narrowed. "What changed your mind?"

I sighed. "The threefold future."

"What?"

"What could be. Might be. Would be." I shook my head bleakly. "I never wanted this . . . *none* of this nonsense. But Staal-Ysta gave me a lump of iron and forced me to Make it. To blood and key a *jivatma*—"

"But not requench in Chosa Dei! No one made you do that!"

I smiled sadly. "You did, bascha. I'd have lost, otherwise. And Chosa would have had you."

She knew it as well as I. Trapped in Dragon Mountain, penned by the hounds of hoolies, Del had stood no chance. He would have taken her sword, and her, then augmented his own growing power to destroy Shaka Obre's wards.

Del lowered her blade slightly. Progress. "What is to happen next? What of this threefold future?"

I shrugged. "Images. I saw death, and life. Beginnings and endings. Bits. Pieces. Fragments. Shattered dreams, and broken *jivatmas*."

"Do we die?"

"In one future. In another, we both survive. In yet another, one of us dies. In another, the other does."

"That's four," she said sharply. "Four futures, Tiger. You called it *three*fold."

"Multiple futures," I clarified. "Only three possibilities for any of them: it could be, it might be, it will be." I spread hands in futility, knowing how it sounded. "But each future shifts constantly, altering itself the instant I look at it—even *think* about it. If you look straight at it, it changes. It's only if you let it slide away and look at the edges . . ." Hoolies, it was worse when I tried to explain it! "Anyway, that's what happened last night, when the hustapha cast the sands." I smoothed tangled hair on the back of my neck, rubbing away tension. "I saw everything. It moved, everchanging. Squirmed, like a bowl of worms." I tried to find the words, the ones that would make her see, so she could explain it to me. "I saw everything there was, wasn't, will be. And you and I smack in the middle."

Del's face was pale. She seemed as overwhelmed as I.

"I don't *like* it!" I snapped. "I don't like it at all—I'd just as soon not have anything to do with any of this . . . but what am I to do? I'm stuck with this sword, and *it's* stuck with Chosa Dei! Not a whole lot I can do about it, is there? Except feel helpless." I sighed, backhanding sweat-sticky hair from forehead. "I didn't want the hustapha to cast the sand in the first place. . . ."

Her voice was rusty. "Because you knew what you might see?"

"I just—didn't." I shrugged. "I didn't have much chance to think about the future when I was a Salset chula. Slaves learn not to think about much at all, except staying alive." I hitched shoulders again in a half-shrug, disliking the topic. "I'd just as soon find out what my future holds when I'm in the middle of it."

Del nodded absently. Then smiled a little, going back to something seemingly inconsequential, because it was a thing she *could* grasp, banishing helplessness. "Then—we stay together. And nothing I do and say now will alter anything."

"Oh, it might. It could. It would." I spread my hands, laughing feebly in frustration. "Do you see, Delilah? There is no knowing the truth, because the truth is everchanging. The moment one truth becomes another, the old truth becomes a lie."

Del wiped away the dampness stippling her upper lip. "I don't understand you. You're not the man I knew."

I forced a grin. "Don't you take credit for that? Isn't it what a woman wants?"

She spat a Northern curse. "I don't know what to say. You have twisted me all up."

"*Me*," I said, with feeling. Then, before she could stop me, I closed my hand on Boreal's blade. "I am not Chosa Dei. A piece of him is in me, but most of me is *me*." I paused. "Could Chosa Dei do this without swallowing her up? Without swallowing you?"

She gazed down at the hand upon the blade. At flesh-colored forearms, fuzzed with fine, sunbronzed hair, and normal fingernails.

"I know her name," I said. "She's mine, if I want her. If I were Chosa Dei."

"And me?" she asked. "Am I yours, if you want me?"

Slowly, I shook my head. "I'd never make that choice for you. You've taught me better than that."

A long moment passed. Then, "Let go, Tiger." When I did, she sheathed the sword.

I sat down on our bedding, glad that was over. Too much aqivi for wits confused by new and complex truths. "What *I* want to know is, how did you drink so much aqivi without passing out?"

Del smiled. "Part of training on Staal-Ysta."

"Training. In drinking?"

She knelt, crossed legs, leaned against the wall. "It is believed liquor makes sword-dancers careless; I have told you that often."

"Yes. Very often. Go on."

"Therefore it is a lesson we must learn *before* we risk ourselves."

"What?"

"We are made to drink through the night. Then again through the next day."

"All night—and all *day?*"

"Yes."

"Hoolies, you must have been sick!"

"That is the point."

"To make you sick?"

"To make us so sick we have no desire to drink again."

"But—you drank. Tonight."

"Drunkenness destroys balance."

"That's *one* of the things."

"So we are made drunk. Several times each year of our training, to increase our tolerance. So that should we drink too much, we do not lose the dance."

I thought about it. Twisted as it was, it made a kind of sense. "I've been drinking a lot of years . . . what about *my* tolerance?"

"Mine was perfected through discipline. Control. Yours—is merely *yours*, and subject to certain weaknesses in self-control."

"Northern pompousness." I thought about it some more. "So all that business about being able to drink more than me . . ." I let it trail off.

"I can," Del said softly.

I smiled, smug. "But I can *piss* farther."

She froze, and then she thawed. "I will forfeit that victory."

"Good." I stood up. "Now why don't you get some sleep while I go check on the horses?"

"I can go with you."

I smiled. "I know you're not drunk, bascha. But I *did* hit you pretty hard, and I'm betting your head hurts."

She put her hand to her jaw. "It does. I wasn't expecting that." Brows slanted downward. "I should repay you for it."

"You will," I declared. "With your tongue, if not your fist." I smiled, blunting it. "Get some sleep, bascha." I headed toward the curtain. "Oh—one more thing . . ."

Del lifted brows.

"What in hoolies possessed you to challenge that Punja-mite?"

"Which one?"

"The rich one. The one who wanted to buy you."

"Oh. Him." She scowled. "He made me very angry."

I eyed her suspiciously. "You were enjoying yourself."

Del grinned. "Yes."

"Go to sleep." I turned.

"Tiger?"

I paused, turned back. "What?"

Del's eyes were steady. "If you drew a binding circle to keep Chosa Dei in, why did you not leave your sword?"

"My sword?" And then I understood. "I could have."

"And Chosa would have been trapped."

I nodded.

Del frowned blackly. "Is that not what we're trying to do? Find a way to keep him trapped?"

I nodded again. "There *is* a way. I found it. My *jivatma* is the key."

Blue eyes blazed. Her words were carefully measured, as was her emphasis. "Then why not simply *do* it and be *done* with this foolishness?"

"Because," I answered simply.

"Because? Because *what?*"

I smiled sadly. "I'd have to stay in the circle."

"You—?"

"He's *in me*, bascha. There's more to do now than discharge a sword—there's also *me* to discharge."

Del's face went white. "Oh, hoolies . . ." she murmured.

"I thought you might see it my way." I turned back and went out of the room.

Chapter 27

I didn't go to check on the horses. I went to see the old man.

Mehmet's aketni had set up camp in what had become the caravan quarter. Originally it had been a sprawling bazaar, in the days when Quumi was bustling, and caravans had encamped outside the city. But as Quumi's strength and presence faded, borjuni took to preying on caravans and travelers outside the walls. The bazaar, slowly deserted as Quumi died, altered purpose. Now it housed small caravans on the way to Harquhal and the North.

The sunbleached, dome-canopied wagons were easy to find, even in starlight and the crescent moon's dim luminescence. I made my way across the dust-layered, open-air bazaar and went looking for the hustapha's wagon.

In his typical uncanny way, the old man was waiting for me.

Or else he was simply awake, and made it *look* that way.

He was alone, seated on the ground on his cushion at the back of his wagon. Dun-colored danjacs, dyed silver and saffron by pale light, were hobbled a distance away, whuffling and snuffling in dust as they lipped up grain and fodder. Immense, tapered ears flicked this way and that; frazzled tails snapped a warning to inquisitive insects.

Bright black eyes glittered as I came to stand before him. "Did you see this?" I asked. "Me coming here?"

He smiled, stretching wide the wrinkled lips accustomed to folding unimpeded upon a toothless mouth.

I knelt down, drew my knife, drew patterns in the packed dirt of the bazaar. Not words; I can't read or write. Not even runes, though I have some understanding of those. Nor symbols, either, denoting water, or blessing, or warning.

Just—lines. Some straight, some curving, some with intersections. And then I put away my knife and looked at the old man.

For some time he didn't even look at the drawings. He just stared at me, into my eyes, as if he read my mind. I knew he couldn't do that—well, maybe he could; but a sandcaster usually only reads sand—so I assumed he was looking for something else. Some sort of sign. A confirmation. Maybe acknowledgment. But I didn't know what to give him, or even if I could.

At last he looked at my drawings. He studied them a long moment, moving eyes only as he followed the lines. Then he leaned down, wheezing, and slapped the flat of his fragile, palsied hand into the middle. It left a cloudy, fuzzy-edged print that obscured most of the patterns. Then he took his hand away and drew a line across his brow.

Which told me a whole lot of nothing.

Or maybe a lot of *something;* the gesture in his aketni referred to the jhihadi.

I drew in an exquisitely deep breath, filling my head with air. "*Am* I the jhihadi?"

He stared back at me: an old, shriveled man with a streak of grit across his forehead.

"If I am," I persisted, "what in hoolies do I do? I'm a *sword-dancer,* not a holy man . . . not a messiah with the ability to change sand to grass!" I paused, arrested, thinking about alternate possibilities. And feeling silly for it. "Or—is it supposed to be changed to *glass?*"

Black eyes glittered. In accented Desert he told me his aketni comported itself solely in expectation of Iskandar's prophecy coming true.

Ah, yes. Iskandar. The so-called jhihadi who got himself kicked in the head, and died before he could do any of the miraculous things he said he'd do.

Of course, *before* he died he also said he'd come back, one way or another. Apparently, if Jamail—in his Oracle guise—was correct, it didn't necessarily mean Iskandar *himself* would be back, but someone assuming his role.

I had no plans to assume *anyone's* role, thank you very much.

Without warning, consciousness flickered. Memories bubbled haphazardly to the surface of my awareness: alien, eerie, *sideways* memories painting pictures of a land as yet lush and green and fertile. I recognized it with effort, blotting out my own far different version: Chosa's recollections of the South before the disagreement with his brother.

Thanks to Chosa, I "recalled" very well Shaka Obre declaring he would find a way to restore it—he would find some*one* to restore it—no matter what Chosa did.

And it was possible he had, in Iskandar the jhihadi. No one knew much about him, except the city was named after him, and his own horse kicked him in the head—which is enough to get most messiahs remembered, irrespective of holiness. So Iskandar the man might not have *been* a man, not as we reckon men.

After all, no one really knows how magic works, where it comes from, or how it can be controlled. Not entirely. Not *absolutely*. They just borrow *pieces* of it, and hope they do it right.

Which meant, odd as it sounds, Iskandar might have been a construct, an aspect of Shaka's magic, meant to restore the South by changing the sand to grass.

Construct. A man *Made* for something, as Chosa Dei Made things. It seemed entirely possible Shaka Obre could Make things, too, even men—

I stood up abruptly, shaken to the marrow. A whole new possibility unfolded itself before me. And I didn't like it one bit.

"No," I declared.

The hustapha sat on his cushion, grit glittering on his brow.

"No," I repeated, with every bit of determination in my Chosa-remade body.

The old man shrugged, renouncing his intention to tell me anything.

Or was it he didn't know?

Breath came faster. "I'm a man," I said urgently. "A *man* man, not a construct. Not a conjured *thing*—"

Mehmet came around the wagon and stopped, staring at me in mild surprise, which altered quickly enough as he took in the tableau. His expression reproached me for taxing the old man.

"What *is* a jhihadi?" I asked Mehmet intently. "Messiah?—or magicked man conjured by a wizard for reasons of his own?"

He was scandalized. "The jhihadi is the most holy of all!"

"Not 'the' jhihadi—*a* jhihadi," I clarified in something approaching desperation. It hurt to breathe through the constriction of chest and throat. "Do you know where one comes from?"

Mehmet shrugged. "Does it matter? A past is not necessary—only the present and future. What he *does* is important, not what he *is*."

I swallowed painfully. Then turned on my heel and strode rapidly away from them both.

Away from the possibility—no, the *im*possibility—I didn't want to acknowledge.

I broke one of the most important rules a sword-dancer can ever have beaten into his brain—and body—by tongue-lashing, wooden practice swords, *and* real blades.

That is: not to be so distracted by your thoughts, no matter how chaotic, that you neglect to take note of your surroundings.

Especially if those surroundings decide for some unknown reason to become hostile.

Which my surroundings did.

To my pronounced—and painful—regret.

I never even made it out of the bazaar into the sidestreets, alleys, and passageways. Not completely, at any rate; I got about halfway, just on the verge of trading open space for the confinement of warrenlike streets, when a whole army of men converged upon me.

Well, maybe not an army. It just felt like one.

Maybe half.

Usually, when you get ambushed in a city, it's by one or two—

or three or four—opportunistic thieves who want your money. If they're that open about everything, they arrive one by one like gathering wolves, trying to intimidate by numbers and attitude. It works with a lot of people. But with a man trained as a sword-dancer, such tactics serve only to give him the time to unsheathe his blade. And once there's a weapon in the hands of a trained, skilled sword-dancer, there's not a whole hoolies of a lot the attackers can do. Because usually one of them loses a hand, an arm—maybe even a head, if he insists—and the others generally decide they have something better to do.

Usually. But these friendly folk were not thieves. At least, I don't think they were. They didn't use thieflike tactics. They just *descended*, en masse, swarming over me all at once. I wound up smack on my back in the middle of the street, spitting sand, dung, blood, and cursing.

Lying *on* my sheathed sword, I might add.

Hoolies, how embarrassing.

Once I was there, arms and legs spread-eagled, they were actually rather restrained. A few kicks, a couple of snatches, pinches, rabbit punches; no more.

Until someone quietly reminded them I was neither predictable nor to be trusted, and that if they lost me, none of them would survive. That *he* would have them killed, if I didn't do it myself.

Which did a good job of convincing them they ought not to waste any more time, and then someone whacked me in the side of the head with something very hard.

I woke up in the dimness, swearing, aware my kidneys were killing me. And my head, but that was nothing new. The kidneys, though; that's pretty cold-blooded. Also effective: a man doesn't feel much like struggling when every move tells him it'll hurt like hoolies, and make him piss blood the next couple of days.

Inside. A room of some kind. It was dry, musty, and dusty, stinking of rats and insects and stale urine. I seemed to be near a wall or some sort of partition, because I sensed a blockage behind me. I lay on my right hip and shoulder, bundled up like a rug merchant's wares. From behind me came a dim, nacreous glow. Sickly yellow-green. It illuminated very little, but I caught a glimpse of something—or some*one*—across the room, hidden in deeper shadows.

I stopped swearing when I realized I wasn't alone, and when I discovered it was rather difficult to make any sound at all, because something very taut and painful was looped around my throat. Wrists were tied behind me, and a length of something—wire? rope?—ran from them to the binding around my ankles. An excessively *short* length; my legs were bent up so that heels nearly touched buttocks. It was highly uncomfortable.

Which didn't make me very confident about the situation.

"Sandtiger."

So much for wondering if they—or he—knew who I was. On one hand, it made me feel like this had been done for a reason. On the other, it made me feel like I was in more trouble than just a random, if violent, robbery.

Especially since I heard the few coppers in my pouch rattle as I shifted, testing bonds.

"Sandtiger."

I stilled. The back of my neck itched, and forearms. My belly felt queasy.

"Do me a favor?" I asked. "Give us a little more light, so I can see what party I've been invited to."

Nothing. And then the voice asking, with a trace of mild amusement, if I was *sure* I wanted light. "Because if you see me, will you not then have to be killed?"

A cultured, authoritative voice; the kind that appears ineffective, until you demand proof of strength. The slight accent was of the Border country, with a twist of something else. It sounded vaguely familiar, but I couldn't place it.

I expelled a breathy, cynical grunt. "Hoolies, you'll kill me regardless—if *that's* what this is all about. If it isn't, you don't really care one way or another." I worked my wrists a little, found no give at all. If anything, the binding tightened.

Silence. And then light.

I swore in spite of the loop around my throat.

"Precisely," he agreed. "Now, shall we discuss once more what kind of payment you would like for the Northern woman?"

I told him what he could do with himself.

"I intend to," he said mildly. "I'm quite depraved, you know. It's part of my reputation. Umir the Ruthless, they call me."

I gritted teeth. "Is that why you want Del?"

"Is that her name?"

I swore again. This time at myself.

"No." The light came from a crude clay lamp set into a window sill. He stood in front of it, which threw him mostly into silhouette and limited its effectiveness, but the pale glow from behind me balanced the illumination and allowed me to see the characteristic dark Southron face with high-arched nose, sharp cheekbones, thin lips and deep sockets, but the eyes in them were an unusual pale gray. Borderer, I decided, in view of the accent. Rings and studded belt glinted. "I want—*Del*—for the very reasons I gave you before: I collect differences."

"What in hoolies is *that* supposed to mean?"

He gestured. "Some people collect gemstones, golden ornaments, horses, women, men, rugs, silks . . ." Again the smooth gesture illustrative of the obvious. "I collect many different things. I collect things that interest me by their very different*ness.*"

"So you want her."

"She is a remarkably beautiful woman, in a very dangerous, deadly sort of way. Most women—*Southron* women—are soft, accommodating things, all tears and giggles—depending on their moods, which are innumerable. She is most decidedly *not* soft. She is hard. She is sharp. She is edged, like steel. Like glass." His smile was faint in the thick shadows. "So keenly honed she would part the flesh with no man the wiser, and let him bleed to death at her feet, smiling all the while."

"As she'll part yours," I promised. "She's a *sword-dancer,* borjuni . . . a fully trained, *jivatma*-bonded sword-dancer. Do you have any idea what that means?"

"It means I want her more than ever." He smiled. "And I'm not a borjuni. I'm a tanzeer."

"In *Quumi?*"

He shrugged. "With proper management, Quumi could become profitable again. But it has only lately come into my possession. I have annexed it to my domain." He pointed northerly. "Harquhal."

"Harquhal is *yours?*" I frowned. "Harquhal hasn't belonged to a tanzeer for years. It's a border town—a *Borderer* town. You can't just walk in there and take it over."

"It's when people believe you can't that you *can.*" He made a sharp gesture. "But we're not here to discuss annexations. We're not here to discuss anything, really—I just thought you might like to know that even as we speak, my men are abducting the woman for me."

I tried to break the bindings and succeeded only in nearly choking myself into unconsciousness. Shaking with anger, I subsided. "So much for offering to *buy* her."

"I pride myself on being a judge of men. When I learned who you were, I knew it was unlikely you would give in. *You* have something of a reputation, Sandtiger . . . there is talk that imprisonment in Aladar's goldmine changed you." He paused. "And the woman."

"How?" I spat. "Are you trying to say *I'm* soft, like the Southron women?"

"To the contrary—although some undoubtly *would* argue that; but then, they have no idea what motivates a man." He smoothed the rich silk-shot fabric of his nubby, slubbed burnous, rings glittering. "Those who understand men—or understand *you*—say the mine and the woman have made you more focused. More deadly than ever. Before, you cared mostly for self-gratification . . . now that life and freedom mean so much more to you—now that there is the woman—you are not so lackadaisical."

"Lackadaisical?" It was about the last word I'd choose to characterize myself.

"Men who are nomads—or once were—drift with the Punja, Sandtiger. Where they go matters little, so long as there is a job, or women, or wine." He smiled. "You were blessed with unusual size, strength and quickness, and a great natural ability . . . why should a man so talented waste his strength unnecessarily? No, he merely flicks the insect aside instead of squashing it, because he knows he *can* . . . and that if he should choose to squash it, his will be the quickest foot any insect has ever known."

He stopped speaking. I stared at him, unsettled by his summation. By his ability to judge so easily, and speak with such certainty.

I lay unmoving, cognizant of bindings. "Let her alone."

"No." He moved a single step closer. "Do you understand what I have just said? You are a man who cannot be bought. An anomoly, Sandtiger—a different kind of sword-dancer, whose whole lifestyle *is* to be bought. Slavery of a different sort."

I bit back anger, putting up a calm front. "So, am I to join your collection, too?"

"No. Sword-dancers are a copper a dozen . . . admittedly, *you* might be worth more than that, but not so much that you're worthy of my collection. No," he said thoughtfully, "were I to add a sword-dancer, it would be Abbu Bensir."

I blurted it without thinking. "Abbu!"

"I want the most unique, Sandtiger. That is the *point*. You are very good—seventh-level, I believe?—but Abbu is . . . well, Abbu is Abbu. Abbu *Bensir*."

I know. I know. It was stupid to feel even remotely jealous, in view of the circumstances. But it grated. It *rankled*. Because while it's bad enough to be trussed up and dumped in a stinkhole because you're inconvenient, being told you're not worth as much as your chief rival makes it even worse.

I scowled blackly. "Ever heard of Chosa Dei?"

He smiled faintly, brows lifted in amused perplexion. "Chosa Dei is a Southron legend. Of course I have."

I grunted. "He collected things, too. Mostly magic, though."

The tanzeer laughed softly. "Then we are very alike, the legend and I. I have acquired a bit of magic lore over the years."

Magic *lore*, not magic itself. I thought the distinction important. "What happens next, tanzeer? Am I to be left here as rat food, or do you have something in mind?"

"What I have in mind is the woman." He smiled as my muscles instantly knotted against the bindings. "I would not try quite so hard to break free, Sandtiger. That is not rope imprisoning you, but magic."

I froze. "Magic?"

"Runelore, to be precise." He shrugged. "I have a grimoire."

"A grim-*what?*"

"Gri-moire," he enunciated. "A collection of magical spells and related enchantments. The *Book of Udre-Natha*, it is called. The Book of the Swallowed Soul." The tanzeer smiled. "My soul is quite intact, as yet . . . but certainly bartered." He reached inside his burnous and drew out something that glowed dull gray-brown in muted illumination. "This is but a sample, a fragment left over—do you see?" He spoke a single word under his breath, and the thing he held flared into life. It glowed a sickly yellow-green. "There. Runelore. The *Book of Udre-Natha* is full of such small magics, as well as larger." He came closer, bending slightly to dangle the length before my eyes. "Do you see the runes? Hundreds of them, all woven together into a single strand of knotted, unbreakable binding, stronger than rope, or wire. That is what imprisons you, Sandtiger. At throat, wrists, ankles." He gestured. "Skill or no skill, sword or no sword, even you cannot break free of *magic.*"

Transfixed, I stared at the abbreviated length dangling from his fingers. Dim, pulsing light; runes knotted together to form a bizarre, living rope thick around as a woman's smallest finger.

He tucked the runes away. "I would not struggle too much," he warned. "Part of runelore, once set to bind, is to constrain such attempts. If you fight too heartily, the loop around your throat could quite easily strangle you. And I would hate to have that happen."

"Why?" I asked rustily. "What use am I to you?"

"Not to me. To Sabra."

Every muscle froze.

"*I* don't want you," he said, "but she does. And since I am not averse to making a profit, I'm pleased to be able to rid myself of you while also earning coin—*and* Sabra's gratitude. One never knows when such gratitude can come in handy."

"She's a woman," I said, looking for an edge. "You'll deal with a woman tanzeer?

"I'll deal with anyone I must to secure the things I want." He shrugged. "I am a pragmatist, Sandtiger . . . for now, Sabra rules her father's domain, but that will change. It always does, eventually."

He shook out the folds of his heavy sleeves. "By now they should have the woman—Del?" He nodded. "So I take my leave." He turned to the lamp, blew it out. The nacreous glow of binding runes cast sickly light upon his stark, shadowed face. "Sabra should arrive from Iskandar in a day or two. Until then, you'll have to make shift where you can. And if you think to shout for help, recall you are in my domain. I have promised the people I will restore her to her former glory—and I have *also* told them they are not to meddle in my affairs."

I lurched, then stiffened as rune-bindings tightened. "*Wait—*"

He moved to the door and put his hand upon the latch. "I am not a murderer, borjuni, or rapist. I acquire things to *admire* them. It may please you to know I have no intention of harming the woman."

It was something. But as he shut the door and latched it, I wondered if he lied.

Lied about *everything*.

Chapter 28

No light, save for the ghostly glow of rune-bindings. I lay in pallid darkness, bathed by sickly shadows, and wondered how far I could test the bonds without strangling myself. Umir the Ruthless had been clever; by also running the single length of rune-rope through loops at wrists and ankles, he made certain any sort of testing would tighten the noose snugging my throat.

Hoolies take him.

Then, again, I reflected, he seemed to think his soul was already compromised by his ownership of the *Book of Udre-Natha*, or whatever the hoolies it was.

I scowled into darkness. By refusing to think about magic most of my adult life, it seemed I'd missed out on a lot of knowledge and forgone conclusions. It seemed the South was *riddled* with magical items, grim-whatevers, would-be sorcerers, afreets . . . ah, hoolies, I don't care what they say, it's all tricks and nonsense.

Except Umir's "nonsense" was doing a fine job of keeping me out of action.

I lay very still and did a meticulous examination of my physical condition. My kidneys still ached unremittingly, and undoubtedly would for a day or two; a few bruises here and there, abrasions; a couple of painful gouges; a sore lump on the side of my head.

And a cramping discontent across my spine that told me something else: they'd left me my sword. Still sheathed and hooked to harness, which I still wore.

A question occurred: Why?

Then again, why not? Without my arms free, the sword did me no good. And for all I knew, Sabra had requested its presence as pointedly as my own.

And also something else: What if someone had *tried* to take my sword, and Samiel had repulsed him?

If you didn't know his name, he could be downright testy. It was a *jitvatma's* first line of defense; the second being its ability to do incredible, magical things.

Magic.

I chewed the inside of my cheek thoughtfully. Hadn't I used magic the day before, to repair injured knee, and restore arms and fingernails?

Hadn't I bent Chosa Dei—well, a *piece* of him—to my will?

I shivered. The binding tightened at throat, on wrists, on ankles.

I lay in the dust-smeared darkness and sweated stickily, trying to swallow without giving the noose a reason to snug itself any tighter. Trying to figure a way of undoing Umir's magic.

Trying not to think of what they were doing to Del, who—drunk or not—had swallowed much too much aqivi, and received a tap on the jaw from a none-too-gentle fist.

I slept, and woke up with a jerk that snugged the noose a step tighter. Now it was *really* uncomfortable. I cocked my head back, trying to put slack into the tautness; rapped my skull against the upstanding hilt of my sword and swore, hissing the oath in disgust, despair, desperation.

"Stupid . . ." I muttered hoarsely. "Your shodo would hold you up to ridicule—"

But I broke it off. I didn't really want to think about my shodo right about now. Twelve years dead, he still exerted a powerful influence over my behavior. Much as I hated to admit it. Much as I got sloppy and depended on size, strength, quickness and natural ability to win my dances, instead of the precise techniques my shodo had labored seven years to teach me.

Just as Umir had said.

Ah, hoolies. Might as well give it a try.

Shut my eyes. Thought about magic. And power. And need.

Thought about Del, and how if I didn't get loose Umir might bind her up in rune-ropes and haul her off to a lair every bit as impregnable as Dragon Mountain, and tuck her away behind wards I couldn't break no matter *how* much magic I summoned, because he had a grim-something.

Thought about me, left to lie here in a stinking, rat-infested, dusty, musty, dry-rotted room with no breathable air to speak of, and certainly no food or water, or even a way of relieving myself—

(—which would hurt too much, anyway, because someone—or several someones—had planted feet in the small of my back, somewhere in the general vicinity of my kidneys—)

—until Aladar's vengeful daughter arrived from Iskandar by way of Harquhal, and hauled *me* off to a lair every bit as impregnable as . . .

Ah, *hoolies.*

"Magic," I muttered grimly, "and let's be quick about it."

But quickness is not something that goes very well with magic. Especially if you have a renegade sorcerer—well, a *piece* of him—stuck inside you somewhere.

And the rest of him in your sword.

Thought about runes, and sickly light, and undoing all the knots.

Umir had taken the last bit of rune-rope from inside his burnous. It had been nothingness, a stringy patch of darkness. Until he spoke a single word.

What in hoolies had he said?

I thought about it. Hard. Until my head ached along with everything else, and sweat stung my eyes, and the cramps in neck, arms, and legs made me seriously consider moving even against my better judgment, because if I didn't move soon, the pain would become unbearable.

Umir the Ruthless. Who'd said Sabra might arrive in a couple of *days.*

Who'd said he didn't really want to kill me. But who had un-

doubtedly known that I'd be dead inside of two days anyway, because a combination of the slackness of sleep and the spasms of
muscular cramps would cause me to move, and the bindings to
constrict.

Until I choked to death.

Which meant that unless I myself engineered it—as soon as
possible—I'd be dead of "natural causes" before Sabra arrived to
collect me.

Magic. I shut my eyes and thought about it, willing myself to
relax.

And fell asleep.

I came to with a jerk, gagging, and spat out a word. *The* word, recalling how the syllables fit together, and how Umir had pronounced them. A tongue-tangling, gnarled word, like the unruly
spine of the stud when he humps and hops and squeals. But I knew
it, and I said it—

And nothing happened.

Ah, hoo—

No. Something *did* happen: the glow brightened.

Not what I had in mind.

I tried again, altering intonation.

Nothing.

Yet again. Only this time, the pressure *increased*.

"*No*—" Desperately, I pressed my skull more fiercely against the
sword, trying to escape the tautness. Spine arched, legs cramped,
buttocks tightened. Kidneys blared discontent.

"*Un*do . . ." I gagged. "—not—do . . . *un*do—"

I summoned the word again, saw its shape inside my head,
tried one more time.

This time I said it backward.

Light winked out. The pressure didn't slacken, but it didn't
tighten, either.

For now, that was enough.

I said the word—*backward*—again.

Nothing.

"Undo—" I muttered. And thought about knots untying.

Nothing.

Swearing, I concentrated. Visualized rune-bindings I couldn't see, had never seen, except for a brief glimpse in Umir's hand.

Dangling from his fingers: a tangle of glowing runes, like a four-plaited Salset rein.

Memory wandered nearer.

—*think*—

Had it. Saw the lines, the patterns, the knots. Thought about my *own* lines and patterns and knots; the welts graven in flesh, slicing whitely through two-day stubble; the intersections I'd carved into sand and dust before the old hustapha; the interlaced layers of knot on knot: double, triple, quadruple, wrapped twice and thrice, then knotted again, then braided; then joined by one and two and three and four—

Displaced by my panting, a gout of dust blew up into my face. Irritated eyes teared. Runnels channeled cheeks, reminding me of Mehmet's face when first I'd seen him, dust- and sand-caked, thirsty, exhausted; Mehmet, whose aketni harbored a hustapha, a sandcaster, who cast the sands for me and called me a jhihadi—

Or had he?

A ripple swarmed over my flesh. At least the runes didn't tighten in immediate response, but it still didn't feel *good*.

Flesh tingled. Every inch itched. And I couldn't do a thing.

"—don't think—about that—"

But I did. Because a warping chill wracked my limbs, setting my joints to aching. Weirdly, it reminded me of the North, wrapped in winter's breath.

Nausea invaded my belly.

Hoolies, not *now!*

I swore against the ground. I sweated, then shivered convulsively, in the two-faced touch of fever.

Now is not the *time*—

A sour belch worked its way up from the unhappy contents of my belly.

What I need *now* is magic, not this—

Magic.

Which always made me sick.

Hoolies, maybe it *was* working!

With renewed determination—and a still discontented belly—I returned with increased vigor to my attempts at dispelling Umir's bindings.

I panted. Sweated. Ground teeth. Thought about runes: Southron, Northern, Borderer. Thought about knots untied, unlaced, undone.

Thought of everything *backward*.

Slackness.

Eyes popped open. Breath was thunderous in my ears. I thrust myself upright, chest heaving. Ash slipped free of neck, of wrists, of ankles. I brayed a hoarse laugh of triumph that combined unexpectedly with a throttled belch, then doubled over and fell sideways, sucking air and dirt and blood.

Ah, hoolies. I hate magic. It makes me *feel* bad.

Cramps eventually subsided to a manageable level. I lay there panting a moment longer, drying in the darkness, then pressed myself up again.

Del.

Oh, bascha. Give me a chance—I'm coming.

I got up, staggered to the door, wrenched it open crookedly on sun-rotted leather hinges.

And fell through into the dawn.

Chapter 29

I stumbled into the shadow-curtained room, rebounded from the doorframe when I misjudged its nearness, and rousted Akbar's nephew. "Where is she? Where did they take her? Which way did they go?"

The nephew gaped, duly rousted.

One-handed—the other was full of sword—I caught a knot of cloth beneath his chin and jerked him off his pillow. "I said, *where is she?*"

"The woman?" he managed.

"No, I mean the *mare*." I let go of his nightrobe. "There were men here earlier—"

He tugged at his twisted attire. "Yes, but—"

"Which direction did they go?"

"Toward the North gate, but—"

"Did they hurt her?"

"No—but—"

"Harquhal," I muttered intently. "They'd take her to Harquhal—unless there's somewhere else—"

The voice came from the doorway. "Where in hoolies have you been?"

I jumped, spun, stared. "What are you doing *here?*"

Stalemate. Del knitted brows. Lovely pale brows, set obliquely in a flawless, familiar forehead—unmarred by all save bad temper.

But never mind that. "I mean—" I frowned back. Then, rather lamely, feeling more than a little foolish, "Didn't they come for you?"

Boreal gleamed in her hands. "Those men? Yes."

"But . . ." I sat down—no, *collapsed*—on the edge of Akbar's nephew's bed. "I don't understand."

"They came," Del clarified. "Happily, I wasn't in the room. I was in the stable, looking for you."

Uh-oh. "For me?"

"Yes. The last thing you said to me was you were going to check on the horses." The scowl deepened; pointed reproach. "When you didn't come back, I went to look for you." She shrugged. "I heard them come. I stayed where I was. In the stall, with the stud." She scrutinized me. "You look worse now than you did two days ago."

I felt worse, too. Then, it was head and knee. Now it was everything else. "I *thought*," I began, with great dignity, "that I would rescue you."

"I'm fine." Then her expression softened. "Thank you for the thought."

Akbar's nephew stirred. "May I go back to sleep now?"

"Oh." I stood up, rubbed numbly at filthy cheek, then tried to arrange my back so my kidneys didn't hurt. Well, didn't hurt so *bad*. "We'd better get out of here."

Del stepped aside as I made my way by her into the common room, then followed. "Are you so sure they'll be back? They came here once and didn't find what they wanted. Sometimes a room already searched makes the best hiding place."

"They'll be back." I fought my way through tables, kicking stools aside grumpily, and headed for our room. "I have the feeling Umir won't give up."

"Who?"

"Umir. The Ruthless. The man who wanted to buy you."

"*Him?*"

"Now he wants to steal you." I yanked cloth out of the way and leaned against our doorsill. "Do I seem real to you?"

Brows shot up. "What?"

"Never mind." I waved a limp hand. "Just—get our things. I'll see about the horses."

"Our things are *with* the horses." Del studied me. "After those men left, I packed and readied them."

"Readied—?"

"Saddled, bridled . . . with pouches already in place." Her expression was exquisitely bland, as if she didn't want to insult me but knew any comment would. "With all the botas filled."

I must look *really* bad.

"Well, then . . ." I straightened up, winced. "I guess we should leave."

Blandness was replaced with the faintest trace of dry concern. "You do not appear to be in condition to go anywhere."

"It never stopped me before." Grinding teeth, I pressed a hand against my spine. "Let's go, bascha. Sabra's on her way, and Umir will be back."

We repaired to the stable with due haste and brought the mare and the stud out, whereupon the stud took to lashing his tail and peeling back his lip. A shrill, imperative whinny—meant to impress the mare—pierced the pale new light. *And* my right ear, much too close to the stud's mouth. Horses can be loud.

I whopped him on the nose. "Not now, lackwit . . ."

Del swung up on her mare, assembling folds in the slack burnous. Boreal's hilt above her shoulder glinted in the dawn. "If you are in such a hurry . . ."

"I'm coming. I'm *com*—oh, hoolies, horse, did you have to do that?" I wiped a glob of slobbery slime from the filthy ruin of my left cheek. "The mare goes," I declared, "as soon as we reach a settlement that has a *gelding* for sale." I planted my left foot in the brass stirrup, catching hold of the stud's sparse mane—I keep it clipped—and dragged myself upward. To the detriment of my kidneys. "They went out the main gate, which means we should try the other one." I turned the stud and headed him around the corner of the cantina. "Umir doesn't know where we're going, and since I know he knows *we* know Sabra is after us, Julah is the last place he'd expect us to go."

"Won't he have dispatched men to the other gate?"

"The walls are falling down, in case you hadn't noticed. We'll look for one of the breeches." We rounded the cantina into the street proper. "I don't think—"

But what I didn't think never got said. A man stepped out of fading darkness and caught hold of my rein, pulling the stud up short. "I challenge you," he declared, "to formal combat in the circle."

"Nezbet," I gritted, "we don't have *time* for this."

"Shodo's Challenge," he clarified. "Or will you once again plead injury in place of cowardice?"

Del took a stab at it. "Just kill him, Tiger."

"*Shodo's Challenge*," Nezbet hissed, still gripping the rein.

"Later," I suggested. "Right now we're sort of busy—"

"Tiger." Del's voice, stirred from equanamity into something more intense. "Others are coming."

"Umir's men? No." I answered it almost as soon as it was asked because I saw the others.

"Sword-dancers," Nezbet said. "Osman. Mahoudin. Hasaan. Second- and third-level. Honorable men, all." He smiled. "Will you say no before *them*, Sandtiger the Coward?"

I tossed the free rein to Del. "Hold him," I said. "This won't take very long."

Surprise flickered in Nezbet's dark eyes. Then pride, and sudden pleasure. Lastly, recognition: he'd finally gotten his dance with the South's greatest swordsman.

Unless, like Umir the Ruthless, he tacked that title on Abbu.

I stripped out of my burnous, suppressing a wince of pain from kidneys, and draped it across my saddle. "Let's go," I said briefly. "We're burning daylight, here."

Nezbet let go of the rein. "Do you mean it?"

I bared even teeth. "Shodo's Challenge, is it not? To put me in my place?" I waved a commanding hand. "Hurry up and draw the circle."

Brows arched. "But *you* are the Challenged. *You* have the right—"

I spread fingers across my heart, inclining head. "I give the honor to you. Just *draw* the thing, Nezbet!"

"—isn't right," he muttered, but stepped away from me into the street to begin the proper circle.

I glanced down the street at the three approaching sword-dancers. Looked the other way. Fidgeted with a buckle on my harness. Glanced at the trio again. Finally looked at Del. "Maybe you should just go on. I can catch up."

"No."

"It's *you* Umir wants, not me. If you hang around just for this—"

"I'm staying." Del smiled. "You need someone to hold your horse."

I sighed. Bent to untie and unlace sandals. "Waste of time," I muttered. "Stupid would-be panjandrum . . ." I jerked the sandals off. "Ought to know better than to turn this into a challenge . . . stupid Punja-mite should have been taught never to make it personal." I unhooked arms from my harness, sliding free of straps. "Thrice-cursed son of a goat—who does he think he is?"

Del, from atop her mare, with amused curiosity, "Do you ever hear yourself?"

"Hear myself? Of course I hear myself. I'm not deaf. How could I *not* hear myself?"

The smile blossomed, unrestrained. "Then perhaps one day you should *listen*."

"Don't have the time," I growled. Glared back into the street. "Is that thing finished *yet?*"

Nezbet straightened. Showed me white teeth against a dark Southron face. "Step into the circle."

"About time." I unsheathed, dumped the harness on top of the sandals and strode out into the street. Saw from the edge of my eye Nezbet's three witnesses range themselves against the cantina wall. *My* witness, on horseback, jabbed a sandal into the stud's nose to remind him of his manners. I reflected, belatedly, I might have put him somewhere else. He *was* a stud, after all, and the mare was a mare. "All right, Nezbet." I stopped at the circle. "Shodo's Challenge, you say."

"Yes." He continued smiling.

"Death-dance," I told him, then stepped into the circle.

Nezbet lost his smile. "*Death*-dance!"

I stood in the precise center of the circle, the Chosa Dei-infested blade a diagonal slash across my chest from hip to shoulder. "You drew the circle. I choose the dance."

"But—" He broke off, realizing his blunder.

"See?" I smiled, lifting brows guilelessly. "If you had *learned* from the shodo, you'd have known better than to fall for that trick."

"This was not to be to the death," he hissed, dark color ebbing to gray. "I was hired to find you, *defeat* you—bring you back to Sabra!"

"Plans go awry." I beckoned with a triple snap of fingers. "Step into the circle."

The edges began to fray. "This isn't the way it's supposed to *be!*"

I hunched an idle shoulder. "Life often isn't, Nezbet. But then third-level sword-dancers *know* that already."

Elegant nostrils pinched. He flicked a white-rimmed glance at Osman, Mahoudin, and Hasaan slouched against the cantina. Then looked back at me. "You said—" Splotchy color stained his face. "You said—any man may refuse a dance."

"I said it. It's true. But generally the man who refuses is the chall-*enged*, not the challeng-*er*; it would be pointless—and somewhat foolish—if the challenger withdrew after begging for the dance." I shrugged again. "And a Shodo's Challenge, accepted, can never be renounced, or the skill level is lost, along with all the honor. Especially before witnesses." I flicked the blade in new light. "A man such as yourself—*third-level*, no less!—would never do such a thing. It would besmirch his honor to even contemplate it."

Nezbet was gray. "I may renounce the terms."

"I don't think so." I squinted past him at the trio. "But if you like, you can put it before your friends. They might be talked into lying for your sake."

"Lying!"

"The circle codes," I mentioned, "say something about other sword-dancers bearing witness against a man who reneges on a proper challenge."

"But—" Nezbet ground teeth. "You *want* me to renounce it!"

"I don't care *what* you do." I lowered the sword a notch. "I'm a little busy, Nezbet—would you please make up your mind?"

Jaw muscles flexed violently. Then he tore off his burnous, ripped thongs loose on his sandals, jerked arms out of his harness. And stepped into the circle.

"Better," I commended, and put my sword down in the middle.

It surprised Nezbet. Some of the tension and desperation drained from eyes and body. "I thought—" But he didn't finish. Smiling faintly, he set his sword next to mine.

"Who's arbiter?" I asked. "Which of your friendly trio?"

He was, abruptly, magnanimous. "Let the woman do it."

"Del," I called.

Nezbet and I retreated directly opposite one another to the perimeter of the circle. We would run, scoop up sword, commence. A true Southron challenge, with footspeed part of the dance.

"Prepare," she said calmly.

Nezbet stared at me. He was swift, young, and agile, vibrant with life, prepared to spring and snatch up the sword. He knew he could beat me. *Knew* he could beat me. I was old. Big. Slow.

And my knee could not have healed since our last confrontation.

Stupid Punja-mite.

Nezbet smiled.

"Dance," Del said.

Chapter 30

I wanted nothing more than to teach the boy a long, lazy lesson, beginning with sheer power and ending with endurance. But I didn't have the time.

So instead, I settled for speed.

He gaped inelegantly as I snatched up Samiel, hooked the tip beneath Nezbet's blade, and sent it sailing out of the circle before he could even reach it. Hands closed on sand. I pinned the left with a swordtip, lending it just enough weight to sting.

I leaned down over the boy, who knelt out of awkward deference to the steel biting into his hand. "The woman beat you," I hissed. "What makes you think *I* can't?"

Nezbet called me a name.

The sword tip pricked more deeply. "That isn't very nice. Where'd you learn that kind of language?"

So of course he repeated it.

I lifted the tip from his hand, traced a steel path up a bare arm, tapped him repeatedly under the chin to add emphasis to each word. "Not nice at all."

"Chula," he spat. "Everyone knows the truth."

"*Do* they, now?" I rested the blade on his left ear. "Can an earless man still hear gossip?" Now to the mouth. "Can a *tongueless* man repeat it?"

Black eyes glittered. "Jhihadi-killer. You have no honor left."

"No, I suppose I wouldn't—if it were true I'd killed the jhihadi. But we've had this discussion before, and I don't care to repeat myself." I took the sword away, indicated his. "There it is, Nezbet. Fetch it back, if you like . . . the dance has hardly begun."

A trickle of blood smeared the back of his left hand as he rose. "You would allow—?"

"I'm polite," I said lightly. "Jhihadi-killer or no, I remember the seven years I spent with my shodo, and all the lessons learned."

Stiffened jaw flexed. "You will say I have forfeited if I step out of the circle."

"Not if I give you permission. That's in the codes, too."

Nezbet jerked around to face the trio in the shade. "You hear him!" he called. "He permits me to retrieve my sword without forfeiting!"

Stupid, stupid Nezbet. Have you no sense at all? Have you no idea of what personal dignity and self-control are all about?

Stupid me for asking.

I put down my sword once again and went barehanded to my side of the circle. My kidneys hurt like hoolies, I needed to eat something, and I wanted very badly to find a nightpot.

But first things first.

Nezbet came back with his sword, then paused just inside as he saw my relinquished blade. "But—again? To run?"

It wasn't required. We'd begun. It was most definitely out of place, but not disallowable.

"There." I pointed. "That was a bad start for you. Why not try again?"

He stared at me for a long moment, unable to read my intentions. Then, frowning, Nezbet slowly set his sword next to mine. Retreated to his side of the circle.

"Dance," Del said.

This time he reached his sword and actually picked it up. But by the time he did, I was waiting for him. Samiel's tip teased his throat.

I tongue-clucked sympathy. "Sorry, Nezbet. You must have slipped in the sand." I bent and put down my sword. "Let's try one more time."

One of Nezbet's friends stirred against the cantina wall. Osman, or Mahoudin, or Hasaan; I didn't know which. "Kill him," he suggested.

"I think he's trying," I said.

The other flashed a grin. "No, Sandtiger. I mean you should kill *him*."

"Ah." I looked at Nezbet. "I believe they're getting bored."

Nezbet, who had *not* put down his sword, lunged directly at me. Thereby forfeiting any shred of honor, but I don't think honor—or even victory—was on his mind anymore.

Now he wanted to kill.

The steel sang, arcing out of the rising sun. A black slash of blade, silhouetted against whitening light. I sidestepped slightly, caught the wrist and broke it, then hooked Nezbet's ankle and sat him on his rump.

Meanwhile catching his sword before it hit the sand.

I gazed down pitilessly on the stupid Punja-mite. "I hate repeating myself, but this time I think I will." I bent down close. "You're too stupid to kill."

Nezbet, shaking, was mute. And about time, too.

"Where is she?" I asked. "How far behind?"

The boy still said nothing. Tears of shock and humiliation welled in dark eyes.

"Where is she?" I repeated.

"Coming," he muttered. "She and all her men."

"How far behind?"

He shrugged. "A day, maybe. She rides like a man."

No time to waste. I fetched my own sword, then stepped out of the profaned circle and walked over to his friends. Osman. Mahoudin. Hasaan. Or maybe the other order. "Which of you is next?"

Three faces were very still. Then one of them smiled.

I tossed him Nezbet's sword. "Which one are you?"

"Mahoudin. Third-level." He handed the blade to the young sword-dancer next to him. *All* of them were young. "You do me honor, Sandtiger. But I have learned the lesson: any man may refuse a dance."

I looked at the next. "You?"

In silence, he shook his head.

"You." The third and final man.

"Hasaan," he said simply. "And the price is not enough."

"Oh?" I lifted brows. "Any price is enough if there is a level to be attained."

Hasaan demurred. "Death is not the level I aspire to."

"Hoolies, boy, I'm not about to *kill* you! How can you spread word of my deeds if your guts are all over the ground?"

White teeth shone briefly. "May the sun shine on your head."

"It is." I glanced up, judged the time, angled a shoulder away. "Another time, then. When the price is worth the risk."

Mahoudin briefly spread fingers against his heart. "You should have killed him. He's lost his sword, and honor—the circle is closed to him. What is there left to live for?"

I paused. "The chance to learn some sense."

The second—Osman?—shook his head. "You've made him bor-juni. Better to have killed him."

"Nezbet made himself." I turned and walked away, heading for Delilah.

Behind me, three quiet voices, intended to be private: "Big," one of them murmured. "Strong," from another. Followed by the third, "*Fast* for a man so old."

You can't win for losing.

Riding. Again. Hurting, again. And Del noticed it.

"What's the matter?" She reined the mare a sideways step from the stud. "You look sort of—gray."

"Need to—stop—" I gritted.

Del pulled up at once. "Why didn't you say something?"

"Because—we needed—to *go*—"

"That was hours ago." She watched me in concern as I bent in half over the stud's neck. "What's *wrong*?"

"I just—need to get down . . . for a bit . . . something I should do—" I slid out of the saddle, managed to find the ground, hung onto the stud. "Walking, at the moment, is not my idea of enter-tainment . . . do you mind?"

Del stared blankly.

"Then watch," I muttered. "Right now, I don't much care."

"What do you—*oh*."

Oh, indeed. I hung onto the stud and got my business done, swearing all the while. The results were as expected, with kidneys as sore as mine.

Once decent, I dragged myself back into the saddle. Del heard the creaking, the swearing, and turned back to face me. "What did they do to you?"

"Generally beat me up." I pressed a hand into my back. "Someone had big feet."

"We should find a place to stop and rest. At once."

I grunted. "We're in the middle of the Punja."

"There are oases, are there not? And settlements? And wells?"

I squinted. "No settlement close by. But water's not the problem. That can wait until tomorrow evening. Right now, we can't stop." I set the stud moving. "I don't trust Umir."

Del followed, clucking to the mare. "Surely he will not come so far. For me? So far into the Punja?"

"I got the feeling Umir would go anywhere he needed to, to *acquire* whatever he wants." I glanced at her. "You don't see yourself the way others do. You are—different. And that's what he collects."

"No one sees himself the way others do. You don't."

"No," I agreed sourly. "And not as Osman and Hasaan and Mahoudin do either, apparently."

Del was blank. "What do you mean?"

"Nothing." I slanted her a glance. "How do *you* see me?"

"Me?"

Echoing myself: "I don't mean the mare."

Del glared. Then it faded, replaced by thoughtfulness. "I see the underparts."

"The *what?*"

"Underparts." She chewed a lip, thinking, brows tangled together. "The things not on top."

I laughed, and scrubbed at my face. "I forget sometimes—you are Northern, after all . . . the language is not the same."

"I am reminded of that, myself, when *you* sometimes talk."

So bland. I nodded acknowledgment of the point. "So, what is this underpart you see? The things not on top."

"The man inside the skin."

Something cold tapped a fingernail against my spine. It nearly made me squirm. "What about the *outside?*"

Del frowned. "What do you mean?"

"Do I look—" I paused, "—different?"

"Of course."

Colder yet. "*How* different?"

"Not like anyone else."'

"Del—"

"What do you think?" she asked indignantly. "You are taller than all Southroners, but not so tall as most Northerners. You are darker than me; than every Northerner, but not so dark as a *Southroner.* Your eyes are green, not blue or brown, or even the occasional gray. And you are brown-haired, not black-; *not* fair, either." She sighed. "Is this enough for you?"

"No."

She muttered in uplander. "Your nose, then."

"My *nose?*"

"It curves upside down."

"My nose is *upside down?*"

Expressions warred in her face as she fought for the best explanation. Finally she settled for example. "You have seen Abbu's nose."

"Abbu's has a notch in it. Abbu's was broken. Mine never was."

"But you can see what it was, Abbu's nose. And many others. All shaped like this." She hooked a finger downward, bowing the knuckle out.

I tested mine. "I don't have a hook."

"No. Yours is much straighter, though not as straight as some tribes I have seen. Yours is more like a Northerner's. And your cheeks are not so sharp, so arched." Del studied me. "We have discussed this before. You are both, and neither. There are things of the South in you, and also things of the North. Like a Borderer."

I nodded impatiently. "Do I look *real* to you?"

"Real!" She frowned. "You asked that before."

"Just—do I look real?"

Pale brows arched. "Do you mean to ask, are you the man of my dreams?"

"*No!*" I glared. "Can't you be serious?"

"Not at the moment," she murmured, and burst out laughing.

Which only goes to prove you can't *talk* to a woman.

Camp, such as it was, was established with little fanfare: two blankets spread on the ground, wadded—in *her* case, folded—burnouses for pillows. Nothing at all for a fire: we lay on our blankets and chewed steadily at dried cumfa. Staring up at the stars.

"You meant it," she murmured.

"Sometimes." I lay very still. It was better not to move.

"Earlier. About seeming real."

"Just wondered."

"If you were real?"

I thought about it deeply, eventually dredging up an answer. "You wouldn't understand."

"I promise not to laugh."

"Oh, I don't know . . . I enjoy hearing you laugh."

"So long as it's not at you." Del smiled at the sky. "Sometimes, there is cause." She rolled toward me, settling her head into a spread hand on the end of a braced arm. "Do you not feel real?"

"My kidneys convince me I am."

"Then you have proof. Pain means you are real."

"But—" I frowned, chewing violently on the last bite of cumfa. "I don't know anything about me. I have no past."

The amusement died in her eyes. "You have too much of a past."

"I don't mean that. I mean I have no history. Only an upside down nose, and color like a brown burnous left too many years in the sun."

"So do most Borderers. Look at Rhashad: he has *red* hair."

"I don't look anything like Rhashad."

"Most Borderers do not look like one another. The dye lots are always mixed." Del smiled. "I don't mean to tease. But you do not strike me as the kind of man to *need* a past. You make your own of the future."

That cut too close to bone. "They said the jhihadi was—*is*—a man of many parts."

Del's gaze sharpened. She stopped chewing cumfa.

I scratched a patch of bruise. "Nobody knows much about Iskandar, either."

"He died."

I counted. "It's been eight days."

"Since?—oh." Del shrugged. "I think you will outlive Iskandar's ten days."

"Not if Sabra has anything to say about it. Or maybe Umir. The Ruthless."

"They must catch you, first."

"Umir caught me."

"And you got free." Del's brow wrinkled. "*How* did you get free? You have told me nothing."

I shrugged. "Nothing to tell."

"But they beat you, and you got free."

"I wouldn't have, if I hadn't used—" I stopped.

Del waited. And then realization sharpened her gaze. She pushed herself upright. "Magic," she finished.

I heaved a heavy sigh. "The sorriest day of my life was getting involved with magic."

"But it got you free of Umir. You just said so."

"It's also got me lugging around an infested sword. One I didn't want in the first place, but *now* . . ." I sighed again, very tired, letting it go. "Hoolies, it's not important."

Del lay down again. "You humiliated him."

"Who? Oh. Him." I sucked a tooth. "Nezbet got what he deserved."

"You might have beaten him fairly."

"I *did* beat him fairly! I gave him a chance to quit before we started, and *two* chances to give up. What did you want me to do—cut off his head, like you did Ajani's?"

Her tone was flat. "No. But—"

"But? Did you *want* me to kill him?"

Del said nothing.

"*Did* you?" I persisted.

She sighed. "It seems to me you left him injured and angry and humiliated. Some people, with nothing but that to think on, come to trouble you later. They make bad enemies."

"*Nezbet?*"

"You don't know he wouldn't."

I snickered. "With enemies like Nezbet, I'll live forever."

"I heard them. What they said. A borjuni. Why?"

"Why did I make him one? Or how did it come to be?"

"Both."

"I didn't make him one. It was his choice. And he *made* that choice by relinquishing his honor, according to the codes." I dug a cumfa string from between two teeth. "You know about codes. You know about honor."

"Yes."

"When a shodo-trained sword-dancer knowingly relinquishes honor merely to win, or kill, he relinquishes himself. He exiles himself from the circle." I shrugged. "He doesn't *have* to become a borjuni. But I don't know of a single sword-dancer who would be content to raise goats, or scratch a crop from the Southron desert."

"There are other things."

"Caravan guard, yes. But caravan-serais prefer to hire the real thing, not a dishonored man. They can't be certain of his allegiance—what if he *was* a borjuni, and leading them into a trap?" I shook my head. "There is no greater, truer freedom than being a sword-dancer. And no greater dishonor than breaking the codes. It follows you for life, mocking you every day. Until all you can think to do is become a borjuni, because none of them care. They just want you to be like them: to kill quickly and effortlessly."

"And you made Nezbet one."

"Nezbet is young. Nezbet came from somewhere. He *could* petition to reapprentice, starting all over again—but if he's smart, he'll go back where he came from and forget about the circle. He wasn't suited for it."

"Is that why you broke his wrist?"

"No. Well, maybe. Mostly, I did it because I knew I didn't have another chance to give him. If he'd tried one more time, he might have succeeded."

Del grunted. "No."

I smiled. "Misplaced faith."

"You are the best I have ever seen."

"Except for Abbu?"

Silence.

"Well?" I prodded.

"Abbu is—good."

"Umir says he's the best."

Del rolled onto her side. "Do you listen to the word of a man who would steal a woman?"

"A man's morals—or lack of—don't affect his judgment of *sword*-dancing."

She muttered something in uplander.

"Of course, he hasn't *seen* me dance. Only heard about me." I paused. "I think."

"Vanity," she murmured. "Vanity—and pride."

I was tired, and sleepy. I rolled onto my side carefully, showing her my back. "You've got your own share of both."

No answer.

I drifted, sliding toward the edge.

Then she touched my back, tracing the line of my spine with a single soothing finger. "Real," she said softly. "Am I not proof of that?"

"You?" I asked sleepily.

"I am not an afreet. If you were not real, what then could share your bed *except* an afreet?"

I smiled into darkness. "How do I know you're not? *Your* say-so? A bit biased, *I* would say."

The finger departed my spine. Then prodded a sore spot gently. "If I were an afreet, I'd have neither pride nor vanity."

I grunted. "Then I guess we're both real."

Del turned onto a hip, bumping against me. "Go to sleep."

"Stop nattering, then."

The night was filled with silence.

Unless I snored, of course.

Del swears I do. But *I* never hear it.

Chapter 31

*I*nside me, something—*rustled*. It rummaged around in my mind, stirring up old memories, and replaced them with its own.

It was Shaka. Shaka's fault. He twisted childhood truths and made them over into falsehoods, because he was jealous of me. Of the things I had learned to do. The magic I could wield.

The things I had learned to Make.

It was all Shaka's fault.

And my task to put it right—

I sat up, choking, and spat out a clot of—something.

Beside me, Del roused also, levering up on an elbow. "Are you all right?"

Breathing steadied. The world righted itself.

I looked at her, scratching at the stubble I hated. "—'m all right. Just got something caught in my throat." I hacked, cleared it, spat. "Sorry."

She scrutinized the morning. "Dawn," she announced. "We may as well get up. As you would say: we are burning daylight."

"Not yet. The sun's not even up."

"Close enough." Del moved over, knelt in sand, began folding her blanket. "We should be on our way."

"We should," I agreed. "But that means I have to move."

The answering smile was crooked. "Can you not heal yourself again? Restore all your aching bones?"

I snorted in derision, then thought about the suggestion. If there was a chance I *could* do such a thing. . . . "Tempting," I agreed thoughtfully. "You know—"

But it was gone.

Just—*gone.*

Something else was in its place. Not a thought; a *lack* of thought. A sort of absence of anything.

Except for Chosa, knocking at my door; rapping on my gate; tapping at my soul.

Do it. *Do* it.

Do it NOW.

Oh, hoolies, bascha . . . he's here. He's back—

I squinched my eyes shut and willed him away. Willed him to go, to leave me alone. After all, there was only a little piece of him inside me. Tucked away somewhere. I was much bigger, much stronger.

If I concentrated on what Del had said, maybe I could give him the slip. If I tried what she suggested—

No.

I vividly recalled the last time I'd done it. Something flared, promising much; something else waited impatiently. Wanting me to do it, because then he would have power.

My belly rolled. I shivered away from the image. "I—don't think so. I think I'd probably better leave well enough alone."

"But if you can *do* such a thing . . ." She shrugged, going about her business. "Imagine what kind of legend you could become if no matter how badly you were injured in the circle, you came back the next day as good as you were before."

"Imagine," I muttered, massaging a stiff shoulder. "Imagine what else they might say—maybe call me a sorcerer?" I shook my head. "No thanks. I've already got a magical sword. I don't need a magical *me.*"

Del began packing saddle-pouches. "I only meant you look like you hurt this morning. I just thought, if there were a way—"

"I know. But I don't want to—" I left it at that, biting off the end of the sentence I'd meant to say: "—risk it." No need to tell Del

I felt odd, disoriented, and somehow unbalanced. Let her think I just didn't want to do it, period. Somehow it seemed safer.

I got up very slowly, moving in sections, biting my lip on curses. I was bruised and stiff and sore from the ambush by Umir's men. Kidneys were afire. "Right now I just want to take things slowly, and get on our way." I made my way toward the stud, who would provide a measure of privacy.

Del had to be content with what I was willing to give her. *I* had to be content with knowing something more: that Chosa wasn't gone. Chosa wasn't quiet. Chosa was growing *impatient.*

I slung an arm across the stud's brown rump and leaned, shutting my eyes. The bruises would fade, I knew. The pain would diminish. The kidneys would remember what it was to do their task without producing blood. But Chosa would remain.

And continue trying, with brute force and intricate subtlety, to leech me of my will until I had none left, so he could claim the body.

If I used any more magic, I gave him the means to succeed. Because every bit I summoned, no matter the intention, gave *him* that much to play with.

Chosa Dei, collector—much like Umir the Ruthless—who gathered all kinds of magic so he could "melt" it down and remake it in his image.

As he would remake me.

Del tapped the mare a step away from the stud. "How much farther to the oasis?"

I glanced around, squinting. "Not much farther. Two or three hours."

"And then Rusali tomorrow?"

"Depending on how hard we want to push the horses." I scrubbed the back of a hand across my forehead. "And how hard we want to push ourselves."

Del's brows knitted as she assessed my expression. "Is it your kidneys?"

I scowled. "Kidneys are fine."

"You're lying."

"Yes, well . . ." I shifted in the saddle. "Nothing a little rest won't cure."

Her frown deepened. "We could stop for a while."

"Can't afford to stop," I said brusquely. "Our best bet is to keep on going as long as we can, and put as much room between Umir and us as we can."

"Yes, but—"

"Just *ride*," I snapped irritably. "We're wasting time even discussing it."

Del offered no reply. She just shook up her reins and rode on.

Time—blurred. I sat atop the stud, who pulled at reins in irritation: he wanted to go after the mare, but I was holding him back.

I didn't know why.

Del, ahead, twisted in the saddle to glance back. Frowned. "What's the matter?"

I wanted to tell her "nothing." But it wasn't the proper answer. "Tiger?"

I just sat there, shivering.

Del turned the mare, heading her back toward me. Her tone sharpened abruptly. "Are you all right?"

No. I felt—thick. Heavy. My skin felt stretched and tight.

Inwardly, I asked it: *Is that you, Chosa?*

Inwardly, Chosa giggled.

Oh, hoolies. The sun hurt my eyes.

Del reined in the mare before the stud could quite reach her. Her assessment was intense. "What's wrong?"

Something cold ran down my spine. *Let her go,* Chosa suggested. *You don't need HER.*

"I don't—" I shook my head. "Nothing. Just—tired."

She swore between her teeth. "Do you think I am blind? Your color is terrible. You're sort of a greenish-gray, in between all the bruises."

Let her go, Chosa said. *Right now, I only want you.*

I wondered if maybe I should. He'd been very clear about wanting Del before, to collect the magic in her sword as well as Del herself. I knew it was safer if she was somewhere else, where he couldn't hurt her.

But how do I tell *her* that?

Del's voice was unrelenting. "There is a way, Tiger. You could call on the magic again."

No, bascha. I don't dare.

"It's *stupid* to ignore the chance to heal yourself. Why turn your back on a gift?" The tone grew more pointed. "And if you don't, you'll never make it across the Punja."

I gritted teeth. "I *said* I'm just tired. Sore. It'll pass, Del. I've had worse."

"Then why are you sitting here?"

I managed a lopsided grin. "It seemed the easiest thing to do."

Her jaw tightened. "I don't believe you. Not a bit."

"Too bad for you," I jeered.

Eyes flickered. Mouth tightened. "If you wish to be so foolish . . . very well. But if you need to stop, say so. The oasis is not so far."

I shivered. I felt—*swollen*. "Then let's go on."

Let her go, Chosa said. *I'm beginning to lose my patience.*

I tapped heels to the stud and let him go on with the mare.

Mistake, Chosa whispered. *I don't like mistakes.*

I shivered. But I kept riding.

Del's legs approached. Stopped before me. I saw them at knee level. It hurt too much to look up from where I sat slumped on the blanket.

"How much longer?" she asked tautly. A dropped bota slapped sand by the hand braced to support my arm, braced to support me. "It has been two days since the dance with Nezbet, three since Umir's attack, and you are worse."

Much worse. "I don't know," I mumbled.

Frustration and fear made her strident. "You can't even ride, Tiger! How are we to escape the threat you say is coming if you can't even ride?"

I tilted my head back, setting my jaw against the pain. "What in hoolies do you want me to do? Pray? It'll pass, Del—I just got beat up worse than I thought. It'll pass."

Deep inside, Chosa gloated.

"Will it?" She squatted. Her face was a travesty, stretched tight and pale and thin, but the words were brutal. "The bruises are worsening—you are black and blue and swollen, because you are bleeding under the skin. And from the *inside*, also—do you think I haven't seen it when you spit?"

"So maybe a rib broke loose. . . ." I gathered myself, shifted. "Look, bascha—"

"*You* look!" she retorted. "If it goes on like this, you could die. Is that what you want? To fulfill Iskandar's fate, so everyone knows you really *are* the jhihadi?"

"I just need some time to heal. All this running . . ." I let it go, summoning the strength to stand. "All right—just give me a moment."

Del's voice was glacial, as it is when she is very angry—or very frightened. "You are still passing blood."

I stood exquisitely still, giving my body no reason to protest. "Because someone—or several someones—kicked and punched me in the kidneys," I rasped. "What in hoolies do you expect?"

"I have seen a man die from that."

I stopped testing things. "What?"

"I have seen a man die from it."

Anger flared, burning away what little strength remained. "There's *nothing I can do!*"

"You can tend to yourself," she said. "You have the magic—*use* it!"

It was all I could do to answer. "I told you why I won't."

"No, you didn't. You just said you won't. Nothing more." Del stood up stiffly. Her face was tight and pale. "I think you've given up. I think you *want* to die."

I wavered on my feet. "Oh, in the name of—"

"So you can die as the jhihadi, and be better than Abbu that way."

"*What?*"

Her mouth was rigid. "He's only a sword-dancer. *You* are the jhihadi."

No, no, bascha—it's because I feel so bad.

But why tell her that?

"Del—"

"If you can't beat him in the circle, you will beat him in your death."

I managed a laugh. "You're sandsick."

"Am I?"

"Do you really think I want to *die* to prove myself better?"

"More," she said bitterly. "To prove yourself *more*."

"Sandsick," I muttered. Hoolies, couldn't the woman see I just needed to rest? To lie down again, and sleep, and *rest*, and let the body recover?

Let her go, Chosa said. *For now, I only need you. She will come later.*

It was easier to give in. "Go on," I croaked. "If you feel that strongly . . . look, I need to rest. Go on to the oasis. I can catch up later."

Clearly, it surprised her. "I don't want that. I want us *both*—"

"Go on. You. Go on."

"The oasis isn't much farther. You can reach it, *then* rest."

"Go on without me. I'll catch up."

The line of her shoulders was impossibly taut. "If you would simply use the magic . . ." She gritted teeth. "You only refuse because you hate it so much. Because you won't admit you need more than yourself."

I laughed once. Sat down very carefully. Tented my knees and rested my brow against them. "You don't understand at all—you have no idea what kind of toll magic takes—"

Self-control frayed. "It makes you sick," she snapped. "So? Too much aqivi does the same, but that does not dissuade you."

I mumbled something against my thighs.

Del swore. I heard her walk smartly through the sand, pause—muttering—then come back again. "I *will* go," she declared. Part threat. Part plea. But also a familiar conviction I knew better than to dismiss.

I dragged my head up. Something deep inside me flared from apathy into fear.

Del's face was cold as ice. Blue eyes glittered. She spat it out all at once, almost sing-song, acquiring determination with every syllable. "You have given me leave, though I take it anyway. And so I say this: If you will do nothing—if you make no attempt to *try*—then I will not stay here to see it. The death of the jhihadi will have no witnesses. And so his body will be consumed by the Punja until only bones are left, and they will be scoured in time, and carried away, and scattered unto dust . . . until there is nothing left. No jhihadi. No sword-dancer. And nothing at all of Tiger."

Stung, I applied a rather uncomplimentary term to her.

"Yes," Del agreed, and marched away to the mare.

I watched her go. I watched her saddle the mare; split the botas, leaving me half; then mount. She reined the mare up short. "I will be at the oasis until dawn. If you are not there by then, I go on."

She didn't mean it. I knew she didn't mean it.

Del's face twisted briefly. Then she spun the mare and left.

I watched Del *go*.

"Hoolies," I croaked, "she *meant* it."

Sand drifted in her passage, dusting me with grit.

Dull anger flared anew. "She's only doing this to make me come after her."

Of course she was. She'd tried everything else.

Anger died to ash. No one—and nothing—answered. Inside me, Chosa was silent.

There is a time to set pride aside. I sighed deeply, nodding. "All right, bascha . . . I'm coming." I pressed myself to my knees, prepared to try for my feet.

The world turned upside down, spilling me like meal.

Fear punched into my belly: what if I *couldn't* reach her?

"Wait—" I rasped. "Del—don't go *yet*—"

But Del, meaning well, was already gone.

Chosa Dei was not.

Fear faded. Replacing it was a dull, colorless surprise, that Chosa could do so much when I wasn't even looking.

"Punja-mite," I croaked.

It occurred to me to wonder, as I sprawled across the blanket, if Shaka Obre's construct was coming apart at the seams. Unraveling from inside out, because Chosa was cutting into pieces the fabric of my begetting.

"Iskandar," I muttered. "Is this how it happened with you?"

Hands. They invaded burnous, belt, unbuckling and stripping away. A hand lingered on my rib cage, then withdrew.

"Dead," a man said.

"Or dying," said another.

Then a voice I knew. "Take the horse and the sword, and any coin he might have. Leave the rest for Sabra. I don't care about him. I just want the woman."

Tentatively: "He is—the Sandtiger."

Umir, impatient: "What do I care about that? He's not worthy of my collection."

No. Abbu was.

Hands again. The belt was yanked from under me, leaving me bare from chest to dhoti. Coppers rattled briefly; someone cursed. If I could have, I would have smiled: a nearly empty pouch. Small pickings from the legend.

Sound: movement. A hand at my throat, grasping sandtiger claws. "Leave that," Umir ordered. "We want to make certain Sabra knows who he was."

"There is his face," someone said. "The scars . . ."

"Vermin may eat his face—and the *rest* of him—before Sabra arrives. Leave the necklet. Abbu Bensir himself may choose to make it a keepsake."

Abbu? Abbu—with Sabra?

"Water." Another voice.

"Put it on the horse. We'll take it all." Umir strode away. "Waste no more time recalling legends. His is finished now, and I want the woman."

I heard the stud snort. Then the urgent, rumbling nicker that wasn't greeting, but warning. Southron voices called out. Then the stud screamed. Then a man did.

Ah. Good boy.

Voices, gabbling about the stud. He had crushed a man's head.

"Leave him," Umir snapped. "You won't get close to him now."

Someone by me, bending. He picked up the harness, the scabbard. Paused. Through sealed lids, I could see it: The man looking upon it. The legendary sword. His hand so very close—why not unsheathe the blade and see what the balance is like? The *Sandtiger's* sword—

He screamed. Long and loud and horrified, as the magic ate into his bones.

Stupid Punja-mite.

Gabbling again, all around me. The man still screamed.

"Kill him," Umir said. "I will not have such noise."

In a moment, the screaming stopped.

Silence. A gathering of others as they contemplated the sword. "Pick it up," Umir ordered.

One man protested that it was a magicked blade, and no one knew the spell.

"Pick it up," Umir repeated. "Use something to shield yourself—here, use the blanket."

They ripped it from under me, spilling limbs and head awry. Stupid Punja-mite. A *blanket* against Samiel?

A second man shrieked, called on his (deaf) god, then fell into sobbing. Dispassionately, Umir the Ruthless ordered him killed, too, because he did not like the noise.

"Leave it," he said curtly. "Magicked blade it may be, but I won't lose the woman. If no one can pick it up, it will be here when we return."

"But—what if Sabra herself—?"

Umir laughed. "Let us hope she tries. A woman has no business attempting to rule in a man's stead."

Retreat. Horses remounted. Men riding off.

I lay slack-limbed on the sand and wondered if it was worth it.

Maybe *I* wasn't. But Del was worth everything.

The merest breath of sound hissed through dry, unmoving lips. "Chosa?" I whispered.

Inside me, something rustled. Then flared into life, gibbering exaltation: the battle had been won.

Now there was the war.

"Ah, hoolies," I mumbled, "I *really* don't want to do this."

Chapter 32

I hunched beside the sword: obscene, unintended obeisance. But my bones were so brittle I expected them to shatter and crumble into dust even inside my living flesh.

Mottled, discolored flesh, but living nonetheless.

I stretched out a hand. Fingers trembled. The nails were bluish again; the forearms streaky black, tinged with violet, outlined luridly with traceries of yellow. What had begun as normal—if painful—bruising had spread to swallow me whole. The skin was puffy and squishy, swollen by leaking fluid.

Hoolies, I was a mess. No wonder Del got mad.

Because she was scared, too.

Pain centered in the small of my back. Fire burned brilliantly, climbing the length of my spine, then out along each of the ribs to curve around my chest and meet at the breastbone, where more pain lived. My whole body was a pyre.

Time to put it out.

The sword lay bare in the sand. I was very grateful; had Umir's man dropped it *in* its sheath, someone could have picked it up and carried it away. The blanket was no shield—nor anything else so plain—but the runes worked into the leather muted the weapon's bite. While sheathed in my harness, touching only the straps or scabbard, anyone could steal it.

"—song—" I croaked. "Hoolies, I hate singing—"

I wavered, nearly fell. I'd made no promises to Chosa—wouldn't keep them anyway—and he knew it well. He was taking no chances. By summoning the healing, I opened the door for him. And he would try to snatch it and tear it away from the wall, rushing in to fill the room that doubled as my body.

I didn't like the risk. I didn't like it at all.

But Umir was after *Del*.

I summoned my little song. Croaked it into the day. Reached down and caught the sword, then dragged it into my lap.

—circle, Tiger. Don't forget the circle—

Inside me, Chosa stirred.

He'd wanted me to forget.

On knees and one hand, I swung-dragged the tip of the sword in a ragged circle, taking care to seal the ends together. There could be no break, no crack in the drawn line, or Chosa would find and use it.

Circle. I hunched within the confines, cradling the sword, and sang my little song.

What a waste of—

Power reached out and caught me. It shook me from head to toe, rattling every bone, then threw me down again.

Belly climbed up my gullet. Chosa, crawling out?

"—*sick*—" I gulped. "—worse than aqivi—"

Every bone was wracked, twisting in sockets, pulling free of tendons.

"—*wait*—"

Blood broke from my nose.

"I take it back—" I mumbled. "—don't want it after all—"

Power dug into my hair and jerked my head up straight. I have a tough scalp, but this was too much.

"—s-ss*stop*—"

The sword glowed dully black. Inside me, Chosa answered.

I panted. Labored to swallow. Twitched from Chosa's touch, sensing his invasion. Tried to shut it—*him*—off, to deny him entrance.

But trying to deny Chosa also denied the magic.

Power had no patience. I'd sent it an invitation, and it was bringing friends.

"I *take it back*—" I shouted. "Forget I said anyth—"

Power bent very low and looked into my eyes, as if to judge the truth. As if to judge *me*.

"I'm just—a sword-dancer. . . ."

Power disagreed. It dangled me from its hand, as Umir had dangled the runes.

Blood ran down my chin. I lacked the strength to wipe it away; to do anything but breathe.

Hoolies, what have I done? What have I unleashed?

So much for the binding circle.

But it was meant to keep Chosa *in,* not keep Power out.

And who would even try?

"I just—need—to be better . . . to go—and help Delilah—"

The little piece of Chosa played hop-rock with my heartbeat. It waxed and waned, like the moon.

The spasm wracked my body. Power shook me again. Then released my hair.

The sword spilled from lax hands and out of elbow crooks. I fell on top of it.

The edge snicked into one arm, shaving hair from flesh. All I could do was laugh, stirring dust and sand with my breath.

Then the laughter died.

Because Chosa was very angry.

Chosa would take his revenge, one way or another.

I lay in the sand, on the sword. Wondering what in hoolies I was.

Wondering what I could *do*.

And what Chosa Dei would try.

Oasis. Near dusk, with the sun painting everything orange. Palm trees in sharp silhouette sprouted haphazardly, dangling beards and dates. Below, around the water, ranged Umir and his men.

One body lay on the ground, with a fallen sword nearby. I wondered if Del had killed him; or Umir, for his noise.

She stood on foot, and braced, with naked blade in her hands. Blood ran down the steel, regulated by runes, carried off the hilt before it could stain her hands. Although some would argue the stain was on her soul.

Umir, I realized, was hampered by his greed, as well as his up-bringing. He wanted her unscathed, unharmed, for addition to his collection. No matter how unique her vocation, she *was* a woman, and he a Southroner. He certainly hadn't reckoned on Del herself taking steps to refuse him so violently.

It was almost laughable. But nobody was laughing.

I reined up quietly before anyone noticed me, putting Umir and his men between Del and me. They outnumbered us, but we had the major advantage. Umir wanted her whole. Del and I were not so picky with regard to Umir's men.

She looked past them. Saw me. Didn't so much as flick an eye-lash. Returned her attention to Umir before anyone even noticed.

I began to smile, anticipating the surprise, the overwhelming shock . . . then the stud took a hand in the game by whinnying im-peratively to the mare, who answered with shrill welcome.

"Hoolies," I muttered, disgusted, and yanked the sword free of sheath as Umir and company whirled, swordblades glinting in sun-set.

Mouths dropped open, gaping. Widened eyes displayed whites. Someone muttered a prayer to the god of apparitions.

Umir the Ruthless just scowled.

A flutter of pleasure tautened my belly. I leaned forward with grave deliberation, perfectly at ease; perfectly prepared. "Some-one," I said lightly, "has my belt and my money. Care to give them back?"

"Kill him," Umir ordered.

Nobody moved a muscle. Until one man did just barely, drop-ping belt and pouch.

I grinned. I knew very well what I looked like: me. *Me* me, which all on its own can be rather threatening, since I have prac-ticed for many years. The legend in the flesh—firm, swift, *danger-ous* flesh—not the puffy, mottled, discolored body Umir's men had discovered. "Dead, am I?" I asked. "*Near* dead, maybe? Or maybe neither one, merely the deviser of a trap—or of great and powerful magic."

And for once I wasn't lying.

Well, half, maybe. It had never been a trap, but why tell them that?

Umir's men stirred. But no one obeyed his repeated order to kill me. Who could kill a man who was already dead?

I waggled the naked blade. "Anyone else care to take my sword? I think he's still hungry."

"Fools," Umir snapped. "He's a man like any of you. Don't let him goad you—*kill* him!"

"Go home," I said softly, "before I lose my temper."

Umir's men went home. Or *some*where; nonetheless, they all departed, making ward-signs against great magic. Leaving Umir by himself.

I walked the stud up to him, slowly and purposefully. Flicked a glance at Del. Then pinned Umir with a stare. "You made three mistakes," I explained. "First, you bound me with magic, and challenged me to escape. Second, you left me for dead, which I consider an insult. You wouldn't do that to *Abbu*."

Umir, eloquently unruffled, folded his hands in wide, gem-weighted sleeves. "What is the third?"

I pointed with the blade. "You discounted *her*."

He didn't even look. "Perhaps I underestimated you. Perhaps you *are* better than Abbu Bensir, and perhaps I *should* reconsider."

I grinned. "That's better." A glance at Del. "Do you want to kill him?"

She hunched a shoulder. "I've killed one man today. Another would be surfeit."

I nodded as she bent to clean her blade on the dead man's burnous. "Then I will tend to it."

Umir paled, but only slightly. "I could have killed you twice. I left you the chance to escape . . . and both times you succeeded."

"And I'll leave *you* a chance." I sheathed the sword with a snap, jumped off the stud, approached Umir the Ruthless. "Your hands," I said gently.

Thin lips smiled. "You must take what you will have."

"All right." I caught his wrists, squeezed; hands spasmed rigidly as he gasped, and stabbed out of the heavy sleeves. Still squeezing, I made him sit. Then shut the wrists in one large hand, drew my knife with the other, nicked him to free the blood.

Umir grayed. "Do you mean me to *bleed* to death?"

"I don't mean you to do anything, except sit here." I shot the knife home again, then carefully smeared blood all over both wrists. "Nice bracelets," I commented. "Now, a little piece of advice . . ."

Umir's lips were pale. "What do you—?" He winced.

Del came over. She stood next to me and watched, one hand gripping her sword. I heard her indrawn breath.

"There." I released his wrists. Both were bound tightly by thick, twined ropes of rune-wrought blood, red-black in the setting sun. "Now, for that advice . . ." I leaned down close to Umir. *"Never annoy a man whose magic is greater than yours."*

Chapter 33

"Come on," I said to Del. "No need to stay here."

She stared after me as I turned back to the stud. I swung up smoothly, gathered reins, saw the tension in her shoulders; the questions in her eyes. But she asked none of them, because she knew better: you do not put even a small weapon into the hands of the enemy. She simply sheathed her newly-cleaned blade and went to her own mount.

Umir's mouth opened. "You're leaving?"

I shrugged as the stud danced, wanting to go to the mare. "No reason to stay. I don't like the company."

"But—" He lifted his blood-bound hands. "What about this?"

"Good color on you." I angled the stud southerly, discussing matters through reins. "You ought to make it a habit."

"You can't *leave* me here!"

"Of course I can. You have water, don't you?—right there in the basin. Binding your hands doesn't mean you can't drink. As for food, well . . ." I shrugged, bunching the stud under me. "Guess you'll just have to wait for Sabra."

"But—" He broke it off.

I took a deeper seat in the saddle and stilled the stud deftly, leaning forward toward Umir. "Unless you've lied. Unless she isn't coming at all."

Indecision warped his features. Then grimness settled. "She's coming," he said flatly. "From Iskandar to Julah. She will have left Quumi by now."

"Good. She can feed you when she gets here." The stud danced again as I gave him rein and glanced at Del. "You ready?"

Mutely, she nodded.

"Good. Then let's ride. We're burning the last little bit of daylight." But even as Del rode off, I reined the stud back once more. He didn't like it a bit, snorting and tossing his head. "Umir," I said quietly, "I wouldn't struggle too much. Those runes won't strangle you, but they might cut off your hands."

Umir sat very still.

I turned the stud loose and went after Del, laughing into the stud-born wind.

The amusement was short-lived. Del, as expected, did not allow me to get very far before taxing me with questions. The trouble was, she had too many, even for *her* mouth; she started out fine, but ended up in a Northern tangle.

"Start over," I suggested.

Del stared at me hard, teeth clenched. "*You* start," she ordered.

"I didn't die." I arched eyebrows at her expression. "I did what you wanted me to, so why are you complaining?"

Teeth remained clenched. "Because you might have done it *before*."

"Before what? Umir's arrival? Hoolies, it worked out very well. Now his men are hightailing it back to Quumi telling tales of a Sandtiger fetch . . . should add something to the legend, and save us a bit of hide."

"How?"

"Some would-be captors may decide not to try their luck."

She thought about it. "But you felt it was necessary to drive me away—"

"No." The humor died. "I felt it necessary to give nothing to Chosa Dei. *That* is why I refused to summon the magic again."

She stared angrily, weighing the truth. Assessing my expression; the sincerity of my tone. Her expression eventually softened, but doubt remained paramount. "But you *did* summon it."

"Yes. But not for me."

"If it was such a risk, as you say, then why—?" She let it die. Realization blanched her pale as her hair, plaited off her face. "But not for you," she said numbly.

I did not pursue that topic. "As for why I wanted us to leave Umir where he was, and in such haste, it's because I don't know how long in hoolies those rune-ropes will last. For all I know, he's already loose."

Brows lanced down. "How did you do that? How did you make them? What did you do to him?"

"Borrowed a little trick from Chosa Dei."

Del jerked the mare to a halt. She is not ordinarily heavy-handed, and the mare has a soft mouth. Gape-mouthed, the mare stopped, dark eyes rolling. I also reined in the stud. "What have you done?" Del asked. Her eyes searched my face. "What have you done to yourself?"

I shrugged.

Pupils spread in blue eyes, altering them to black. She studied everything in my face with avid intensity. Then some of the tension faded. Now she looked for something else; for a different kind of truth. "Umir's men didn't kill you because they thought you were dead already. That's why you scared them off."

I shrugged again. "Close enough."

It clearly unsettled her. "Did you fail to come after me because of pride? Or because you *couldn't?*"

I grinned. "Close enough." But I wasn't as good as I'd hoped. Blood drained from her face. The look in her eye scared me. "I wouldn't have—*died*," I told her hastily. "Not from Chosa's devising. *Umir's* men might have killed me, but Chosa wouldn't have. He wants the body too much."

Her voice was oddly toneless. "If he had won, you wouldn't be Tiger anymore."

I twisted shoulders. "Probably not."

Del swallowed tightly. "I left you to force your hand."

"I know that."

"I thought you would come."

"I know that, too."

"But you might have died, anyway . . . because you *couldn't* come." Del's expression was despairing. "What have I done to you?"

"Nothing." I tapped heels to the stud. "It's done, Del. None of this matters because I'm all healed and I'm still me."

"Are you?"

I arched a single brow. "I'll prove it to you later."

She didn't smile at the suggestive tone. "Tiger—"

I sighed. "I just learned a couple of tricks."

"Did *he?*" she demanded as I rode by the mare. "Did Chosa learn tricks, too?"

I shook my head, jerking the stud's back around as he looked for the mare. "He already knows them all."

It was a cool, soft night, and we treated it as such. I lay on my back, contemplating the stars and moon, slack-limbed in satiation. I was bare except for the dhoti, the dampness of exertion drying slowly on my body. I felt wondrously relaxed, gazing sleepily at the sky, but Del was wide awake. I never have understood how a woman, thoroughly satisfied, wants to discuss the state of the world, while I'd just as soon let the world drift right on by, taking me with it.

Her thigh was stuck to mine, as was a shoulder blade angled slightly against my chest. Del unstuck us both by rolling onto a hip, dragging her burnous to drape across exquisitely long, bare legs, as well as the hips and taut rump above them. Pale hair was loose and tousled: silver beacon in the darkness.

"What are you thinking about?"

Hoolies. They always ask.

I contemplated lying. But Del was not overly romantic—not like most other women—and the truth would not disturb her. "About Abbu."

She stiffened. "Abbu Bensir? *Now?*"

Maybe she wanted less truth after all. "Just—never mind."

But she went slack again. One hand touched my chest and began counting scars. It was a habit of hers, to which I never objected, because her touch felt good. "You want to beat him *so* badly."

"Didn't used to." I pillowed my head on one bent arm. "Well, that's not entirely true—I've *always* wanted to beat him—but it never mattered so much before."

"And now it does, because of what Umir said?"

"Umir says whatever he thinks will get him what he wants." I scowled faintly, considering. "I think it has more to do with Sabra."

"Why? You know nothing about her."

"I know something. I know she's a woman tanzeer, and she's managed to hold her place."

"It won't last. You've said so."

"It won't. But if Abbu is riding with her, after telling us he wasn't . . ." I freed a pale ribbon of hair as it tangled in my necklet. "He is not the kind to lie."

Del shrugged, still counting scars. "Perhaps he changed his mind later. Perhaps Sabra convinced him."

"Nor is he the kind to be won by a woman's blandishments."

"You don't know that. Have you ever slept with him?"

I grunted. "Do I seem like the kind?"

"One should not judge." Del's voice was languorous. "I only mean that many men will do many things, depending on a bedding."

"You sound uncommonly knowledgeable."

"*You* know better than that."

"I only know what you've told me."

She considered getting testy but discarded it out of apathy. "I say again, men can be persuaded of many different things."

"I never thought of Abbu as a man to be bought by a bedding." I paused. "Nor *myself,* I might add."

"I have too little coin." Del shifted closer. "If she is a beautiful woman, he may have been persuaded to take up her cause. Or for the other reason."

"What other reason?"

"The chance to dance against you. He wanted it in Iskandar, before the stud kicked you in the head."

I smiled. "Maybe he weighs himself against my reputation."

"As you do against his?"

I shrugged. "Maybe."

"Yes."

I gave in. "Yes."

"Well, I think this will be settled between you one day. Perhaps not for years, but one day." Her fingers found and stilled on the fist-deep, fibrous fissure carved below the short ribs on the left side of my chest. I could barely feel the pressure through the whorls of scar tissue. "I'm sorry," she whispered.

She said it every time. Meant it every time. And every time recalled how she'd very nearly killed me, in the circle on Staal-Ysta.

"Could have been worse," I said. "Could have been—*lower*—" I rolled over and atop her, crooking a leg across her hips, "—and then we'd *both* be sorry."

Del's laugh is smoke. It curled its way around me and drifted into the night.

When I am with this woman, the doubts all spill away. Because even if I am *not* real, at least I have this much.

Chapter 34

*I*ce, all around. Wreaths of it, riming rocks, glittering in saffron sunlight; in the warmth of a Southron day—

Wait, I said to myself. Ice? In the South?

Even deep in sleep, I knew better than that.

Which, of course, woke me up.

Del rolled over as I pushed myself upright and scowled fiercely into morning. A hand through tousled hair did nothing to rid myself of the afterimage, nor did a violent rubbing of squinting, sleep-begummed eyes. The impression was very clear: ice, in the South.

"Must be sandsick," I muttered, and reached for the nearest bota.

Del yawned, stretched, squinched up her face against pale new sunlight, peering at me one-eyed. "Why?"

I shrugged, sucking water.

The other blue eye came open. "I don't necessarily disagree, but I am curious as to why *you* would say so."

I swallowed and lowered the bota. "One need not explain one's dreams if one does not desire it."

"Ah." She put out a hand for the bota. "Unless one is the jhihadi."

"Jhihadis don't need to explain themselves, either. Jhihadis just—are."

"Like the Sandtiger."

"Yet more proof." I stripped aside blankets, stood up. I felt amazingly good for a man taken to task by a certain unspecified power, and later left for dead in the midst of the Punja. I felt *intensely* good—

And then recalled how I'd been healed, or remade, or whatever you want to call it.

Which meant the *real* me was just as battered and bruised, and no younger than before.

Or whatever me I was.

Scowling, I looked down at Del. "How was I last night?"

Pale brows shot up. Del blinked feigned astonishment at me. I realized her interpretation of the question, in view of the intimacy we'd shared, was not to be unexpected.

I rephrased it, waving a hand. "Not that. I don't need reassurances about *that*. I just meant . . ." I trailed off. "I'm not doing this very well."

Del, somewhat bemused, slid a foot into one sandal and began lacing the cross-garter thongs to her knees. "What are you trying to say? Or ask? Or—whatever?"

"Did I seem—*real*—to you?"

A number of expressions took turns upon her face. Amusement, curiosity, bafflement; also a flicker of uncertainty. At last, as she looked up at me, an unfamiliar tranquillity, as if she knew how much her answer meant, and was pleased to be utterly honest. "Indisputably."

I didn't let up; not yet. "You never doubted for once it was me?"

She stopped knotting sandal laces. "*Should* I have?"

"No. I don't think so. I mean, I felt like me to *me*." I scratched viciously at stubble. "Never mind. I just—never mind."

"Tiger." Del finished the knot and smiled up at me. Fair hair curtained shoulders. "You were as you always are. I have no complaints. I doubt Elamain would, either . . . or any of the other thousands of women who've shared a night with you."

No, Elamain had never had any complaints, before she nearly got me castrated. Neither had any of the other women (not *thousands*; Del exaggerated), but I wasn't really concerned about them.

What concerned me was that Del might—or might not—see any kind of *difference* in me. Anything that might indicate I was something of Shaka Obre, with a bit of Chosa, as well.

I felt like the same old me. But the same old me was—who?

"Sandsick," I muttered again, and went off to water the dirt.

Del's purposefully idle tone drifted in my wake. "And men say *women* are fanciful."

Which is because they are.

But I was a bit too busy to explain it to her.

Rusali was much as we'd left it, which was a year or so before. A typical Southron town. A typical *Punja* town in a typical Punja domain—except when we'd left it, its tanzeer was newly dead because a Northern sword-dancer had killed him in order to requench a *jivatma*.

Not Del. Theron. Who'd come hunting her for the death of the *an-kaidin* Baldur, whom Del had killed to blood her blade.

In hindsight, the explanation for both of them sounded similar. But Del's situation had been different. Theron had *requenched* against all Northern taboos, in order to gain an edge. Lahamu, Rusali's tanzeer, dabbled a bit in magic, and had some experience with sword-dancing techniques. Theron decided to requench in order to have a better chance against Del in the circle, because by requenching in Lahamu he gained the Southron style, which she didn't know.

He'd nearly beaten her, too, but I'd figured out something was wrong and forcibly pulled Del from the circle. Ordinarily it would have forfeited the dance to Theron, but Del had quickly realized what he'd done. Theron's transgression made the dance invalid, except I'd decided, on my own, to teach him a lesson.

And I had. I'd killed him.

Meanwhile discovering just what it was to wield a *jivatma*, when one knows its name.

Ah, yes. Theron. Brother to Telek, son to old Stigand; both of whom, on Staal-Ysta, had conspired first to exile Del, then to kill us both by playing one against the other in the deadliest dance of all, because each of us wanted—*needed*—to win: Del, to gain a year with her daughter; me to win back my freedom from an oath-sworn, binding service Del had tricked me into.

Hoolies, so much had happened. Look at us *now*.

Look at *me* now.

Then again, don't. You might see something neither one of us likes.

Rusali. Empty of Lahamu, but also now of Alric, transplanted Northern sword-dancer, and Lena, his Southron wife, and all their mixed-blood girls.

We rode through the haphazard outskirts and into the city proper. Del was strangely bemused. "What?" I asked.

"Remembering," she answered. "We barely knew each other then . . . look at us now."

It echoed my own thought. Glumly, I said, "Now we know too much."

She smiled. "Sometimes."

"Then, again, there's a lot I don't know about you—and a lot you don't know about me."

That earned me a sidelong glance. "That may be—but there's a lot about you that *you* don't know."

I grunted. "I know enough."

"Then why do you keep asking me if I think you're real?"

I reined the stud around an overturned basket spilling refuse into the narrow, dusty street. "Don't you ever wonder if *you're* not real?"

"No."

I ducked a low-hanging awning, bumping left knee against Del's right as the narrowing of the street squeezed us closer to-gether. "You never once wondered if maybe you weren't some sort of—construct?"

"Construct?"

I groped for the best explanation. "A conjured person. A *mag-icked* person, created by sorcery for a particular purpose." Like changing the sand to grass?

Del frowned. "No. Why would I?"

I tried to figure out the easiest way of explaining, without re-ally explaining. "Didn't you think, when you realized how good you could be with the sword, that maybe you were something out of the ordinary?"

Del smiled faintly. "My kinfolk *always* told me I was out of the ordinary."

I scowled. "That's not what I mean. I mean—when you knew, in your heart, you were better than everybody. Did you think there might be a reason?"

Brows quirked upward. "Better than *every*body?"

"Well, not me. That hasn't been established."

She laughed softly. "No, I never wondered. When I was young, and my brothers and uncles and father began to teach me weaponry, it was simply something to do. Everyone else did it. My mother had the great good sense not to forbid me the chance, and the other women had the great good sense not to criticize my mother for that. And when, on Staal-Ysta, I knew I could be *this* good—well . . ." The tone died out. When it resumed, the inflection had altered from idle recollection to grim acknowledgment. "By then, I merely wanted to be as good as was required to do what I had to do, in order to destroy Ajani. I did not think again on anything else, nor to question the good fortune that gifted me with the skill."

"Oh," I said at last.

"So no, I never wondered if I was a—construct?" She waited for my nod. "I have always been what I am. What I was required to be."

I said nothing. It had never occurred to me, either, until I squatted before the old hustapha and thought, for the first time, that all the natter about jhihadis and sand and grass might have some foundation in fact.

I shivered uneasily. Felt the weight of *jivatma* across my back, and the sorcerer it housed.

We took a room in a small, mostly empty inn whose proprietor was so glad for the custom that he gave us his very best. Which didn't mean much, really, but at least the bed was longer. For once my heels hit the end of the frame, instead of hanging over the edge.

Del knelt on the packed dirt floor and sorted out botas, untangling thongs from saddle-pouch buckles. "We can't stay long."

"Overnight." I loosened a knot in one of my sandal laces. "We can pick up provisions now, or wait until morning."

"I'll go now. You can bathe first." She rose, settling pouches beside me on the bed. "Assuming you *want* to bathe."

"And *I* assume, by your tone of voice, you think I should."

Del smiled. "Yes." And walked toward the curtain door.

"Where are you going?"

Elaborate clarity: "To buy provisions; I said so."

"We can do that together."

She shrugged. "No need. I'll be back by the time you're done, and use your water."

All in all I thought it somewhat odd. While Del was perfectly capable of provisioning us on her own, we usually did it together simply to make things easier. But I saw no reason to protest. Maybe she needed time to herself; women are like that.

Especially when they spend money.

My turn to shrug. "All right. If I'm not in here, I'll be in the common room."

"Sucking down aqivi; where else?" Del pulled aside the tattered fabric curtaining the door and was gone.

I ordered a bath brought in; the proprietor acquiesced by rolling in a warped half-cask, then lugging in buckets of water. Not many; not enough. But it was better than nothing. There were bathhouses in Rusali, but with them there's no telling how many bodies the water's washed. At least this way Del got mine, and me she already knew.

Not enough soap, either, but I made do, and left enough for Del. Then I took my freshly washed self into the common room, where I ordered aqivi, and spent some time drinking it.

Del eventually came back bearing burdens, nodded at me, then disappeared into our room. I contemplated wandering in to witness her bath, then decided she might not get bathed at all, in view of what sometimes happened when she was bare of clothes and wet, and stayed where I was. Drinking.

The aqivi ran out. I didn't order more. I went in to see what in hoolies was taking Del so long.

She sat with her back to me, swathed in a hooded burnous. I

opened my mouth to ask her what in hoolies she was doing, when she turned, startled, and stared wide-eyed.

Struck dumb, I stared back. We neither of us moved.

All I saw were blue eyes. The bluest, brightest eyes. They were her same old eyes, with the same old color and clarity, but everything else was different.

I managed at last to speak. "What have you done to yourself?"

Her answer was very forceful, as if she tried to convince herself as well as me. "Made myself someone else."

I moved, finally. Stopped beside the bed. Put out a tentative hand and pushed the hood from head to shoulders. "All of it?"

Del arched a dyed-black eyebrow. "Blonde *and* black hair would make me even more obvious than I already was."

"But—I like you blonde."

She scowled. "It will wash out."

"What about this?" I touched one darkened cheek.

"That, too." A black-haired, dark-skinned Del, glowering, was oddly different from the usual fairer version, even with the same expression. "Do I look very Southron?"

"Not with *those* eyes."

She put a hand up, then let it drop back. "I'm a Borderer."

"Hah."

"You will say so, of course."

I studied her. Formerly white-blonde hair, sunbleached, was now a dull black, still wet and slick. Darkened eyebrows were more pronounced, harshening her expression, and she'd even tipped eyelashes. The skin was a uniform brown several shades lighter than Southron color, not so far from my own—except she lacked the coppery tint.

I frowned. Stepped back. Chewed a lip as I considered.

I felt—odd. I had never before seen her as anyone but herself: pale-haired, blue-eyed Delilah, shaped by a cooler sun. She had been Northern from the outset, indisputably foreign, and all the more striking for the difference. But now she was, in color, more Southron than anything else; now looking much like other women, Del lost much of the distinctiveness that attracted every male eye. She was still strikingly beautiful, but in a much different way. In an oddly *familiar* way, since coloring as much as bone and flesh affects a woman's appearance.

Comparing the old Del to the new one underscored how men felt when the familiar became something else. Something more tantalizing.

Was this how Umir felt? Attracted to differences?

She was still remarkably beautiful. Skin stain and hair dye could not erase the clarity of her features, the flawlessness of the bones, nor the subtle self-awareness and elegant physical power that set her apart from others.

The dye was very bad. The skin stain muddy. But underneath the dulled exterior lay the gleam of glorious steel.

"Why?" I asked.

She lifted her chin. "I am a Southron woman—a *Borderer* woman—being escorted to Julah by a hired sword."

I squinted a little. "Why?"

"Because no one is *looking* for that; why do you think?"

"Oh, and am *I* supposed to dye my hair, too?"

She shrugged. "You don't have to. It's *me* who stands out."

I nodded thoughtfully. "Didn't we discuss the fact I'm not exactly unknown in these parts? That there are certain physical differences that also set *me* apart?"

"They will ask for you, of course . . . but they will also ask for a fair-haired Northern bascha who carries—and uses—a sword." Del didn't smile. "Not a proper Borderer woman who buys a sword-dancer for protection, instead of wielding a *jivatma*."

"And you think that will throw them off."

"Either that, or we must split up."

"No." I didn't even waste a moment considering it. "It's true they'll ask for the Northern bascha . . . this might confuse them a little. But only a very little."

"If it earns us the freedom to reach Julah without being molested—and wherever else we must go—it will have served its purpose."

I smiled faintly, still assessing a black-haired, dark-skinned Del. "Is this your way of testing my—interest?"

"No," she answered dryly. "As *interested* as you are—and as often—I think I could be bald."

I grunted disagreement. "Bald women don't excite me."

Del was speculative. "You could shave your head."

Aghast: "What *for?*"

"To see if bald men excite *me*."

"Close your eyes," I suggested firmly. "And then you can just *pretend*."

Del's smile was still Del's smile, in spite of dye and stain.

So was my response.

Chapter 35

I was cold, cold as ice . . . cold as stone in Northern mountains wracked by a Northern wind. The air was sharp as a knife, bathing bare flesh in rippling pimples of protest. I shivered, wrapped myself more tightly in the threadbare coverlet—

—and realized I was awake, in the South, and sweating because of the warmth.

I threw back the coverlet, cursing sleepily, and realized the bed was empty of Del.

I cracked eyelids and saw her across the room, sitting against the wall opposite the bed. Just—sitting. And staring at her naked sword, which she held before her face in a level, horizontal bar.

It was an unusual posture, particularly for someone sitting in an otherwise relaxed position. She wasn't singing for one of her little rituals. Wasn't honing the steel. Just staring. From my angle, the sword blade blocked her eyes. I saw a chin, a mouth, a nose, and the upper part of her forehead.

I hitched myself up on one elbow. "What are you doing?"

"Looking at my reflection." Del lowered the blade to rest across her thighs. One hand touched dyed black hair, now dry and luster-less. Her gaze was fixed and unwavering, centered somewhere other than here. It was an eerie, unfocused expression. The hand fell away from hair, landed slackly on tunicked thighs. "Do you know what I have done?"

Awareness sharpened. "What do you mean? The dye? I thought you said it would wash out."

Del stared blindly at me. "What I have done," she murmured. And then slumped against the wall with the sword across her knees. Her face was an odd mixture of realization and relief; weary recognition and a transcendent discovery she clearly was uncertain could bring her any peace. She closed her eyes, shivered once, then laughed softly to herself. Murmuring something in uplander incomprehensible to me.

I sat up, swinging legs over the edge of the bed, planting bare feet on packed dirt. "Del—"

Blue eyes opened and stared back. "It's done," she said intently. "Don't you see?"

"What's done?"

She laughed out loud. Cut it off. Then laughed again, half choked, splaying both hands against her face in a peculiarly vulnerable, feminine gesture. "Ajani," she said through her fingers.

I blinked. "That was almost two weeks ago. Are you only just *now* realizing he's dead?"

Glazed blue eyes stared fixedly at me over stained fingertips. "Dead," she echoed. And then tears welled up without warning and Del began to laugh.

Awash with helplessness, I stared warily back at her. That she cried out of something other than sadness was obvious, because it didn't warp her features with grief. She just laughed, and cried, and eventually cradled a sword against her breasts as a woman does a child.

"Done," she said huskily, when the laughter died away. "My song is truly ended."

Tears still stained her face, muddying her efforts at making herself Southron. But at the moment that appeared to be the least of her concerns. "Bascha—"

"I had not allowed myself to think about it," she said. "Do you see? There was no time. There were people after us—"

"They still are."

"—and never any time to think—"

"Not much more now; we ought to get moving."

"—nor any time to consider what I must vanquish *now*."

That stopped me. "Vanquish?" Oh, hoolies, what now?

Del smiled sadly. "Me."

I gazed blankly back at her.

"You asked me so many times, Tiger . . . and each time I gave you no answer, putting off the consideration for another time."

"Del—"

"Don't you see? I have finally come to myself. I know what I have done . . . but not what I will *do*." She smiled crookedly. "You said it would come to this. I chose not to listen."

It was not, I decided, the proper time to rub it in. Instead, I pointed her to another topic infinitely more important. "At the moment we're sort of in the middle of something else."

The diversion didn't work. "All those years," she said reflectively. "I gave him all those years, with nothing left for myself."

I waited, deciding she didn't need my comments.

"He took from me everything I knew in the space of one morning—kinfolk, lifestyle, virginity. With steel and flesh alike he shredded me inside and out—" She leaned her head into one rigid, splay-fingered hand, knotting dull black hair. "And do you know what I did?"

"Escaped," I said quietly. "Collected blood-debt for your kinfolk, according to Northern custom."

Del smiled. Such a sad, despairing smile, cognizant of accomplishment as well as recognition of what the task had required. "More," she said hollowly. "And I gave it to him willingly, all those years on Staal-Ysta, and the others spent searching for him. *I* gave it to him—Ajani did not insist. He did not *require* it." She leaned her head against the wall, combing black hair with darkened fingers. "I did what most people, even men, might have refused to do, or given up along the way when the doing became too demanding."

"You honored the oaths you swore."

"Oaths," she said wearily, "oaths can warp a soul."

I gazed steadily back. "But oaths are what we live by. Oaths are food and water when the belly cramps on emptiness and the mouth is dry as bone."

Del looked at me. "Eloquent," she murmured. And then,

somberly, "We both of us have known too much of that. And allowed our oaths to consume us."

I sat very still. She spoke of herself, but of more; of me, also, putting faith into oaths meant to get me through the night, or through the day beyond. A chula makes his own future when the truth is too bleak to face.

"It's over," I said. "Ajani is dead. And if you waste your breath on regrets—"

"No." She cut me off. "No, no regrets—that much I do not acknowledge . . . I have sung my song as I meant to, and the task is at last accomplished. Honor is satisfied . . ." Briefly, a glorious smile. "But I am only just realizing—now, *this moment*—that I am truly free at last. Woman or man, I am completely free for the first time since I was born to be whatever I choose, instead of having it chosen for me."

"No," I said quietly. "As long as you stay with me while there is a price upon my head, you are free of nothing."

She sat against the wall holding the sword that had been sweet deliverance as well as harsh taskmaster. And then she smiled, and reached for the harness, and put the sword away. "That choice was made long ago."

"Was it?"

"Oh, yes. When you came with me to Staal-Ysta. When, in my obsession, I made the man into coin to be bartered to the *voca*."

I shrugged. "You had your reasons."

"Wrong ones," she said, "as you were at pains to tell me." She rose, began to gather up pouches and collect scattered gear. "After all you gave to me, in the midst of my personal song, do you think I could leave you?"

"You," I said clearly, "are eminently capable of doing anything you please."

Del laughed. "That is the best kind of freedom."

"And the kind you couldn't know if you hadn't killed Ajani."

She paused. Turned to look at me. "Are you making excuses for me?"

I shrugged negligently. "If I started doing that, I'd have no time for anything else."

"Hah," Del retorted. But accepted the bone with grace. She, as well as I, is uncomfortable with truths when they border on the soul.

The problem arose when I suggested it was a good idea if I kept Del's sword with me.

"Why?" she asked sharply.

"Because you said it yourself: you're a Borderer woman who's hired a sword-dancer to escort her to Julah."

"That doesn't mean you need to carry my *jivatma*."

"It means someone other than *you* should; who in hoolies else is there?"

We stood outside in the morning sunlight, saddled horses at hand, pouches secured. All that wanted doing was us to mount and ride—only Del wasn't about to.

"No," she declared.

I glared. "You don't trust me."

"I trust you. I don't trust your sword."

"It's *my* sword . . . don't you think I can control it?"

"No."

I bit back an expletive, kicked out at a stone, sucked teeth violently as I stared at the ground, the horses, the horizon; at everything but Del. Finally I nodded tightly. "Then you may as well wash out the dye and the stain."

"Why?"

"Because you toting around that sword will draw all sorts of attention, regardless of your color."

"I'll carry it on my horse," she said. "Here—I'll wrap it in a blanket, tie it onto the saddle . . . no one will know what it is."

I watched her strip a rolled blanket off the mare, spread it on the ground, then place harnessed *jivatma* in its folds. She tucked ends, rolled up the blanket, tied the bundle onto the back of her saddle.

"Can't get at it," I observed.

"You're supposed to protect me."

"And when have you ever allowed it?"

Del's smile was fleeting: white teeth flashed in a muddy face. "Then I guess we'll both have to learn something new."

I grunted. "Guess so." And climbed up onto the stud.

*　*　*

The Punja thinned as we neared the Southron Mountains jutting
up beyond Julah. The sand was now pocked with the rib cage of
the South's skeleton, the knobs of a spine all broken and crumbly
and dark. Wispy vegetation broke through to wave spindly stems,
and spiky, twisted sword-trees began to march against the horizon,
interspersed with tigerclaw brush. Even the smell began to change,
from the acrid dust-and-sand of the Punja to the bitter tang of vegetation and the metallic taste of porous smokerock, lighter by far
than it looked. The colors, too, were different. Instead of the pale,
crystalline sands in shades of ivory, saffron and silver, there were
deeper, richer hues: umber, sienna, tawny gold, mixed with the
raisin-black of crumbly smokerock and the olive-ash of vegetation.
It made the world seem cooler, even if it wasn't.

"So," Del said, "what do we do once we reach Julah?"

I didn't answer at once.

She waited, glanced over, lifted brows. "Well?"

"I don't know," I muttered.

"You—don't know?" She slowed the mare a pace. "I thought
you said we had to go to Julah."

"We do."

"But . . ." She frowned. "Do you have a reason? Or was this ar-
bitrary?"

"It's where we're supposed to go."

"Is Shaka Obre somewhere in Julah?"

"I don't know."

She let a long moment go by. "I do not mean to criticize—"

"Yes, you do."

"—but if we are to go into the dragon's maw once again, don't
you think there should be a purpose?"

"There is a purpose." I slapped at a bothersome fly trying to
feast upon the stud's neck. "The purpose is to find Shaka Obre."

"But you don't know—"

"I will." Definitively.

"How do you know you'll know?"

"I just will."

"Tiger—"

"Don't ask why, Del. I don't have an answer. I—just know this is what we have to do."

"In spite of the danger."

"Maybe *because* of the danger; how should I know?"

"You don't think it's odd that you've brought us down here with no certainty of our task?"

"I think everything's odd, bascha. I think everything we've done in the past two years is odd. I don't even know why we've done it, or are *still* doing it . . . I just know we have to." I paused. "*I* have to."

She digested that a moment. "Is this all part of the sandcasting the old hustapha did?"

"Partly." I left it at that.

"What else?"

"You wouldn't understand."

"I might."

"No, you wouldn't."

"How do you know?"

"I just—know."

"Like you 'just know' we should go to Julah."

I scowled. "You don't have to."

Del gritted teeth. "That's not the point. I'm here, am I not? I just want to know what we may be facing. Is that so bad? Is it not appropriate? I am a sword-dancer, after all—"

"Del, just let it go. I can't give you the answers you want. All I can say is we're supposed to go to Julah."

"And where after that?"

"How in hoolies should *I* know?"

"Ah," Del murmured.

Which contented neither of us, but was the best I could do.

Dark, ragged rock, all chewed and twisted and jagged, glittering with ice. Cold air bathed bare flesh; fogged a rune-scribed jivatma; flowed through the narrow throat into the mouth beyond and wisped away into warmer breath. Not the dragon near Ysaa-den, but an older, smaller place, all twisted and curdled and fissured: dark hollowness rimed with frost—

"Tiger?"

I twitched in the saddle. "What?"

"Are you all right?"

"I'm just thinking. Isn't that allowed?"

She arched a single blackened brow. "Forgive me my intrusion. But it is nearing sunset, and I thought perhaps we should stop for the night."

I waved a hand. "Fine."

Del scrutinized me. "You've been awfully quiet the last few hours."

"I *said* I was thinking."

She sighed, aimed the mare in a diagonal line toward a cluster of tigerclaw brush, said nothing more. Disgruntled by my own snappishness and Del's questions, I followed. Dropped off the stud and began to undo buckles and thongs.

Stopped. Stared blankly at my hands: wide-palmed, scar-pocked hands, showing the wear and tear of slavery as well as sword-dancer calluses. But as I stared the scars faded, the palms grew narrow, the flesh a darker brown. Even the fingers were changed: longer and narrower, with a sinewy elegance.

"Tiger?"

I glanced up. I knew it was Del, but I couldn't see her. I saw the land instead: a lush, green-swathed land, undulant with hills.

—I will unmake what you have made, to show you that I can—

"Tiger." Del snagged the mare's reins into tigerclaw brush and took a step toward me. "Are you all right?"

—I will destroy its lush fertility and render it into hoolies, just to prove I CAN—

Del's hand was on my arm. "Ti—"

—I will change the grass to sand—

I twitched at her touch, then shuddered. Stepped away, shaking my head, and rubbed at the place she had touched me. My hands were my own again, with no trace of what I'd seen.

No trace of what I'd heard.

Del's blue eyes, in a dark face, were avidly compelling. "Where do we go?" she asked. "Where is Shaka Obre?"

Without thought, I pointed.

She turned. Stared. Glanced back at me, measuring my mood. "You're sure?"

"Yes—*no.*" I frowned. Slowly lowered my hand. "When you asked, I knew. But now—" I shook my head to shed disorientation. "It's gone. I have no idea what I meant."

"You pointed that way, toward the mountains beyond Julah."

I shrugged. "I don't know, bascha. It's gone."

She chewed at a lip. "Perhaps . . ." She let it go, then sighed. "Perhaps you should ask Chosa Dei."

"Chosa Dei has had entirely too much to say of late, thank you. I'd just as soon keep it that way."

"But he would know. He is the one who imprisoned Shaka Obre." Her expression altered. "Is that how you know we must go to Julah? Because of him?"

Unsettled, I hunched shoulders. "Some things I just—sense."

Pensively, she nodded. "There is that part of him in you—"

I turned back to the stud, undoing buckles again. "For the moment, he's being quiet."

"Is he?"

"He isn't trying to unmake me, if that's what you mean. I'd know about that." I pulled down pouches and saddle, stepping away from the sweat-drenched stud to set things damp-side up to dry in the sun. "I promise: I'll let you know."

"Do," Del said pointedly, and turned back to her mare.

I sat bolt upright in the middle of the night, then thrust myself up and ran two stumbling steps before I stopped, swearing, and scrubbed sweat from my face. As expected, Del was awake also. Waiting.

I turned back, blew out a deep breath of disgust and self-contempt, walked back to the blankets. Stood aimlessly in the sand, feeling its coolness between my toes. Saw the gleam of Del's *ji-vatma:* three feet of naked steel.

I waved a hand. "No."

After a moment, she put it away. And waited.

I squatted. Picked up a chunk of smokerock. Flipped it into darkness and excavated for more. "Cold," I said finally. "Cold—and closed *in.*"

"Is it Chosa's memories?"

"And mine. They're all tangled, layered one on top of another.

I saw Aladar's mine. And Dragon Mountain. And some place I don't know, but I know that I *should* know it."

"Chosa," she murmured grimly.

I shivered, moved to sit on the blanket, drew the burnous over bare legs. "You know what happened to me. You saw. When Aladar threw me in the mine."

"I know."

I tasted bitterness. "It doesn't go away."

"Someday it will."

"It was bad enough when we were with the Cantéada, in their canyon caves . . ." I shivered. "Dragon Mountain wasn't much better, but at least Chosa made me think about something else. Once he had you, I didn't think of it at all. I just knew I had to kill him."

Her hand settled on my right leg, smoothing burnous and flesh. "What was it tonight?"

"A cold, small place. Funnels and tunnels and pockets . . ." I frowned. "And I was *in* it."

"Well, perhaps it was just a dream. A nightmare."

"I don't dream anymore."

It startled her. "What?"

"I don't dream anymore. I haven't for a few weeks."

"What do you mean? Everyone dreams. You did before."

I shrugged. "It's not the same. What I see are *memories* now, not dreams. Over and over again. Shaka and Chosa, but Chosa's always blurred. As if—" I broke it of with the flop of a hand.

"As if you and he are one?"

I grimaced. "Not quite. Chosa's still Chosa, and I'm still me. But the memories are tangled. I see mine, and I see his—and sometimes I can't tell the difference."

Del's hand tightened on my leg. "It will end. It will be over. We will find Shaka and discharge the sword as well as your memories."

"Maybe," I said grimly. "But if we purge me of Chosa, how much of me goes, too?"

Chapter 36

*B*eyond reared the mountains: raisin-black, dusty indigo, tumbled croppings of dark smokerock. Before them clustered Julah, a crude, ragged encampment of lopsided hovels—

No.

Julah?

Julah was a *city*, a full-fledged domain city, rich from mines and slave-trade.

I blinked. Frowned. Rubbed eyes. Glowered at the city again, as the Chosa-memory and mine traded places. This time it *was* a city.

Del's tone was grim. "I hoped never to come here again."

"No more than I," I agreed, recalling our subterfuge. Del, chained like a slave, with a collar around her neck, walking behind the stud.

It had been the only way. I took her to a known slaver, saying I wanted to breed her, and that I needed a Northern male; he, in turn, had sent me to the tanzeer's agent, who had agreed she deserved a proper partner. It had been designed to flush out her brother, stolen five years before and sold on the slaveblock; in the end, it had gone wrong, putting her in Aladar's hands and me in Aladar's mine.

We'd both of us escaped. But Del had killed the tanzeer, and now his daughter ruled in his place with vengeance on her mind.

Julah was a warren of close-built dwellings toppling one

against the other, if you looked from certain angles. Narrow streets were choked with stalls, wares, livestock, refuse, turning passages into bazaars. The Merchant's Market proper was in the middle of the city, but bargains were best had in shaded corners tucked away from the heat of the day, and the rituals of the Market. Julah smelled of wealth, but stank of the means to gain it. The city was the largest slave market in the South, thanks to dead Aladar, whose mines ate living people and vomited bodies.

I'd nearly been one of them.

We rode through the variegation of midday, blocks of shadow and sunlight falling in angled, sharp-edged slants across adobe dwellings huddling one against another, laddering packed dirt streets. Awnings drooped over windows and doors, all deep-cut against the glare; one could tell how prosperous the family by the condition of awnings and paint. Bright, fresh-sewn awnings and clean pale-painted adobe boasted a successful family. Those of lesser luck trusted to the sun not to rot through fabric too quickly. And if the luck was truly poor, there were no awnings at all.

We wound our way through the outskirts into the crowded inner city, regimented by thick block buildings and the narrow streets cutting skeins in all directions. Dark-eyed children ran everywhere, chattering and shrieking, ducking beneath the stud's head, and the mare's; goats and fowl and cats and dogs added to the racket.

"What do we do?" Del asked over the noise.

"What we always do. Find a cantina with rooms, rent one, have a drink or two while sitting in the *shade*." I smiled. "I'd also suggest a bath, but it would wash out your Borderer blood."

Del shrugged. "I have more dye and stain."

The stud sidled over toward the mare, swished a lifted tail, opened his mouth to bite until I reminded him *I* was in charge and reined him away again. "We forgot to trade the mare in on a gelding in Rusali."

"She's not so bad."

"We'll get rid of her here."

"Or you could get rid of the stud."

That did not deserve an answer. "We can cut through this alley here and head for Fouad's cantina," I suggested, pointing the way. "It's a clean, decent place, well up to your standards—" I grinned. "And Fouad knows me."

Del arched a darkened brow. "In our present circumstances, I'm not certain that's wise."

"Fouad's a *friend*, bascha, from the old days . . . besides, I doubt anyone down here knows about our troubles. Too far from Iskandar."

"They *will* know, once Sabra returns."

"We're ahead of her."

"For how much longer? She was a day behind us, Nezbet said—"

"Umir said two."

Del shrugged. "Either way, we have little time. We would do better to conduct our business quickly. . . ." She slid a sidelong glance at me as we slanted mounts across the road toward the narrow alley I'd indicated. "If you know what business there is to conduct."

"Chosa knows," I said grimly. "He knows all too well."

Del looked uneasy. "I wish we knew what to do. What it will take to discharge the sword."

"*And* me."

"And you." She guided the mare around a pile of crudely-woven rugs piled in rolls against the wall. "Your sword is Northern-made, using Northern rituals, blessed by Northern gods—I can only hope Shaka Obre understands we mean him no dishonor."

"We don't even know if he's still alive."

She sounded a bit annoyed. "Then you can ask that of Chosa, when you ask him where to go."

I grinned. "A lot of people in this world can *tell* me where to go. But it isn't to Shaka Obre."

Del's mouth tightened. "Where is this cantina?"

"Right up ahead. See the purple awning?"

Del looked. "It *is* purple. And the bricks are painted yellow."

"Fouad likes color."

Del's silence was eloquent.

"You just don't appreciate the finer things in life, bascha. Here. Fouad has boys to take mounts—you can hand the mare off."

I reined in, jumped down, waited for the swarm of dark-eyed Southron boys all clamoring for the job of taking the horses to livery. The streets were much too narrow and choked to add anything more, and so Fouad had begun the practice of hiring boys to stable mounts at the end of the block, between two dwellings.

They came, as expected. Brown-skinned, black-haired boys wearing thin tunics and gauze dhotis, with brown, callused bare feet. They all vied for the job, promising better care than the next boy could give.

I chose a likely looking hand, set the reins into it. "Bring the pouches back," I said. "We'll be taking a room."

"Yes, lord," the boy said. He was nearly identical to all the others.

"He can be testy," I warned.

"Yes, lord."

It was all I could get out of him. I gave him a copper, watched Del abstractedly select a boy for her mare, and grinned when she finally turned toward me, wading through the boys. "Isn't it nice to see helpful, ambitious children?"

Del grunted. "*Isn't* it?"

"It keeps them out of trouble."

She had tucked the blanketed sword bundle beneath one arm, unwilling to part with Boreal. "Is your friend to be trusted?"

"Fouad knows everyone, and he knows what everyone's done. If he sold out his friends, he'd be dead already." I gestured toward the deep-cut, open doorway. "I'll get us a room. If you want to sleep first, go ahead; I'm going to sit down in the shade for a bit and relax with aqivi and food."

Del shrugged, passing by. "I'm hungry, too."

Indoors, it was cool, cavernous, shady. I sighed, stripped off harness, found the perfect table near the door, and hooked out a chair. "Fouad!" I shouted gustily. "Aqivi, mutton, cheese!"

As expected, Fouad came out of his back room and threw open welcoming arms. "Sandtiger!" he cried. "They said you were dead!"

Del, pausing, looked meaningfully at me.

I ignored her. "Do I look dead to you?"

The Southroner laughed. "I didn't think it was true. They *always* say you're dead."

I shrugged, settling back against the wall as Del acquired a stool. "Hazards of the profession. One of these days I suppose it *will* be true, but not for a long time."

Fouad stopped by the table. He was short, small-boned, friendly, with gray streaking black hair. He wore a vivid yellow burnous and a scarlet underrobe. Dark eyes glittered avidly as he smiled down at Del. "And is this the Northern bascha?"

Del did her best not to give the game away. But Fouad wasn't buying it. He grinned as she explained she was a Borderer who had hired the Sandtiger for escort. And he nodded, agreed politely, then shot a bright-eyed glance at me full of amusement and understanding as he moved away to fill my order.

"It's not working," I mentioned. "I just thought you should know."

Her mouth hooked sideways. "You might have chosen a cantina where the proprietor doesn't know you." She paused. "If such a place exists."

I sighed noisily. "Right now, I'm content. You may as well relax, too. By morning I'll know what to do, so we may as well enjoy the rest of the afternoon."

She'd hooked elbows on the table, but now sat more upright. "By morning?"

I glanced around the room, marking a few men here and there, dicing, drinking, talking. Glumly, I murmured, "You may have the right idea. About asking Chosa. It's time I gave him his chance to punish his brother."

"That's what you'll tell him?"

I snorted. "Let's just say I'll let him know I won't oppose him. I don't think Chosa can ignore the chance to punish Shaka, so he'll have to tell me where he is."

Her brow puckered. "Just like that?"

Some of the amusement faded. "Nothing to do with Chosa is 'just like that.' Given a choice, I'd never talk to him again—but in order to *get* that choice, I *have* to talk to him." I scowled gloomily. "Let's talk about something else."

Fouad arrived with aqivi, mutton, cheese, and set everything down on the table. "Bascha," he said respectfully, "may the sun shine on your head."

Del smiled faintly. "And on yours, Fouad."

Content with that, he left. I poured us both full cups—accepting no protests from Del—and pushed hers across the table. "Watch the accent," I suggested.

"I'm a Borderer," she murmured. "Borderers *have* accents."

"Border accents, yes. Yours is uplander."

"They won't know the difference, down here."

"Fouad does. But Fouad doesn't matter." I lifted the pewter cup. "To the end of a quest, and to a future of adventure."

Del's mouth crimped a little, but she tapped her cup against mine. "The quest is hardly ended, and the adventure is growing old."

"Oh, now, let's not be down in the mouth about it. Look at all we've accomplished."

Del sipped, nodding. "Indeed, look. We are both of us panjandrums—but I'm not so certain it's good."

I drank half a cup, then grinned. "Neither of us is the sort to do anything without stirring up attention. It's the kind of people we are."

Del swallowed more aqivi, then set the cup down. "And shall we alter our habits when your sword is finally free of its inhabitant?"

"I don't know. Should we?"

She leaned forward on one elbow, cupping chin in hand. "Short of changing the sand to grass, there is nothing you can do to convince anyone of the truth: that you are the jhihadi. If indeed that *is* the truth." She sat back, sighing, picking dyed hair out of her eyes. "Will we always be running away?"

"Not always." I shrugged. "You accomplished your goal. Ajani's dead, and now you have another future. I still have to accomplish *my* goal, and then I'll decide mine."

"The 'threefold future,'" she quoted.

Uneasily, I stirred on my stool. "Let's worry about that later. Right now I just want to eat a little, drink a lot, and sleep in a decent bed." I glanced up idly as a man halted by the table, standing behind Del. I was accustomed to them staring at her, poking companions with eloquent elbows, or stopping to get a closer look. But this man stared at *me*.

He said something. Don't ask me what; it was incomprehensible. Clearly it wasn't any kind of Southron; just as clearly neither was he. He was too big, too broad, too light-eyed, with hair a russet-brown shade close to mine. I shrugged my ignorance of his tongue as Del turned to look up at the man. Her idle scrutiny sharpened.

He stopped speaking, seeing my blank expression. Frowning faintly, he switched to heavily accented Southron. "Forgive me," he said briefly. "I mistook you for Skandic." He spread eloquent hands, smiling inoffensive apology, then took himself out of the door.

"Whoever *he* is," I murmured, lifting my cup again.

Del, pensive, stared after the man. Then the pensiveness faded as she turned back to me. "Do you know him?"

"No. Or Skandic either, whoever he is."

Del sipped aqivi. "I thought he looked a little like you."

"Who? Him?" I glanced at the doorway, empty of foreigner. "I don't think so."

Del shrugged. "A little. The same height, the same kind of bone, the same kind of coloring. . . ."

I stared again at the doorway, sluggish interest rising. "You really think he looked like me?"

"Maybe it's just that he doesn't look Southron." She smiled faintly. "Or maybe it's just that I have grown accustomed to looking at you."

I grunted. Then chewed at a lip, considering. I glanced yet again at the doorway.

Del smiled, seeing my indecision as well as the temptation. She lifted her pewter cup. "Go ask," she suggested. "Go find him and ask. You don't know. I do not suggest he is kin, but if you resemble this Skandic, this man might know something of the people you came from."

I tensed to rise, relaxed. "No. I don't think so."

She regarded me over the cup. "You don't know anything about your history," she said quietly. "Sula's dead. You may never have another chance. And he *does* look like you. As much as Alric looks like me."

Something pinched my belly. There was merit in what she proposed, but— "This is silly."

Del shrugged. "Better to ask than to wonder."

I chewed my lip again, undecided.

"Go," she said firmly. "I'll wait here for our things."

"This is *stupid*," I muttered, pushing back the stool. But I went out of Fouad's cantina wondering if Del could be right.

Wondering if, in my heart, I wanted her to be.

Chapter 37

I paused outside the cantina, peering in either direction. The twisty street was crowded, keeping its own secrets. I hesitated, muttered an epithet, started to turn back. Then I saw the horseboys squatting against the building, waiting for the next customer.

I pulled a copper out of my pouch. Four boys arrived instantly. "Big man," I said. "A lot like me. He came out a moment ago."

One boy pointed immediately: to the right. Three other faces fell. I flipped the boy the copper with a quick word of thanks and went after the big foreigner Del thought looked like me.

I felt—odd. I had spent most of my life despairing of ever knowing anything about myself except for what I had won in the circle, or stolen from the dreams I'd dreamed as a child, chula to the Salset. But two or three weeks before there had been a chance, a slight chance, that I could learn the truth. That chance had died with Sula, who said she didn't know. I had castigated myself for even hoping, charging myself with the task of setting such hopes aside.

But hopes die hard, even in adulthood.

Now there was another chance. It was almost nonexistent, but worth a question or two. Julah was the first domain and city of any size beyond the Southron Mountains if you came up from the ocean-sea; it was not impossible that the stranger who looked like me could be from a neighboring land, coming inland from the seaport city, Haziz.

Yet I wondered. There were enough Borderers, mostly half-bloods, who resembled me. Cross big-boned, fair-haired Northerners with smaller, darker Southroners, and people like me result.

Still.

"Stupid," I muttered, making my way through the throng. "You'll never find him in the city, and even if you do, chances are he can't tell you anything. Just because he mistook you for someone else . . ."

Hope flared, then died, tempered by caution and contempt.

"Stupid," I repeated. And stumbled into a one-eyed man standing guard over a basket of melons.

I apologized for my clumsiness, patted him once on the arm, then turned to continue my search. And realized, as I turned, my limbs felt sluggish and cold.

I stopped. Sweated. Shivered. Blinked as vision blurred.

Chosa?

No. He didn't work this way. Chosa was not so subtle. Besides, I'd grown accustomed to anticipating his attempts to exert more power. This was not one of them.

Then what—?

Hoolies, the *aqivi*—which both of us had drunk.

I swore, swung around, staggered three steps and fell to one knee as numb legs failed. Pulled myself up and staggered again, tripping over a cat as it ran between a dozing danjac's legs. The danjac woke up as I fell against its ribs, grabbing handfuls of scraggly mane to hold myself upright.

A female. She shifted, turned her head, spat a glob of pungent cud. It landed on my thigh, but by then I didn't care. By then I wanted my sword, Chosa Dei or no.

I slapped weakly at the danjac's mouth as she bared teeth in my direction, trying to unsheath the *jivatma* with a hand nearly dead on the end of my arm. I staggered as the danjac turned her hip out from under me, but caught my balance spread-legged as the sword at last came free.

"Bascha—" I mumbled. "Hoolies, Del—it's a trap—"

Eyes. They stared, shocked and fearful and wary: a man in obvious straits swayed off-balance in the street, holding a black-charred blade with perilous control. I didn't really blame them. Sword-dancer or no, at the moment I was a danger to anyone who came near. Even if I didn't mean it.

"—bascha—" But even my mouth was numb.

Vision wheeled. The street fell out from under me; hip and elbow dug dirt. I managed, as I landed, to thrust the sword to arm's length, so I wouldn't cut myself.

Up. Blade chimed dully as I dragged it along the ground, thrusting myself to unsteady knees. Everyone hugged the walls, or went in and shut their doors.

Except for the men with swords, all swathed in dark burnouses rippling as they walked out of shadows into sunlight.

So. Now I would know.

To my knowledge, I have never employed a sword in any method save the one for which it was intended. But now I did. I dug the tip into the ground, leaned my weight upon it, levered myself to my feet.

The men stopped approaching.

I smiled. Laughed a little. Heaved the sword upright into position and balanced very delicately with feet spread too far apart. If someone spat, I'd fall down. But a reputation comes in handy.

That, and Samiel.

The danjac was still beside me, whuffling discontent. Then a dark-clad, quick-moving body slipped beneath the belly, came up from under it with a knife; smoothly and efficiently sliced into the softer flesh of the underside of my forearm.

I dropped the sword, of course. Which was exactly what he intended.

And then he dropped *me* with a hook of agile ankle around one of my wobbly ones.

I landed painfully, flat on my back, banging a lolling head against hard-packed dirt. I bit my lip, swallowed blood; felt more flowing out of my arm.

But only for a moment. Everything went numb.

He gestured to the others. They came, putting away their swords. One man moved closer, then leaned forward to inspect me.

I saw, through fading vision, the notched Southron nose. Heard, in thundering ears, the familiar broken voice.

"Why is it," Abbu began, "that every time I see you, you're wallowing in the dirt?"

Weakly, I spat blood. "So much for your oaths."

Dark brows rose. "But I have honored my oath. With Sabra as my witness."

Sabra. I looked. No woman. Only men, in Southron silks and turbans.

And then I saw her. The small, quick body which had slid beneath a danjac to cut the sword from me. The one I'd thought was a man.

She stripped the sandshield from the lower half of her face, letting the cloth hang free to dangle from the turban. I saw the small, dark face, infinitely Southron; the black, expressive eyes, infinitely elated; the dusky flush of her cheeks and the parted curve of a lovely mouth. Infinitely *aroused.*

Sabra knelt. She was tiny, slender, sloe-eyed: an exquisite Southron beauty. Mutely she reached for my wounded arm, closing fingers around the flesh. Blood still flowed freely, staining her palm. She let go of my arm, stared intently at her bloodied hand, then looked into my eyes.

Her voice was very soft. "I gave the woman to Umir."

I twitched once. It was all I could manage. "Hoolies take you," I croaked, "and your broken-nosed bedpartner, too."

The bloodied hand flashed out and caught me full across the face, leaving sticky residue. Vision winked.

Went out.

—a fissure in the ground . . . a cracked opening that splits the ground apart, all blackened and curled awry like a mouth opened to scream. Inside, something glitters, ablaze like Punja crystals, only it isn't Punja crystals, but something else instead. Something white and bright and cold—

Deep inside me, Chosa rustled.

The mountains are familiar, tumbled ruins of sorcerous warfare; brother pitched against brother in a waste of strength and power. Shaka

Obre means to protect, but Chosa Dei is determined to destroy whatever he can.

The warfare escalates until even the land protests, rising up to defy them both. Flesh falls away, but it isn't flesh of man; the flesh is the flesh of the land. Grasslands peel away, leaving bare rock and wasted earth.

Inside me, Chosa laughed.

"I can unmake it all, merely to make it again—"

The mountains tremble, and fall, forming new chains of peaks and hillocks.

Chosa raises his arms. The words he chants are strange, unknown even to Shaka. Meadows become a desert. A necklace of freshwater lakes becomes an ocean of sand.

Shaka Obre screams, to see his creation destroyed.

His brother merely laughs. "I TOLD you I could do it!"

"Then I'll hurt YOU!" Shaka shouts.

Deep inside the mountains, the last bastion of Shaka's making is warded against permanent summer, and the unyielding eye of the sun.

"I'll show YOU!" Shaka mutters.

But by then it is too late. Chosa has made a prison.

"Begone!" Chosa shouts, and points imperatively to the nearest hunch-shouldered mountain.

A rent appears in it: gaping mouth curls awry. Deep inside, it glitters.

"Go there," Chosa commands. "Go there and live your life without sun or sand or stars."

"Go THERÉ!" Shaka points: north, away from himself. A thin ruby haze issues from his fingers and encapsulates Chosa Dei. "There!" Shaka repeats. "Inside his own new-made mountain—"

And Shaka Obre is gone, sucked through the gaping mouth into the fastness inside the mountain, a necklet of pockets and hollows riddling the new-made mountain.

"You see?" Chosa says. "You don't have the proper magic."

And then he also is gone, escorted by brilliant wards to the far fastness of the new north, so different from the south.

That once was a single land, lush and green and fertile.

I twitched, then slackened again. Saw the patterns and whorls and grids, and the hustapha's gnarled hand slapping flat against spit-dampened sand.

Inside me, Chosa stirred.
Lines drawn in the sand—

The hand thrust itself into my groin and closed. I bucked, tried to
shout; realized I was gagged. Realized I was stretched spine-down
on a splintery wooden bench in a small, slant-shadowed room that
boasted a single slot of a window, with arms and legs pulled taut to
the floor, chained to rings. All I wore was a dhoti; little shield
against Sabra's hand. I twisted away as best I could even as she
laughed.

"Do you want to keep them?" she asked. And squeezed a little
harder. "What should I do with you, to repay you for his death?"

I could make no answer through the gag. It was leather, once
dampened, now dried into painful stiffness. There was more in my
mouth: a hard, smooth roundness that threatened to make me retch.

Sabra let go. Black eyes were pitiless. "I could do much worse."

Undoubtedly she could. Undoubtedly she would.

Del. With Umir.

Sabra laughed as I tensed. Iron rattled dully, sweeping me back
to Aladar's mine. Sweat bathed my face. This was Aladar's
daughter.

"I had a brother," she said lightly. "He would have inherited.
But when he was nine—and I was ten—I had him murdered. It
was done with perfect skill, and no one ever knew. But none of the
harem girls ever bore a boy again . . . or else they gave them away,
so no more accidents would occur."

She had put off the black burnous and turban and wore a long-
sleeved, calf-length white linen tunic instead, draped over baggy
carnelian trousers. Tiny feet were leather-shod; the toes were
tipped in gold. Sleek black hair hung unbound to her knees, rippling as she moved. On the bench, I tensed.

She was dusky Southron perfection, exquisite elegance. No
wasted motion. No wasted thought. A lock of hair brushed my ribs,
then slid downward toward abdomen. I nearly choked on the gag.

"He expected to live longer," she said. "He expected to have
other sons. But all he had were girls, and I the oldest of all. The
others were unworthy."

A small hand touched the fissure Del's sword had left in my ribs. Paused. Traced the scar, much as Del herself had so many times before. But the gesture now was obscene. I wanted to spit at her.

Reflectively, Sabra said, "You must be hard to kill."

I swallowed convulsively. Then wished I hadn't, as the gag tickled my throat.

Wished I had my sword.

My—sword?

Sabra's hand lingered, still tracing the scar. Then drifted to the others, including the ones on my face. "*Very* hard to kill."

What had happened to Samiel? I recalled with clarity what had become of Umir's men when they had tried to touch him before. Had Sabra left the *jivatma* lying in the street?

"I hated him," she said. "I was glad you killed him. But I can't tell anyone that. There are appearances . . . I should thank you, but I can't. It would be a weakness. I dare not afford a weakness. I am a woman tanzeer—the men would pull me down. They would rape me to death." The hand moved away from my face to my ribs once more, finger-walked each one, then crawled to the edge of my dhoti. Nails stirred coppery hair, slipping beneath the leather. "Would you rape me, Sandtiger?"

Is that what Abbu did?

Small teeth were displayed oh so briefly. "Should I castrate you, so you can't?"

Hoolies, the woman was sandsick.

Fingers found the thong drawstring. "He bought you for me, you know. That silly Esnat of Sasqaat. He wanted to impress me, so I would consider his suit. So I would marry him." Quietly, Sabra laughed. "As if I would marry a man when I have a domain of my own."

The memory awoke. Esnat of Sasqaat, Hashi's heir, hiring me to dance so he could impress a woman. He'd told me her name: Sabra. But I hadn't known her, then. I'd known nothing at all about her.

Esnat, you don't want her. The woman would eat you alive.

Sabra undid the thong, loosened it. Yanked the dhoti aside, unheeding of my flinch. "It would interest Abbu," she said thoughtfully, "to see how you compare."

Hoolies, she *was* sandsick!

Sabra laughed softly. "In the *circle*, you fool; is this all you think about? Like every other man?" She flipped the dhoti back over my loins contemptuously. "Men are predictable. Umir. Abbu. You. Even my own father. They think with this, instead of with their heads. It is so *easy* to make a man do whatever I want him to do . . . when one doesn't care about these—" she touched genitals once more "—or *these*—" now she caressed her own breasts "—it's so easy to get what you want. Because you have no stake in the flesh." Black eyes shone brightly. "Sleeping with a man is such a small matter. But it binds him more certainly than anything else could—and then he does what I tell him."

I wondered about Abbu.

Sabra thrust fingers into her hair and scooped it back from her face, unconsiously seductive for a woman who didn't care what a man's response might be. Or maybe she knew, and *did* care; the woman was unpredictable, even as she claimed men otherwise.

She let the hair fall, sheeting down her back. "I don't care about the jhihadi," she continued calmly. "He meant nothing to me, nor his Oracle. But it was useful, that death. And the Oracle's. It inflamed all the tribes and made you easier prey." She smiled, stroking her bottom lip with a long fingernail. "Once my people killed the Oracle, they whispered it came of you and the woman, using blackest sorcery. So the Oracle couldn't unmask you; you destroyed him to keep him from it. So now you are hated for that, too." Sabra laughed throatily. "Clever, am I not? It made them all angrier. It made it all very easy."

The Oracle. Dead. Del's brother. Dead again?

"Jhihadi-killer," she said. "Murderer of my father."

I had killed neither man. But now it didn't matter.

Sabra shrugged. Silken hair rippled. "Eventually, I would have had him assassinated so I could have the domain. You saved me some trouble. If I could reward you, I would. But there are appearances." She tossed a curtain of hair behind a slender shoulder. "Rest the night, Sandtiger. In the morning you will dance."

Sweat trickled from temples.

She moved close again, dragging fingernails across my bare chest. Beneath it, flesh rippled. It wasn't from desire, but increasing trepidation. The woman unsettled me. "Abbu wants you," she told me. "He said he always has. When I asked him what he wanted as payment for his assistance, he said he wanted the dance. The final dance, he said. The true and binding test of the shodo's training."

A tiny spark lighted. Abbu and I were rivals, but never enemies.

"I agreed," Sabra said. "But there must be *provisions*."

The newborn spark went out.

Aladar's daughter left.

Chapter 38

Near dawn, men came. One of them was Abbu Bensir, who had put off his sword. He waited silently just inside the door as the others unlocked the manacles, took away the gag, bound up the crusted knife slice in my right arm, left me food and drink.

They departed, closing the door. Abbu remained behind, leaning against the wall. He wore a bronze-brown burnous, a weave of heavyweight silk and linen that shone oddly metallic, even in poor illumination. It was far better than his usual garb, which was generally understated; I knew it had to be Sabra.

Light from the narrow slot of a window slanted across the room. He shifted out of its path so he wouldn't have to squint. "For the dance," he said, nodding toward the food.

I sat on the splintery bench, retying the dhoti thong, and didn't say a word.

"She has your sword, too. I told her what it was . . . she wanted it, of course. So she had Umir bring Del. The bascha didn't like it much, but she sheathed it for us. She said something about it was better for us to have it than some innocent child in the street."

I made no answer.

The husky voice was calm. "You know it has to be settled, one way or another."

I flexed the forearm, tightening and relaxing a fist to test flesh and muscle. The wound stung, as expected, but the bleeding had stopped, and the binding would protect it. It wouldn't interfere.

"It's how legends are made, Sandtiger. You know that. To all the young sword-dancers, it's what you *are*."

I lifted my head finally and looked at him directly. My voice croaked from disuse; my mouth hurt from the gag. "Does it matter so much to you?"

Abbu's shoulders moved in a shrug beneath the burnous. "What is there, save the legend? It's what people buy when they hire a sword-dancer. The man, the skill, *the legend*."

"You could have asked," I told him. "We could have had our own private dance, just the two of us, and settled it once and for all. No need for all of this."

He smiled, creasing a Southron face nearly ten years older than my own. Light glinted briefly on threads of silver in dark hair. Older, harder, wiser. Legend in the flesh, much more so than I. "What benefit in asking, Sandtiger? I meant to once, and found you beset by what Del claimed was Chosa Dei. Could I ask then?" He made a dismissive gesture. "And when you were recovered, you had no time for a true dance, according to the codes. There was Sabra, and all the others, hunting the murderer. And I knew you would never stop, never enter a circle against me, unless I forced your hand."

Dim light shadowed his features. I saw the steady, pale brown eyes, the seamed scar bisecting his chin, the quiet readiness. He was and had always been something I was not: a man secure in himself. A man so good at what he did it colored all his life.

In the circle, I was as good. Possibly even better, though we couldn't know that yet. But I was not and had never been secure within myself.

I just didn't tell anyone.

Abbu waited in silence. That he respected me, I knew: he had put off his sword. I thought it unnecessary. I had been chained all night. As quick as he was, I could attempt very little before he could counter me.

I looked into his face and saw banked expectancy.

Belly tautened abruptly "It was *you*," I declared. "She was a day, two days behind. And then suddenly she was here, waiting at Fouad's."

He grinned. "There is a disadvantage to being a legend, Sandtiger. People begin to expect things. When we realized you and Del had left Quumi, I told Sabra—and Umir, once we met up with him at the oasis—that you were bound for Julah. I didn't know why, but I knew where. It's where you always go: Fouad's. So I suggested they double up on mounts and water and beat you here to Julah, so the trap could be laid."

I recalled Fouad's unfeigned friendliness, his courtesy toward Del. "Fouad?"

Abbu hitched a shoulder. "You have no idea how determined Sabra is. She is—not like other women. What Sabra wants, she gets. Julah is her domain; she is free to do as she likes, and *to* any person who happens to strike her fancy: man, woman, child. You know what Aladar was like—I heard what he did to you. The daughter is worse. The daughter is—different. Fouad would have been a fool to refuse her."

"What happens to Del?"

He shrugged. "She's Umir's, now. He'll do whatever he likes."

I sought something in his face. He had known, admired, desired Del. "Doesn't that bother you?"

Abbu Bensir laughed his husky, broken laugh. "Have you no faith in the bascha? Umir underestimates her—I know better. He beds boys, not women . . . and he wants merely to *collect* her. Collectors cherish their icons." He shifted against the wall, rubbing absently at the notched bridge of his nose. "Del is hardly helpless. I doubt he'll keep her long."

"Which brings us back to me." I picked up the cup of water, drank.

"It's simple, Tiger. We dance."

I nodded thoughtfully as I lowered the cup. "Sabra mentioned certain *provisions*."

Something jumped briefly in the flesh beneath one brown eye. "She promised me the dance. I didn't ask for provisions, merely the chance to settle it according to the codes. Nothing more than that."

I grunted. "Sabra may have other ideas."

"Sabra is ruthless," he agreed. "Far more ruthless than Umir, but—"

"But you trust her."

His mouth thinned. He pushed himself from the wall and walked to me, then around me, peering briefly out the slit serving as window. I heard his step behind me; the rasp of his broken voice, distinct and oddly tight. Each word was emphasized, and very deliberate: "Listen to me."

I didn't say a word.

Silence. Then, very quietly, with infinite clarity: "Sabra needs to show her power to all the male tanzeers, as well as the men of her domain. To prove herself. To hold them all with whatever means it takes, because she is a *woman*. She will do whatever she has to do. Left to her own desires, she might have had you flayed alive—have you ever seen that done?" He didn't wait for me to answer. "A man trained by our shodo, a seventh-level sword-dancer, deserves to die in the circle."

"Don't do me any favors." I set the cup down. "Once, we might have settled this in a circle where death was not required."

"Once," Abbu agreed. "In Iskandar . . . but a horse interfered. And also in the Punja, but then Chosa Dei interfered. And now it's much too late." Steps gritted again as he came around to face me. No more amusement. No more quiet goading. He was perfectly serious. "It will be quick, and clean, and painless. It will be an honorable death."

The words rose unbidden. "*You're* sure of yourself."

The flesh at the edges of eyes creased. He didn't—quite—smile. "I admire your bravado. But be sensible, Sandtiger . . . I am *Abbu Bensir*—"

Very quietly, I told Abbu Bensir where to go. Also when, how fast, and in what condition.

The recoil was faint, but present. And then he did smile. "Steel, this time. No more wooden blades."

I looked at the scar in this throat. "I nearly killed you then. I was seventeen years old, utterly lacking in skill . . . it's twenty years later, Abbu. And you're that many years older. Slower. Stiffer. *Older.*"

"Wiser," Abbu said softly. "And the Sandtiger is not so young as *he* once was."

No. And he'd also spent a muzzy-headed night chained to a splintery bench, thinking about Delilah.

I looked again at his throat. "Funny thing, Abbu—I never thought you were the kind for revenge."

The tone snapped sharply. "Don't confuse me with Sabra."

I looked at him more alertly.

"This isn't for revenge. What do I care about that? What do I care about *you?*" He angled a shoulder toward the door. "I just want to dance."

I sought another edge. "Is she that good in bed?"

Abbu swung back, laughing. "Old trick, Sandtiger."

I shrugged. "At least it's a reason."

"She is—inventive. Uninhibited. But a woman, all the same, much like any other." He gestured. "I gave you my reason. I dance for the joy, the *challenge* . . . do you realize how long it's been since I danced with a worthy opponent?"

Sourly, I said, "I'd just as soon not."

"Too late." He turned, moved toward the door, looked back. "There is one more thing."

I waited.

Brown eyes glittered in sunlight. "I *am* older, even as you say . . . and growing older daily. There is in me now a desire to leave behind something of myself, if I am to leave the world. A name, if nothing else." The husky tone took on a quality I'd never heard in Abbu: intense, decided virulence. "Old men are flaccid in spirit, dying drunk in a filthy cantina, losing wits to huva dreams, or pissing in their beds. I'd rather die in the circle. I'd rather die honorably." He put his hand on the latch. "And if it's meant to happen, I'd just as soon have the Sandtiger do it than some Punja-mite of a boy who caught me on a bad day."

I stared blankly at the door as it shut slowly behind him, latch falling into place. I wanted to call him a fool. But I thought about what he'd said. Applied it to myself. And realized he was right.

I'd sooner have Abbu kill me now than Nezbet do it later.

Of course, given a choice. . . .

Without any further ado, I ate the food they'd left and finished off the water. Then got up from the bench, stretched, and began to loosen up.

Abbu Bensir. At last.

The smallest flicker of anticipation lit a bonfire in my belly.

Chapter 39

ead Aladar's impressive palace was very much as I recalled it: white-painted adobe; tiled, elegant archways;
palm and citrus trees planted for shade, and looks. Even the stableyard boasted layers of cream and copper gravel.

I was barefoot. The gravel was small and fine, but gravel
nonetheless; I scowled faintly, assessing footing, thinking ahead to
the dance. As yet the day was still cool, which meant the footing
would also be cool, but I preferred packed sand or dirt to a circle
drawn in gravel.

The stableyard was filled with spectators, except for the circle
and a narrow perimeter around it. They stood against walls, squatted in gravel, sat upon benches and stools, dependent upon their
status. All men, of course. Most, I assumed, were guards or merce-
naries Sabra had hired to maintain a hold on Julah; the richly-
dressed men were merchants and the politicians of the city, who
would fight to snatch it away; others were trained sword-dancers
who'd come down from Iskandar. I knew many of the latter, by
name or by face. As one they stared at me, as I stood flanked by a
knot of guards, and then at Abbu Bensir as he came out of the airy,
elegant palace into the bright stableyard.

It was, I thought, silly. So much fanfare for a dance. But it was
Sabra's idea, of course: she intended to see me killed before a mul-
titude of witnesses, so no doubt could be attached to her part in the

matter. What she meant was plain: she alone had caught the Sandtiger, killer of father, jhihadi, and Oracle, when *all others* had failed; see now as she meted out justice!

Hoolies, what a farce.

I wore only brief dhoti and necklet, naked of sandals, burnous, harness. It's the usual attire for a man entering a circle; extra clothing can foul the dance. Many of the sword-dancers had seen me dance before in identical garb, but none had seen me dance properly since coming back from the North.

Except, of course, for Abbu. He was unsurprised. But I saw and heard the reaction as everyone else saw the hideous scar left by Del's *jivatma*.

Yet something else for the legend. I found it a little amusing.

As I waited in my knot of guards, Abbu quietly stripped out of burnous, harness, sandals. Like me, he wore a dhoti; unlike me, there was no necklet, nor a fist-sized, lumpy fissure eaten out of still-living flesh. He was a spare, sinewy man several years beyond forty, seamed by knicks and slices gone pale pink or white with age. He was Southron, and therefore smaller, but Abbu Bensir lost nothing at all by boasting less bulk; nothing at all by giving up height to a lower distribution of weight.

Surreptitiously, I sucked in a substantial breath that lifted and spread ribs, giving me room to breathe, then released it slowly and evenly. I yawned once, twice; shook out arms and hands; felt the tingle in thighs and groin. Felt the rippled, ticklish clenching deep in my belly that always presaged a dance.

Umir the Ruthless had named me a gut-level dancer, a man whose quickness, power, and skill had never truly been tested to prove or disprove the legend. This time, I knew, was different. This time I would find out *exactly* what—and who—I was.

I thought of Sula. I thought of Del. I thought of the nameless mother who had birthed me in the sands, then left me there to die. All those years ago: thirty-six, thirty-seven, thirty-eight.

Hoolies, who cares?

It was *Abbu Bensir* I faced.

It began as a ripple. Then a quiet murmur. And at last a splitting of bodies: Sabra, Aladar's daughter, came out of her father's magnificent palace. With her came white-clad eunuchs carrying cushions, fans, gauzy screens quickly erected to shade her from the sun as she settled upon piled cushions. She wore vivid, bloody crimson: tunic, trousers, turban, and the palest wisp of modesty veil weighted with tiny gold tassels. Leather slippers were also red; the tissue-thin soles were glossy gold with freshly gravel-torn foil. It was, I decided wryly, Sabra's way of proving her wealth *and* her disdain for poorer people, even the rich ones gathered here.

She lifted a small, graceful hand, and everyone fell silent. Her voice rang throughout the courtyard, carrying even into corners. She knew how to pitch it properly. "Honored guests, today I bring you the justice of a powerful yet humble new tanzeer as personified in the circle, the South's greatest tradition. Let there be no question as to who the dancers are: Abbu Bensir, whom you know, and also the Sandtiger."

I sighed and cocked a hip as a murmuring filled the stableyard. This might take a while.

"Abbu Bensir," she repeated, "who is accorded the honor of being the South's greatest sword-dancer, trained by the most honorable and most revered shodo of Alimat, where only the best of the best are privileged to be trained."

Everyone knew that.

"And the Sandtiger, also trained at Alimat and was taught by the same shodo, but who repudiated the training, his honor, and codes by turning to basest infamy. He murdered three men: my father, Aladar, former tanzeer of Julah—" Her voice broke artfully a moment, then she recovered a perfect composure, "—and also the jhihadi, long promised to the South by prophecy and legend as the man who would save us all by changing the sand grass."

"Or maybe *glass*," I muttered.

"And lastly, the man who by blackest sorcery murdered the Oracle, the one sent to all of us to prepare the way for the jhihadi, so we could honor and welcome him."

"Anything else?" I murmured.

Sabra placed a hand across her heart, inclining her head modestly. "I am only a woman, and unworthy . . . but I have done this thing. For Julah, and all of the South—I *give you retribution for the deaths of three whom we loved!"*

Hoolies, what a performance.

"And so," she said quietly, "today I bring you justice. Today I bring you a dance that will never again be equaled. A dance to the death. A true and binding dance shaped of true and binding oaths, as taught at Alimat. All of the codes shall hold. The traditions shall be honored."

"It might be fairer," I shouted, "if somebody gave me a sword!"

It did what I expected: broke Sabra's hold; shocked merchants and politicians; made the sword-dancers laugh. The tension she worked to build was abruptly dissipated.

She didn't like it one bit.

"Here!" Sabra snapped, and one of her guardsmen muscled me over to her cushions. Black eyes were livid, but red-painted lips smiled sweetly behind the sheer red veil. "A sword?" she inquired. "But of course there will be a sword. A very special sword." Sabra snapped her fingers. "Surely you will know it. It is all a part of the legend."

For a moment, a moment only, I thought it was to be Samiel. And then, as quickly, I knew better than to hope it. Sabra was not stupid. If she had known nothing about *jivatmas* before setting out after me, Abbu would have told her by now. He knew enough about them to respect and be wary of them. He had seen Del's, and he'd also seen mine. Abbu knew better.

So, not Samiel, full of Chosa and Southron magic. Brief hope died.

A eunuch came forward bearing an oblong purple cushion. Displayed upon it was a sword, a Southron sword. A very familiar sword: shodo-blessed, blued-steel blade, with beadwire-wrapped hilt.

Strength, like sand, ran out. *"Where did you get this sword?"*

"You were careless," she said, "and heedless of the legend. Which makes it all the sweeter." Her eyes dwelled avidly on my face, weighing my expression. What she saw pleased her; Sabra smiled, and laughed. Maliciously, she whispered, "I restore what has been lost, to make the legend complete."

I gritted teeth tightly. "It broke," I hissed curtly. "Singlestroke *broke*."

"And so you discarded it." Sabra shrugged. "The halves were found, and recognized. I had them brought to me, and repaired. So I could restore it to you."

"Hoolies, woman—you're *sandsick*. Steel once broken . . ." But I let it go, seeing the glint in black eyes. She knew. As well as I. As well as anyone, though she took no pains to tell them.

Steel once broken will always break again. No matter how skillful the mending.

Which, of course, is what she wanted.

Sabra gestured expansively, showing small white teeth. "Take it, Sandtiger. So the legend is whole again."

I was getting downright sick of hearing myself called a legend. First Abbu, now Sabra. I was a sword-dancer, nothing more. A good one, I'll admit; I'll even say I'm great (which I've been known to do anyway) . . . but real legends are usually dead. And I wasn't. Yet.

I put out a hand. The cushion was snatched away.

"Ah!" Sabra laughed and coyly touched her breast. "So I am reminded . . . there are the oaths to be sworn, first!" She gestured to Abbu, raising her voice so all could hear again. "Will you come forward? All must be witnessed. All must be done properly, according to the honor codes of Alimat. Both of you must be bound into a blessed circle."

I wondered sourly how much she'd already known. How much Abbu had told her.

Sabra laughed again as Abbu came forward. "*Still* I forget—how like a woman!" Another graceful gesture. "I have special guests. There—do you see?"

We looked, of course, as she meant us to. Directly across the circle another sunshade affair was erected, cushions laid out carefully as eunuchs gathered with fans. Umir the Ruthless stood there. By his side was a hooded woman well-swathed in Southron silk.

Singlestroke. And Del. What more could I ask for?

Freedom for both of us.

Hoolies, what a mess.

Umir brought her forward to the edge of the circle. Close enough for me to see her wrists were bound before her. Close enough for me to see her face and the expression upon it. Clearly she was unhurt; just as clearly she was annoyed. But she lacked *jivatma* and freedom, even as I did. And as we each of us gazed at each other, seeking truth behind mutual masks, we knew there was no way out.

Umir had worked his own brand of magic. She wore white samite, the costly Southron silk that only tanzeers could wear, because all others were forbidden save by a tanzeer's permission. Plain, unadorned samite, too bright in the light of the sun; a hooded, loose-fitting burnous that grazed the tops of bare toes, neither belted nor fastened. It hung open from hood to hem in heavy, unmoving folds.

Umir smiled at me. "Subdued, is she not? As is her attire?"

I scowled, thinking him foolish.

"I prefer simplicity in all things; in the things I show to the world. Surface understatement can be *so* effective . . . but underneath that surface, the complexion is much different. In people—*and* in attire." He put a hand on Del's shoulder, sinking fingers into samite. "This burnous is a part of my collection, worth the price of three domains. Worthy of *her*, I think."

Umir caught cloth abruptly and pulled the burnous open with a skilled flourish, draping it inside out across his left arm like a cloth merchant showing off wares. The severe white burnous was abruptly something else; something incredibly *more*: a lurid Southron sunset awash in morning light. All the yellows, and the oranges; all the lurid reds—and everything in between—of a simoom-birthed sunset boiling out of the Punja's horizon bloomed against costly samite, and an even costlier woman.

Umir spread a hand across the brilliant lining. "Beads," he whispered softly. "Hundreds and hundreds of beads, colored glass and gold and brass . . . and feathers, *all the feathers*, from a hundred thousand birds not even known to the South . . ." He smiled fatuously, caressing the sunset lining gently as a man caresses a woman's breast. Beads glittered, rattled. Delicate feathers fluttered. "Worth three domains," he repeated. "And now a woman to wear it."

Deftly, Umir slipped the hood. It, too, was lined with beads of glass, and myriad vivid feathers. But I didn't care about that. Now her face was naked for everyone to see. Behind me, I heard the rustle; the murmur of Southron men looking upon a Northern woman.

She was blonde once again, and the skin was honey-fair. She wore white also beneath the burnous: a Northern-style tunic of soft-worked, pristine suede cut to mid-thigh. Legs and feet were bare, emphasizing her pronounced, powerful grace as well as Umir's victory; no Southron man ever saw so much of a woman— or displayed her so blatantly—unless he slept with that woman, or paid money for her.

Del did not smile. She didn't so much as blink. But then, she didn't have to. She was, in the sunlight, daylight to Sabra's night. Steel to Sabra's silk. And everyone there knew it, including Aladar's daughter.

Especially Aladar's daughter.

A small but worthy revenge.

Chapter 40

Sabra stood in a welter of cushions beneath a gauzy sunscreen. "You will swear," she declared, leaving no room for question. "Swear the oaths of Alimat, that you will honor all the codes as your shodo taught you to."

I slanted a sidelong look at Abbu, standing next to me. "Don't you just love these people who think they know everything?"

One corner of his mouth twitched, which told me a thing or two. He might be in Sabra's pay as well as in her bed, but he didn't necessarily approve of her overacting.

Sabra's black eyes glittered. "I know what I know." She put out a slim, beckoning hand. A small, short-bladed knife was set into her palm. "*Elaii-ali-ma,*" she said coolly, "as I've taken pains to learn."

My amusement dropped away. A second more intent glance at Abbu showed me companion consternation in the faint frown and tautening mouth. I assumed he'd taught her the things she knew about Alimat and oaths. But what she touched on now was a private, personal thing only rarely ever addressed once the ritual was done, and then very obliquely.

She spoke now for the two of us, quietly and with conviction. "I am Aladar's daughter in all things, save one: I am alive. One day I will die, by assassin or murderer if I do not take certain measures, but for now I am alive. For now I am *tanzeer,* irrespective of gender.

Aladar's power is mine—" She paused, marking our attentiveness; satisfied, she continued, "—as are all his resources, including certain scrolls extolling the virtues of many things, and spelling out the magic necessary to accomplish every goal." Behind the sheer crimson veil with its weight of golden tassels her young face was coolly tranquil, frightening in itself. "That magic, that power, is knowledge. Because of the scrolls and my father's prescience, I have that in abundance . . . and so the power is mine. I choose to wield it now to put order into your lives."

Abbu shifted weight slightly. "Sabra—"

Black eyes blazed abruptly. "You will be silent, Abbu Bensir. We have begun *elaii-ali-ma.*"

I stirred in defense, shaking my head. "Only the shodo—"

"In this, I *am* the shodo."

Abbu and I exchanged a look. Then Sabra made a gesture. Massive eunuchs with knives in their hands stepped up behind us both, impressing upon us—even in silence—that we should mind our manners.

Clearly, Abbu's role had altered. He didn't look very happy. But then, neither was I.

If Abbu grew *very* unhappy . . . anticipation fluttered. The two greatest sword-dancers should quench even Aladar's daughter, who was, I thought grimly, becoming more of a threat with every passing moment.

Not stupid, Aladar's girl. And very dangerous.

"*Elaii-ali-ma,*" she repeated, "is required to seal the circle against outside profanation. To seal the dancers inside, until the dance is done."

"We know what it is," I muttered.

Abbu nodded agreement. "Let's get on with it."

"Then give me your blood," she ordered.

I displayed my cloth-wrapped forearm. "Already gave my share."

"Then this will take little effort." She gestured sharply, and two eunuchs grabbed my arm. One of them tore the bandage free and bared the five-inch slice Sabra had put there herself.

Before I could protest, the little knife flashed out. I swore as it cut in at an angle across the crusted slice. Fresh blood welled. Sabra dipped fingers into it, then dabbed three dots onto Abbu's forehead. "By the honor of your shodo; by the codes of Alimat: you will not step out of the circle until the dance is finished and one of you lies dead. If you revoke this, if you renounce your personal honor and the honor of your shodo, you are henceforth denied the grace of a shodo-blessed sword-dancer's circle, whether true or of your own making."

A muscle ticked in Abbu's jaw. "According to the codes, which I swore to live by thirty years ago before the shodo himself, I accept the dance. It shall be as you require, in accordance with all the oaths."

She nodded once, then put out a hand. Without the aid of eunuchs, Abbu bared his forearm and watched dispassionately as Sabra sliced into it. He bled less than I had, since he was lacking a prior wound. For myself, I still dripped sluggishly; Abbu's blood ran in a single runnel until Sabra put fingers in it.

Three dots on my brow, too, beneath the disheveled hair. "For you, the same," she declared. "Do you understand the oath?"

"I suppose I could say no—" But I broke it off abruptly, no longer disposed to humor her in any fashion. "There is one little thing. You mentioned certain *provisions*."

"Ah." Sabra smiled. "You might call it incentive. I want the dance to be the best there has ever been, with neither man holding back out of old friendships and rivalries. Such things can hamper the effort." Black lashes lowered briefly, then she looked at Abbu Bensir. "You are to kill him," she said clearly, "as artistically as you can. I want it to last a *long* time. Cut him to bits, if you like . . . carve him apart like rarest meat—but do not waste my time with protestations of loyalty, or a personal need to be merciful by killing him with one stroke." Her tone went soft, languid. In another woman I'd have said it belonged in bed; I began to wonder if this meant as much to her, or perhaps even more. "I think you know me well enough now to realize what might happen if you don't do as I say."

She was dead serious. Abbu didn't even blink, but the line of his mouth went tight and pale. He didn't look at me, because I don't think he could. He had accepted the dance in accordance with his oaths. Regardless of Sabra's bloodthirsty designs upon it, he couldn't forsake the dance, or he would forsake everything he lived for. And Abbu wasn't the type.

I opened my mouth to comment, but Sabra was now staring at me. "Hear me," she said quietly. "I am vengeful and vindictive. I am everything they—and you—have said of me; do you think I'm unaware?" She gripped the knife in one hand, dark knuckles turning pale. "I don't *care* about you . . . not about *either* of you. Do you understand? I want this for myself, and I will have it *my way.*"

I stared back at her, offering nothing. She was in complete control, with the hirelings—and large, attentive eunuchs—to back her up.

She bared small teeth. "I could kill you out of hand, before every man here—and that woman; would that satisfy you?" When I gave her no answer, she went on without inflection. "Well, it does not satisfy me. I prefer a greater *effort.*" She held out the knife; one of the eunuchs took it from her. "Hear me, Sandtiger, as I tell you my provisions: Abbu Bensir is to kill you. But *you* are to kill him."

I nodded sagely. "That's the way a dance to the death *usually* works: each man tries to kill the other."

Sabra smiled coolly, unperturbed by my insolence. "If you kill him, I will free you."

I wanted to spit, but didn't; settled for laughing out loud. "I don't believe you for a moment! The entire *point* of this dance is to execute me."

"Is it?" She shook out a fold in her veil. "No, I think not. It's merely to *entertain* me—and to prove to all the others I am worthy of my station."

I gritted teeth so hard my jaw protested. "Then why—"

She laughed lustily in amusement, tossing her turbaned head."You fool—I want a good dance. I want a dance of *passion:* two men within a circle, servicing one another with steel instead of with flesh." The amusement faded abruptly, replaced by avid intensity. "Kill him, and you go free. But if he fails to execute *you*, he shall be killed in your place. I will see to it myself."

"You said that already."

Sabra's eyes glinted. "If you fail to entertain me, if you prevaricate to goad me—*or* dally to conserve your strength—I will stop this dance at once and do worse than have you killed."

I laughed. "What is worse?"

"First, I will geld your horse."

It caught me completely off-guard. "My—horse?"

"Then I will castrate you—and throw you into the mine." Sabra smiled complacency. "I have your horse. I have your sword—even the magical sword—and also I have you. I learned when I was a child men value their maleness most of all, and that of living possessions . . . you will lose yours if you fail to entertain me sufficiently, and be left to die in the mine." A tiny, malicious smile. "I believe you know the mine. You *visited* it once before."

I tasted metal in my mouth. "Leave my horse alone."

It was sufficient to make her laugh. And then the laughter died. "You will accept the dance according to the codes you swore to obey. You will uphold the binding vows you made before your shodo."

Oh, hoolies, bascha—and you thought *your* codes were tough!

I shrugged false negligence. "What else can I do?"

"Complete the ritual!" she snapped.

Hoolies, she *does* know it all. . . .

Once again I shrugged. Then said the words she wanted so much, the words Abbu had said as they applied to me, and knew the circle sealed.

Along with my future. But I don't know as that mattered so much anymore; Abbu, given his way, would make it very short.

Or excruciatingly long, depending on your viewpoint.

I bared my teeth at Sabra. "I'll see you in hoolies."

Sabra smiled back. "You'll see it before *I* do."

Chapter 41

Sabra herself took Abbu's sword and Singlestroke out to the circle. Abbu and I both watched, but neither of us saw. We didn't have time for it.

I had loosened up as best I could in the room before being brought out into the courtyard. It wasn't enough after a night spent chained up with no food or water until morning, but I'd done what I could. Overall, I was physically prepared: my once-sore knee was sound, the scar tissue was stretched, shoulders and thighs were loose. And although I didn't like gravel much, it wouldn't bother me; the soles of a sword-dancer's feet are always toughened from years of dancing barefoot.

I felt pretty good, save for the nagging sting of the freshly reopened slice in my forearm and the smaller cut Sabra had added. But I'd forget all about them once the dance began. You can't afford to think about anything save the dance itself once you've been set into motion.

I glanced sidelong at Abbu. His eyes were very clear, his expression perfectly calm, betraying no concern with what was about to happen. The Southron body was in good proportion, and the flesh was taut, lacking the telltale signs of liquor or huva abuse. He was older, but still exceedingly fit, with no excess weight or softness or dullness. I knew better than to hope he wasn't as prepared;

Abbu Bensir had not lived this long—or defeated so many men—by being lazy about preparation.

But he *was* older. Older than me, of course, but also *old;* at least for a sword-dancer. It had to be in his mind. And although he'd said more than once I'd changed over the last couple of years; that the North had altered intensity and fitness, a glance at me now would dispel that. (And he had more than glanced, though he'd been very casual about it.) Between my getting sharper from being on the run, and the assistance of Chosa Dei in restoring a battered body, I was hardly a poor opponent. And I was a *younger* one.

I smiled. Shook out long, muscled arms; flopped big hands. Laughed a little, very softly, as I briefly worked broad shoulders, tweaking thick neck from side to side. "Should be interesting," I murmured. "Too bad we didn't get a chance to lay a wager."

"I did," he retorted. "I'll let you guess which way I bet."

I snickered. "Wise money goes on me."

"Not with that sword."

"I don't need a sword."

He smiled grimly. "Do you plan to dance with your tongue?"

"I outweigh you by nearly one hundred pounds."

Abbu nodded sagely. "Should slow you down."

"Never has before."

He watched blood-colored, silken Sabra kneel to lay out his sword. "I'm as fit as I ever was."

"*I'm* as fit as I was at seventeen years old, when I shattered your guard and nearly crushed your throat—does it still hurt? Or ever bother your breathing?—except now I'm a little older, a little wiser—" I paused, "—and a whole lot *better.*"

Abbu made no answer.

I drew in a breath, laughing softly. "Who does she think she is—ordering *us* to entertain her? Hoolies, Abbu—we've done nothing *but* entertain for—what?—fifty years between us?" I snickered again. "I figure we ought to be pretty flashy for—oh, two engagements?—and then we'll begin to dance." I paused. "*Dance* dance, I mean . . . the kind from which legends are made."

Abbu's gaze was steady as he looked at me. "He told me one day it would come to this."

"Who?"

"The shodo. At Alimat, one day. When I watched a clumsy chula pretend to be a man."

I laughed outright. "Save the games, Abbu. It's not your style— and anyway, you already told me you were one of the first to suggest I might be better than good."

He shrugged. "You are. But so am I. I am Abbu Bensir." Very slowly, he smiled. "I am the legend against which others measure themselves. Even Sandtigers."

Politely, I disagreed. "You're old," I said gently. "Old men are slower than young ones, and prone to make mistakes once tired limbs begin to fail. You're a legend, all right . . . but the light of that legend usually begins to dim along with an old man's vision."

Abbu's mouth tightened.

Before he could respond, I jumped in again. "I'm glad you helped her out so much, telling her all our secrets regarding oaths, and whatnot. Another kind of dance—the *normal* sort of dance—would have been much too boring. At least this way we get a chance to show Sabra—and everyone else—just what kind of men we are." I shrugged. "After all, how many sword-dancers can brag about being trained at Alimat? How many of us actually swore the proper oaths?" I nodded. "All that secrecy serves no purpose . . . after all, there's no sense in trying to live up to a single shodo's expectations. Who cares?" I shrugged. "It's a good thing you brought it all out into the open."

The Southron face darkened. "I said *nothing*—"

But Sabra's return cut him off. "Go to the circle," she snapped curtly, and sat down upon her cushions.

Abbu gazed blankly at her, still too bound up in what I'd said, and the need to tell me the truth. "Wait—"

"No." She pointed. "Waste no more time."

"Sabra—"

"*Go*," she hissed, "or I'll have you carried out there!"

Laughing quietly, I turned and walked out to the circle. I stopped this side, letting Abbu walk all the way around, still thinking about what I'd said. I wanted him to think about it as long as he could. A fractured concentration can come in very handy—so long as it isn't yours.

I nodded. Assumed stance, arms hanging slack at my sides. I focused eyes, ears, body, narrowing *my* concentration to just one thing: the opening maneuver. I knew the parameters of the circle, the placement of Sabra's cushions, the positions of eunuchs and onlookers. Had already judged how fast I could run in gravel, how many steps to the swords, how soon I could scoop mine up.

Poised, I waited in stillness, quietly gathering strength and the sheer physical power that had served me so many years. If she wanted entertainment—

I laughed without making a sound.

Hoolies, what a farce. A single initial parry between Abbu Bensir and me would offer more entertainment than she had a right to see.

I nodded again, still smiling. Focused on the sword. Refused to look beyond Abbu to Del, who stood across from me in the shade of Umir's sunshade. I saw the blur of blinding samite, but didn't look at it. Instead, I thought about the dance. Thought about Abbu. Thought about the move I'd made so many years before, that had nearly crushed his throat.

Sabra's voice: "Prepare!"

I grinned across at Abbu. "Did you teach her that, too?"

"Dance!" Sabra shouted.

I was already moving.

But so was Abbu.

A true circle for a true dance—as this one was—is fifteen paces in diameter. That means a man can cross one in fifteen strides; seven and a half, to the center. But there's one thing a lot of Southron sword-dancers forget, when they dance against me: my legs are longer than theirs.

Abbu, as expected, took seven and a half strides to the center of the circle. I took five.

I tore the sword from the ground. "Entertain us," I said, and laughed to see his face.

Singlestroke lay in the gravel. I had taken *his* sword.

"Not only younger," I taunted, "but also *smarter* than you. Not to mention faster—"

He snatched up Singlestroke: a sword is a sword, and no weapon is disdained. I let him grip the beadwire hilt; watched his expression alter; marked the shift in posture. The shock of seeing the sword had faded. Singlestroke had been "dead" to me for too long. Now he was merely a chance for me to upset the dance.

"Two engagements," I said. "Then all hoolies breaks loose."

Abbu didn't flick an eyelash. He just came in with Singlestroke.

He was good. *Very* good; I sucked in breath, ducked away, twisted his steel off my own. This was just the beginning—what would happen at the end?

Gravel hissed and chattered. Abbu drove me back, straight back, teasing me with steel. I caught the blows, turned them; threw steel back at him. His deftness and speed was incredible.

Back— I thought. Almost—

Blade scraped blade. Quillons caught, hung up, broke free as we wrenched them apart. All around us people murmured.

Almost— I thought. Two more steps—

I let him drive me back. Then countered his pattern, responded with my own.

"That's enough," I said.

Abbu's eyes flickered.

I grinned. Laughed. Stared straight at the scar that punched a hole in the flesh of his throat, then rotated a hip, shifted stance, lifted elbows and twisted wrists, giving him what he expected. What he had recalled so many times, in the darkness of his dreams; the memory of the maneuver that had nearly ended his life.

Let him remember it all.

Let him make himself ready.

Let him prepare the defense; consider the proper riposte—

Then take it away from him—from *them*—by purposely breaking the pattern.

By purposely breaking the sword.

By purposely breaking the oaths.

Exactly eight paces—my legs are much longer than theirs—and I was out of the circle.

I was *in* Sabra's shade, marking quickness as she sprang up. Judging how far she could get. Hearing her garbled call for guards as she tripped over cushions and silks.

Then Sabra was in my arms.

But I didn't intend to kiss her.

Chapter 42

I knocked the turban off her head, sank a fist into thick black hair, and yanked her head back roughly to expose the fragile throat. Then settled my left arm across it, pressing a hard-muscled wrist into the taut-stretched windpipe.

One throttled outcry escaped her, and then she clawed at my arms. I shut off her breath easily with a slight increase in pressure. "Your choice," I told her.

She wavered, sagged minutely, then allowed slackened arms to drop back to her side.

"Better." I looked out into the courtyard, noting opened mouths and staring eyes, as well as stiffened postures. Saw Abbu still standing in the circle, broken Singlestroke in one hand; saw Umir across the way with a white-clad woman next to him, poised to move; saw—and felt—the tension in Sabra's hirelings as they considered options. "Five things," I said clearly. "Two horses immediately—and one of them better be mine . . . two Northern swords—leave them sheathed, if you please . . . and one Northern bascha." I looked across at Umir. "Cut her loose *now*."

For a long moment no one did anything. And then Abbu threw down Singlestroke. His own sword lay in gravel just outside the circle, where I had dropped it on my way to Sabra. I didn't need steel. I wanted my hands upon her.

The chime of steel on gravel released everyone. They began to stir, to mutter; Umir cut Del's wrists free, and she moved away quickly. Someone came up from a stable block with the stud and Del's mare. Someone else approached me with two Northern *jivatmas*. Sheathed, as requested.

"On the horses," I said.

It was done. Del moved to mare, mounted, hooked arms through harness straps. Loose sleeves fouled on leather and buckles, but she jerked the fabric loose, yanking it into place even as Umir blurted a protest. Then she reached down and took the reins to the stud, turning him broadside to me.

I smiled. "Your turn," I said to Sabra.

She was perfectly rigid, barely breathing, trembling with tension and anger. I could feel it through crimson silk; in the rigidity of her neck; in the minute curving of stiffened fingers.

"*Elaii-ali-ma!*" I shouted. "Every single sword-dancer here knows what that means!"

Abbu's face was ashen. "Do *you?*"

"Three days," I told him. "It's in the honor codes: you all owe me three days."

"Those of us who are sworn, yes—"

"Doesn't matter," I told him. "I'm taking Sabra with me. That ought to make the others think twice."

Slowly he shook his head. "Such a fool, Sandtiger."

I smiled over Sabra's head. "One thing I have learned is that in order to stay alive, one must make sacrifices."

"*This?*"

"This," I confirmed. "Do what you have to do. Everything's different now . . . I can't afford to care."

Abbu thrust a fist into the air. "*Elaii-ali-ma!*" he shouted. "The oaths of honor are broken! There is no more Sandtiger among us, to enter the true circle in the name of Alimat! *Elaii-ali-ma!*"

Those who were sword-dancers echoed the cry. Then all, led by Abbu, turned their backs on me.

"Now," I rasped to Sabra, and walked her across the gravel to the restive, waiting stud.

Del, strangely white-faced, pulled him up short so he couldn't sidestep. A glance showed me she appeared to be unhurt, as did the stud. Then I turned my attention back to Sabra, still rigid in my arms.

"Time to go," I told her. Sabra opened her mouth. I immediately made a fist and chopped her just under the jaw, snapping her head back. It would hold her for a while.

She sagged. I scooped her up, threw her facedown across the front of the saddle, clambered up behind her. Grabbed a handful of raven hair and jerked her head up, displaying the slack face. "Not dead," I told her eunuchs. "But she will be soon enough if anyone follows us."

I dropped her head back down. She was dead weight across the saddle, arms and legs dangling. I pressed one hand into the small of her back, caught up the reins with the other, and nodded at Del.

She swung the mare and left at a trot. I followed at the same pace, hearing gravel hiss beneath hooves.

Hearing also the echoing cry that had filled the entire courtyard: *"Elaii-ali-ma!"*

We wasted no time. Our long-trot through narrow streets scattered passersby and earned us curses, but that was the least of our worries. All I wanted to do was get out of Julah as soon as possible; as far from Sabra's hirelings as we could, before they at last roused into action.

Del dropped back. "Where?"

"Up into the mountains."

She studied my face. "Are you all right?"

"I will be, once we're out of here."

She nodded, slackened rein, fell back behind the stud as we wound our way through canyons of adobe dwellings and ramshackle shelters built out of city refuse.

We left the inner city for the outer, where the streets were a little wider and less clogged. Now I tapped the stud out of a trot into a lope, guiding him through the crooks as I pressed Sabra one-handed down into the saddle and the stud's withers. It was not the most comfortable way I'd ever ridden, but I'd been left with little choice. I'd sincerely doubted Sabra was the kind of woman to do as I told her, even in the face of threats; she'd have spat in my eye and dared me to kill her. Since I didn't really want to do that, it was easier just to knock her out and carry her away.

"This way," I said, and reined the stud into an alley that led us through looming shadows to daylight again. "Keep riding," I said over the clatter of hooves. "Straight up into the mountains."

"How long are we going to keep her?"

"Not much longer. I have a plan for her." I patted Sabra's rump. "She's going to buy us safe passage to the place we need to go."

Del twisted in the saddle. "*Where* do we need to go?"

"Don't worry about it, bascha. I know what I'm doing."

Fair brow creased a little. "I've learned to be concerned whenever you say that."

I grinned, oddly content. "I see Umir made you bathe."

Del grinned back. "I see Sabra didn't bother."

Which was enough for the time being; things were normal again.

Up. Out of sandy hardpan into real dirt and webby grass, sprawling in clusters across the ground. Catclaw, tigerclaw, scrubby greasewood trees; beanpods dropped from feathertrees scattered pebbled ground. We chipped and gouged earth as we climbed, negotiating clinking rectangles of shale, and gray-green granite rubble.

Up. Over hillocks and shoulders and elbow bends out onto jagged escarpments, then in against sharp-cut walls. We left behind the first flank and went over across the second. Shale and granite were interspersed with smokerock, crumbling beneath shod hooves.

"How much farther?" Del asked. "There is no trail—do we keep climbing?"

"Keep climbing. We'll rid ourselves of Sabra any old time, then head higher."

"What are you going to do with her?"

"You'll see."

Del said nothing as the mare worked her way up the mountain. Both horses stumbled, staggered, splayed legs; slid back, recovered, climbed. Beneath me the stud heaved himself upward, head dropped and rump bunching. Shoulders strained, driving legs down through loose footing to firmer ground beneath. He grunted rhythmically.

Sabra's slack body slipped to one side. I caught a handful of hair and crimson silk, dragged her up, balanced her more securely.

"Is she dead?" Del asked.

"No. What good would a body do us?"

"What good does she do us at all?"

"Be patient. You'll see. As a matter of fact . . . wait a moment. Pull up." I halted the stud, tore strips of tough silk from Sabra's tunic, tied her wrists together. "No sense in making it easier." Then I prodded the stud out. "All right. Keep climbing."

It wasn't much farther before Sabra roused. She came to with a jerk and a twitch, then arched her back as she tried to counterbalance her head-down posture.

I patted her on the rump. "Careful now, tanzeer—or I'll dump you on your head."

Loose hair sheathed her face. Her words were muffled, but not the tone of voice. "Stop this horse. Untie me. Let me *go*."

I chuckled. "Not a chance."

She twisted mightily. I caught handfuls of hair and cloth before she went over. "Let me *go*," she repeated.

I stopped the stud. Tipped her off backward. Silk hooked and tore. Bound hands caught on the harness and hilt. Strung up, she dangled against the stud. Toes barely scraped the ground.

"If you insist . . ." I grabbed hair, pulled her upright, unhooked trapped wrists and dropped her to the ground. Legs buckled and she sat, crying out at the impact. "Now," I said calmly, "perhaps you'd rather walk."

She spat out a string of rather foul expletives, all designed to make me blush. Except I don't blush easily. Then she stopped swearing and began speaking more clearly, if with no less conviction.

"You broke them. You *broke* them. You made a mockery of the oaths and honor codes."

"I did what I needed to do."

"Now you'll *die!*" she shrieked. "Do you think I don't know? Do you think I don't know *how?*" Sabra laughed stridently, tossing hair out of her face. "They'll forgo paying dances to kill you, all of those sword-dancers . . . you're meat to them now. They'll kill you first chance they get—"

"*Elaii-ali-ma.*" I nodded. "I know all about it, Sabra."

"You're not a sword-dancer anymore. You have no honor. You broke the codes. You repudiated your shodo, and the honor of Al-imat. Do you think I don't *know?*"

Wearily, I sighed. "I don't care what you know."

"You're a borjuni!" she spat. "Sandtiger the borjuni . . . how will you live *now?* How will you find work? No one will hire you . . . no one will ask you to dance. You're nothing but a borjuni, and you'll live by borjuni rules!"

"I'll live by my *own* rules."

"Tiger." It was Del. "We have company."

I glanced up. Nodded. "I wondered what took them so long."

Sabra, still sitting in shale and smokerock, twisted her head to look behind us. She saw what we saw: four leather-kilted Vashni warriors wearing human fingerbone necklets, mounted on small dark horses.

She scrambled up and moved close to the stud. "Vashni," she hissed. "Do you know what you've done?"

"Pretty much. It's the one reason I came up here."

"*Vashni,* you fool! They'll kill us all!"

"They won't kill any of us. Well . . . I suppose they might kill you, if you don't do what they want." I dug a rigid toe into her spine and prodded her off the stud. "Don't crowd him, Sabra. He might take a bite of your face."

Del sat quietly. Equally quietly, she asked, "Do you know what you're doing?"

I grinned. "Pretty much."

"Oh, good," Del muttered. "I guess I need not worry."

"Not yet." I reached down, caught a handful of shiny black hair, pulled Sabra up short. "This is Julah's tanzeer."

The four warriors sat impassively on their horses. Bare-chested save for the pectorals; also bare-legged. Dark skin was greased. Black hair was oiled smooth and slicked into single fur-bound plaits.

I smiled at the warriors. "This is *Aladar's* daughter."

Dark eyes glittered. Single-file, four men rode down the mountain. Sabra called me names.

"It's not my fault," I told her. "Blame your father. He double-crossed them in the treaty, and then he snatched a few young Vashni and put them to work in the mine. Vashni don't take kindly to that sort of bad manners . . . I wonder what they'll do to you."

She exercised her tongue a little more, until the four warriors pulled up close by. Then she fell silent, twisting wrists against silk bonds. Brilliant crimson finery was torn, soiled, befouled. Tangled hair obscured half of her face. The paint on her lips had smeared. She was altogether a mess.

"Sabra," I told them. "Aladar's daughter, now tanzeer in his place. Any business you have with Julah can be tended by this woman."

They ignored Sabra completely, concentrating on me. Del earned a quick assessment, being a woman and obviously foreign, but me they measured more closely. Then one of them made a gesture, and put a finger on his cheek. "You are the Sandtiger."

I nodded.

"You and that woman came here before, looking for a not-Vashni boy, one of Aladar's slaves."

"That woman" said nothing, but I sensed her sharpened awareness. Again, I nodded. "He remained with the Vashni," I said. "It was his own choice."

The warrior flicked a glance at Del, marking fair hair, blue eyes, the sword. He made another quick gesture I didn't understand, but his fellow warriors did. The three rode down slowly to Del and surrounded her, cutting her off from me. I stiffened in the saddle, aware of sudden tension, but the leader's eyes forbade me to move.

Each of the three warriors reached out and touched Del's shoulder. One touch only, then a half-hidden sign. Without saying a word, they reined back and turned their horses, rejoining the fourth warrior.

He nodded. "Bloodkin to the Oracle; may the sun shine on your head."

The common Southron blessing sounded incongruous coming

from a Vashni. But it put me at ease. If they respected Del, they weren't about to kill us.

"Jamail," she said. "Is he with you again?"

Something pinched the pit of my belly. I recalled with sick realization that Del hadn't been present when Sabra had told me her men had killed Jamail.

"Bascha—"

But the Vashni overrode me. "The Oracle is dead."

Del, shocked, opened her mouth. Shut it. Shock was transformed to acknowledgment; her mouth to a grim, tight line. The flesh at her eyes was pinched. "Then I will have to sing his song, when I am free to do so."

"I'm sorry," I said quietly. "I meant to tell you myself."

"What is this?" Sabra asked. "Grief for a worthless fool? Did you *believe* all that nonsense about Oracles and jhihadis?"

I shrugged. "Doesn't matter anymore, does it?"

The Vashni looked at me. "Will you kill Aladar's daughter as you killed Aladar?"

I grinned. "I thought I'd let the Vashni have her, as recompense for the warriors Aladar stole."

Del spoke before they could say anything. She was, at long last, making sure everyone got it right. "Tiger didn't kill Aladar," she said clearly. "*I* did."

"You!" Sabra tried to wrench her hair free of my grasp. She failed, then gave it up, transfixed by new information. "*You* killed my father?"

"Recompense," Del spat. "For Tiger. For my brother. For all the others." Cold eyes glittered. "Your father deserved to die. I was grateful for the chance to see the color of his guts."

Sabra was rigid. "You," she whispered. "You—*not* him."

"No," I agreed. "But she just beat me to it. He wasn't a popular man."

Sabra stared at Del. "You," she repeated.

Then she reached up and clasped the grip of my sword, trying to tear it down from the saddle.

Chapter 43

The stud spooked violently, lurching sideways. I swore, grabbed rein and harness; felt Sabra's frenzied jerking. The harness came free of the saddle.

"*Hoo—*" I lunged, leaned, grabbed hold; felt the stud bunch, then cut loose with a buck that nearly lost me my seat. As it was, my position was more than a little precarious.

Sabra was shouting. Both hands were locked on the hilt, tugging it free of sheath. I hung onto harness, tugging back, but the stud's violence distracted me. He stumbled, staggered, nearly fell. I was halfway out of the saddle, trying to jerk the harness and sheath away from Sabra. Sabra jerked back.

Overbalanced, I came off. One foot caught briefly in brass stirrup, then pulled free as the stud leaped aside and I twisted in midfall. I landed hard, one leg bunched under me, then threw myself full-length and flopped belly-down as Sabra dragged at the harness, trying to jerk it out of my hands.

I called her a nasty name, but she wasn't listening. By then she had the sword halfway out of the sheath.

"Tiger!" It was Del. I saw the glint of Boreal as she unsheathed the *jivatma*.

"Kill her—" I said hoarsely. "Don't let her get the sword."

But Sabra *had* the sword.

I pushed up, dove, caught silk. Felt the bite of steel in flesh as the tip dragged across one forearm. I reached to grab for the hilt; to peel her hands away. "Sabra—Sabra *don't* . . . you don't know what it is."

But Sabra didn't care.

"Get away!" Del shouted. "Tiger—you're too close."

"Hoolies, she's got the *jivatma*—"

Something inside me flared. Chosa Dei, scenting power, swarmed out of the dark little corner he'd used as a place to live, biding his time patiently. Now the time had come.

Sabra screamed. She scrambled through loose shale and tumbling smokerock, kicking dirt and debris and stone as she tried now to escape the sword a moment before she'd wanted so badly. Wet blackness ran up the blade, darkening twisted runes, then danced along the quillons and began to tickle the grip. Began to caress her fingers.

"Let it go—" I rasped. "Sabra—let it *go*—"

But Sabra didn't. Or couldn't.

A convulsion cramped my body. I tied up, spasmed, retched; blurted a grunt against the pain.

Sabra kept on screaming.

Hoolies, shut her up—

Blackness charred her fingers. Reached her wrists. Then, sensing unrestricted opportunity, engulfed her entire body.

The screaming abruptly stopped.

Within me, Chosa moved. No more tentative testing. No more anticipation. He went straight for the heart, and squeezed.

Sabra's mouth hung open, but made no sound. She sat upright, clutching the sword. Rocking back and forth, with black eyes stretched so wide the whites showed all around them.

Chosa Dei was in her. Part of him, at least. The rest was still in me.

Sabra's features began to soften. The skin began to droop. The nose slid sideways as the mouth slackened to shapelessness. A keening moan bubbled from her throat.

She bled from nose and ears. The hands on the sword swelled until the flesh split like a melon. Chosa Dei had filled her utterly, and found she wasn't enough.

Breath came in heaves and gusts: sucked in, then held, then expelled. I crawled across the ground and reached for Aladar's daughter. Caught the quillons in one hand, both tiny wrists in the other. "Let her go," I grated. "There isn't enough of her!"

The Chosa in me lunged the length of my arms, trying to pour himself into Sabra, whom he saw as a means to escape. I felt him swarm into the quillons, up the grip, then to her fingertips.

I wrenched her hands loose. "No," I said hoarsely. "I said there wasn't enough!"

"Let him go!" Del shouted. "Let him go into her!"

"She'll die—she'll *die* . . . and he'll be loose. Do you really want him loose?"

"Better than in you!"

Nice sentiment, bascha.

Then Chosa came surging back. The tiny body was clearly unsuitable; I offered much better. Bigger. Stronger. *Alive.*

At least, for the moment.

"Tiger—let go of the sword!"

In leaps and bounds, he came, flowing out of Sabra's body. I scrambled backward, thrusting the sword away, but realized I'd left it too late. The blade was black again, but so were my hands. Even as I swore, the blackness invaded forearms and climbed up to elbows.

"Drive him back!" Del shouted. "You've done it before—*do it again—*"

Legs flailed impotently as I scrambled to get up. My right knee failed. Belly knotted itself, then spewed out its contents. I grasped the hilt and clenched it in both hands, straining to force him back.

It would be so easy if I simply let him have me.

I lunged up onto my knees and hoisted the sword into the air. Brought it down against shale and granite, splintering dark smokerock.

Again and again and again. Steel rang a protest.

"Go back—" I husked, "—*go back—*"

Tried to focus myself. Tried to beat Chosa Dei back as I methodically beat the steel against the hard flesh of Southron mountains.

"go back—"

"*go back*—"

"GO BACK—"

Del's voice, strident: "Stop . . . Tiger, *stop*—"

"—go back—go back—go back—"

"Tiger—no more!"

"—back—" I gasped. "*Go back*—"

A litany. A chant. The kind learned at Alimat, to focus concentration.

In the North, they sang. In the South, we don't.

"Tiger—*let go*—"

"Go. Back," I commanded.

Someone hit me over the head.

"I'm sorry," Del whispered.

But I didn't care anymore.

I came to in grave discomfort, aware of constant movement, and blood pounding in my head. "What have you done to me?"

Del rode ahead on the mare, leading the stud. "Tied you onto your horse."

That part I could tell. "Hoolies, bascha—you might have let me ride *normally,* instead of throwing me over the saddle like a piece of meat!"

"It's what you did to Sabra."

I shifted. Swore. I was exceedingly uncomfortable, sprawled belly-down across the saddle just as Sabra had. Wrists and ankles were tied to stirrups. "Do you mind if we stop?" I croaked.

"We don't have any time."

"Time for what? What are you talking about? Del—what in hoolies do you mean?"

"Shaka Obre," she said.

"Shaka—" My belly cramped. "Del, for pity's sake—"

"It's for your own good."

"*How* is it for my own good?"

"Look at your hands," she said.

I looked. Saw the pallid, hairless flesh, all flaky and scaly. The crumbling, discolored fingernails. "Not again," I muttered.

"They told me where to go."

"*Who* did? What are you talking about?"

"The Vashni. They told me how to get there. So that's where we're going."

"Told you how to get *where?* What are you talking about?"

"Shaka Obre."

I spasmed. "You *know* where he is?"

"I told you: they told me."

"How do the Vashni know where Shaka Obre is? And why tell *you?*"

She twisted in the saddle and looked back at me. Her face was very white. "They know because they have always known; it's never been a secret among the Vashni. But no one ever cared, and no one bothered to ask. They told *me* because I am the Oracle's sister. They also told me because you are Chosa Dei—or so they believe." She shrugged. "I am to take you there, to imprison you in the mountain."

"Imprison me!" I flailed. "But I'm *not* Chosa Dei. I'm *me*. Didn't you tell them that?"

"You didn't see what happened. They did, and they're superstitious."

I gritted teeth, trying to keep from shouting. "I didn't see it—I was *in* it."

"I'm sorry," she said. "It was the only way they would let me take you. Otherwise they meant to kill you on the spot . . . I explained why we needed to find Shaka Obre, and they agreed to let me take you."

"You could untie me *now*. There aren't any Vashni around."

"They said they'd watch, to make sure I got you there safely." She paused. "Also myself."

"So you're just going to *leave* me this way?"

"They said they'd be *watching*, Tiger."

"Do they really know where he is?"

"They said they did. They gave me directions." She was quiet a moment, letting the mare climb. "They said they took Jamail there once."

It chilled me. "Jamail."

"He'd been having dreams. Since he had no tongue, he couldn't explain anything." She shrugged. "They took him to Shaka Obre. When he came back, he could speak. He had no tongue, but he could speak."

"*How?*"

"I don't know. But you said you heard him talk in Iskandar."

"Yes, but . . ." I was fascinated. "How could that happen?"

The mare climbed steadily. So did the stud. "The Vashni said Shaka Obre caused him to speak again so he could carry word of the jhihadi throughout the South. To prepare the way." Del looked back at me. "If Shaka can do that, surely he can discharge your sword."

"We had better hope so." I frowned. "Was it you who hit me?"

"I had to. You were trying to break your sword."

"I was?"

"And it would have made things worse. Chosa was already back in the *jivatma*—but you just kept banging the blade into the mountainside, trying to break it. If you had, it would have freed Chosa."

I frowned. "I don't remember that part."

"At that point, I doubt you remembered your name." Del reined the mare around a tumble of boulders. "So I hit you with my sword hilt."

"Thank you very much."

"And now I'm taking you to Shaka Obre, where you can discharge your sword."

"And me."

"And you."

"But can't we do this with me riding *upright?*"

Del's tone was flat. "I don't want to take a chance with the part of Chosa that's in you."

"Hoolies, bascha—I'm not Chosa, if that's what you mean."

"Not now, maybe."

"*Del—*"

She interrupted. "You don't understand. The Vashni told me. The closer we get to Shaka, the stronger Chosa becomes."

That shut me up.

I hung slackly over the saddle and contemplated my state. Blackened nails, dead skin . . . a bruised knee (*again*) . . . general discomfort. I felt sick and cold and tired. I needed some aqivi. I needed a hot bath. I needed a healthy body that hosted no part of Chosa.

"Hoolies," I muttered wearily. "When will this all be over?"

"Soon," Del answered.

It made me feel no better.

Chapter 44

Del took one look at my face. "Are you all right?"

I cleared my throat pointedly, rubbing wrists with elaborate attention. "It's what happens when you're forced to ride slung across your own saddle on your own horse."

"No, it's not," she retorted. "But if that's your answer, you must be all right." Lines creased her brow when I didn't respond. "Are you *really* all right?"

"No," I answered truthfully. "You want me to go *in* there, don't you?"

"There" was the mouth I'd seen inside my head as I lay chained in Sabra's palace. The blackened, peeled-away opening; a hole leading into the mountain.

Del and I had left the horses down below, in a sandy, level area with a little bit of grazing, if you like Southron drygrass. We'd climbed up a little ways because Del said it was what we were supposed to do; now we stood facing a hole. The hole I'd seen in my mind, all mixed up with Chosa's memories of what he'd done to his brother. Like it or not, Shaka Obre was near.

Or what was left of him.

Del slid a step, flung out arms, caught her balance. "This is where Shaka's supposed to be. They said it looked just like this: all broken, choppy smokerock, gaping open like a mouth. See? There are the lips—and just inside it looks like teeth."

A ripple tickled my spine. "I don't like it, bascha."

"It starts out small, then opens up," she persisted. "They've all been inside the first chamber."

I ignored the pinching in my belly. "The *first* chamber?"

She shrugged. "They didn't go any farther."

"But *we're* supposed to, right?"

Another shrug. "If we're to find Shaka Obre, we'll have to do what we must."

I sucked in a deep breath, held it, blew it out gustily. Scratched at a prickling scalp. "It's a lot like the mine."

"Aladar's—? *Oh.*" Now she understood. "Do you want me to go first?"

"No, I don't want you to go first. I don't want *either* of us to go."

"Then I guess we'd better leave." Del turned on her heel, slid down a step, then began to pick her way laboriously down the slope.

"*Del*—"

She stopped. Looked back. "Your choice," she said. "You're the one with a piece of Chosa trapped inside."

I kicked a rock aside. "I went into the Canteada hidey-holes. And into Dragon Mountain—where I rescued you. If you'll just give me a *moment*, I'll go in here, too."

She climbed back up the slope, slipping and sliding through rolling pebbles and crumbling smokerock. "If you want—"

"Never *mind*, Del." I ducked my head way down and squeezed my way through into the first chamber, scraping past the "lips."

The "mouth" was small. Very small. And very, very cold. I stopped just inside and felt the hairs rise on my neck. The ones on my arms tried to, too—except Chosa Dei had burned them away.

Deep inside me, something quivered. Trouble was, I couldn't tell if it was Chosa, or just my normal discomfort when faced with cave or tunnel.

"Tiger?" Del ducked through, blocking out the light. "Is this—it?"

I drew in a breath. "Seems to be." With two of us, it was cramped. I edged back toward the daylight as Del moved through. "So—now we've done it. I guess we can go . . ."

"This can't be *it*," she murmured, looking around. "One little two-person cave?"

"I'm cold. It's dark. We're done."

"Wait." She put a hand on my arm. "It *is* very cold."

"I said that. Let's go."

"But why? This is the South. Why should it feel like the North?"

"It's confused, maybe." I edged away from the restraining hand. "There's nothing for us to do here—"

"Tiger, wait." She knelt, pressed a hand against the floor. "It's cold . . . cold and *damp*."

"So?" I peered around impatiently. The chamber was little more than a privacy closet, with a low rock roof. If Del and I linked hands and stretched out either arm, we'd knock knuckles against both sides. "There *is* water in the South, bascha . . . or none of us would be here."

She moved her hand along the wall. The damp stone was pocked with hollows and holes, falling away into darkness. Del followed it to the back, then blurted in surprise.

I stiffened. "What?"

"Move."

"Do what?"

"*Move*. You're in the light."

Reluctantly, I moved away from the opening. The absence of my body allowed sunlight into the tiny chamber. Then I saw what Del meant.

The first chamber was exactly that: the first. Cut into the back wall, hidden in shadow when a body blocked the opening, was a narrow passageway leading deeper into the mountain.

Hairs stirred on neck and in groin. "I don't think so," I blurted.

Del, still kneeling in Umir's priceless burnous, looked up at me in assessment. "How are you feeling?"

"Pretty sick of all this."

"No. How are you *feeling*?"

I sighed, summoned a smile. "He's being very quiet."

Del frowned. "We should be close to Shaka, and the Vashni said Chosa would grow stronger. I wonder why he's being so quiet."

"I don't. I'm just happy he is." I took a single step, reached down to catch a sleeve. "Let's go, bascha."

She pulled sleeve—and arm—free. "I'm going deeper. Stay or go, as you like . . . or maybe you'd rather come with me."

"You don't know what's *in* there."

In muted light, she smiled. "Shaka Obre," she said. And turned to go through the door.

In a moment, bright white samite was swallowed by the darkness. So was Del.

"Oh, hoolies," I muttered. "Why does she always do this?"

A muffled echo came back to me. "You'll have to take off your harness. There isn't very much headroom."

"Or much room inside *your* head."

But I didn't say it loudly. I just slipped free of straps, wound them around the sheath, followed Del into darkness.

Swearing all the while.

She was all hunched up when I made my way to her, sitting on the rock floor with doubled up knees jutting roofward. One arm cradled harness-wrapped sheath and sword. The other was stretched out, picking at crevices cut into the walls.

"Ice," she said briefly.

"Ice?"

"Feel it yourself."

I sat down next to her, easing myself past outcroppings that threatened to snatch at bare flesh. All I wore was a dhoti, and no sandals, either. I sat for only a moment, then shifted hastily to a squat. "Hoolies! It'll freeze my *gehetties* off!"

Del smiled. "Ice." She dug into a crevice, then pulled her hand out and displayed fingertips.

I inspected. Touched. Ice, all right. Frowning, I scraped my own share out of the crevice. It was gritty, frozen hard. Not in the slightest mushy. "Like Punja crystals—hard and sharp and glittery."

"Only this is real ice." Del rubbed fingertips together. "Like the ice-caves near Staal-Ysta."

"But this is the South."

She shrugged. "A sixth-month ago, I would have said there

could be no such thing. But that same sixth-month ago, I'd have said there would be no need to find a Southron sorcerer in order to discharge a sword."

I grunted. "We don't seem to be doing much other than sitting here discussing ice."

"It *is* odd," she growled. "An ice-cave in the South?"

"So maybe it's a holdover from when there was no Southron desert, or Northern snowfields . . . maybe the world they made was nothing but a world, with no divisions at all." I shifted, rose carefully, rubbed at a stiffened neck. "Are we going on?"

Del got up, bent, kept going.

I stopped moving, because I had to. Held my posture, all bent over, with the wrapped sheath in one hand. Felt the uneven thumping in my chest.

I couldn't *breathe*.

"Bascha—"

Del was murmuring up ahead. She didn't know I'd stopped.

I shut my eyes. Gritted teeth. Scrubbed sweat off my face, and banged an elbow into rock. Swore beneath my breath, then set a hand against broken stone and tried to retain my senses.

He knew. Chosa *knew*.

I was light-headed. Dots filled my eyes, already straining to see. If I could see, and breathe—

"Tiger?" It echoed oddly from somewhere ahead. She'd realized I wasn't behind her. I heard scraping, a hissed invective; she came back to my side, rubbing the top of her head. "What's wrong?"

In choppy gasps, I expelled it. "He's here. Somewhere. Shaka."

She stopped rubbing her head, looking more alertly into my eyes. "Which way?"

"There's only—one way to go—unless we head out again—" I swallowed heavily. "Hard—to breathe—in here."

Frowning, she moved closer. "Can you go on?"

"Have to," I muttered.

She didn't say anything. Then put a hand on my arm. "I swear, I won't leave you again. What I did in the Punja was wrong. I left for the oasis because I thought it would make you follow—and I knew it wasn't far. Tiger—" Her face was strained. "I want you purged of Chosa, so you can be you again. But I don't want to hurt you. If this is too hard—"

"No." I sucked in a breath. "I've done harder things. It's just—everything. This place—Chosa . . . and Shaka. All the weight pressing down . . ." I scrubbed sweat from my face. "If I could *breathe* again . . ."

She touched my chest. "Slow down," she said softly. "We need be in no hurry."

Breathlessly, I nodded. Then motioned her to go on. "I'll be right behind."

Light glowed dimly. It glittered off bits of ice and leached shadows from crevices.

"Ahead," Del said.

I clutched the sheathed *jivatma*, dripping sweat as I moved. I wondered absently if the droplets would freeze to ice. My feet were so cold they ached, but I didn't say anything. Del was barefoot, too.

She stopped. White samite glowed. She turned her face back to shadow; to me. "It's a crack in the rock," she said. "Wide enough for a body . . . it runs up through the roof. There's light, and fresh air. Do you want to go through first?"

"You don't understand," I said thickly. "I'm not afraid, bascha—that passed some time ago. This is—different. This is—*power.*"

She tensed. "Power?"

"Don't you feel it?"

"I feel . . . odd."

I nodded. "Power."

"Are you sick?"

"You mean—like usual?" I shrugged. "I'm so cold I can't tell."

She smiled. "Poor Tiger. At least I have Umir's burnous. I could share—"

I grunted. "Keep it. I'm not much for feathers and beads, no matter how much they cost."

"Do you want to go first?"

"Fine." I squeezed past her, moved into the narrow crack, stepped out into daylight.

And into Shaka Obre.

"*Hoo*lies—" I fell to my knees. Retched. Dropped harness and sheath and sword. "Oh, gods—*Del*—"

She was through. She took a step, then froze. Murmured something in awed uplander.

"—get out—" I gasped. "—got to—get *out*—"

Shaka Obre was everywhere.

Pressure flattened me. I tried to get up again, but my scrabbling earned me nothing. I lay sprawled belly-down with my cheek pressed into pale, gritty sand, while blazing ice crystals blinded me. Because I couldn't shut my eyes.

My guts knotted. Squeezed. My belly turned inside out.

"—*bascha*—"

Del didn't move.

It was nearly bright as day. It *was* day, inside; the place we had come into was open to the sky. But I couldn't look up to see it, because I couldn't move.

Fingers twitched. Hands spasmed. Toes dug fruitlessly.

"It's Shaka," Del breathed.

I knew that already.

"Shaka's *everywhere*."

I knew that, too.

"I can't see him, but he's here. I can feel all the power—" She sucked in an audible breath. "Is this what it's like to taste the magic?"

How in hoolies did *I* know? I was too busy trying to breathe to think about how things tasted.

Del knelt down next to me. "It's Chosa, isn't it?"

"Shaka," I gasped hoarsely. "He knows . . . he knows about Chosa—"

A hand was on my back. "Can you get up?"

"I'm too tired to try."

"Here." The hand closed on my shoulder, pressing against rigid flesh. "I'll help—"

It did help. I heaved myself up, managed to sit, then collapsed against the wall. The rock was very cold, but I was too limp to move. I drew up both knees and pressed an arm across my abdomen. My whole body wanted to cramp.

"We brought him here," I rasped. "Chosa—we brought him *here*."

"We had to," she said.

I rolled my skull against sharp rock. "We made a mistake. They'll tear me to bits, both of them . . . hoolies, it's a mistake . . ."

"Tiger." She touched a knee. "It had to be done. You couldn't spend the rest of your life fighting a sword. One day, you would have failed, and Chosa would have had you."

"He has me now. He has me now, and Shaka has *him*—" I grimaced. "Don't you see? One of them has to lose—and I'm caught in the middle."

The hand tightened. "I can't believe Shaka would put you at risk. He caused Jamail to speak."

"Then why not restore *me?*" I scraped myself off rock and sat fully upright, tipping my head back to stare up through the massive mountain chimney to the blue sky overhead. "Restore me, Shaka! So I can fight Chosa, too!"

The echo died away. Mutely, I looked at Del.

She rose. Went to the very center of the chimney. Tipped her head back and stared up, squinting against the glare. Sunlight bathed samite. She was white in the light of the day.

Her gaze came down. Frowning, she looked around. Assessed the wide-bottomed chimney. Then bent and scooped up pale sand, testing it in her hand before she let it fall back to the floor. "Punja sand," she said. "Fine, and full of crystals . . ." She looked around again. "This is a circle."

I grunted. "No. Just a natural chimney. See?" I pointed. "Just a part of the mountain."

"A circle," she said again, and paced to the far wall. "Six and one half," she murmured.

"See? It's not accurate. A proper one is fifteen." Some of the pressure and discomfort had passed. I heaved myself up, cursing, staggered to my fallen harness, but didn't pick it up. I was too busy watching Del.

She rounded the chimney, testing cracks and crannies with deft, questing fingers. "A proper *Southron* one is fifteen; my legs are longer than that."

I stared at her. Braced legs and tipped my head back again,

looking up. Dizzy, I squinted. The chimney *looked* natural, but maybe it wasn't. Magic had put Shaka here. Magic, then, had made it.

It was, as Del said, a little more than fifteen paces in diameter, which made it a bit larger than a true circle. The bottom portion of the chimney was widest, curving smoothly into roundness. It was smokerock dark, but ice lined crevices and coated knobby protrusions, glittering in the light. The rounded chimney was striated by faceted ribs of stone spiraling toward the sky. It was hardly symmetrical, and it lacked a certain preciseness, being hacked out of sharp-angled rock. But the floor was properly sandy, and the circumference was round *enough*. One need only take up a sword and draw a formal circle.

Which I couldn't do anymore.

She dug into a crevice, judging its depth and width. Then withdrew her fingers. She stood very still, as if lost in thought.

"What are you doing?"

"I thought so," Del breathed, ignoring me altogether. "If he could be *lured* out . . ."

I looked at her more sharply. "Del—"

She shook her head. Lips were compressed. She squeezed eyelids together for a brief, tension-filled moment, then opened them again. The line of her jaw was grim. "How are you feeling?"

I countered dubiously. "How are *you* feeling?"

She looked through me, not at me. Murmured something beneath her breath in an uplander dialect I didn't know. She bit into her bottom lip, turned it white a moment, then let it go again. The blood flowed back.

"Done," she said softly.

"Bascha . . ." But I let it go. She wasn't listening. "Yes, I'm feeling better. Why?"

Del unsheathed her sword and tossed the harness and sheath against the wall. With deft preciseness, she set the blade tip into the sand and began to draw a circle. She spoke quietly to herself, never pausing an instant. When she joined the ends at the far side, across from the narrow crack, she lifted her *jivatma*.

"What are you doing?" I asked, for about the thousandth time.

Del stood very still. The light from above bathed her, setting hair and samite to glowing. Slowly the sword came up until it was in a familiar position: hilt at left hip, double-gripped; left elbow out for balance and dexterity; rune-scribed blade a diagonal slash lined up with her right shoulder, tipped outward slightly in precise, eloquent challenge.

"Take up your sword," she said.

I realized I stood very nearly in the middle of the circle Del had drawn. "Are you *sandsick?*"

"Take it up," she said.

I nearly laughed. "You yourself said we should never dance against one another with these swords. You always swore it was dangerous."

"It is." She didn't blink. "Take up your sword, Tiger. This is a true dance."

It was curt. "I can't."

"Yes, you can."

"*Elaii-ali-ma.* I broke all my oaths, bascha—I renounced my personal honor." Abruptly I was angry, because it hurt so much. "I thought it was plain enough. To *you* most of all."

"This dance has nothing whatsoever to do with any of that. Here, in this place, *elaii-ali-ma* is as nothing. This dance is the beginning. This dance is the ending."

Hairs stirred on the nape of my neck. "I don't like the sound of that."

Her tone was firm and sure. "Take up your sword, Sandtiger. We will settle it once and for all."

"You're sandsick," I whispered.

A wind hissed through the crack from the passageway beyond. It snatched tumbled fair hair and blew it back, baring the flawless face. Then rippled and caught the burnous, gusting beneath poised elbows. Heavy folds billowed, curled back; samite slapped ribbed walls. The full panoply of intricate sunset lining blazed forth within the chimney: all glass and brass and gold, and myriad brilliant feathers. Umir's costly burnous set the bastard circle alight, as well as the woman who wore it.

Ice glittered behind her, catching fire from sun and sword. "Dance with me, Chosa Dei. I stand proxy for your brother."

Chapter 45

I scooped up the harness and sword. Then turned and stalked out of the circle—

Tried to stalk out of the circle. Something blasted me back at the boundary, flinging me back inside. I sprawled rather inelegantly, dumped flat on my back in the sand.

When the dust had settled and I could see again, let alone breathe, I sat up. Spat grit. Scowled at the crooked slot I had intended to enter on my way back out of the chimney, but obviously wasn't meant to.

"You can't," Del said. "We came through the wards when we entered, but clearly we can't go out again. At least—*you* can't."

I twisted my head to glare at her. "Chosa didn't set wards around a *circle*."

"No. I did that. Or rather, Shaka did." She shrugged. "Did you expect him to give Chosa leave to simply walk out again, while Shaka remains behind?"

"I didn't expect anything. Except maybe a little more *re*spect. And besides, how do we really know Shaka Obre's *here*, and that there are wards at all? I don't see anything."

"Not all power is visible. Weren't you the one telling me Shaka knew you were here, and that you knew *he* was here?"

Annoyed, I brushed sand off my chin. "I just don't see how you managed to ward the circle."

"I invoked Boreal. I think Shaka Obre is willing to use whatever avatar he can, since he obviously lacks a body. Just as Chosa does, which is why he wants you."

I grunted. "I'll reserve an opinion."

Del didn't answer. She just lowered her sword, stabbed it down into sand to sheathe it briefly, then stripped out of the burnous. She dropped it onto her harness into folds of Southron sunset, then pulled the sword out of the sand and stepped across the line.

Now two of us were bound. Me by wards and sword; Del by honor and oaths.

Barefoot, both of us, as was proper. I wore dhoti and necklet, Del wore Northern tunic. And each of us had a sword.

I stood up. Pulled Samiel free of sheath and tossed the harness aside. Turned to face Delilah. "The last time we did this, both of us nearly died."

Del smiled a little. "We were young and foolish then."

"*I'd* like to get older and wiser. But you may not give me a chance."

Del's voice was soft. "No more delays, Tiger. We came to discharge your *jivatma*. Let us purify the blade, so it may be free of taint."

"And me," I muttered.

"And you," she agreed.

I took two steps away, turned. "Then let's get it done!" I snapped, and brought Samiel into position without benefit of preparation.

It was an ugly beginning, lacking elegance or power. We each of us tested the other, tapping blades, then disengaging; sliding steel across steel, then snatching respective blades away before the intimacy increased. It was slow, disjointed, amateurish; nothing of what we knew, save both of us were afraid.

We dug divots in the sand, kicking showerlets of glittering crystal. Blades clashed, fell away; tapped again for a brief moment before wrists turned them aside. Then Del, muttering something, began to sing a song.

I stiffened. "Wait—"

But Del didn't.

Hoolies, if she keys her sword . . . oh, bascha—don't do that. Because then the dance will be real . . . and I don't *want* it to be— I don't want to relive Staal-Ysta—

Del sang very softly. Silver blade took on the faint glow of palest salmon-silver.

Steel chimed, then screeched apart. I felt her pattern tighten; the increased power in the turn of wrists. Saw the tracery left in the air; an afterglow of *jivatma* forged and blessed in Northern rituals as binding as those I knew: the oaths of Alimat.

"Dance," Del hissed. "Come on, Chosa—*dance*—"

"Tiger," I said. "Tiger."

"Dance, Chosa. Or can't you?"

I snapped my blade against hers, felt the power in her counter, jerked mine away again. "Do you *want* to summon him?"

A faint trace of sweat sheened her face. "Come out and dance, Chosa. Or have you no power to do it? No skill to guide the sword? No grace to create the patterns?"

"He's not a sword-dancer, he's a *sorcerer*—"

"Sorcerers can dance. Chosa Dei remakes. Can't he remake himself in your image? Can't he use your body as his? Can't he dance against a *woman?*"

"Hoolies, bashcha—" I hop-skipped, ducked a pattern, came up and caught blade with blade. Steel screamed. I broke her pattern easily, practically throwing her sword back at her from the force of my riposte. "What are you trying to do?"

"Dance," she said. "Just—dance. But I don't think Chosa can."

And Del began to sing again, coloring her blade.

Vision blurred. Overlaid with my own present memory was one of a past time. Of a sorcerer blasting sorcerer with power of such magnitude it could remake mountains.

Inside me, Chosa laughed.

"Don't *do* this!" I shouted.

Delilah's song increased. And Chosa, in me, heard it.

"Don't, bascha—" I choked, recognizing familiar cramps. Sweat ran down my chest to dampen the top of the dhoti. "Don't do this to me—don't make me *do* this—"

Her pattern grew intricate, tying up my own, then sliding out of the knot. I trapped her, twisted, banged the blades apart.

They met again almost at once, clanging within the chimney. If this was what she wanted—

Inside me, Chosa took notice.

Boreal glowed salmon-silver. With every knot and swoop, Del smeared color in the air. A glowing afterimage of runes and blade and power.

I was irritated. I hadn't wanted this dance. Hadn't wanted this confrontation. I had not even thought about it, because each time I began to I recalled the dance on Staal-Ysta, when Del and I had been matched through trickery and deceit. We each of us had danced then using every bit of skill, because so much—*too much*— was at stake. In the end, the dance had won, because so many years of training can thwart even the strongest of wills. You just *dance,* because you have to. Because the body won't let you stop, and pride won't let you give up.

We danced, Delilah and I. Teased one another with steel, flicking tips at noses and throats to promise we could do better, knowing we didn't dare. This was not a dance to the death, not as it had been for Abbu and me, but a dance to the *ending,* when Chosa would be defeated and the sword would be purified.

We sweated. Cursed. Danced. Taunted one another. Bit lips and spat blood. Dug deeper divots in crystalline sand, bracing muscled thighs and hips to translate power into arms. I exerted physical strength into the finesse of her patterns, beating her back with sheer power, until she darted in with quickness and grace and teased me into openings she was more than prepared to exploit.

Del slammed blade into blade, scraping edge against Northern runes. In the chimney, the noise was deafening, echoes increased fourfold.

I caught the blade with my own, twisting, and wrenched the steel apart, hissing invective at her for bringing us to this pass. I had long ago given up wondering, even a little, which of us was better. It simply didn't matter. Of course we *said* it did, merely to tease one another, but I knew in my heart of hearts we neither of us knew.

Del came at me, singing. Northern steel flashed in chimneyed sunlight, throwing slashes against ribbed walls. Clustered crystals of sand and ice glittered in cracks and crannies. The sun gazed down upon us, benificent arbiter.

Steelsong filled the chimney, spiraling upward along smoke-rock ribs. We hammered at one another, knowing each blow would be caught, and turned, and blunted. Because neither of us wanted to die. We simply wanted an ending: Del, to discharge the blade *and* me; me, to be free of the blackness of spirit that had nothing to do with Chosa, and everything to do with dishonor.

Elaii-ali-ma is what you make it, binding those who wish to be bound. And I had bound myself by completing the training and rit-uals, by accepting the oaths of blood before the legendary shodo of Alimat, knowing myself worthy in spite of my heritage. I had made something of myself, banishing the chula in the circle, giving birth to the Sandtiger.

And I had killed him also, by stepping out of Sabra's circle and shattering all my oaths.

Elaii-ali-ma. Making this the final circle.

"Dance," Del hissed, cleaving air, then stopping short to twist, and turn, and snap.

Such tiny, intricate patterns, requiring incredible skill as well as powerful, flexible wrists. I broke the patterns as best I could, slicing through salmon runeglow, then saw the blackened shimmer corr-uscate up my blade.

"No!" I jerked it aside, felt Del's blade slide by, licking through broken pattern to sting me across the forearm. Blood welled, dribbled.

Chosa was *awake*.

"Dance!" Del shouted, using my inattention to nick my arm again.

I stumbled back, then held my ground, beating away her hun-gry blade. Saw the blackness rising higher, splashing onto quillons, licking at fingers and grip.

I staggered. Nearly went down. My guts twisted inside out.

"Yes!" Del shouted. "Come out and dance, Chosa!"

The sorcerer, thus invited, surged out of his hidden corner. Ate his way through bones even as I cried out.

"Come out and dance," she hissed.

"Del—no—"

"It's Shaka Obre, Chosa. Do you remember him?"

I shook. Power ran down my arms to the blade. In my hands the sword was black; the sword was *entirely* black.

Without warning, I was empty.

I fell to one knee, struggled up. Blade met blade, held. Del cried out in extremity.

"Let go!" I cried hoarsely.

Boreal was abruptly extinguished, swallowed by Chosa's blackness.

"No!" I shouted. "Bascha—*let go!* Drop your sword! Don't let Chosa near it!"

Del didn't let go. Del didn't drop it.

Chosa Dei, who'd made it clear from the start he wanted sword *and* woman, swarmed up the steel toward flesh.

"*Yes!*" Del cried.

"Bascha—*let go*—"

She broke the final pattern, letting my blade slip through to slice across one wrist, and staggered to the edge of the circle. Blood ran from the wound, dripping onto crystalline sand. Where it dripped, smoke rose.

"Expunge—" she murmured dazedly.

"Drop it!" I shouted.

Blood fell onto the line she'd drawn in the sand. Black Boreal trembled in Del's hand. "It's me, Shaka—" she whispered.

The line, and smoke, wisped away. Del staggered through, thrust Boreal into the ice-crusted crevice she had inspected so carefully . . . jammed the blade into the slot . . . jerked the hilt to the left so violently the steel snapped in two.

I dropped Samiel even as Del dropped Boreal. "Bascha—*no*—"

Chosa was free of the sword. Chosa was free of me. Chosa was free of everything except Shaka Obre.

Chapter 46

Sand began to fly. It was scooped up from the floor, thrown piecemeal into the circle, then hurled against ribbed walls. Through slotted crack came a howling wind, buffeting flesh and rock. It wailed like a Northern banshee-storm, whistling across ice-rimed smokerock corrugated by Chosa's magic.

I spat, thrust up a shielding hand, fell to my knees as the blast howled into the circle. The dhoti was little protection; nearly every inch of me, bared, was painfully vulnerable to howling wind and stinging sand.

"Del!" She made no answer. For the sand, I couldn't see her. "Bascha—where are you?"

But the howling swallowed my words. I heard them myself, barely, only because I knew what they were.

My eyes were crusted shut. I hunched there in the circle, my back to the slotted crack, and felt ice and Punja crystals worrying at my spine.

In my mind's eye I saw where Del had been as she wedged Boreal into the crevice and snapped the blade in two. Slowly, meticulously, I made my way across the circle, then touched a taut-muscled leg.

"Del!"

"Tiger?" Hands caught me, hung on. "Tiger—I can't see!"

"Neither can I. Come on—*hang* on . . . we need to find Umir's burnous . . . ah, *here!*"

I dragged the priceless garment to us both, then huddled close to Del as I dragged it over shoulders and heads. It muffled the shrill keening and allowed us to open our eyes, peering out through a hooded opening.

"It's spinning," Del shouted over the noise. "The sand—it's *spinning!*"

"Dust demon," I said. "Whirlwind. It happens sometimes near the Punja . . . don't know why, but it does. They blow themselves out eventually, but *this* one—" I shook my head. "I don't think this is natural, and it's awfully big."

The shrill keening increased. Eerie sparkling lights crackled and snapped as spinning sand was sucked up chimney walls in a maelstrom of pressure, whistling along the ribs. Aching ears popped; I clapped both hands over them. Blood broke from my nose.

"It's them—" Del said. "It's Shaka Obre and Chosa Dei—"

"A minor argument, maybe?" I hunched in the burnous. "I don't care who it is—I just wish they'd stop." I blotted my nose in irritation. Pulled the burnous more tightly around one shoulder as the wind snatched at fabric, snapping it furiously.

"Look."

"I can't *see* anything, bascha!"

"Look," she repeated.

I looked, squinting and cursing. Saw sand, still flying; crystals still yanked upward through ribs and pockets and whorls, sucked out through the chimney hole glowing sunbright and fair far over our heads.

Something else was flying. Something orange, and red, and yellow, and all the colors in between. "What?" And then I began to laugh. Reached out and caught a feather. "Umir's burnous is shedding!"

Del's head came out of folds. "Is it? It *is!* Oh, Tiger, no—"

I just kept laughing.

"Tiger, all the workmanship—work*woman*ship, more like!" A yellow feather caught in Del's tangled hair. "All the care and effort . . ."

"Not as much care and effort as went into your *jivatma*." I stuck my head out farther. "The wind is dying down."

It was. The keening howl faded. The dust demon blew itself out. The floor was now of rock, ice-free, dark-brown smokerock, lacking even a grain of sand. The only things left in the chimney were Del and me and feathers.

And two Northern *jivatmas,* one of which was broken.

I pulled Del up from the floor, shrugging out of the molting burnous. "About Boreal—" I began.

Del clapped a hand over my mouth. "Listen!"

I listened. Peeled fingers away. "It's quiet."

"*Too* quiet."

"After all that howling, *anything* would seem too quiet."

"*Listen!*" she hissed.

A piece of rib cracked off and fell next to us, shattering on the floor. Followed by another.

"Out!" I blurted, shoving her toward the slot. "Hoolies, get *out* of here!" The ribbing of the chimney crumbled.

Del ran, ducked, twisted, sliding through the narrow slot. I started to follow, paused; looked back at my *jivatma*.

"Tiger!" She had a hand and tugged hard, scraping my right shoulder into an outcropping.

"Samiel—"

The chimney fell into itself, collapsing into bits and pieces of smokerock large enough to squash a horse.

"Tiger—come *on*!"

"Wait," I mumbled tonelessly, staring back into the chamber even as it collapsed. "Wait—I *saw* this—"

"Tiger! Don't waste your only chance!" She tugged again at my arm.

"But I *saw* this . . . it's part of the threefold future—"

"You also saw us die, or you, or me. Come *on*—"

The vision snapped. "All right. I'm coming, Del—let *go*—"

Del let go. Hunching, twisting, ducking, we scrambled through the passageway as the mountain around us remade itself. The chimney was gone, I knew, filled up with tumbled rubble. If we weren't quick about it, the rest of the place might fall down.

I banged elbows, knees; stubbed toes; smacked my head once or twice. But Del did much the same, so I didn't complain about it. We scrambled through the smokerock bowels and at last reached the chamber; burst out of the passageway into dim light; out of that into the day.

We did not, in our haste, take time to judge the footing. We simply ran, taking the shock into knees and ankles, steadying balance with stiffened arms and splayed hands, landing on rumps if we overbalanced. Cursing, spitting grit, sobbing for breath, we slid-scrambled down the mountainside, scraping rock and rubble and dirt.

The tumbling slide ended eventually, spilling us out onto the flat where we had left the horses. We landed, sucked air, twisted onto bellies, staring up at the ruined mountain.

Dust still hung in the air. A few feathers drifted down: red and yellow and orange.

We waited, holding breath. Dust—and feathers—settled. The day was bright, and quiet.

I flopped facedown in the dirt, sucking in great gulps of air, then heaving them out again. It dusted my face with grit, but I didn't care. I was alive to notice; there's something to be said for dirt.

Del patted my shoulder limply, then stretched out on her back. A lock of littered hair fell across my elbow. "Done," she croaked. "The *jivatma* is free of taint."

For a moment, too busy breathing, I didn't bother to answer. When I did, it was half-laugh, half-gasp. "—course, we can't *get* it, now—"

"But it's purified. It's clean." Del breathed noisily a moment. "And *you're* clean, too."

"Actually, I'm pretty filthy."

She slapped a shoulder weakly. "Clean of Chosa Dei."

I felt a little better. Managed to turn over; even to sit up, hooking elbows over knees. Peered out at the Southron day, picking grit off a bloodied lip. Then glanced sidelong at Del, still sprawled on her back, and laughed huskily.

"What?"

"You. There are feathers stuck to you." I picked one off, displayed it. "A filthy, sweaty sandhen all ready for the plucking."

Del sat up. "Where?"

"In your hair, mostly. Here." I unstuck another.

Muttering, she began to inspect her hair, yanking feathers out of tangles.

I twisted and looked back at the mountain, twitched prickling shoulders. "Shaka Obre and Chosa Dei . . ." Another prickle ran down my spine. "What do you think happened?"

"I think they blew themselves out, as you said dust demons do." Del glanced up, squinting against the brightness. "You are the one who is sensitive to magic. Tell me: are they there?"

I stared up at the hollow mountain. Waited for hair to rise, for belly to grow queasy. Nothing at all happened. I was dusty, tired, and sore, but I felt perfectly fine. "I don't think so."

"Where might they have gone?"

I shrugged. "Wherever magic goes when it has no home."

Del looked sharply at me. "Magic without a home . . ."

It sounded as odd to me, but it made a strange sort of sense. Then I frowned. Pointed. "Look way off there in the distance, along the horizon."

Del looked. "Lightning."

"It's not the right time of year. In the summer, every night, heat lightning lights up the sky, but that's not what that is."

She studied it more closely. "Do you think—?"

I shrugged. "I don't know. But they were both reduced to *essences* . . . maybe nothing more than the memory of power. And that's the end result: a crackle in the air and a flash of light now and then."

Del shivered. "Why did Chosa have a body in Dragon Mountain? Shaka didn't here."

"I don't know. But seeing how Chosa worked, luring villagers to the mountain to serve his own purposes, I imagine he *stole* a body. Shaka wouldn't do that."

Del looked at me. "Was this part of the threefold future?"

I smiled crookedly. "One of the futures I saw, all mixed up with the others. But it's hard to see it clearly when you're right in the middle of it . . . and then when Chosa's memories kept interfering with mine—" I shrugged. "I never knew which was which, or whose was whose. But from the looks of things, I'd predict our future is rather quiet." I reached out and caught a wrist as she dug idly in dirt. "Now. Why did you break Boreal?"

Del's brows knotted. "It was the only chance. And only that: a chance. I thought if Chosa were loosed behind the wards, even his own wards, Shaka might destroy him, or at least overpower him. But I knew as long as Chosa was in you, needing you so much, you wouldn't be able to break Samiel. So—that left Boreal." She shrugged defensively. "I wanted to lure him out, tease him into *my* sword during the dance . . . and then break her."

"But—your *jivatma*—"

Del dug a deeper hole. "I don't need her anymore. My song is finished. Now I start a new one."

"Bascha—"

"Leave it," she said softly.

I nodded, respecting her wishes. Then heaved myself to my feet, muttered as knees cracked, limped my way to the stud.

"So, old son, couldn't leave me yet." I patted a sweat-crusted shoulder. "Even in the midst of that, you waited here for me."

The stud shook his head and snorted, showering me with dampness.

"Thank you," I said gravely. "What happened to the mare?"

The stud didn't tell me, but I had a good idea. She'd probably broken her rein and headed down the mountain when the chimney collapsed, or when the howling began. We'd find her down below, waiting for a person. Horses are like that.

I patted the shoulder again. "We've sure been through some times. . . ." I rubbed a scraped shoulder. "Most, I'd like to forget."

"Tiger?" Del. "We have company."

I spun and looked up at her. "Where?"

She pointed. "There."

I moved around the stud, one arm across his rump, wishing I had a sword; *any* sword—then saw I wouldn't need one.

"Mehmet!" I blurted. "What are *you* doing here?"

Mehmet grinned. He wore dusty saffron burnous and equally

dusty white turban. "Sandtiger," he said. "May the sun shine on your head."

I squinted very hard. "Am I sandsick? Or dead?"

"Neither. I am I, and here."

Frowning, I nodded. "That's something, I guess. But—*why* are you here?"

"The old hustapha is dead."

Which baffled me even more. "I—uh—I'm sorry. I mean—" I gestured helplessness. "He was a nice old man . . . I'm sorry."

"He was old, and his time was done." Mehmet climbed up the slope that lipped over onto the flat. "I have left the aketni below."

"You brought *them* here, too?"

"The hustapha said I must. It's here it all begins."

"What begins?"

He grinned. "You are to give me a message."

I touched my breastbone. *"Me?"*

Mehmet nodded. "The hustapha said: the jhihadi."

"But—" I stopped. Glanced upslope at Del, who continued picking feathers as if there was nothing else as important. Frowning, I looked back at Mehmet. "I have no message for you."

He was perfectly serene. "The hustapha cast the sand. He saw it would be this way. He sent us here to find you, so you could give us the message."

"I don't *have* a message—ah, hoolies, horse—do you have to do that here?"

The stud spread back legs and began to water the dirt. I moved quickly, avoiding the deluge; found myself stepping this way and that as he splattered. We stood on the lip of the slope—Mehmet, the stud, and I—and water runs downhill . . . so do other things.

"How much do you have?" I asked crossly, as the stud continued to flow.

"The message," Mehmet mentioned.

"I told you. I don't have any—" I stared at the urine as it ran down the slope. I watched the flow split, diminish; watched it channeled by dip and pocket; saw it diverted by bits of smokerock too big to dislodge on its own.

Patterns in the dirt. Channels and runnels and funnels. Lines filled, and overflowing; diverted in other directions.

"Water," I said blankly.

Mehmet waited politely.

"Water," I repeated. Then looked around intently, found the proper twig, bent down to draw in the dirt.

"Tiger." Del, from upslope. "What *are* you doing?"

I heard her come down, scraping dirt and pebbles as she moved. But I didn't give her an answer, too busy with the task. Consumed by the pattern.

She stopped next to me. Didn't say a word.

Eventually I looked up. Saw two pairs of eyes staring: one pair blue, one black.

I laughed up at them both. "Don't you understand?"

In unison: *"No."*

"Because you're both blind. We've *all* been blind." I stood up, tossing the twig aside. "Look at that. *Look* at that. What do you see?"

"Piss in dirt," Del said.

"I said you were blind. What else?"

"Lines."

"And piss *in* the lines. Don't you see?" I stared at them both intently. "All you have to do is put *water* in the lines. Only make the lines big. Make the lines deep. Put pullies at the cisterns. Dig channels in the dirt. There's water in the North—just bring it down from *there!*"

Del was astonished. "Bring water from the North?"

"Bit by bit. Divert the rivers, the streams . . . build patterns to bring it *here*." I grinned, shrugging scraped shoulders. "And turn the sand to grass."

Mehmet fell to his knees. He spat into his hand, slapped it flat against the ground, then striped a line across his brow. "Jhihadi," he croaked.

I shrugged. "It's all a matter of viewpoint."

Del looked at me. Then she looked at the stud. Then picked another feather from her hair—this one was red—and blew it into the air. "I think you're sandsick," she said.

"Jhihadi," Mehmet repeated.

I grinned hugely at Del. "That wasn't so hard, after all."

She arched a skeptical brow. "If you are so wise, O jhihadi, tell us what we should do *now?*"

My grin died away. "We'll have to think of something."

Mehmet scrambled up. "Come with us!" he cried. "Come with the aketni. If we are to go North, to bring the water down—"

I put up a silencing hand. "Wait. First of all, it won't be that easy. You can't do it by yourselves. You'll need people. *Lots* of people. You'll need to dig more cisterns, find more water . . . build ditches to channel the water . . . but you'll mostly need to convince the tribes, tanzeers, and everyone else that this is the way to do it."

Mehmet nodded. "It begins with a single person. It has begun with the jhihadi. There will be more who believe."

Del was dubious. "It would take a very long time."

"We have time. And now we have a future." Mehmet touched his heart. "May the sun shine on your head."

"*Second,*" I said, "we can't come with you. Del and I have a little—problem. We have to leave the South."

"Leave?" Del echoed.

I kept talking to Mehmet. "So we can't go with you."

Del wasn't finished. "Where are we going, then? We can't go to the North. Where are we supposed to go?"

I kept talking to Mehmet. "So you'll just have to take your aketni and do the best you can. Talk to some people. Go to other tribes. Tell them what I told you." I paused. "What the *jhihadi* said."

"Tiger—" Rather more insistently, "—where in hoolies do we go?"

I clapped Mehmet on the arm. "He wasn't such a bad old man. I'm glad I got to know him." I turned to the stud, untied him. "Give greeting to the aketni."

"*Tig*er!"

I climbed aboard the stud. "Are you coming? Have a stirrup."

Del stared up at me from the ground, hands on hips. "When you tell me where we're going."

"Right now, over-mountain. South to the ocean-sea. There's a city called Haziz." I reached down to catch a hand. "Come on up, bascha. We're burning daylight, here."

Chapter 47

I n my line of work, I've seen all kinds of women. Some beautiful. Some ugly. Some just plain in between. But when *she* walked into the hot, dusty cantina and slipped the hood of her white burnous, I knew nothing I'd ever seen could touch her.

Everyone else in the common room stopped talking. Stopped moving. They all just stared.

The vision in the white burnous looked across the room directly at me with eyes as blue as Northern lakes. *This* time, I knew what a Northern lake was.

I stretched legs. Grinned. Sighed in appreciation as she crossed the cantina to my table. "I sold the mare," she said. "I have booked passage on a ship. And laid in provisions." She looked at the plump botas piled on the table. "I will let you bring the aqivi."

"I'd planned on it." I stood up, hooked thongs over shoulders, motioned for her to precede me out of the cantina. "Where are we going?"

"To the ship."

"No—I mean, where are we *sailing?*"

"Oh." Del made her way through the throng of fisherfolk. "You said you didn't care."

"I don't *care* . . . I was just curious."

"The only ship sailing tomorrow is one bound for a place called Skandi."

"Where?"

"Skandi."

"Never heard of it."

"Neither have I."

I bumped shoulders with a man, apologized, moved around a crippled woman. "Skandi?"

"Yes."

"The *word* sounds familiar." I took two long steps, caught up and fell in next to her. "Isn't that what the man called me in Julah? The one you said looked like me?"

"He said Skan*dic*. He asked if you were Skandic." Del stopped and looked at me. "We thought he meant a person . . . do you suppose he meant a *place?* That he thought you were from his homeland?"

I stared back at her a long moment, examining possibilities. There were too many to consider, so I gave up. Shrugged. "Oh, well. I guess we'll find out, if it's where we're going anyway." I peered over her shoulder to the docks and the mass of sail. "Is that our ship?"

She looked. "No. The one next to it."

I scowled, chewing a lip. I wasn't sure about any of this.

"Come on," she said. "It will be all right."

At sundown, we stood side by side on the dock, contemplating our future as it floated in black water. Del's voice was muted. "Are we doing the right thing?"

I shrugged. "I don't know. Seems like we don't have much choice."

She sighed. "I suppose not."

I summoned false gaiety. "Besides, think of all the places we'll see. People we'll meet. Adventures we'll have."

She looked sidelong at me. "It's the last one *you're* interested in."

I put a hand on my heart. "That hurts my feelings," I told her. "You just *assume* things about me without giving me the benefit of doubt."

Del snickered. "I know better."

Having gotten that far out of nerves, we fell into uneasy silence. The ship was tied up at the dock, creaking and rocking and rubbing. A tongue of wood connected it to the dock, waiting for dawn; for Del and me to climb it to the ship.

I scratched idly at my cheek, rubbing a blackened thumbnail against claw marks. "Look at it this way—it'll be a chance to start over."

"You won't like it," she declared.

I arched an imperious brow. "How do *you* know?"

"I know. You've been 'the Sandtiger' for too long—how will you deal with anonymity?"

"Ano-what?"

Del smiled. "No one knowing who you are."

"Oh, hoolies, who cares about that? I've been a panjandrum and a jhihadi. Neither one got me much, except to make me a target." And now a borjuni, but I didn't say that.

Del looked into my face, then gripped my elbow a moment. "I'm sorry, Tiger. I wish it might have been different."

I shrugged dismissively. "The aqivi's been spilled . . . and anyway, it was my choice. No one stuck a knife in my back and *told* me to break the circle. I did it on my own. And no one can deny it didn't do the trick."

She looked away. "No."

"And besides—" I broke it off.

She waited. Then, gently, "What?"

"This isn't—*home*. Not anymore. It's not the same, the South . . ." Something occurred. "Or maybe it *is*, and I can't live with it anymore. I just know that when we came down from the North, before Iskandar, I felt good. I was home. And then Iskandar happened, and the old hustapha and his sandcasting, and then Abbu and Sabra and everything else. . . ." I sighed. "I'm no messiah. I just had an *idea*. Maybe it'll work, and maybe it won't, this channeling of the water—but that's all it is. An idea. Anyone could have had it. It just happened to be me." I shrugged. "And now it's over. The jhihadi isn't anything special, or holy . . . just a beat-up, battered sword-dancer who no longer can enter a true circle—" I cut it off abruptly, staring at the creaking ship for a long, intense moment. Until the topic was bearable. "Besides, you lost more," I told her finally. "You lost Jamail again."

Her jaw tautened. "Yes."

"And also a *jivatma.*"

She ducked it. "So did you."

I shook my head. "You know that sword never meant as much to me as yours did to you. You *know* that, bascha."

She gazed blindly at the ship. Didn't say a word. Just turned and walked away.

I let her go without protest, because sometimes it's for the best.

In the darkness, in the silence, I heard the indrawn breath. It caught itself, soft and fleeting: a self-stifled, private moment. She'd turned as I lay sleeping, so we touched at rumps and shoulders.

I twisted, turned over. Snaked an arm beneath her loose one and scooped her against my chest, hugging powerfully.

"It's stupid," she whispered.

"No."

"It's only a *sword.*"

"That's not what you're crying about."

She gulped a choked laugh. "*What,* then? I sang my song for Jamail; that part is done. That part I understand. I've given him his passing." She swallowed noisily. "Why do I cry for the sword?"

"I told you: you aren't. Not for Boreal. You're crying for *Delilah* . . . for the loss of what you knew." I shifted a trifle closer, stroking a lock of hair from her face. "All your oaths are complete. Your vows are executed. Your songs have all been sung."

"I don't understand."

"You're crying for Delilah, because you don't know who she is."

In poignant vulnerability, she hitched a single shoulder. "I'm just—me."

"You don't know what that is. Trust me, bascha—I've felt that way myself."

"But . . ." She thought about it. "Who am I, then?"

I spoke gently into her ear. "An honorable woman."

Half-sob, half-laugh. "What is *that* worth in the place we're going?"

"I don't know. Something. We'll let them decide a price."

"Them," she murmured reflectively. Then, very softly, "It's all I've been for *seven years* of my life. A vengeful, obsessed woman, bent on killing men. Now all those men are dead. All the blood is spilled. What honor is there in that?"

"The honor is in the oaths, and your commitment to them."

Del twisted abruptly, turning to face me. I could see the shine of her eyes. "What about you?"

I shrugged easily. "It never meant the same to me. That sword—or the honor."

"*Don't lie.*" Vehemently. "I know you better than that."

I smiled. "Maybe. But if honor meant as much to me as it does to you, I'd never have broken my oaths."

"And you'd be dead."

I grinned into her face, all of inches from my own. "You're *that* certain Abbu would have won?"

She didn't answer at first. Then, "That's not fair."

"Of course it's fair. If you really think he'd have won, you can tell me."

Silence. Then, "No, I can't."

"*Do* you think he'd have won?"

"See?"

"Do you?"

Del laughed. "We'll never know, will we?"

"*That's* not fair."

"Life often isn't." She lay quietly a long moment. "She was everything I was. My blooding-blade. *Everything.* She was my talisman, my surety . . . as long as I had Boreal, I could be anyone. I could survive the worst."

"You'll survive the worst now, no matter what happens."

Del sighed. "I don't know."

I poked her in the breastbone. "You sound just like a woman."

She stiffened. "What does *that* mean?"

"Nothing. I just wanted to get a rise."

She relaxed. The teasing had done its job. "We'll need to buy swords."

"Tomorrow. When we get a chance, we'll have new ones made.

Properly made; none of this Northern fol-de-rol that sucks souls out of people into steel. I want an old-fashioned sword, like Single-stroke was."

She touched my cheek, stroking scars. "I'm sorry about him, too."

I shrugged away the sorrow. "He was dead already."

Her tone was as empty. "So was Jamail."

I kissed her on the forehead. "Go to sleep, bascha. Tomorrow we set sail for the rest of our lives."

She was very still a moment. "I hope you don't get seasick."

I snorted. "Save the sentiment for yourself."

Epilogue

We sailed at first light. Neither of us was sick, unless you count the discomfort of second thoughts. Standing at the rail, we watched Haziz fall away. Our past fall away. Doubts riddled us, but neither of us would admit it. Not that easily. Not to one another.

Del raked back hair and locked it behind ears. Then clutched the rail again, white-knuckled. Her eyes watched avidly as the rim of known land dropped below the horizon.

Helpfully, I suggested, "You could jump overboard. I can't, of course, because I don't know how to swim. But you could swim back to Haziz. We're not that far."

"Far enough," she mourned. Then shifted against the rail, leaning a hip into mine. "We're doing the right thing."

"I answered that already."

"It wasn't a question. It was a statement."

"Didn't sound like it." I turned my back to the water, hooking elbows over the rail. Changed the topic on purpose. "Why don't we get married?"

Del gaped. *"What?"*

"Get married." I shrugged idly, watching her expression sidelong. "We might as well."

"Next you'll want a family!"

I laughed. "I don't think we have to go that far."

Del's expression was a mixture of bafflement and curiosity. "Why do you want to get married?"

I waited a moment, purposefully abstracted. "What?—oh. I don't know." I shrugged. "It was just a passing fancy. It passed."

Del was very quiet. She still leaned against the rail, but no longer touched me. "I never thought about it. Not since I went to Staal-Ysta. Marriage?" She shook her head. "I am not the kind."

What had begun merely as a method of distracting her from our uneasy departure suddenly took on a new complexion. Even if I wasn't serious, Del was. And now I was curious. "Why not?"

"There is too much expected."

I challenged her. "No more than what we have."

She mulled that over, lines creasing her brow. "I just . . . I don't think so. Not for me. I had not thought to swear *that* oath. Not with you."

Unexpectedly, it stung. Now it was *personal*. "Why not? I'm not good enough?"

"That isn't what I mean."

"Or is it just that you're afraid of making any sort of commitment?"

Del sighed. "No."

"Then why not? What's wrong with the idea?"

"I'm not ready."

"No. What you mean is, you just don't want to grow up."

"That has nothing to do with it!"

"Of course it does."

She scrubbed a hand across her face, muttering in uplander.

"See?" I prodded.

Del took her hand away from her face. "It is not that I think you unworthy, or that I don't care. It is only I'm not ready."

"That's just an excuse. You'd rather make no commitment so that if things ever get tough, you can just walk out of the hyort."

Del gazed at me speculatively. "We're not in the South anymore. There wouldn't be a hyort."

"You're avoiding the subject."

"No." She laughed, shaking her head. "Ask me again later, when I have recovered myself."

It didn't matter anymore that I'd never intended the topic—or the question—to be serious. "Oh, *I* see. It was a stupid idea. Is that it?"

"Not stupid. Odd."

Odd? I scowled fiercely. "You don't fool me. You just want the aqivi without having to pay for it."

Del studied me expressionlessly. Her tone was exquisitely bland. "Believe me, I pay."

I couldn't hold onto the irritation. Laughing, I gestured surrender with both hands raised. "All right. I give up. It was a stupid idea. How silly of *any* man to want something he can count on. Someone to come home to."

As expected, she was ablaze instantly. "Come home to? Is that what you think I'll be? Someone to 'come *home* to'?" She pressed herself off the rail. "You know me better than that. I am not a docile Southron woman staying home to cook kheshi and mutton, emptying your slops bucket when you are sick from too much aqivi. I will be a companion walking *beside* you every step of the way, or even running or riding; stitching your wounds and tending your fevers, when you are foolish enough to get hurt. I will shirk no part of my duty, nor lay down my sword for you. And if *that* is not wife enough, then I want no part of you; nor should you want it of me!"

Waves slapped at the ship. After a moment, I nodded. "That should be enough."

"Then be content with it!"

I grinned. "Oh, bascha, I am. I just wanted to hear it from you."

Hot-eyed, she glared. "And are you satisfied, then, that I have spewed so much tripe?"

I laughed out loud. Hooked an arm around her neck. "You spew prettier tripe than anyone I know."

Unmollified: *"Hunh."*

I squinted beyond her, pointing with the arm slung over her shoulder. "Look at the sun on the water. Like sunglare off the Punja."

After a moment, she laughed. An odd, throttled laugh of rueful discovery. "You meant none of it!"

"None of what?"

"Getting married!"

I laughed. "I'm not the marrying kind."

Del's expression was exquisite: a blend of concern, relief, contemplation. "I feel odd."

"Why odd? Aren't you glad? You're not cut out for it any more than I am."

"Am I not?"

"You *said* you weren't! You've told me several times, at various dramatic moments in various dramatic ways over the past couple of years—including a few moments ago—that you were not suited to marriage. I didn't think you'd changed your mind quite *that* quickly, woman or no." I paused. "Why do you feel odd?"

"I think I feel *happy*."

"Happy? That we're not getting married?"

"That we don't have to. That there are no expectations. That we are what we are."

"Oh." I wasn't sure I understood exactly what she meant, but didn't feel like pursuing it any longer. Instead, I held her very close, setting my temple against hers as sea-salted wind ruffled our hair. Like Del, I felt happy. "We're free, bascha. Both of us. For the first time in a very long time."

"Free?"

"Of songs and oaths. Free of blood-born swords. Freed of who we *were;* to become whatever—and whoever—we choose." I sighed, feeling younger, and much relieved. "I think we'll like it, bascha . . . everything will be different."

Deep below in the hold, the stud rang a hoof off wood.

Muttering disgust, I buried my face in her hair. "Maybe not *everything*."

Delilah, laughing, hugged me, as we sailed into the sunrise.

Author's Note

What Comes Next?

I have, in my professional life, written books that were "easy," and books that were difficult—though of course "easy" is a matter of degree and context. Though at eight volumes the Cheysuli series was a lengthy task, it also offered escape from college classes (I was an adult student), and part-time work. I lost myself in an "alternate universe," if you will, and, being an organic writer, discovered much of the tales as I went along, just as readers did. Every free moment I had was spent creating the worlds, the characters, and stories of the Cheysuli. But in the midst of writing the series, *Sword-Dancer* appeared in my head. It arrived completely out of the blue one summer evening and more or less wrote itself in a burst of white-hot creative energy; it was what many authors call an "attack book." *Sword-Dancer* came pouring out of my typewriter over two weeks of twelve- to fifteen-hour days. Tiger had a story to tell, and I was his chosen scribe. I had so much fun I went on to write five more novels featuring Tiger and Del.

Then there was *The Golden Key,* a collaboration with Melanie Rawn and Kate Elliott. I said from the beginning that no one of us could have written that massive, complex novel. All of our brainstorming on world, customs, characters and plotlines was interconnected, and we critiqued one another's work along the way. We each of us was responsible for writing our specific sections (me,

Part I; Melanie, Part II; and Kate, Part III), but they were born out of many three-party discussions via phone, e-mail, and fax machine. *The Golden Key* was a huge undertaking and an immensely challenging task, but it was also a creative "high" and made all of us better writers. To this day I am extremely proud of that novel.

Authors always have ideas bubbling away on the back-burners of the brain, and eventually there came a day when I told my agent I had an idea for an entirely new fantasy universe unrelated to the Cheysuli and *Sword-Dancer* series. By saying it, I made it real. Now I had to write it. And so in fits and starts and bumps along the way, I embarked on a new fantasy journey.

It was the first brand-new universe and cast of characters that I, as a solo author, had created since 1983, when I wrote *Sword-Dancer*. *Karavans* wasn't another volume in an existing series with people, places, and plots already in place, but a wholly new undertaking. And I knew I wasn't the same person, much less the same writer, that I was in the early to mid-'80s when the Cheysuli and *Sword-Dancer* series debuted. *Karavans* became, in fact, the most challenging fantasy novel I'd ever written. Afterall, in keeping with traditions of the time, the first several Cheysuli novels and *Sword-Dancer* arrived on the bookshelves without fanfare. I was a completely unknown author. But *Karavans* would be published *with* fanfare. I knew readers would have expectations. And I had expectations about those expectations. (Never let it be said that authors don't speculate about what their fans will think!)

I've been most fortunate to have two fantasy series, both markedly different from one another (and both published by the same publishing house), become very successful. It allowed me the luxury, with DAW's blessing, of alternating between worlds, writing styles, and plots and characters instead of living in the same universe day in and day out, something that can make an author— and her work—go quite stale.

Now, with *Karavans*, I begin all over again once more, some twenty-eight years after I began writing about a race of shapechangers and their magical animals, and twenty-six since Del walked through the door of a Southron cantina and into Tiger's heart. With those experiences behind me, I have high hopes for the new world and an eclectic slew of characters.

In the aftermath of a bitter, brutal war waged by ruthless neighboring warlord, many residents of Sancorra Province have turned refugee, fleeing the destruction of farmsteads and settlements to begin new lives in another province. But it is very late in the karavan season with the rains due any day, and the roads are made even more dangerous by opportunistic bandits and the warlord's vicious armies and patrols. Also threatening the safety of the refugees is the land called Alisanos, a living hell-on-earth that changes location at will, swallowing everything—and every*one*—in its path. Infamous as the dwelling place of demons, devils, gods and demi-gods and countless other horrors, Alisanos wreaks tragedy on entire villages or single individuals. Few humans, once taken into Alisanos, ever escape—and those who do have been terribly altered in mind and body by the poisonous magic of Alisanos, fated to be shunned by the human race they were once a part of.

I invite readers to join karavan guide Rhuan and his cousin, Brodhi, a courier, both born of a legendary race called the Shoia; Ilona, the karavan diviner who reads in the hands of others the dangers and griefs facing them, but cannot read her own; demons Darmuth and Ferize, hiding true forms and secrets; and a farmstead family desperate to reach Atalanda Province before the new baby is born, each on a perilous journey along dangerous roads much too close to the living evil threatening them all as Alisanos prepares to go active.

Karavans will be published in hardcover by DAW Books in April 2006.

Watch out for

KARAVANS

*Jennifer Roberson's first all-new
fantasy universe in twenty years*

Coming in hardcover in April 2006

Read on for a special introduction
to the series: the short story that
debuted the world of *Karavans*

Ending and Beginning

Four had died. Killed ruthlessly. Uselessly. Three, because they were intended as examples to the others. The fourth, merely because he was alone, and Sancorran. The people of Sancorra province had become fair game for the brutal patrols of Hecari soldiers, men dispatched to ensure the Sancorran insurrection was thoroughly put down.

Insurrection. Ilona wished to spit. She believed it a word of far less weight than war, an insufficiency in describing the bitter realities now reshaping the province. *War* was a hard, harsh word, carrying a multiplicity of meanings. Such as death.

Four people, dead. Any one of them might have been her, had fate proved frivolous. She was a hand-reader, a diviner, a woman others sought to give them their fortunes, to tell their futures; and yet even she, remarkably gifted, had learned that fate was inseparably intertwined with caprice. She could read a hand with that hand in front of her, seeing futures, interpreting the fragments for such folk as lacked the gift. But it was also possible fate might alter its path, the track she had parsed as leading to a specific future. Ilona had not seen any such thing as her death at the hands of a Hecari patrol, but it had been possible.

Instead, she had lived. Three strangers, leaving behind a bitter past to begin a sweeter future, had not. And a man with whom she had shared a bed in warmth and affection, if not wild passion, now rode blanket-wrapped in the back of the karavan-master's wagon, cold in place of warm.

The karavan, last of the season under Jorda, her employer, straggled to the edges of the nameless settlement just after sundown. Exhausted from the lengthy journey as well as its tragedies, Ilona climbed down from her wagon, staggered forward, and began to unhitch the team. The horses, too, were tired; the karavan had withstood harrying attacks by Sancorran refugees turned bandits, had given up coin and needed supplies as "road tax" to three different sets of Hecari patrols until the fourth, the final, took payment in blood when told there was no money left with which to pay. When the third patrol had exacted the "tax," Ilona wondered if the karavan-master would suggest to the Hecari soldiers that they might do better to go after the bandits rather than harassing innocent Sancorrans fleeing the aftermath of war. But Jorda had merely clamped his red-bearded jaw closed and paid up. It did not do to suggest anything to the victorious enemy; Ilona had heard tales that they killed anyone who complained, were they not paid the "tax."

Ilona saw it for herself when the fourth patrol arrived.

Her hands went through the motions of unhitching without direction from her mind, still picturing the journey. Poor Sancorra, overrun by the foreigners called Hecari, led by a fearsome warlord, was being steadily stripped of her wealth just as the citizens were being stripped of their holdings. Women were widowed, children left fatherless, farmsteads burned, livestock rounded up and driven to Hecari encampments to feed the enemy soldiers. Karavans that did not originate in Sancorra were allowed passage through the province so long as their masters could prove they came from other provinces—and paid tribute—but that passage was nonetheless a true challenge. Jorda's two scouts early on came across the remains of several karavans that the master knew to be led by foreigners like himself; the Hecari apparently were more than capable of killing anyone they deemed Sancorran refugees, even if they manifestly were not. It was a simple matter to declare anyone an enemy of their warlord.

Ilona was not Sancorran. Neither was Jorda, nor one of the scouts. But the other guide, Tansit, was. And now his body lay in the back of a wagon, waiting for the rites that would send his spirit to the Land of the Dead.

Wearily Ilona finished unhitching the team, pulling harness from the sweat-slicked horses. Pungent, foamy lather dripped from flanks and shoulders. She swapped out headstalls for halters, then led the team along the line of wagons to Janqueril, the horse-master. The aging, balding man and his apprentices would tend the teams while everyone else made their way into the tent-city settlement, looking for release from the tension of the trip.

And, she knew, to find other diviners who might tell a different tale of the future they faced tomorrow, on the edge of unknown lands.

Ilona delivered the horses, thanked Janqueril, then pushed a fractious mass of curling dark hair out of her face. Jorda kept three diviners in his employ, to make sure his karavans got safely to their destinations and to serve any of his clients, but Tansit had always come to her. He said he trusted her to be truthful with him. Hand-readers, though not uncommon, were not native to Sancorra, and Tansit, like others, viewed her readings as more positive than those given by Jorda's other two diviners. Ilona didn't know if that were true; only that she always told her clients the good and the bad, rather than shifting the emphasis wholly to good.

She had seen danger in Tansit's callused hand. That, she had told him. And he had laughed, said the only danger facing him were the vermin holes in the prairie, waiting to trap his horse and take him down as well.

And so a vermin hole *had* trapped his horse, snapping a leg, and Tansit, walking back to the karavan well behind him, was found by the Hecari patrol that paused long enough to kill him, then continue on to richer pickings. By the time the karavan reached the scout, his features were unrecognizable; Ilona knew him by his clothing and the color of his blood-matted hair.

So Tansit had told his own fortune without her assistance, and Ilona lost a man whom she had not truly loved, but liked. Well enough to share his bed when the loneliness of her life sent her to it. Men were attracted to her, but wary of her gift. Few were willing to sleep with a woman who could tell a lover the day of his death.

At the end of journeys, Ilona's habit was to build a fire, lay a rug, set up a table, cushions, and candles, then wait quietly for custom. At the end of a journey clients wished to consult diviners for advice concerning the future in a new place. But this night, at the end of this journey, Ilona forbore. She stood at the back of her wagon, clutching one of the blue-painted spoke wheels, and stared sightlessly into the sunset.

Some little while later, a hand came down upon her shoulder. Large, wide, callused, with spatulate fingers and oft-bruised or broken nails. She smelled the musky astringency of a hard-working man in need of a bath; heard the inhaled, heavy breath; sensed, even without reading that hand, his sorrow and compassion.

"He was a good man," Jorda said.

Ilona nodded jerkily.

"We will hold the rites at dawn."

She nodded again.

"Will you wish to speak?"

She turned. Looked into his face, the broad, bearded, seamed face of the man who employed her, who was himself employed several times a season to lead karavans across the wide plains of Sancorra to the edge of other provinces, where other karavans and their masters took up the task. Jorda could be a hard man, but he was also a good man. In his green eyes she saw grief that he had lost an employee, a valued guide, but also a friend. Tansit had scouted for Jorda more years than she could count. More, certainly, than she had known either of them.

"Yes, of course," she told him.

Jorda nodded, seeking something in her eyes. But Ilona was expert at hiding her feelings. Such things, if uncontrolled, could color the readings, and she had learned long before to mask emotions. "I thank you," the master said. "It would please Tansit."

She thought a brace of tall tankards of foamy ale would please Tansit more. But words would have to do. Words for the dead.

Abruptly she said, "I have to go."

Jorda's ruddy brows ran together. "Alone? Into this place? It's but a scattering of tents, Ilona, not a true settlement. You would do better to come with me, and a few of the others. After what happened on the road, it would be safer."

Safety was not what she craved. Neither was danger, and certainly not death, but she yearned to be elsewhere than with Jorda and the others this night. How better to pay tribute to Tansit than to drink a brace of tall tankards of foamy ale in his place?

Ilona forced a smile. "I'm going to Mikal's wine-tent. He knows me. I'll be safe enough there."

Jorda's face cleared. "So you will. But ask someone to walk you back to your wagon later."

Ilona arched her brows. "It's not so often I must *ask* such a thing, Jorda! Usually they beg to do that duty."

He understood the tone, and the intent. He relaxed fractionally, then presented her with a brief flash of teeth mostly obscured by his curling beard. "Forgive me! I do know better." The grin faded. "I think many of us will buy Tansit ale tonight."

She nodded as the big man turned and faded back into the twilight, returning to such duties as were his at the end of a journey. Which left her duty to Tansit.

Ilona leaned inside her wagon and caught up a deep-dyed, blue-black shawl, swung it around her shoulders, and walked through the ankle-deep dust into the tiny tent-city.

She had seen, in her life, many deaths. It rode the hands of all humans, though few could read it, and fewer still could interpret the conflicting information. Ilona had never *not* been able to see, to read, to interpret; when her family had come to comprehend that such a gift would rule her life and thus their own, they had turned her out. She had been all of twelve summers, shocked by their actions because she had not seen it in her own hand; had she read theirs, she might have understood earlier what lay in store. In the fifteen years since they had turned out their oldest daughter, Ilona had learned to trust no one but herself—though she was given to understand that some people, such as Jorda, were less likely to send a diviner on her way if she could serve their interests. All karavans required diviners if they were to be truly successful; clients undertaking journeys went nowhere without consulting any num-

ber of diviners of all persuasions, and a karavan offering readings
along the way, rather than depending on itinerant diviners drifting
from settlement to settlement, stood to attract more custom. Jorda
was no fool; he hired Branca and Melior, and in time he hired her.

The night was cool. Ilona tightened her shawl and ducked her
head against the errant breeze teasing at her face. Mikal's wine-
tent stood nearly in the center of the cluster of tents that spread
like vermin across the plain near the river. A year before there
had been half as many; next year, she did not doubt, the popula-
tion would increase yet again. Sancorra province was in utter disarray, thanks to the depredations of the Hecari; few would wish
to stay, who had the means to depart. It would provide Jorda with
work as well as his hired diviners. But she wished war were not
the reason.

Mikal's wine-tent was one of many, but he had arrived early
when the settlement had first sprung up, a place near sweet water
and good grazing, and not far from the border of the neighboring
province. It was a good place for karavans to halt overnight, and
within weeks it had become more than merely that. Now merchants put up tents, set down roots, and served a populace that
shifted shape nightly, trading familiar faces for those of strangers.
Mikal's face was one of the most familiar, and his tent a welcome
distraction from the duties of the road.

Ilona took the path she knew best through the winding skeins
of tracks and paused only briefly in the spill of light from the tied-
back door flap of Mikal's wine-tent. She smelled the familiar odors
of ale and wine, the tang of urine from men who sought relief
rather too close to the tent, the thick fug of male bodies far more interested in liquor than wash water. Only rarely did women frequent
Mikal's wine-tent; the female couriers, who were toughened by experience on the province roads and thus able to deal with anything,
and such women as herself: unavailable for hire, but seeking the
solace found in liquor-laced camaraderie. Ilona had learned early on
to appreciate ale and wine, and the value of the company of others
no more rooted than she was. Tansit had always spent his coin at
Mikal's. Tonight, she would spend hers in Tansit's name.

Ilona entered, pushing the shawl back from her head and

shoulders. As always, conversation paused as her presence was noted; then Mikal called out a cheery welcome, as did two or three others who knew her. It was enough to warn off any man who might wish to proposition her, establishing her right to remain unmolested. This night, she appreciated it more than usual.

She sought and found a small table near a back corner, arranging skirts deftly as she settled upon a stool. Within a matter of moments Mikal arrived, bearing a guttering candle in a pierced-tin lantern. He set it down upon the table, then waited.

Ilona drew in a breath. "Ale," she said, relieved when her voice didn't waver. "Two tankards, if it please you. Your best."

"Tansit?" he asked in his deep, slow voice.

It was not a question regarding a man's death, but his anticipated arrival. Ilona discovered she could not, as yet, speak of the former, and thus relied upon the latter. She nodded confirmation, meeting his dark blue eyes without hesitation. Mikal nodded also, then took his bulk away to tend the order.

She found herself plaiting the fringes of her shawl, over and over again. Irritated, Ilona forcibly stopped herself from continuing the nervous habit. When Mikal brought the tankards, she lifted her own in both hands, downed several generous swallows, then carefully fingered away the foam left to linger upon her upper lip. Two tankards upon the table. One: her own. The other was Tansit's. When done with her ale, she would leave coin enough for two tankards, but one would remain untouched. And then the truth would be known. The tale spread. But she would be required to say nothing, to no one.

Ah, but he had been a good man. She had not wished to wed him, though he had asked; she had not expected to bury him either.

At dawn, she would attend the rites. Would speak of his life, and of his death.

Tansit had never been one known for his attention to time. But he was not a man given to passing up ale when it was waiting. Ilona drank down her tankard slowly and deliberately, avoiding the glances, the stares, and knew well enough when whispers began of Tansit's tardiness in joining her.

There were two explanations: they had quarreled, or one of them was dead. But their quarrels never accompanied them into a wine-tent.

She drank her ale, clearly not dead, while Tansit's tankard remained undrunk. Those who were not strangers understood. At tables other than hers, in the sudden, sharp silence of comprehension, fresh tankards were ordered. Were left untouched. Tribute to the man so many of them had known.

Tansit would have appreciated how many tankards were ordered. Though he also would have claimed it a waste of good ale that no one drank.

Ilona smiled, imagining his words. Seeing his expression.

She swallowed the last of her ale and rose, thinking ahead to the bed in her wagon. But then a body blocked her way, altering the fall of smoky light, and she looked into the face of a stranger.

In the ocherous illumination of Mikal's lantern, his face was ruddy-gold. "I'm told the guide is dead."

A stranger indeed, to speak so plainly to the woman who had shared the dead man's bed.

He seemed to realize it. To regret it. A grimace briefly twisted his mouth. "Forgive me. But I am badly in need of work."

Ilona gathered the folds of her shawl even as she gathered patience. "The season is ended. And I am not the one to whom you should apply. Jorda is the karavan-master."

"I'm told he is the best."

"Jorda is—Jorda." She settled the shawl over the crown of her head, shrouding untamed ringlets. "Excuse me."

He turned only slightly, giving way. "Will you speak to him for me?"

Ilona paused, then swung back. "Why? I know nothing of you."

His smile was charming, his gesture self-deprecating. "Of course. But I could acquaint you."

A foreigner, she saw. Not Sancorran, but neither was he Hercari. In candlelight his hair was a dark, oiled copper, bound back in a multiplicity of braids. She saw the glint of beads in those braids, gold and silver; heard the faint chime and clatter of ornamentation.

He wore leather tunic and breeches, and from the outer seams of sleeves and leggings dangled shell- and bead-weighted fringe. Indeed, a stranger, to wear what others, in time of war, might construe as wealth.

"No need to waste your voice," she said. "Let me see your hand."

It startled him. Arched brows rose. "My hand?"

She matched his expression. "Did they not also tell you what I am?"

"The dead guide's woman."

The pain was abrupt and sharp, then faded as quickly as it had come. *The dead guide's woman.* True, that. But much more. And it might be enough to buy her release from a stranger. "Diviner," she said. "There is no need to tell me anything of yourself, when I can read it in your hand."

She sensed startlement and withdrawal, despite that the stranger remained before her, very still. His eyes were dark in the frenzied play of guttering shadows. The hand she could see, loose at his side, abruptly closed. Sealed itself against her. Refusal. Denial. Self-preservation.

"It is a requirement," she told him, "of anyone who wishes to hire on with Jorda."

His face tightened. Something flickered deep in his eyes. She thought she saw a hint of red.

"You'll understand," Ilona hid amusement behind a businesslike tone, "that Jorda must be careful. He can't afford to hire just anyone. His clients trust him to guard their safety. How is he to know what a stranger intends?"

"Rhuan," he said abruptly.

She heard it otherwise: *Ruin.* "Oh?"

"A stranger who gives his name is no longer a stranger."

"A stranger who brings ruination is an enemy."

"Ah." His grin was swift. He repeated his name more slowly, making clear what it was, and she heard the faint undertone of an accent.

She echoed it. "Rhuan."

"I need the work."

Ilona eyed him. Tall, but not a giant. Much of his strength, she thought, resided beneath his clothing, coiled quietly away. Not old, not young, but somewhere in the middle, indistinguishable. Oddly alien in the light of a dozen lanterns, for all his smooth features were arranged in a manner women undoubtedly found pleasing. On another night, *she* might; but Tansit was newly dead, and this stranger—Rhuan—kept her from her wagon, where she might grieve in private.

"Have you guided before?"

"Not here. Elsewhere."

"It is a requirement that you know the land."

"I do know it."

"Here?"

"Sancorra. I know it." He lifted one shoulder in an eloquent shrug. "On a known road, guiding is less a requirement than protection. That, I can do very well."

Something about him suggested it was less a boast than the simple truth.

"And does anyone know *you?*"

He turned slightly, glancing toward the plank set upon barrels where Mikal held sovereignty, and she saw Mikal watching them.

She saw also the slight lifting of big shoulders, a smoothing of his features into a noncommittal expression. Mikal told her silently there was nothing of the stranger he knew that meant danger, but nothing much else either.

"The season is ended," Ilona repeated. "Speak to Jorda of the next one, if you wish, but there is no work for you now."

"In the midst of war," Rhuan said, "I believe there is. Others will wish to leave. Your master would do better to extend the season."

Jorda had considered it, she knew. Tansit had spoken of it. And if the master did extend the season, he would require a second guide. Less for guiding than for protection, with Hecari patrols harrying the roads.

Four people, dead.

Ilona glanced briefly at the undrunk tankard. "Apply to Jorda," she said. "It's not for me to say." Something perverse within her flared into life, wanting to wound the man before her who was so vital and alive, when another was not. "But he *will* require you to be read. It needn't be me."

His voice chilled. "Most diviners are charlatans."

Indeed, he was a stranger; no true-born Sancorran would speak so baldly. "Some," she agreed. "There are always those who prey upon the weak of mind. But there are also those who practice an honest art."

"You?"

Ilona affected a shrug every bit as casual as his had been. "Allow me your hand, and then you'll know, won't you?"

Once again he clenched it. "No."

"Then you had best look elsewhere for employment." She had learned to use her body and used it now, sliding past him before he might block her way again. She sensed the stirring in his limbs, the desire to reach out to her, to stop her; sensed also when he decided to let her go.

It began not far from Mikal's wine-tent. Ilona had heard its like before and recognized at once what was happening. The grunt of a man taken unawares, the bitten-off inhalation, the repressed blurt of pain and shock; and the hard, tense breathing of the assailants. Such attacks were not unknown in settlements such as this, composed of strangers desperate to escape the depredations of the Hecari. Desperate enough, some of them, to don the brutality of the enemy and wield its weapon.

Ilona stepped more deeply into shadow. She was a woman, and alone. If she interfered, she invited retribution. Jorda had told her to ask for escort on the way to the wagons. In her haste to escape the stranger in Mikal's tent, she had dismissed it from her mind.

Safety lay in secrecy. But Tansit was dead, and at dawn she would attend his rites and say the words. If she did nothing, would another woman grieve? Would another woman speak the words of the rite meant to carry the spirit to the Land of the Dead?

Then she was running toward the noise. "Stop! *Stop!*"

Movement. Men. Bodies. Ilona saw shapes break apart; saw a body fall. Heard the curses meant for her. But she was there, telling them to stop, and for a wonder they did.

And then she realized, as they faded into darkness, that she had thought too long and arrived too late. His wealth was untouched, the beading in the braids and fringe, but his life was taken. She saw the blood staining his throat, the knife standing up from his ribs. Garotte to make him helpless, knife to kill him.

He lay sprawled beneath the stars, limbs awry, eyes open and empty, the comely features slack.

She had seen death before. She recognized his.

Too late. Too late.

She should go fetch Mikal. There had been some talk of establishing a Watch, a group of men to walk the paths and keep what peace there was. Ilona didn't know if a Watch yet existed; but Mikal would come, would help her tend the dead.

A stranger in Sancorra. What rites were his?

Shaking, Ilona knelt. She did not go to fetch Mikal. Instead she sat beside a man whose name she barely knew, whose hand she hadn't read, and grieved for them both. For them all. For the men, young and old, dead in the war.

In the *insurrection.*

But there was yet a way. She had the gift. Beside him, Ilona gathered up one slack hand. His future had ended, but there was yet a past. It faded already, she knew, as the warmth of the body cooled, but if she practiced the art before he was cold, she would learn what she needed to know. And then he also would have the proper rites. She would make certain of it.

Indeed, the hand cooled. Before morning the fingers would stiffen, even as Tansit's had. The spirit, denied a living body, would attenuate, then fade.

There was little light, save for the muddy glow of lanterns within a hundred tents. Ilona would be able to see nothing of the flesh, but she had no need. Instead, she lay her fingers gently upon his palm and closed her eyes, tracing the pathways there, the lines of his life.

Maelstrom.

Gasping, Ilona fell back. His hand slid from hers. Beneath it, beneath the touch of his flesh, the fabric of her skirt took flame.

She beat it with her own hands, then clutched at and heaped

powdery earth upon it. The flame quenched itself, the thread of smoke dissipated. But even as it did so, as she realized the fabric was whole, movement startled her.

The stranger's hand, that she had grasped to read, closed around the knife standing up from his ribs. She heard a sharply indrawn breath, and something like a curse, and the faint clattered chime of the beads in his braids. He raised himself up on one elbow and stared at her.

This time, she heard the curse clearly. Recognized the grimace. Knew what he would say: *I wasn't truly dead.*

But he was. Had been.

He pulled the knife from his ribs, inspected the blade a moment, then tossed it aside with an expression of distaste. Ilona's hands, no longer occupied with putting out the flame that had come from his flesh, folded themselves against her skirts. She waited.

He saw her watching him. Assessed her expression. Tried the explanation she anticipated. "I wasn't—"

"You were."

He opened his mouth to try again. Thought better of it. Looked at her hands folded into fabric. "Are you hurt?"

"No. Are *you?*"

His smile was faint. "No."

She touched her own throat. "You're bleeding."

He sat up. Ignored both the slice encircling his neck and the wound in his ribs. His eyes on her were calm, too calm. She saw an odd serenity there, and rueful acceptance that she had seen what, obviously, he wished she hadn't seen.

"I'm Shoia," he said.

No more than that. No more was necessary.

"Those are stories," Ilona told him. "Legends."

He seemed equally amused as he was resigned. "Rooted in truth."

Skepticism showed. "A living Shoia?"

"Now," he agreed, irony in his tone. "A moment ago, dead. But you know that."

"I touched your hand, and it took fire."

His face closed up. Sealed itself against her. His mouth was a grim, unrelenting line.

"Is that a Shoia trait, to burn the flesh a diviner might otherwise read?"

The mouth parted. "It's not for you to do."

Ilona let her own measure of irony seep into her tone. "And well warded, apparently."

"They wanted my bones," he said. "It's happened before."

She understood at once. "Practitioners of the Kantica." Who burned bones for the auguries found in ash and grit. Legend held Shoia bones told truer, clearer futures than anything else. But no one she knew of used *actual* Shoia bones.

He knew what she was thinking. "There are a few of us left," he told her. "But we keep it to ourselves. We would prefer to keep our bones clothed in flesh."

"But I have heard no one murders a Shoia. That anyone foolish enough to do so inherits damnation."

"No one *knowingly* murders a Shoia," he clarified. "But as we apparently are creatures of legend, who would believe I am?"

Nor did it matter. Dead was dead, damnation or no. "These men intended to haul you out to the anthills," Ilona said. Where the flesh would be stripped away, and the bones collected for sale to Kantic diviners. "They couldn't know you are Shoia, could they?"

He gathered braids fallen forward and swept them back. "I doubt it. But it doesn't matter. A charlatan would buy the bones and *claim* them Shoia, thus charging even more for the divinations. Clearer visions, you see."

She did see. There were indeed charlatans, false diviners who victimized the vulnerable and gullible. How better to attract trade than to boast of Shoia bones?

"Are you?" she asked. "Truly?"

Something flickered in his eyes. Flickered red. His voice hardened. "You looked into my hand."

And had seen nothing of his past nor his future save *maelstrom.*

"Madness," she said, not knowing she spoke aloud.

His smile was bitter.

Ilona looked into his eyes as she had looked into his hand. "Are you truly a guide?"

The bitterness faded. "I can be many things. Guide is one of them."

Oddly, it amused her to say it. "Dead man?"

He matched her irony. "That, too. But I would prefer not." He stood up then; somehow, he brought her up with him. She faced him there in the shadows beneath the stars. "It isn't infinite, the resurrection."

"No?"

"Seven times," he said. "The seventh is the true death."

"And how many times was this?"

The stranger showed all his fine white teeth in a wide smile. "That, we never tell."

"Ah." She understood. "Mystery is your salvation."

"Well, yes. Until the seventh time. And then we are as dead as anyone else. Bury us, burn us . . ." He shrugged. "It doesn't matter. Dead is dead. It simply comes more slowly."

Ilona shook out her skirts, shedding dust. "I know what I saw when I looked into your hand. But that was a shield, was it not? A ward against me."

"Against a true diviner, yes."

It startled her; she was accustomed to others accepting her word. "You didn't believe me?"

He said merely, "Charlatans abound."

"But you are safe from charlatans."

He stood still in the darkness and let her arrive at the conclusion.

"But not from me," she said.

"Shoia bones are worth coin to charlatans," he said. "A Kantic diviner could make his fortune by burning my bones. But a *true* Kantic diviner—"

"—could truly read your bones."

He smiled, wryly amused. "And therefore I am priceless."

Ilona considered it. "One would think you'd be more careful. Less easy to kill."

"I was distracted."

"By—?"

"You," he finished. "I came out to persuade you to take me to your master. To make the introduction."

"Ah, then *I* am being blamed for your death."

He grinned. "For this one, yes."

"And I suppose the only reparation I may pay is to introduce you to Jorda."

The grin flashed again. Were it not for the slice upon his neck and the blood staining his leather tunic, no one would suspect this man had been dead only moments before.

Ilona sighed, recalling Tansit. And his absence. "I suppose Jorda might have some use for a guide who can survive death multiple times."

"At least until the seventh," he observed dryly.

"If I read your hand, would I know how many you have left?"

He abruptly thrust both hands behind his back, looking mutinous, reminding her for all the world of a child hiding booty. Ilona laughed.

But she *had* read his hand, if only briefly. And seen in it conflagration.

Rhuan, he had said.

Ruin, she had echoed.

She wondered if she were right.